The Editor

KATHRYN L. LYNCH is Katharine Lee Bates and Sophie Chantal Hart Professor of English at Wellesley College. She is the author of *The High Medieval Dream Vision: Poetry, Philosophy, and Literary Form* and *Chaucer's Philosophical Dream Visions* and editor of *Chaucer's Cultural Geography*. Her articles have appeared in, among other publications, *The Chaucer Review*, *Studies in the Age of Chaucer*, and *Speculum*.

W. W. NORTON & COMPANY, INC.
Also Publishes

A NORTON CRITICAL EDITION

Geoffrey Chaucer
DREAM VISIONS
AND OTHER POEMS

AUTHORITATIVE TEXTS
CONTEXTS
CRITICISM

Selected and Edited by
KATHRYN L. LYNCH
WELLESLEY COLLEGE

W • W • NORTON & COMPANY • *New York* • *London*

W. W. Norton & Company has been independent since its founding in 1923, when William Warder Norton and Mary D. Herter Norton first published lectures delivered at the People's Institute, the adult education division of New York City's Cooper Union. The Nortons soon expanded their program beyond the Institute, publishing books by celebrated academics from America and abroad. By mid-century, the two major pillars of Norton's publishing program—trade books and college texts—were firmly established. In the 1950s, the Norton family transferred control of the company to its employees, and today—with a staff of four hundred and a comparable number of trade, college, and professional titles published each year—W. W. Norton & Company stands as the largest and oldest publishing house owned wholly by its employees.

The text of this book is composed in Fairfield Medium
with the display set in Bernhard Modern.
Composition by Binghamton Valley Composition.
Manufacturing by the Courier Companies—Westford Division.
Production manager: Benjamin Reynolds.

Library of Congress Cataloging-in-Publication Data

Chaucer, Geoffrey, d. 1400
[Poems. Selections]
Geoffrey Chaucer : dream visions and other poems : authoritative texts, contexts,
criticism / selected and edited by Kathryn L. Lynch.
p. cm. — (Norton critical edition)
Includes bibliographical references.
ISBN-13: 978-0-393-92588-3 (pbk.)
ISBN-10: 0-393-92588-9 (pbk.)

I. Lynch, Kathryn L., 1951– II. Title.

PR1852.L96 2006
821'.1—dc22
2006046641

W. W. Norton & Company, Inc., 500 Fifth Avenue, New York, N.Y. 10110-0017
www.wwnorton.com
W. W. Norton & Company Ltd., Castle House, 75/76 Wells Street, London W1T 3QT

6 7 8 9 0

for Michael and Rachel
"Al this mene I by Love."

Contents

Criticism

Preface

This Norton Critical Edition is intended both for students just beginning their acquaintance with Chaucer and for those coming to what are sometimes referred to as his "minor poems"—his dream visions, short lyrics, complaints—for a deeper knowledge of the poet after reading his masterworks, the *Canterbury Tales* and *Troilus and Criseyde*.[1] Because beginning readers of Middle English form an important part of my audience, I provide extensive glosses of all unfamiliar words, expressions, and constructions, and translate both first and subsequent uses of difficult words unless they are found within a few lines; sometimes I offer more than one translation of a specific word to give the reader a sense of its semantic range and context. When there is no modern equivalent for a Middle English construction (for example, the distinction between the formal "you" and the familiar "thou"), I have preferred modern usage, but whenever it was possible I have stayed as close to Chaucer's literal meaning as I could. My aim has been to provide whatever help is possible to an inexperienced reader. As Chaucer's lexicon becomes more familiar, readers may find they are increasingly able to ignore the glosses, but the help is there whenever it is needed, and consequently reading can begin at any point and with any poem. A full translation of all the dream visions has not been made since Brian Stone's Penguin edition over twenty years ago, and his is a poetic rather than a literal translation.[2] This heavily glossed edition should make it possible for even the beginning reader to experience Chaucer in his own words.

The first section presents the text. I have tried to construct a trustworthy text that does not offer unnecessary hardship to the reader who is first encountering a Middle English poem. My textual method can be summed up briefly: moderately conservative in respect to substance; moderately liberal in respect to spelling. To elaborate, my copy-text is W. W. Skeat's late nineteenth-century edition of Chaucer's complete poetry.[3] Despite being a somewhat enthusiastic reviser of the text, especially when he could improve a manuscript's metrical regularity, Skeat had editorial instincts that are hard to match, which is the main reason for the tremendous influence of his work on subsequent editors. But Skeat sometimes falls victim to what one critic calls "a degree of emendatorial impetuosity."[4] I have

---

1. The rubric "minor poems" is sometimes used only to refer to the short, lyric poems; but W. W. Skeat, in his edition, included the *Book of the Duchess* and the *Parliament of Fowls* in this group. Despite my hesitation in using the term, I prefer it here to "early poems" because the dating of Chaucer's works is more fundamentally uncertain than many earlier critics have acknowledged; the term "early poems" prejudges questions of dating that I will take up in these pages. The short lyric "The Complaint of Chaucer to His Purse" was most likely the latest of all his poems.
2. Geoffrey Chaucer, *Love Visions*, trans. Brian Stone (New York: Penguin, 1983).
3. *The Complete Works of Geoffrey Chaucer*, ed. Walter W. Skeat, 6 vols. (Oxford: Clarendon P, 1894).
4. A. S. G. Edwards, "Walter Skeat (1835–1912)," in *Editing Chaucer: The Great Tradition*, ed. Paul G. Ruggiers (Norman, OK: Pilgrim Books, 1984), 184.

thus taken care to compare his readings with those of all the original man-
uscripts, available in facsimiles and transcriptions, and to consult the work
of other modern editions, listed in the Selected Bibliography at the end of
this Norton Critical Edition. I have not followed Skeat when his emen-
dations are clearly in conflict with the best manuscript evidence, even
when his reading yields a smoother line.

The present moment is an especially exciting time for editorial work on
Chaucer. Great strides have been made recently in editorial procedure and
in our understanding of the history of Middle English dialects and scribal
practice. The recent identification of Chaucer's scribe offers an example
of the kind of breakthrough that makes working on Chaucer right now so
exciting.[5] Computer applications are accelerating the pace of discovery and
expanding the database of readings, allowing scholars to make ever more
precise comparisons among different manuscript groups. The work being
done on the *Canterbury Tales* by "The Canterbury Tales Project" <*www
.cta.dmu.ac.uk/projects/ctp/index*> provides an especially thrilling example
of the possibilities of technology in this area. This project makes available
in electronic form all the manuscripts and early printed editions of the
Canterbury Tales, enabling its creators to reconstruct a manuscript history
or family tree more fully and reliably than has been done previously. We
are thus on the verge of many new insights into Chaucer's texts, some of
which have implications for the minor poems.

Chaucer's minor poems, however, differ from the *Canterbury Tales* in
some important ways that affect editorial practice. There are many more
manuscripts of the *Canterbury Tales* than of the dream visions, and the
best of these are very early (increasingly, scholars are coming to think that
the Hengwrt manuscript of the *Tales* may have been produced during the
poet's lifetime and even perhaps supervised by Chaucer himself). There
are far fewer manuscripts of Chaucer's minor poems, and some of the short
poems—for example, "Merciless Beauty"—exist in only a single manu-
script copy. Moreover, what manuscript evidence we have for Chaucer's
minor poems is mostly later than that available for the *Canterbury Tales*.
Although the manuscript commonly known as Gg (Cambridge University
Library Gg 4.27), which contains texts of the *Parliament of Fowls*, the
Legend of Good Women, and several of the shorter poems, can be dated
to the first quarter of the fifteenth century, it is written in an East Anglian
dialect quite different from the rest of the manuscript tradition.[6] And the
other important manuscripts of these poems come from the middle of the
century (e.g., perhaps the most important single manuscript for many of
them, Fairfax 16, Bodleian Library) or even later, which means that their
grammatical and lexical forms and spellings, produced decades after Chau-
cer's death, are quite unlikely to have been his own.

Furthermore, because they sometimes include material not found in the
manuscripts, early print editions of the minor poems take on an impor-
tance that they do not have for the *Tales*. Consider, for example, the *Book
of the Duchess*, a poem that appears in only three manuscripts, none before
the second quarter of the fifteenth century. All three of these manuscripts
are defective, lacking lines 31–96, which first appear in the 1532 edition

5. Linne Mooney, "Chaucer's Scribe," *Speculum* 81 (2006): 97–138.
6. M. B. Parkes and Richard Beadle, *Poetical Works, Geoffrey Chaucer: A Facsimile of Cambridge
   University Library MS Gg.4.27*, vol. 3 (Norman, OK: Pilgrim Books, 1980), 46–56.

of William Thynne, suggesting to some scholars that Thynne may have had access to a manuscript that no longer survives. Yet other readings in Thynne are manifestly inferior to those found in the manuscripts. What status are we then to give Thynne's printed text, published more than one hundred years after Chaucer's death? Can we trust its additions?[7] The complex and somewhat chaotic manuscript and printing history of Chaucer's early poems means that any edition must proceed by a series of critical judgments about such matters that cannot be fully verified. While each poem has a "best text" (which I will indicate in the individual introductions), the readings of that text must be evaluated in light of the entire manuscript tradition. In the case of the *Book of the Duchess*, I have included the lines from Thynne's edition as the best solution to the problem of the missing lines in the manuscript witnesses, but even a beginning student needs to keep in mind that a medieval poem does not have the editorial stability of a modern book. Print gives the book the look of a fixed and determinate object—one copy is the same as another. But the original manuscripts, with their gaps and disagreements, are far more variable and discontinuous. The difference can be experienced by spending some time with a hypertext edition that permits the reader, with the click of a mouse, actually to see the manuscripts in their glorious diversity; happily, an excellent one is available for the *Book of the Duchess*, done by Murray McGillivray and listed in the Selected Bibliography.

Chaucer was himself quite aware of the danger of entrusting his text to the copying skills of even a trained scrivener, as he reveals in his excoriation of his own scribe in "Words to Adam, His Own Scribe," included here among his Short Poems. Errors introduced because of manual copying were only the beginning, however, as Chaucer also recognized, for English in the late fourteenth century was far from a standardized language, and change could be introduced even as a poem was "translated" from one regional dialect of English to another. As Chaucer writes fearfully of his great historical romance *Troilus and Criseyde*, "And for ther is so gret diversite / In Englissh and in writyng of oure tonge, / So prey I God that non myswrite the, / Ne the mysmetre for defaute of tonge" ("And because there is so much variation / in English and in the way our language is written / therefore I pray God that no-one make mistakes in writing you / Nor foul up your meter due to [their] linguistic deficiency"; 5.1793–96). But variation was not limited to translation from one dialect to another. Such "miswriting" and "mis-metering" occurred also because of changes in the spelling system, as inflectional endings were lost during the late fourteenth and the fifteenth centuries, and as writers increasingly adopted the comparatively standardized spelling of administrative documents, known as "Chancery English." Patterns of immigration into London also liberalized the forms that were used there, and for much of the late fourteenth century "standard English" in London allowed for an unusual amount of that "diversity" of which Chaucer complains, making it nigh upon impossible for a modern editor to determine Chaucer's original spellings and sometimes word forms.

Again, this problem of reconstruction is more acute for Chaucer's minor poetry than for his major works, the *Canterbury Tales* and *Troilus and*

---

7. These problems are explored by Norman F. Blake, in "The Textual Tradition of *The Book of the Duchess*," *English Studies* 62 (1981): 237–48.

Criseyde, as the surviving manuscripts are appreciably further in time from the author's originals, which he wrote, for the most part, in the early part of his career—the 1360s–1380s. Moreover, for all his brilliance, the Chaucer of the dream visions is in some ways an inexperienced, apprentice-poet, just developing the metrical repertoire that would carry him through the *Troilus* and the *Tales*. Not only is his meter likely more irregular than it would be later (whether from inexperience or as he experimented with novel metrical approaches to the four-beat line that he favored in some of his earliest poems); he is also more prone to reach back for a rhyme to archaic or remote forms. For example, he uses a Northern verb ending "es" to produce the rhyme "telles / elles" in lines 73–74 of the *Book of the Duchess*; the more standard form in London English, which he would adopt consistently in his later poetry, is "eth."[8] In general, therefore, Chaucer's spelling and metrical practices are less predictable and harder to reconstruct in the early poems than in the later ones. On the one hand, an editor wishes to present the reader with a text that conforms to manuscript evidence; on the other hand, the manuscript evidence, in this case, is certain to generate spellings and forms that are unChaucerian.

This Norton Critical Edition offers a compromise by restoring some of the most obvious fourteenth-century forms, while remaining as true as possible to the substantive readings in the manuscripts. At the same time, while restoring spellings, I have no illusion that I am able to reproduce the specific repertoire of Chaucer's forms and spellings. I have lightly regularized these so that the inexperienced reader will not have to confront the extreme variability of medieval spelling. Although somewhat unusual, this policy is not fundamentally at odds with modern editorial practice. Virtually all modern editions of Chaucer, including my nineteenth-century copy-text, make many concessions to a normalized modern English, for example, by excising archaic orthography, distinguishing between i/j and u/v according to modern practice, and introducing modern customs of punctuation and capitalization. While I have punctuated this edition less heavily than my copy-text (in accord with the lack of punctuation in the manuscripts), I have accordingly retained and extended Skeat's normalization of spelling. For clarity, I have also kept his hyphen after the y-prefix before past participles.

Even so, consistency itself is not an entirely Chaucerian quality. Neither Chaucer nor any of his contemporaries had a stable, fixed system of spelling, of the kind a modern reader has come to expect. For all his complaints about the diversity of his language, Chaucer takes advantage of this feature, as I have noted, to produce rhymes that might only be possible in one regional dialect, but not in another. Scribes often underscored these rhymes by spelling them alike, making them "eye" as well as "sound" rhymes; this is a practice that I also have followed even when it has yielded a spelling that is different from other instances of the same word. In sum, decisions about a specific spelling amount, as always, to an act of editorial judgment; I have exercised such judgment in an effort to balance historical plausibility with the needs of the modern reader, for whom a consistent spelling system is a real convenience. The result, I hope, is a text that,

---

8. The example is provided by Simon Horobin, *The Language of the Chaucer Tradition* (Cambridge: D. S. Brewer, 2003), 29. This book is an excellent resource for the student who wants to learn more about Chaucer's linguistic background and the state of current research.

while it may not match any single manuscript, represents a version that Chaucer and his readers would themselves have recognized and one that incorporates the best substantive readings available.

The second section of this Norton Critical Edition provides many of Chaucer's "Contexts." I might have called these texts "Backgrounds," but for a quibble discussed below. This section begins with the imaginative and speculative opening of Ruth Evans's essay "Chaucer in Cyberspace" (2003), which presents a fantasy version of Chaucer sitting at his computer, windows open on his screen to the myriad of texts that he would be drawing on as he created his own phantasmagoric mnemonic palace, the "House of Fame." My hope is that this picture itself reminds readers of both the differences and similarities between the textual culture of the Middle Ages and our own. Although Chaucer of course had no computer, he virtually (in all senses of that word) lived in a world of competing authorities, which he knew intimately and struggled to represent and reconcile in his art. They were as present to him in his memory as sources on the Internet are to the modern student.

This reminder should help make more immediate the relevance of the "backgrounds" that follow; these are not the spaces that stand *behind* Chaucer's art, the "background" against which his real interests are by contrast represented. Chaucer's sources—Cicero, Virgil, Boethius, Dante, Boccaccio, and others—are in a very important way the central subjects of his dream poems; their insights, confusions, and disagreements the very objects that he was trying to come to grips with in his art. In his Prologue to the *Legend of Good Women*, Chaucer raises concerns about knowledge and authority: "What do we know of heaven or hell?" he asks provocatively; "nothing" by direct experience. We must, as he says, resort "to bookes [where] we finde / . . . olde thinges [that] been in minde" (17–18). Books, however, are subject to various and competing interpretations. In large part, then, Chaucer's dream visions represent an attempt to sort these out, giving special urgency to the written authorities that shaped his imagination. The interpretation of Aeneas's desertion of Dido offered by Ovid, excerpted here from the *Heroides*, is quite different from Virgil's explanation of Aeneas's dilemma in Book 4 of the *Aeneid*, also included. These are essential contexts for understanding both the *Legend of Good Women* and the *House of Fame*, where Chaucer rehearses that story from multiple perspectives.

In short, the Contexts section "teaches the conflicts" medieval-style. "Criticism," the third section, teaches the modern conflicts, for here we move forward to modern authorities on Chaucer who are themselves often in disagreement in ways that I think would have both surprised and delighted Chaucer. This part of the volume begins with a chapter from Charles Muscatine's groundbreaking study *Chaucer and the French Tradition* (1957), which puts some of the poet's sources themselves into context by analyzing the poet's characteristic turn to comic realism as he adapted the style of French and Italian contemporaries to an English idiom. In the next excerpt, the discussion of the *Parliament of Fowls* from A. C. Spearing's influential study *Medieval Dream-Poetry* (1976), the critical field of reference is expanded further, freeing Chaucer to move beyond the category of the literary to converse with the ancients on topics as varied as the nature of dreams to the order of society. As Spearing suggests,

Chaucer's concern with the relationship between nature and culture in the *Parliament of Fowls* is one of universal importance, encompassing even the insights of modern anthropology. At the same time, it is easy to forget that Chaucer, for all of his imaginative and intellectual freedom, exercised his poetic talent within the social constraints of a specific court setting, as R. T. Lenaghan reminds us in the third excerpt, "Chaucer's Circle of Gentlemen and Clerks" (1983). Lenaghan discusses Chaucer's relationship to his audience and his sophisticated narrative voice, as the poet negotiates social and political distance in some of his short, lyric pieces.

The next two essays—Richard Firth Green's "Chaucer's Victimized Women" (1988) and Elaine Tuttle Hansen's "The Feminization of Men in Chaucer's *Legend of Good Women*" (1989)—are imagined as a pair, taking opposed sides in the modern critical controversy over whether or not Chaucer intended the *Legend of Good Women* to be construed literally or ironically. Green argues eloquently from contemporary evidence that Chaucer straightforwardly resists the medieval double standard that cynically turned a blind eye to male duplicity as long as the victim was female. Just as powerfully, Hansen maintains that Chaucer's sympathy for the ladies in the poem is ironic and that his real interest lies in establishing a bond between men that reinforces their masculinity. Interestingly, while both Green and Hansen draw upon modern gender criticism, it is the male critic who focuses on and defends womanhood and the female critic whose interest lies in definitions of manhood. My hope is that these two essays will lead to interesting classroom discussion and student writing opportunities. The final piece of criticism is Steven Kruger's "Medical and Moral Authority in the Late Medieval Dream" (1999), an essay that focuses on philosophical and scientific theories of dreaming as they apply to the *Book of the Duchess*, ultimately connecting these again to the morbid and feminine passivity of the dreaming narrator in this poem. Kruger's essay thus links up with Hansen's by providing a different kind of gloss on the feminized male in Chaucer's poetry.

Both Spearing's and Kruger's contributions also place Chaucer's dream poetry within the important medieval genre of the "dream vision," perhaps the most popular literary form of the Middle Ages and one at which virtually every serious poet tested his hand. Perhaps the best known as well as the most complex and ambitious dream vision of the medieval period is Dante's *Divine Comedy*, a poem that Chaucer clearly admired and imitated. Most simply, a dream vision is a literary text that recounts a narrator's experience of a dream or even a waking vision. But there were many different subgenres of the form during the thousand years of its popularity. The Boethian or "philosophical" vision, for example, based on a work that Chaucer translated—the *Consolation of Philosophy* by the late classical writer Boethius—confronted a grieving or confused narrator with an allegorical figure able to guide him out of his troubles. In contrast the love vision, a form popular with many of Chaucer's contemporaries, for example the French master of the form Guillaume de Machaut,[9] typically explored a love problem or situation without an obvious solution. The rhetorical purposes of the Boethian form—philosophical instruction and moral

9. Selections from Dante's *Divine Comedy*, Boethius's *Consolation of Philosophy*, and Guillaume de Machaut's *Fountain of Love* are included in this Norton Critical Edition in the Contexts section.

improvement—are thus in many ways incompatible with the courtly desire to entertain that characterizes the love vision.

Yet in the hands of a skilled writer like Chaucer, the two subgenres could be combined into a complex and pleasing new creation. Chaucer's most important early poems—the *Book of the Duchess*, the *House of Fame*, the *Parliament of Fowls*, and the Prologue to the *Legend of Good Women* are all classic dream visions, but Chaucer worked within the form with considerable flexibility and independence. Not only did he marry the love vision to the Boethian or "philosophical" vision; he also brought an unusually light and often comical sensibility to the presentation of the narrator, and introduced a number of innovations that would influence his own fifteenth-century imitators—for example, a more elaborate frame before the dream section of the poem in which the narrator reads a related story before falling asleep. As the work by Spearing and Kruger also shows, Chaucer was able to build features of dream psychology itself, especially the conjunction of dream and imagination, into the visionary structure of his poetry.

In the last fifty years, there has been a great deal of excellent and thought-provoking modern commentary on Chaucer's dream visions and shorter poems, very little of which can be accommodated in any specific collection. I have tried to select criticism spread across several decades in order to give the reader a sense of the evolution of scholarly inquiry, which has taken a variety of approaches, from New Critical (close reading) to (New) Historical, to gender theory. In these essays, the reader can see the relationship of Chaucer's poetry to a range of influences, from French love poetry, to classical and Christian philosophy and science, to contemporary court culture. I also have chosen writings that focus on different texts, so that the reader should be able to find some discussion, usually by more than one writer, about each one of the major texts presented here. Muscatine discusses the *Book of the Duchess*, the *House of Fame*, and the *Parliament of Fowls*; Spearing the *Parliament of Fowls*; Lenaghan several of the short lyrics; Hansen and Green the *Legend of Good Women* (with Green also alluding to "Anelida and Arcite" and the *House of Fame*); Kruger the *Book of the Duchess*; and Evans the *House of Fame*. Space limitations prevent me from including criticism that touches on every part of each text presented here or on all of the individual shorter lyrics. The Prologue to the *Legend of Good Women*, especially, has been a source of great critical controversy, as readers cannot even agree which of two versions of the Prologue has greater authority; although I summarize some of the issues in my introduction to that poem, unfortunately there was not space to represent the controversies in the Criticism section. The reader who wishes to go further is invited to consult the section of the Selected Bibliography devoted to the *Legend*.

Chaucer's "minor poems" are indeed dwarfed by the monumental accomplishments of the *Canterbury Tales* and *Troilus and Criseyde*. But these early poems have their own interest too, which goes beyond their foreshadowing of those later Chaucerian achievements. The pieces included here reflect their medieval origins in their use of traditional forms, but simultaneously they are highly experimental. In these poems, one sees used, for the first time in English, major metrical forms, like an early version of iambic pentameter, and stylistic devices, like fast-paced dialogue, autobiographical asides, or the familiar ironic, self-deprecating Chaucerian narrator, predecessor of the unreliable narrator of the modern novel. The profound medievalism of Chaucer's poetry offers a glimpse of an earlier and much different world, but one that is seen through the eyes of an intelligent and detached persona who seems uncannily modern. In the dream visions and other poems, for example, we find many issues that still have relevance—the difficulty of accepting the finality of death, the vagaries of fame, the war between the sexes, the class issues involved in choosing a spouse, even the problem of getting by on one's pension—but reflected through a range of traditional poetic genres that were popular over six hundred years ago. These poems thus mediate between past and present and offer us entry to a world that seems at once forbiddingly distant and hauntingly present.

My thanks go to many helpers in the making of this Norton Critical Edition. The list must begin with the teacher who first introduced me to Chaucer, V. A. Kolve, whose lucid and elegant instruction provided an indispensable framework for understanding and a model of teaching I can emulate but never achieve. It must also include the wonderful Wellesley College students who have inspired me in my classroom over the years, and without whose curiosity and common sense I would not have known where to begin in choosing supplementary texts or in glossing Chaucer's language. Several student research assistants have additionally given me particular assistance at various stages in the preparation of this book: Jessica Mankus, Bijou Mgbojikwe, Simran Thadani, Adrienne Odasso, and Taline Boghosian. My thanks also go to the kind and capable staff at W. W. Norton, especially Carol Bemis and Brian Baker, and to the authors, translators, and publishers who so graciously allowed their work to be reprinted. I am grateful also to the patience of my family, especially to the trinity of father, husband, and youngest son, who have shared their domestic space with Chaucer more than was comfortable, but with hospitality and good cheer worthy of their guest.

A Quick Course in Chaucer's Language

Middle English in Historical Context

The history of the English language is conventionally divided into three periods. The first, "Old English" (or "Anglo-Saxon"), is the language of *Beowulf,* covering the period of English up to about 1100. The second, "Middle English," is the language of Chaucer, and extends to about 1500. English after 1500 is generally referred to as "Modern English." Just as the writing of John Updike or Toni Morrison is radically different from the writing of Shakespeare, Middle English evolved significantly over its four-hundred-year history. It was also spoken in a number of different regional dialects that could likewise diverge as dramatically from each other as the English of the British Isles today differs from that spoken in the United States or Australia. Chaucer wrote in the language of London, which itself evolved into standard English as we know it, making his poetry easier for modern readers than the Middle English that originated in other parts of England like the Northern or Midlands regions.

There are nonetheless many fascinating and complex grammatical and phonological differences between and within each of the three broad historical periods in the English language. A student wishing to learn more about these can consult the sources listed in the section on "Language, Recordings, and Editing," in the Selected Bibliography at the end of this Norton Critical Edition. Indeed, it is my hope that acquaintance with the beauty of Chaucer's poetry will spark the interest of students, prompting them to go further in studying the language in which his poems were written. The standard editions of Chaucer's complete works, such as the *Riverside* or others listed in the Selected Bibliography, also include useful introductions to Chaucer's Middle English. This Norton Critical Edition does not attempt to duplicate these more comprehensive treatments, and the information offered in this "quick course" should not be mistaken for full understanding.

Fortunately, though, unlike Old English (which is truly a foreign language to the speaker of Modern English), Middle English can be understood without comprehensive grammatical instruction. The extensive glossing in this edition should reduce the immediate need for such instruction; the reader will quickly pick up such differences as are found, for example, in the pronoun system (where one pronoun "hir(e)" does double duty for both "her" and "their" and "his" for "his" and "its"). A few additional tips to help get started: Middle English word order can be a little tricky, for the object precedes the verb much more frequently than in Modern English, or the verb may be separated from the subject by other kinds of modifying phrases (as in line 95 of the *Book of the Duchess*—"Such sorrow this lady to herself took"). Several rules of Modern English do not apply to Middle English. Verb tense, for example, is often inconsistent. Also, rather than canceling itself out, the double negative has the rhetorical effect of intensification; for example, *Legend of Good Women* 5–8—"ther nis noon dwelling in this contree / that either hath in heven or helle y-be"—would be translated in modern English "there is nobody who dwells in this country / who has been in hell or heaven" rather than literally "there is not nobody. . . ." The lack of modern punctuation in medieval manuscripts should also be kept in mind, as phrases and clauses frequently refer forward as well as backward in a much more flexible construction of meaning than we are accustomed to in Modern English texts.

Pronunciation of Vowels and Consonants

Even a student reading silently should be trying to "hear" the poetry in Chaucer's verse. Otherwise, the experience of Chaucer will be regrettably incomplete. Reading Chaucer aloud does require a little special training. While a full appreciation of the differences between the sounds of Modern and Middle English is a matter for years of study, the beginning reader willing to make a small investment of time can make a start without too much difficulty. The biggest difference between the sound system of Modern English and that of Middle English comes in the vowels, for over the course of the fifteenth century a linguistic event known as "The Great Vowel Shift" gradually but profoundly altered the value of the "long vowels" in English. Because the long vowels shifted their value in a systematic way, we can approximate Chaucer's original pronunciation by working "backward" from the long vowel sounds of Modern English to reconstruct their predecessors in Middle English. Happily, since most of the "short vowels" did not change significantly, there are a relatively limited number of sound changes that the modern reader needs to master.

Most Middle English consonants also are not considerably different from those in Modern English. Notably, however, consonants that are silent in Modern English *were* pronounced in Middle English, with the exception of the "gn" in French loan words. Thus, in the word "know," the "k" sound is pronounced in Middle English, but in the word "sign," the "g" sound is nasalized as in French but not pronounced. Also silent in French loan words, and in some common short Middle English words, is initial "h," as in "honour" or "his." In contrast, the consonant combination "gh" *is* pronounced as a guttural similar to the German "ich" (there is no Modern English equivalent), and the Middle English "r" is trilled. Also pronounced in Middle English was the final "e" (pronounced "uh" as in the first and last syllables of "America," and called by linguists a "schwa") at the end of a line of poetry or when needed for meter. A final "e" is generally required by the meter as an unstressed syllable to complete an iambic foot. For example, in line 4 of the *Parliament of Fowls*, transcribed below, a final "e" would not be required in the words "mene" or "Love," because the regular ten-syllable line of iambic pentameter is complete without additional syllables; nor would a final "e" be required at the end of this line, where it is not written in the word "feling." In contrast, in the first line of the *Legend of Good Women* ("A thousand tymes have I herd men telle"), the "e" in "tymes" *would* be pronounced, to fill out the meter, as would the final "e" as written at the end of the line.

Table of Sound Changes

In the interests of simplicity, I have listed in the table below *only* those vowels that differ significantly between Middle and Modern English. For convenience, I have also included diphthongs (vowel sounds that glide between two different values). Unlike most such charts, this one puts Modern English on the left side, so that the student can work back from the speech values that he or she already knows. This table should be viewed as a study aid. It does not pretend to cover all the finer nuances of Middle English pronunciation. Again, the reader is directed to the sources in the Selected Bibliography at the end of this Norton Critical Edition. Especially useful are recordings of professional scholars reading Chaucer aloud, like those produced by The Chaucer Studio (and included in the Selected Bibliography).

Vowel Sound Changes, Working "Backward" from Modern to Middle English

Modern English Sound	Modern English Spelling	Middle English Spelling	Middle English Sound
a, as in "cat," "after"	a	a	"not," "hot" (American)
a, as in "fame," "wake"	a	a,[aa]	"fall," "father"
a, as in "day," "they"	ai, ay, ei, ey	ai, ay, ei, ey	between "day" and "die"
aw, as in "law," "cause"	au, aw	au, aw	"house," "town"
e, as in "sweet"	e, ee, ie	e, e, [ie]	"wake," "break"
i, as in "I," "tile"	i, y	i, y	"feet," "be"
o, as in "loan," "go"	o, oa	o, oo	"trod," "saw"
o, as in "do," "boot"	o, oo	o, oo	"doe," "boat"
ow, as in "how," "round"	ou, ow	ou, ow	"too," "moon"

In addition to the major changes listed above, several more subtle changes and features should be noted and observed when possible. In general, even the short vowels in Middle English are slightly more open than those in Modern English, so that the word "but" rhymes with "put" (as opposed to "putt") and the word "tongue" rhymes with "song." Middle English is also influenced more strongly than Modern English by the

French "u," as in recent loan-words like "vertu." "U" is also lightly pronounced in some "eu," "ew" glides (e.g., "fewe," "lewed," "shewe," and "shrewe") and "ou," "ow" (in words that do not have the Modern English "ow" sound). Bracketed spellings in the table are those not represented in this edition.

Opening Verse of the *Parliament of Fowls* Represented Phonetically

This phonetic transcription follows the verse in its original spelling. Spellings in the transcription are designed to approximate Modern American Pronunciation while avoiding the International Phonetic alphabet as unfamiliar to many students; the result should be a rough approximation of Middle English. This exercise is meant to get a student started quickly with the important experience of feeling the language in mouth and ear, not to replace listening to tapes and studying other sources to improve language performance. The "o" in the words "so" and "sore" should be slightly relaxed, between Modern English "so" and "saw"; italicized "r" is a reminder to trill. Through the following online link to Francis De Vries reading this verse for the Chaucer Studio, a student can find a quick point of reference and comparison: <http://english.byu.edu/chaucer/early.htm.>

> The lyf so short, the craft so long to lerne,
> Th'assay so hard, so sharp the conquering,
> The dredful joy alwey that slit so yerne,
> Al this mene I by Love, that my feling
> Astonyeth with his wonderful werkyng
> So sore ywis that whan I on him thinke
> Nat wot I wel wher that I flete or sinke.

> The leef so shorrt, the crroft so long toe lerrn-uh,
> Thassaiy so harrd, so sharrp the konkwerring,
> The drredful joy alwaiy thot slit so yerrn-uh,
> Al this main Ee bee Lov, thot mee failing
> Astonyeth with is wonderrful werrking
> So sorr ee-wiss thot whan Ee on im think-uh
> Not wot Ee wel wherr thot Ee flait or sink-uh.

The Texts of
DREAM VISIONS
AND OTHER POEMS

The Book of the Duchess

The *Book of the Duchess* occupies an important position at the head of Chaucer's poetic canon. His earliest significant narrative poem, it bears marks of the poet's youth and inexperience—in its comparatively ragged meter, for instance, and in its sometimes jarring mixture of courtly and comical themes—but at the same time it is a poem of undeniable emotional power, which skillfully draws upon classical sources and medieval French models. Although Chaucer does not present himself as a known poet at court, as he would in his later works, his narrative *persona*—untutored, self-deprecating, even foolish—is fully realized and consistent. He moves within the conventional form of the dream vision with the confidence and originality of a master poet. Chaucer innovates within the form by having his narrator fall asleep over a classical story that itself contains a dream that foreshadows the one he is about to experience. Then, like a series of cleverly constructed Chinese boxes, the black knight's story of his lady's loss nestles inside a parallel narrative of a h(e)art hunt, which rests within the dreamer's untold story of his mysterious affliction. The complexity of the poem's form is in meaningful tension with the simplicity of its message: death is final, and the grief it causes unspeakable.

These features are remarkable considering the likely early date of the *Book of the Duchess*. Of all Chaucer's poems, it is the one most securely linked to a specific occasion, the death of John of Gaunt's wife, Blanche of Lancaster, from the plague on September 12, 1368.[1] Although early editions titled the poem "The Dreame of Chaucer," in the Prologue to the *Legend of Good Women* (418), the poet himself calls it "the Deeth of Blaunche the Duchesse." Blanche is thus clearly the identity of the lady "Whyte," described at length by the man in black within the poem. More word play confirms this identification later, when we are told that a king rides, at the conclusion of a hunt, to "a longe castel with walles whyte, / By Seynt Johan, on a riche hille" (1318–19). Critics agree that John is here identified as John of Gaunt, Earl of Richmond ("riche mont" is French for "riche hille") and Duke of Lancaster (imaginatively derived from "longe castel"). These references have implications, of course, for the poem's date. Since the *Book of the Duchess* commemorates Blanche after her death, it cannot have been written earlier than 1368, and most scholars believe that it is unlikely to have been written after 1372, when Gaunt would no longer have held the title Earl of Richmond, though there is less than unanimous agreement about this second date. An early date is also suggested by the fact that the poem is written in a four-beat line, rather than the five-beat line Chaucer favored in his later verse. At all events, the poem was most likely written when Chaucer was a relatively young and untested poet, probably just in his mid twenties. His patron, John of Gaunt, would also have been a young man, only twenty-eight at the time of his wife's death.

The young poet took on a difficult and ambitious theme. Death is hard to to accept at any point in life; the death of a young person is especially painful, and even though the Middle Ages was a time of political marriages among the

---

1. J. J. N. Palmer, "The Historical Context of the *Book of the Duchess*," *The Chaucer Review* 8 (1974): 253–61.

3

nobility, nothing suggests that John of Gaunt did not care deeply about his lovely young wife. Two marriages later, one a union of deep affection to Chaucer's own sister-in-law, Katherine Swynford, Gaunt still specified, in the burial instructions that formed part of his will, his wish that he be laid to rest beside his "most dear late wife Blanche."[2] But Blanche not only died young; she fell to a frightening and gruesome disease. The plague that swept through Europe in the late fourteenth century, wiping out one third of its population, brought mortality in an especially terrifying form. Consolation must have been hard to formulate. Furthermore, in presuming to offer comfort to the highly placed John of Gaunt, son of Edward III and a man later acknowledged as the most powerful political force in England, Chaucer, a comparative nobody at court, set himself a particularly challenging task. The human side of the *Book of the Duchess* is thus important to keep in mind. Far from a sterile exercise, the poem weaves its art from threads of real life and death.

It is easy to forget this important point, because the *Book of the Duchess* is also a highly literary and conventional piece. In it, Chaucer reaches back to the canonical works of the Latin past, like Ovid's *Metamorphoses* and Virgil's *Aeneid*. These he recasts in a dream vision form popularized by some of the greatest European poets of the Middle Ages, especially in the French tradition. The narrator's dream is literally refracted through this double lens as he awakens inside his dream to find the sun streaming down upon him through stained glass images of the story of Troy and the widely known thirteenth-century French dream vision the *Romance of the Rose*, representing the universal literary themes of war and love. Less directly, Chaucer pays homage to a French writer from the generation just ahead of him, Guillaume de Machaut (ca. 1300–1377), whose *dits amoureux* (tales of love, sometimes cast in visionary form) the *Judgment of the King of Bohemia, Fortune's Remedy*, and the *Fountain of Love* deeply inform its structure, language, and imagery.[3]

In addition to being a poem of great literary sophistication, the *Book of the Duchess* draws on other texts and fields of learning as well: Aristotelian epistemology, Boethian philosophy, the dream theory of Macrobius,[4] medical practice and physiology derived from Galen and Hippocrates, the Bible, and the rules of chess. But all this erudition is easy to miss in the presence of a narrator as artfully obtuse as the one here. His dream experience progresses as a series of misreadings, beginning with his interpretation of his bedtime story, Ovid's tale of Ceyx (the Chaucerian Seys) and Alcyone, as a prophylactic against insomnia and continuing through his literalization of the chess allegory used by the grieving man of black, whom he enounters in a lush dream landscape, to convey the loss of his queen to the goddess Fortune. "What are you so upset about?" exclaims the dreamer; "no sane person would wax suicidal over the loss of a few chess pieces" (721 ff.)! But if the dreamer is guilty of over-literalizing in these cases, at other times he seems unable to grasp even the most tangible and obviously stated truth. The first words, for example, that he hears out of the mysterious black knight's mouth are lamentations over the loss of his "lady bright" who is "fro me deed" (477, 479). Nonetheless, as the man in black repeatedly observes, the dreamer's subsequent conversation shows that he knows little about the nature of the knight's loss, which is far greater than the dreamer understands it to be (743–44, 1137–38, 1305–06).

The dreamer's slowness creates the narrative space that permits the knight to rehearse the history of his relationship with the lady Whyte and to celebrate

---

2. Sydney Armitage-Smith, *John of Gaunt* (New York: Barnes and Noble, 1964), 78; also 420.
3. Of the works listed in this paragraph, relevant sections from Ovid's *Metamorphoses* (the story of Ceyx and Alcyone), the *Romance of the Rose*, and Machaut's *Fountain of Love* are included in the Contexts section of this Norton Critical Edition.
4. Selections from Boethius's *Consolation of Philosophy* and Macrobius's *Commentary on the Dream of Scipio* are included in the Contexts section.

and finally to commemorate her physical and moral beauty. The catharsis comes near the end of the poem, in lines 1309–10, when the knight is pressed to acknowledge his loss without art or equivocation—"She is deed"—and the dreamer to produce the only comfort possible in such circumstances, a simple expression of fellow feeling—"By God, it is routhe [pitiable]." To grant this much, however, is only to approach the mystery at the center of the poem; it is not to solve it. Readers continue to disagree about the extent and intent of the dreamer's clumsiness. Does he merely pretend to ignorance as a strategy for drawing out the ailing knight? Is he offering, as perhaps lines 553–54 might suggest (". . . to make yow hool / I wol do al my power hool . . ."), an opportunity for a talking cure? Or, alternatively, are we meant to take the dreamer's obtuseness straight? Is the bumbling dreamer perhaps Chaucer's vehicle for tactfully expressing comfort and counsel to his noble patron?

A related question is just how comforting the message of the poem truly would have been. Notably absent from the world of "Kynde" or nature that the poet describes is any mention of the Christian afterlife, leading some readers to speculate that Chaucer remains critical of the response of both the dreamer and the man in black to the lady's death. The dreamer's exclamation of pity seems to these and other readers insufficient to the enormity of the loss described in the poem. Are either or both of these two characters ultimately seen as lacking, spiritually, morally, or socially? Or is the slippage in the poem a feature of the poet's own artistic immaturity? Perhaps he had not yet learned how to harmonize such comic moments as the awakening of Morpheus in the cave of sleep with the serious themes of love and death; there are many such odd disjunctions in the poem, extending even to its bathetic final line: "This was my sweven [dream]; now it is doon" (1334). With his promise to put his curious dream into rhyme (1330–33), the narrator returns us to the poem's opening, but without having resolved any of the key questions raised there or having indicated whether the dreamer has made progress in addressing his lassitude and insomnia. As with any great but imperfect poem, part of the delight in reading the Book of the Duchess lies in exploring such unanswerable questions. Even the cause of that lassitude—the narrator's cryptic eight-year sickness—ultimately remains obscure.

Recent readers have extended critical inquiry to the poem's celebration of the beautiful lady Whyte and its commitment to the feminine values she represents. In a poem whose ostensible purpose is to eulogize a woman, real women are notably absent. Whyte herself remains something of a cipher, beautiful, elusive, difficult to interpret; for all her presence in the poem, it is her absence that remains significant. Recollected and interpreted by others, the only word she actually utters is the one-word negative, "Nay" (1243), and even that is reported speech. Her abstract beauty is balanced by the equally stereotyped treachery of the goddess Fortuna, who embodies the wiliness and faithlessness commonly associated with women in medieval misogynist literature. It is a decidedly negative view of woman barely kept at bay here by the praise of the knight's lost lady, who often seems good only because she does not engage in the "knakkes smale" ("petty tricks") that come so easily to other craftier females. Although the dreamer's Ovidian bedtime story suggests through the character of Alcyone that a woman's sorrow and desire can be as urgent and deeply felt as a man's, Alcyone, like Whyte, dies, and the relationship that finally takes over the poem is the one between the two men, the dreamer and the man in black. The realm of the female, ostensibly the poem's subject, is all but effaced. One might even say, as Steven Kruger does in an essay included here in the Contexts section, that the poem is not just about men but about masculinity.[5] To the extent that the dreamer is passive, mel-

5. "Medical and Moral Authority in the Late Medieval Dream," in Reading Dreams: The Interpretation

ancholic, confined to his bedchamber, he is feminized and in need of correction. His dream gives him access to a naturalized, courtly world where he can again take charge as a man helping a friend come to terms with the loss of his wife. Thus, the ambivalent attitude toward women so pervasive in Chaucer's later work—for example, in the *Legend of Good Women*—emerges even here, in his first major poem.

To some extent that ambivalence is inevitable; it is a feature of Chaucer's time period and of the language available to him to describe the relationship between the sexes. The very form in which he worked—the philosophical dream vision—carried assumptions about the right subordination of imaginative and bodily experience to a unitary spiritual truth that was bound to work ultimately against an over-valuation of romantic love. The ultimate prototype of this kind of poem was the *Consolation of Philosophy* by the late classical philosopher Boethius, in which the allegorical figure of Lady Philosophy comes to the suffering writer, imprisoned and victimized by political persecution, to banish from his soul any attachment to the capricious world of Fortune. Compared to many other medieval poems that similarly worked within the Boethian tradition, the *Book of the Duchess* finally demonstrates an admirable originality and independence in its use of the form. Although framed within a very specific aristocratic world with values much different from our own, it is not only a humanist poem, but a human one. For in this poem, no figure of Philosophy (or as she is styled in other texts, Reason or Nature) comes to guide the dreamer out of his quandary or to explain to the black knight why he should give up his grief. Instead, with uncommon poignancy, two mortal men struggle to find a way to console each other. Their communication at once dignifies poetic tradition and exposes its limitation—its silence in the face of Fortune's ultimate weapon and the final blow that Nature has in store for all her creatures.

The text here is based chiefly on the version found in the Fairfax manuscript (Fairfax 16, Bodleian Library).

The Book of the Duchess

I have gret wonder, by this light°	daylight *(a mild oath)*
How that I live,° for day ne night	*stay alive*
I may nat° slepe wel nigh nought,°	*cannot / nearly at all*
I have so many an ydel° thought	*pointless, meaningless*
5 Purely° for defaute° of slepe	*Simply / lack*
That, by my trouthe,° I take no kepe°	*honestly / do not care*
Of nothing,° how it cometh or goth,°	*about anything / comes or goes*
Ne me nis nothing leef nor loth.	
Al is yliche good to me,[1]	
10 Joye or sorwe,° wherso it be,°	*sorrow / whichever it may be*
For I have feling in° nothinge,	*emotions about*
But as it° were a mased° thing	*(I) am like / dazed*

---

of Dreams from Chaucer to Shakespeare, ed Peter Brown (Oxford: Oxford UP, 1999), 51–83; a similar discussion of feminization and male homosocial relationships, though not in the *Book of the Duchess*, is also offered by Elaine Tuttle Hansen in another essay in the Contexts section: "The Feminization of Men in Chaucer's *Legend of Good Women*," in *Seeking the Woman in Late Medieval and Renaissance Writings: Essays in Feminist Contextual Criticism*, ed. Sheila Fisher and Janet E. Halley (Knoxville: U of Tennessee P, 1989), 51–70; Hansen specifically discusses the *Book of the Duchess* in *Chaucer and the Fictions of Gender* (Berkeley: U of California P, 1992), 58–86.

1. Nor is anything pleasing or displeasing to me. Everything is equally desirable to me (that is, I am without desire for any of it).

Alwey in point to° falle adoun,   *about to*
For sorwful imaginacioun
15 Is alwey hooly in my minde.[2]
    And wel ye wote,° ageynes kynde°   *know / against nature*
It were to liven in this wyse,°   *manner*
For nature wolde nat suffyse°   *permit*
To noon erthely° creature   *any earthly*
20 Nat longe tyme to endure
Withoute slepe and be in sorwe;°   *(so much) sorrow*
And I ne may,° ne night ne morwe,°   *cannot / morning*
Slepe, and thus melancolye[3]
And drede° I have for to dye;°   *fear / die*
25 Defaute° of slepe and hevinesse°   *Lack / dullness, dejection*
Hath slayn° my spirit of quiknesse,°   *Have deprived / liveliness*
That° I have lost al lustihede.°   *So that / enjoyment (of life)*
Swiche° fantasies ben° in myn hede   *Such / are*
So° I noot° what is best to do.   *That / do not know*
30   But men myght axe° me, why so   *ask*
I may nat slepe, and what me is?[4]
But natheles,° who aske° this   *nevertheless / whoever asks*
Leseth° his asking° trewely.   *Gains nothing from / question*
Myselven° can nat telle why   *I myself*
35 The sooth,° but trewely as I gesse,°   *In truth / guess*
I holde it be° a siknesse°   *to be / sickness*
That I have suffred this eight yere,°   *for eight years*
And yet my bote° is never the nere;°   *cure / no nearer*
For ther is phisicien but oon,°   *only one*
40 That may me hele,° but that is doon.° *heal / over and done with*
Passe we over until efte;
That wil nat be, mot nede be lefte;
Our first matere is good to kepe.[5]
    So whan I saw I might nat slepe
45 Til now late this other night,°   *just the other night*
Upon my bedde I sat upright
And bad oon recche° me a booke,   *someone fetch*
A romaunce,[6] and he it me tooke°   *brought*
To rede and dryve the night awey,°   *pass the time*
50 For me thoughte it better pley

2. For sorrowful imagination entirely dominates my mind. (The imagination was a specific faculty in the mind in classical and medieval psychology, responsible for processing the images perceived in daily life and for producing the images seen in dreams; these images are also called "phantasms" or "phantasies"—see line 28.)
3. In medieval physiology, the emotional state of sorrow and anxiety brought on by an excess of the natural humor of black bile. Melancholy could produce a disordered imagination.
4. I cannot sleep, and what is the matter? (Lines 31–96 are not found in any of the three surviving manuscripts of the poem; they first appear in the 1532 edition of William Thynne. For additional discussion, see the Preface of this Norton Critical Edition.)
5. Let's skip over (that part) until later; that which will never be must be left behind. Better to stick to our original topic. (This cryptic passage has excited many different interpretations. What is the poet's mysterious eight-year illness? Is he lovesick, or is his malady moral or spiritual in nature? He promises to return to the subject "eft" [i.e., at another time], but never does explain the cause of his melancholy.)
6. The original of the book that the narrator takes up to read here is Ovid's *Metamorphoses* (11.411–748), but the generic term "romance" would be more appropriate to Guillaume de Machaut's *Fountain of Love*, which also recounts the story of Ceyx and Alcyone (544–698). Both sources are included in the Contexts section of this Norton Critical Edition.

Than pleyen either at chesse or tables.[7]
And in this book were wryten fables°   *fictional stories*
That clerkes° hadde, in olde tyme,   *scholars, writers*
And other poets, put in ryme°   *rhyme*
55   To rede and for to be in minde°   *preserve for memory*
Whyl° men loved the lawe of kinde.[8]   *A time when*
This book ne spake but° of swiche° thinges,   *spoke only / such*
Of quenes lyves and of kinges
And many othere thinges smale.°   *of little importance*
60   Amonge al this I fonde a tale
That me thought a wonder° thing.   *wonderful, amazing*
       This was the tale: There was a king
That hight° Seys, and hadde a wyf,   *was named*
The beste that mighte bere lyf,°   *could exist*
65   And this quene hight Alcyone.
So it befel° therafter sone°   *happened / soon*
This king wol wenden over see.°   *travel across the sea*
To tellen shortly, whan that he
Was in the see thus in this wyse,°   *manner*
70   Swich a tempest° gan to ryse°   *Such a storm / arose*
That brak hir mast° and made it falle   *their (ship's) mast*
And clefte° hir ship and dreynt hem° alle,   *split apart / drowned them*
That° never was founden,° as it telles,   *So that / there found*
Borde° ne man ne nothing elles.°   *Board, plank / else*
75   Right thus° this king Seys loste his lyf.   *Just so*
       Now for to speke of Alcyone his wyf:
This lady that was left at home
Hath wonder,° that the king ne come   *was perplexed, worried*
Hoom,° for it was a longe terme.°   *Home / time*
80   Anoon° hir herte began to erme,°   *Soon / grieve*
And for that hir thoughte° evermo   *because it seemed to her*
It was nat wel he dwelte so,°   *stayed away so (long)*
She longed so after° the king   *for*
That certes° it were° a pitous° thing   *truly / would be / pitiful*
85   To telle hir hertely sorweful lyf°   *deeply sorrowful existence*
That she had, this noble wyf,
For him, allas, she loved alderbest.°   *best of all*
Anoon° she sente° bothe est and west   *Immediately / sent messengers*
To seke him, but they founde nought.°   *nothing*
90   "Allas!" quod° she, "that I was wrought!°   *said / created*
And wher my lord, my love, be deed?
Certes, I nil never ete breed,
I make a vowe to my god here,
But I mowe of my lord here!"[9]
95   Swich sorwe° this lady to hir took   *Such sorrow*

---

7. Than to play either chess or backgammon (or a similar board game).
8. The "lawe of kinde" or natural law governed virtuous pagans in ancient times; it was distinct from but not incompatible with Christian law.
9. And is my lord, my love, dead? Indeed, I will never again eat bread, so I vow to my god here, unless I may hear (something regarding) my lord. (The word "wher" is a form of the conjunction "whether"; the fact that Alcyone does not know whether or not Seys is dead causes her to fast in order to persuade her special goddess, Juno, to bring her knowledge of his fate.)

That trewely I that made this book
Had swich pitee and swich routhe°   *compassion*
To rede° hir sorwe, that, by my trouthe,°   *In reading about / truly*
I ferde° the worse al the morwe°   *got on / morrow (morning, day)*
100 After, to thinken on° hir sorwe.°   *from thinking about / sorrow*
    So whan this lady coude here° no word   *hear*
That no man mighte finde hir lord,
Ful ofte she swowned° and seyd "Allas!"   *swooned, fainted*
For sorwe ful nigh wood° she was,   *almost crazy*
105 Ne she coude no reed but oon,[1]
But doun on knees she sat anoon,°   *at once*
And weep, that pitee was to here.°   *(she) wept piteously*
    "A mercy, swete lady dere!'
Quod° she to Juno, hir goddesse;   *Said*
110 "Help me out of this distresse,
And yeve° me grace my lord to see   *give*
Sone,° or wite wherso° he be,   *Soon / know where*
Or how he fareth,° or in what wyse,°   *how he is doing / manner*
And I shal make yow sacrifyse,
115 And hooly° youres become I shal   *completely*
With good will, body, herte, and al;
And but thou wilt this, lady swete,[2]
Send me grace to slepe and mete°   *dream*
In my slepe som certeyn sweven,°   *a trustworthy dream*
120 Wherthurgh that° I may knowe even°   *Through which / simply*
Whether my lord be quik or ded."°   *is alive or dead*
With that word she heng doun the hed,°   *lowered (her) head*
And fil a-swown° as cold as stoon.°   *swooned, fainted / stone*
Hir women caught° hir up anoon°   *lifted / at once*
125 And broughten hir in bed al naked;
And she, forweped and forwaked,
Was wery, and thus the dede slepe
Fil on hir er she tooke kepe,[3]
Thurgh° Juno, that had herd hir bone°   *Caused by / prayer*
130 That made hir to slepe sone.°   *quickly to fall asleep*
    For as she preyde, right° so was doon°   *just / it done*
In dede;° for Juno right anoon°   *In deed, in fact / immediately*
Called thus hir messagere°   *messenger*
To do hir erande, and he com nere.°   *approached closer*
135 Whan he was come, she bad° him thus: *asked, commanded*
"Go bet,"° quod° Juno, "to Morpheus,[4]   *quickly / said*
Thou knowest hym wel, the god of slepe;
Now understond wel, and tak kepe.°   *pay attention*
Sey thus on my halfe,° that he   *behalf*

---

1. Nor was she able to come up with any solution except for one (i.e., the solution of praying to Juno, traditionally the goddess of married women).
2. And if you wish to do only this, sweet lady.
3. And she was exhausted from weeping and sleeplessness, and thus a deathly sleep fell upon her before she knew it. (The prefix "for" is an intensifier. As reflected in line 125, it was common practice during the Middle Ages to sleep without clothing; also 176, 293.)
4. In Ovid's *Metamorphoses* (11. 633–72), Morpheus is one of the sons of Somnus, god of sleep; Morpheus's special skill is his ability to assume specific human form. In contrast, Chaucer makes Morpheus himself the god of sleep and has him re-animate Seys's literal dead body (see 144–45).

140 Go faste° into the Grete See,°	quickly / i.e., the Mediterranean
And bid° him that, on alle thing,°	instruct / above all else
He take up Seys body the king°	the body of King Seys
That lyth° ful pale and nothing rody.°	lies / not at all ruddy
Bid him crepe into° the body,	creep inside
145 Aud do it goon° to Alcyone	cause it to go
The quene, ther° she lyth° alone,	where / lies
And shewe hir shortly,° it is no nay,°	quickly / beyond denial
How it was dreynt° this other day;	drowned
And do° the body speke right° so	make / just
150 Right as it was woned to do°	used to do
The whyles° that it was alyve.	During the time
Go now faste, and hye thee blyve!"°	hurry along quickly
This messager took leve° and wente	took his leave
Upon his wey and never ne stente°	stopped
155 Til he com° to the derke valey	Until he came
That stant° bytwene roches twey,°	stands / two rock formations
Ther° never yet grew corne° ne gras,	Where / grain
Ne tree, ne nothing that ought° was,	amounted to anything
Beste,° ne man, ne nought elles,°	Beast / anything else
160 Save° ther were a fewe welles	Except that
Came renninge° fro the cliffes adoun,°	Which came flowing / down from
That° made a deedly slepinge soun,°	(And) which / soporific sound
And ronnen° doun right by a cave	they ran, flowed
That was under a rokke y-grave°	hollowed out
165 Amid° the valey wonder depe.°	In the middle of / wondrously deep
There these goddes laye and slepe,°	slept
Morpheus, and Eclympasteyre,[5]	
That was the god of slepes heyre,°	heir
That slepe° and did noon° other werk.	Who slept / no
170 This cave was also as° derk	just as
As helle pit overal aboute;°	throughout, everywhere
They had good leyser° for to route°	plenty of leisure time / snore
To envye° who might slepe beste;	compete as to
Some henge hir chin° upon hir breste	hung their chins
175 And slepe upright,° hir heed y-hed,°	(sitting) upright / slumped forward
And some lay naked in hir bed°	in their beds
And slepe whyles° the dayes laste.	as long as
This messager come fleeinge° faste	flying
And cryed, "O how,° awake anoon!"°	O ho! / at once
180 It was for nought;° ther herde him noon.°	to no avail / nobody
"Awak!" quod° he, "Who is lyth° there?"	said / is it who lies
And blew his horne right in hir ere°	their ears
And cryed "awaketh!" wonder hye.°	incredibly loudly
This god of slepe, with his oon eye°	one of his eyes
185 Cast° up and axed,° "Who clepeth° there?"	Looked / asked / calls
"It am I," quod this messagere;	
"Juno bad thou shuldest goon"°—	asked that you go
And tolde him what he shulde doon°	should do

5. Although Ovid's *Metamorphoses* names four of the thousand sons of the god of sleep, Eclympasteyre is not among them; the name is taken from Jean Froissart's poem *The Paradise of Love*.

As I have tolde yow heretofore°— *before this*
190 It is no nede reherse it more°— *repeat it again*
And wente his wey whan he had seyd.° *after he had spoken*
    Anoon this god of slepe abreyd° *awakened, started up*
Out of his slepe and gan to goon,° *began to get going*
And did as he had bede him doon:° *asked him to do*
195 Tooke up the dreynte° body sone° *drowned / straightway*
And bar° it forth to Alcyone, *carried*
His wif the quene, theras° she lay, *where*
Right even a quarter bifore day,[6]
And stood right at hir beddes fete,° *the foot of her bed*
200 And called hir, right as she hete,° *was called*
By name, and seyde, "My swete wyf,
Awak! Let be° your sorweful° lyf, *Give up / sorrowful*
For in your sorwe there lyth no reed,° *can be found no remedy*
For certes, swete, I am but deed.[7]
205 Ye shul me never on lyve y-see.° *(again) see me alive*
But good swete herte, look° that ye *take care*
Bury my body, for swich a tyde° *at such and such a time*
Ye mowe° it finde the see besyde;° *may / next to the sea*
And farewel, swete, my worldes blisse!
210 I preye God your sorwe lisse;° *relieve, lessen your sorrow*
Too litel whyl° our blisse lasteth!" *short a time*
    With that hir eyen up she casteth,
And sawe nought.° "Allas!" quod° she for sorwe, *nothing / said*
And deyde° within the thridde morwe.° *died / three days*
215 But what she seyde more in that swowe° *swoon*
I may nat° telle yow as nowe;° *cannot / at this time*
It were too longe for to dwelle;
My first matere I wil yow telle
Wherfore I have told this thinge[8]
220 Of Alcyone and Seys the kinge.
    For thus moche dar° I sey wel: *this much dare*
I had be dolven everydel
And deed right thurgh defaute of slepe,[9]
If I ne had° red and take kepe° *had not / taken heed*
225 Of this tale next bifore.° *just preceding*
And I wol telle yow wherfore:° *the reason*
For I ne might,° for bote ne bale,° *could not / good or bad*
Slepe er° I had red this tale *before*
Of this dreynte° Seys the kinge *drowned*
230 And of the goddes of sleping.
    Whan I had red this tale wel
And overlooked it everydel,° *looked it over fully*
Me thoughte wonder° if it were so,° *it a marvel / true*
For I had never herde speke er tho° *heard tell before then*

6. At exactly three hours before daybreak. ("Quarter" refers to one quarter of a twelve-hour night; according to standard medieval dream theory, dreams that occur in the early hours of the morning, just before dawn, are the most trustworthy.)
7. For certainly, (my) sweet, I am quite dead.
8. It would delay (us) too long. I will return to our first topic—the reason I am narrating the story.
9. I would have been dead and buried simply for lack of sleep.

235 Of no goddes° that coude make — *any gods*
    Men to slepe ne for to wake,° — *awaken*
    For I ne knewe never God but oon.[1]
    And in my game° I seyde anoon°— — *playfully / at once*
    And yet me list right evel to pleye[2]—
240 "Rather than that I shulde deye° — *die*
    Thurgh defaute° of sleping thus, — *the lack*
    I wolde yive thilke° Morpheus — *would like to give this same*
    Or his goddesse, dame Juno,
    Or som wight elles, I ne rought who,[3]
245 To make me slepe and have som reste,
    I wil yive° him the alderbeste° — *give / very best*
    Yift° that ever he abode° his lyve, — *Gift / received during*
    And here onwarde,° right now as blyve,° — *as a pledge / at once*
    If he wol make me slepe a lyte,° — *little*
250 Of downe of pure doves whyte° — *pure white doves*
    I wil yive him a fether bed,
    Rayed° with golde and right wel cled° — *Decorated / wrapped*
    In fyn blak satin doutremere, — *from overseas*
    And many a pilow, and every bere° — *pillowcase (to be made)*
255 Of clothe of Reynes, to slepe softe;
    Him thar nat nede to turnen ofte.[4]
    And I wol yive him al that falles° — *is fitting*
    To a chambre; and al his halles
    I wol do peynte° with pure golde — *have painted*
260 And tapite hem ful many folde
    Of o sute;[5] this shal he have,
    If I wiste° wher were his cave, — *knew*
    If he can make me slepe sone,° — *soon*
    As did the goddesse° Alcyone. — *As the goddess (Juno) did for*
265 And thus this ilke° god Morpheus — *same*
    May winne of° me mo fees° thus — *gain from / more payments*
    Than ever he wan;° and to Juno, — *won (previously)*
    That is his goddesse, I shal so do,° — *do so (much) that*
    I trow° that she shal holde hir payde."° — *believe / herself pleased, satisfied*
270   I hadde unnethe° that word y-sayde° — *scarcely / uttered*
    Right thus as I have told it yow,
    That sodeynly,° I niste° how, — *Than suddenly / do not know*
    Swich a lust anoon° me tooke — *desire abruptly*
    To slepe, that right upon my booke
275 I fil aslepe, and therwith even° — *thereupon directly*
    Me mette° so inly° swete a sweven,° — *I dreamed / thoroughly / dream*
    So wonderful that never yit° — *yet, to this day*

1. For I never knew about any God except for one (that is, the Christian God). (This observation underscores the distinction between the ancient age of "kind" or nature, when the Ovidian story takes place, and the narrator's time period, the Christian Middle Ages. Despite his religious and philosophical advantages, however, the narrator brings a comically literal mind to his interpretation of the story.)
2. And yet I really did not feel in a playful spirit.
3. Or some other being, I'm not particular as to whom.
4. Of cloth from Rennes, (to cause him) to sleep softly. He will not be forced to toss and turn. (Rennes, in Brittany, was known for its production of fine linen.)
5. And hang them with a multitude of tapestries, all in one pattern.

I trow° no man had° the wit — *believe / has had*
To conne° wel my sweven rede;° — *to know how / to interpret*
280 No, nat Joseph, withoute drede,
Of Egipte, he that red so
The kinges metinge Pharao,
No more than coude the lest of us;
Ne nat scarsly Macrobeus,
285 He that wroot al th'avisioun
That he mette, King Scipioun,
The noble man, the Affrican—
Swiche mervailes fortuned than—
I trowe arede my dremes even.[6]
290 Lo, thus it was, this was my sweven.° — *dream*
   Me thoughte thus: that it was May,
And in the dawning° I lay, — *dawn*
Me met° thus, in my bed al naked, — *I dreamed*
And looked forth,° for I was waked° — *around / had been awakened*
295 With° smale foules° a grete hepe° — *By / birds / crowd*
That had affrayed° me out of my slepe — *startled*
Thurgh° noyse and swetnesse of hir° songe; — *By (their) / their*
And, as me mette,° they sate amonge° — *I dreamed / sat together*
Upon my chambre-roof withoute,° — *bedroom roof outside*
300 Upon the tyles overal aboute,° — *everywhere on the roof-tiles*
And songen everich in his wyse° — *each in his fashion*
The moste solempne° servyse — *solemn, ceremonious*
By note° that ever man, I trowe,° — *in song / believe*
Had herde, for som of hem song lowe,° — *low notes (in pitch)*
305 Som high, and al of oon acorde.° — *in perfect harmony*
To telle shortly, at o worde,° — *in a word*
Was never y-herd so swete a steven° — *voice*
But° it had be° a thing of heven; — *Unless / been*
So mery a soun,° so swete entewnes,° — *sound / such sweet melodies*
310 That certes, for the toune of Tewnes,
I nolde but I had herd hem singe,[7]
For al my chambre gan to ringe° — *rang out, resounded*
Thurgh singing of hir armonye.° — *their harmony*
For instrument nor melodye
315 Was nowher herd° yet half so swete, — *Has not been heard anywhere*
Nor of acorde° half so mete,° — *concord / agreeable*

---

6. No, without a doubt, not Joseph of Egypt, he who interpreted the dreams of the (Egyptian) Pharoah—he could no more (interpret my dream) than could the least (skilled reader of dreams). Hardly could Macrobius (himself), I believe, interpret my dream properly—he who wrote the whole vision that was dreamed by King Scipio, that noble man, the African—such marvels happened in those days. (For the story of how Joseph interpreted the Pharoah's dreams, see Genesis 41:1–36. "Macrobius" was the author of a famous fifth-century commentary on Cicero's "Dream of Scipio," the conclusion of Cicero's *De re publica*; Chaucer here conflates Macrobius with Cicero, the author of the dream proper, perhaps suggesting a lack of direct familiarity with the primary texts at this point in his career. "King Scipioun" is the Roman general Publius Cornelius Scipio the Younger, whose dream about his distinguished grandfather, Publius Cornelius Scipio the Elder, is also described, more accurately, by Chaucer in the *Parliament of Fowls*, where it is the elder Scipio who is called "Affrican." Both the "Dream of Scipio" by Cicero and a section from the beginning of Macrobius's *Commentary* are included in the Contexts section of this Norton Critical Edition.)
7. That truly I would not trade the town of Tunis for the experience of hearing them sing. (Tunis, in North Africa, was probably chosen for the rhyme, but the city was also known for its wealth and culture.)

[margin: Room became beautifully decorated — he could hardly look]

For ther was noon of hem° that feyned°	*not one of them / pretended*
To singe, for ech° of hem him peyned°	*each / took pains*
To finde out° mery crafty° notes;	*invent / skillful*
320 They ne spared nat hir throtes.°	*i.e., they did not hold back*
And, sooth to seyn,° my chambre° was	*truth to tell / bedroom*
Ful wel depeynted,° and with glas	*beautifully decorated, painted*
Were al the windowes wel y-glased,°	*glazed*
Ful clere,° and nat an hole y-crased,°	*Very clear / broken*
325 That° to beholde it was gret joye.	*So that*
For hooly al the story° of Troye	*the entire story*
Was in the glasinge y-wrought° thus,	*worked in stained glass*
Of Ector and of Kinge Priamus,	
Of Achilles and Kinge Lamedoun,	
330 Of Medea and of Jasoun,	
Of Paris, Eleyne, and Lavyne.	
And al the walles with colours fyne	
Were peynted, bothe text and glose,	
Of al the Romaunce of the Rose.[8]	
335 My windowes weren shet echoon,°	*each shut*
And thurgh the glas the sonne shoon°	*sun shone*
Upon my bed with bright bemes,°	*beams*
With many glade gilde stremes;°	*golden streams (of light)*
And eek the welken° was so fair;	*also the sky*
340 Blew,° bright, clere was the air,	*Blue*
And ful atempre, for soothe,° it was;	*truly very mild*
For nother° too cold nor hot it nas,°	*neither / was not*
Ne in al the welken° was a cloude.	*the whole sky*
And as I lay thus, wonder° loude	*wondrously, incredibly*
345 Me thoughte° I herde an hunte° blowe	*It seemed to me / huntsman*
T'assaye° his horn and for to knowe°	*To test / to find out*
Whether it were clere or hors of soune.°	*hoarse, rough-sounding*
And I herd goinge, both up and doune,	
Men, hors,° houndes, and other thinge,°	*horses / things*
350 And al men speke° of huntinge,	*all the men spoke*
How they wolde slee the hert° with strengthe,	*slay the hart*
And how the hert had upon lengthe°	*after a while*
So moche embosed,° I noot° now what.	*become exhausted / do not know*
Anonright° whan I herde that,	*Immediately*
355 How that they wolde on hunting goon,°	*go*
I was right° glad and up anoon°	*very / at once*

[margin: He heard hunters & noise]

8. Text and gloss mean literally the script of the story and commentary on it; in this context, probably pictures and captions. The figures listed each have some connection to the story of Troy: Hector and Paris were the sons of the Trojan king Priam, and Lamedon was his father. Achilles was a great Greek warrior who fought against Troy. Helen was the Greek queen whose abduction by Paris was the cause of the Trojan war. Lavinia was the Trojan Aeneas's bride later in Latium. The ill-fated lovers Jason and Medea, though not participants in the ancient story of Troy, are described in medieval Trojan romances; Medea helped Jason win the Golden Fleece and was later betrayed by him; Chaucer tells their story in the *Legend of Good Women* 1580–1679. The *Romance of the Rose* was a famous thirteenth-century allegory of love by Guillaume de Lorris, continued by Jean de Meun; many details of Chaucer's description of the *locus amoenus* (the beautiful place) he now finds himself are taken from the description of the Garden of Love in this poem; included in the Contexts section of this Norton Critical Edition are lines 1347–1410, which include trees, birds, and other forest animals such as are found in passages coming up.

Tooke my hors,° and forth I wente.   *horse*
   Out of my chambre° I never stente°   *bedroom / stopped (going)*
Til I com to the feld withoute.°   *field, open country outside*
360 Ther overtook I a grete route°   *company, crowd*
Of huntes° and eek of foresteres,°   *hunters / also game trackers*
With many relayes and lymeres,°[9]
And hyed hem° to the forest faste,   *they hurried*
And I with hem.° So at the laste   *them*
365 I asked oon, ladde° a lymere,   *one who led*
"Sey, felow, who shal hunte here?"
Quod° I, and he answerd ageyn;°   *Said / back*
"Sir, th'emperour Octovyen,"[1]
Quod he, "and is° here faste by."°   *he is / nearby*
370 "A Goddes halfe,° in good tyme," quod I,   *For God's sake*
"Go we° faste!" and gan° to ryde.   *Let's go / we began*
Whan we came to the forest syde,°   *edge*
Every man dide, right anoon,°   *right away*
As to hunting fil to doon.°   *as required by the hunt*
375 The maister hunte° anoon, fote-hote,°   *chief huntsman / very quickly*
With a gret horne blew three mote°   *notes*
At the uncoupling° of his houndes.   *unleashing*
Within a whyl the herte founde is,
Y-halowed° and rechased° faste   *chased with shouts / pursued*
380 Longe tyme;° and so at the laste   *for a long time*
This hert rused° and stal° awey   *retraced his steps / crept*
Fro° al the houndes a privy wey.°   *From / to a hidden place*
The houndes had overshote hem alle°   *all passed up (the hart)*
And were on a defaute y-falle;°   *had lost the scent*
385 Therwith° the hunte wonder faste°   *With that / huntsman very quickly*
Blew a forloyn° at the laste.   *the note of recall*
   I was go walked fro° my tree,   *had gone walking from*
And as I wente ther cam by me
A whelp,° that fauned° me as I stood,   *puppy / fawned on*
390 That hadde y-folowed° and coude no   *followed me*
   good.°   *didn't know better*
It come and crepte to me as lowe°   *low to the ground*
Right as° it hadde me y-knowe,°   *Just as if / knew me*
Held doun his hede and joyned° his eres°   *brought together / ears*
And leyde al smothe doun his heres.°   *fur*
395   I wolde have caught it, and anoon° *but all at once*
It fledde and was fro me goon,°   *gone away from me*
And I him folwed, and it forth wente
Doun by a floury° grene wente°   *flowery / path*
Ful thikke of° gras, ful softe and swete,   *Very thick with*
400 With floures fele,° faire under fete,°   *many flowers / feet*

---

9. Lymeres: hounds led on a leash who track game by scent. Relayes: hounds positioned in advance
   on the probable course of the hunt to replace dogs grown tired.
1. The Roman Emperor Augustus Caesar (63 B.C.E.–14 C.E.), the adopted heir of Julius Caesar, was
   born Gaius Octavius. He was the first and one of the most important and famous Roman emperors.
   Octavian also figures in Christian interpretations of the poem, as he was the ruler of Rome at the
   time of the birth of Christ.

And litel used, it seemed thus;°   *so it seemed*
For bothe Flora and Zephirus,[2]
They two that make floures growe,
Had made hir° dwelling ther, I trowe;°   *their / believe*
405   For it was on to beholde°   *to look upon*
As though th'erthe envye wolde°   *the earth wanted to compete*
To be gayer° than the heven,°   *more beautiful / the sky*
To have mo floures swiche seven°   *seven times the flowers*
As in the welken° sterres be.°   *sky / are stars*
410   It had forgete° the povertee   *forgotten*
That winter thurgh his colde morwes°   *with its cold mornings*
Had made it suffre, and his sorwes.°   *its sorrows*
Al was forgeten, and that was sene°   *apparent*
For al the wode was waxen° grene;   *had grown*
415   Swetnesse of dewe had made it waxe.
    It is° no need eek° for to axe°   *There is / also / ask*
Wher° ther were many grene greves°   *Whether / groves*
Or thikke of° trees so ful of leves;   *a multitude of*
And every tree stood by himselve°   *itself*
420   Fro other° wel ten feet or twelve.   *Away from the others*
So grete trees, so huge of strengthe,
Of fourty or fifty fadme lengthe,
Clene withoute bough or stikke,
With croppes brode, and eek as thikke[3]—
425   They were nat an inche asonder°—   *apart*
That it° was shadwe overal under;°   *So that there / everywhere underneath*
And many an hert and many an hinde
Was both bifore me and bihinde.
Of founes, sowres, bukkes, does
430   Was ful the wode, and many roes,[4]
And many squirels that sete°   *sat*
Ful high upon the trees and ete°   *ate*
And in hir° maner made festes.°   *their / had feasts*
Shortly,° it was so ful of bestes°   *Briefly / beasts, animals*
435   That though Argus,[5] the noble countour,°   *mathematician*
Sete to rekene° in his countour,°   *calculate / counting house*
And rekene with his figures ten°—   *i.e., the Arabic numerals*
For by tho° figures mowe al ken,°   *those / all may know*
If they be crafty,° rekene and noumbre°   *skillful / enumerate*
440   And telle° of every thing the noumbre—   *tally*
Yet shulde he faile to rekene even°   *exactly*
The wondres me mette° in my sweven.°   *I dreamed / dream*
    But forth they° romed wonder° faste   *i.e., the deer / wondrously*

2. Respectively, the goddess of flowers and of the west wind.
3. Such great trees, so very strong, forty to fifty fathoms in height, (their trunks) clear of branch or twig, their tops wide and likewise full. (A fathom is a measurement of about six feet, based on the distance between a man's fingertips when his arms are extended.)
4. The list of deer includes harts (mature male red deer), hinds (female red deer), fawns (male fallow deer, one year old), "sowres" (male fallow deer, four years old), bucks (mature male fallow deer), does (female fallow deer), and roes (roe deer).
5. Muhammad ibn-Musa al-Khwarizmi, a ninth-century Arab mathematician and author of astronomical tables; his name here is taken from the Old French "Algus," in the *Romance of the Rose* 12760.

Doun° the wode, so at the laste — *through*
445 I was war° of a man in blak — *became aware*
That sat and had y-turned his bak° — *with his back turned*
To an oke,° an huge tree. — *oak*
"Lord," thoughte I, "who may° that be? — *can*
What aileth him° to sitten here?" — *What is the problem causing him*
450 Anonright° I wente nere;° — *Immediately / nearer*
Than fond° I sitte even upright° — *found / sitting up straight*
A wonder wel-faringe° knight, — *handsome, well formed*
By the° maner me thought so,° — *In his / seemed so to me*
Of good mochel° and right yong therto,° — *size / also quite young*
455 Of the age of foure and twenty yeer.[6]
Upon his berde° but litel heer,° — *beard / little hair*
And he was clothed al in blak.
I stalked even unto° his bak, — *walked quietly right up to*
And ther I stood as stille as ought,° — *anything*
460 That,° sooth to seye,° he saw me nought, — *So that / truth to tell*
Forwhy° he heng his hede° adoune. — *Because / hung his head*
And with a deedly sorweful soune° — *deathly sorrowful sound*
He made of° ryme ten vers° or twelve — *composed in / ten verses, lines*
Of a compleynt° to himselve,° — *complaint, lamentation / himself*
465 The moste pite,° the moste rowthe,° — *pitiful / moving*
That ever I herde; for, by my trowthe,° — *in honesty*
It was gret wonder that nature
Might suffre° any creature — *allow*
To have swich sorwe° and be nat deed. — *experience such sorrow*
470 Ful pitous,° pale, and nothing reed,° — *pitiful / not at all ruddy*
He seyde a lay,° a maner° song, — *short narrative poem / kind of*
Withoute note,° withoute song,° — *musical notes / melody*
And was this,° for ful wel I can — *here it is*
Reherse° it; right thus° it began: — *Repeat / just so*
475 "I have of sorwe so grete woon° — *such great abundance*
That joye gete I never noon,° — *any at all*
Now that I see my lady bright,
Which I have loved with al my might,
Is fro me deed and is agoon,
480 And thus in sorwe lefte me aloon.[7]
Allas, Deeth, what aileth thee° — *ails you*
That thou noldest° have taken me — *did not want to*
Whan thou took my lady swete
That was so fair, so fresh, so free,° — *generous*
485 So good that men may wel y-see° — *see, perceive that*
Of al goodnesse she had no mete!"° — *equal*
Whan he had made thus his complaynte,° — *lament*

---

6. The man in black's prototype, the English prince John of Gaunt, would have been twenty-eight at the time of his wife's death in 1368; the discrepancy in age may be due to miscopying.
7. Has died and left me and gone away, and thus abandoned me to sorrow. (Although the man in black makes it clear that his lady has died, the narrator mysteriously does not seem to take his meaning; explanations for this misunderstanding vary from the narrator's tact to his obtuseness, or perhaps the dreamer takes the knight's expression here to be mere poetic convention. Line 480 first appears in the 1532 edition of William Thynne and so may not be original to Chaucer; see also the note to lines 31–96.)

His sorweful herte gan faste faynte,°   *quickly became faint,*
And his spirites wexen dede;
490 The blood was fled, for pure drede,
Doun to his hert to make him warm[8]—
For wel it feled° the hert had harm—   *felt that*
To wite eek° why it was adrad,°   *find out also / frightened*
By kinde,° and for to make it glad,   *nature*
495 For it is membre principal°   *the chief organ*
Of the body. And that° made al   *i.e., that process*
His hewe° chaunge and wexe° grene   *complexion / grow, become*
And pale, for ther no blood is sene
In no maner lime° of his.   *any of his limbs*
500   Anoon therwith° whan I saw this,   *At the very moment*
He ferde thus evel there° he sete,   *got on so badly there where*
I wente and stood right at his fete°   *feet*
And grette° him, but he spak nought,°   *greeted / said nothing*
But argued with his owne thought,
505 And in his witte° disputed faste°   *mind / intently*
Why and how his lyf might laste;°   *could continue*
Him thoughte° his sorwes were so smerte°   *It seemed to him / painful*
And lay so colde upon his herte;
So, thurgh his sorwe and hevy thought,°   *gloom, sadness*
510 Made him that he ne herde me nought,°   *not at all*
For he had wel nigh° lost his minde,   *almost entirely*
Though Pan,[9] that men clepe° god of kinde,°   *call / nature*
Were° for his sorwes never so wrooth.°   *might be / angry*
  But at the laste, to seyn right sooth,°   *quite truly*
515 He was war° of me, how I stoode   *became aware*
Bifore him, and dide of myn hoode,°   *doffed my head covering*
And grette him,° as I best coude.°   *greeted / knew how*
Debonairly° and nothing° loude.   *Graciously / not at all*
He seyde, "I prey thee, be nat wrooth,°   *angry*
520 I herde thee nat,° to seyn the sooth,   *did not hear you*
Ne I saw thee nat,° sir, trewely."   *Nor did I see you*
  "A goode sir, no fors,"° quod° I,   *no problem / said*
"I am right° sory if I have ought°   *very / in any way*
Destroubled° yow out of your thought;   *disturbed*
525 Foryive me if I have mistake."°   *done wrong, made a blunder*
  "Yis, th'amendes is light° to make,"   *amends are easy*
Quod he, "for ther lyth noon° therto;   *there are none*
Ther is nothing misseyd nor do."[1]
Lo, how goodly spak° this knight,   *becomingly spoke*

8. And his (animal) spirits deadened; the blood had fled, from absolute fear, down to his heart to make it warm. (Chaucer describes a specific Galenic physiology of swooning; the man's vital spirits, which regulate what we would call his "central nervous system," gather at his heart—the organ where he is suffering—to bring it assistance, causing a loss of consciousness by depriving the brain and limbs of energy and motion.)
9. Pan, Mercury's son and the classical god of shepherds, was known in the Middle Ages as the general god of nature. The sense is that the man in black gives himself up to grief even though the god of nature would be angry with him for this abandonment of natural balance in his emotions.
1. You have not said or done anything wrong. (Throughout this exchange note how the difference in status between the dreamer and the man in black is registered in the pronouns they use to address one another: The dreamer uses the formal "you" and the knight the familiar "thou.")

530 As it° had been another wight;°	As if / a different person
He made it nouther tough ne queynte,²	
And I saw that, and gan m'aqueynte°	feel on friendly terms
With him, and fond him so tretable,°	receptive, agreeable
Right wonder skilful° and resonable,	Most amazingly rational
535 As me thoughte, for al his bale.°	suffering
Anonright° I gan finde a tale°	At once / thing to say
To him, to look wher° I might ought°	see whether / in any way
Have more knowing of° his thought.	knowledge about
"Sir," quod° I, "this game° is doon;	said / sport (i.e., the hunt)
540 I holde that this hert be goon;°	hart has gone (away)
These huntes° conne him nowher see."	hunters
"I do no fors therof,"° quod he;	don't care about that
"My thought is theron never a del."°	not about that at all
"By our Lord," quod I, "I trow° yow wel,	believe
545 Right so me thinketh by° your chere.°	so it seems from / face
But, sir, o° thing wol ye here?°	one / hear
Me thinketh in gret sorwe° I yow see;	sorrow
But certes,° good sir, if that ye	truly
Wolde ought discure me° your wo,	reveal to me any of
550 I wolde, as wis God° help me so,	the wise God may
Amende it, if I can or may;°	know how or am able
Ye mowe preve° it by assay.°	may test / trying (me)
For, by my trouthe,° to make yow hool,°	honestly / bring you health
I wol do al my power hool.°	whole
555 And telleth me of your sorwes smerte;°	sharp, grievous
Paraventure° it may ese° your herte,	Perhaps / bring ease to
That semeth ful seke° under your syde."	very sick
With that he looked on me asyde,°	askance
As who seyth,° "Nay, that wol nat be."	Like a person who says
560 "Graunt mercy,° goode frend," quod° he,	Pardon me / said
"I thanke thee that thou woldest so,°	you want (to do) so
But it may never the rather be do;³	
No man may my sorwe glade,°	turn to gladness
That maketh my hewe to falle and fade,°	complexion grow pale and dim
565 And hath myn understonding lorn,°	ruined
That me is° wo that I was born!	So that I have
May nought° make my sorwes slyde,°	Nothing can / pass away
Nought al the remedies of Ovyde,	
Ne Orpheus, god of melodye,	
570 Ne Dedalus, with pleyes slye;	
Ne hele me may no phisicien,	
Nought Ypocras ne Galien;⁴	

2. He behaved neither arrogantly nor with exaggerated politeness. (His courtesy and kindness make it hard for the dreamer to recognize the man who was so recently entirely overcome with grief.)
3. But it cannot be done the more quickly. (I.e., despite your wish to help me, my recovery will not happen any faster.)
4. The "remedies" of Ovid are tongue-in-cheek countermeasures against love described in the *Remedia Amoris*; the mythic Orpheus charmed the rulers of the underworld with the music of his lyre to win back his wife Eurydice; Daedalus was famous in classical mythology for his inventions ("pleyes slye"), most prominently for the wings he built to enable himself and his son Icarus to escape from danger in Crete; Ypocras (Hippocrates) and Galien (Galen) were respectively doctors in the fifth century B.C.E. and second century C.E., known for founding the practice and science of medicine.

Me is wo° that I live houres twelve.   *Woe is me*
But whoso wol assaye° himselve   *whoever wishes to test*
575 Whether his hert can have pitee
Of° any sorwe, lat him see me.   *On*
I wrecche,° that deeth hath mad al   *miserable one*
  naked°   *wholly deprived*
Of al the blisse that ever was maked,°   *there was*
Y-worthe° worste of al wightes,°   *(I have) become / creatures*
580 That hate my dayes and my nightes;
My lyf, my lustes be me loothe,°   *pleasures are hateful to me*
For al welfare and I be wrooethe.°   *are at odds*
The pure deeth° is so ful my fo°   *death itself / fully my foe*
That I wolde° deye, it wolde nat so;   *wish to*
585 For whan I folwe° it, it° wol flee;   *follow / i.e., death*
I wolde° have him, it nil nat° me.   *want to / does not want*
This is my peyne withoute reed,°   *remedy*
Alwey deynge° and be nat° deed,   *to be dying / not to be*
That Tesiphus, that lyth in helle,
590 May nat of more sorwe telle.[5]
And whoso wiste° al, by my trouthe,°   *whoever knew / truly*
My sorwe, but he hadde routhe°   *unless he had compassion*
And pitee of° my sorwes smerte,°   *pity for / painful sorrows*
That man hath a feendly herte.°   *fiendish, devilish heart*
595 For whoso seeth° me first on morwe°   *whoever sees / in the morning*
May seyn° he hath met with sorwe;°   *say that / sorrow*
For I am sorwe and sorwe is I.
 Allas, and I wol telle thee why:
My song is turned to pleyning,°   *lamentation*
600 And al my laughter to weping,
My glade thoughtes to hevinesse,°   *sadness*
In travaile° is myn ydelnesse°   *Turned to labor / leisure*
And eek° my reste; my wele is wo,°   *also / joy is (turned to) woe*
My goode is harm, and evermo
605 In wrathe is turned my pleying,[6]
And my delyt° into sorwing.°   *delight / sorrowing*
Myn hele° is turned into seknesse,°   *health / sickness*
In drede° is al my sikernesse.°   *anxiety / (sense of) security*
To derke is turned al my light,
610 My wit° is foly,° my day is night,   *reason, understanding / foolishness*
My love is hate, my slepe waking,
My mirthe and meles° is fasting,   *meals*
My countenaunce° is nicete,°   *self-possession / silliness, folly*
And al abawed° wherso° I be,   *rattled, confounded / wherever*
615 My pees,° in pleding and in werre.°   *peace / arguments and conflicts*
Allas, how mighte I fare werre?°   *worse*
  My boldnesse° is turned to shame,   *courage*

---

5. To the extent that Tesiphus, who lies in hell, cannot recount greater sorrows than can I. (Tesiphus appears to be a conflation of Tityus, punished in Tartarus by a vulture tearing at his entrails, and Sisyphus, whose infernal punishment was repeatedly to roll a stone up a hill, only to have it slide down again.)
6. The good things in my life have come to grief, and at all times my merrymaking has turned to anger.

For fals Fortune⁷ hath pleyd a game
At the chesse° with me, allas, the whyle!°   *chess / the time*
620 The traiteresse fals and ful of gyle,°   *guile, deceit*
That al behoteth° and nothing   *promises everything*
   halte;°   *holds to, delivers*
She goth° upryght and yet she halte,°   *walks / limps*
That baggeth° foule and looketh faire,°   *squints / casts lovely glances*
The dispitouse debonaire°   *disdainful courteous one*
625 That scorneth° many a creature!   *casts scorn upon*
An ydole of fals portraiture⁸
Is she, for she wil sone wryen;°   *turn away, become unresponsive*
She is the monstres° hed y-wryen,°   *monster's / covered over*
As filth over y-strawed° with floures.°   *strewn, spread / flowers*
630 Hir moste worship° and hir flour° is   *honor / crowning achievement*
To lyen, for that is hir nature,
Withoute feyth, lawe, or mesure.°   *moderation*
She is fals, and ever laughinge
With oon° eye, and that other° wepinge.   *one / other (eye)*
635 That° is brought° up, she set al doun.   *All that / raised*
I lykne° hir to the scorpioun,   *liken, compare*
That is a fals, flateringe beste,°   *beast, animal*
For with his hede° he maketh feste,°   *head / acts in friendly manner*
But al amid° his flateringe   *in the middle of*
640 With his taile he wol stinge
And envenyme,° and so wol she.   *poison*
She is th'envyouse charite°   *spiteful benevolence*
That is ay° fals and seemeth wele;°   *always / good*
So turneth she hir false whele
645 Aboute,° for it is nothing° stable—   *Around / not at all*
Now by the fyre, now at table;
For many oon° hath she thus y-blent.°   *a one / blinded*
She is pley° of enchauntement,   *a trick of*
That semeth oon° and is nat so,   *to be one thing*
650 The false theef! What hath she do,°   *done*
Trowest thou?° By our Lord, I wol thee sey.   *(What) do you think?*
At the chesse° with me she gan to pley;°   *chess / began to play*
With hir false draughtes divers°   *various false moves*
She stal° on me and took my fers.°   *stole up / queen*
655 And whan I saw my fers awey,°   *i.e., had been taken*
Allas, I couthe no lenger° pley,   *could no longer*
But seyde, "Farewel, swete, ywis,°   *darling, indeed*
And farwel al that ever ther is!"
Therwith Fortune seyde, "Chek° here!"   *Check*

---

7. The goddess Fortune governs earthly power and mutability. Many featues of her description here are taken from popular medieval convention, especially the description of the wheel that she operates (see 644), on which she elevates the rich, powerful, and lucky in love as a prelude to plunging them into mischance and adversity. The most famous and influential source of the medieval idea of Fortune is Boethius's *Consolation of Philosophy*, where she is described in opposition to the figure of Philosophy, whose stoicism and eye to higher values offers an antidote to Fortune's miseries; relevant passages from the *Consolation* and also from the thirteenth-century *Romance of the Rose* are printed in the Contexts section of this Norton Critical Edition.
8. An idol (to be worshipped like a god) deceptively pictured.

660 And "Mate!"° in mid° pointe of the   *Checkmate / central*
     chekkere°   *chess board*
     With a poune erraunt,° allas!   *mating pawn*
     Ful craftier to pley she was
     Than Athalus,⁹ that made the game
     First of the chesse; so was his name.
665 But God wolde° I had ones or twyes°   *I wish to God / once or twice*
     Y-coud and knowe° the jeupardyes°   *i.e., studied and learned / pitfalls*
     That coude° the Greke Pictagores,°   *knew / Pythagoras*
     I shulde have pleyd the bet° at ches   *better*
     And kept my fers° the bet therby.   *guarded my queen*
670 And though wherto?° For trewly,   *yet to what purpose?*
     I hold° that wish nat worth a stree!°   *consider / straw*
     It had be never° the bet for me,   *could never have been*
     For Fortune can so many a wyle,°   *knows so many tricks*
     Ther be but fewe can hir begyle,°   *who can outwit her*
675 And eek° she is the lasse° to blame;   *also / less*
     Myself I wolde have do° the same,   *done*
     Bifore God, had I be as she;°   *i.e., in her shoes*
     She oughte the more excused° be,   *more easily excused*
     For this I sey yet more therto:°   *in addition, about that*
680 Had I be° God and mighte have do°   *been / done*
     My wille, whan she° my fers caughte,°   *i.e., Fortune / captured*
     I wolde have drawe° the same draughte,°   *made / chess move*
     For, also wis God yive me reste,¹
     I dar wel swere° she took the beste.   *make bold to swear*
685   But thurgh that draughte° I have lorne°   *through that move / lost*
     My blisse; allas, that I was borne!
     For evermore, I trowe° trewly,   *believe*
     For° al my wille, my lust hooly°   *Despite / pleasure wholly*
     Is turned,° but yet what to° done?   *overturned / is to be*
690 By oure Lord, it is to deye sone.°   *die soon*
     For nothing I leve° it nought,   *believe in*
     But live and deye right° in this thought.   *I live and die simply*
     For there nis° planet in firmament,°   *is no / the heavens*
     Ne in aire ne in erthe noon element,
695 That they ne yive me a yift echoon
     Of weping whan I am aloon.²
     For whan that I avyse me° wel,   *think it over*
     And bethinke° me everydel°   *remember / everything*
     How that ther lyth in rekeninge
700 In my sorwe for nothinge,³
     And how ther leveth° no gladnesse   *remains*
     May glade° me of° my distresse,   *gladden, cheer / out of*

---

9. Named by the *Romance of the Rose* (6631–6726) as the inventor of chess in an allegorical passage (concerning a battle between Manfred of Sicily and Charles of Anjou and Provence) that provides many of the details of the chess game mentioned here.
1. For, as surely as (I hope for) God to give me rest.
2. Nor do any of the elements that compose the air or earth not bestow upon me the gift of weeping when I am alone.
3. How there is nothing on account (on the positive side of the ledger) to balance against (the deficit) of my sorrow.

And how I have lost suffisaunce,°   *satisfaction, contentment*
And therto° I have no plesaunce,°   *also / pleasure, delight*
705   Than may I sey I have right nought.°   *absolutely nothing*
And whan al this falleth in my thought,°   *comes to mind*
Allas, than am I overcome,
For that is doon is nat to come.
I have more sorwe than Tantale."[4]
710   And whan I herde him telle this tale
Thus pitously,° as I yow telle,   *movingly, pitifully*
Unnethe mighte° I lenger dwelle,°   *Scarcely could / stay (there)*
It dide° myn hert so moche wo.   *caused*
      "A! goode sir," quod° I, "sey nat so.   *said*
715   Have some pitee° on your nature°   *leniency / (human) nature*
That formed yow to° creature.   *as a*
Remembre yow of° Socrates,   *Remember*
For he ne counted nat three strees°   *didn't give three straws*
Of nought° that Fortune coude do."   *For anything*
720   "No," quod he, "I can nat so."
      "Why so, good sir? Yis, pardee!"° quod I,   *by God, indeed*
"Ne sey nought° so, for trewly,   *Do not say*
Though° ye had lost the ferses twelve,° *Even though / twelve (chess) queens*
And° ye for sorwe mordred yourselve,°   *If / murdered yourself*
725   Ye sholde be dampned° in this cas°   *would be damned / situation*
By as good right as Medea was,
That slow hir children for Jasoun;
And Phyllis also for Demophoun
Heng hirself, so welaway,
730   For he had broke his terme day
To come to hir. Another rage
Had Dido, the quene eek of Cartage,
That slow hirself for Eneas
Was fals, which a fool she was!
735   And Ecquo dyed for Narcisus
Nolde nat love hir, and right thus
Hath many another foly don.
And for Dalida died Sampson,
That slow himself with a pilere.[5]
740   But ther is noon alyve° here   *nobody living*
Wolde for a fers° make this wo!"   *Who would for a (chess) queen*
      "Why so?' quod° he; "it is nat so,   *said*

---

4. For what is gone will never come again. I have more sorrow than Tantalus. (Tantalus was a mythological figure whose punishment in hell was lying near a tree of fruit and a pool of water just out of his reach.)

5. By as proper a justice as was Medea, who killed her children for Jason, and Phyllis also who, for Demophon, hung herself, alas, because he had delayed past the promised time he had agreed to return to her. Another (similar kind of) madness had Dido, the Queen of Carthage, who killed herself because Aeneas was false to her—what a fool she was! And Echo died because Narcissus did not love her, and just so have many other (lovers) foolishly done. And for Delilah died Samson, who killed himself with a pillar. (Medea revenged herself on Jason when he was false to her by killing their two children [see the *Legend of Good Women* 1580–1679]; the story of Phyllis and Demophon is told in the *Legend of Good Women* 2394–2561; Dido killed herself after having been betrayed by Aeneas [see the *Legend of Good Women* 924–1367]. Echo died because Narcissus did not return her love; and the biblical Samson perished by pulling the pillars of a hall down upon himself after he had been betrayed by Delilah [see Judges 16].)

Thou woste ful litel° what thou menest;   *know very little*
I have lost more than thou wenest."°   *think, comprehend*
745   "Lo, howe that may° be," quod I,   *can that*
"Good sir, telle me al hooly°   *completely, the whole story*
In what wyse,° how, why, and wherfore°   *manner / the reason*
That ye have thus your blisse lore."°   *lost*
      "Blythly,"° quod he, "come sit adoun;°   *Happily / down*
750   I telle thee up a° condicioun   *will tell you on one*
That thou shalt hooly° with al thy wit°   *completely / mind*
Do thyn entent° to herken° it."   *your best / attend to*
"Yis, sir." "Swere thy trouthe therto."°   *Take an oath to that*
"Gladly." "Do than holde herto!"°   *keep that promise*
755   "I shal right blythly,° so° God me save,   *quite gladly / as*
Hooly° with al the witte I have,   *Entirely*
Here° yow as wel as I can."   *Listen to*
      "A Goddes half!"° quod he, and began: *For God's sake*
"Sir," quod he, "sith° first I couthe°   *since / was able to*
760   Have any maner wit fro° youthe   *kind of intelligence from*
Or kindely° understondinge   *natural*
To comprehende,° in any thinge,°   *To perceive, grasp / aspect*
What love was, in myn owne wit,
Dredeles,° I have ever yit   *Doubtless*
765   Be tributary° and yive rente°   *Been a vassal / paid tribute*
To Love hooly° with goode entente,°   *entirely / intention*
And thurgh plesaunce° become his thral°   *pleasure / servant, slave*
With good will, body, hert, and al.
Al this I putte in his servage°   *service*
770   As to my lorde and did homage;
And ful devoutly I preyde him to°   *to him that*
He shulde besette° myn herte so°   *bestow / in such a way*
That it plesaunce to him were,
And worship° to my lady dere.   *honor*
775   And this was longe,° and many a yeer   *for a long time*
Er that° myn herte was set o-wher,°   *Before / committed anywhere*
That I did thus, and niste° why;   *did not know*
I trowe° it cam me kindely.°   *believe / to me naturally*
Paraventure I was therto most able
780   As a whyt wal or a table,
For it is redy to cacche and take
Al that men wil therin make,
Whether so men wol portreye or peynte,
Be the werkes never so queynte.[6]
785   And thilke° tyme I ferde right° so: *at that / behaved just*
I was able to have lerned tho°   *then*
And to have coud° as wel or better,   *come to understand*
Paraunter other° art or letter.°   *Perhaps another / subject of study*
But for° love cam first in my thought,   *because*

---

6. Perhaps I was most receptive (to Love), (being) like a white wall or a (blank) tablet, for it is ready
   to take and receive all that men want to put there, whether men wish to draw or paint (and) no
   matter how elaborate (the design). (The Aristotelian image of the untutored mind as a blank slate
   was widely known in medieval philosophy, in writers from Boethius to William of Ockham; it also
   appears in secular texts, like Guillaume de Machaut's *Remède de Fortune*.)

790   Therfore I forgat it nought.
      I chees° love to° my firste craft,   *chose / to be*
      Therfor it is with me y-laft.°   *remains with me*
      Forwhy I took it of so yong age
      That malice hadde my corage
795   Nat that tyme turned to nothinge
      Thurgh too mochel knowlechinge;[7]
      For that tyme Youthe, my maistresse,°   *mistress, instructor*
      Governed me in ydelnesse,
      For it was in my firste youthe,
800   And tho ful litel good I couthe;[8]
      For al my werkes° were flittinge,°   *activities / always changing*
      And al my thought varyinge.°   *thoughts (were) unsettled*
      Al° were to me y-liche° good,   *All things / equally*
      That I knew tho,° but thus it stood: *then*
805   It happed° that I came on a day   *happened, chanced*
      Into a place ther that° I say,°   *where / saw*
      Trewly, the fairest companye
      Of ladies that ever man with eye
      Had seen togedres° in o° place.   *together / one*
810   Shal I clepe° it hap other° grace   *call / luck or*
      That brought me there? Nay, but Fortune,
      That is to lyen ful comune,°   *a notorious liar*
      The false traiteresse pervers,°   *wicked, perverted*
      God wolde I coude clepe hir° wers!   *call her something*
815   For now she worcheth° me ful wo,°   *causes / great woe*
      And I wol telle sone why so.
        Amonge these ladies thus echoon,°   *each one*
      Sooth° to seyn, I sawe oon°   *Truth / one*
      That was lyk noon° of the route,°   *like none / crowd*
820   For I dar° swere, withoute doute,°   *dare / a doubt*
      That as the someres sonne bright
      Is fairer, clerer,° and hath more light   *brighter*
      Than any other planete in hevene,
      The mone° or the sterres sevene,°   *(Than) the moon / i.e., the Pleiades*
825   For al the worlde so had she
      Surmounted hem° al of° beaute,   *Surpassed them / in*
      Of maner° and of comlinesse,°   *In manners / in loveliness*
      Of stature° and of wel set° gladnesse,   *form / fitting*
      Of goodlihede° and so wel beseye°— *excellence, virtue / beautiful*
830   Shortly,° what shal I more seye?   *In short*
      By God and by his halwes twelve,°   *the twelve apostles*
      It was my swete,° right al hirselve!° *sweetheart / her very self*
      She had so° stedfast countenaunce,° *such / bearing, composure*
      So noble port° and meyntenaunce.° *deportment / conduct, behavior*

---

7. Because I took to (Love) at such a young age that malice had not yet reduced my heart to rubbish
from knowing too much. (The word "malice" is hard to interpret. Does Chaucer suggest that more
knowledge and experience of life leads a lover to malice—i.e., to wickedness? Or does the man in
black imply that age and experience subject one to the malice of others—i.e., to suffering? The
Middle English Dictionary supports both readings, but the moral implications for the poem's treat-
ment of Love are quite different.)
8. And then I had little idea how to behave.

835 And Love, that had herd my bone,°   *prayer, request*
    Had espyed° me thus sone,°   *found / so quickly*
    That she ful sone in my thought,°   *into my thoughts*
    As helpe me God, so was y-caught°   *caught up*
    So sodeinly° that I ne tooke   *suddenly*
840 No maner reed but at° hir looke   *kind of instruction except from*
    And at myn° herte; forwhy° hir eyen   *from my (own) / because*
    So gladly, I trow,° myn herte seyen°   *believe / saw*
    That purely tho° myn owne thought°   *absolutely then / my own mind*
    Seyde it were bet° serve hir for nought° *would be better to / nothing*
845 Than with another to be wel.°   *get on well, be successful*
    And it was sooth,° for everydel°   *true / in all respects*
    I wil anonright° telle thee why.   *at once*
        I saw hir daunce so comcely,°   *gracefully*
    Carole° and singe so swetely,   *dance or sing in a round*
850 Laughe and pley so womanly,°   *in such a womanly way*
    And looke so debonairly,°   *graciously*
    So goodly speke° and so frendly   *speak so courteously*
    That certes,° I trow,° that evermore°   *certainly / believe / never*
    Nas seyn° so blisful a tresore.°   *has been seen / glorious treasure*
855 For every heer upon hir hede,°   *hair on her head*
    Sooth° to seyn, it was nat rede,°   *truth / red*
    Ne nouther° yelow ne broun it nas;°   *Nor either / was not*
    Me thoughte most lyk gold it was.
    And which eyen° my lady hadde!   *such eyes*
860 Debonair,° goode, glade, and sadde,°   *Gracious / steadfast, true*
    Simple,° of good mochel,° nought too wyde; *modest / size*
    Therto° hir looke nas nat asyde°   *Also / was not sidelong*
    Ne overthwert,° but beset so wele,°   *nor askance / so well directed*
    It drew° and took up everydele°   *attracted / completely charmed*
865 Al that° on hir gan beholde.°   *All who / looked upon her*
    Hir eyen° semed anoon° she wolde   *eyes, gaze / soon*
    Have mercy°—fooles wenden so°—   *i.e., in love / believed that*
    But it was never the rather do.°   *nevertheless not so*
    It° nas no countrefeted thing;°   *i.e., her gaze / pretense, affectation*
870 It was hir owne pure° looking,   *perfect, genuine*
    That the goddesse, dame Nature,
    Had made hem° opene by mesure,°   *i.e., her eyes / moderately*
    And close; for, were she never so glad,° *however happy she was*
    Hir looking was nat foly sprad,°   *foolishly open-eyed*
875 Ne wildely, though that she pleyde;°   *was having fun*
    But ever, me thought,° hir eyen seyde,   *it seemed to me*
    "By God, my wrathe is al foryive!"⁹
    Therwith hir liste so wel to live,°   *life so pleased her*
    That dulnesse° was of hir adrad.°   *boredom / afraid*
880 She nas° too sobre° ne too glad;°   *was not / serious / cheerful*
    In alle thinges more mesure°   *moderation*

---

9. By God, I forgive any cause of anger! (The man in black interprets his lady's demeanor in the
   terms of courtly love, where haughtiness or anger was part of the game of aloofness that made the
   lady ever more appealing; this is a misinterpretation, however, for he learns his lady is not playing
   love games and bears a virtuous affection toward all mankind.)

Had never, I trowe,° creature.   *I believe, any*
But many oon° with hir looke° she herte,°   *a one / glance / wounded*
And that sat hir ful litel at herte,°   *little concerned her*
885 For she knew nothing of hir thought;°   *about their thoughts*
But whether she knew or knew it nought,
Algate° she ne roughte of hem a stree!°   *Anyway / didn't give a straw*
To gete hir° love no neer° was he   *win / nearer, closer*
That woned at hoom° than he in Inde;°   *dwelled at home / India*
890 The formest° was alwey behinde.   *first*
But goode folk over al other°   *above all others*
She loved as man may do his brother;
Of whiche love she was wonder large°   *wondrously generous*
In skilful° places that bere charge.°   *well chosen / were worthy*
895 But which a visage° had she therto!°   *what a (beautiful) face / also*
Allas, myn herte is wonder wo°   *woeful, distressed*
That I ne can descryven° it!   *am not able to describe*
Me lakketh° bothe Englissh° and wit   *I lack / i.e., the language*
For to undo it at the fulle,°   *disclose, explain it fully*
900 And eek° my spirits be so dulle°   *also / wits are too slow*
So greet a thinge for to devyse.°   *describe*
I have no witte that can suffyse°   *is adequate*
To comprehende° hir beautee;   *put into words*
But thus moche dar I seyn, that she
905 Was whyte, rody,° fressh, and lyvely hewed,°   *rosy / i.e., sparkling*
And every day hir beautee newed.°   *renewed itself*
And nigh hir face was alderbest,[1]
For certes,° Nature had swich lest°   *certainly / took such pleasure*
To make° that fair° that trewly she   *In creating / beautiful one*
910 Was hir cheef patron of° beautee   *most important pattern for*
And cheef ensample° of al hir werke°   *illustration / works*
And moustre;° for, be it never so derke,   *the model, exemplar*
Me thinketh° I see hir evermo.°   *It seems to me / always*
And yet moreover, though alle tho°   *those*
915 That ever lived were now alyve,
Ne sholde have founde to descryve
In al hir face a wikked signe,[2]
For it was sad, simple, and benigne.°   *steadfast, innocent, and kind*
And which° a goodly, softe speche°   *what a / way of speaking*
920 Had that swete,° my lyves leche!°   *sweet one / healer, protector*
So frendly and so wel y-grounded,°   *based*
Up° al resoun so wel y-founded,°   *Upon / established*
And so tretable° to alle goode,°   *receptive / everything good*
That I dar° swere by the roode°   *dare / (Christ's) cross*
925 Of eloquence was never° founde   *has never been*
So swete a souninge facounde,°   *Such sweet-sounding fluency*
Ne trewer tonged, ne scorned lasse,
Ne bet coude hele, that by the masse
I durste swere, though the Pope it songe,

---

1. And her face was approaching perfection.
2. (Nobody) would have been able to discover in her face (anything he could) describe as a sign of wickedness.

930 That ther was never yet thurgh hir tonge	
Man ne woman greetly harmed;	
As for hir, ther was al harm hid,³	
Ne lasse flateringe° in hir worde,°	*less flattery / words*
That° purely hir simple recorde°	*So that / testimony*
935 Was founde as trewe as any bonde°	*covenant, commitment*
Or trouthe° of any mannes honde.	*pledge*
Ne chyde° she coude never a dele,°	*scold, nit-pick / not at all*
That knoweth al the world ful wele.	
But swich° a fairnesse of a nekke°	*such / neck*
940 Had that swete that boon° nor brekke°	*bone / blemish*
Nas° ther noon sene that missat.°	*There was / was unbecoming*
It was whyte, smothe, streight, and pure flat,°	*completely smooth*
Withouten hole° or canel-boon,°	*hollow / collar bone*
As by seming,° had she noon.	*So that it seemed*
945 Hir throte, as I have now memoire,°	*memory*
Semed a round tour of yvoire,⁴	
Of good greetnesse,° and nought too grete.°	*size / large*
And goode faire Whyte she hete,°	*was called*
That was my lady name right.°	*lady's proper name*
950 She was bothe fair and bright;	
She hadde nat hir name wronge.	
Right faire shuldres,° and body longe°	*beautiful shoulders / tall*
She had, and armes; every lith°	*limb*
Fattissh, flesshy,° nat greet° therwith;	*Rounded, plump / (too) large*
955 Right whyte handes and nailes rede,°	*reddish*
Rounde brestes, and of good brede°	*width*
Hir hippes were, a streight flat bakke.°	*back*
I knew on hir noon other lakke°	*no other defect*
That al hir limes nere pure sewing,	
960 In as fer as I had knowing.⁵	
Therto° she coude so wel pley°	*In addition / have fun*
Whan that hir liste,° that I dar sey,	*it pleased her*
That she was lyk to torche° bright,	*like the candle, torch*
That every man may take of light°	*take light from*
965 Ynough,° and it hath never the lesse.	*Plentiful, sufficient*
Of° maner and of comlinesse°	*In (her) / beauty*
Right° so ferde° my lady dere,	*Just / fared*
For every wight of° hir manere	*person from*
Might cacche° ynough if that he wolde,°	*take / wished*

3. Nor (anyone) more likely to speak the truth or less likely to scorn others, nor (anyone) who could bring more comfort, so much so that I would venture to swear by the (holy) mass, even if it were sung by the Pope (himself), that through her tongue no man or woman was ever greatly harmed. As far as she was concerned, no harm was in evidence. (The last probably means that she never slandered or spoke anything to harm others.)

4. The image of a "round tower of ivory" has its ultimate source in the biblical Song of Solomon 7:4, and was used in medieval times as an image of the virgin Mary. It may also recall the chess imagery from earlier in the poem. The color of ivory and the lady's name (Whyte, 148) are used here in remembrance of the historical Blanche (French for "white") of Lancaster, John of Gaunt's wife (see my introduction to the poem).

5. That would result in her limbs being anything other than perfectly proportioned, inasmuch as I had knowledge. (The man in black here completes his physical description of the lady with the decorous, though somewhat coy, admission of what, in honor, he cannot know at this point about the extent of her beauty. The description of the lady "Whyte" has followed the standard rhetorical format of the "blazon" or "effictio," which itemizes female beauty from head to toe.)

970 If he had eyen° hir to beholde.	*eyes*
For I dar swere wel, if that she	
Had amonge ten thousand be,°	*been*
She wolde have be at the leste°	*least*
A cheef mirour of° al the feste,°	*model for / the party*
975 Though they had stonde° in a rowe	*stood*
To mennes eyen° coude have knowe.	*In the eyes of men (who)*
For wherso° men had pleyd or waked°	*wherever / stayed up (partying)*
Me thoughte the felawship as naked°	*was as lacking*
Withouten hir, that° saw I ones,°	*as that which / once*
980 As a coroune° withoute stones.°	*crown / gems*
Trewly she was to myn eye	
The soleyn fenix of Arabye,⁶	
For ther liveth never but oon,°	*one (at a time)*
Ne swich° as she ne know I noon.	*such*
985 To speke of goodnesse, trewly she	
Had as moche debonairte°	*grace*
As ever had Hester⁷ in the bible	
And more if more were possible.	
And, sooth° to seyne, therwithal°	*truth / besides*
990 She had a wit° so general,°	*mind, understanding / liberal*
So hoole° enclyned to alle goode°	*completely / benefit of others*
That al hir wit was set, by the roode,°	*(Christ's) cross*
Withoute malice° upon gladnesse;°	*ill will / happiness*
Therto° I saw never yet a lesse	*Also*
995 Harmful° than she was in doing.°	*Mischievous, injurious person / action*
I sey nat that she ne had knowing°	*the knowledge of*
What harme was, or elles° she	*else*
Had coud no good,° so thinketh me.	*Wouldn't have understood virtue*
And trewly, for to speke of trouthe,°	*honor, honesty*
1000 But° she had had,° it had be routhe.°	*Unless / possessed (it) / a pity*
Therof she had so moche hir dele,°	*portion, share*
And I dar seyn° and swere it wele,	*dare say*
That Trouthe himself, over al and al,°	*over and above all others*
Had chose his maner principal°	*main residence*
1005 In hir, that was his resting place.	
Therto° she hadde the moste grace°	*Also / greatest favor*
To have° stedfast perseveraunce	*Of possessing*
And esy atempre governaunce°	*temperate self-control*
That ever I knew or wiste yit,°	*was aware of to date*
1010 So pure suffraunt° was hir wit.°	*utterly tolerant / understanding*
And reson gladly she understoode,	
It folowed wel she coude goode.°	*knew what was best*
She used gladly to do wel;	
These were hir maners everydel.°	*in every respect*
1015 Therwith she loved so wel right,°	*what was proper, just*
She wrong do wolde° to no wight;°	*intended wrong / person*
No wight might do hir no° shame,	*could bring upon her any*

---

6. The solitary phoenix of Arabia. (The phoenix is a mythical Arabian bird, only one of which can exist at a time; when one phoenix dies, the new one arises out of its ashes.)
7. The biblical Esther was a model of womanliness and sacrifice on behalf of others.

She loved so wel hir owne name.°	*reputation*
Hir lust° to holde no wight in honde,°	*She wished / toy with*
1020 Ne, be thou siker, she wolde nat fonde°	*try*
To holde no wight in balaunce°	*any person in suspense, uncertainty*
By half word° ne by	*verbal insinuation*
countenaunce,°	*outward expression*
But if° men wolde upon° hir lye;	*Unless / about*
Ne sende men into Walakye,	
1025 To Pruyse, and into Tartarye,	
To Alisaundre, ne into Turkye,	
And bidde him faste anoon that he	
Go hoodless into the Drye See,	
And come hoom by the Carrenare;⁸	
1030 And seye, "Sir, be now right ware°	*take particular care*
That I may of yow here seyn°	*hear said*
Worship er° that ye come ageyn!"	*A favorable report before*
She ne used no swich knakkes smale.°	*such petty ruses*
But wherfor that I° telle my tale?	*why do I*
1035 Right on this same,° as I have seyde,	*this very same (lady)*
Was hooly° al my love leyde,°	*entirely / laid, placed*
For certes,° she was, that swete wyfe,°	*certainly / woman*
My suffisaunce,° my lust,° my lyfe,	*contentment, satisfaction / desire*
Myn happe,° myn hele,° and al my blisse,	*good fortune / health*
1040 My worldes welfare, and my goddesse,	
And I hooly° hires, and everydel."°	*entirely / in every way*
"By our Lord," quod° I, "I trowe° yow wel.	*said / believe*
Hardely° your love was wel beset,°	*Assuredly / placed*
I noot° how ye might have do bet."°	*don't know / done better*
1045 "Bet? Ne no wight so wel!"° quod he.	*man (had done) as well*
"I trowe it, sir," quod I, "pardee."°	*indeed, by God*
"Nay, leve° it wel!" "Sir, so do I;	*Believe*
I leve yow wel, that trewly	
Yow thoughte° that she was the beste	*It seemed to you*
1050 And to beholde the alderfaireste,°	*most beautiful*
Whoso° had looked hir with° your eyen."	*Whoever / seen her through*
"With myn? Nay, alle that hir seyen°	*who saw her*
Seyde and swore it was so.	
And though° they ne had,° I wolde tho°	*even if / had not / then*
1055 Have loved best my lady free,°	*noble, generous*
Though I had had al the beautee	
That ever had Alcipyades	
And al the strengthe of Ercules,	
And therto had the worthinesse	
1060 Of Alisaundre and al the richesse	
That ever was in Babiloyne,	
In Cartage or in Macedoyne,	

8. The locations listed are, in order, Walachia (in southern Romania), Prussia, Outer Mongolia (land of the Tatars), Alexandria (in Egypt), Turkey, the Gobi Desert (in Outer Mongolia), and the Qara Na'ur ("Black Lake" on the far side of the Gobi). All were areas either of Christian/Muslim conflict or distantly situated on the medieval trade route to the Far East, and are here mentioned as far-away and dangerous regions, not suitable for a romantic quest. Going to any of them "hoodless" or without head protection would be particularly foolish.

      Or in Rome, or in Ninive,
      And therto also hardy be
1065 As was Ector, so have I joye,
      That Achilles slow at Troye—
      And therfor was he slayn also
      In a temple, for bothe two
      Were slayn, he and Antilegius,
1070 And so seyth Dares Frigius,
      For love of Polixena—
      Or ben as wys as Minerva,[9]
      I wolde ever,° withoute drede,°   *always / without a doubt*
      Have loved hir, for I most nede!°   *needs must (do so)*
1075 Nede? Nay, trewly, I gabbe° now,   *speak nonsense*
      Nought 'nede,' and I wol telle how,
      For of good wille myn herte it wolde,°   *wished for, desired*
      And eek° to love hir I was holde°   *also / obliged*
      As for° the fairest and the beste.   *to*
1080 She was as good, so have I° reste,   *as I may have*
      As ever was Penolopee of Grece
      Or as the noble wyfe Lucrece,
      That was the beste—he telleth thus,
      The Romayne Tytus Livius—
1085 She was as good, and nothing lyke,[1]
      Though hir° stories be autentyke;°   *their / trustworthy, authoritative*
      Algate° she was as trewe as she.°   *In any case / i.e., as Lucrece*
      But wherfor° that I telle thee   *why is it*
      Whan I first my lady sey?°   *saw*
1090 I was right yong,° sooth to sey,°   *quite / truth to tell*
      And ful greet need° I had to lerne;°   *a very great deal / learn*
      Whan my herte wolde yerne°   *eagerly longed*
      To love, it was a greet empryse.°   *undertaking, enterprise*
      But as my wit° coude best suffyse,°   *understanding / suffice*
1095 After° my yonge childly° wit,   *In accord with / childish*
      Withoute drede,° I besette° it   *Without a doubt / applied*
      To love hir in my beste wyse,°   *fashion*
      To do hir worship° and servyse   *the honor*
      That I tho coude,° by my trouthe,°   *then knew how / faith*
1100 Withoute feyning outher slouthe.°   *pretense or sloth*
      For wonder fain° I wolde° hir see,   *wondrously gladly / wished to*
      So mochel° it amended° me,   *much / cheered, restored*

---

9. Alcibiades, the son of an Athenian general and statesman in the fifth century B.C.E., was renowned for his beauty; the mighty Hercules was legendary for his strength; by the time of his death in 323 B.C.E. at the age of thirty-three, Alexander the Great controlled an empire that reached from Greece to India; Babylon, Carthage, Macedonia, Rome, and Nineveh were all cities or regions known for their extraordinary wealth; "hardy" (brave) Hector, slain on the battlefield by Achilles, was the eldest prince and preeminent warrior of Troy; Achilles and Antilochus were slain together, in revenge for Hector's death, as they attempted to woo the Trojan princess Polyxena in a medieval retelling of the Trojan story by Dares Frygius; Minerva was the goddess of wisdom.
1. She was as good (as they), and (at the same time really) nothing like (them). (The man in black consistently stresses his lady's uniqueness even as he elevates her through conventional comparisons. Penelope, the steadfast wife of Odysseus, was a standard example of wifely truth and forbearance; Livy (Tytus Livius) tells the story of the Roman noblewoman Lucretia (sixth century B.C.E.), who chose suicide rather than dishonor after being raped, and Chaucer retells it in the *Legend of Good Women* 1680–1885.)

That, whan I saw hir first a-morwe,°   *in the morning*
I was warisshed° of al my sorwe°   *healed, relieved / sorrow*
1105 Of al° day after til it were eve;°   *For the whole / was evening*
Me thoughte° nothing mighte me greve,°   *It seemed / grieve, injure*
Were my sorwes never so smerte.[2]
And yet° she sit° so in myn herte   *still / dwells, remains*
That, by my trouthe,° I nolde noughte,°   *faith, honor / would not want*
1110 For al this worlde, out of my thought
Leve° my lady; no, trewly!"   *to give up, let go*
   "Now, by my trouthe, sir," quod° I,   *said*
"Me thinketh ye have swich a chaunce
As shrifte withoute repentaunce."[3]
1115   "Repentaunce! Nay, fy,"° quod he;   *fie, phooey*
"Shulde I now repente me°   *repent*
To love? Nay, certes° than were I wel° *certainly / would I be much*
Wers than was Achitofel,
Or Anthenor, so have I joye,
1120 The traitour that betraysed Troye,
Or the false Genelloun,
He that purchased the tresoun
Of Rowland and of Olyvere.[4]
Nay, whyl I am alyve here°   *as long as I live*
1125 I nil foryete hir nevermo."°   *will never forget her*
   "Now, good sir," quod I tho,°   *then*
"Ye han° wel told me herbifore°—   *have / earlier*
It is° no nede reherse° it more—   *There is / to repeat*
How ye sawe hir first and where.
1130 But wolde ye telle me the manere
To hir which was your firste speche°—   *of your first words*
Therof I wolde yow beseche°—   *beseech, beg*
And how she knewe first your thought,°   *state of mind*
Whether ye loved hir or nought,
1135 And telleth me eek° what ye have lore;°   *also / lost*
I herde yow telle herbifore."°   *talk (about that) before*
   "Ye," seyde he, "thou nost° what thou menest; *do not know*
I have lost more than thou wenest."°   *think, comprehend*
   "What losse is that?" quod I tho;°   *I said then*
1140 "Nil she nat° love yow? Is it so?   *Will she not*
Or have ye ought doon amis,°   *done something wrong*
That° she hath left yow? Is it this?   *So that*
For Goddes love, telle me alle."
   "Bifore God," quod he, "and I shalle.

---

2. No matter how painful my sorrows might be.
3. It seems to me that you are taking a chance on confession without (first) undergoing penance. (The penitential comparison here is obscure, and admits of several alternative interpretations in addition to the translation above: It could also mean that the man in black wants to get off easily— to be shriven [absolved] without repenting first. Or it could mean that he is sorrowing even though he has nothing to repent.)
4. Nay, certainly, then I would be much worse than was Achitofel or Antenor, as I may have joy, the traitor who betrayed Troy, or the false Ganelon, he who brought about the treason against Roland and Oliver. (The biblical Achitophel attempted to betray David by advising his son Absalom to rebel against him [2 Samuel 15–17]; in various medieval sources, the Trojan Antenor was responsible for Troy's fall to the Greeks; Ganelon sold the battle position of the French heroes Roland and Oliver to the Saracen enemy in the Old French *Song of Roland*. All were notorious traitors.)

1145	I sey right° as I have seyde,	*just*
	On hir was al my love leyde,°	*laid, placed*
	And yet she niste° it nat never a del,°	*did not know / not a bit*
	Nought longe° tyme, leve° it wel.	*for a long / believe*
	For be right siker,° I durste° nought	*quite certain / dared*
1150	For al this worlde telle hir my thought,	
	Ne I wolde have wratthed° hir, trewly.	*angered*
	For wostow° why? She was lady°	*do you know / i.e., mistress*
	Of the body; she had the herte,	
	And who hath that, may nat asterte.°	*be eluded*
1155	But, for to kepe me fro° ydelnesse,	*from*
	Trewly I did my besynesse°	*acted diligently*
	To make songes, as I best coude,	
	And ofte tyme° I songe hem loude,°	*often / them aloud*
	And made songes thus a grete del,°	*deal*
1160	Although I coude nat make so wel	*compose as*
	Songes, ne knowe the art al	
	As coude Lamekes sone Tubal,	
	That fond out first the art of songe,	
	For, as his brothres hamers ronge	
1165	Upon his anvelt up and doun,	
	Therof he took the firste soun.	
	But Grekes seyn Pictagoras,	
	That he the firste finder was	
	Of the arte; Aurora telleth so.	
1170	But therof no fors of hem two.[5]	
	Algates° songes thus I made	*At any rate*
	Of° my felinge, myn herte to glade;°	*About / gladden, comfort*
	And lo, this was alderferst,°	*first (song) of all*
	I noot wher that° it were the werst:°	*don't know whether / worst*
1175	'Lord, it maketh myn herte light,°	*i.e., happy*
	Whan I thinke on that swete wight°	*being, creature*
	That is so semely on to see;°	*pleasing to look upon*
	And wisshe° to God it might so be,	*I wish, hope*
	That she wolde holde° me for° hir knight,	*take / as*
1180	My lady, that is so fair and bright!'	
	Now have I told thee, sooth to saye,°	*truthfully*
	My firste song. Upon a daye°	*One day*
	I bethoughte me° what wo	*considered*
	And sorwe° that I suffred tho°	*sorrow / had suffered then*
1185	For hir, and yet she wiste it nought,°	*knew nothing about it*
	Ne telle hir durste I nat° my thought.	*Nor dared I tell her*
	'Allas!' thoughte I, 'I can no rede°°	*know no way out*
	And, but° I telle hir, I nam but dede;°	*unless / am simply dead*
	And if I telle hir, to seye soothe,°	*truly*

---

5. Nor (did I) know the art as well as did Lamech, the son of Tubal, he who first invented the craft of composing songs, for as his brother's hammers rang out, going up and down on the anvil, from that Lamech took the first (musical) sound. But the Greeks say that Pythagoras was the first inventor of that art; so says Aurora. But pay no mind to those two. (One of the sons of the biblical Lamech was Jubal, reputed inventor of music; another son Tubalcain invented brass and iron [Genesis 4:16–24]. The *Aurora* [shorthand for a work by the twelfth-century Peter of Riga] names both Jubal and Pythagoras as founders of music.)

1190	I am adred° she wol be wroothe;°	*afraid, terrified / angry*
	Allas! What shal I thanne° do?'	*then, in this case*
	In this debat° I was so wo°	*inner turmoil / distraught*
	Me thoughte° myn herte braste atweyne!°	*It seemed / would burst in two*
	So atte laste, sooth to seyne,°	*truth to tell*
1195	I bethought me° that nature	*considered, thought*
	Ne formed never° in creature	*Had never formed*
	So moche beautee, trewly,	
	And bountee,° withoute mercy.	*goodness, benevolence*
	In hope of that, my tale I tolde	
1200	With sorwe, as that I never sholde,	
	For nedes, and maugree my heed,	
	I moste have told hir or be deed.[6]	
	I noot° wel how that I began,	*do not know*
	Ful evel reherse it I can;	
1205	And eek, as helpe me God withal,	
	I trowe it was in the dismal,	
	That was the ten woundes of Egipte,[7]	
	For many a word I overskipte°	*skipped, stumbled over*
	In my tale, for pure fere°	*fear*
1210	Lest my wordes missete were.°	*be unsuitable, misplaced*
	With sorweful herte and woundes dede,°	*deadly*
	Softe° and quaking for pure drede	*Softly*
	And shame, and stinting° in my tale	*halting*
	For ferde,° and myn hewe° al pale,	*fear, dread / complexion*
1215	Ful ofte I wex° bothe pale and rede.°	*often I grew / flushed*
	Bowing to hir, I heng the hede;°	*hung my head*
	I durste nat ones° looke hir on,°	*dared not once / upon*
	For wit, manere,° and al was gon.	*manners, proper conduct*
	I seyde 'mercy,' and no more;	
1220	It nas no game,° it sate me sore.°	*joke / moved me to pain*
	So at the laste, sooth to seyne,°	*truth to tell*
	Whan that myn herte° was come ageyne,°	*heart, inner self / had returned*
	To telle shortly° al my speche,	*recount briefly*
	With hool° herte I gan hir beseche°	*(my) whole / asked, prayed her*
1225	That she wolde be my lady swete,	
	And swore, and gan hir hertely hete°	*earnestly, fervently promised*
	Ever to be stedfast and trewe	
	And love hir alwey fresshly newe°	*anew*
	And never other lady° have	*any other lady to*
1230	And al hir worship° for to save°	*honor / protect, preserve*
	As I best coude; I swore hir this:	
	'For youres is al that ever ther is	
	For evermore, myn herte swete!	
	And never to false° yow but I mete,°	*be false to / unless I'm dreaming*
1235	I nil,° as wisse° God helpe me so!'	*will not / surely as*

6. In expectation of (her mercy), I told my story in sorrow, as one who would never have spoken unless forced, and so in spite of myself, I had to (reveal my secret) to her or I would have died.

7. Quite badly can I repeat it now; and also, so help me God, I believe that it happened during the unlucky days (the "dismal," probably from the French "evil days"), which constitute the ten wounds of Egypt. (In this complex reference, Chaucer connects the medieval superstition that some days are unlucky with biblical allusions—see Exodus 9, 12—to the plagues [or "wounds"] of Egypt.)

    And whan I had my tale y-do,° — *done, finished*
    God wote,° she acounted nat a stree° — *knows / didn't give a straw*
    Of° al my tale, so thoughte me.° — *For / it seemed to me*
    To telle shortly right° as it is, — *briefly just*
1240 Trewly hir answere, it was this;
    I can nat now wel countrefete° — *repeat exactly*
    Hir wordes, but this was the grete° — *gist, upshot*
    Of hir answere: she seyde, 'Nay'
    Al utterly. Allas, that day
1245 The sorwe° I suffred and the wo! — *sorrow*
    —That° trewly Cassandra, that so — *So much that*
    Bewailed° the destruccioun — *lamented*
    Of Troy and of Ilioun,[8]
    Had never swich° sorwe as I tho.° — *such / had at that time*
1250 I durst° no more sey therto° — *dared / about that*
    For pure fere, but stal away.° — *I slipped away*
    And thus I lived ful many a day,
    That° trewly, I hadde no nede — *(In such state) that*
    Ferther than my beddes hede° — *bed's head*
1255 Never a day to seche sorwe;° — *to seek out sorrow*
    I fonde it redy every morwe,° — *morning*
    Forwhy° I loved hir in no gere.° — *Because / light, changeable fashion*
    So it befel,° another yere, — *came about*
    I thoughte ones° I wolde fonde° — *once (more) / attempt*
1260 To do° hir knowe and understonde — *make*
    My wo; and she wel understoode
    That I ne wilned° nothing but goode° — *desired / goodness*
    And worship° and to kepe hir name° — *honor / preserve her reputation*
    Over° al thing, and drede hir° shame, — *Above / protected her from*
1265 And was so besy° hir to serve; — *eager, attentive*
    And pitee were I shulde sterve,
    Sith that I wilned noon harme ywis.[9]
    So whan my lady knewe al this,
    My lady yaf° me al hooly° — *gave / unreservedly*
1270 The noble yifte° of hir mercy, — *gift*
    Saving° hir worship by° al weyes; — *Preserving / honor in*
    Dredles,° I mene noon other weyes.° — *Fear not / nothing otherwise*
    And therwith° she yaf° me a ringe; — *with that / gave*
    I trowe° it was the firste° thinge. — *believe / earliest, also foremost*
1275 But if myn herte was y-waxe° — *(then) became, grew*
    Glad, that is no need to axe!° — *ask*
    As° helpe me God, I was as blyve° — *So / quickly*
    Reysed as fro° deeth to lyve,° — *from / life*
    Of alle happes° the alderbeste,° — *fortunes / the very best*
1280 The gladdest and the moste at reste.° — *contented*
    For trewly, that swete wight,° — *creature, person*
    Whan I had° wrong and she the right, — *was in the*

8. Cassandra was the Trojan princess whose prophecy of Troy's destruction was doomed to be ignored. Her lament over the fall of Troy is included in medieval versions of the story by Guido delle Colonne and Benoit de Sainte Maure. Ilioun (for Latin "Ilium") was the citadel in Troy; see also the *Legend of Good Women* 936, and the *House of Fame* 158.
9. And it would have been a pity if I were to die since I truly meant no harm.

	She wolde alwey so goodely°	*pleasingly, courteously*
	Foryeve° me so debonairely.°	*forgive / graciously*
1285	In al my youthe, in al chaunce,°	*cases, events*
	She tooke me in hir governaunce.°	*under her guidance, care*
	Therwith° she was alwey so trewe,	*Also*
	Our joye was ever yliche newe;°	*unfailingly fresh*
	Our hertes weren so even a paire°	*evenly matched*
1290	That never nas that oon° contraire	*was (the wish) of one*
	To that other, for no wo.°	*whatever the sad (circumstance)*
	For soothe,° yliche° they suffred tho°	*truly / alike / then*
	O° blisse and eek o sorwe° bothe;	*One / also one sorrow*
	Yliche° they were bothe gladde and wrothe.°	*Equally / angry, vexed*
1295	Al was us oon,° withoute were.°	*We were united / quarrel*
	And thus we lived ful many a yere	
	So wel, I can nat telle how."°	*fully convey it*
	"Sir," quod° I, "where is she now?"	*said*
	"Now?" quod he, and stinte anoon.°	*stopped at once*
1300	Therwith° he wex° as deed as stoon,	*With that / grew*
	And seyde, "Allas that I was bore!°	*born*
	That was the los° that herbifore°	*loss / earlier*
	I tolde thee that I had lorne.°	*suffered*
	Bethinke° how I seyde herbiforne,	*Remember, consider*
1305	'Thou wost ful litel° what thou menest;	*know very little*
	I have lost more than thou wenest.'°	*think, comprehend*
	God wot,° allas, right that was she!"	*knows*
	"Allas, sir, how? What may that be?"°	*What do you mean?*
	"She is deed." "Nay!" "Yis, by my trouthe."°	*faith, honor*
1310	"Is that your los? By God, it is routhe."°	*a cause for pity*
	And with that worde, right anoon°	*all at once*
	They gan to strake forth. Al was doon,	
	For that tyme, the herte hunting.[1]	
	With that, me thoughte that this king	
1315	Gan quikly hoomward for to ryde	
	Unto a place was ther besyde,	
	Which was from us but a lyte:	
	A longe castel with walles whyte,	
	By Seynt Johan, on a riche hille,	
1320	As me mette; but thus it fille.[2]	
	Right thus me mette,° as I yow telle,	*dreamed*
	That in the castel was a belle,	
	As it had smyte° houres twelve,°	*(And) as it struck / midnight?*
	Therwith° I awooke myselve,°	*With that / awakened*

1. They began to blow the notes on the horn that sounded the end of the hunt. For the moment, the hart hunt was done.
2. With that, it seemed to me that this king quickly rode homeward, to a place quite near, only a small distance away: a tall castel with white walls, situated—by Saint John—on a splendid hill, as I dreamed; but thus it happened. (In these lines Chaucer gives us the most pointed clues to the poem's occasion. "Seynt Johan" on a "riche hille" [French "riche mont"] is most likely a reference to John of Gaunt, also the Earl of Richmond; the "longe castel" with "walles whyte" to his wife Blanche of Lancaster, who died in 1368 of plague [John was also the Duke of Lancaster; see my introduction]. The specific identity of the "king" is open to debate, for it could simply allude back to Octavian [368], or it could suggest John of Gaunt or his father, Edward III. Some critics also see in Saint John an allusion to the Book of Revelations 21–22, where the Evangelist's vision of the New Jerusalem, another city on a hill, is described.)

1325 And fonde me° lying in my bed;   *found myself*
And the booke that I had red
Of Alcyone and Seys the kinge
And of the goddes of slepinge,
I fond it in myn honde ful even.°   *just like that*
1330   Thought I, "This is so queynt a sweven°   *strange, curious a dream*
That I wol, by processe° of tyme,   *in the course*
Fonde° to putte this sweven in ryme°   *Strive / rhyme*
As I can° best, and that anoon."°   *am able, know how / at once*
This was my sweven; now it is doon.

The House of Fame

If the chief focus of the *Book of the Duchess* is human emotion, specifically the power of grief, the *House of Fame* forms a distinctive contrast: It is a highly intellectual and literary poetic performance, skeptical if not lighthearted in tone. As one reader calls it, this "most bookish of Chaucer's books"[1] puts Chaucer's learning on display. In the guise of bewilderment, the dreaming narrator launches into the major theories of the origins and interpretation of dreams themselves. He draws knowledgeably upon biblical dreams and themes; he retells the ancient story of Dido and Aeneas from the conflicting perspectives of Virgil and Ovid; he demonstrates a wide-ranging knowledge of classical and medieval literary traditions from Homer (whom he could only have known indirectly) to the great Italian visionary poet Dante; and he even shows a respectable understanding of medieval astronomy, physics, and acoustics. Although the poem wears its learning lightly—indeed, it mocks erudition and artistic pretense—it is an ambitious and bravura demonstration of its author's increasing confidence in his craft. It is probably the poem that his fifteenth-century admirer and imitator, John Lydgate, called "Dante in Inglissh."[2]

At the same time, the *House of Fame* presents something of a paradox: Far from "bookish," its nervous, confiding narrator offers us glimpses into what seems to be the poet's "real life." To some extent, this impression is a function of Chaucer's growing ability to capture the pace and movement of dialogue in the engaging conversation of the eagle and his fretful charge: 'Don't you *want* to learn anything about the stars?' the bird asks the squirming poet he carries in his claws higher and higher into the heavens. "Nay, certeynly," the dreamer replies, "right nought." "And why?" "For I am now too old" (993–95). When the eagle plays upon his passenger's fear of falling, drawing attention to how troublesome he is to carry (see 574, 660, 737–46), the reader recalls medieval portraiture of a small, plump Chaucer and the other places in his poetry where he represents himself as a "popet" (a little doll) with a wide waist (see the Prologue to Sir Thopas, the *Canterbury Tales* 7.700–701). Like those other, later "Chaucers," this one is presented as a poet—one who has composed "bookes, songes, dytees" in honor of Love (622). Who, one wonders, is the person (the "oon I coude nevene [name]," 562) of whom he is reminded by the eagle barking out the command "Awake"? Many have conjectured that it is the poet's wife, Philippa Chaucer, a surmise reinforced by the seeming verisimilitude of the poem's description of late nights reading, after a day spent laboring over the "rekeninges" or accounts that would have been Chaucer's very real responsibility in his job as customs controller (see 652–60). Indeed, the eagle goes so far as to address Chaucer by his given Christian name: "Geffrey" (729)—the only time in all his poetry where he is addressed with this kind of familiarity.

But it is important to remember that such gestures are at the same time highly conventional. Beatrice also called Dante by name at a similar moment

1. A. J. Minnis, *Oxford Guides to Chaucer: The Shorter Poems* (Oxford: Oxford UP, 1995), 183.
2. John Lydgate, *Fall of Princes*, ed. Henry Bergen, EETS OS 121 (London: Oxford UP, 1924), 1.Prol.303, p. 9.

in the *Divine Comedy* (*Purgatorio* 30.55), to mark a moment of spiritual transition. In the *House of Fame*, the theme of identity, reputation, name (a word that appears twenty-three times just in Book 3) is central to the poem's meaning. Chaucer is thus not so much self-revealing here as he is deploying the notion of privacy as part of a complex investigation of different kinds of truth, both personal and public. In the end, the *House of Fame* remains stubbornly skeptical about the validity of human communication, both written and oral, and the narrator dissatisfied with the kinds of revelations he discovers in either the palace of the goddess Fame or the contiguous spinning House of Rumor. Rather than conferring authority on Fame, the narrator declares that he does not intend to seek meaning in literary or social reputation ("I wot myself best how I stonde"; 1878), and he expresses frustration with the news he finds in her realm: "[T]hese be no swiche tydinges / As I mene of" (1894–95). Given what he has observed, his conclusions are unsurprising. The only law that governs Fame's distribution of renown is that of complete arbitrariness; worth and desert have nothing to do with the reward of good or bad fame, as individuals in precisely equal positions receive from the goddess opposite results (see, for example, 1771–82).

On the level of form, the poem registers its skepticism in its parody of the traditional dream vision. From its temporal and physical setting (December 10, rather than the conventional springtime; a sandy desert, an icy palace rather than a lush garden) to the lore and science provided by its garrulous avian guide-figure, the *House of Fame* systematically frustrates the reader's visionary expectations. Chaucer repeatedly reminds us of all the aspiring visionaries of literary, mythological, and biblical history to whom he should *not* be compared. "I am not Enoch," he asserts, "nor Elijah, Romulus, or Ganymede" (588–89), echoing Dante's "I am not Aeneas, I am not Paul" (*Inferno* 2.32). But, whereas for Dante such protests called attention to the poet's visionary aspiration, for Chaucer they offer repeated opportunities to undermine it, especially as he draws failed fellow travelers, like Icarus and Phaeton (920, 942), into his circle. The eagle, himself a transplant from Dante's *Purgatorio* (9.13–33), may soar into the stratosphere, but his science is decidedly pedestrian and peculiarly material, as for instance when he informs the narrator that, in the principality of Fame, sounds assume the bodily form of the person who uttered them "[b]e it clothed red or blake" (1078). Similarly, the invocations to Books 2 and 3, based on invocations in the *Divine Comedy*, fall flat, with the poet's repeated expressions of doubt in his own ability ("if any vertu in thee be"; 526) as with his plan to kiss the next laurel he sees if only Apollo will assist him (1106–1108). Such parodic moments are less likely to put one in mind of Dante than of the hapless dreamer in the *Book of the Duchess* when he promises a feather-bed to Juno, Morpheus, or 'any other person, I don't care who' (242–44), if provided with the gift of sleep.

It is difficult even to be sure what *kind* of vision the *House of Fame* is supposed to be. There are many clues that it will be a love-vision: The chief location of the first book, which explores different interpretations of the love affair between Dido and Aeneas, is the Temple of Venus; Book 2 begins with an invocation to the goddess of Love; and the eagle there promises the dreamer recompense for his service of Venus and Cupid (613–19). But the theme of love is more intermittent than consistently developed, and there is certainly no sustained attempt to follow earlier medieval authors like Alain de Lille, Jean de Meun, or Dante in building a serious philosophical discussion on the framework of earthly love. Ultimately, the poem seems determined to avoid a coherent synthesis of topics, or any philosophical or literary position beyond a bantering mockery of earthly fame. This posture certainly has implications for understanding what is probably the greatest puzzle posed by the *House of Fame*, its lack of an ending.

While the poem's first editor, the fifteenth-century bibliophile William Caxton, solved the problem expeditiously with a twelve-line wrap-up (included here in a footnote) that awakens the poet who marvels briefly at his dream and determines to understand it better in the future, later readers have offered more elaborate theories. The "man of great authority," who suddenly appears at the poem's end to be on the point of delivering much-awaited news and closure, has been variously identified. Perhaps he is a member of Chaucer's audience (whether John of Gaunt, a foreign messenger bringing a report on a highly anticipated marriage, or the master of revels at a seasonal celebration), a literary-historical figure (maybe Boethius or Boccaccio), the allegorical figure of "Amor," or Jesus Christ himself.[3] Of course, such identifications assume that Chaucer *had* a specific figure in mind, a premise that many readers, especially more recent ones, argue the poem does not support. Indeed, during the past two decades, most critics have turned from the task of identifying the "man of great authority" to discussing the significance to the world-view of the poem of his absence. His is an authority that, as the poem's penultimate line suggests, only "seems to be." Thus, rather than driving forward toward resolution in the form of a unitary truth imparted at the poem's conclusion, the poem's structure is labyrinthine or circular.[4] For no advance on its opening discussion of dreams has been achieved, and nowhere does it establish any basis for a secure or definitive conclusion, as is suggested as well by the multiplication of truths in Book 3, almost as long as Books 1 and 2 combined. In the end, the whirling wicker House of Rumor, where the dreamer ends his travels observing the inevitable compounding of truth and falsehood, offers a fitting architectural image for the restless, tentative world of texts that Chaucer represents in this poem.

Like her sister-goddess Fortune (see 1547), Fame, of course, also conveys the contingency and instability of earthly renown. Chaucer draws his description of Fame chiefly from two passages of classical literature: first, her characterization in Virgil's *Aeneid* 4.173–97 as the last of Mother Earth's daughters, a swift and shape-shifting monster covered with feathers that conceal watchful eyes, blabbing mouths, and ears pricked up for the slightest news; second, her mountaintop location in Ovid's *Metamorphoses* 12.39–63, midway between "the land and seas and the celestial regions," in a dwelling with countless entrances and openings and visited by mobs of liars and tale-tellers who fill her hall with a roar like that of the sea (both passages are included here in the Contexts section). Chaucer is alert to the differences between Virgil and Ovid elsewhere in the poem. In Book 1, lines 143–467, their conflicting perspectives on the story of Dido and Aeneas help the poet to (dis)organize his own complex reading, which veers from word-for-word citation of Virgil to over-identification with Dido and back again to Virgil and Aeneas's victories in Italy. The placement of Virgil, carrying "[t]he fame of Pius Eneas" (1485), next to Ovid, "Venus clerk" (1487), in Fame's hall in Book 3, coyly reminds us that neither alone offers a full or verifiable account. If they concur about nothing

---

3. Space prevents a comprehensive enumeration of the many critics who have participated in this debate, but a partial list would include Larry Benson, "The 'Love Tydynges' in Chaucer's *House of Fame*," in *Chaucer in the Eighties*, ed. Julian N. Wasserman and Robert J. Blanch (Syracuse: Syracuse UP, 1986), 3–22 (marriage news); R. J. Shoeck, "A Legal Reading of Chaucer's *House of Fame*," *University of Toronto Quarterly* 23 (1954): 185–92 (seasonal celebration); John M. Steadman, "*The House of Fame*: Tripartite Structure and Occasion," *Connotations* 3.1 (1993): 1–12 (seasonal celebration); Paul G. Ruggiers, "The Unity of Chaucer's *House of Fame*," *Studies in Philology* 50 (1953): 16–29 (Boethius); R. C. Goffin, "Quiting by Tidings in the *House of Fame*," *Medium Aevum* 12 (1943): 40–44 (Boccaccio); Pat Trefzger Overbeck, "The 'Man of Gret Auctorite' in Chaucer's *House of Fame*," *Modern Philology* 73 (1975): 157–61 ("Amor"); B. G. Koonce, *Chaucer and the Tradition of Fame: Symbolism in the House of Fame* (Princeton: Princeton UP, 1966), esp. 266–75 (Christ).
4. As suggested by Penelope Reed Doob, *The Idea of the Labyrinth from Classical Antiquity through the Middle Ages* (Ithaca: Cornell UP, 1990), 307–39, and Rosemarie P. McGerr, *Chaucer's Open Books: Resistance to Closure in Medieval Discourse* (Gainesville: UP of Florida, 1998), 61–78.

else, however, Virgil and Ovid provide a vision of Fame herself—her inconstancy, perfidy, and general monstrousness—that is remarkably consistent. They agree, paradoxically, only that there is no authoritative textual basis for agreement—that is, for validation of a unitary truth. And linguistically, Chaucer pushes their rupture even further. In distinguishing between the dwellings of Fame and Rumor, Chaucer draws a contrast that would not have been present in his Latin sources (where the word "Fama" means both "Fame" and "Rumor").

In every way, then, the lady Fame—and all her queendom—produces an unsettling, even frightening, portrait of caprice and inconstancy. It is somewhat ironic to find this essentially misogynist icon in a poem that had earlier introduced examples of female resistance to male transgression. Here, perhaps for the first time—through brief retellings of the misfortunes of Dido, Phyllis (389–96), Ariadne (405–26), and others—Chaucer undertakes to represent the woman's point of view, a theme that will occupy many of his future poems. Compared to the *Book of the Duchess*, which praises the lady Whyte without ever inhabiting her perspective, the *House of Fame* shows a genuine, if comic, interest in female agency and subjectivity. It also interestingly includes the non-human animal voice, in the eagle-guide and indeed in feather-covered Fame herself.[5] Certainly, this blurring of boundaries—across genders and species—is not experienced as entirely positive; it contributes to the sense of danger and uncertainty that surrounds Fame, but the poem's fluidity also suggests that not all truths will be found in the determinate textual tradition underwritten by male authority. The *House of Fame* grants significant power to the oral/aural distributing of information over which Fame presides and to which the narrator-poet is referred for material for his art.

The relationship of the *House of Fame* to Chaucer's later poetry, and especially to the *Parliament of Fowls*, the dream vision that most critics believe he turned to next, is thus complex. Again in the *Parliament*, Chaucer will show a realm ruled by a goddess or two, if one counts the seductive figure of Venus; again, he will explore a way to represent female agency; again, the animal world will be represented in the parliament of birds. Because the *Parliament* brings greater unity and closure to these and other disparate elements—and because it uses verse forms associated more closely with Chaucer's later career—editors and critics traditionally have assigned the *House of Fame* an earlier date, usually between 1378 and 1380. Although no theory as to the poem's specific occasion has ever won favor, there is little doubt that it post-dates the *Book of the Duchess*; it demonstrates a more flexible and adept metrical sense, and the pervasive influence of Dante argues for a date after Chaucer's first trip to Italy in 1372–73.

But little certainty can be had about whether the *House* comes before or after the *Parliament*, usually dated 1380–82. Although its four-beat line makes it metrically more similar to the *Book of the Duchess* than to the rest of Chaucer's poetry, which works in a five-beat line, some of the short lyrics, also composed in complex pentameter verse forms (for example, "An ABC" or "The Complaint to Pity"), are usually assigned an early date, complicating any simple division of Chaucer's career solely on the basis of metrics. In fact, many scholars and editors register some uncertainty about the date of the *House of Fame*. Among other arguments, Helen Cooper notes the extensive influence of Boethius's *Consolation of Philosophy*, which Chaucer probably translated in the early 1380s, as a reason to date the *House of Fame* after the *Parliament of Fowls*.[6] While the *Oxford Guide to the Shorter Poems* affirms the earlier date,

---

5. See Lesley Kordecki, "Subversive Voices in Chaucer's *House of Fame*," *Exemplaria* 11 (1999): 53–77.
6. Helen Cooper, "The Four Last Things in Dante and Chaucer: Hugolino and the House of Rumour," *New Medieval Literatures* 3 (1999): 59.

it does so only tentatively: "[T]here seems to be no compelling reason to abandon the dating of 1379–80. Yet there seems to be no utterly compelling reason in favour of it either."[7] And, on the basis of the poet's representation of his art in a state of crisis, John Fisher's edition locates the *House* between the *Parliament* and poems like *Troilus and Criseyde* and the *Canterbury Tales* that would strike out in a new direction. The poem is placed here between the *Book of the Duchess* and the *Parliament of Fowls* in deference to tradition. If, however, we take its own words to heart, we will be skeptical of all claims to certainty where literary tradition is concerned.

The text here is based chiefly on the version found in the Fairfax manuscript (Fairfax 16, Bodleian Library).

The House of Fame

Book 1

	God turne us every drem° to goode!	*make every dream turn*
	For it is wonder,° by the roode,°	*a marvel / (Christ's) cross*
	To my wit what causeth swevenes°	*dreams*
	Either on morwes° or on evenes,°	*in the mornings / evenings*
5	And why the effect folweth of some°	*some come true*
	And of some it shal never come;°	*some do not*
	Why that is an avisioun	
	And this a revelacioun,	
	Why this a drem, why that a sweven,	
10	And nought to every man liche even;	
	Why this a fantom, why these oracles	
	I noot;[1] but whoso° of these miracles	*whoever*
	The causes knoweth bet° than I,	*better*
	Devyne he,° for I certeinly	*Let him pronounce (upon them)*
15	Ne can hem nought,° ne never thinke	*Do not know them*
	Too besily° my wit to swinke°	*Too diligently / work, apply*
	To knowe of hir signifiaunce	
	The gendres, neither the distaunce	
	Of tymes of hem,[2] ne the causes,	
20	Or why this more than that cause is;	
	As if folkes complexiouns	
	Make hem dreme of reflexiouns,[3]	

(margin: categories, lines 7–12)

---

7. Minnis, 171.
1. Why that one is a vision, and this one a revelation; why this one is a nightmare, why that one a dream, and they don't come equally to all people; (and) why this one is an hallucination, why those are prophecies, I do not know (any of this). (In the opening lines of the poem, Chaucer introduces the confusing topic of dream classification, derived ultimately from such writers as Artemidorus [second century C.E.] and Macrobius [ca. 400 C.E.; selections included in the Contexts section]. Different systems suggested slightly divergent, though overlapping terminology for the various categories of dream experience; "swevens" and "drems," for example, are basically synonymous. Because early writers and thinkers did believe in prophecy and dream prognostication, their most difficult task was to distinguish between true and false dreams; no system offered a foolproof way of accomplishing this. Dreams that occur in the early morning [see line 4] were believed more likely to be true than those experienced earlier in the night.)
2. To know about the different kinds of meanings (they hide), nor the intervals of time (when they happen).
3. I.e., I don't know if their physical constitutions are reflected in the dreams that different people have. (Medieval dream theory attributed some unreliable dreams to the dreamer's temperament, which was constituted from his physical humors—blood, phlegm, choler, and black bile. This

Or elles° thus, as other sayn,°   *else / others say*
For to° greet feblenesse of hir brayn,°   *Because of too / their brains*
25 By abstinence,° or by seknesse,°   *Due to asceticism / sickness*
Prison, stewe,° or greet distresse;   *confinement*
Or elles by disordinaunce°   *pathological disorder*
Of naturel acustomaunce,°   *(one's) normal habits*
That° som man is too curious°   *Such that / zealous, obsessed*
30 In studie, or melancolious,[4]
Or thus, so inly° ful of drede,°   *inwardly / fear, anxiety*
That no man may him bote bede;°   *help him, offer relief*
Or elles that devocioun°   *the religious devotion*
Of some and contemplacioun
35 Causeth swiche° dremes ofte;°   *such / often*
Or that the cruel lyf unsofte°   *fierce and painful existence*
Which these ilke° lovers leden°   *same, very / lead*
That hopen over moche° or dreden,   *excessively*
That purely hir impressiouns°   *their emotions alone*
40 Causeth hem avisiouns;°   *them to have visions*
Or if that spirites have the might°   *power*
To make folk to dreme a-night,°   *at night*
Or if the soule, of propre kinde°   *in its own nature*
Be so parfit,° as men finde,°   *perfect / learn, discover*
45 That it forwot that° is to come   *foresees what*
And that it warneth alle and some
Of everiche° of hir° aventures   *each one / their*
By avisiouns or by figures,°   *apparitions, phantoms*
But° that our flesh ne hath no might°   *Except / ability*
50 To understonde it aright,
For it is warned too derkly—
But why the cause is, nought wot I.
Wel worthe of this thing grete clerkes
That trete of this and other werkes,[5]
55 For I of noon opinioun
Nil as° now make mencioun,   *Will not for*
But only° that the holy roode°   *Except to (pray) / cross*
Turne us every drem to goode!   *see line 1*
For never, sith that° I was born   *since*
60 Ne no man elles° me biforn,°   *any other man / before*
Mette,° I trowe stedfastly,°   *Dreamed / truly believe*
So wonderful a drem as I
The tenthe day now of Decembre,[6]

---

theory, for example, is expressed by the hen Pertelote in Chaucer's Nun's Priest's Tale [*Canterbury Tales* 7.2923–38].)
4. Melancholy was the temperament dominated by black bile and characterized by anger and gloom.
5. Because the information provided is too obscure. But what the cause is (of the different kinds of dreams), I do not know. May those great scholars who write about this and other activities get along well (i.e., good luck to them!). (In line 52, Chaucer finally brings to a close the long paratactic sentence about dream theory with which he begins the *House of Fame*; the "cause" of 52 reaches all the way back to the "causes" in 13, to repeat once again emphatically that the narrator does not comprehend the inspiration that lies behind different kinds of dreams. The meandering and confusing sentence imitates the confusion of the dream categories themselves.)
6. See also 111. The winter date is a little unusual but not entirely unprecedented for a dream vision, most of which are set in the spring. Its specificity has suggested to some readers that Chaucer is writing for a special occasion, perhaps a wedding, but no particular occasion has ever prevailed.

	The which,° as° I can now remembre,	*i.e., the dream / as much as*
65	I wol yow tellen every dele.°	*give you all the details*

THE INVOCATION

	But at my ginninge,° trusteth wele,	*beginning*
	I wol make invocacioun[7]	
	With special devocioun	
	Unto the god of slepe anoon,°	*at once*
70	That dwelleth in a cave of stoon°	*stone*
	Upon a streem that cometh fro Lete,	
	That is a flood of helle unswete	
	Besyde a folk men clepe Cimerie.[8]	
	Ther slepeth ay° this god unmerie°	*forever / dull, somnolent*
75	With his slepy thousand sones	
	That alwey for to slepe hir wone° is.	*their custom, way of life*
	And to this god that I of rede°	*am discussing*
	Prey I that he wol me spede°	*give me success*
	My sweven° for to telle aright,°	*dream / properly*
80	If every drem stonde in his might.[9]	
	And he that mover° is of al	*creator (i.e., God)*
	That is and was and ever shal,°	*shall be*
	So yive hem° joye that it here°	*give them / listen to it*
	Of° alle that they dreme to-yere,°	*In / this year*
85	And for to stonden alle in grace	
	Of hir loves, or in what place	
	That hem wer levest for to stonde,	
	And shelde hem fro poverte and shonde[1]	
	And from unhappe° and eche° disese,	*misfortune / each, every*
90	And sende hem al° that may hem plese	*them everything*
	That take° it wel and scorne it nought	*(To) those who understand*
	Ne it misdemen° in hir° thought	*misjudge, condemn / their*
	Thurgh malicious entencioun.°	*intention, inclination*
	And whoso,° thurgh presumpcioun°	*whoever / arrogance*
95	Or hate or scorne or thurgh envye,	
	Dispyt° or jape° or vilanye,° *Disdain, contempt / joking / churlishness*	
	Misdeme° it, preye I Jesus God	*condemn*
	That—dreme he° barefoot, dreme he	*whether he dreams*
	shod°—	*with shoes*

The proximity of the date to the winter solstice—the date furthest from spring—may be humorous, or the season may have religious significance as a time when heavenly tidings are made manifest to humanity or as a date in the liturgical calendar appropriate to speaking of judgment.)

7. Each one of the three books of the *House of Fame* is introduced by an "invocation"—a summoning up of authority or inspiration before embarking on a poetic project. The invocations to Books 2 and 3 are taken from Dante; this one, according to F. N. Robinson, echoes Jean Froissart's *Treasure of Love* (see the *Riverside Chaucer*, Explanatory Note, p. 979).

8. Above a stream that comes from Lethe, which is a bitter river of hell, next to a people whom men call the Cimmerians. (Lethe was the River of Forgetfulness in the ancient underworld; it is mentioned, along with the Cimmerians and the god of sleep with his thousand sons in the description of sleep's kingdom in Ovid's *Metamorphoses* [Book 11, passage included in the Contexts section of this Norton Critical Edition and also incorporated into the *Book of the Duchess* 153–77].)

9. If (indeed) he does have power over all dreams. (The classical god of sleep provides yet another theory for how dreams are generated to add to the plethora of such theories that the dreamer has already described.)

1. And (may those who attend to my dream) stand in the good graces of those they love, or (at least) stand wherever it is that they wish to be. And protect them from poverty and harm.

That every harm that any man
100 Hath had, sith° the world began,   *since*
Befalle him therof er° he sterve,°   *for that before / dies*
And graunte he mote° it ful deserve,°   *that he may / fully attain*
Lo, with swich a conclusioun°   *such an ending, outcome*
As had of his avisioun°   *from his vision*
105 Cresus, that was king of Lyde[2]
That high upon a gebet dyde!°   *gallows died*
This prayer shal he have of me;
I am no bet° in charite!   *better*
Now herkneth,° as I have yow seyde,   *hear listen to*
110 What that I mette er I abreyde.°   *dreamed before I awoke*

THE DREAM

Of° Decembre the tenthe day   *On*
Whan it was night, to slepe I lay
Right ther as I was wont to done°   *accustomed to do*
And fil on slepe° wonder sone°   *fell asleep / amazingly quickly*
115 As he that wery was forgo°   *wiped out by weariness*
On pilgrimage myles two
To the corseynt Leonard,
To make lythe of that was hard.[3]
   But as I slept, me mette° I was   *I dreamed*
120 Within a temple y-mad of glas°   *constructed of glass*
In whiche ther were mo images°   *more statues*
Of gold, stondinge in sondry stages,°   *various platforms, tiers*
And mo riche tabernacles,°   *more canopied niches*
And with perre mo pinacles,°   *more jeweled spires*
125 And mo curious portreytures,°   *ornate pictures*
And queynte maner° of figures   *intricate kinds*
Of olde werke° than I saw ever.   *craftsmanship*
For certeynly, I niste never°   *had no idea*
Wher that I was, but wel wiste° I   *knew*
130 It was of Venus redely°   *clearly, plainly*
The temple, for, in portreyture,
I saw anonright° hir figure   *immediately*
Naked fletinge in a see.°   *floating in the sea*
And also on hir heed, pardee,°   *by God, indeed*
135 Hir rose garlond whyt and reed,°   *red*
And hir comb to kembe hir heed,°   *comb her hair*
Hir doves, and Daun° Cupido   *Lord, Sir (an honorific)*
Hir blinde sone, and Vulcano,
That in his face was ful broun.°[4]   *quite brown, swarthy*

2. Croesus, King of Lydia (sixth century B.C.E.), foresaw his own death figuratively in a dream; the
story is related in the Monk's Tale (*Canterbury Tales* 7.2727–60) and in the Nun's Priest's Tale
(*Canterbury Tales* 7.3138–40).
3. From taking a two-mile pilgrimage to the (shrine of) Saint Leonard, (in an attempt to) ease what
was difficult. (St. Leonard, the patron saint of prisoners, was associated in the thirteenth-century
Romance of the Rose [8836] with the shackles of marriage, perhaps offering a clue to the difficulty
described here in 118. As Brian Stone points out [*Love Visions*, p. 237], three churches dedicated
to St. Leonard were located near Chaucer's house, making the estimate of two miles realistic.)
4. This description of Venus—floating on her birthplace, the sea; wearing a rose garland; holding a
comb and surrounded by doves; accompanied by her blind son Cupid and her husband Vulcan,

140	But as I romed° up and doun,	roamed, wandered
	I fond° that on a wal ther was	found
	Thus wryten on a table° of bras:	tablet, slate
	"I wol now say, if that I can,	
	The armes and also the man	
145	That first cam, thurgh his destinee,	
	Fugitif of Troy contree,	
	In Itaile with ful moche pyne	
	Unto the strondes of Lavyne."⁵	
	And tho° began the story anoon,°	then / at once
150	As I shal telle yow echoon.°	all
	First saw I the destruccioun	
	Of Troye, thurgh the Greke Sinoun,⁶	
	That with his false forsweringe°	perjury
	And his chere° and his lesinge,°	outward show / lying
155	Made the hors° brought into Troye	Caused the horse to be
	Thurgh which Troyens° loste al hir joye.	the Trojans
	And after this was grave,° allas,	engraved
	How Ilioun° assailed was	tower of Ilium (Troy)
	And wonne, and King Priam y-slayn,°	slain
160	And Polites his sone, certayn,°	truly
	Dispitously of° Daun Pirrus.⁷	Fiercely, cruelly by
	And, next that,° saw I how Venus,	next to that
	Whan that she saw the castel brende,°	castle burn
	Doun fro the° hevene gan descende°	from / descended
165	And bad° hir sone Eneas° flee;	directed, urged / Aeneas to
	And how he fledde and how that he	
	Escaped was from al the pres,°	press of combat
	And took° his fader Anchises	how he took
	And bar° him on his bakke away,	carried
170	Cryinge, "Allas" and "Welaway!"°	i.e., exclamation of woe
	The whiche Anchises in his honde	
	Bar the goddes of the londe,	
	Thilke° that unbrende° were.⁸	Those / unburnt
	And I saw next, in alle this fere,°	group, company
175	How Creusa, Daun Eneas° wyf,	Lord Aeneas'
	Which that° he lovede as his lyf,	Whom
	And hir° yonge sone Julo	their

---

the blacksmith god—is drawn from standard iconography. Many of these details also appear in her description in the Knight's Tale (*Canterbury Tales* 1.1955–66).

5. I will now speak, if that I can, about the arms and the man who, as a fugitive from the country of Troy, followed his destiny (to arrive finally) in Italy, upon the shores of Lavinium. (Loose translation of the opening lines of Virgil's *Aeneid*; some editors read "sing," as in Virgil, for "say" [manuscripts allow for either], but Chaucer is more likely mocking the narrator's tentativeness here, as reflected also in the concessive "if that I can." "Arms" is Virgilian metonymy for Aeneas's prowess as a warrior. Lavinium was an ancient city in the region of Italy where Aeneas and his descendants would found Rome.)

6. In the *Aeneid* 2.1–354, Sinon is the treacherous Greek who persuades the Trojans that he is on their side and that they should accept the gift of the gigantic wooden horse, defeating by stealth those who could not be vanquished in battle.

7. Priam was the King of Troy, Polytes one of his sons; in Book 2 of the *Aeneid*, both are killed by Pyrrhus (here Daun or Lord Pyrrhus), when the Greeks sack Troy.

8. According to the *Aeneid* (2.717–20), Aeneas gives his father Anchises the household gods, important for the honor and protection of the family, because his own hands are stained with blood from the recent battle.

And eek° Ascanius also,   *in addition*
Fledden eek with drery chere,°   *sorrowful or frightened faces*
180 That it was pitee for to here;°   *hear*
And in a forest as they wente,
At a turninge of a wente,°   *path*
How Creusa was y-lost, allas,
That° deed, noot° I how, she was;   *So that / don't know*
185 How he hir soughte and how hir gost°   *ghost, spirit*
Bad° him to flee the Grekes ost,°   *Urged / army*
And seyde he most unto Itaile,°   *must (go) to Italy*
As was his destinee, sauns° faile;   *without*
That it was pitee for to here,°   *hear*
190 Whan hir spirit gan appere,°   *appeared*
The wordes that she to him seyde,
And for to kepe hir° sone him preyde.⁹   *protect their*
Ther saw I graven eek° how he,   *engraved also*
His fader eek, and his meynee,°   *retainers, company*
195 With his shippes gan to saile°   *set sail*
Toward the contree of Itaile,
As streight as that they mighte go.
    Ther saw I thee, cruel Juno,
That art Daun Jupiters° wyf,   *Lord Jupiter's*
200 That hast y-hated al thy lyf
Al the Troyanisshe blood,°   *race of Trojans*
Renne° and crye as thou were wood°   *Run / like a madwoman*
On Eolus, the god of windes,
To blowen out, of alle kindes,
205 So loude, that he shulde drenche
Lord and lady, grome and wenche
Of al the Troyan nacioun
Withoute any savacioun.¹
    Ther saw I swich tempeste° aryse,   *such a storm*
210 That every herte might agryse°   *shudder with fear*
To see it peynted on the walle.
    Ther saw I graven eek withalle,°   *engraved also*
Venus, how ye, my lady dere,
Wepinge with ful woful chere,°   *face, expression*
215 Preyen Jupiter an hye°   *on high*
To save and kepe° that navye   *protect*
Of the Troyan Eneas,
Sith that° he hir sone was.   *Since*
    Ther saw I Joves Venus kisse,
220 And graunted of the tempest lisse.²

9. According to Virgil, Julus and Ascanius (177–78) are actually different names for a single son of Aeneas and his wife Creusa, as reflected in Creusa's use of the singular "son" in 192. The events portrayed here, including the loss and reappearance of Creusa as a monitory spirit, are adapted from Book 2 of the *Aeneid*.
1. To Aeolus, the wind-god, to blow out (winds) of all different sorts, so violently that he would drown lord and lady, groom and wench, all the Trojan nation, without saving anyone. (Juno hates the Trojans because the Trojan prince Paris chose Venus over her in the contest for the golden apple meant for the most beautiful of all the goddesses.)
2. Then I saw Jupiter kiss Venus and agree to calm the storm. (By long tradition, Aeneas is the son of Anchises and Venus. This relation explains Venus's protection of Aeneas in Book 1 of the *Aeneid*

Ther saw I how the tempest stente°   storm ceased
And how with alle pyne he° wente   with great difficulty he (Aeneas)
And prively took arrivage°   secretly came ashore
In the contree of Cartage;°   Carthage
225 And on the morwe,° how that he   next day
And a knight hight Achate°   named Achates
Metten with Venus that day,
Going in a queynt aray°   an elaborate costume
As° she had been an hunteresse,   As if
230 With wind blowing upon hir tresse;°   hair
How Eneas gan him to pleyne,°   began to lament, complain
Whan that he knew hir, of his peyne°   about his hardship
And how his shippes dreynte° were,   sunk
Or elles° lost, he niste° where;   else / did not know
235 How she gan him comforte tho°   comforted him then
And bad° him to Cartage go,   urged, directed
And ther he shulde his folke° finde   i.e., his retainers
That in the see° were left behinde.   sea
     And, shortly of this thing to pace,°   to make a long story short
240 She made Eneas so in grace°   to win the grace, stand in favor
Of Dido, quene of that contree,
That, shortly° for to tellen, she   briefly
Becam his love and let him do
Al that wedding longeth to.°   is proper to marriage
245 What shulde I speke more queynte³
Or peyne me° my wordes peynte°   take pains / adorn
To speke of love? It wol nat be;
I can° nat of that facultee.°   know / field of knowledge
And eek° to telle the manere   also
250 How they aqueynteden in fere,°   got to know each other
It were a long proces° to telle,   would make a long story
And over long for yow to dwelle.°   keep you here
     Ther saw I grave° how Eneas   engraved
Tolde Dido every cas,°   event
255 That him was tid° upon the see.   happened to him
     And after grave was how she
Made of him shortly,° at o word,°   soon / in a word
Hir lyf, hir love, hir luste,° hir lord,   delight, pleasure
And dide him al the reverence
260 And leyde on him al dispence°   spent all the money
That any woman might do,°   could (possibly) do
Weninge° it had al be° so   Believing / everything was
As he hir swoor;° and hereby demed°   swore to her / judged
That he was good, for he swich° semed.   such
265 Allas, what harm doth apparence°   outer appearance

---

and deepens the rivalry between Venus and Juno; see above, note 1, p. 48. Although Venus takes
many actions to promote and protect Aeneas in Virgil's epic, in this instance Neptune alone calms
the storm; see *Aeneid* 1.124–56.)
3. Why should I speak more euphemistically. (The line also may contain bawdy word play on the
word "queynte," which can also mean female genitalia; the rite of marriage Chaucer alludes to
implies sexual intercourse.)

Whan it is fals in existence!° *in fact, in truth*
For he to hir a traitour was,
Wherfor° she slow° hirself, allas! *For which reason / killed*
   Lo,° how a woman doth amis ° *Behold / amiss, wrong*
270 To love him that unknowen is,
For, by Crist, lo, thus it fareth:° *so it goes*
It is nat al gold, that glareth.° *glitters*
For, also brouke I wel myn heed,° *as I (hope to) keep my head*
Ther may be under goodliheed° *a fine appearance*
275 Kevered° many a shrewed° vice; *Concealed / corrupt, terrible*
Therfor be no wight so nice,
To take a love only for chere,[4]
Or speche, or for frendly manere;
For this shal every woman finde:
280 That som man of his pure kinde
Wol shewen outward the faireste,
Til he have caught that what him leste,
And thanne wol he causes finde[5]
And swere how that she is unkinde,° *cruel, disloyal*
285 Or fals, or privy double° was. *secretly two-timing*
  Al this sey I by° Eneas *about*
And Dido and hir nice lest,° *foolish (love-)longing*
That loved al too sone a gest;° *quickly a guest, stranger*
Therfor I wol sey a proverbe,
290 That "he that fully knoweth th'erbe° *i.e., used as a medicine*
May saufly ley° it to his eye"; *safely apply*
Withoute drede,° this is no lye. *fear*
    But let us speke of Eneas,
How he betrayed hir, allas,
295 And lefte hir ful unkindely.
So whan she saw al utterly° *completely, in every way*
That he wolde hir of trouthe faile° *fail in (his) loyalty to her*
And wende fro° hir to Itaile,° *(he) traveled from / Italy*
She gan° to wringe hir hondes two. *began*
300 "Allas!" quod° she, "what me is wo! ° *said / woe is me*
Allas, is every man thus trewe,
That every yere wolde have a newe° *(he) desires a new (lover)*
If it° so longe tyme dure,° *i.e., his love / lasts, endures*
Or elles three, paraventure?° *else three (lovers), perhaps*
305 As thus: of oon° he wolde° have fame *from one / wishes to*
In magnifying° of his name,° *enhancing / reputation*
Another for frendship, seith he;° *(so) he says*
And yet ther shal the thridde° be, *third*
That shal be taken for delyt,° *sensuous pleasure*
310 Lo, or for singuler profyt."° *personal benefit*
    In swiche° wordes gan to pleyne° *such / began to lament*
Dido of hir grete peyne,° *pain, suffering*

---

4. Therefore, let no person be so simpleminded as to take a lover only on the basis of outward appearance.
5. For this shall every woman find: that it is the essential nature of a certain kind of man to exhibit his fairest side (just) until he has gotten what he wanted, and then he will invent justifications (for betraying the woman who has trusted him).

As me mette redely;°   *I dreamed certainly*
Noon° other auctour alegge° I.   *No / author allege, claim*
315 "Allas!" quod° she, "my swete herte,   *said*
Have pitee on my sorwes smerte,°   *painful sorrow*
And slee° me nat! Go nat away!   *slay*
O woful Dido, welaway!"
Quod she to hirselfe tho.°   *then*
320 "O Eneas, what wol ye do?
O that your love ne your bonde°   *nor your pledge*
That ye have sworn with your right honde,
Ne my cruel deeth," quod she,
"May holde° yow stille here with me!   *keep*
325 O, haveth of° my deeth pitee!   *have on*
Ywis,° my dere herte, ye   *Truly*
Knowen ful wel that never yit,°   *yet, to this time*
As ferforth as I hadde wit,°   *insofar as I was able*
Agilte I° yow in thought ne dede.   *Have I wronged*
330 O, have ye men swich goodlihede°   *such excellence*
In speche, and never a deel of° trouthe?   *not a bit of*
Allas, that ever hadde routhe°   *compassion, pity*
Any woman on any man!
Now see I wel and telle can,
335 We wrecched women can noon art;⁶
For, certeyn,° for the more part   *certainly*
Thus we be served everichone.°   *are we all (mis)treated*
How sore that ye men can grone,
Anoon as we have yow receyved
340 Certeinly we been deceyved;
For, though your love laste a sesoun,
Waite upon the conclusioun,
And eek how that ye determynen,
And for the more part diffynen.⁷
345   O, welawey° that I was born!   *woe is me*
For thurgh yow is my name lorn°   *reputation lost*
And alle myn actes° red and songe°   *deeds / told and sung*
Over al this lond, on every tonge.°   *tongue*
O wikke° Fame,⁸ for ther nis°   *wicked / is*
350 Nothing so swift, lo, as she is!
O, sooth is° every thing is wist°   *truth is that / known*
Though it be kevered with the mist.°   *concealed by mist*

6. We miserable women do not know how to play the game (of love). (Perhaps a reference to the "arts of love," derived from Ovid's *Ars Amatoria*; a medieval example is Andreas Capellanus's *Art of Courtly Love*.)

7. However sorely (convincingly) you men are able to groan (i.e., moan and complain), just as soon as we have accepted you (as lovers), certainly (that is the moment when) we will be deceived. For, though your love may last for a season, wait for the result, and (see) also then what you conclude and on the whole determine as an outcome. (The scholastic diction speculatively employed by men here is in dramatic contradiction to the emotional realism of the woman's feelings of betrayal in love.)

8. For the goddess Fame, first named here, and described in more detail later, see Virgil's *Aeneid* 4.173–97 and Ovid's *Metamorphoses* 12.39–63, the two, often opposing sources for Chaucer's presentation of the tale of Dido and Aeneas. Both passages are included in the Contexts section of this Norton Critical Edition. Although Virgil and Ovid differ about many aspects of the story, they do seem to agree on the waywardness of Fame ("Fama"), which in Latin also meant "Rumor" (see my introduction).

Eek,° though I mighte duren ever,°   *Also / live forever*
That I have doon, rekever I never
355   That I ne shal be seyd, allas,
Y-shamed be thurgh Eneas[9]
And that I shal thus juged be:
'Lo, right° as she hath doon,° now she   *just / has done*
Wol do eft-sones, hardely';°   *again, assuredly*
360   Thus seyth the peple prively.°   *privately*
But that° is doon, nis nat to done."°   *that which / cannot be undone*
But al hir compleynt ne al hir mone,°   *moaning, lamenting*
Certeyn, availeth hir nat a stre.[1]
And whan she wiste sothly° he   *knew truly that*
365   Was° forth unto his shippes goon,   *Had*
She into hir chambre° wente anoon,°   *bedchamber / at once*
And called on hir suster Anne°   *sister Anna*
And gan hir° to compleyne thanne,   *to her began*
And seyde that she cause was
370   That she first loved him, allas,
And thus counseilled hir therto.[2]
But, what,° whan this was seyd and do,°   *no matter / done*
She roof° hirselfe to the herte,   *stabbed*
And deyde° thurgh the wounde smerte.°   *died / bitter wound*
375   But al the maner how she deyde,
And al the wordes that she seyde,
Whoso° to knowe it hath purpos,°   *Whoever / has the aim*
Reed Virgile in Eneidos,
Or the Epistle of Ovyde
380   What that she wroot er that she dyde;[3]
And nere it° too long to endyte,°   *would it not take / narrate*
By God, I wolde it here wryte.
But, welaway,° the harm, the routhe°   *alas / the suffering*
That hath betid° for swich untrouthe,°   *occurred / such faithlessness*
385   As men may ofte° in bookes rede,°   *often / read about*
And al day see it yet in dede,°   *in deeds, in fact*
That for to thinken it, a tene is.[4]
Lo,° Demophon, Duk° of Athenis,   *Behold / Duke*
How he forswoor him° ful falsly   *perjured himself, was forsworn*
390   And traysed° Phillis wikkedly,   *betrayed*
That Kinges doughter was of Trace,

9. That which I have done, (my reputation will) never recover (from it); it will always be said, alas, that I was dishonored by Aeneas.
1. Truly, it does her not a straw of good.
2. In Virgil's *Aeneid* 4.31–53, Anna counsels Dido to accept Aeneas as her wooer. The passage is included in the Contexts section of this Norton Critical Edition. In the *Legend of Good Women*, where Chaucer retells the story, Anna resists the courtship; see 1182–88.
3. Read Virgil in the *Aeneid* or (read) what she wrote before she died in the *Epistles* of Ovid. (Here Chaucer explicitly names his two sources. Dido's death is described in detail in *Aeneid* 4.474–705; the letter she wrote to Aeneas is Epistle 7 in Ovid's *Heroides* [also called the *Epistles*]. Both sources, which differ significantly in their points of view, are included here in the Contexts section. Broadly speaking, in Virgil, Aeneas's conduct is justified by his imperial mission; Ovid tells the story exclusively from Dido's point of view. Accordingly many details vary in the two accounts. Chaucer again draws on both when he recounts the story in the *Legend of Good Women* 924–1367.)
4. Just thinking about it is painful.

And falsly gan his terme pace;[5]
And whan she wiste° that he was fals,   *knew*
She heng° hirself right by the hals,°   *hung / neck*
395 For he had do hir swich untrouthe;°   *proved so faithless*
Lo, was nat this a wo and routhe?°   *cause for woe and pity*
   Eek° lo! how fals and reccheles°   *Also / callous*
Was to Breseida Achilles,
And Paris to Enone;
400 And Jasoun to Isiphile;
And eft Jasoun to Medea;
And Ercules to Dyanira;
For he left hir for Iole,[6]
That made him cacche his deeth, pardee.°   *led to his death, by God*
405   How fals eek° was he, Theseus,   *also*
That, as the story telleth us,
How he betrayed Adriane;[7]
The devel be his soules bane!°   *destroyer*
For had he laughed, had he loured,°   *scowled*
410 He moste have be al° devoured,   *would have been entirely*
If Adriane ne had y-be!°   *had not existed*
And, for° she had of° him pitee,   *because / on*
She made him fro° the deeth escape,   *from*
And he made° hir a ful fals jape;°   *played on / joke, trick*
415 For after this, within a whyle°   *certain time*
He lefte hir slepinge in an yle,°   *on an island*
Deserte,° aloon, right in° the see,   *uninhabited / in the midst of*
And stal° away and let hir be,°   *he stole / left her (alone)*
And took hir suster Phedra tho°   *sister Phaedra then*
420 With him, and gan to shippe go.°   *boarded (his) ship*
And yet he had y-swoor to here°   *sworn to her*
On al that ever he mighte swere,
That, so° she° saved him his lyf,   *if / i.e., Ariadne*
He wolde have take hir to° his wyf,   *take her as*
425 For she desyred nothing elles,°   *else*
In certeyn,° as the book us telles.   *truth*
    But to excusen Eneas
Fulliche° of al his greet trespas,   *entirely*
The book° seyth, Mercurie, sauns° faile,   *i.e., the Aeneid / without*
430 Bad him° go into Itaile,   *Commanded him to*
And leve Affrikes regioun,°   *i.e., Carthage*
And Dido and hir faire toun.

5. Who was the daughter of the King of Thrace, and (how) he failed to keep the promised date (of his return to her). (The betrayal of Phyllis, Queen of Thrace, by Demophon of Athens, son of Theseus and Phaedra, is told by Ovid in the *Heroides* 2, and again by Chaucer in the *Legend of Good Women* 2394–2561.)
6. These are all stories told in Ovid's *Heroides*: Briseis (Briseida) laments Achilles' abandonment of her in *Heroides* 3; the nymph Oenone chastizes Paris, who has deserted her for Helen, in *Heroides* 5; Hypsipyle complains to Jason in *Heroides* 6, when he has thrown her over for Medea, who for her own part, condemns Jason's betrayal of her in *Heroides* 12. Deianira reproaches both Hercules and herself in *Heroides* 9: Jealous because of a rumor that he loved Iole, Deianira unintentionally poisoned her beloved Hercules by sending him a garment she believed would win back his love; for this story, see also Ovid's *Metamorphoses* 9.134–210.
7. Ariadne advised Theseus on how to defeat the Minotaur; after promising to marry her, Theseus deserted her on an island for her sister Phaedra. Chaucer tells the story in the *Legend of Good Women* 1886–2227. It is also the subject of Ovid's *Heroides* 10 and *Metamorphoses* 8.169–82.

	Tho° saw I grave,° how to Itaile	*Then / engraved*
	Daun° Eneas is goon to saile,	*Lord*
435	And how the tempest° al began	*storm*
	And how he loste his steresman,°	*helmsman, pilot*
	Which that the stere er he took kepe	
	Smot over bord, lo, as he slepe.[8]	
	And also saw I how Sibyle°	*the Sibyl*
440	And Eneas, besyde an yle,°	*next to an island*
	To helle° wente, for to see	*i.e., the underworld*
	His fader,° Anchises the free.°	*father / noble one*
	How he ther fond° Palinurus	*found*
	And Dido and eek° Deiphebus;[9]	*also*
445	And every torment eek° in helle	*other punishment*
	Saw he, which is° long to telle.	*would take too*
	Which whoso willeth° for to knowe,	*whoever wishes*
	He mote° rede many a rowe°	*must / line (of verse)*
	On° Virgile or on Claudian	*In*
450	Or Daunte, that it telle can.[1]	
	Tho° saw I grave° al the arivaile°	*Then / engraved / arrival*
	That Eneas had in Itaile,[2]	
	And with King Latyne° his tretee,°	*Latinus / negotiations*
	And alle the batailles° that he	*battles*
455	Was at himself and eek° his knightes,	*also*
	Er° he had al y-wonne° his rightes;	*Before / won, established*
	And how he Turnus refte° his lyf	*deprived, robbed Turnus of*
	And wan Lavyna to° his wyf,	*had won Lavinia as*
	And al the mervelous signals°	*heavenly signs*
460	Of the goddes celestials;	
	How, maugre° Juno, Eneas,	*in spite of*
	For al hir sleighte° and hir compas,°	*trickery / subtlety, cunning*
	Acheved al his aventure,°	*quest, venture*
	For Jupiter took of him cure°	*care*
465	At the prayere° of Venus,	*request*
	The which° I prey alwey° save us	*Who / will always*
	And us ay° of our sorwes lighte.°	*always / relieve our suffering*
	Whan I had seen al this sighte	
	In this noble temple thus,	
470	"A Lord!" thoughte I, "that madest us,	
	Yet° saw I never swich noblesse°	*Never before / magnificence*
	Of images, ne swich richesse°	*such wealth, abundance*
	As I saw graven° in this chirche;	*engraved*
	But nat wot I° who did hem wirche,°	*I do not know / fashioned them*
475	Ne wher I am, ne in what contree.	

8. Who was thrown overboard by the rudder before he knew (what was happening), as he was sleeping. (The helmsman is Palinurus, whom Aeneas sees in the next verse paragraph in his journey to the underworld; see *Aeneid* 5.827–871.)

9. Aeneas's journey to the underworld, guided by the Sibyl, is described in Virgil's *Aeneid* 6; he sees there his father, his helmsman Palinurus, Dido, the Trojan prince Deiphebus, and others.

1. In addition to Virgil's *Aeneid* (see above), descriptions of the underworld are also included in Claudian's *The Rape of Proserpine* and Dante's *Inferno*.

2. In the lines that follow, Chaucer quickly narrates the events of the final six books of the *Aeneid*, including Aeneas's arrival in Latium, his treaty with King Latinus, and his defeat of Lavinia's betrothed Turnus, which involved the cooperation of the gods.

But now wol I go out and see,
Right at the wiket,° if I can   *small gate*
See o-wher° any stering° man   *anywhere / stirring, animate*
That may° me telle wher I am."   *Who might be able to*
480   Whan I out at the dores cam,°   *came outdoors*
I faste° aboute me behelde;°   *eagerly / looked around*
Than saw I but° a large felde,   *nothing but*
As fer° as that I mighte see,   *far*
Withouten toun or hous or tree
485   Or bush or gras or eryd° londe;   *plowed, cultivated*
For al the feld nas but of° sonde   *was nothing but*
As smal° as man may see yet lye   *finely ground*
In the desert of Libye;°   *Libya*
Ne I no maner° creature   *kind of*
490   That is y-formed° by Nature   *formed, created*
Ne saw, me for to rede or wisse.°   *to advise or instruct me*
"O Crist," thought I, "that art in blisse,°   *i.e., in heaven*
Fro fantom° and illusioun   *From delusion*
Me save!" and with devocioun
495   Myn eyen to the heven I caste.°   *i.e., looked up*
Tho° was I war,° lo, at the laste   *Then / aware*
That faste by° the sonne, as hye°   *close to / high*
As kenne mighte I° with myn eye,   *I was able to discern*
Me thoughte I saw an egle³ sore,°   *soar*
500   But° that it semed moche more°   *Except / much larger*
Than I had any egle seyn.°   *any eagle I had seen*
But this as sooth° as deeth, certeyn:°   *as sure / certainly*
It was of golde and shoon so brighte°   *shone so brightly*
That never saw men swich° a sighte,   *such*
505   But if° the heven hadde y-wonne°   *Unless / gained*
Al newe of gold another sonne;°   *a second sun*
So shoon the egles fethres bright,
And somwhat dounward gan it light.°   *it descended*

Book 2

THE INVOCATION

Now herkneth,° every maner man   *listen*
510   That Englissh understonde can,
And listeth° of my drem to lere;°   *pay attention / learn*
For now at erste° shul ye here°   *for the first time / hear*
So sely° an avisioun,°   *excellent, fine / vision*
That Isaye, ne Scipioun,
515   Ne King Nabugodonosor,
Pharo, Turnus, ne Elcanor,¹

3. The episode of the eagle, here and below, is based on Dante's *Purgatorio* 9.13–33, which is
included in the Contexts section of this Norton Critical Edition.
1. The vision of Isaiah is referenced in Isaiah 1:1. Scipio's dream, recounted by Cicero in the sixth
book of the *De re publica*, was the subject of an important fifth-century commentary by Macrobius
(excerpts from both are included here in the Contexts section); he is also mentioned later in the
poem (line 916), in the *Book of the Duchess* 286–87, and in the *Parliament of Fowls*. Nebuchad-
nezzar's dream is described in Daniel 2. Pharoah's dream, and Joseph's interpretation of it, are

Ne mette swich° a drem as this!   *never dreamed such*
Now faire blisful,° O Cipris,°   *happy, also blessed / Venus*
So be my favour° at this tyme!   *benefactor, helper*
520 And ye, me to endyte and ryme
Helpeth, that on Parnaso dwelle
By Elicon the clere welle.[2]
    O Thought, that wroot al that I mette,
And in the tresorie it shette
525 Of my brayn,[3] now shal men see
If any vertu° in thee be   *strength*
To tellen al my drem aright;°   *properly*
Now kythe° thyn engyne° and might!   *show / talent, imaginative skill*

THE DREAM

    This egle, of which I have yow tolde,
530 That shoon with fethres as of° golde,   *like*
Which that so high gan to sore,°   *began to soar*
I gan beholde° more and more   *gazed (upon him)*
To see the beautee and the wonder;
But never was ther dint° of thonder,   *clap, stroke*
535 Ne that thing that men calle foudre,°   *lightning, thunderbolt*
That smoot° somtyme a tour to poudre,°   *reduced / tower to rubble, dust*
And in his swifte coming brende,°   *approach burned*
That so swythe gan descende,°   *swiftly descended*
As this foul° whan it behelde   *fowl, bird*
540 That I a-roume° was in the felde;   *out in the open*
And with his grim pawes° stronge,   *hideous claws*
Within his sharpe nailes° longe,   *talons*
Me, fleinge in a swappe he hente,
And with his sours ageyn up wente,
545 Me caryinge in his clawes starke[4]
As lightly as° I were a larke,   *easily as if*
How high I can nat telle yow,
For I cam up, I niste° how,   *did not know*
For so astonied and asweved°   *stunned and overwhelmed*
550 Was every vertu in my heved,°   *power in my head*
What with his sours° and with my drede,°   *upward flight / fear*
That al my feling gan to dede,°   *deadened, stupefied*
Forwhy° it was too greet affray.°   *Because / frightening an assault*
    Thus I longe° in his clawes lay,   *for a long time*

---

described in Genesis 41 and also mentioned by Chaucer in the *Book of the Duchess* 280–82.
Turnus's dream is related in *Aeneid* 7.413–60. The reference to Elcanor is uncertain: The most
likely possibilities include the prophet Samuel's father Elkanah (1 Samuel 1–2) or Helcana, a
princess from an Old French romance, *Cassiodorus*, who appears to her lover in dreams.
2. And help me to compose and versify, you who dwell on Parnassus by the clear well of Helicon.
   (Parnassus was a mountain range in Greece sacred to the Muses; although Helicon is a mountain
   in the Parnassus, Chaucer treats it as a sacred well; see also "Anelida and Arcite" 17.)
3. Oh Thought, which inscribed all that I dreamed, and enclosed it in the treasury of my brain. (The
   poem's second invocation is based on Dante's *Inferno* 2.7–9; "Thought" is an English translation
   for Dante's "mente"; memory, which occupies physical space in medieval faculty psychology in a
   lobe at the back of the brain, was often referred to as a "treasury.")
4. Swooping down, he seized me, and in his upward flight sailed up again, carrying me in his sturdy
   claws.

555 Til at the laste he to me spak°	*spoke*
In mannes vois° and seyde, "Awak!	*the voice of a man*
And be nat agast so,° for shame!"	*so frightened*
And called me by my name,	
And, for I sholde the bet abreyde,°	*so I would awaken more easily*
560 Me mette° "Awak" to me he seyde	*I dreamed*
Right in the same vois and stevene°	*intonation*
That useth oon I coude nevene;⁵	
And with that vois, soth for to seyne,°	*truth to tell*
My minde cam to me ageyne,	
565 For it was goodly seyd to me,	
So nas it never wont to be.⁶	
And herewithal I gan to stere,°	*stir, come to life*
And he me in his feet to bere	
Til that he felte that I had hete°	*warmth*
570 And felte eek tho° myn herte bete.	*then also*
And tho gan he° me to disporte°	*then he began / console me*
And with wordes to comforte	
And seyde twyes,° "Seynte Marie,	*said twice*
Thou art noyous° for to carie,	*annoying, troublesome*
575 And nothing nedeth it, pardee!°	*unnecessarily so, indeed*
For also wys God° helpe me	*as the wise God may*
As thou noon harm shalt have of° this;	*shall not be harmed by*
And this cas that betid° thee is,	*event that has befallen*
Is for thy lore° and for thy prow.°	*education / benefit*
580 Let see, darst thou° yet look now?	*do you dare*
Be ful assured, boldely,°	*for a certainty*
I am thy frend." And therwith° I	*with that*
Gan for to wondren° in my minde.	*began to muse*
"O God," thoughte I, "that madest kinde,°	*who created the natural world*
585 Shal I noon other weyes dye?°	*i.e., is this how I'm going to die*
Wher Joves wol° me stellifye,°	*Will Jupiter / make a star, constellation*
Or what thing may this signifye?	
I neither am Enok, ne Elye,	
Ne Romulus, ne Ganymede	
590 That was y-bore° up, as men rede,°	*carried / read*
To hevene with Daun Jupiter	
And made the goddes boteler."⁷	
Lo, this was tho° my fantasye!	*then*
But he that bar° me gan espye°	*carried / discerned, noticed*
595 That I so thoughte and seyde this:	
"Thou demest of thyself amis;°	*are mistaken about yourself*
For Joves is nat theraboute°—	*anywhere around here*
I dar wel putte thee out of doute°—	*Let me reassure you*

5. That a person I know well might use (possibly Chaucer's wife).
6. I regained my sense of self, for (that phrase) was spoken kindly to me, in such a way that I was not accustomed to hear it.
7. A"boteler" or butler was the servant put in charge of serving drink at court. Chaucer echoes but alters Dante's "I am not Aeneas, I am not Paul" (*Inferno* 2.32). Enoch (Genesis 5:24) "walked with God," and Elijah (2 Kings 2:11) was carried up to heaven in a whirlwind. Romulus was rewarded with translation to the heavens in the *Metamorphoses* 14.805–28, and Jupiter stole Ganymede up to the heavens to be his cupbearer (or butler) in the *Metamorphoses* 10.155–61 (also, Dante, *Purgatorio* 9.22–24).

To make of thee as yet a sterre.[8]
600 But er I bere° thee moche ferre,°   *before I carry / much farther*
     I wol thee telle what° I am,   *who*
     And whider thou shalt° and why I cam   *where you are going*
     To do this, so that thou take
     Good herte,° and nat for fere quake."°   *courage / shake with fear*
605 "Gladly," quod° I. "Now wel," quod he.   *said*
     "First, I that in my feet have thee,
     Of which thou hast a fere and wonder,°   *have fear and amazement*
     Am dwellinge with the god of thonder,
     Which that men callen Jupiter,
610 That dooth me flee° ful ofte fer°   *makes me fly / far*
     To do al his comaundement.
     And for this cause he hath me sent
     To thee; now herke,° by thy trouthe.°   *listen / on your honor*
     Certeyn,° he hath of thee routhe,°   *Truly / has pity on you*
615 That thou so longe trewely
     Hast served so ententifly°   *earnestly, diligently*
     His blinde nevew° Cupido   *nephew*
     And faire Venus also,
     Withoute guerdoun ever yit,°   *any reward to date*
620 And nevertheles has set thy wit°—   *you've set your mind*
     Although that in thy hede ful lyte is[9]—
     To make° bookes, songes, dytees,°   *write / poems (often sung)*
     In ryme or elles in cadence,°   *else in rhythm*
     As thou best canst° in reverence   *to the best of your ability*
625 Of° Love and of his servants eke,°   *About / also*
     That° have his servise sought, and seke;°   *Those who / (still) seek*
     And peynest thee° to preyse his art   *you strive, take pains*
     Although thou haddest never part;°   *portion, share (in love)*
     Wherfor,° also God° me blesse,   *Therefore / as God may*
630 Joves halt° it greet humblesse°   *considers / humility*
     And vertu eek,° that thou wolt make   *also*
     A-night ful ofte° thyn hede to ake,°   *Often at night / ache*
     In thy studie so thou wrytest
     And evermo of° love endytest°   *constantly about / compose (poems)*
635 In honour of him and in preysinges,°   *praise, veneration (of Love)*
     And in his folkes furtheringes,
     And in hir matere al devysest
     And nought him nor his folk despysest
     Although thou mayst go in the daunce
640 Of hem that him list nat avaunce.[1]
          "Wherfor,° as I seyde ywis,°   *Therefore / indeed*
     Jupiter considereth this

---

8. About to turn you into a star (just) yet. (In classical literature, for example Ovid's *Metamorphoses*,
   it was common for the gods to transform mortals into stars, flowers, birds, and other objects in
   nature.)
9. Although your head is filled with very little. (The self-deprecating narrator here represents himself
   as a love-poet, albeit a poor one lacking direct experience of his subject.)
1. And your work advances the cause of (Love's) followers, and is all about the subject (of Love),
   and you do not disparage him or his servants, despite the fact that you are in the group of those
   whom Love chooses not to favor.

And also, beau sir,° other thinges: *kind sir*
That is, that thou hast no tydinges°   *news*
645 Of Loves folk, if they be glade,
Ne of nought elles° that God made;   *anything else*
And nought° only fro fer contree°   *it's not / from far-off lands*
That ther no tyding comth to thee,
But of thy verray° neighebores   *very own*
650 That dwellen almost at thy dores,°   *at your door*
Thou herest neither that ne this;
For whan thy labour doon al is,°   *is done (at the day's end)*
And hast y-made rekeninges,[2]
In stede of reste and newe thinges,
655 Thou gost hoom to thy hous anoon;°   *straightway*
And, also domb° as any stoon,   *as speechless, dumbfounded*
Thou sittest at another booke
Til fully daswed° is thy looke   *dazed, stupefied*
And livest thus as° an hermyte   *in the manner of*
660 Although thyn abstinence is lyte.[3]
    And therfor Joves, thurgh his grace,
Wol° that I bere° thee to a place   *Wishes / carry*
Which that hight° the Hous of Fame   *is called*
To do° thee som disport and game°   *give / fun and amusement*
665 In som recompensacioun°   *repayment*
Of° labour and devocioun   *For the*
That thou hast had, lo, causeles,°   *i.e., without encouragement*
To Cupido, the reccheles.°   *uncaring, callous*
And thus this god thurgh his meryte°   *divine power*
670 Wol° with som maner thing thee quyte,° *Wishes / to requite, reward*
So that thou wolt be of good chere.°   *happy, cheerful*
For truste wel that thou shalt here,°   *hear*
Whan we be comen ther I seye,°   *have arrived where I've said*
Mo wonder° thinges, dar I leye,°   *More amazing / I avow*
675 Of° Loves folke mo tydinges,°   *About / more news*
Both sothe sawes° and lesinges,°   *statements of truth / lies*
And mo° loves newe° begonne   *(about) more / just*
And longe y-served° loves wonne,   *(after) long service*
And mo loves casuelly
680 That been betid, no man wot why,
But as a blind man stert an hare;[4]
And more jolytee° and fare°   *gladness / celebration*
Whyl that° they finde love of stele,°   *when / (unbreakable) steel*
As thinketh hem,° and overal wele;°   *they believe / joy, well-being*
685 Mo discords,° mo jelousyes,   *More quarrels*
Mo murmours° and mo novelryes,°   *muttering / contrivances*
And mo dissimulaciouns°   *deceptions, dishonesty*
And feyned reparaciouns,°   *pretenses at making up*

2. You have finished your accounts. (From 1374–1386, Chaucer served in the position of Controller of the Wool Custom, whose duties he may be describing here.)
3. Although your abstinence is minimal. (An allusion to the characteristic rotundity of Chaucer's narrator, which also becomes a matter of fun in 574 and 737–46.)
4. And (about) more loves that happen by (pure) chance, nobody knows why, but (they come about in the same way) as a blind man (accidentally) flushes a hare (out of hiding).

And mo berdes in two houres	
690 Withoute rasour or sisoures	
Y-made, than greynes be of sondes;⁵	
And eke mo° holdinge in hondes°	also more / offering of false hope
And also mo renovelaunces°	renewals
Of olde forleten° aqueyntaunces,	forsaken, neglected
695 Mo love-dayes⁶ and acordes°	agreements
Than on instruments be cordes,°	are chords
And eek of loves mo eschaunges°	exchanging, swapping
Than ever cornes were in graunges.°	grain (stored in) barns
Unnethe maistow trowen° this?"	Are you ready to believe
700 Quod° he. "No, helpe me God so wis,"°	Said / wise
Quod I. "No? why?" quod he. "For it	
Were° impossible to my wit,°	Seems / understanding
Though that Fame hadde al the pyes°	magpies (i.e., informers)
In al a realme and al the spyes,	
705 How that yet she shulde here° al this,	could hear
Or they espye it."° "O yis, yis!"	find it out
Quod he to me, "that can I preve°	prove, demonstrate
By resoun° worthy for to leve,°	arguments / of belief
So° that thou yeve° thyn advertence°	Provided / give / attention
710 To understonde my sentence.°	teachings
First shalt thou here° wher she dwelleth,	hear
And so thyn owne book° it telleth;	Ovid's Metamorphoses (see l.349 note)
Hir paleys stant,° as I shal seye,	palace stands
Right even in middes° of the weye	Exactly in the middle
715 Betwixen° hevene, erthe, and see,°	Between / the sea
That,° what so ever in al° these three	So that / any of
Is spoken, either privee° or aperte,°	Secretly / openly
The wey therto is so overte°	accessible, unobstructed
And stant eek° in so juste° a place	also / perfectly situated
720 That every soun mot to it pace,°	sound must travel there
Or what so° comth fro° any tonge,°	whatever / from / tongue
Be it rouned,° red,° or songe,	whispered / spoken
Or spoke in seurtee° or in drede,°	with confidence / with fear
Certeyn, it mote thider nede.°	needs must go there
725 Now herkne wel° forwhy° I wille	listen up / because
Tellen thee a propre skille,°	excellent argument
And a worthy demonstracioun°	logical proof
In myn imagynacioun.⁷	
Geffrey, thou wost right° wel this,	know quite
730 That every kindly° thing that is,	natural
Hath a kindly stede ther° he	natural place where

5. And more beards (shaved) in two hours, without the use of razor or scissors, than there are grains of sand. (To "make someone's beard" is to play a humiliating trick on him, especially of a sexual nature; the most famous example in Chaucer—or perhaps anywhere—is the climactic moment in the Miller's Tale when a misdirected kiss involves the misconstrual of a lady's beard, leading to beard-making of several kinds; see *Canterbury Tales* 1.3736–43.)

6. A "love-day" was a time formally set aside for reconciliation or arbitration of a dispute.

7. According to my imagination. (In medieval faculty psychology, however, the imagination was likely to offer a phantasm as the basis for a logical proof; see the note to line 15 in the *Book of the Duchess*.)

May best in it conserved° be;[8]   *itself sustained*
Unto which place every thing,
Thurgh his kindly enclyning,°   *its natural inclination*
735 Moveth for to° come to°   *in order to / there*
Whan that it is awey therfro;°   *from that place*
As thus, lo, thou mayst al day° see   *can always*
That any thing that hevy be,°   *is heavy*
As stoon or lede° or thing of wighte,°   *lead / (great) weight*
740 And ber it never° so hye on highte,   *If you carry it ever*
Lat go thyn hand, it falleth doun.
    Right° so seye I by° fyre or soun°   *Just / about / sound*
Or smoke or other thinges lighte,°   *i.e., in weight*
Alwey they seke° upward on highte;°   *tend to move / altitude*
745 Whyl ech of hem° is at his large,°   *them / at large, free*
Light thing upward,° and dounward charge.°   *goes up / heavy (thing)*
    And for this cause° mayst thou see   *same reason*
That every river to the see
Enclyned° is to go, by kinde,°   *Disposed, inclined / nature*
750 And by these skilles,° as I finde,   *for these reasons*
Hath fissh dwellinge° in floode° and see,   *their habitat / river*
And trees eek° in erthe be.   *also*
Thus every thing, by this resoun,°   *argument*
Hath his° propre mansioun,°   *its / dwelling place*
755 To which it seketh to repaire,°   *return*
As ther° it shulde nat apaire.°   *to the place / deteriorate*
Lo, this sentence° is knowen couthe°   *science / widely known*
Of° every philosophres mouthe,   *From*
As Aristotle and Daun Platon°   *the Honorable Plato*
760 And other clerkes many oon.°   *many other scholars*
And to confirme my resoun,°   *argument*
Thou wost° wel this, that speche is soun°   *know / sound*
Or elles° no man mighte it here;°   *else / hear*
Now herke° what I wol thee lere.°   *listen to / teach you*
765   Soun is nought but air y-broken,°   *nothing but broken air*
And every speche that is spoken,
Loud or privee,° foul or fair,   *quietly*
In his° substaunce is but air;   *its*
For as flaumbe° is but lighted° smoke,   *a flame / kindled*
770 Right° so soun is air y-broke.°   *Just / broken*
But this may be in many wyse,°   *(different) ways*
Of which I wil thee two devise,°   *describe two to you*
As° soun that comth of pipe or harpe.   *I.e., first the*
For whan a pipe is blowen sharpe°   *vigorously*
775 The air is twist° with violence   *split*

---

8. Line 729 marks an important moment: Nowhere else does Chaucer refer to himself by his first name; the naming of the visionary is a gesture that marks a significant transition in other poems. See, for example, Beatrice's naming of Dante in *Purgatorio* 30.55 or Venus's naming of John Gower in *The Lover's Confession* 8.2908. The eagle now launches into an exposition of classical and medieval physics, including an early version of the theory of gravity; his science derives ultimately from Aristotle, and was conveyed to the Middle Ages through such authors as Boethius and Dante. Despite his learning, however, the eagle speaks with comical repetition and prolixity.

And rent;° lo, this is my sentence.°   *torn apart / proposition*
Eek° whan men harpe-stringes smyte,°   *Also / strike*
Whether it be moche or lyte,°   *hard or lightly*
Lo, with the strook the air to-breketh;°   *breaks apart, shatters*
780 Right so it breketh whan men speketh.
Thus wost thou° wel what thing is speche.   *you know*
   Now hennesforth° I wol thee teche°   *starting now / teach*
How every speche or noise or soun,
Thurgh his multiplicacioun,°   *its amplification*
785 Though it were piped of° a mouse,   *squeaked out by*
Mot nede° come to Fames House.   *Needs must*
I preve° it thus—tak hede° now—   *prove / pay attention*
By experience,° for if that thou   *With (this) evidence*
Throwe on water now a stoon,°   *stone*
790 Wel wost thou° it wol make anoon°   *You know well / at once*
A litel roundel as° a cercle,   *ripple (shaped) like*
Paraventer brode as a covercle;⁹
And right anoon° thou shalt see weel°   *right away / well*
That wheel° wol cause another wheel,   *circular ripple*
795 And that the thridde,° and so forth, brother,   *third*
Every cercle causinge other,°   *another*
Wyder than himself was;°   *Bigger than the last*
And thus, fro roundel to compas,
Ech aboute other goinge,
800 Causeth of othres steringe,¹
And multiplying evermo,°   *continuously*
Til that it be so fer y-go°   *has progressed so far*
That it° at bothe brinkes° be.   *i.e., the ripple / banks, edges*
Although thou mowe it nat y-see°   *cannot see*
805 Above, it goth yet alwey under,°   *submerged*
Although thou thinke it a greet wonder.°   *marvel*
And whoso seith of trouthe I varie,°   *depart from the truth*
Bid him° proven the contrarie.   *Ask him to*
And right thus° every word ywis°   *just so / indeed*
810 That loude or privee° spoken is   *quietly*
Moveth first an° air aboute,°   *a body of / around*
And of this moving,° out of doute,°   *from this motion / undoubtedly*
Another air anoon is meved.°   *is straightway moved*
As I have of° the water preved°   *(with the example) of / proven*
815 That every cercle causeth other,°   *another*
Right so of° air, my leve° brother;   *Just so with the / dear*
Everich° aire other stereth°   *Each (bit of) / sets in motion*
More and more, and speche up bereth,°   *carries upward*
Or° vois or noise or word or soun,   *Either*
820 Ay thurgh multiplicacioun°   *Through continuous amplification*
Til it be atte° Hous of Fame;   *Until it is at the*
Tak it in ernest° or in game.°   *seriously / fun*

---

9. About the size of the lid of a cup or a pot. (I.e., an imprecise but generally small measurement; see the *Middle English Dictionary*.)
1. And thus, from the first circular ripple to the outer rim (of the pool), one concentric ripple sets another in motion.

Now have I told, if thou have minde,°   *remember*
How speche or soun, of pure kinde,°   *in its very nature*
825 Enclyned is° upward to meve°—   *Tends / move*
This, mayst thou fele, wel I preve°—   *I've proven well*
And that same stede ywis°   *place truly*
That every thing enclyned to is
Hath his kindeliche stede.°   *its (own) natural resting place*
830 That sheweth it,° withouten drede,°   *It is plain / doubt*
That kindely° the mansioun°   *naturally / dwelling place*
Of every speche,° of every soun,   *spoken word*
Be it either foul or faire,
Hath his kinde° place in aire.   *its natural, proper*
835 And sin that° every thing that is   *since*
Out of his kinde place, ywis,°   *truly*
Moveth thider° for to go   *(back) there*
If it awey be therfro°—   *from that place*
As I bifore have preved° thee—   *proven to*
840 It seweth° every soun, pardee,°   *follows that / by God, indeed*
Moveth kindely to pace°   *Naturally tends to travel*
Al up into his kindely° place.   *its natural, proper*
And this place of which I telle,°   *speak*
Ther as° Fame list° to dwelle,   *Where / chooses*
845 Is set amiddes of° these three,   *midway between*
Heven, erthe, and eek the see,°   *also the sea*
As most conservatif° the soun.   *able to preserve*
Than is this the conclusioun:
That every° speche of every man,   *all the*
850 As I thee telle first began,
Moveth up on high to pace°   *travel*
Kindely° to Fames place.   *Naturally*
Telle me this feithfully,°   *truthfully*
Have I nat preved° thus simply,   *proven*
855 Withouten any subtiltee°   *undue complexity*
Of speche, or greet prolixitee°   *superfluity*
Of termes of philosophye,
Of figures of poetrye,
Or colours of rethoryke?°   *rhetorical devices*
860 Pardee,° it oughte thee to lyke,°   *Indeed / please you*
For hard langage and hard matere°   *difficult subject matter*
Is encombrous° for to here   *troublesome*
At ones;° wost thou nat° wel this?"   *(Both) at once / don't you know*
And I answerd and seyde, "Yis."
865 "A ha!" quod° he, "lo, so I can   *said*
Lewedly to a lewed° man   *Simply to an uneducated*
Speke and shewe him swiche skilles,°   *such arguments, proofs*
That he may shake hem° by the billes,°   *them / beaks*
So palpable they shulden be.°   *i.e., evident are they*
870 But tell me this, now prey I thee,
How thinkth thee° my conclusioun?"   *What do you think of*
"A good persuasioun,"°   *persuasive case*
Quod° I, "it is, and lyk to be°   *Said / likely to be (true)*

Right so° as thou hast preved° me."   *Just / demonstrated to*
875 "By God," quod he, "and as I leve°   *trust*
Thou shalt have yet, er it be eve,°   *before nightfall*
Of every word of this sentence°   *science, teaching*
A preve by experience,°   *evidentiary proof*
And with thyn eres° heren wel   *your (own) ears*
880 Top and tail, and everydel°   *every bit*
That every word that spoken is
Comth into Fames Hous ywis,°   *in truth*
As I have seyd; what wilt° thou more?"   *do you want*
And with this word upper to sore°   *to soar upward*
885 He gan,° and seyde, "By Seynt Jame,[2]   *began*
Now wil we speken al of game."°   *mirth, fun*
    "How farest thou?"° quod he to me,   *are you doing*
"Wel," quod° I. "Now see," quod he,   *said*
"By thy trouthe, yond adoune,°   *down over there*
890 Wher that° thou knowest° any toune   *Whether / recognize*
Or hous or any other thinge.
And whan thou hast of ought knowinge,°   *recognize anything*
Look that° thou warne° me,   *See that / advise*
And I anoon° shal telle thee   *immediately*
895 How fer° that thou art now therfro."°   *far / from it*
    And I adoun gan looken tho°   *looked then*
And beheld feldes and plaines,
And now hilles and now mountaines,
Now valeys, now forestes,
900 And now unnethes grete bestes,°   *barely (could discern) big animals*
Now riveres, now citees,
Now tounes and now grete° trees,   *large*
Now shippes saillinge in the see.
    But thus sone in a whyle° he   *after a short time*
905 Was flowen fro° the grounde so hye,°   *Had flown from / high*
That al the world as to myn eye
No more semed than a prikke,°   *pin-point*
Or elles° was the air so thikke°   *else / foggy, thick*
That I ne mighte nat discerne.°   *see through (it)*
910 With that he spak to me as yerne°   *earnestly, eagerly*
And seyde, "Seest thou° any toun   *Do you see*
Or ought° thou knowest yonder   *anything*
     doun?"°   *you recognize down there*
I seyde, "Nay." "No wonder nis,"°   *that is*
Quod° he, "for half so° high as this   *Said / as*
915 Nas° Alexander Macedo,   *Was not*
Ne the king, Daun° Scipio,   *Lord*
That saw in dreme, at point devys,°   *perfectly, completely*
Helle and erthe and paradys,
Ne eek° the wrecche° Dedalus,   *Nor also / miserable*
920 Ne his child, nice° Icarus,   *foolish*
That fleigh° so hye that the hete°   *(Who) flew / heat (of the sun)*

2. Saint James of Compostella, probably chosen as a saint cherished by pilgrims and travelers; see Nicholas R. Havely, *The House of Fame* (1994), p. 158.

His winges malt,° and he fel wete°	*melted / (becoming) soaked*
In mid° the see, and ther he dreynte,°	*the middle of / drowned*
For whom was maked moch compleynte.°[3]	*lamentation*
925 Now turn upward," quod he, "thy face,	
And behold this large place,	
This air, but looke° thou ne be	*take care that*
Adrad of hem° that thou shalt see;	*Afraid of them*
For in this regioun, certeyn,°	*truly*
930 Dwelleth many a citezeyn°	*inhabitants*
Of which that speketh Daun Plato.°	*i.e., in the Timaeus*
These been the airissh bestes,[4] lo!"	
And so saw I al that meynee°	*company*
Bothe goon° and also flee.°	*walk / fly*
935 "Now," quod he tho,° "cast up thyn eye;°	*then / eyes*
See yonder, lo, the Galaxye,	
Which men clepeth° the Milky Wey,	*call*
For° it is whyt: and some parfey°	*Because / indeed*
Callen it Watlinge Strete,[5]	
940 That ones° was y-brent with° hete,	*once / burnt by*
Whan the sonnes sone the rede,	
That highte Pheton, wolde lede	
Algate his fader cart and gye.	
The carte hors gan wel espye	
945 That he ne coude no governaunce	
And gan for to lepe and launce[6]	
And beren° him now up, now doun,	*carried*
Til that he saw the Scorpioun,°	*i.e., in the Zodiac*
Which that in heven a signe is yit,°	*even now*
950 And he for ferde° loste his wit	*fear*
Of° that, and let the reynes goon°	*Because of / reins go*
Of his hors;° and they anoon°	*horses / immediately*
Gan up to mounte° and doun descende	*ascend upward*
Til° bothe the air and erthe brende,°	*Until / were scorched*
955 Til Jupiter, lo, atte laste,	
Him slow,° and fro the carte° caste.	*killed / from the chariot*
Lo, is it nat a greet mischaunce,°	*calamity*
To lete a fool han governaunce°	*have control*

3. The eagle cites a series of figures who had attempted or achieved flight above the earth: In medieval romances, Alexander the Great (of Macedonia) tried to ascend the heavens in a flying machine. Scipio—though he did not see hell—was taken up and shown the tiny point of the earth from the heavens by his grandfather in the sixth book of Cicero's *De re publica* (included here in the Contexts section; see above line 514; also, the *Book of the Duchess* 286, and the *Parliament of Fowls* 29 ff.). Daedalus built wings for flying, which his son Icarus used on an ill-fated trip that soared first too close to the sun, scorching the wings, and then plunged Icarus to his death in the sea.
4. Demons of the air. (Possibly the creatures that make up the signs of the Zodiac, but more likely intermediate beings that haunted the atmosphere, according to classical and medieval writers from Plato to Augustine to Alain de Lille; for more detail, see the *Riverside Chaucer*, Explanatory Note, p. 984.)
5. As Skeat points out (*Complete Works*, vol. 3, p. 263), the Milky Way looks like a road in the night sky, and hence in classical and medieval texts was frequently compared to various throroughfares. Watling Street was an ancient road that ran the length of England.
6. When the son of the glowing sun, namely Phaeton, wanted to take control of steering his father's chariot. The chariot's horse began to notice that (Phaeton) didn't know how to control (him), and (so the horse) began to leap and jump about. (The story of Phaeton, taken from Ovid's *Metamorphoses* 1–2, was widely known in the Middle Ages.)

Of thing that he can nat demeyne?"°   *is not able to govern*
960   And with this word, soth for to seyne,°   *truth to tell*
He gan alwey upper° to sore   *higher and higher*
And gladded me ay° more and more,   *comforted me ever*
So feithfully° to me spak° he.   *earnestly, sincerely / spoke*
    Tho° gan I looken under° me,   *Then / beneath*
965 And beheld the airissh bestes,°   *see line 932*
Cloudes, mistes, and tempestes,°   *storms*
Snowes, hailes, raines, windes,
And th'engendring in hir kindes,[7]
And al the wey thurgh whiche I cam.
970 "O God," quod° I, "that made Adam,   *said*
Moche° is thy might and thy noblesse!"°   *Great / nobility*
    And tho° thoughte I upon Boece,°   *then / Boethius*
That wryt,° "A thought may flee so hye°   *Who wrote / fly so high*
With fethres° of philosophye   *feathers*
975 To passen everich° element;   *as to travel beyond each*
And whan he hath so fer y-went,°   *gone so far*
Than may be seen behind his bak
Cloud[8] and al that I of spak."°   *spoke of (earlier)*
    Tho gan I wexen in a were,°   *to grow anxious*
980 And seyde, "I woot° wel I am here;   *know*
But wher° in body or in gost°   *whether / spirit*
I noot ywis,° but God, thou wost!"°[9]   *do not know truly / know*
For more clere entendement°   *understanding*
Nas° me never yet y-sent.°   *Has to / been sent*
985 And than thoughte I on Marcian,
And eek° on Anteclaudian,[1]   *also*
That sooth was hir° descripcioun   *true was their*
Of al the hevenes regioun
As fer as that I saw the preve;°   *evidence, proof*
990 Therfor I can hem now beleve.
    With that this egle gan to crye,
"Lat be,"° quod he, "thy fantasye;°   *Get over / deluded state*
Wilt thou lere of° sterres ought?"°   *learn from / anything*
"Nay, certeynly," quod I, "right nought."°   *absolutely nothing*
995 "And why?" "For° I am now too old."   *Because*
"Elles° I wolde thee have told,"   *Otherwise*
Quod he, "the sterres° names, lo,   *stars'*
And al the hevenes signes therto,°   *also the Zodiacal signs*
And which they been." "No fors,"° quod I.   *Not a problem*
1000 "Yis, pardee,"° quod he; "wostow° why?   *indeed / do you know*
For whan thou redest poetrye,°   *in poems, fables*
How goddes gonne stellifye°   *turned into stars*
Briddes,° fissh, beste,° or him or here,   *Birds / animals*
As° the Raven or either Bere,°   *Such as / Bear*

---

7. I.e., how such natural events are engendered or created.
8. The source for this passage from Boethius's *Consolation of Philosophy*, the opening lines of Book 4, meter 1, is included here in the Contexts section.
9. A parody of Saint Paul, 2 Corinthians 12:2–3.
1. Martianus Capella's *Marriage of Mercury and Philology* and Alain de Lille's *Anticlaudianus*.

1005	Or Ariones° harpe fyne,°	*Arion's / excellent*
	Castor, Pollux, or Delphyne,	
	Or Athalantes° doughtres sevene,	*Atlas's*
	How al these are set in hevene;[2]	
	For though thou have hem° ofte on honde,°	*them / ready, at hand*
1010	Yet nostow nat° wher that they stonde."°	*you don't know / are located*
	"No fors,"° quod I, "it° is no nede;	*No problem / there*
	I leve° as wel, so God me spede,°	*believe / God help me*
	Hem° that wryte of this matere,°	*Those who / subject matter*
	As though I knew hir° places here;	*had direct knowledge of their*
1015	And eek° they shynen here so bright,	*also*
	It shulde shenden al my sight°	*destroy my eyesight*
	To look on hem."° "That may wel be,"	*at them*
	Quod° he. And so forth bar he° me	*Said / he carried*
	A whyl, and than he gan° to crye,	*began*
1020	That never herde I thing so hye,°	*loud*
	"Now up thyn hede,° for al is wel;	*lift up your head*
	Seynt Julyan,[3] lo, bon hostel!°	*good lodging*
	See here the Hous of Fame, lo!	
	Maistow° nat heren that° I do?"	*Can you / what*
1025	"What?" quod I. "The grete soun,"	
	Quod he, "that rumbleth up and doun	
	In Fames Hous, ful of tydinges°	*pieces of news, reports*
	Bothe of fair speche and chydinges,°	*fault-finding, loose talk*
	And of fals and sooth compouned.°	*truth combined*
1030	Herke° wel; it is nat rouned.°	*Listen / whispered*
	Herestow nat° the grete swough?"°	*Don't you hear / roar*
	"Yis, pardee,"° quod I, "wel ynough."°	*indeed / enough*
	"And what soun is it lyk?" quod he.	
	"Peter!—Beting of the see,"	
1035	Quod I, "ageyn the roches holowe,[4]	
	Whan tempest° doth the shippes swalowe,°	*storm / swallows up*
	And lat a man stonde, out of doute,	
	A myle thens, and here it route;[5]	
	Or elles lyk° the last humblinge°	*like / rumbling*
1040	After the clappe of o thundringe,°	*a single clap of thunder*
	Whan Joves hath the aire y-bete;°	*struck the air*
	But it doth° me for fere swete."°	*makes / sweat with fear*
	"Nay, dred thee nat thereof,"° quod he,	*Don't be afraid of that*
	"It is nothing wil byten° thee;	*that will bite*
1045	Thou shalt noon harme have, trewely."	

2. The eagle's syntax here is characteristically loose. He describes in his casual and pedestrian way the variety of divine transformations chronicled in classical mythology, where the raven was transformed from white to black; an Arcadian nymph was changed first into a bear and later, along with her son, stellified—"either Bear" likely means either the constellation of *Ursa major* or *Ursa minor*; Arion's Harp is the constellation Lycra; Castor and Pollux, Helen's twin brothers, form the Zodiacal sign of Gemini; Delphyne is the constellation of the dolphin that rescued Arion; and Atlas's seven daughters form the Pleiades, seven stars in the constellation of Taurus.
3. Patron saint of hospitality.
4. "By Saint Peter!—(It sounds like the) crashing of the sea," I said, "(echoing) in rocky caves." ("Peter" was a common oath, used elsewhere in Chaucer, but particularly appropriate here; as Brian Stone notes [*Love Visions*, p. 240], the Latin word for rock is "petra.")
5. (Even) to the man who stands, sure enough, a mile away (from Fame's castle), listening to it roar.

And with this word bothe he and I
As nigh° the place arryved were   *close to*
As men may casten with° a spere.   *reach by throwing*
I niste° how, but in a strete   *don't know*
1050 He sette me faire° on my fete   *squarely, precisely*
And seyde, "Walke forth a pas,°   *for a while*
And tak thyn aventure or cas°   *fortune or chance*
That thou shalt finde in Fames place."
      "Now," quod° I, "whyl we han space°   *said / time*
1055 To speke, er that° I go fro° thee,   *before / from*
For the love of God, tell me
In sooth that° wil I of thee lere,°   *Truly something / learn*
If this noise that I here
Be, as I have herd thee tellen
1060 Of° folk that doun in erthe dwellen   *From*
And cometh here in the same wyse°   *manner*
As I thee herde er this devyse;°   *you describe earlier*
And that ther lyves body nis°   *is no living body*
In al that hous that yonder is
1065 That maketh al this loude fare?"°   *disturbance, commotion*
"No," quod he, "by Seynt Clare,[6]
And also° wys God rede° me!   *as / guides, advises*
But o° thinge I wil warne° thee   *one / inform*
Of the which° thou wolt have wonder.   *About which*
1070 Lo, to the Hous of Fame yonder
Thou wost° how cometh every speche,°   *know / utterance*
It nedeth nought° thee eft° to teche.   *It's not necessary / again*
But understond now right° wel this: *very*
When any speche y-comen is°   *has arrived*
1075 Up to the paleys,° anonright°   *i.e., of Fame / all at once*
It wexeth lyk° the same wight,°   *becomes / the same person*
Which° that the word in° erthe spake,°   *Who / on / spoke*
Be it° clothed red or blake;°   *Whether it be / red or black*
And hath so verray his° lyknesse   *such a true likeness*
1080 That spake° the word, that thou wilt gesse   *Of the person who spoke*
That it the same body be,°   *is the very same body*
Man or woman, he or she,
And is nat this a wonder° thing?"   *an amazing*
"Yis," quod I tho,° "by heven king!"°   *then / heaven's king*
1085 And with this worde, "Farwel," quod° he,   *said*
"And here I wol abyden° thee,   *wait for*
And God of hevene sende thee grace
Som° good to lerne° in this place!"   *Something / learn*
And I of him took leve anoon,°   *took leave immediately*
1090 And gan° forth to the paleys goon.°   *began / to walk, proceed*

---

6. Founder of the Franciscan order of "poor clares," which taught silence and simplicity.

Book 3

THE INVOCATION

	O god of science° and of light,	*knowledge, learning*
	Apollo,[1] thurgh thy grete might	
	This litel laste book thou gye!°	*guide*
	Nat that I wilne,° for maistrye,°	*aspire / the prestige*
1095	Here° art poetical be shewed,°	*That here / exhibited*
	But, for° the rym is light and lewed,°	*because / slight and awkward*
	Yet make it somwhat agreable°	*pleasing*
	Though som vers faile in° a sillable;	*verses are lacking*
	And that° I do no diligence°	*i.e., though / am not trying*
1100	To shewe craft° but o sentence.°	*show off skill / only meaning*
	And if, divyne vertu,° thow	*power*
	Wilt helpe me to shewe° now	*reveal*
	That° in myn hede y-marked° is—	*What / conceived, formed*
	Lo, that is for to menen this,°	*that is to say*
1105	The Hous of Fame for to descryve°—	*describe*
	Thou shalt see me go, as blyve,°	*without delay*
	Unto the nexte laure° I see	*laurel tree*
	And kisse it for it is thy tree.[2]	
	Now entreth in° my brest anoon!°	*enter into / at once*

THE DREAM

1110	Whan I was fro° this egle goon,°	*had from / departed*
	I gan beholde° upon this place.	*began to gaze*
	And certeyn,° er I ferther pace,°	*truly / before I move on*
	I wol yow al the shap devyse°	*describe the appearance*
	Of hous and citee,° and al the wyse°	*(walled) city / manner*
1115	How I gan to this place aproche	
	That stood upon so high a roche;°	*rocky crag*
	Hyer stant° ther noon in Spaine.	*Higher stands*
	But up I clomb° with alle paine,°	*climbed / great effort*
	And though to climbe it greved me,°	*was difficult, painful for*
1120	Yet I ententif° was to see	*eager*
	And for to pouren wonder low°	*bend down and peer*
	If° I coude any weyes know	*(To see) if*
	What maner stoon° this roche was,	*kind of stone*
	For it was lyk alumed glas,[3]	
1125	But° that it shoon ful more clere,°	*Except / far more brightly*
	But of what congeled matere°	*congealed, compacted material*
	It was, I niste redely.°	*assuredly did not know*
	But at the laste espyed I°	*examined (it)*

1. This invocation to Apollo, god of wisdom, music, and poetry, parodies Dante, *Paradiso* 1.13–27, included here in the Contexts section.
2. According to Ovid, Apollo adopted the laurel as his tree in honor of Daphne, a nymph he was pursuing, who eluded him when she was transformed into a laurel by her father Peneus; see the *Metamorphoses* 1.452–567.
3. For it was like glass limned with light. (I am following Kathy Cawsey's suggested reading, which connects the brilliant glass here to the gilding and illumination of medieval manuscripts and stained glass, thus linking the fragility of ice to the fragility of manuscript transmission; " 'Alum de glas' or 'Alymed glass'? Manuscript Reading in Book III of *The House of Fame*," *University of Toronto Quarterly* 73 [2004]: 972–79.)

And found that it was everydeel   *entirely*
1130 A roche of yse° and nat of steel.°   *ice / steel*
Thoughte I, "By Seynt Thomas of Kent,°4   *Thomas à Becket*
This were a feble fundament°   *is a weak foundation*
To bilden on a place hye!°   *for such a tall building*
He ought him litel glorifye°   *should not boast*
1135 That° hereon bilt, God so° me save!"   *Who / as God may*
  Tho° saw I al the half y-grave°   *Then / one side engraved*
With famous folkes names fele°   *aplenty*
That had y-been in mochel wele°   *enjoyed great prosperity*
And hir° fames wyde y-blowe.°   *their / widely disseminated*
1140 But wel unnethes° coude I knowe°   *only scarcely / make out*
Any lettres for to rede
Hir names by, for out of drede°   *without a doubt*
They were almost of-thowed,° so   *thawed away*
That of the lettres oon° or two   *one or two*
1145 Was molte° away of every name,   *had melted*
So unfamous was wexe hir° fame;   *had grown their*
But men seyn, "What may ever laste?"
  Tho gan I° in myn herte caste,°   *Then I began / to consider*
That they were molte° awey with hete°   *had melted / from heat*
1150 And nat awey with stormes bete,°   *pummeled by storms*
For on that other syde I sey°   *saw*
Of this hille, that northward ley,
How it was writen° ful of names   *engraved, inscribed*
Of folk that hadden grete fames   *achieved great fame*
1155 Of° olde tyme, and yet° they were   *from / still*
As fresshe as° men had writen hem there   *as if*
The selfe° day, right er° that houre   *That very / just before*
That I upon hem° gan to poure.°   *them / peered*
But wel I wiste° what it made;°   *knew / caused this*
1160 It was conserved with° the shade—   *protected by*
Al this wrytinge that I sye°—   *saw*
Of a castel that stood on hye,°   *high*
And stood eek on° so cold a place   *also in*
That hete mighte it nat deface.°   *obliterate*
1165   Tho gan I up the hille to goon,
And fond° upon the coppe a woon,°   *found / top a dwelling*
That al the men that been on lyve
Ne han the cunning to descryve
The beautee of that ilke place,
1170 Ne coude casten no compace
Swich another for to make
That mighte of beautee be his make,
Ne so wonderliche y-wrought
That it astonieth yet my thought
1175 And maketh al my wit to swinke
On this castel to bethinke,5

4. Archbishop of Canterbury, martyred in 1170, whose church was the destination of the pilgrimage in the *Canterbury Tales* (see 1.17–18).
5. Such that no man who has ever lived would have the skill to describe the beauty of that place,

So that the grete beautee,
The cast,° the curiositee° *design / elegance*
Ne can I nat to yow devyse,° *describe*
1180 My wit ne may me nat suffyse.° *is insufficient (to the task)*
But natheles° al the substaunce° *nonetheless / gist*
I have yet° in my remembraunce;° *still / memory*
Forwhy° me thoughte,° by Seynt Gyle, *And so / it seemed to me*
Al was of stoon of beryle⁶
1185 Bothe castel and the tour° *tower*
And eek° the halle° and every bour,° *also / great hall / all the rooms*
Withouten peces° or joininges;° *sections / joints*
But many subtil compassinges,° *contraptions*
Babewinnes° and pinacles,° *Gargoyles / spires*
1190 Imageries° and tabernacles° *Sculptures / canopied niches*
I saw, and ful eek° of windowes *so full also*
As flakes falle in grete snowes.
And eek in ech° of the pinacles *each*
Weren sondry habitacles° *various niches*
1195 In whiche stooden, al withoute,° *on the outside*
Ful the castel, al aboute,° *Entirely encircling the castle*
Of alle maner of minstrales° *musicians*
And gestiour, that° tellen tales *entertainers, minstrels who*
Bothe of weping° and of game,° *sorrow / delight*
1200 Of al that longeth unto° Fame. *is appropriate to*
Ther herde I pleyen on an harpe,
That souned° bothe wel and sharpe,° *sounded / loud, piercing*
Orpheus ful craftely,° *skillfully*
And on° his syde, faste by,° *by / quite near*
1205 Sat the harper Orion,
And Eacides Chiron,
And other harpers many oon,° *a one*
And the Bret Glascurion;⁷
And smale harpers with hir glees° *musical instruments*
1210 Saten under hem° in divers sees,° *below them / various seats*
And gonne on hem upward to gape° *stared, gaped up at them*
And countrefete hem° as an ape *copied them*
Or as craft countrefeteth kinde.° *art imitates nature*
Tho° saw I stonden hem behinde, *Then*
1215 Afer fro° hem, al by hemselve,° *Far away / themselves*
Many thousand tymes twelve
That maden loude menstralcyes° *music*
In cornemuse° and shalmyes,° *On bagpipes / woodwinds*
And many other maner pipe,° *kinds of pipes*

---

nor would he be able to come up with a blueprint to build such another that might equal this in beauty or be constructed with such intricate detail that even yet it astounds me and makes my brain weary to think upon it.

6. A greenish-blue precious stone, with various properties—from amorous to religious—that may be significant in the context; in 1288–92, beryl has the property of magnifying whatever is reflected there. St. Giles (or Aegidius) was a follower of St. Francis known for his pilgrimages and travels to far-off places.

7. Using his lyre, Orpheus charmed the guardians of the underworld to win back his wife Eurydice; Chiron, descended from Eacus, was a centaur notable for his musical abilities; Orion/Arion (see also 1005) was a mythological poet annd songster; the Breton Glascurion was a Welsh bard.

1220 That craftely° began to pipe	*skillfully*
Bothe in doucet° and in rede,°	*on flutes / reeds*
That been at festes° with the brede;°	*are at feasts / meat*
And many floute° and lilting-horne°	*flutes / clarions*
And pipes made of grene corne,°	*plants*
1225 As han these litel herde-gromes°	*these little shepherds have*
That kepen bestes° in the bromes.°	*guard livestock / fields*
Ther saw I than Atiteris,	
And of° Athenes Daun° Pseustis,	*from / Lord*
And Marcia that lost hir skin,	
1230 Bothe in face, body, and chin,	
For that° she wolde envyen,° lo,	*Because / compete*
To pipen bet° than Apollo.[8]	*better*
Ther saw I famous olde and yonge	
Pipers of the Duche tonge,°	*German tongue, language*
1235 To lerne° love-daunces, springes,°	*teach / lively dances*
Reyes,° and these straunge° thinges.	*Round-dances / such unusual, foreign*
Tho° saw I in another place	*Then*
Stonden in a large space,	
Of hem that° maken blody° soun	*those who / a warlike*
1240 In trompe, beme, and clarioun,°	*i.e., different kinds of trumpets*
For in fight and blood-shedinge°	*on the battlefield*
Is used gladly clarioninge.°	*customarily trumpeting*
Ther herde I trompe° Messenus	*blow the trumpet*
Of whom that speketh Virgilius.	
1245 Ther herde I trompe Joab also,	
Theodomas and other mo,°	*others in addition*
And al that used° clarion	*all those who played*
In Cataloigne and Aragon,	
That in hir° tyme famous were	*their*
1250 To lerne,° saw I trompe there.[9]	*to learn (from or about)*
Ther saw I sitte in other sees,°	*seats*
Pleyinge upon sondry glees°	*various musical instruments*
Whiche that I can nat nevene,°	*am not able to name*
Mo° than sterres been in hevene,	*More*
1255 Of whiche I nil° as now nat ryme,°	*don't wish / make rhymes about*
For ese of° yow and losse of° tyme:	*To accommodate / to save*
For tyme y-lost, this knowen ye,	
By no way may recovered be.	
Ther saw I pley jogelours,°	*conjurers*
1260 Magiciens and tregetours,°	*illusionists*
And phitonesses,° charmeresses,°	*spiritualists / enchantresses*

8. The list is of failed musicians: Atiteris is obscure, but possibly an oblique reference to Tityrus, a Virgilian shepherd, or to Tyrtaeus, a famous battle poet named by Horace (the "a" in both cases could suggest negation, as in "not-Tityrus"); Pseustis (Greek for "lie"), mentioned next, was defeated in a poetry contest against Alithia (Greek for "truth") in the *Eclogue* of Theodulus; Marcia is Marsyas, from Ovid's *Metamorphoses*, who was tricked into losing a music contest with Apollo.
9. Misenus, described by Virgil in the *Aeneid*, was the son of the wind god Aeolus and trumpeted for Hector and Aeneas; Joab, a warrior for King David, blew the trumpet on three occasions in 2 Samuel after victories over his enemies; Theodamas (also mentioned along with Joab in the Merchant's Tale, *Canterbury Tales* 4.1719–20) was a warrior named by Statius in the *Thebaid* in proximity to the blowing of trumpets; references to Catalonia and Aragon, in Spain, parallel the earlier references to German musicians (1234), allowing Chaucer to include contemporary figures from various regions abroad known for their specific skills as musicians or entertainers.

Olde wicches, sorceresses,
That use exorsisaciouns°   *incantations*
And eek° these fumigaciouns,°   *also / aromatic smoke (for magic)*
1265 And clerkes eek, which conne wel°   *are well versed in*
Al this magyke naturel,[1]
That craftely doon hir ententes°   *endeavor*
To make, in certeyn ascendentes,°   *astrological configurations*
Images,° lo, thurgh which magyk   *effigies, figures*
1270 To° make a man been hool or syk.°   *(They strive) to / healthy or sick*
Ther saw I thee, quene Medea,
And Circes eek, and Calipsa;
Ther saw I Hermes Ballenus,
Lymote, and eek Simon Magus.[2]
1275 Ther saw I, and knew hem° by name,   *them*
That by swich art doon men han° fame.   *such arts win their*
Ther saw I Colle tregetour[3]
Upon a table of sicamour°   *sycamore wood platform*
Pleye an uncouthe thing to telle;[4]
1280 I saw him carien° a wind-melle°   *place / windmill*
Under a walsh-note shale.°   *walnut shell*
    What° shuld I make lenger tale°   *Why / go on longer*
Of° al the peple that I say,°   *About / saw*
Fro hennes into° domesday?   *From now until*
1285   Whan I had al this folk beholde
And fond me loos° and nought y-holde°   *at liberty / detained*
And eft y-mused° longe whyle   *had again contemplated*
Upon these walles of beryle,
That shoon ful lighter than a° glas   *more brightly than*
1290 And made wel more than it was
To semen every thing ywis,
As kinde thing of Fames is,[5]
I gan forth romen° til I fond   *began to wander forth*
The castel-yate° on my right hond,   *castle gate*
1295 Which that so wel corven° was   *carved*
That never swich° another nas,°   *such / has existed*
And yet it was by aventure°   *in a haphazard way*
Y-wrought,° as often as by cure.°   *fashioned / careful design*
It nedeth nought° yow for to tellen,   *It's not necessary*
1300 To make yow too longe dwellen,°   *i.e., at great length*
Of this yates florisshinges,°   *gate's ornamentation*

---

1. "Magyke naturel," or natural magic, uses invisible natural forces to perform feats that might otherwise be considered supernatural—e.g., the use of astrology to make predictions, or of images (effigies), as described here, to effect a cure for disease.
2. Medea was known to the Middle Ages as a great enchantress; most famously, with her magical powers, she helped Jason win the Golden Fleece and rejuvenated his ailing father Aeson. Circes and Calypso are taken from the story of Odysseus; the first attempted, but failed, to turn Odysseus into a beast, and the second detained him on her island. Hermes Ballenus was a follower of the founder of alchemy Hermes Trismegistus (see the Canon's Yeoman's Tale, *Canterbury Tales* 8.1434). Limote is possibly Elymas, a sorceror encountered by St. Paul at Paphos (Acts 13:6–12). Simon Magus, also the founder of the sin of simony, was a sorceror in Samaria who was converted to Christianity (Acts 8:9–24).
3. Possibly one Colin T., mentioned in a French courtesy handbook as a magician; see the *Riverside Chaucer*, Explanatory Note, p. 987.
4. Perform an unusual trick, (difficult) to describe.
5. And made everything seem much larger than it really was, as is the nature of Fame.

	Ne of compasses,° ne of kervinges,°	*the designs / the carvings*
	Ne how they hatte in masoneries,°	*are called in masonry*
	As corbetz° fulle of imageries.°	*decorated braces / sculptures*
1305	But Lord, so fair it was to shewe,°	*behold*
	For it was al with gold behewe!°	*gilded with gold (leaf)*
	But in I wente and that anoon;°	*straightway*
	Ther mette I crying many oon,°	*individuals*
	"A larges, larges,° hold up wel!°	*generosity / keep it up*
1310	God save the lady of this pel,°	*castle*
	Our owne gentil° lady Fame,	*noble*
	And hem that wilnen° to have name°	*those who desire / win renown*
	Of° us!" Thus herde I cryen alle,°	*From / (them) all cry out*
	And faste comen° out of halle,	*they came*
1315	And shoken nobles and sterlinges.[6]	
	And some corouned° were as kinges,	*crowned*
	With crounes wrought° ful of losinges;°	*fashioned / diamond shapes*
	And many riban,° and many fringes°	*ribbons / ornamental borders*
	Were on hir° clothes trewely.	*their*
1320	Tho° atte laste espyed I°	*Then / I perceived*
	That pursevauntes and heraudes°	*heralds and (their) assistants*
	That cryen° riche folkes laudes,°	*sound / the praises of*
	It° weren alle; and every man	*I.e., they*
	Of hem,° as I yow tellen can,	*them*
1325	Had on him throwen a vesture°	*garment*
	Which that men clepe a cote-armure,°	*call a coat of arms*
	Enbrowded wonderliche riche,°	*Embroidered amazingly richly*
	Although they nere nought yliche.°	*none were the same*
	But nought nil I,° so mote I thryve,°	*I'm not / as I may thrive*
1330	Been aboute to descryve°	*describe*
	Al these armes° that ther weren,	*heraldic arms, insignia*
	That they thus on hir cotes beren,°	*wear on their tunics*
	For it to me were impossible;	
	Men mighte make of hem a bible°	*collection of books*
1335	Twenty foot thikke, as I trowe.°	*so I believe*
	For certeyn,° whoso coude y-knowe,°	*truly / whoever could identify (them)*
	Mighte ther alle the armes seen	
	Of famous folk that han y-been°	*have lived*
	In Affrike, Europe, and Asye,°	*Asia*
1340	Sith° first began the chevalrye.	*Since*
	Lo, how shulde I° now telle al this?	*could I (possibly)*
	Ne of the halle eek° what nede is°	*also / need is there*
	To tellen yow that every wal	
	Of it, and floor, and roof and al	
1345	Was plated half a fote thikke	
	Of° gold, and that nas nothing wikke,°	*With / not poor quality*
	But, for to° prove in alle wyse°	*(likely) to / all ways*
	As fyn° as ducat in Venyse,°	*pure / Venetian gold coin*
	Of whiche too lyte° al in my pouche° is?	*too few / purse*
1350	And they wer set as thikke of nouchis	

---

6. And they scattered nobles and sterlings. (The noble was a coin worth six shillings, eight pence, and the sterling the English silver penny.)

Fulle of the fynest stones faire,
That men rede in the Lapidaire,
As greses growen in a mede;[7]
But it were° al too longe to rede°   *would take / to narrate*
1355   The names, and therfore I pace.°   *pass over, omit (them)*
     But in this riche lusty° place   *delightful*
That Fames halle called was,
Ful moche prees° of folk ther nas,°   *A large crowd / was not*
Ne crouding for too mochil prees.°   *a mob too big*
1360   But al on hye,° above a dees,°   *high / daïs*
Sat in° a see imperial,°   *Set upon / majestic throne*
That made was of a rubee al°   *entirely of ruby*
Which that a carbuncle is y-called,
I saw, perpetually y-stalled,°   *enthroned*
1365   A feminyne creature;
That never, formed by nature,
Nas swich° another thing y-seye.°   *has such / been seen*
For alderfirst,° sooth for to seye,°   *first of all / truth to tell*
Me thoughte° that she was so lyte,°   *It seemed to me / small*
1370   That the lengthe of a cubyte°   *approx. 18–21"*
Was lenger° than she semed be;   *longer, taller*
But thus sone in a whyle,° she   *a short time later*
Hir tho° so wonderliche streighte°   *then / wondrously stretched*
That with hir feet she th'erthe reighte,°   *reached the earth*
1375   And with hir heed she touched hevene
Ther as° shynen sterres sevene.[8]   *Where*
And therto eek,° as to my wit,°   *in addition / in my opinion*
I saw° a gretter wonder yit°   *found it / still*
Upon hir eyen to beholde;
1380   But certeyn I hem never tolde,°   *never counted them*
For as fele eyen° hadde she   *many eyes*
As fethres upon foules be,°   *are on birds*
Or weren on the bestes foure
That Goddes trone gonne honoure,
1385   As John writ in th'Apocalips.[9]
Hir heer, that oundy° was and crips,°   *wavy / curly*
As burned° gold it shoon to see.   *Like burnished*
And sooth° to tellen, also she   *truth*
Had also fele upstonding eres°   *as many ears sticking up*
1390   And tonges° as on bestes heres,°   *tongues / are hairs on animals*
And on hir feet wexen° saw I   *had grown*
Partriches[1] winges redely.°   *assuredly*

7. And (the walls) were covered with clusters of gems, full of beautiful stones of the highest quality, which one can read about in the *Lapidary* (a treatise on precious stones), as many (gems) as blades of grass (that) grow in a meadow.
8. The seven planets of the Ptolemaic universe. In addition to borrowing from Virgil's description of Lady Fame here (see 349 note), Chaucer also includes details that liken her to Lady Philosophy from Boethius's *Consolation of Philosophy* Book 1, prose 1 (included here in the Contexts section), making her an ambiguous figure indeed.
9. Or as there were (eyes) on the four beasts who honored God's throne, as John writes in the Book of Revelation (4:6–9).
1. Explanations for the "partridge" here range from its speed in running to its inability to fly; Skeat suggests Chaucer simply mistranslated a similar-looking word from *Aeneid* 4.180 (*Complete Works*, vol. 3, p. 276).

	But Lord, the perry° and the richesse°	*jewelry / splendor*
	I saw sitting on this goddesse!	
1395	And Lord, the hevenissh° melodye	*heavenly*
	Of songes, ful of armonye°	*harmony*
	I herde aboute hir trone y-songe,°	*sung around her throne*
	That° al the paleys walles ronge;°	*So that / resounded*
	So song° the mighty Muse, she	*sang*
1400	That cleped° is Caliopee,²	*called*
	And hir eighte sustren eke,°	*sisters also*
	That in hir face° semen meke.°	*their faces / meek*
	And evermo, eternally,°	*always (and) forever*
	They singe of Fame, as tho° herde I:	*then*
1405	"Heried° be thou and thy name,	*Praised*
	Goddesse of renoun or of fame!"	
	Tho° was I war,° lo, atte laste	*Then / aware*
	As I myn eyen gan° up caste,	*began to*
	That this ilke° noble quene	*same*
1410	On hir shuldres° gan sustene°	*shoulders / was bearing*
	Bothe armes° and the name	*the coats of arms*
	Of tho that° hadde large° fame:	*those who / great*
	Alexander,° and Hercules	*Alexander the Great*
	That with a shert his lyfe les.³	
1415	And thus fond I sitting this goddesse	
	In nobley,° honour, and richesse,°	*majesty / splendor*
	Of which I stinte° a whyle now	*(will) stop for*
	Other thing to tellen yow.	
	Tho saw I stonde on either syde,	
1420	Streight doun to the dores wyde	
	Fro° the dees,° many a pilere°	*From / daïs / pillar*
	Of metal that shoon nat ful clere;°	*not very brightly*
	But though they nere of no richesse,°	*not opulent*
	Yet they were made for greet noblesse,°	*honor*
1425	And in hem° greet sentence.°	*them / significance*
	And folkes of digne° reverence,	*worthy of*
	Of whiche I wol yow telle fonde,°	*undertake to tell*
	Upon the piler saw I stonde.	
	Alderfirst,° lo, ther I sighe,°	*First of all / saw*
1430	Upon a piler stonde on highe	
	That was of lede° and yren fyne,°	*lead / pure iron*
	Him of secte Saturnyne,°	*Saturnine faith*
	The Ebrayk° Josephus, the olde,	*Hebrew*
	That of Jewes gestes° tolde,	*chronicles*
1435	And he bar° upon his shuldres hye°	*bore, supported / high*
	The fame up of the Jewerye. °	*Jewish people*
	And by him stooden other sevene,°	*seven others*
	Wyse and worthy for to nevene,°	*name, mention*
	To helpen him bere up the charge,°	*burden*
1440	It was so hevy and so large.⁴	

2. The muse of epic poetry, Calliope, one of the nine Muses.
3. Hercules who lost his life by means of a shirt. (See above, 402–403 and note.)
4. The Jewish religion is characterized as "Saturnine" because its founding was believed to have

And for° they writen of batailes° — *because / about battles*
As wel as other olde mervailes,° — *ancient marvels*
Therfor was, lo, this pilere
Of° which that I yow telle here — *About*
1445 Of lede and yren° bothe ywis,° — *Made of lead and iron / truly*
For yren Martes° metal is, — *of Mars*
Which that god is of bataile,° — *combat*
And the lede, withouten faile,° — *undoubtedly*
Is, lo, the metal of Saturne
1450 That hath a ful large wheel° to turne. — *i.e., his heavenly orbit*
Tho stooden forth on every rowe,
Of hem which that I coude knowe
Though I hem nought be ordre telle,
To make yow too long to dwell
1455 These, of whiche I gonne rede.[5]
　　Ther saw I stonden out of drede,° — *indeed*
Upon an yren piler° strong — *iron pillar*
That peynted was al endelonge° — *from end to end*
With tygres blood in every place,
1460 The Tholosan that highte Stace,
That bar of Thebes up the fame
Upon his shuldres, and the name
Also of cruel Achilles.[6]
And by him stood withouten les,° — *truly (lit. without lie)*
1465 Ful wonder hye° on a pilere — *Extremely high*
Of yren, he the greet Omere,
And with him Dares and Tytus
Bifore,° and eek he° Lollius, — *in front / also*
And Guido eek de Columpnis,
1470 And Englissh Gaufride[7] eek ywis;° — *truly*
And ech° of these, as have I joye, — *each*
Was besy for to bere° up Troye. — *industriously lifting*
So hevy therof was the fame
That for to bere it was no game.° — *no laughing matter*

---

occurred under the conjunction of the planets Jupiter and Saturn; see the *Middle English Dictionary*, "secte," 2a. Also Judaism is the ancestor of Christianity, as Saturn is the father of the gods. Josephus was a first-century author of several books on the history of the Jews; his seven helpers remain unidentifed.

5. Loosely translated: Then there appeared lined up in rows many figures that I recognized, though I am not going to speak about them in detail, in order to save time for those that I am going to describe.

6. Statius, the first-century author of the an unfinished life of Achilles, the *Achilleid*, and an epic treatment of the matter of Thebes, the *Thebaid*, was erroneously held to be "Tholosan" (i.e., from Toulouse in France).

7. Each of the authors listed here wrote on the subject of Troy: The work of Homer ("Omere") on the Trojan War was known in the Middle Ages by reputation; Dares Phrygius and Dictys ("Tytus") Cretensis were believed to have authored first-hand (but conflicting) accounts of the Trojan War; Guido delle Colonne wrote the thirteenth-century *History of the Destruction of Troy*; Lollius, mentioned as a source by Chaucer in *Troilus and Criseyde* 1.394 and 5.1653, is of disputed origin (among the many possibiities are a special name for Chaucer's contemporary, Giovanni Boccaccio, or a man mentioned by Horace in the *Epistles* 2.1–5 and linked there to an authority on Troy); the "Englissh Gaufride" is usually taken to be Geoffrey of Monmouth, who in the twelfth-century *History of the Kings of Britain* traced the founders of Britain back to the Trojans, but another possibility is Chaucer himself, assuming that he had already begun writing *Troilus and Criseyde* (see Helen Cooper, "Four Last Things in Dante and Chaucer: Ugolino in the House of Rumour," *New Medieval Literatures* 3 [1999]: 39–66). The plethora of disputed and conflicting authorities raises the problem, central to the *House of Fame*, of literary and historical truth.

1475	But yet I gan ful wel espye,°	*perceived quite well*
	Betwix hem° was a litil envye.°	*Between them / enmity, ill will*
	Oon° seyde Omere made lyes,°	*One / told lies*
	Feyninge° in his poetryes,°	*Making things up / poems*
	And was to Grekes favorable;°	*favored the Greeks*
1480	Therfor held he it but fable.°	*just a fable, fiction*
	Tho° saw I stonde on a pilere	*Then*
	That was of tinned yren clere°	*bright tin-plated iron*
	That Latin poete Virgyle	
	That bore hath up a longe whyle°	*for a long time*
1485	The fame of Pius Eneas.°	*Pious (devoted, honorable) Aeneas*
	And next him on a piler was,	
	Of coper, Venus clerk° Ovyde,[8]	*Venus's acolyte, scholar*
	That hath y-sowen° wonder wyde	*scattered, spread*
	The grete god of Loves name,	
1490	And ther he bar up wel his fame	
	Upon his piler also hye°	*as high*
	As I might see it with myn eye,	
	Forwhy° this halle of whiche I rede°	*Because / tell, speak*
	Was woxe° on highte,° lengthe, and brede°	*Had grown / height / breadth*
1495	Wel more,° by a thousand del,°	*Much larger / times*
	Than it was erst,° that saw I wel.	*before*
	Tho saw I, on a piler by,°	*nearby*
	Of yren wrought ful sternely,°	*sturdily*
	The grete poete Daun° Lucan,	*Lord*
1500	And on his shuldres bar up° than	*he supported*
	As highe as that I mighte see	
	The fame of Julius and Pompee.[9]	
	And by him stooden alle these clerkes,°	*writers*
	That writen of Romes mighty werkes,	
1505	That° if I wolde hir° names telle	*(So many) that / their*
	Al too longe mot I dwelle.°	*must I continue*
	And next him on a piler stood	
	Of soulfre,° lyk as he were wood,°	*sulfur, brimstone / mad, agitated*
	Daun Claudian, the sooth° to telle,	*truth*
1510	That bar up° al the fame of helle,	*supported*
	Of Pluto and of Proserpyne,[1]	
	That quene is of the derke pyne.°	*hell (place of punishment)*
	What shulde I more telle of this?	
	The halle was al ful, ywis,°	*truly*
1515	Of hem° that writen olde gestes°	*those / tales of heroic deeds*
	As been° on trees rokes° nestes;	*there are / rooks'*
	But it a ful confus° matere	*very confusing*
	Were° al the gestes for to here°	*Would be / hear*

8. Virgil, the author of the *Aeneid*, and Ovid, the great classical love poet and author of the *Heroides*, the *Metamorphoses*, and other famous works, represented opposite perspectives, especially in their presentation of the story of Aeneas and Dido. Excerpts from both tellings of this story are included in the Contexts section of this Norton Critical Edition. See also the note to line 349.
9. The greatest poem of the first-century author Lucan was the *Pharsalia*, which presents the struggle between Julius Caesar and Pompey (Gnaeus Pompeius).
1. Claudian (ca. 400 C.E.) wrote the *Rape of Persephone*, about Pluto's abduction of the heroine to the underworld.

That they of write or how they hight.° — *what they are called*
1520 But whyl that I beheld this sight,
I herde a noise aprochen blyve° — *quickly*
That ferde° as been doon° in an hyve, — *i.e., sounded / bees do*
Ageyn hir° tyme of out-fleyinge;° — *Just before / flying out*
Right swich° a maner murmuringe, — *Just such*
1525 For al the world, it semed me.° — *to me*
   Tho gan I° look aboute and see — *Then I began to*
That ther come° entring in the halle — *came*
A right greet company withalle,° — *indeed*
And that of sondry° regiouns, — *from various*
1530 Of alleskinnes condiciouns,° — *from all walks of life*
That dwelle in° erthe under the mone,° — *on / moon*
Pore° and ryche. And also sone° — *Poor / as soon*
As they were° come into the halle, — *had*
They gonne doun on knees falle° — *fell on (their) knees*
1535 Bifore this ilke° noble quene, — *same*
And seyde, "Graunte us, lady shene,° — *beautiful*
Ech° of us, of thy grace, a bone!"° — *Each / boon, favor*
And some of hem° she graunted sone,° — *them / quickly*
And some she werned wel and faire,° — *refused kindly and courteously*
1540 And somme she graunted the contraire° — *(complete) opposite*
Of hir axing° utterly; — *their request*
But thus I seye yow trewely,
What hir cause° was, I niste.° — *reasoning / don't know*
For of this folk, ful wel I wiste,° — *knew*
1545 They had good fame ech° deserved, — *each*
Although they were diversly served,° — *treated differently*
Right° as hir suster, Dame Fortune,[2] — *Just*
Is wont° to serven in comune.° — *accustomed / in general*
   Now herkne° how she gan to paye° — *Listen to / pleased, alt. paid*
1550 That° gonne hir of hir grace praye, — *Those who*
And yet, lo, al this° companye — *this entire*
Seyden sooth,° and nought a lye. — *Told the truth*
   "Madame," seyde they, "we be
Folk that here besechen thee° — *beg of you*
1555 That thou graunte us now good fame
And let our werkes han that name;° — *i.e., good fame*
In ful recompensacioun° — *repayment*
Of° good werk, give us good renoun."° — *For / renown, reputation*
   "I werne° yow it," quod° she anoon,° — *deny / said / at once*
1560 "Ye gete of° me good fame noon,° — *(will) get from / none*
By God, and therfor go your wey."
   "Allas," quod they, "and welaway!° — *woe!*

---

2. Like her sister Fame, the goddess Fortune is a classical figure linked to the vanity and unreliability of worldly power and success. The most famous aspect of her iconography is the wheel on which she elevates the rich, powerful, and lucky in love as a prelude to plunging them into mischance and adversity. For more details, see also Chaucer's description of the lover's chess game with Fortune in the *Book of the Duchess* 618–84. The medieval idea of Fortune derives largely from Boethius's *Consolation of Philosophy*, where she is placed in opposition to the more wholesome figure of Philosophy; relevant passages from the *Consolation* and also the *Romance of the Rose* are printed in the Contexts section of this Norton Critical Edition.

Telle us, what may your cause° be?" — reason, justification
"For me list it nought,"° quod she; — Because I don't want to
1565　"No wight shal speke of° yow, ywis,° — say anything about / truly
Good ne harm,° ne that ne this." — Good or bad
And with that word she gan to calle° — called, summoned
Hir messager that was in halle
And bad° that he shulde fast goon, — commanded
1570　Upon peyn to be blinde anoon,[3]
For Eolus,° the god of winde: — To (fetch) Aeolus
"In Trace° ther ye shul him finde, — Thrace
And bid him bringe his clarioun
That is ful dyvers° of his soun,° — quite various / its sounds
1575　And it is cleped Clere Laude,° — Glorious Renown
With which he wont° is to heraude° — accustomed / celebrate
Hem° that me list° y-preised be; — Those / it pleases me
And also bid him how that he
Bringe his other clarioun
1580　That highte Sclaundre° in every toun, — is called Slander
With which he wont is to diffame° — dishonor, disgrace
Hem° that me list, and do hem° shame." — Those / bring them
　This messager gan fast to goon
And found wher, in a cave of stoon
1585　In a contree that hight Trace,° — was called Thrace
This Eolus, with harde grace,° — bad luck for him!
Held the windes in distresse° — in check
And gan° hem under him to presse,° — did / squeeze, compress them
That they gonne as beres rore,° — roared like bears
1590　He bond and pressed hem so sore.° — tormented them so sorely
　This messager gan fast° crye, — eagerly, earnestly
"Rys up," quod° he, "and fast hye° — said / hurry
Til that° thou at my lady be,° — Until / arrive
And tak thy clariouns eek° with thee, — also
1595　And speed thee forth." And he° anon° — i.e., Aeolus / at once
Took° to a man that hight Triton[4] — Gave
His clariouns to bere tho,° — carry then
And lete a certeyn wind to go° — go free
That blew so hidously and hye,° — violently and swiftly
1600　That it ne lefte nat a skye° — a cloud, a mist
In al the welken° longe and brode. — sky
　This Eolus nowher abode° — delayed
Til he was come to Fames fete,° — feet
And eek° the man that Triton hete,° — also / was called
1605　And ther he stood as still as stoon.
And herewithal ther com anoon° — came at once
Another huge companye
Of gode folk, and gonne° crye, — who began to
"Lady, graunte us now good fame,
1610　And lat our werkes han that name° — have that (same) reputation

---

3. Or he would suffer the penalty of being immediately struck blind.
4. The son of the sea god Neptune, Triton is frequently portrayed blowing on a conch shell like a trumpet.

Now, in honour of gentilesse,°   *nobility*
And also God your soule blesse!°   *as God bless you*
For° we han° wel deserved it,   *Because / have*
Therfore is right° that we been quit."°   *it is just / be rewarded*
1615   "As thryve° I," quod° she, "ye shal faile;   *may prosper / said*
Good werkes shal yow nought availe°   *not help you*
To have of me good fame as now.
But wite ye what?° I graunte yow   *do you know what*
That ye shal have a shrewed° fame   *bad, evil*
1620 And wikked loos° and worse name,°   *fame / reputation*
Though ye good loos have wel deserved;
Now go your wey, for ye be served.°   *you've gotten what's coming*
And thou, Daun Eolus," quod she,
"Tak forth thy trompe anoon,° let see,   *trumpet immediately*
1625 That is y-cleped Sclaunder light,°   *called foolish Slander*
And blow hir loos, that° every wight°   *their fame so that / person*
Speke of hem harm and shrewednesse°   *(Will) speak ill of them*
In stede of good and worthinesse.°   *honor*
For thou shalt trompe al the contraire°   *opposite*
1630 Of that they han doon wel or faire."°   *the good they have done*
"Allas," thoughte I, "what aventures°   *vicissitudes, mischances*
Han° these sory° creatures,   *Have / pitiful, miserable*
For they, amonges al the pres,°   *the whole crowd*
Shal thus be shamed, gilteles!
1635 But what! It mote nedes be."°   *needs must be*
What did this Eolus, but he°   *except (to)*
Tok° out his blake trompe of bras   *Take*
That fouler° than the devil was,   *filthier, more evil, rotten*
And gan° this trompe for to blowe   *began*
1640 As° al the world shulde overthrowe,°   *As if / were ruined*
That thurghout every regioun
Wente this foule trompes soun°   *sound of this foul trumpet*
As swifte as pelet° out of gonne°   *ball / cannon*
Whan fyr is in the poudre ronne.°   *ignites the gunpowder*
1645 And swich° a smoke gan out-wende°   *such / came out*
Out of his foule trompes ende,
Blak, blo,° grenissh, swartissh rede,°   *bluish gray / dark red*
As doth° wher that men melte lede,°   *is created / lead*
Lo, al on high fro the tuel!°   *from the chimney pipe*
1650 And therto o° thing saw I wel,   *another*
That the ferther that it ran
The gretter wexen it began,°   *larger it grew*
As doth the river from a welle,°   *wellspring*
And it stank as the pit of helle.
1655 Allas, thus was hir shame y-ronge°   *loudly sounded, proclaimed*
And giltelees on every tonge!°   *tongue*
Tho° cam the thridde° companye   *Then / third*
And gonne up to the dees to hye,°   *hurried to the daïs*
And doun on knees they fille anoon°   *at once*
1660 And seyde, "We been everichoon°   *every one (of us)*
Folk that han ful trewely

Deserved fame rightfully,°   *justly, fairly*
And pray yow it mot be knowe°   *may be known*
Right° as it is, and forth y-blowe."°   *Just / blown, proclaimed*
1665 "I graunte," quod° she, "for me liste°   *said / I feel like it*
That now your good werkes be wiste,°   *be known*
And yet ye shul have better loos,°   *fame*
Right in dispyt of° alle your foos,°   *In order to spite / foes*
Than worthy is,° and that anoon.°   *you deserve / immediately*
1670 Lat now," quod she, "thy trompe goon,°   *trumpet be put aside*
Thou Eolus, that is so blake,
And out thyn other trompe take
That highte Laude,° and blow it so   *Renown*
That thurgh° the world hir fame go°   *throughout / their fame will go*
1675 Al esely° and nat too faste,   *leisurely*
That it be knowen atte laste."°   *eventually*
    "Ful gladly, lady myn," he seyde,
And out his trompe of golde he breyde°   *pulled, yanked*
Anoon, and set it to his mouthe
1680 And blew it est and west and southe
And north, as loude as any thonder,
That every wight° hadde of it wonder,   *So that every creature*
So brode° it ran er than it stente.°   *far / before it stopped*
And certes° al the breeth° that wente   *certainly / wind*
1685 Out of his trompes mouthe smelde
As° men a pot-ful bawme° helde   *As if / of aromatic balsam*
Among° a basket ful of roses;   *Within*
This favour dide he til hir loses.°   *to their reputations*
    And right with this I gan espye,°   *noticed*
1690 Ther cam the ferthe° companye,   *fourth*
But certeyn° they were wonder° fewe,   *certainly / marvelously*
And gonne stonden in a rewe°   *(they) stood in a row*
And seyden, "Certes,° lady brighte,   *Certainly*
We han doon° wel with al our mighte;   *have done*
1695 But we ne kepen have no° fame.   *don't care about having*
Hyd° our werkes and our name,°   *Hide / reputations, renown*
For Goddes love, for certes we
Han certeyn° doon it for bountee,°   *truly / benevolence, altruism*
And for no maner other thing."
1700 "I graunte yow al your asking,"°   *request*
Quod° she; "let your werk be dede."°   *Said / dead, i.e., unknown*
    With that aboute I clew° myn hede   *scratched*
And saw anoon° the fifte route°   *at once / crowd, company*
That to this lady gonne loute°   *began to bow down*
1705 And doun on knes anoon to falle,
And to hir tho besoughten alle°   *then they all begged*
To hyde hir° goode werkes eke,°   *their / also*
And seyde they yeven nought a leke°   *didn't give a leek*
For no fame nor swich° renoun,   *such*
1710 For they, for° contemplacioun   *as a result of*
And Goddes love, hadde y-wrought;°   *done (good works)*
Ne of fame wolde they nought.°   *did they desire*

"What?" quod she, "and be ye wood?° — *are you crazy*
And wene ye° for to do good — *do you expect*
1715 And for to have of° that no fame? — *for*
Have ye dispyte° to have my name? — *Are you too haughty*
Nay, ye shul liven everichoon![5]
Blow thy trompe and that anoon,"° — *immediately*
Quod she, "thou Eolus, I hote,° — *command*
1720 And ring these folkes werk by note[6]
That° al the world may of it here." — *So that*
And he gan blowe hir loos so clere° — *their fame so loudly*
In° his golden clarioun — *On*
That thurgh° the world wente the soun — *throughout*
1725 Also kenely° and eek so softe,° — *(Both) sharply / slowly*
But atte laste it was on lofte.° — *in the air, abroad*
Tho° cam the sexte° companye, — *Then / sixth*
And gonne faste° on Fame crye. — *earnestly began to*
Right verrayly° in this manere — *Exactly*
1730 They seyden: "Mercy, lady dere!
To telle certein, as it is,° — *To be honest*
We han doon° neither that ne this, — *have done*
But ydel° al our lif y-be.° — *idle, lazy / (we) have been*
But natheles,° yet prey we, — *nevertheless*
1735 That we mowe° have so° good a fame — *may / as*
And greet renoun and knowen° name — *famous, well known*
As they that han doon° noble gestes° — *who have done / deeds*
And acheved alle hir lestes° — *their desires*
As wel of love as° other thing, — *in love as (in)*
1740 Al was us never broche ne ring,
Ne elles nought, from women sent,
Ne ones in hir herte y-ment
To make us only frendly chere,
But mighte temen us on bere.[7]
1745 Yet lat us to the peple seme° — *seem to (other) people*
Swich° as the world may of us deme° — *Such / judge*
That women loven us for woode.° — *madly, wildly*
It shal doon us as moche goode,
And to our herte as moche availe° — *bring as much benefit*
1750 To countrepese ese and travaile° — *To balance labor with comfort*
As° we had wonne it with labour;° — *As if / hard work*
For that is dere bought honour
At regard of our grete ese.[8]
And yet thou most° us more plese: — *must*
1755 Let us be holden eek therto° — *in addition*
Worthy, wyse, and goode also,
And riche, and happy unto love.° — *fortunate in love*
For Goddes love, that sit° above, — *who sits (i.e., God)*

---

5. (The renown) of each one of you will survive.
6. Ring out the deeds of these folk in harmony.
7. Although women have never sent us brooch nor ring nor any other (love token), nor did (women) ever intend, from their hearts, to show us anything more than friendship, but would rather have seen us dead (literally, on our biers).
8. For the honor that costs us our great material comfort comes at too high a price.

Though we may nat the body have
1760 Of women, yet, so God yow save,°   *God save you!*
Let men glewe on° us the name;°   *attach to / reputation (of lovers)*
Sufficeth° that we han the fame."   *It's enough*
      "I graunte," quod° she, "by my trouthe!°   *said / on my honor*
Now, Eolus, withouten slouthe,°   *sloth, delay*
1765 Tak out thy trompe of gold,° let see,   *golden trumpet*
And blow as they han axed° me,   *have requested of*
That every man wene hem at ese,°   *think them comfortable*
Though they gon in ful badde lese."⁹
This Eolus gan it so blowe°   *began to blow it thus*
1770 That thurgh° the world it was y-knowe.°   *throughout / known*
      Tho° cam the seventh route anoon°   *Then / group immediately*
And fel on knees everichoon°   *each one (of them)*
And seyde, "Lady, graunte us sone°   *quickly*
The same thing, the same bone,°   *boon, favor*
1775 That ye this nexte folk han doon."°   *gave these last people*
"Fy° on yow," quod she, "everichoon,   *Fie, Phooey*
Ye masty swyn,° ye ydel° wrecches,   *overfed swine / lazy*
Ful of roten slowe tecches!°   *slothful vices*
What, false theves, wher ye wolde
1780 Be famous good, and nothing nolde
Deserve why, ne never ye roughte?
Men rather yow to hangen oughte!¹
For ye be lyk the sweynte° cat   *lazy*
That wolde° have fissh, but wostow° what?   *wants to / do you know*
1785 He wolde nothing° wete his clowes.°   *doesn't want to / claws*
Evel thrift come to your jowes²
And eek° to myn if I it graunte   *also*
Or do yow favour yow to avaunte!°   *to praise, extol you*
Thou Eolus, thou king of Trace,°   *Thrace*
1790 Go, blow this folk a sory grace,"°   *miserable fate*
Quod she, "anoon,° and wostow° how?   *at once / do you know*
As I shal telle thee right now:
Sey: 'These been they that wolden° honour   *those who desired*
Have,° and do noskinnes° labour,   *To possess / no kind of*
1795 Ne do no good and yet han laude,°   *still to have praise*
And that men wende that bele Isaude
Ne coude hem nought of love werne,
And yet she that grint at a querne
Is al too good to ese hir herte.' "³
1800   This Eolus anoon up sterte,°   *jumped up straightway*
And with his blake clarioun

---

9. Although they graze in a bad pasture (i.e., are not doing well at all).
1. Oh, you false thieves, do you want to be famous for goodness, and yet you would (do) nothing to deserve it, and don't even care? You ought sooner to be hung (from the gallows)!
2. May bad luck befall your jaws (i.e., bad luck to you!).
3. And (they want other) men to think that the beautiful Isolde was unable to refuse them her love, whereas (the peasant girl) who grinds (grain or spices) on a hand-mill is too good to comfort their hearts. (Isolde was the famed Irish beauty married to King Mark of Cornwall and adored with a tragic passion by his nephew Tristan; their story was told or alluded to in many medieval romances. Fame's point is that such aspiring lovers have as much chance of wooing the local milkmaid as they do the noble and unattainable Isolde.)

He gan to blasen out a soun°   *began to sound a blast*
As loude as beloweth° wind in helle.   *loudly as roars the*
And eek therwith,° sooth° to telle,   *also / truth*
1805 This soun was so ful of japes°   *jokes, pranks*
As ever mowes° were in apes.   *grimaces*
And that wente al the world aboute,°   *around*
That° every wight° gan on hem shoute°   *So that / person / to jeer*
And for to laughe as° they were wood;°   *as if / crazy, mad*
1810 Swich game fonde they in hir hood.[4]
    Tho cam another companye,
That had y-doon the traiterye,°   *committed the (greatest) treason*
The harm,° the gretest wikkednesse   *(worst) injury*
That any herte couthe gesse,°   *could guess*
1815 And preyed hir to han good fame
And that she nolde hem doon° no shame,   *would bring on them*
But yeve° hem loos° and good renoun,   *give / praise*
And do it blowe in° clarioun.   *trumpeted by the*
"Nay, wis!"° quod° she, "it were° a vice;   *truly / said / would be*
1820 Al be ther° in me no justice   *Although there is*
Me listeth nat° to do it now   *It doesn't please me*
Ne this nil° I graunte yow."   *Nor do I wish*
    Tho cam ther lepinge in a route,°   *group, crowd*
And gonne choppen° al aboute   *began to hit, strike*
1825 Every man upon the croune°   *the tops of their heads*
That° al the halle gan to soune,°   *So that / resound*
And seyden,° "Lady, lefe° and dere,   *they said / beloved*
We been swich° folk as ye mowe here,°   *are such / may hear about*
To tellen al the tale aright,°   *truth*
1830 We been shrewes,° every wight,°   *scoundrels / one (of us)*
And han delyt° in wikkednesse   *take as much pleasure*
As good folk han in goodnesse,
And joye° to be knowen° shrewes,   *we rejoice / known as*
And° ful of vice and wikked thewes,°   *And (we are) / qualities*
1835 Wherfor we preyen yow, a-rowe,°   *each in turn*
That our fame swich be knowe°   *be known (as) such*
In alle thing right° as it is."   *just*
    "I graunte it yow," quod she, "ywis.°   *certainly*
But what art° thou that seyst° this tale   *who are / tells*
1840 That werest on thy hose° a pale°   *leggings, stockings / stripe*
And on thy tipet swich° a belle?"   *hood such*
"Madame," quod he, "sooth° to telle,   *truth*
I am that ilke shrewe, ywis,°   *same scoundrel truly*
That brende° the temple of Isidis   *burned*
1845 In Athenes, lo, that citee."[5]
"And wherfor° didest thou so?" quod she.   *why*
"By my thrift,"° quod he, "madame,   *prosperity (a mild oath)*
I wolde fain han had a° fame,   *gladly have won*

4. I.e., such cause for merriment they found in their situation (literally, "in their hoods").
5. A reference to Herostratus's burning of the temple of Diana (erroneously here Isis) in the fourth-
century B.C.E., described by various medieval authors. The arsonist is here dressed in the garb of
a court fool, a role that may also explain the batting about the head in 1824–25, which might
have been done using a "fool's stick," as Nick Havely explains (*The House of Fame* [1994], p. 182).

As other folk hadde in the toun,
1850 Although they were of greet renoun
For hir vertu and for hir thewes;°   *their virtues and (good) qualities*
Thoughte I, as greet a fame han shrewes,°   *have rogues*
Though it be but for shrewednesse,°   *only for wickedness, depravity*
As good folk han for goodnesse,
1855 And sith° I may nat have that oon,°   *since / one (kind of reputation)*
That other nil I nought forgoon.°   *will I not forgo, sacrifice*
And for to gette of° Fames hyre,°   *from / (a) reward*
The temple sette I al a-fyre.°   *on fire*
Now do our loos° be blowen swythe,°   *fame / trumpeted swiftly*
1860 As wisly be thou° ever blythe."   *(And) may you truly be*
    "Gladly," quod° she; "thou Eolus,   *said*
Herestow nat° what they preyen° us?"   *Do you not hear / ask of*
"Madame, yis, ful wel," quod he,
And I wil trompen it, pardee!"°   *trumpet it indeed*
1865 And took his blake trompe faste,
And gan to puffen and to blaste,
Til it was at the worldes ende.
    With that I gan aboute wende,°   *turn around*
For oon that° stood right at my bak   *one who*
1870 Me thoughte goodly° to me spak°   *graciously, amicably / spoke*
And seyde, "Frend, what is thy name?
Artow come hider° to han fame?"   *Have you come here*
"Nay, forsooth,° frend," quod I.   *Truthfully no*
I cam nought hider,° graunt mercy,°   *here / thank you*
1875 For no swich cause,° by my hede.°   *such reason / i.e., a mild oath*
Sufficeth me, as I were dede,
That no wight have my name in honde.[6]
I wot myself° best how I stonde;   *myself know*
For what I drye° or what I thinke,   *feel, experience*
1880 I wol myselfe al it drinke,°   *i.e., deal with it myself*
Certeyn° for the more part,   *Truly*
As ferforth° as I can myn art."°   *Insofar as / have the craft*
"But what dost thou° here than?" quod he.   *are you doing*
Quod I, "That wol I tellen thee,
1885 The cause why° I stonde here: *reason*
Som newe tydings° for to lere°   *information, news, gossip / learn*
Som newe thing, I noot° what,   *don't know*
Tydinges, other° this or that,   *News of either*
Of love or swiche thinges glade.°   *such happy tidbits*
1890 For certeynly he° that me made   *i.e., the eagle*
To comen hider° seyde me   *here*
I shulde bothe here and see,
In this place, wonder° thinges;   *amazing, wonderful*
But these be no swiche° tydinges   *are no such*
1895 As I mene of."° "No?" quod he,   *was intending*
And I answerde, "No, pardee!°   *by God, indeed*
For wel I wote ever yet,°   *have always known*

6. It's enough for me, when I'm dead, that nobody bandies my name about (literally, has my name in hand).

Sith that° first I had wit,°	*Since / understanding*
That som folk° han desyred fame	*different people*
1900 Dyversly,° and loos° and name;°	*Differently / renown / reputation*
But certeynly I nist° how	*did not know how*
Ne wher that Fame dwelte er° now,	*before*
Ne eek° of hir descripcioun,	*also*
Ne also hir condicioun,°	*personal character*
1905 Ne the ordre of hir dome,°	*pattern of her decision-making*
Unto° the tyme I hider° come."	*Until / here*
"Why than be looth these tydinges	
That thou now hider bringes,	
That thou hast herd?" quod he to me.[7]	
1910 "But now, no fors,° for wel I see	*it doesn't matter*
What thou desyrest for to here.	
Com forth, and stond no longer here,	
And I wol thee, withouten drede,°	*fear not*
In swich another° place lede,°	*another sort of / lead*
1915 Ther° thou shalt here many oon."°	*Where / i.e., desired news*
Tho gan° I forth with him to goon	*Then began*
Out of the castel, sooth to seye.°	*truth to tell*
Tho° saw I stonde in a valeye,	*Then*
Under° the castel faste by,°	*Below / right next to it*
1920 An hous, that Domus Dedaly,	
That Laborintus cleped is,	
Nas made so wonderliche ywis,	
Ne half so queynteliche y-wrought.[8]	
And evermo,° so swift as thought,	*constantly*
1925 This queynt° hous aboute wente°	*cunning, remarkable / twirled around*
That nevermo still it stente.°	*it was never still*
And therout com so greet a° noise,	*such a loud*
That, had it stonde upon Oise,°	*a river in northern France*
Men mighte it han herd esely°	*easily have heard it*
1930 To° Rome, I trowe sikerly.°	*in / truly believe*
And the noise which that I herde	
For al the world right so it ferde°	*proceeded (i.e., sounded)*
As doth the routing° of the stoon	*whizzing, whirring*
That from th'engyn° is leten goon.	*war machine (for hurling stones)*
1935 And al this hous of whiche I rede°	*tell, speak*
Was made of twigges, falwe,° rede,	*dusky yellow*
And grene eek,° and som weren whyte,	*also*

7. "Why, then, is this unwanted, this news that you have heard and that you now bring here to me?" he asked me. (I am following the suggested emendation of "lo" in this line to "looth," suggested by A. S. G. Edwards, "Chaucer's *House of Fame*, lines 1709, 1907," *English Language Notes* 26 [1988]: 2.)

8. A house, such that the House of Daedalus, called the Labyrinth, was not of such wondrous construction nor half so ingeniously designed. (In *Metamorphoses* 8.152–68, Ovid tells the story of King Minos's employment of the architect-engineer Daedalus to build the Labyrinth, where Minos confined his wife's monster-child the Minotaur. Chaucer's description, however, is more detailed than either Ovid's or Virgil's [see *Aeneid* 5.588–91], and also borrows from Ovid's description of the "House of Rumor [Latin *Fama*]" in the *Metamorphoses* 12.39–63, included here in the Contexts section. An intermediate source is the comparison of Daedalus's House to impenetrable philosophical argumentation in Boethius's *Consolation of Philosophy*, Book 3, prose 12, 154–59, which Chaucer translated using language similar to the present description. Elsewhere, Chaucer describes the Labyrinth in the story of Ariadne in the *Legend of Good Women*; see especially 2012–14.)

Swiche° as men to these cages thwyte,° *Such / whittle into bird-cages*
Or maken of these paniers,° *into wicker hampers*
1940 Or elles° hottes or dossers;⁹ *else*
That, for the swough° and for the twigges, *because of the rushing wind*
This hous was also ful of gigges° *squeaking, creaking*
And also ful eek of chirkinges° *grating, creaking*
And of many other werkinges;° *motions*
1945 And eek this hous hath of entrees° *entrances*
As fele as of leves° been on trees *as many as leaves*
In somer whan they grene been;
And on the roof men may yet seen° *also see*
A thousand holes, and wel mo,° *considerably more*
1950 To leten wel the soun out go.
And by day, in every tyde,° *at all times*
Been al the dores open wyde,
And by night echoon unshette;° *each one (still) open*
Ne porter° ther is non to lette° *gatekeeper / prevent*
1955 No maner° tydings in to pace;° *Any kind of / from entering*
Ne never reste is in that place
That it nis° fild ful of tydinges, *When it is not*
Other° loude or of whispringes; *Either*
And over alle the houses angles° *nooks, corners*
1960 Is ful of rouninges° and of jangles° *whispering / gossip*
Of werres,° of pees,° of mariages, *war / peace*
Of reste, of labour, of viages,° *journeys, travels*
Of abode,° of deeth, of lyfe, *staying in one place*
Of love, of hate, acorde,° of stryfe, *friendliness, agreement*
1965 Of loos,° of lore,° and of winninges,° *fame / loss / success*
Of hele,° of sekenesse,° of bildinges,° *health / sickness / construction*
Of faire windes, and eek of tempestes,° *also of storms*
Of qualme of° folk, and eek of bestes,° *pestilence in / animals*
Of dyvers transmutaciouns° *various reversals*
1970 Of estats,° and eek of regiouns,° *rank / (power over) kingdoms*
Of trust, of drede,° of jelousye, *fear*
Of wit,° of winninge, of folye, *understanding, wisdom*
Of plentee, and of greet famyne,
Of chepe,° of derth,° and of ruyne, *abundance / dearth, scarcity*
1975 Of good or mis-governement,
Of fyr, and of dyvers accident.° *variable fortune*
And lo, this hous of whiche I wryte,
Siker be ye,° it nas nat lyte,° *You can be sure / small*
For it was sixty myle of° lengthe; *in*
1980 Al° was the timber of no strengthe, *Although*
Yet it is founded to endure
Whyl that it list to Aventure,° *is pleasing to Chance*
That is the moder° of tydinges, *mother*
As the see° of welles and of springes; *ocean (is)*
1985 And it was shapen lyk a cage.
"Certes,"° quod° I, "in al myn age,° *Certainly / said / life*

9. Two kinds of baskets commonly carried on one's back; citations in the *Middle English Dictionary* suggest that "hottes" were used to transport earth, stone, mortar, or grain.

Ne saw I swich° a hous as this."   *I never saw such*
And as I wondred me, ywis,°   *marveled indeed*
Upon this hous, tho war was I°   *then I became aware*
1990 How that myn egle, faste° by,   *close*
Was perched hye upon° a stoon;   *on the top of*
And I gan streight to him goon°   *went straight over to him*
And seyde thus: "I preye thee
That thou a whyle abyde° me   *wait for*
1995 For Goddes love, and let me seen
What wondres in this place been,°   *there are*
For yet, paraventure,° I may lere°   *perhaps / learn*
Som good theron° or somwhat here°   *from that / hear something*
That leef me were er that° I wente."°   *would please me before / left*
2000   "Peter!°—that is myn entente,"°   *i.e., a mild oath / intention*
Quod he to me; "therfore I dwelle;°   *stay, wait (here for you)*
But certeyn,° oon° thing I thee telle: *certainly / one*
That, but° I bringe thee therinne,°   *unless / inside (the house)*
Ne shalt thou never cunne ginne°   *figure out a way*
2005 To come into it, out of doute,°   *without a doubt*
So faste it whirleth, lo, aboute.°   *around*
But sith that Joves,° of his grace,   *Since Jupiter*
As I have seyd, wol° thee solace   *wishes to*
Fynally with these thinges,
2010 Uncouthe° sightes and tydinges,   *strange, novel*
To passe with thyn hevinesse°—   *counteract your depression*
Swich routhe° hath he of° thy distresse   *Such pity / on*
That thou suffrest debonairly,°   *humbly, graciously*
And wost thyselfen° utterly   *you know yourself to be*
2015 Disesperat° of alle blis,   *deprived*
Sith that Fortune hath made amis
The fruit of al thyn hertes reste
Languisshe and eek in point to breste[1]—
That he,° thurgh his mighty meryte,°   *i.e., Jupiter / divine power*
2020 Wol do thee ese,° al be it lyte,°   *give you comfort / small*
And yaf° in expres° commaundement,   *(he) gave / explicit*
To whiche I am obedient,
To further° thee with al my might   *advance*
And wisse° and teche thee aright°   *guide / properly*
2025 Wher° thou mayst most tydinges here;   *About where*
Shaltow here anoon many oon lere."[2]
With this worde he, right anoon,°   *suddenly*
Hente° me up bitwene his toon,°   *Seized / toes*
And at a windowe in me broughte,
2030 That in this hous was° as me thoughte,°   *(I) was / so it seemed*
And therwithal° me thoughte it stente,°   *with that / stayed still*
And nothing it aboute wente,°   *i.e., it stopped spinning*
And me sette in° the floore adoun.°   *(he) set me on / down*
But which° a congregacioun   *such / gathering, crowd*

1. Since Fortune has wrongly caused your heart's desire to fail and, indeed, to be on the point of destruction.
2. Here you will soon learn many a (tidbit of news).

2035 Of folk as I saw rome aboute,	
Some within° and some withoute,°	*inside / outside*
Nas never° seen, ne shal been eft;°	*Has never been / again*
That certes in the world nis left	
So many formed by Nature	
2040 Ne deed so many a creature;[3]	
That° wel unnethe° in that place	*So that / scarcely*
Hadde I a foote brede° of space;	*foot's breadth*
And every wight° that I saw there	*person*
Rouned everich° in others° ere	*Each whispered / another's*
2045 A newe tyding prively,°	*tidbit of news secretly*
Or elles tolde° al openly	*else spoke*
Right thus° and seyde: "Nost nat thou°	*Just so / Don't you know*
That is betid,° lo, late er now?'°	*What happened / just now*
"No," quod° he, "tell me what";	*said*
2050 And than he tolde him this and that,	
And swoor therto° that it was sooth:°	*to it / true*
"Thus hath he seyd" and "Thus he dooth,"	
"Thus shal it be," "Thus herde I seye,"	
"That shal be found," "That dar I leye"°—	*dare I claim, allege*
2055 That° al the folk that is alyve°	*So that / who are alive*
Ne han the cunning to descryve°	*skill to describe*
The thinges that I herde there,	
What aloude and what in ere.°	*(whispered in my) ear*
But al the wondermost° was this:	*greatest wonder, marvel*
2060 Whan oon° had herd a thing ywis,°	*one / truly*
He com forth right° to another wight°	*went right over / person*
And gan° him tellen anonright°	*began / immediately*
The same that to him was told	
Er it a furlong-way was old,[4]	
2065 But gan somwhat for to eche°	*add something*
To this tyding° in this speche	*news*
More than° it ever was.	*(Making it) greater than*
And nat so sone° departed nas	*no sooner had (the second man)*
Tho fro° him, that he ne mette°	*Then from / before he met*
2070 With the thrid;° and er he lette°	*a third / before he slowed up*
Any stounde,° he tolde him als;°	*For a moment / also*
Were the tyding sooth° or fals,	*Whether the news was true*
Yet wolde he telle it nathelees,°	*in any case*
And evermo° with more encrees°	*always / added*
2075 Than it was erst.° Thus north and southe	*there was at first*
Went every mote fro° mouth to mouthe,	*speck (of news) from*
And that encresing evermo°	*always increasing*
As fyr is wont to quik and go°	*usually ignites and spreads*
From a sparke spronge amis°	*blown astray*
2080 Til al a° citee brent° up is.	*Until an entire / burnt*
And whan that was ful y-spronge,°	*had spread completely*

3. Truly, there do not remain in the world (alive today) as many people created by nature, nor are there as many who have (already) died (as were in that hall). (An echo of Dante, *Inferno* 3.55–57.)

4. Before the amount of time had passed that it takes to walk a furlong (220 yards or about 201 meters).

And woxen° more on every tonge°		*had grown / tongue*
Than ever it was, it wente anoon°		*rapidly*
Up to a windowe out to goon;		
2085	Or, but it mighte° out ther pace,°	*if it could not / pass, escape*
	It gan out crepe at som crevace,°	*through some crack*
	And fleigh° forth faste for the nones.°	*flew / at that time (a filler)*
	And somtyme saw I tho at ones°	*at the same time*
	A lesing° and a sad sooth sawe°	*falsehood / the sober truth*
2090	That gonne of aventure drawe°	*arrived by chance*
	Out at a windowe for to pace,°	*pass, escape*
	And, whan they metten in that place,	
	They were a-chekked° bothe two,	*blocked*
	And neither of hem mote out go°	*them could get out*
2095	For° other, so they gonne croude°	*Because of the / crowded, pushed*
	Til eche of hem° gan cryen loude,°	*Until each of them / loudly*
	"Lat me go first!"—"Nay, but let me!	
	And here I wol ensuren° thee,	*promise, assure*
	With the nones° that thou wolt do so,	*On the condition*
2100	That I shal never fro° thee go,	*away from*
	But be° thyn owne sworen brother!	*(I will) be*
	We wil medle us ech° with other,	*each of us join, unite*
	That no man, be he never so wrothe,°	*however fierce*
	Shal han that oon of two,° but bothe	*(just) one of (us) two*
2105	At ones,° al besyde his leve,°	*once / whatever he wishes*
	Come we a-morwe° or on eve,°	*in the morning / evening*
	Be we cryed° or stille y-rouned."°	*shouted / quietly whispered*
	Thus saw I fals and sooth compouned°	*mixed, compounded*
	Togeder flee for o° tydinge.	*fly as one*
2110	Thus out at holes gonne wringe°	*squeezed*
	Every tyding° streight to Fame,	*piece of news*
	And she gan yeve eche° his name	*gave to each*
	After hir disposicioun,°	*According to their characters*
	And yaf° hem eek duracioun,°	*gave / also lifespans*
2115	Some to wexe and wane sone,°	*quickly grow and dwindle*
	As dooth the faire, whyte mone,°	*moon*
	And let hem gon.° Ther might I seen	*them pass away*
	Winged wondres faste fleen,°	*flying*
	Twenty thousand in a route,°	*in a group, a swarm*
2120	As Eolus hem blew aboute.°	*blew them around*
	And Lord, this hous in° alle tymes	*at*
	Was ful of shipmen° and pilgrymes	*sailors*
	With scrippes bretful of lesinges°	*satchels brimful of lies*
	Entremedled° with tydinges,	*Interspersed*
2125	And eek° alone by hemselve;°	*also / themselves*
	O, many a thousand tymes twelve	
	Saw I eek of these pardoneres,[5]	
	Currours,° and eek messageres,°	*Couriers / messengers*

---

5. The association of pilgrims and tale-telling is strong, forming the background to the collection of tales in the *Canterbury Tales*, which also specifically includes a storytelling shipman and pardoner—itself a quasi-clerical profession easily corrupted into mendacity by the practice of selling Christian pardons for cash.

	With boistes° crammed ful of lyes	*boxes, cases*
2130	As ever vessel was with lyes.°	*sediment, the lees (of wine)*
	And as I alderfastest° wente	*fastest of all*
	Aboute° and dide al myn entente°	*Around / gave my attention*
	Me for to pleyen° and for to lere,°	*amuse myself / learn*
	And eek a tyding° for to here	*also some news*
2135	That I had herd of° som contree	*from*
	That shal nat now be told for° me—	*revealed by*
	For it no nede is, redely;°	*it's truly not necessary*
	Folk° can singe it bet° than I,	*(Other) people / better*
	For al mot out,° other late or rathe,°	*must come out / sooner*
2140	Al the sheves in the lathe°—	*sheaves (of grain) in the barn*
	I herde a grete noise withalle°	*at that time*
	In a corner of the halle,	
	Ther° men of love tydings tolde,°	*Where / talked about love*
	And I gan thiderward beholde,°	*looked over there*
2145	For I saw renninge every wight°	*every person running*
	As faste as that they hadden might;°	*were able*
	And everich° cryed, "What thing is that?"	*each one (of them)*
	And som seyde, "I noot never what,"°	*have no idea*
	And whan they were al on an hepe,°	*(piled) in a heap*
2150	Tho behinde° gonne up lepe°	*Those in the back / leapt*
	And clamben up on othere° faste	*climbed over the others*
	And up the nose° and eyen caste	*their noses*
	And troden faste on othere° heles,	*they stepped on each others'*
	And stampen as men doon after eles.[6]	
2155	At the laste I saw a man,	
	Which that I nevene nat ne can,°	*Whose name I cannot give*
	But he semed for to be	
	A man of greet auctoritee° . . . [7]	*authority*

[UNFINISHED]

6. Eels could be captured for food by stamping behind them, driving them into traps; see Skeat, *Complete Works*, vol. 3, pp. 286–87, and the *Riverside Chaucer*, Explanatory Note, p. 990.
7. Whether or not Chaucer finished or intended to finish the *House of Fame* remains a source of intense critical controversy, which hinges to some extent on the identity (or obscurity) of the mysterious "man of great authority" named here but not identified. For more discussion of the poem's inconclusiveness, see my introduction. The poem's first editor, William Caxton (1483), apparently frustrated by the lack of an ending, appended his own twelve-line conclusion as follows:

And with the noyse of them wo°	*that distress*
I sodeynly awoke anon tho°	*then all at once*
And remembryd what I had seen	
And how hye and ferre° I had been	*high and far*
In my ghoost° and had grete wonder	*spirit*
Of that° the god of thonder°	*what / i.e., Jupiter*
Had lete me knowen and began to wryte	
Lyke as ye have herd me endyte;°	*compose*
Wherfor° to study and rede° alway	*Therefore / read*
I purpose° to doo day by day.	*intend*
Thus in dremyng and in game	
Endeth thys lytyl book of Fame.	

The Parliament of Fowls

The *Parliament of Fowls* is Chaucer's most polished dream vision. Half the length of the *Book of the Duchess* and one third as long as the *House of Fame*, this dazzling little poem, like a multifaceted gem, deftly brings together disparate literary and philosophical traditions without ever losing its artistic poise or integrity. Unlike the *House of Fame*, which expands toward a conclusion it can never quite achieve, the *Parliament* ends in formal harmony with chosen birds singing a roundel in honor of spring and Saint Valentine, whose celebration-day the poem is sometimes credited with inventing (see line 309).[1] Unlike Chaucer's other early vision poems, which were set in unadorned iambic tetrameter couplets, the *Parliament* uses the more complex and demanding form of rhyme royal (seven-line stanzas of iambic pentameter rhyming ababbcc). The poem contains some of Chaucer's most beautiful and memorable verse, and is especially notable for its skill at blending aphoristic generalization with narrative and allegorical set pieces. At the same time, Chaucer's distinctive ability to individualize voices in dialogue is also in evidence. These many stylistic virtues lead most critics to date the poem after *Duchess* and *Fame*, though dating the *Parliament* remains somewhat speculative.

While the *Parliament* cannot be as securely tied to a specific occasion as the *Book of the Duchess* (ca. 1368–72), several literary historians have linked details of the poem's situation to negotiations for the marriage of the young English king Richard II and Anne of Bohemia, which began in 1380 and culminated in the couple's marriage in 1382. According to the most persuasive discussions of the matter, these parallels suggest a likely date of about 1380 for the *Parliament of Fowls*, and identify Richard with the royal tercel eagle (line 393); Friedrich of Meissen, whose protracted engagement to Anne was broken by her betrothal to Richard in 1381, with the long-suffering second tercel; and the third tercel eagle with the future Charles VI of France, a latecomer to the courtship competition.[2] An interest in the dynamics of parliament also might place the poem in the early to mid 1380s, a time of social unrest during which the relations between the English parliament and the crown were becoming increasingly strained. All that is known for certain is that the poem was written before the Prologue to the *Legend of Good Women*, usually not dated before 1386, where it is referred to by name (F-version 419). As noted in my discussion of the *House of Fame*, most scholars argue, chiefly on the basis of stylistic evidence, that the *House* preceded the *Parliament*. But no hard and fast evidence exists for this order. One might even imagine the poet moving back and forth between these two very different pieces, trying out different solutions for similar kinds of artistic and philosophical problems, such as the relationship of books to experience, the proper focus of poetry, and the nature of true authority.

For a poem of such dexterity and sophistication, the *Parliament* remains

---

1. Most fully and forcefully argued by Henry Ansgar Kelly, *Chaucer and the Cult of Saint Valentine* (Leiden: E. J. Brill, 1986).
2. See especially Larry D. Benson, "The Occasion of *The Parliament of Fowls*," in *The Wisdom of Poetry: Essays in Early English Literature in Honor of Morton W. Bloomfield* ed. Larry D. Benson and Siegfried Wenzel (Kalamazoo, MI: Medieval Institute, 1982), 123–44.

surprisingly elusive. It is hard even to pin down its main subject, as one can see from a brief summary of the plot. The very first stanza—which looks at first like a discussion of poetic art—shifts abruptly to encompass the workings of Love, which themselves stymie the poet, who, he admits, lacks direct experience of his subject. He turns then to books, specifically the last book of Cicero's *De re publica*, where he discovers the story of Scipio's Dream, a narrative about the cosmic rewards of social justice, or as it is called here "commune profit" (47, 75), which formed the basis of a famous philosophical commentary on dreams by the late Roman Macrobius. After reading about Scipio the Younger's vision of the heavens as his grandfather Scipio Africanus reveals them to him, Chaucer falls asleep to experience his own dream. The structure of the poem—reading followed by dreaming—is one Chaucer had experimented with before in the *Book of the Duchess*, and here again there seems to be a connection between the book and the dream, both of which concern the ordering of society for the benefit of all. And like Scipio, Chaucer is guided by Africanus, though not to the macrocosmic vision of the universe that had been his visionary predecessor's, for the affairs of state are replaced here by affairs of the heart.

In Chaucer's dream, Africanus shoves his reluctant charge through the gates of a lush garden presided over by the pagan goddess Nature. Within Nature's garden he finds the libidinally overheated temple of Venus, where the goddess of Love herself reclines in a state of inviting undress. The appearance of Venus re-introduces the theme of Love, which is taken up again in the final movement of the poem, when an assembly of birds comes to celebrate Valentine's Day by choosing their mates. The most important of these is a noble female eagle who must select her consort from three eagle suitors. Their courtship of the lady eagle takes up so much time that the other birds become impatient, bringing about a "parliament" that allows the different classes of birds to express opposing opinions about which of the three eligible birds deserves the eagle-bride. No closer to a determination after hearing the birds' increasingly contentious arguments, Nature gives the choice to the female eagle. She in turn asks for a year's respite before having to decide, and the poem concludes, as mentioned previously, with a celebratory song.

Before it ends in the female eagle's delay—signaling a suspension of temporality—the poem's structure is one that, by stages, attends increasingly to the demands of time. First, we have Scipio Africanus's references to his grandson's "immortality" (73) and to the universal "Great Year" (which returns the heavens to their starting point over many thousands of years; lines 67–70). Second, the domain of ideal Nature is initially presented as the land of eternal May, where nobody ages or becomes sick (see 130, 207); seasonal references, though, raise the question of temporality, and indeed the sun does set on Venus's Temple (266). Finally, the rowdy and impatient parliament of birds, eager for consummation of their avian desires, vigorously bring the demands of time and mortal life back into the picture. Analyzed stylistically, the poem similarly falls out into three distinct sections: the report of Scipio's dream, sober in tone and centered on science and universal public values (lines 15–91); the description of the Garden of Nature and the Temple of Venus, leisurely, courtly and highly literary in tone and focus (120–371); and the competition for the female eagle's hand, lively, raucous, and comical (372–665). Robert W. Frank characterizes the three parts as, in order, "expository," "descriptive," and "dramatic."[3]

Is the *Parliament*, then, about philosophy, love, or politics? All three topics take center stage at one point or another, and one might add to them the

---

3. Robert W. Frank, Jr., "Structure and Meaning in the *Parlement of Foules*," *PMLA* 71 (1956): 530.

subject of art itself, never far from Chaucer's mind in his dream visions. This eclectic brew of topics is at least partly an effect of the variety of sources upon which Chaucer is drawing here, and drawing on much more unobtrusively than, say, in the *House of Fame*, where the poem's lineage is indeed its very subject and reason for being. Chaucer does mention Cicero (31), Macrobius (111), and Alain de Lille (316) as sources respectively for his dream, its interpretation, and the goddess Nature. But many more of his debts go unacknowledged, and are thus woven into the fabric of the poem as if seamlessly. For example, the Italian writers Dante and Boccaccio provide important precedents, the first for the inscription over the gate to Nature's garden and the second for the description of Venus and her temple, but neither is ever mentioned by name, nor is the classical philosopher Boethius, whose meditation on the evanescence of worldly contentment provides the source for lines 90–91: "For bothe I hadde thing which that I nolde, / And eek I ne hadde that thing that I wolde."[4] Does the pedigree of these lines insure that Chaucer's real interest is in the higher moral and philosophical values that would have earned Boethius's approval, or might Chaucer simply be showing here that he has an ear for a felicitous phrase wherever he might find it? The *Parliament*'s diversity of interests and tones makes it difficult to tell.

In its literary genre as well, the *Parliament* is a composite, working simultaneously within the conventions of the dream vision, where a determinate conclusion of sorts would have been expected, and the more open form of debate poetry.[5] As in the famous late twelfth- or thirteenth-century debate-poem *The Owl and the Nightingale*, birds often were featured as protagonists in such literary disputations. And the question of which eagle-husband the lady-bird should select, while perhaps not as infinitely debatable as some questions of love, is structurally parallel to the traditional question or "demande" around which such poems conventionally revolved. Indeed, the poem reaches back to earlier poems like the *Owl*, while simultaneously engaging with contemporary literary tradition, and creating imitators in the future. For example, the *Parliament* bears a striking resemblance to other contemporary French love poems, especially to another Valentine's Day poem by Chaucer's contemporary Oton de Graunson, the *Saint Valentine Dream*. Like another late fourteenth-century avian debate-poem, the *Book of Cupid*, by John Clanvowe, Graunson's poem may have been an imitation rather than a source of the *Parliament*, though the relationship between the two poems has never been firmly established.[6] Chaucer, at any rate, has a dialogic relationship with contemporary literary culture, and his many literary alliances and allusions complicate our sense of what he was up to in this poem.

The critics, in response, while agreeing that the *Parliament* presents a puzzle, have reached little consensus about its solution or even about whether it finally brings concord to the different elements it includes. Thus, essays about the *Parliament*, for much of its critical history, have had titles like "The Harmony of Chaucer's *Parliament*," "The Harmony of Chaucer's *Parliament*: A Dissonant Voice," "Antithesis as the Principle of Design in the *Parlement of Foules*," "The Question of Unity and the *Parlement of Foules*,"[7] and many others along

---

4. Adapted from Boethius's *Consolation of Philosophy*, Book 3, prose 3, 33–36.
5. See Thomas L. Reed, Jr., *Middle English Debate Poetry: The Aesthetics of Irresolution* (Columbia: U of Missouri P, 1990), esp. 294–362.
6. The French title of Graunson's poem, *Le Songe Saint Valentin*, is more commonly used; the poem is translated into modern English by Barry Windeatt in *Chaucer's Dream Poetry: Sources and Analogues* (Woodbridge, Suffolk: D. S. Brewer, 1982), 120–24. The *Book of Cupid* is anthologized in *Chaucerian Dream Visions and Complaints*, ed. Dana M. Symons (Kalamazoo, MI: Medieval Institute, 2004), 19–41.
7. For specific bibliographic references, see McCall, Leicester, Kelley, and Jordan in the *Parliament of Fowls* section of the Selected Bibliography at the end of this Norton Critical Edition.

similar lines, each reader weighing in on the question of the poem's coherence and each offering a theory about what, if anything, unifies the various themes and concerns. Often the key to interpretation is located in a specific character or figure, frequently Nature, since she seems to mediate between the moral aspiration of the poem's opening and the libidinal disorganization of Venus and the parliament itself. Another possibility is to find the poem's unity in a repeating theme, for example, philosophical theories of will or desire or, alternatively, models of the good society.

Recent readers, however, have come increasingly to embrace and appreciate the ambiguity in the poem, looking past it to the psychological and anthropological issues that may be concealed by its attempts to yoke political, philosophical, and literary culture to the mating habits of birds under the control of the female goddess Nature. In such readings, the Dreamer's hesitation, often perceived as parallel to that of the reluctant female eagle, takes on a new importance, as he moves through the different spaces of the poem, defined in psychological and gendered terms.[8] Compared to the *Book of the Duchess* and the *House of Fame*, the *Parliament* allows more scope to commonly marginalized voices—to the female Nature who takes over from the masculine Africanus to replace the male political realm with a garden of romantic love; to the nonhuman bird-world, which is both like and unlike the human world; and even to the lowest classes among the birds, who get a chance to critique the overly idealized constructions of aristocratic courtly behavior held by their social betters. Indeed, in its textual "unconscious," the poem may even be seen as entertaining the possibility of same-sex desire.[9] Perhaps most remarkably, Chaucer here permits the female eagle to control the time and manner of her union with her male counterpart, a perquisite even the noble Emelye will not achieve in similar circumstances in the Knight's Tale in the *Canterbury Tales*.

At the same time, the *Parliament* stops short of being truly radical. The female eagle's ultimate submission to the demands of Nature is delayed but not denied, and the poem's sexual and social hierarchies are never finally in doubt. The most that can be said is that it creates the space to explore multiple points of view. In this way, it serves as a transition poem to Chaucer's later works, where the voice of the woman will be heard more audibly in the *Legend of Good Women* and the competition of social classes will form an important structural principle in the *Canterbury Tales*. As ever, though, Chaucer gestures toward a more inclusive poetic without fully declaring his allegiances. Paradoxically both restless and self-contained, the *Parliament of Fowls* ends as it began, with the search for certainty in the authority of texts, rather than in the experience of life or of dreams: "and thus to rede I nil nat spare" (699).

The text here is based chiefly on the version found in the Fairfax manuscript (Fairfax 16, Bodleian Library).

---

8. See Russell A. Peck, "Love, Politics, and Plot in the *Parlement of Foules*," *The Chaucer Review* 24 (1990): 290–305; Kathryn L. Lynch, "Diana's 'Bowe Ybroke': Impotence, Desire, and Virginity in Chaucer's *Parliament of Fowls*," in *Menacing Virgins: Representing Virginity in the Middle Ages and Renaissance*, ed. Kathleen Coyne Kelly and Marina Leslie (Newark: University of Delaware Press, 1999), 83–96.
9. See Britton J. Harwood, "Same-Sex Desire in the Unconscious of Chaucer's *Parliament of Fowls*," *Exemplaria* 13 (2001): 99–135.

The Parliament of Fowls

The lyf so short, the craft so long to lerne,[1]
Th'assay° so hard, so sharp the conquering,°   *attempt / difficult the struggle*
The dredful° joy alwey that slit so yerne,°   *fearful / slides away so swiftly*
Al this mene I by° Love, that my feling°   *about / feeling, senses*
Astonyeth° with his wonderful werkyng   *Stuns, dazes*
So sore ywis° that whan I on him thinke   *violently indeed*
Nat wot I wel wher° that I flete° or sinke.   *I do not know whether / float*

For al be that° I knowe nat Love in dede°   *although / firsthand*
Ne wot° how that he quyteth° folk hir hyre,°   *know / pays / for their services*
Yet happeth me° ful ofte in bookes rede°   *I happen / to read*
Of his miracles and his cruel yre.°   *ire, anger*
Ther rede I wel he wol be lord and syre;
I dar nat seyn,° his strokes° been so sore,   *dare not say (more) / blows*
But "God save swich° a lord!" I can° no more.   *such / can say (alt. know)*

Of usage,° what for luste° what for lore,°   *By habit / pleasure / learning*
On bookes rede I ofte, as I yow tolde.
But wherfor° that I speke al this? Nat yore°   *why is it / Not long (ago)*
Agon, it happed me° for to beholde   *I happened*
Upon a book, was wryte with° lettres olde;   *written in*
And therupon, a certeyn thing to lerne,[2]
The longe day ful faste° I redde and yerne.°   *intently / eagerly*

For out of olde feldes,° as men seith,   *fields*
Cometh al this newe corn fro° yeer to yere;   *grain from*
And out of olde bookes, in good feith,
Cometh al this newe science° that men lere.°   *knowledge / learn*
But now to purpos° as of this matere°—   *(the) point / discussion*
To rede forth° it gan° me so delyte,   *read on / did*
That al the day me thoughte but a lyte.°   *seemed only a little (time)*

This book of which I make mencioun,
Entitled was al ther, as I shal telle,
"Tullius of the dreme of Scipioun";[3]
Chapitres seven° it hadde of° hevene and helle   *Seven chapters / about*
And erthe and soules that therinne dwelle,

---

1. The life so short, the art so long to learn. (This often-quoted truism [in Latin, *ars longa, vita brevis*] has been traced back to Hippocrates [see the *Riverside Chaucer*, Explanatory Note, p. 994, and Brewer, *Parlement of Foulys*, p. 101].)
2. And upon (this book), in order to learn a certain thing. (The meaning of the word certain is itself somewhat *un*certain: It could mean a specific or particular "certain" thing, or it could mean a thing that is "certain," i.e., firm or reliable.)
3. Was given the title there, as I shall tell (you), (of) "Tullius of the Dream of Scipio." (Tullius is Marcus Tullius Cicero, and the work to which Chaucer refers is the sixth and final book of Cicero's *De re publica*. Relevant sections of this text as well as an excerpt from the famous fifth-century commentary on it by Macrobius appear in the Contexts section of this Norton Critical Edition. In the *De re publica*, Cicero describes a dream experienced by Scipio [Publius Cornelius Scipio the Younger] during a visit he paid to Massinissa, King of Numidia in 149 B.C.E. [see line 37]. Scipio's illustrious grandfather [Publius Cornelius Scipio the Elder] appears to him in the traditional role of guide figure in this vision [see "Affrican" in 41, 44, etc.], a role he then duplicates in Chaucer's own dream; see below, 96, 107, etc.)

Of which, as shortly° as I can it trete,°   *briefly / write about it*
35   Of his sentence° I wol yow seyn the grete.°   *its meaning / most important part*

First telleth it whan Scipion was come
In Affrik,° how he mette Massinisse,°   *Into Africa / Massinissa (see note 3 above)*
That him for joye in armes hath y-nome.°   *embraced*
Than telleth it hir° speche and al the blisse   *their*
40   That was betwix hem° til the day gan misse,°   *them / came to an end*
And how his auncestre, Affrican°   *Scipio Africanus the Elder (see note 3 above)*
   so dere.
Gan° in his slepe that night to him appere.   *Did*

Than telleth it that, from a sterry° place,   *starry*
How Affrican hath him Cartage shewed,°   *shown him Carthage*
45   And warned him bifore° of al his grace,°   *in advance / fortune*
And seyde° him, what man, lered other lewed,°   *told / learned or ignorant*
That loveth comun profit, wel y-thewed,[4]
He shal unto a blisful place wende,°   *go*
Ther as° joye is that last° withouten ende.   *Where / lasts, endures*

50   Than asked he, if folk that here be dede°   *dead*
Have lyf and dwelling in another place;
And Affrican seyde, "Ye, withoute drede,"°   *without a doubt*
And that our present worldes lyves space°   *lifetime*
Nis but a maner° deth, what wey° we trace,   *Is only a kind of / path*
55   And rightful° folk shal go after they dye   *just, virtuous*
To heven; and shewed° him the galaxye.°   *showed / the Milky Way*

Than shewed he him the litel erthe that here is
At regard of° the hevenes quantite;°   *In comparison to / size*
And after° shewed he him the nyne speres,°   *then / nine spheres*
60   And after that the melodye herde he
That cometh of thilke speres thryes three,°   *three times three*
That welle° is of musyk and melodye   *wellspring, source*
In this world here, and cause of armonye.°[5]   *harmony*

Than bad he° him, sin° erthe was so lyte,°   *he asked / since / small*
65   And ful of torment and of harde grace,°   *fortune*
That he ne shulde him in the world delyte.°   *take delight in*
Than tolde he him, in certeyn yeres space,
That every sterre shulde come into his place
Ther it was first, and al shulde out of minde
70   That in this worlde is doon of al mankinde.[6]

---

4. Who loves the common good (and is) well mannered, virtuous. ("Common profit," first introduced here, is an important unifying concept in the poem, as many critics have noted, helping to harmonize the seemingly disparate themes of love and politics.)
5. In the medieval Ptolemaic universe, the earth sits motionless at the center encircled by nine revolving spheres, containing first the seven planets, then in the eighth sphere the fixed stars, and finally the outermost Primum Mobile. The heavenly motion of these revolving spheres creates the musical harmony described here by Chaucer, also known as the Music of the Spheres.
6. Then he told him that, after a period of some years, every star would return to the place where it was first, and all (human things) would pass out of mind, (everything) that is done by mankind in this world. (A reference to the concept of the "Great Year," actually a period of many thousands

Than preyed him Scipioun° to telle him al   *Scipio entreated him*
The wey to come into that hevene blisse;
And he seyde, "Know thyself first immortal,°   *(to be) immortal*
And look ay besily thou werke and wisse
To comun profit,[7] and thou shalt nat misse
To comen swiftly to that place dere,
That ful of blisse is and of soules clere.°   *shining, unsullied*

But brekers of the lawe, sooth to seyne,°   *truth to tell*
And lecherous folk, after that they be dede,°   *after they are dead*
Shal whirle aboute th'erthe° alwey in peyne°   *the earth / pain*
Til many a world be° passed, out of drede,°   *an age has / fear not*
And than, foryeven° alle hir wikked dede,°   *forgiven / their wicked deeds*
Than shal they come unto that blisful place,
To which to comen God thee sende his grace!"[8]

The day gan failen,° and the derke night   *began to fail*
That reveth bestes from hir besynesse[9]
Berafte° me my book for lak of light,   *Took from*
And to my bedde I gan me for to dresse°   *prepare*
Fulfild° of thought and besy hevinesse,° *Full / anxious depression*
For bothe I hadde thing which that I nolde,
And eek I ne hadde that thing that I wolde.[1]

But fynally my spirit at the laste
Forwery of° my labour al the day   *Tired out from*
Took rest, that made me to slepe faste,°   *deeply*
And in my slepe I mette° as I lay   *dreamed*
How Affrican,° right in the self aray°   *Scipio the Elder / same dress*
That° Scipioun him saw bifore that tyde,°   *In which / time*
Was comen° and stood right at my bedes syde.°   *Had come / bedside*

The wery° hunter slepinge in his bed   *weary*
To wode ageyn° his minde goth anoon;° *Back to the woods / straightway*
The juge dremeth how his plees been sped;° *lawsuits are gettting along*
The carter dremeth how his cartes goon;
The riche, of gold; the knight fight with his foon;°   *fights with his foes*
The seke met° he drinketh of the tonne;° *sick person dreams / barrel, cask*
The lover met he hath his lady wonne.

---

of years, after which all the stars and planets will have rotated back to their original positions; described by both Cicero and Macrobius; e.g., see p. 263 in the Contexts section of this Norton Critical Edition.)

7. Look that you busily (industriously) work and instruct others (in how to work) toward the common good.
8. And then, forgiven all their wicked deeds, shall they come into that blissful place, to arrive at which may God send you his grace.
9. That relieves beasts of their labor.
1. For I both had (that) thing that I did not want, and also I did not have that thing that I wanted. (Chaucer here echoes a passage from Boethius's *Consolation of Philosophy*, Book 3, prose 3, 33–36, suggesting the poet's broad philosophical concern with higher values rather than a specific material desire.)

Can I nat seyn if that the cause were
For I had red of Affrican biforne,
That made me to mete that he stood there;[2]
But thus seyde he, "Thou hast thee so wel borne°   *conducted yourself so well*
110 In looking of° myn olde book to-torne,°   *looking over, studying / frayed*
Of which Macrobie roughte nat a lyte,[3]
That somdel° of thy labour wolde I quyte."°—   *for some part of / repay (you)*

Citherea,° thou blisful lady swete   *Cytherea (i.e., Venus)*
That with thy fyrbrond dauntest whom thee lest
115 And madest me this sweven for to mete,[4]
Be thou my help° in this, for thou mayst best;°   *helper / are most able*
As wisly as I sawe thee north-north-west,[5]
Whan I began my sweven° for to wryte,   *dream*
So yif me might° to ryme and endyte!°   *give me the power / compose*

120 This forseyd° Affrican me hente anoon,°   *aforementioned / grabbed at once*
And forth with him unto a gate broughte
Right of a parke walled with° grene stoon;   *encircled by a wall of*
And over the gate, with lettres large y-wroughte,
Ther were vers y-wryten as me thoughte
125 On either halfe of ful greet difference,
Of which I shal yow sey the pleyn sentence.[6]

"Thurgh me men goon into that blisful place
Of hertes hele° and deedly° woundes cure;   *heart's healing / deadly, mortal*
Thurgh me men goon unto the welle of Grace
130 Ther° grene and lusty° May shal ever endure;°   *Where / delightful, fertile / last*
This is the wey to al good aventure;°   *fortune*
Be glad, thou reder,° and thy sorwe of-caste,°   *reader / cast off sorrow*
Al open am I; passe in, and sped thee faste!"[7]

"Thurgh me men goon," than spak that other syde,
135 "Unto the mortal strokes° of the spere,°   *blows / spear*
Of which Disdayn and Daunger is the gyde,[8]
Ther tre° shal never fruyt ne leves bere.°   *Where the tree / bear*

2. I cannot say if reading about Affrican (Scipio Africanus the Elder) was what made me dream he stood there.
3. About which Macrobius cared not a little. (Using the literary trope of litotes, Chaucer here suggests by negation that Macrobius respected Cicero's Dream of Scipio a great deal. As indicated above [see the footnote to line 31], Macrobius wrote a long and famous commentary on the Dream.)
4. Who with your fiery torch tame whomever you please and (who) made me dream this dream.
5. As surely as I saw you in the north-northwest. (This is a much debated line: Because Venus may not actually have been visible from London in the north-northwest sky, it may be an ironic way of saying "never." But there are other interpretations as well, some perhaps helpful for dating the poem; see *Riverside*, Explanatory Note, pp. 996–97.)
6. And above the gate, fashioned in large letters, it seemed to me there were verses inscribed, (those on) each side very different from the other, the full meaning of which (verses) I shall reveal to you. (The verses written over the gate to Nature's walled garden recall the warning inscription that adorns the gate to Hell in Dante's *Inferno* 3.1–9, which is included here in the Contexts section.)
7. The phrase "sped thee faste" is an injunction to fare well, to prosper greatly; but the phrase is also often used to denote literal speed, for example as a send-off on a journey: "Speed on fast!" Chaucer thus foreshadows the opposition of haste and delay that will become important later in the poem (e.g., 385).
8. Wielded (guided) by Disdain and Haughtiness. ("Daunger" is the traditional courtly standoffish-ness a lady shows her lover.)

This streem yow ledeth to the sorweful were°   *grim trap*
Ther as° the fissh in prison is al drye;   *Where*
Th'eschewing° is only the remedye!"   *Avoidance*

These vers of° gold and blak y-wryten were,   *verses in*
Of whiche I gan° astoned° to beholde,   *began / in confusion*
For with that oon° encresed ay° my fere,°   *one / increased always / fear*
And with that other gan° myn herte bolde.°   *did / grow bold*
That oon me hette,° that other did me colde;°   *heated / chill*
No wit had I, for° errour, for to chese°   *for fear of / choose*
To entre or flee, or me to save or lese.°   *lose (myself)*

Right° as betwixen adamauntes° two   *Just / lodestones, magnets*
Of even might,° a pece of iren set   *equal strength*
That hath no might to meve° to ne fro—   *move*
For what that oon may hale, that other let—
Ferde I, that niste whether me was bet
To entre or leve,⁹ til Affrican my gyde°   *my guide*
Me hente° and shoof° in at the gates wyde,   *grabbed / shoved*

And seyde,° "It stondeth wryten in thy face,   *he said*
Thyn errour, though thou telle it nat to me;
But dred thee nat° to come into this place,   *fear not*
For this wryting is nothing ment by° thee,   *not meant for*
Ne by noon but° he Loves servant be;   *Nor for anyone unless*
For thou of love hast lost thy tast,° I gesse,   *taste*
As sek° man hath of swete and bitternesse.   *a sick*

But natheles,° although that thou be dulle,°   *Nonetheless / you are stupid*
Yet that° thou canst nat do, yet mayst thou see;   *that which*
For many a man that may nat stonde a pulle°   *resist a (wrestling) hold*
Yet lyketh him° at wrastling for to be   *it pleases him*
And demeth yet wher he do bet or he;
And if thou haddest cunning for t'endyte,
I shal thee shewen mater of to wryte."¹

With that, my hond in his he took anoon,°   *at once*
Of ° which I comfort caughte° and went in faste;   *From / took*
But, Lord, so I was° glad and wel begoon!°   *I was so / happy*
For overal wher° that I myn eyen° caste   *everywhere / eyes*
Were trees clad with leves that ay° shal laste,   *always*
Eche in his kinde,° of colour fressh and grene   *its natural form*
As emeraude, that joye was° to sene.°   *it was / behold*

---

9. For what that one (magnet) may attract, that other (magnet) prevents (from moving)—So fared
I, who did not know whether it was better for me to enter or leave. (Chaucer draws here upon a
philosophical conundrum known as the problem of Buridan's ass, which features a donkey posi-
tioned between two identical bales of hay, unable to move because unable to choose between
them. A similar moment occurs in Dante's *Paradiso* 4.1–9, when Dante holds back from ques-
tioning Beatrice, poised between two questions or doubts he needs to resolve.)
1. And have an opinion about whether he (one wrestler) does better or he (another). And if you have
(sufficient) skill to compose (about it), I shall show (give) you subject matter for your writing.

The bilder ook, and eek the hardy asshe;
The piler elm, the cofre unto careyne;
The boxtree piper; holm to whippes lasshe
The sailing fir; the cipres, deth to pleyne;
180 The sheter ew; the asp for shaftes pleyne;
The olyve of pees, and eek the drunken vyne;
The victor palm; the laurer to devyne.[2]

A gardyn[3] saw I ful of blosmy bowes°   *blossoming boughs*
Upon° a river, in a grene mede°   *Above / meadow*
185 Ther as° swetnesse evermore ynow° is,   *Where / always bountiful*
With floures° whyte, blewe,° yelow, and rede,°   *flowers / blue / red*
And colde welle stremes, nothing dede,°   *dead*
That swimmen ful of° smale fisshes light°   *abound in / swift*
With finnes rede and scales silver bright.

190 On every bough the briddes° herde I singe   *birds*
With vois of aungel° in hir armonye;°   *angelic voices / their harmony*
Som besyed hem° hir briddes° forth to bringe; *busied themselves / their fledglings*
The litel conyes° to hir pley gonne hye.°   *bunnies / hurried about*
And further al aboute° I gan espye°   *around / noticed*
195 The dredful roo,° the buk,° the hert° and hinde, *fearful roe-deer / buck / hart*
Squirels and bestes smale° of gentil kinde.°   *small beasts / noble nature*

Of instruments of strenges° in acord°   *stringed instruments / harmony*
Herde I so pleye° a ravisshing swetnesse   *playing with such*
That God, that maker is of al and lord,
200 Ne herde never better, as I gesse;
Therwith a wind, unnethe it might be lesse,
Made in the leves grene a noise softe
Acordaunt to the foules songe on lofte.[4]

The air of that place so atempre° was   *temperate, mild*
205 That never was grevaunce° of hot ne colde;   *there was no discomfort*
Ther wex eek° every holsum spice and gras,°   *grew also / herb*
Ne no man may ther wexe sek° ne ´olde;   *become sick*
Yet was ther joye more a thousand folde°   *a thousand times more*
Than man can telle; ne never wolde it° night   *would it become*
210 But ay clere° day to any mannes sight.   *always bright day*

---

2. The oak tree for building, and also the sturdy ash tree; the elm for making posts (and) coffins for dead bodies; the box-tree for making musical pipes; the holly for making lashes for whips; the fir for sailing (for use in making masts); the cypress for lamenting death; the yew for shooting (making bows); the aspen for making smooth arrows; the olive of peace; and also the drunken (grape) vine; the palm for victory; the laurel for divination.

3. The description of the garden from this point forward to line 294 follows closely the description in Giovanni Boccaccio's *Il Teseide* (*Book of Theseus*) of the ascent of the aspiring lover's prayer to the presence of Venus; for the purpose of close comparison, the full passage is included in the Contexts section of this Norton Critical Edition. The description of the garden more generally draws on courtly love literature and the tradition of the *locus amoenus* (pleasant place) found in such texts as the *Romance of the Rose*; relevant passages from this poem are also provided in the Contexts section, though they do not form as close a parallel as those from *Il Teseide*.

4. In addition, a wind (that might) scarcely be lighter made a soft noise in the leaves in harmony with the birds' song on high.

Under a tree besyde a welle, I say°　　　　　　　　　*saw*
Cupyde our lord his arwes° forge and fyle;　　　　*arrows*
And at his feet his bowe al redy lay,
And Wille his doughter tempred al this whyle
The hedes° in the welle,° and with harde fyle　　　*arrowheads / well(-water)*
She couched hem after as they shulde serve,[5]
Some for to slee° and some to wounde and kerve.°　*slay / cut*

Tho was I war of Plesaunce anonright,[6]
And of Aray,° and Lust,° and Curtesye,　　　　　*Adornment / Desire*
And of the Craft that can° and hath the might　　*has the knowledge*
To doon by force a wight to do folye°—　　　　*person to act foolishly*
Disfigured was she, I nil nat lye°—　　　　　　*will not lie*
And by himself under an oke° I gesse　　　　　　*oak*
Saw I Delyt, that stood with Gentilesse.°　　　*Nobility*

I saw Beautee, withouten any atyr,°　　　　　　*clothes*
And Youthe, ful of game° and jolyte,°　　*merrymaking / jollity, gaiety*
Foolhardinesse,° Flatery, and Desyr,　　　　　*Rashness*
Messagerye,° and Mede,° and other°　*Message-sending / Bribery / another*
　　three—
Hir° names shal nought here be told for° me—　*Their / by*
And upon pilers grete of jasper longe
I saw a temple of bras y-founded stronge.[7]

Aboute° the temple daunceden alway　　　　　　*Around*
Women ynow,° of which some ther were　　*enough, in abundance*
Faire of hemself,° and some of hem were gay;°　*in themselves / richly attired*
In kirtels,° al dischevele,° wente they there—　*in gowns / with hair unbound*
That was hir office° alwey yeer by yere—　　*duty, occupation*
And on the temple, of doves whyte and faire
Saw I sittinge many an hundred paire.

Bifore the temple dore ful soberly
Dame Pees° sat with a curteyn in hir hond:　　*Peace*
And hir besyde wonder discretly,°　　　*discreetly, prudently*
Dame Pacience sitting ther I fond°　　　*found*
With face pale upon an hille of sond;°　　*sand*
And aldernext,° within and eek withoute,°　*very next / also outside*
Behest and Art and of hir folke a route.[8]

Within the temple, of syghes° hote as fyr　*sighs, moans*
I herde a swough° that gan aboute renne;°　*rushing sound / ran around*

5. With a hard file, she notched them so that they would serve (to take the bowstring). (I am following the suggested translation here of John Scattergood, in "Making Arrows, *The Parliament of Fowls*, 211–217," *Notes and Queries* 49 [2002]: 444–47.)
6. Then I suddenly became aware of Pleasure. (The allegorical figures in this passage are somewhat loosely based on those described by Boccaccio in *Il Teseide*.)
7. And upon pillars of jasper, broad and tall, I saw a temple of brass on a strong foundation. (Chaucer's placement of this last couplet in the same stanza with the somewhat questionable allegorical figures associated with Love, such as Rashness and Bribery, casts an ironical light on the soundness of the temple's foundation.)
8. Promise and Cunning and a great number in their company.

Which syghes were engendred with desyr,°   *by desire*
That maden every auter° for to brenne°   *altar / burn*
250   Of newe flaume;° and wel espyed° I thenne   *with new flames / observed*
That al the cause of sorwes° that they drye°   *sorrows / suffer*
Com of° the bitter goddesse Jelousye.   *Came from*

The god Priapus[9] saw I, as I wente
Within the temple, in sovereyn° place stonde   *the preeminent*
255   In swich aray° as whan the asse him shente°   *condition / shamed him*
With crye by° night, and with his ceptre° in honde;   *at / scepter, staff*
Ful besily men gonne assaye and fonde°   *attempted and tried*
Upon his hede to sette, of sondry hewe,°   *various colors*
Garlondes ful of fresshe floures newe.°   *freshly picked flowers*

260   And in a privy° corner in disporte°   *secluded / merrymaking*
Fond I Venus and hir porter Richesse,°   *doorkeeper Wealth*
That was ful noble and hauteyn of hir porte;°   *haughty in her demeanor*
Derk was that place, but afterward lightnesse
I saw a lyte,° unnethe° it might be lesse,   *little / scarcely*
265   And on a bed of golde she lay to° reste   *at*
Til that the hote sonne gan to weste.°   *set in the west*

Hir gilte heres with a golden threde
Y-bounden were, untressed as she lay,[1]
And naked fro° the breste unto the hede°   *from / head*
270   Men might hir see; and soothly° for to say   *truly*
The remenant° was wel kevered to my pay°   *rest / covered to my taste*
Right with a subtil kerchef of Valence;
Ther was no thikker cloth of no defence.[2]

The place yaf° a thousand savours swote,°   *gave off / sweet odors*
275   And Bachus, god of wyn,° sat hir besyde,   *wine*
And Ceres next, that doth of hunger bote;°   *satisfies hunger*
And, as I seyde, amiddes lay Cipryde,[3]
To whom on knees two yonge folk ther cryde
To been hir help;° but thus I let hir lye   *for her to help them*
280   And, ferther in the temple, I gan espye°   *noticed*

That, in despyte of Diane the chaste,[4]
Ful many a bowe y-broke heng° on the wal   *broken bow hung*

---

9. Priapus was the god of gardens and fertility; Chaucer's description of this scene goes back through Boccaccio's *Teseide* to Ovid's *Fasti* 1.415–40 and 6.319–48 where, in separate episodes, the Roman poet portrays Priapus's sexual frustration, first in his approach to the nymph Lotis and then the virgin Vesta; in both cases, the braying of Silenus's ass prevents him from reaching his goal.
1. Her golden tresses were lightly tied by a gold thread, as she lay with her hair hanging loose. (E. T. Donaldson suggests that "untressed" simply means "unbraided"; see *Chaucer's Poetry*, p. 659.)
2. With a lightly woven veil from the town of Valence (in France); there was no thicker cloth to protect (her).
3. Bacchus was the god of wine; Ceres the goddess of food crops (from whom the word "cereal"); the "Cyprian" ("Cipride") is Venus, whose birthplace was traditionally the island of Cyprus. Chaucer draws upon a conventional association between the satisfactions of food, drink, and sex.
4. In contempt of Diana the chaste. (Diana's roles as goddess of chastity and hunting are being evoked here.)

Of maydens swiche as gonne hir tymes waste°   *wasted their time*
In hir° servyse; and peynted overal°   *her (Diana's) / all around*
Ful many a story, of° which I touche shal   *on*
A fewe, as of Calixte and Athalante
And many a mayde of which the name I wante;[5]

Semyramus, Candace, and Hercules,
Biblis, Dido, Thisbe, and Piramus,
Tristram, Isoude, Paris, and Achilles,
Eleyne, Cleopatre, and Troilus,
Silla, and eek the moder of Romulus:
Alle these were peynted on that other syde,[6]
And al hir° love, and in what plyte they dyde.°   *their / circumstances they died*

Whan I was° come ageyn into the place   *had*
That I of spak,° that was so swote° and grene,   *spoke of / sweet*
Forth welk I tho° myselven to solace.°   *I walked then / comfort myself*
Tho was I war° wher that ther sat a quene   *Then I noticed*
That, as of light° the somer sonne shene°   *in brightness / shining*
Passeth the sterre,° right so over mesure°   *Surpasses a star / beyond measure*
She fairer was than any creature.

And in a launde° upon an hille of floures   *grassy clearing*
Was set this noble goddesse Nature;
Of braunches were hir halles and hir boures°   *public and private rooms*
Y-wrought after hir craft and hir mesure;
Ne ther nas foul that cometh of engendrure[7]
That they ne were prest° in hir presence   *ready*
To take hir doom° and yeve hir audience.°   *judgment / listen to her*

For this was on Seynt Valentynes day,[8]
Whan every foul cometh ther to chese his make,°   *choose his mate*

5. A few (stories), like those of Callisto and Atalanta, and many (other) maidens whose names I am lacking. (Callisto and Atalanta were both maidens who, at first determined to preserve their virginities, were later unfaithful in their service to chastity. Callisto became the lover of Zeus, for which crime she was transformed into a bear and then the constellation *Ursa Major*; Atalanta was transformed ultimately into a lion for losing her virginity to Hippomenes, after wagering herself in a footrace, which she lost.)
6. Painted opposite to those whose service to Diana was interrupted are those who served Venus, with similarly catastropic consequences: the incestuous queen Semiramis of Babylon; Candace, probably an Indian queen who seduced Alexander the Great; Hercules, who was betrayed by his wife Deianira when she sent him a poisoned garment; Biblis, who went mad from love for her brother; Dido, betrayed by Aeneas (for her story see Chaucer's *House of Fame* 143–382, and *Legend of Good Women* 924–1367); Pyramus and Thisbe, each of whom committed suicide because Pyramus mistakenly believed that Thisbe was dead (see the *Legend of Good Women* 706–922); Tristan and Isolde, whose disastrous love was prompted by a famous potion; Paris, whose passion for Helen (Eleyne) led to the Trojan War; Achilles, whose love for Polyxena resulted in his own death; Cleopatra, who killed herself after the death of her beloved Antony (see the *Legend of Good Women* 580–705); Troilus, whose doomed love for Criseyde Chaucer immortalizes in *Troilus and Criseyde*; Scylla, who betrayed her father out of unrequited love for Minos; and Rhea Silvia, who was imprisoned for giving birth to the twins Romulus and Remus after being raped by Mars.
7. Built by her art and design; nor was there any naturally created bird.
8. Chaucer is often credited with having created Valentine's Day (the *Oxford English Dictionary* lists this line in the *Parliament* as the first reference). Various saints have been proposed as the honoree of this holiday, and it has been associated both with February 14, when it is currently celebrated, or alternatively with early May due to another reference to Valentine's Day in the Prologue to Chaucer's *Legend of Good Women* (145–46). The tradition that birds choose their mates on Valentine's Day is shared with the *Legend of Good Women* and a poem by Chaucer's contemporary

Of every kinde° that men thinke may,°   *species / can imagine*
And that° so huge a noyse gan° they make,   *And then / did*
That erthe and see, and tree, and every lake
So ful was, that unnethe° was ther space   *scarcely*
315 For me to stonde, so ful was al the place.

And right as Aleyn in the Pleynt of Kinde
Devyseth Nature of aray and face,[9]
In swich° aray men might hir there finde.   *such*
This noble emperesse, ful of grace,
320 Bad° every foul to take his owne place   *Commanded*
As they were wont° alwey fro° yeer to yere,   *accustomed / from*
Seynt Valentynes day, to stonden there.

That is to sey, the foules of ravyne°   *birds of prey*
Were hyest° set, and than the foules smale   *highest*
325 That eten,° as hem Nature wolde enclyne,°   *eat / prompts (them)*
As worm or thing of whiche I telle no tale,°   *better left unsaid*
And water foul sat loweste in the dale;°   *valley*
But foul that liveth by seed° sat on the grene°   *live on seeds / grass*
And that so fele° that wonder was to sene.°   *many / behold*

330 There mighte men the royal egle finde
That with his sharpe look perceth the sonne,[1]
And other egles of a lower kinde°   *breed*
Of which that clerkes° wel devysen conne.°   *scholars / know how to describe*
Ther was the tyraunt with his fethres donne°   *dun, brownish-gray*
335 And greye—I mene the goshauk,° that doth pyne°   *goshawk / harm*
To briddes° for his outrageous ravyne.°   *(other) birds / greediness*

The gentil faucoun° that with his feet distreyneth°   *noble falcon / holds fast*
The kinges hond; the hardy sperhauk eke,°   *sparrowhawk also*
The quailes foo;° the merlion° that peyneth°   *foe / merlin / strains*
340 Himself ful ofte the larke for to seke;°   *to search out*
Ther was the douve° with hir eyen meke;°   *dove / meek eyes*
The jelous swan, ageyns° his deth that singeth;   *at the approach of*
The oule eek,° that of dethe the bode° bringeth;   *owl also / portent*

The crane, the geaunt° with his trompes soune;°   *giant / trumpet-like sound*
345 The theef, the chough; and eek the jangling pye;°   *chattering magpie*
The scorning° jay; the eles foo,° heroune;°   *mocking / eels' foe / the heron*

Oton de Graunson, the *Saint Valentine Dream* (*Le Songe Saint Valentin*). Henry Ansgar Kelly, who has written extensively on the topic in *Chaucer and the Cult of Saint Valentine* (Leiden: Brill, 1986) links the honored saint with the first bishop of Genoa, whose feast day was celebrated in early May.

9. And just as Alanus describes Nature in (her) dress and face. ("Alanus," or Alain de Lille, was a French Neoplatonist of the twelfth century who wrote *The Complaint of Nature* to lament the crimes that humans commit against natural law. An excerpt from his much fuller description of the goddess Nature, which also touches on the moral and human characteristics of many birds, is included in the Contexts section of this Norton Critical Edition. The goddess Nature was widely known from a variety of medieval literary and philosophical texts, including also Jean de Meun's section of the *Romance of the Rose*.)

1. There one could find the royal eagle, who with his keen glance pierces the sun. (It was reported in medieval bestiaries and encyclopedias that the eagle could look directly at the sun.)

The false lapwing ful of trecherye;
The stare,° that the counseyl° can bewrye;° *starling / secret / conceal (alt. divulge)*
The tame ruddok;° and the coward kyte;° *robin / cowardly kite*
The cok,° that orlogge° is of thorpes lyte;° *rooster / clock / for little villages*

The sparow, Venus sone;° the nightingale, *son*
That clepeth° forth the fresshe leves newe; *calls*
The swalow, mordrer of the foules smale° *i.e., bees*
That maken hony of floures fresshe of hewe;° *fresh, colorful flowers*
The wedded turtel° with hir herte trewe; *turtledove*
The pecok with his aungels° fethres bright; *angelic*
The fesaunt, scorner of the cok by night;²

The waker goos; the cukkow ever unkinde;³
The popinjay° ful of delicasye;° *parrot / wantonness*
The drake, stroyer° of his owne kinde;° *destroyer / species*
The stork, the wreker of avouterye;° *avenger of adultery*
The hote cormeraunt of glotonye;⁴
The raven wys;° the crow with vois of care;° *wise / voice of misfortune*
The throstel° olde; the frosty feldefare.° *thrush / wintry field thrush*

What shulde I seyn?° Of foules every kinde *can I say*
That in this world han° fethres and stature,° *have / physical shape*
Men mighten in that place assembled finde
Bifore the noble goddesse Nature,
And eche of hem did his besy cure° *took special care*
Benignely° to chese° or for to take, *With a good will / choose*
By hir acord,° his formel° or his make.° *agreement / female bird / mate*

But to the point: Nature held on hir honde
A formel egle,° of shap the gentileste° *female eagle / noblest*
That ever she among hir werkes fonde,° *found*
The moste benigne° and the goodlieste;° *gracious / most courteous and kind*
In hir was every vertu at his reste° *in its (proper) place*
So ferforth° that Nature hirself had blisse *absolutely*
To look on hir and ofte hir bek° to kisse. *beak*

Nature, the vicaire° of th'almighty Lorde, *deputy, earthly representative*
That hot, cold, hevy, light, moist, and dreye
Hath knit by even noumbre of acorde,⁵
In esy° vois began to speke and seye, *gentle*
"Foules, tak heed of my sentence,° I preye, *judgment*

2. The pheasant, scorner of the rooster at night. (A somewhat obscure reference deriving perhaps from a belief that the pheasant would mate with a hen, or alternately associating the pheasant with the wild cock who, according to authority, "derided" or scorned the domestic cock; see Skeat, *Complete Works*, vol. 1, p. 519.)
3. The vigilant goose, the always unnatural cuckoo. (The explanation for the cuckoo's crime against nature comes later, in 613–14.)
4. The hotly (or passionately) gluttonous cormorant. (The drake's propensity to destroy young ducks, the stork's revenge on adulterers, and the cormorant's gluttony are all proverbial, as are many of the other birds' moral associations.)
5. Who has joined together hot, cold, heavy, light, moist, and dry in harmonious proportion. (See Boethius, the *Consolation of Philosophy* 3, poem 9, relevant excerpts included here in the Contexts section.)

And for your ese,° in furthering of your nede,   *ease*
385 As faste as I may speke, I wol yow spede.°   *help*

Ye knowe wel how, Seynt Valentynes day,
By my statut and thurgh my governaunce,°   *authority*
Ye come for to chese°—and flee° your way—   *choose / fly*
Your makes,° as I prik° yow with plesaunce.°   *mates / excite / desire*
390 But natheles my rightful ordenaunce
May I nat lete, for al this world to winne,
That he that most is worthy shal beginne.[6]

The tercel egle,° as that ye knowen wel,   *male eagle*
The foul royal above° yow in degree,°   *superior to / rank*
395 The wyse and worthy, secree,° trewe as stel,°   *discreet / steel*
The which I formed have, as ye may see,
In every part as it best lyketh me,°   *most pleases me*
It nedeth nought his shap° yow to devyse,°   *physical form / describe*
He shal first chese° and speken in his gyse.°   *choose / his own way*

400 And after him, by° ordre shul ye chese   *in*
After your kinde, everich as yow lyketh,
And, as your hap is, shul ye winne or lese;[7]
But which of yow that love most entryketh,°   *has most entangled*
God sende him hir that sorest° for him syketh."°   *most intensely / sighs*
405 And therwithal° the tercel gan° she calle,   *with that / male eagle did*
And seyde, "My sone, the choys is to thee falle.°   *falls to you*

But natheles, in this condicioun
Mot be the choys of everich that is here,[8]
That she agree to his eleccioun,°   *choice*
410 Whoso he be° that shulde be hir fere;°   *Whoever he is / mate*
This is our usage° alwey, fro yeer to yere;°   *custom*
And whoso may at this tyme have his grace,°   *find favor*
In blissful° tyme he com° into this place."   *At a joyful, blessed / came*

With hed enclyned° and with ful humble chere°   *bowed / expression*
415 This royal tercel spak° and taried nought:°   *eagle spoke / did not delay*
"Unto my sovereyn° lady, and nought my fere,°   *supreme / equal*
I chese,° and chese with wille and herte and thought,   *choose*
The formel° on your hond so wel y-wrought,°   *female / formed*
Whos° I am al° and ever wol hir serve,   *Whose / completely*
420 Do what hir list,° to do me° live or sterve.°   *she pleases / cause me to / die*

Beseching hir of mercy and of grace,
As she that is my lady sovereyne,

6. But nevertheless I may not abandon due process (in this case even) if it were to win the (whole) world, (and that process is) that he that is worthiest shall go first. (From this point on, the poem employs a wide variety of legal and parliamentary terms—like "statute," "plea" [pleading], "dom" [judgment], and other similar vocabulary.)
7. According to your species, each one of you as you please, and according to your luck, you will win or lose.
8. But nonetheless these conditions govern the choices of all who are here.

Or let me dye present° in this place.   *die now*
For certes° long may I nat live in peyne,°   *certainly / in (such) pain*
For in myn herte is corven every veyne;[9]
Having reward° only to° my trouthe,°   *regard / for / fidelity*
My dere herte, have on my wo som routhe.°   *pity*

And if that I be founde to hir untrewe,
Disobeysaunt,° or wilful° negligent,   *Disobedient / willfully*
Avauntour, or in proces love a newe,[1]
I prey to yow this be my jugement,°   *penalty*
That with° these foules I be al torent,°   *by / torn apart*
That ilke° day that ever she me finde   *very*
To hir untrewe or in my gilte unkinde.°   *deliberately inconsiderate*

And sin that noon° loveth hir so wel as I,   *since nobody*
Al be° she never of love me behette,°   *Although / promised*
Than oughte she be myn° thurgh hir mercy,   *to be mine*
For other bond can I noon on hir knette.[2]
For never, for no° wo, ne shal I lette°   *any / cease*
To serven hir, how fer so° that she wende;°   *however far away / travels*
Sey what yow list,° my tale is at an ende."   *wish*

Right° as the fresshe, rede rose newe   *Just*
Ageyn° the somer sonne coloured is,   *In (the light of)*
Right so for shame al wexen gan the hewe°   *i.e., she blushed*
Of this formel whan she herde al this;
She neither answerde wel ne seyde amis,°   *spoke incorrectly*
So sore abasshed° was she, til that Nature   *completely embarrassed*
Seyde, "Doughter, drede yow nought,° I yow assure."   *do not be afraid*

Another tercel egle° spak anoon,°   *male eagle / at once*
Of lower kinde,° and seyde, "That shal nat be. *rank*
I love hir bet° than ye do, by Seynt John,[3]   *better*
Or at the lest° I love hir as wel as ye,   *at least*
And lenger° have served hir in my degree,°   *longer / rank*
And if she shulde have loved for° long lovinge, *in return for*
To me allone had been° the guerdoninge.°   *would have been / reward*

I dar eek sey,° if she me finde fals,   *dare say also*
Unkinde,° jangler,° or rebel in any wyse,   *Cruel / a tale-teller*
Or jelous, do me hongen by the hals!°   *have me hanged by the neck*
And but° I bere me in hir servyse   *unless*
As wel as that my wit can me suffyse°   *I know how*
From point to point° hir honour for to save,   *In every respect*
Tak she° my lyf and al the good° I have."   *Let her take / the worldly goods*

9. I.e., my heart is slashed open and bleeding (by the pain of love).
1. Boastful or, in the course of time, (to) love a new (lady).
2. For I can establish no other claim to her.
3. As Nick Havely points out (*Chaucer's Dream Poetry*, p. 256), this oath fits the context, as St. John was Christ's beloved disciple and his symbol the eagle.

The thridde tercel egle° answerde tho,° *third male eagle / then*
"Now, sirs, ye seen the litel leyser° here; *small (amount of) time*
465 For every foul cryeth out to been ago° *gone*
Forth with his make° or with his lady dere; *mate*
And eek° Nature hirself ne wol nought here,° *also / hear*
For tarying° here, nought° half that I wolde seye; *dawdling / even*
And but° I speke, I mot° for sorwe deye.° *unless / must / die*

470 Of long servyse avaunte I me nothing,° *make no boast*
But as° possible is me° to dye today *it is as / for me*
For° wo, as he that hath been languisshing *from*
These twenty winter,° and wel happen may *i.e., for twenty years*
A man may serven bet° and more to pay° *better / more pleasingly*
475 In half a yere, although it were no more,
Than som man doth that hath served ful yore.° *for a very long time*

I sey nat this by me,° for I ne can *on my own behalf*
Do no servyse that may my lady plese;
But I dar sey I am hir trewest man
480 As to my dom, and fainest wolde hir ese;[4]
At shorte wordes,° til that deth me sese° *Briefly / takes me*
I wol been hires, whether I wake or winke,° *sleep*
And trewe in al° that herte may bethinke."° *every way / imagine*

Of° al my lyf sin° that day I was born, *In / since*
485 So gentil plee° in love or other thing° *noble a complaint / matter*
Ne herde never no man me biforn,° *before, previously*
Who that hadde leyser and cunning
For to reherse hir chere and hir speking;[5]
And from the morwe gan° this speche laste *morning did*
490 Til dounward went the sonne wonder° faste. *very*

The noyse of foules for to been delivered *released*
So loude rong, "Have doon° and let us wende!"° *Finish up / go*
That wel wende° I the wode° had al to-shivered.° *thought / woods / splintered*
"Come of!"° they cryde, "allas, ye wil us shende!° *Hurry up / wreck*
495 Whan shal your cursed pleding° have an ende? *litigation*
How shulde a juge either party leve° *credit*
For ye or nay° withouten any preve?"° *To affirm or deny / proof*

The goos, the doke,° and the cukkow also *duck*
So cryden, 'Kek, kek!' 'Kukkow!' 'Quek, quek!' hye° *loudly*
500 That thurgh myn eres° the noyse wente tho.° *(both) my ears / then*
The goos seyde, "Al this nis nat° worth a flye! *is not*
But I can shape° hereof a remedye, *come up with*
And I wol sey my verdit faire and swythe° *verdict fluently and quickly*
For water foul, whoso be wrooth or blythe."[6]

4. In my opinion, and would take most delight in pleasing her.
5. (As would be obvious if) anyone had the time and skill to represent their manner and their speech.
6. On behalf of water fowl, whomever (the verdict may) anger or gratify.

"And I for worm foul," seyde the fool cukkow,°   *foolish cuckoo*
"For I wol, of myn owne auctorite,°   *on my own authority*
For comune spede take on me the charge now,
For to delivere us is greet charitee."[7]
"Ye may abyde° a whyle yet, pardee!"°   *wait / by God*
Seyde the turtel,° "If it be your wille   *turtledove*
A wight may speke, him were as fair be stille.[8]

I am a seed foul, oon° the unworthieste,   *one of*
That wot° I wel, and litel of kunninge;°   *know / not well educated*
But bet° is that a wightes° tonge reste   *better / creature's*
Than entremeten him of swich doinge°   *meddle in such matters*
Of° which he neither rede° can nor singe.   *About / speak (or advise)*
And whoso doth, ful foule himself acloyeth,
For office uncommitted ofte anoyeth."[9]

Nature, which that alwey had an ere°   *ear*
To murmour of the lewedness behinde,°   *foolishness at the back*
With facound° vois seyde, "Hold your tonges there!   *an eloquent*
And I shal sone, I hope, a counseyl° finde   *plan*
Yow to delivere° and fro° this noyse unbinde;°   *release / from / free you*
I juge,° of every folk° men shal oon° calle   *decree / group / one*
To seyn° the verdit° for yow foules alle."   *announce / verdict*

Assented were to this conclusioun
The briddes° alle; and foules of ravine°   *birds / prey*
Han chosen first by pleyn eleccioun°   *open election*
The tercelet° of the faucon° to diffyne°   *male / falcon / declare*
Al hir sentence, and as him list termyne;[1]
And to Nature him gonne to presente,°   *he presented himself*
And she accepteth him with glad entente.°   *with good will*

The tercelet seyde than in this manere:
"Ful hard were it to preve° it by resoun°   *prove / rational argument*
Who loveth best this gentil formel° here;   *noble female (eagle)*
For everich° hath swich replicacioun°   *each one / such rejoinders*
That noon by skilles° may be brought adoun.°   *nobody by arguments / defeated*
I can nat seen that argumentes availe;°   *avail, succeed*
Than semeth it ther moste be bataile."°   *combat*

"Al redy!' quod° these egles tercels tho.°   *said / male eagles then*
"Nay, sirs!" quod he, "if that I durste it seye,°   *dare to say it*
Ye doon° me wrong, my tale is nat y-do!°   *do / speech is not done*
For sirs, ne taketh nought agref° I preye,   *don't be offended*
It may nought goon as ye wolde° in this weye;   *happen as you wish*

7. For the public welfare (cp. line 47) now take on myself the responsibility (to speak), for rescuing
   us (from this endless argumentation) would be a great act of kindness.
8. (Sometimes) a person might speak who would be better off keeping silent.
9. And whoever does (meddle), does great harm to his own (cause), for service not requested is
   usually an annoyance.
1. The decision of them all, and adjudicate as he wishes.

545 Oures is the vois that han the charge in honde,[2]
    And to the juges dome° ye moten stonde;°   *disposition / must submit*

    And therfor pees!° I seye, as to my wit,°   *peace / in my opinion*
    Me wolde thinke how that the worthieste
    Of knighthode and lengest hath used it,
550 Moste of estat, of blood the gentileste,
    Were sittingest for hir if that hir leste;[3]
    And of these three she wot° hirself, I trowe,°   *knows / believe*
    Which that he be,° for it is light° to knowe."   *Which he is / easy*

    The water foules han hir hedes leyd°   *have laid their heads*
555 Togeder and, of short avysement,°   *(after) brief consultation*
    Whan everich° had his large golee° seyd,   *each one / mouthful*
    They seyden soothly,° al by oon assent,°   *truly / in complete agreement*
    How that the goos, with hir facounde gent,°   *elegant manner of speaking*
    "That° so desyreth to pronounce our nede,°   *Who / deliver our message*
560 Shal telle our tale," and preyde to God hir spede.°   *that she be successful*

    And for these water foules tho° began   *then*
    The goos to speke, and in hir kakelinge
    She seyde, "Pees! Now tak kepe° every man   *take heed*
    And herkeneth which a reson° I shal forth bringe;   *what an argument*
565 My wit is sharp, I love no taryinge;°   *delay*
    I seye, I rede° him, though° he were my brother,   *advise / even if*
    But° she wol love him, lat him love another!' "   *Unless*

    "Lo, here a parfit reson° of a goos!'   *typical assertion*
    Quod the sperhauk,° "Never mot° she thee!°   *sparrowhawk / may / prosper*
570 Lo, swich° it is to have a tonge loos!°   *such / loose tongue*
    Now pardee,° fool, yet were it bet° for thee   *by God / better*
    Have holde thy pees than shewed thy nicete!
    It lyth nat in his wit ne in his wille,
    But sooth is seyd, 'a fool can nought be stille.' "[4]

575 The laughter aroos of gentil foules° alle,   *rose up from the noble birds*
    And right anoon° the seed foul chosen hadde   *immediately*
    The turtel° trewe and gonne hir to hem calle°   *turtledove / called her to them*
    And preyden hir to sey the soothe sadde°   *plain truth*
    Of this matere, and asked what she radde;°   *advised*
580 And she answerde that pleynly hir entente
    She wolde shewe and soothly what she mente.[5]

---

2. Ours is the voice (i.e., of the birds of prey) that has been granted the right (to speak now).
3. It seems to me that the most worthy (representative) of knighthood and (he who) has longest
   practiced (knightly ideals), the highest in rank, the noblest in blood, would be the most suitable
   for her, if she so pleases.
4. To have held your peace than have shown your foolishness! It lies neither in his wit nor in his will
   (i.e, the fool has neither the intelligence nor the desire to remain quiet), but true is the saying "A
   fool cannot be silent."
5. And she answered that she would speak her mind clearly and (say) truly what she meant.

"Nay, God forbede a lover shulde chaunge,"° — *be inconstant*
The turtle seyde, and wex° for shame al rede,° — *grew / red*
"Though that his lady evermore be straunge,° — *aloof, standoffish*
Yet let him serve hir ever til he be dede.° — *until he dies*
For soothe,° I preyse nought the gooses rede,° — *truly / goose's advice*
For though she deyed, I wolde noon other make,[6]
I wol been hires, til that the deth me take."° — *until death takes me*

"Wel bourded!"° quod the doke,° "by my hat! — *Good joke / said the duck*
That men shulde alwey loven° causeles,° — *love forever / unrequited*
Who can a reson° finde or wit° in that? — *argument / the intelligence*
Daunceth he mury that is mirtheles?
Who shulde recche of that is reccheles?"
"Ye quek!" yet quod the doke, "ful wel and faire;
There been mo sterres, God wot, than a paire!"[7]

"Now fy,° cherl!"° quod the gentil tercelet,° — *Shame / peasant / noble eagle*
"Out of the dunghil com that word ful right.° — *comes that statement indeed*
Thou canst nought see which thing is wel beset.° — *well done*
Thou farest by° love as oules doon by° light; — *in respect to / owls to*
The day hem blent,° ful wel they see by night — *blinds them*
Thy kind° is of so lowe a wrechednesse° — *species / vileness*
That what love is, thou canst nat see ne gesse."° — *nor guess*

Tho gan° the cukkow putte him forth in prees° — *Then began / in the crowd*
For foul that eteth worm° and seyde blyve,° — *eat worms / quickly*
"So° I," quod° he, "may have my make° in pees, — *As long as / said / mate*
I recche nat° how longe that ye stryve.° — *do not care / quarrel*
Lat ech of hem be soleyn al hir lyve!° — *single all their lives*
This is my reed,° sin° they may nat acorde;° — *advice / since / agree*
This shorte lesson nedeth nought recorde."° — *does not bear repeating*

"Ye, have the glotoun fild ynough his paunche,[8]
Than are we wel!" seyde the merlioun;° — *the merlin (a small falcon breed)*
"Thou mordrour of the heysogge on the braunche,
That broughte thee forth, thou rewfullest glotoun![9]
Live thou soleyn,° wormes corrupcioun!° — *single / feeder on worms*
For no fors is of lakke of thy nature;[1]
Go, lewed° be thou, whyl° the world may dure!"° — *ignorant / as long as / last*

6. For though she died, I would not wish any other mate. (The turtledove, though female, is imagining herself in the position of the hypothetical male lover.)
7. "Does the person who is miserable dance merrily? (Why should) anyone care about the person who sets no value on himself?" "You quack very well and nicely," said the duck; "there are more than a pair of stars, God knows!" (I.e., there are many stars in the heaven, just as there are many fish in the sea. The passage characterizes the various classes of birds according to the proverbial truths that each espouses, making their discussion a grab bag of commonplaces and colloquialisms.)
8. Yes, as long as the glutton has filled his belly.
9. You murderer of the hedge-sparrow on the branch, who brought you forth, you most contemptible glutton! (Cuckoos were believed to abandon their young to the nests of other birds; the fledgling cuckoos might eject the young they had displaced and even turn against their foster parents; see also above, 358.)
1. (Even) your defects are unimportant.

"Now pees,"° quod° Nature, "I comaunde here!   *peace (silence) / said*
For I have herd al your opinioun,
And in effect yet be we never the nere;°   *no nearer (a resolution)*
620 But fynally this is my conclusioun:
That she hirself shal han hir eleccioun°   *her own choice*
Of whom hir list,° whoso° be wrooth° or blythe,   *she wants / whoever / angry*
Him that she cheest,° he shal hir han as swythe.°   *chooses / as quickly (in return)*

For sith° it may nat here discussed be   *since*
625 Who loveth hir best, as seyde the tercelet,°   *male eagle*
Than wol I doon hir this favour, that she
Shal have right him° on whom hir herte is set,   *the very one*
And he hir that his herte hath on hir knet.²
This juge I, Nature, for I may nat lye;
630 To noon estat° I have noon other eye.   *no condition (other than love)*

But as for counseyl° for to chese a make,°   *advice / mate*
If I were Reson,³ than wolde I
Counseyle yow the royal tercel take,
As seyde the tercelet ful skilfully,°   *very persuasively*
635 As for the gentilest° and most worthy,   *noblest*
Which I have wrought° so wel to° my   *formed / according to*
     plesaunce;°   *pleasure*
That° to yow ought to been a suffisaunce."°   *So that / all you need*

With dredful° vois the formel° hir answerde,   *fearful / female (eagle)*
"My rightful lady, goddesse of Nature,
640 Sooth° is that I am ever under your yerde°   *The truth / authority*
As is everiche° other creature,   *each and every*
And mot° be youres whyle my lyf may dure;°   *must / last*
And therfor graunteth me my firste bone,°   *request*
And myn entente° I wol yow sey° right sone."   *what's in my mind / tell*

645 "I graunte it yow," quod° she, and right anoon°   *said / at once*
This formel egle spak in this degree,°   *manner*
"Almighty quene, unto this yeer be° doon   *until this year is*
I aske respit° for to avysen me,°   *extension (of time) / to consider*
And after that to have my choys al free.
650 This° al and som° that I wolde speke and seye;   *(And) this (is) / sum*
Ye gete no more although ye do me deye.°   *put me to death*

I wol nought serven Venus ne Cupyde
For soothe° as yet, by no manere wey."   *truly*
"Now sin° it may noon other weyes betyde,"°   *since / come to pass*
655 Quod Nature, "here° is no more to sey;   *there*
Than wolde° I that these foules were awey°   *wish / gone*

---

2. And he (will have) her on whom he has fixed his (own) heart.
3. Chaucer here alludes both to the human faculty of reason and to its personifications in allegories like the *Romance of the Rose*.

Ech with his make,° for tarying lenger° here"—	*mate / to avoid longer delay*
And seyde hem° thus, as ye shul after here.	*to them*

"To yow speke I, ye tercelets,"° quod° Nature,	*male eagles / said*
"Beth of good herte and serveth, alle three;°	*all three (of you)*
A yeer is nat so longe to endure,	
And ech of yow peyne him° in his degree°	*take pains / his own way*
For to do wel; for, God wot,° quit° is she	*knows / free*
Fro° yow this yeer; what after so befalle,°	*From / whatever happens later*
This entremes is dressed for yow alle."⁴	

And whan this werk al brought was to an ende,	
To every foule Nature yaf his make°	*gave his mate*
By even acorde,° and on hir° wey they wende.°	*mutual agreement / their / go*
And, Lord, the blisse and joye that they make!	
For ech of hem gan° other in winges take,	*each of them began*
And with hir nekkes° ech gan other winde,°	*their necks / to embrace*
Thanking alwey the noble goddesse of Kinde.°	*Nature*

But first were chosen foules for to singe,	
As yeer by yere was alwey hir usaunce°	*always their custom*
To singe a roundel⁵ at hir departinge°	*their departure*
To do Nature honour and plesaunce.°	*pleasure*
The note,° I trowe,° maked was° in Fraunce;	*melody / believe / composed*
The wordes wer swiche° as ye may here finde	*text was such*
The nexte vers, as I now have in minde.°	*memory*

"Now welcom somer, with thy sonne softe,°	*gentle sun*
That hast this wintres wedres overshake,°	*shaken off this wintry weather*
And driven awey the longe nightes blake!°	*dark nights*

Seynt Valentyn, that art ful hy on lofte;°—	*in heaven above*
Thus singen smale foules for thy sake—	
Now welcom somer, with thy sonne softe,	
That hast this wintres wedres overshake.	

Wel han they cause° for to gladen° ofte,	*have they reason / rejoice*
Sith° ech of hem recovered hath his make;°	*Since / has won his mate*
Ful blisful° may they singen whan they wake;	*joyously*
Now welcom somer, with thy sonne softe,	
That hast this wintres wedres overshake,	
And driven away the longe nightes blake."	

---

4. The intermission is prepared for all of you. (The "entremes" was originally a set of dishes served as part of a courtly entertainment; perhaps Chaucer refers both to the delay that the eagles must endure before the female eagle makes her choice of mate and to a literal "entremes" that will follow the presentation of the poem and allow for a leisurely discussion of its themes.)

5. A "roundel" (or, in French, *rondeau*) is a medieval poetic form that circles back to a refrain and uses only two rhymes. The manuscripts of the *Parliament of Fowls* differ in their inclusion and/or presentation of this "roundel," making the layout and organization of it here and in other editions speculative. This reconstruction is that first offered by Skeat, based on French models of the form (*Complete Works*. vol. 1, p. 359).

And with the shouting, whan hir° song was do,°   *their / finished*
That foules° maden at hir flight away,   *the birds*
695 I wook,° and other bookes took me to°   *awakened / took up*
To rede upon,° and yet° I rede alwey;   *read / still*
I hope ywis° to rede so som day°   *truly / something someday*
That I shal mete som thing for to fare
The bet; and thus to rede I nil nat spare.[6]

6. That will cause me to have a dream that will lead me to better fortune; and thus I will not refrain from reading.

The Legend of Good Women

The *Legend of Good Women* is a hybrid text—a collection of stories introduced by a dream-vision Prologue. While each part of the work can in some ways stand alone, the effect of the poem is far richer when it is seen as a whole. More closely linked in form and content than the individual Canterbury tales, the short "legends" here represent a taxonomy of "good women" whose variety and overlap are the very point of Chaucer's performance. Similarly, the relationship between Prologue and tales is a complex one. Understanding the poem thus requires looking at it from several perspectives at once, in order to see how, on the literal level, it manages the shift from first-person dream narrative to anthology of classical tales; how, more self-consciously, it positions itself in Chaucer's career by developing the identification between the narrator and the poet; and how it links the themes of art, love, and authority to the overarching topic of gender. These different levels of meaning are hard to keep separate, for literal ambiguities in the poem stand for larger themes, which are themselves complicated in ways that cause us to reevaluate the poem's literal meaning.

The Prologue opens with the narrator's brief meditation on the relative merits of book-learning against personal experience. Despite the importance of books, he confesses that he personally prefers to worship nature directly, particularly as embodied in his most beloved flower, the daisy, whom he describes in excessively romantic language; as he claims, "[t]her loved no wight hotter in his lyve" ("No man in all his life ever loved more ardently") (59). His pilgrimage outside to worship the flower takes the place here of the book he sometimes reads in other dream visions before falling asleep, signaling the complex intertwining of experience and authority—or nature and culture—in this poem. Here follows the dream: The narrator returns home, makes up a bed in the garden, and falls asleep, eager for the dawn so that once again he can see the flower open her petals to the sun. She appears to him sooner than he expects, however, in the person of a lady clad just like a daisy—dressed in green with a golden hairnet and a white, petal-shaped crown—walking in a meadow on the arm of the God of Love. She is Alceste, the faithful wife from classical mythology who demonstrated her perfect love by offering to die in the place of her husband. In the narrator's dream, she again shows her kindness and generosity by intervening when the God of Love threatens the narrator; to win back the god's favor, she sets the dreamer the redemptive task of writing about women faithful in love (and the men who betray them). The legends that follow—there are nine of them, the last never completed—attempt to fulfill that assignment.

More so than any other poem that he wrote, Chaucer's *Legend of Good Women* is linked to his entire poetic corpus; it cannot be understood in isolation from his other work, especially the great historical romance *Troilus and Criseyde*, probably completed sometime in the early to mid 1380s. The irate God of Love in the *Legend*-Prologue attacks the poet-narrator for crimes committed in that romance, which in presenting Criseyde's infidelity had made "men to women lasse triste" ("men to put less trust in women") (333). *Troilus*,

117

however, was not Chaucer's only heretical attack against Love, at least according to the angry god. The poet had also translated the thirteenth-century dream vision the *Romance of the Rose*, where the figure of Reason had warned men against enslavement to amorous passion. Nonetheless, as Alceste points out in the poet's defense, he had also written well of love—in hymns, ballads, and other short lyric forms, and in the love visions "the Deeth of Blaunche the Duchesse [the *Book of the Duchess*]," "the Parlement of Foules," and the story of Palamon and Arcite (probably an early version of the Knight's Tale) (418–24). He was moreover the author or translator of such unimpeachably moral texts as Boethius' *Consolation of Philosophy*, a (now lost) treatise on Mary Magdalen, and a life of Saint Cecilia (probably an early version of the Second Nun's Tale) (425–28). If the *Legend* includes allusions to the larger body of Chaucer's poetic work, it was also a poem that he enjoyed making the subject of his allusiveness: In the Introduction to the Man of Law's Tale, he has the *Canterbury Tales* lawyer complain that, in his prolixity, Chaucer had used up all the tales that might have been available to later writers—especially in the "Seintes Legende of Cupide." Complicating this allusion even further, the Man of Law lists there sixteen virtuous ladies of whom Chaucer had supposedly written, seven of whom are not included in the poem as we have it, and omitting three who are (Cleopatra, Dido, and Philomela). Given the tongue-in-cheek tone of this Introduction, Chaucer seems to be using the *Legend* to pose a kind of literary conundrum.

Not only does Chaucer thus self-consciously place the *Legend* in the center of his poetic career; it also turns out to be both formally and substantively a pivotal (or, alternatively, transitional) text. The Prologue, a self-contained dream vision of some mastery, reaches back to his earlier dream visions, from which it takes its naïve and beleaguered narrator, though the narrator of the *Legend*-Prologue exhibits moments of greater self-confidence and artistic awareness. Looking forward, Chaucer here for the first time uses rhyming couplets of iambic pentameter, the verse form that would carry him through most of the *Canterbury Tales*. The legendary, as the collection of stories is called, also points ahead to the frame of the *Canterbury Tales*, though again with a difference, for these legends are composed much more closely according to a formula than the tales of that later work. The *Legend* also develops Chaucer's growing interest in the woman question of his day as a vehicle for exploring ambiguity and narrative subjectivity, which one can see in his briefer rehearsal of stories of betrayed women (most notably Dido) in Book 1 of the *House of Fame*. And through these stories of victimized heroines, Chaucer demonstrates his ability to achieve high pathos in the scope of a short narrative; also inimitably Chaucerian is the knife-edge of irony on which that pathos often rides. For all these reasons—its self-conscious allusions to Chaucer's poetic career, its generic diversity, its rich blend of satire and tragedy, its distanced narrative presentation—the *Legend of Good Women* might be called the most quintessentially Chaucerian of all his poems.

It was a poem that Chaucer probably worked on over a long period of time, as evidenced by the existence of two distinct versions of the Prologue, known as F and G (designated according to the abbreviations of their chief manuscripts). Most scholars today believe that G was the revision, though this opinion is by no means unanimous, and the poem's first modern editors and critics thought that F came after G. The question will probably never be resolved completely, though a rational scheme of dating can be worked up from details in the poem.[1] Because the *Legend* explicitly responds to *Troilus and Criseyde*, it cannot have been written much before 1386; the omission of the reference

1. Sheila Delany provides a useful summary of the history of the problem and a persuasive claim for F as the revision in *The Naked Text: Chaucer's Legend of Good Women* (Berkeley: UC Press, 1994), 34–43.

to the queen at 495–96, suggests to many scholars that the second version of the Prologue was completed sometime after the death of Queen Anne in 1394. The G-version also includes a handful of references to the poet's advancing age (e.g., G 314–16, included here in a footnote), which some critics attribute to the passage of time between the two versions. The F-version, for its part, is fresher and more exuberant in its praise of the daisy, containing some lovely passages that do not appear in the G-Prologue (e.g., 84–96). The G-version, in contrast, presents as Helen Phillips puts it, "a clearer sequence of thought,"[2] and underscores its literary theme with a long passage spoken by the God of Love that details the contents of the poet-narrator's library where he ought to have been able to find subject matter for stories of good women (G 267–316, included here in a footnote).

Whether or not it was the revision, the G-Prologue does not represent an obvious improvement on the F-version. In fact, most readers prefer the lyricism of F, despite the fact that the narrator's guileless investment in loving the daisy is in tension with the poem's real sophistication and with the God of Love's critique of his insubordination. Such ambiguities deepen the poem's meaning, which we will see exploits rather than resolves tension, and are far from a blemish on its achievement. To these reasons for preferring F to G, add the fact that G exists in only a single manuscript while F is the version followed by the eight other manuscripts that include the Prologue in part or whole, plus all early printed editions. Modern editions and translations thus generally follow the F-version, as I have done here, or print both versions alongside each other. While this latter procedure (followed by the *Riverside Chaucer*) offers the reader an easy way to analyze the differences between the two Prologues, it does not provide as coherent a reading experience as focusing on one text and, I think, gives too much priority to a version that lacks full standing in the manuscripts. Rather than setting out both versions in their totality, this Norton Critical Edition indicates the most significant differences between the two versions in footnotes.

The puzzle of the two Prologues is only the first of the many mysteries presented by the *Legend of Good Women*, which is neither the most highly regarded nor the best understood of Chaucer's poems. Early readers often showed sympathy and admiration for Chaucer's project in the *Legend*, even when they thought that Chaucer's feminist partisanship had taken him perhaps too far. Such was the opinion of Gavin Douglas in the Prologue to his early sixteenth-century translation of the *Aeneid*, where he famously called Chaucer "euer, God wait, wemenis frend" ("always, God knows, a friend to women").[3] But later the collection fell out of favor, and for the first part of the twentieth century, it was commonly dismissed as a failed project—one that Chaucer himself gave up in boredom. To be sure, the narrator several times shows mild impatience with the length of the stories he is retelling (e.g., 994–97, 1002–03, 1565, 1679, 1692–93), and as the work draws toward its cut-off point this impatience becomes downright distaste for the unrelenting evil of the villains whose acts he must recount, as in the Legend of Philomela, which he finds loathsome even to read (see 2238–43). More to the point, in the following, penultimate legend—of Phyllis—he represents himself as "agroted" (surfeited, fed up) with writing endlessly about traitors to love (2454; also see 2470–71, 2490–95), and the final legend—of Hypermnestra—actually breaks off with its heroine unjustly imprisoned and her ungrateful husband, whom she has

---

2. Helen Phillips, Introduction to "The *Prologue* to the *Legend of Good Women*," *Chaucer's Dream Poetry*, ed. Helen Phillips and Nick Havely (London: Longman, 1997), 281.
3. See the fifteenth- and early sixteenth-century responses collected in Caroline Spurgeon's *Five Hundred Years of Chaucer Criticism and Allusion, 1357–1900*, vol. 1 (Cambridge: Cambridge UP, 1925); for example, John Lydgate, cited p. 39; Stephen Hawes, cited p. 67; and Gavin Douglas, cited p. 72.

just saved from death, running free. Perhaps Chaucer simply lost his stomach for this endless parade of female misfortune. But this approach, referred to here as the "boredom theory," would be to confuse the fiction of the poem with the reality outside it. Most readers today agree that the "boredom theory" reflects a misunderstanding, informed by an overly literal reading, of the poet's method.[4]

If the stories raise interpretive problems that the narrator is not up to solving, this fact should not startle any experienced reader of Chaucer. Moreover, the narrator's self-conscious abbreviation of his sources constitutes a time-honored rhetorical device, known as *occupatio* (or *occultatio*, in which an author, by stating what he is abbreviating, draws attention to it). Chaucer employs this rhetorical technique in many other works as well—for example, quite extensively in the Knight's Tale and in several other Canterbury tales—which clearly were *not* boring to him. Its use here no more demonstrates that he was truly resistant to the literary project at hand than the fictionalized command that he write it in the Prologue proves that he really composed the poem under duress because the God of Love (or some other personage) was unhappy with him. Yet the *Legend* has frequently elicited just such literal readings, stretching back to John Lydgate's surmise in the fifteenth century that Chaucer crafted the poem at the command of Richard II's queen, Anne; Lydgate was probably extrapolating from Alceste's direction in the Prologue that the narrator should present the finished legends to the queen at the royal residences Eltham or Sheene (497).[5] Modern readers have extended this theory to speculate that, between 1386 and 1394, he wrote one legend a year for Queen Anne, which would explain the nine extant legends and account for their abrupt termination.[6]

It is perhaps not entirely surprising that a poem that so thoroughly collapses the identity of its narrator and its author should excite biographical speculation. But the delicate humor of the Prologue does not depend on such a one-to-one correspondence. Indeed, too close an identification of the flower-besotted narrator of the early Prologue (or the somewhat presuming narrator of the later Prologue and legends) with his biographical self would spoil the joke, just as the recognition of real potentates in the allegorical figures might have exposed the author to the possibly dangerous indignation of his royal patrons. Chaucer's sophisticated narrative method allows us to see an affiliation between the narrator and the author while we are simultaneously aware that the two are not one and the same.

This narrative distance also creates the space for irony, and thus raises the *Legend*'s million-dollar question: How seriously does Chaucer mean us to take the tales of the legendary as examples of the honor and merit of women? On this issue, the critics are divided. On the one hand, some of the women Chaucer describes are fairly unequivocal examples of virtue or at least innocence—for example, Lucrece or Thisbe. When the correspondence is less straightforward, Chaucer takes considerable pains to rehabilitate his heroines and tarnish the men who abuse them—for example, making Dido a more consistently sympathetic victim, while undercutting the imperial mission that gave Aeneas an excuse to leave her. That his women are uniformly meek might not seem a recommendation to a modern reader, but to a medieval audience, the argument goes, the stoic fidelity that these ladies exhibit would have been admirable. The greatest crimes that were committed by the most notorious women-characters

4. The turning point in criticism came in Robert W. Frank, Jr.'s challenge to the "boredom theory" in *Chaucer and the Legend of Good Women* (Cambridge, MA: Harvard UP, 1972).
5. John Lydgate, *Fall of Princes*, ed. Henry Bergen, EETS OS 121 (London: Oxford UP, 1924), 1.Prol.330, p. 10.
6. See Donald R. Howard, *Chaucer: His Life, His Works, His World* (New York: E. P. Dutton, 1987), 395–96.

in the legendary (e.g., Procne and Philomela or Medea) go either unmentioned or unexplored. On the other hand, the very selection of such morally ambiguous exemplars as these last three suggests to a different group of readers that Chaucer's intention was not so forthright.[7] The God of Love's command to begin the legendary with the story of Cleopatra becomes in this context a questionable one, emblematic of the god's comical misunderstanding of the voluptuous Egyptian queen's reputation, which would have been known to at least some of his audience. In short, is the conversion to goodness of such a character as Cleopatra or Medea to be seen as a poetic challenge, one that Chaucer seriously attempted to meet, or is it a literary inside-joke, based on the premise that a "good woman" is a kind of oxymoron?

These alternatives are complicated by the poem's hagiographical framework. According to the *Middle English Dictionary*, the word "legend" means "a written account of the life of a saint," making Chaucer's collection a contribution to the religion of Love that was a popular fiction of courtly literature. The form of real saints' lives clearly contributed to the formula of Chaucer's "legends," which like their prototypes include the heroine's trial and martyrdom. At the same time, Chaucer's chief sources for this poem were secular ones—especially Ovid's *Heroides* (a series of complaints by famous jilted women-lovers), medieval courtly dream visions like the *Romance of the Rose* or Guillaume de Machaut's *Judgment of the King of Navarre*, and the "marguerite" ("daisy") poetry of such French authors as Machaut and Eustache Deschamps. The disjunction between the religious narrative and the secular one inevitably involves some degree of tension. According to different critics, the legends negotiate this intersection of sacred and secular literary types in different ways. For example, Donald Rowe enlists the pagan narratives in the service of a higher Christian truth, while Lisa Kiser argues that Chaucer uses the tension between literary types to explore the nature of poetic art. Both read the legendary, then, to some extent ironically, but for Rowe the poem teaches its readers to exercise their moral freedom, while for Kiser the *Legend* is Chaucer's cry for a poetic that would permit him to convey greater ambiguity and complexity than the one the God of Love has imposed on him.[8] In short, there is no one way to read the legendary, even after the question of irony has been resolved.

It is hard to know even where to seek the center of this complex and asymmetrical poem. Like the labyrinth described in the Legend of Ariadne, it can take a reader in circles. The possibility, raised by Kiser, that Chaucer was concerned less with women *per se* than with poetry or that branch of philosophy known as epistemology receives some support again from the Prologue. The poem begins, as I mentioned earlier, with the question of where true authority can be found—in the words the authors give us or in the things we can see with our own eyes. The narrator's admiration for the daisy, in some ways, seeks to finesse the answer, for, like her *alter ego* Alceste, she "kytheth what she is" (i.e., the truth she displays in appearance reflects her inner truth; 504). The very etymology of her name ("day's eye"; 184) captures the white flower's literal relationship to the sun, to which she opens herself each morning. She thus serves as the ideal mediator between language (or the world of art) and the literal world of experience, just as later Alceste intervenes and mediates on behalf of the dreamer with the God of Love.

But the charge that Alceste then lays upon the narrator is unresponsive to

7. Included in the Contexts section of this Norton Critical Edition are an example of each of these two critical approaches: Richard Firth Green's "Chaucer's Victimized Women" (1988) represents the straightforward or sympathetic approach, and Elaine Tuttle Hansen's "The Feminization of Men in Chaucer's *Legend of Good Women*" (1989) the ironic or cynical view of the poem.
8. See Donald W. Rowe, *Through Nature to Eternity: Chaucer's Legend of Good Women* (Lincoln: U of Nebraska P, 1988), and Lisa J. Kiser, *Telling Classical Tales: Chaucer and the Legend of Good Women* (Ithaca: Cornell UP, 1983).

his true inner poetic intention and so once again opens up the space between experience and authority. In *Troilus and Criseyde* and the *Romance of the Rose*, he insists, "God wot, it was myn entente / To forthren trouthe in love and it cherice" ("God knows, I intended to advance and cherish fidelity in love"; 471– 72). His failure to achieve transparency paradoxically requires him to submit to a form that guarantees that failure in perpetuity: He must vindicate faithful love by telling stories that punish the women who practice it.[9] By thus making a virtue of ambiguity, the last of Chaucer's dream visions dismantles a literary genre that had, for writers like Boethius and Dante, charted a clear path to truth. The tales that follow on the poet's vision, though, do no better. Whatever the "conclusion" he may have intended for Hypermnestra in the final legend, he discovers himself, like her, "fetered" in the prison-house of language (2722– 23). It is this plight that interestingly erases the gender difference between the elusive male poet and the helpless female victim, and that points the way toward a more universal human selfhood. Whether Chaucer intended *that* irony remains an open question.

The text here is based chiefly on the version found in the Fairfax manuscript (Fairfax 16, Bodleian Library).

The Legend of Good Women

Prologue

A thousand tymes have I herd men telle	
That ther is joye in heven, and peyne° in helle,	*pain*
And I acorde° wel that it is so;	*agree*
But natheles,° yet wot° I wel also	*nevertheless / know*
5 That ther nis noon° dwelling in this contree	*is not anyone*
That either hath in heven or helle y-be,°	*been*
Ne may of it noon other weyes witen,°	*know in any other way*
But° as he hath herd seyd, or founde it writen,	*Except*
For by assay° ther may no man it	*direct experience*
preve.°	*prove, demonstrate*
10 But God forbede but men shulde leve	
Wel more thing than men han seen with eye![1]	
Men shal nat wenen° every thing a lye	*believe*
But if himself it seeth or elles dooth;[2]	
For, God wot,° thing is never the lasse sooth,°	*knows / less true*
15 Though every wight° ne may it nat y-see.	*person*
Bernard the monk ne saw nat al, pardee![3]	
Than mote° we to bookes° that we finde,	*must / books*
Thurgh which that olde thinges been in minde.°	*are remembered*
And to the doctryne° of these olde wyse°	*teachings / wise authors*
20 Yeve° credence, in every skilful wyse,°	*give / discerning manner*
That tellen of° these olde approved°	*To those who tell / well tested*
stories,	

9. An extended analysis that makes many of these same points can be found in Florence Percival, *Chaucer's Legendary Good Women* (Cambridge: Cambridge UP, 1998).
1. But God forbid that men believe only that which they can see with their own eyes.
2. Unless he sees or does it himself.
3. Bernard the Monk (likely St. Bernard of Clairvaux) did not see everything, by God!

Of holinesse, of regnes,° of victories,   *kingdoms*
Of love, of hate, of other sondry thinges,
Of whiche I may nat maken rehersinges.°   *repetition*
25 And if that olde bookes were aweye,°   *gone away*
Y-loren were of remembraunce the keye.⁴
Wel ought us than honouren and beleve
These bookes, ther° we han noon other preve.°   *where / proof*
    And as for me, though that I konne but lyte,°   *know little*
30 On bookes for to rede I me delyte,°   *take delight*
And to hem yive I° feyth and ful credence,   *to them I give*
And in myn herte have hem in reverence
So hertely° that ther is game° noon   *wholeheartedly / amusement*
That fro my bookes maketh° me to goon,   *from my books can make*
35 But° it be seldom, on the holyday,°   *Unless / holy day, holiday*
Save,° certeynly, whan that the month of May   *Except*
Is comen, and that I here the foules° singe,   *hear the birds*
And that the floures° ginnen for to springe,° *flowers / begin to spring up*
Farwel my book and my devocioun!
40   Now have I than swich° a condicioun,   *such*
That, of al the floures in the mede,°   *meadow*
Than love I most these floures whyte and rede,
Swiche° as men callen daysies in our toun.   *Such*
To hem° have I so greet affeccioun,   *them*
45 As I seyde erst,° whan comen is the May,   *before*
That in my bed ther daweth me no day°   *no day dawns*
That I nam° up and walking in the mede°   *am not / meadow*
To seen this flour ageyn the sonne sprede,°   *open (its petals) to the sun*
Whan it upriseth erly by the morwe;°   *early in the morning*
50 That blisful sighte softneth al my sorwe,
So glad am I whan that I have° presence   *am in the*
Of it, to doon° it alle reverence,°   *give / due respect*
As she that is of alle floures flour,°   *the flower of all flowers*
Fulfilled of al vertu and honour,
55 And evere ylyke° fair and fressh of hewe,   *the same*
And I love it, and ever ylyke newe,°   *with equally renewed force*
And evere shal til that myn herte dye;
Al swere I nat,° of this I wol nat lye,   *Although I don't swear to it*
Ther loved no wight° hotter in his lyve.   *person, creature*
60   And whan that it is eve,° I renne blyve,°   *evening / run quickly*
As sone° as ever the sonne ginneth weste° *soon / begins to move westward*
To seen this flour, how it wol go to reste
For fere of night, so hateth she derknesse.
Hir chere is pleynly sprad° in the brightnesse *Her face opens up entirely*
65 Of the sonne, for ther it wol unclose.
Allas, that I ne had° Englissh, ryme or prose,   *that I lack the*
Suffisant° this flour to preyse aright!   *Sufficient*
But helpeth, ye that han conning° and might,   *have ability, knowledge*
Ye lovers, that can make of sentement;°   *write about real emotions*

---

4. The key of remembrance would be lost.

70   In this cas oughte ye be diligent
     To forthren me° somwhat in my labour,   *promote, provide for me*
     Whether ye been with the leef or with the flour.[5]
     For wel I wot,° that ye han herbiforn°   *know / before now*
     Of making ropen, and lad awey the corn,[6]
75   And I come after, glening° here and there,   *gleaning, gathering*
     And am ful glad if I may finde an ere°   *ear, kernel (of grain)*
     Of any goodly° word that ye han left.   *pleasing*
     And though it happen me rehercen eft°   *it may happen that I repeat again*
     That° ye han in your fresshe songes sayd,   *What*
80   Forbereth me,° and beth nat evel apayd,°   *Be patient with me / displeased*
     Sin that° ye see I do it in the honour   *Since*
     Of love and eek° in service of the flour   *also*
     Whom that I serve as I have wit or might.
     She is the clerness° and the verray° light   *brightness / true*
85   That in this derke worlde me wynt° and ledeth,   *turns*
     The herte in-with° my sorweful brest yow   *heart within*
       dredeth,°   *fears you*
     And loveth so sore,° that ye been verrayly°   *intensely / are truly*
     The maistresse° of my wit, and nothing I.°   *mistress / not I*
     My word, my werk, is knit so in your bond
90   That, as an harpe obeyeth to the hond
     And maketh it soune after his fingeringe,
     Right so mowe ye out of myn herte bringe
     Swich vois right as yow list, to laughe or pleyne.[7]
     Be ye my gide° and lady sovereyne;   *guide*
95   As to myn erthly god to yow I calle
     Bothe in this werke and in my sorwes° alle.   *sorrows*
       But wherfor that I spak,° to yive°   *for this reason I spoke / give*
       credence
     To olde stories and doon hem° reverence,   *do them*
     And that men mosten more thing beleve
100   Than men may seen at eye or elles preve[8]—
     That shal I seyn whan that I see my tyme;
     I may nat al at ones° speke in ryme.   *at once*
     My besy gost,° that thursteth alwey   *restless spirit*
       newe°   *thirsts always anew*
     To seen this flour so yong, so fressh of hewe,
105   Constreyned me with so gledy° desyre,   *burning a*
     That in myn herte I fele yet the fyre,
     That made me to ryse er it wer° day—   *rise before it was*
     And this was now the firste morwe° of May[9]—   *morning*

5. Regardless of whether you support the flower or the leaf. (Chaucer is alluding here to contemporary courtly debating games that playfully pit defenders of the flower against defenders of the leaf.)
6. Reaped the (best) kernels of poetry-writing, and stored away the grain.
7. My words, my works are so entangled with the bond (that ties me to you) that just as the harp obeys the hand (that plays it) and that controls its pitch by its fingering, so you are able to bring forth from my heart such voice as pleases you, to laugh or to complain.
8. So that men might believe more things than they can see with their eyes or else prove (by experiment).
9. At the corresponding point in an alternative (probably later) version of the Prologue, called the G-text, the poet tells us that it is the last part of May and night is falling; he returns home to his garden, has his bed made up, and falls asleep. The dream in the G-text thus begins before (and

With dredful° hert and glad devocioun, *fearful*
110 For to been at the resureccioun
Of this flour whan that it shuld unclose
Agayn° the sonne, that roos as rede° as rose, *Toward / rose as red*
That in the brest was of the beste° that day *beast*
That Agenores doughter¹ ladde away.
115 And doun on knees anonright° I me sette, *immediately*
And, as I coude, this fresshe flour I grette;° *greeted*
Kneling alwey til it unclosed was,
Upon the smale, softe, swote° gras *sweet*
120 That was with floures swote enbrouded
al,° *all embroidered with sweet flowers*
Of swich° swetnesse and swich odour overal *such*
That for to speke of gomme,° or herbe, or tree, *gum*
Comparisoun may noon y-maked be,
For it surmounteth° pleynly alle odoures, *surpasses*
And of riche beautee alle floures.
125 Forgeten had the erth his pore estat° *its poor condition*
Of winter, that him° naked made and mat,° *i.e., the earth / beaten down*
And with his swerd of cold so sore greved;° *distressed*
Now hath th'atempre sonne al that releved
That naked was, and clad it new again.²
130 The smale foules, of the seson fain,° *glad*
That from the panter° and the net been *bird trap*
scaped,° *have escaped*
Upon the fouler, that hem made awhaped³
In winter and distroyed hadde hir° brood, *their*
In his despyt,° hem thought it did hem° good *scorn / them*
135 To singe of him, and in hir song despise° *insult, revile*
The foule cherl° that, for his covetyse,° *odious ruffian, peasant / greed*
Had hem betrayed with his sophistrye.° *sophistry, deceptiveness*
This was hir song—"the fouler we defye,
And al his craft!" And somme songen clere° *brightly*
140 Layes° of love, and joye it was to here,° *songs / hear*
In worshipinge and preisinge of hir make,° *their mates*
And for the newe blisful somers sake,° *honor of joyful summer*
Upon the braunches ful of blosmes° softe, *blossoms*
In hir delyt,° they turned hem° ful ofte, *delight / turned (to each other)*
145 And songen, "blessed be Seynt Valentyne,
For on his day I chees° yow to be myne,⁴ *choose*
Withouten repenting,° myn herte swete!" *regret*
And therwithal hir bekes gonnen mete,° *touched their beaks together*

---

includes description of) the flowery meadow and the birds' Valentine's Day song, material that occurs outside the dream in the F-text printed here. Some other material (e.g., the reflection on the etymology of the word "daisy") is placed earlier in G, to come before the dream. For the general relationship between the F- and G-texts, see my introduction to the poem.
1. Agenor's daughter, Europa, was seduced by Jove who took the form of a bull. Chaucer here sets the action under the astrological sign of the bull, Taurus.
2. Now the gentle sun has provided relief against all that nakedness and clothed (the earth) anew. (These lines, which metaphorically treat the earth as impoverished and in need of provision, contain a pun on the verb "releved," as the earth's clothing is a literal "re-leaving.")
3. (In disrespect of) the bird hunter who stunned them.
4. For more on the significance of Valentine's Day, see the *Parliament of Fowls* 309 note.

Yelding° honour and humble obeisaunces°   *Bestowing / services due*
150   To love, and diden hir° other observaunces   *their*
That longeth unto° love and to nature;   *belong to, conform to*
Construeth that as yow list,° I do no cure.°   *wish / don't care*
    And tho° that hadde doon unkindenesse°—   *those / unnatural cruelty*
As dooth the tydif,[5] for newfangelnesse—
155   Besoughte mercy of hir° trespassinge,   *for their*
And humblely songen hir repentinge,
And sworen on the blosmes° to be trewe,   *blossoms*
So that hir makes° wolde upon hem   *their mates*
    rewe,°   *take pity on them*
And at the laste maden hir acord.°   *they made up, made peace*
160   Al° founde they Daunger° for a tyme a lord,   *Although / Haughtiness*
Yet Pitee, thurgh his stronge gentil° might,   *noble*
Forgaf and made Mercy passen Right,°   *Mercy subdue Righteousness*
Thurgh innocence and ruled curtesye.°   *courtesy prevailed*
But I ne clepe nat° innocence folye,   *do not call*
165   Ne fals pitee, for vertu is the mene,°   *the mean (between extremes)*
As Etik[6] seith, in swich° maner I mene.   *such*
And thus these foules, voide° of al malice,   *free*
Acordeden° to love and laften vice°   *Agreed / rejected the vice*
Of hate and songen alle of oon acord,°   *in complete agreement*
170   "Welcome, somer, our governour and lord!"
    And Zephirus and Flora gentilly[7]
Yaf° to the floures, softe° and tenderly,   *gave / softly*
Hir swote breth,° and made hem for to   *Their sweet breath*
    sprede,°   *open up*
As god and goddesse of the floury mede;°   *flowery meadow*
175   In which me thoughte I mighte, day by day,
Dwellen alwey, the joly month of May,
Withouten slepe, withouten mete° or drinke.   *food*
Adoun° ful softely I gan to sinke;°   *Down / sank*
And leninge° on myn elbowe and my syde,   *leaning*
180   The longe day I shoop me for t'abyde°   *made a plan to stay*
For nothing elles,° and I shal nat lye,   *nothing else, no other reason*
But for to° look upon the dayesye,   *Than in order to*
That wel by reson° men it calle may   *for good reason*
The "dayesye" or elles the "eye of day,"
185   The emperice° and flour of floures alle.   *empress*
I prey to God that faire mote she falle,°   *she may have good fortune*
And alle that loven floures, for hir sake!
But natheles ne wene nat° that I make°   *do not think / compose poetry*
In preysing of the flour agayn the
    leef,°   *as superior to the leaf (see line 72)*
190   No more than of the corn agayn the sheef,°   *as superior to the sheaf*
For as to me nis lever noon ne lother;°   *neither is better or worse*
I nam withholden yet with never nother.°   *am not a partisan of either*

---

5. Small bird notable for its faithlessness.
6. Possibly Aristotle's *Ethics* or alternatively Horace, the word being taken from the Latin for ethics or the ethical one.
7. The west wind and the goddess of flowers nobly.

Ne I not° who serveth leef ne who the flour;   *Nor do I know*
Wel brouken° they hir° service or labour,   *may they enjoy / their*
195 For this thing is al of another tonne,[8]
Of olde story er swich° thing was begonne.   *before such*
    Whan that the sonne out of the south gan weste,°   *moved westward*
And that this flour gan close and goon to reste°   *closed and went to rest*
For° derknesse of the night, the which she dredde,°   *Because of / feared*
200 Hoom to myn hous ful swiftly I me spedde
To goon to reste, and erly for to ryse,
To seen this flour to sprede,° as I devyse.°   *open / describe, explain*
And in a litel herber° that I have,   *garden*
That benched was on turves fressh y-grave,[9]
205 I bad° men sholde me my couche° make;   *directed / make up my bed*
For deyntee of the newe someres sake,°   *In honor of the new summer*
I bad hem strawen floures° on my bed.   *I instructed them to strew flowers*
Whan I was leyd° and had myn eyen hed,°   *had laid down / closed my eyes*
I fel on slepe within an houre or two;
210 Me mette° how I lay in the medew tho,°   *I dreamed / then*
To seen this flour that I so love and drede.°   *fear*
And from afer com° walking in the mede°   *afar came / meadow*
The god of Love and in his hande° a quene,   *by the hand, on his arm*
And she was clad in real habit grene.°   *clothed in royal green garments*
215 A fret° of gold she hadde next hir   *ornamental hairnet*
    heer,°   *over her hair*
And upon that a whyt coroun she beer°   *she wore a white crown*
With florouns° smale, and I shal nat
    lye,   *flowers, possibly petal-shaped ornaments*
For al the world, right° as a dayesye   *just*
Y-corouned° is with whyte leves lyte,°   *Crowned / little white leaves (petals)*
220 So were the florouns of hir coroun whyte;
For of o perle fyne oriental,°   *one fine oriental pearl*
Hir whyte coroun was y-maked al,°   *fashioned entirely*
For which° the whyte coroun above the grene   *For which reason*
Made hir lyk a daysie for to sene,°   *to appear*
225 Considered eek° hir fret° of gold above.   *As a result also of / hairnet*
    Y-clothed was this mighty god of Love
In silke, enbrouded° ful of grene   *embroidered*
    greves,°   *with green branches*
In-with a fret° of rede rose-leves,   *Intertwined with a design*
The fresshest sin° the world was first bigonne.   *since*
230 His gilte° heer was corouned with a sonne,°   *golden / sun*
In stede of gold, for hevynesse and
    wighte;°   *(to avoid) the heaviness and weight*
Therwith° me thoughte his face shoon so brighte   *For which reason*
That wel unnethes mighte I° him beholde,   *I was almost not able*
And in his hande me thoughte I saw him holde
235 Two firy dartes as the gledes rede,°   *burning arrows red as embers*
And aungelyke° his winges saw I sprede.   *angel-like, angelically*
And al be that° men seyn that blind is he,   *although*

---

8. From an entirely different barrel (i.e., of a much different sort).
9. Fitted out with benches made of freshly cut turf.

Algate° me thoughte that he mighte° see,   *Nevertheless / was able to*
For sternely on me he gan biholde
240 So that his looking doth myn herte colde.°   *made my heart grow cold*
And by the hande he held this noble quene,
Corouned with whyte and clothed al in grene,
So womanly, so benigne,° and so meke,   *gracious, gentle*
That in this world, though that men wolde
    seke,°   *seek (the whole world)*
245 Half hir beautee shulde men nat finde
In creature that formed is by kinde.°   *nature*
And therfor may I seyn, as thinketh me,°   *it seems to me*
This song in preysing of this lady fre.°   *noble, generous*

Balade[1]

Hyd,° Absolon, thy gilte tresses clere;°   *Hide / golden bright locks of hair*
250 Ester, ley thou thy meknesse al adoun;°   *surrender your meekness*
Hyd, Jonathas, al thy frendly manere;
Penolopee and Marcia Catoun,
Make of your wyfhod° no comparisoun;   *with your wifely dignity*
Hyde ye your beautes,° Isoude and Eleyne,   *beauty*
255 My lady cometh, that al this may disteyne.°   *make pale*

Thy faire body, lat it nat appere,
Lavyne; and thou, Lucresse of Rome toun,
And Polixene, that boughten love so
    dere,°   *who paid so high a price for love*
And Cleopatre, with al thy passioun,
260 Hyde ye your trouthe of° love and your renoun;°   *truth in / fame*
And thou, Tisbe, that hast of love swich peyne;°   *such pain*
My lady cometh, that al this may disteyne.

Herro, Dido, Laudomia, alle yfere,°   *together*
And Phyllis, hanging for thy Demophoun,
265 And Canace, espyed by thy chere,°   *distinguished by your expression*

1. In the G-text this *ballade* is not sung by the narrator but by the procession of women that the narrator of the F-text observes later (see below, 282–90); more information on the form of the *ballade* is included in my introduction to the Short Poems. In this song, the narrator compares the lady Alceste to a number of women (and two men), none of whom, however, completely measures up to her virtue or beauty, according to biblical or literary tradition. They include, in the order mentioned, the biblical Absolom, the son of David famed for his beauty; Esther, the Jewish queen notable for wisdom and meekness; Jonathan, David's friend; Penelope and Marcia, steadfast wives respectively of Odysseus and Cato; Isolde and Helen, celebrated adulterous lovers of Tristan and Paris; Lavinia, Aeneas's wife in Latium; Lucretia, a Roman wife who committed suicide after being raped; Polyxena, the faithful mistress of Achilles who was sacrificed after his death; Cleopatra, the notorious lover of Julius Caesar and Mark Antony, who killed herself after Mark Antony's death; Thisbe, the lover of Pyramus and another suicide; Hero, who killed herself after the drowning of her lover Leander; Dido, Aeneas's mistress in Carthage, who killed herself after Aeneas deserted her to found Rome; Laodamia, the wife of the Greek soldier Protesilaus who failed to return from the Trojan War, and another suicide; Phyllis, a Thracian princess who hung herself after being betrayed by her lover Demophon; Canace, killed by her father for her incestuous love of her brother; Hypsipyle, the abandoned lover of Jason; Hypermnestra, who died at her father's hand for refusing to murder her bridegroom; Ariadne, abandoned for her sister by Theseus. Later in the poem, Chaucer tells the stories of eight of these women (Lucretia, Cleopatra, Thisbe, Dido, Phyllis, Hypsipyle, Hypermnestra, Ariadne); of the women he celebrates in the stories of the legendary, only Medea and Philomela are not mentioned here.

Ysiphile, betrayed with° Jasoun,   *by*
Maketh of your trouthe neither boost ne soun;°   *boast nor sound*
Nor Ypermistre or Adriane, ye tweyne;°   *two*
My lady cometh, that al this may disteyne.

270   This balade may ful wel y-songen be,
As I have seyd erst,° by° my lady free,   *before / about*
For certeynly alle these° mow nat   *these (women)*
    suffyse°   *are not deserving*
To apperen with° my lady in no wyse.   *To equal*
For as the sonne wol the fyr disteyne,°   *outshine the fire*
275   So passeth al my lady sovereyne,°   *my sovereign lady surpasses all others*
That is so good, so fair, so debonaire;°   *gentle, mild*
I prey to God that ever falle hir faire!°   *only good fortune befall her*
For, nadde comfort been° of hir   *had I not experienced the comfort*
    presence,
I had been deed,° withouten any defence,°   *dead / remedy (i.e., surely)*
280   For drede° of Loves wordes and his chere;°   *fear / expression*
As, whan tyme is, herafter ye shul here.
    Behind this god of Love, upon the grene,
I saw cominge of ladies nyntene
In real habit,° a ful esy paas;°   *royal clothing / at a comfortable pace*
285   And after hem° com of women swich a   *them*
    traas,°   *such a (large) procession*
That, sin that God Adam had mad of erthe,
The thridde part of mankind, or the ferthe,
Ne wende I nat by possibilitee,
Had ever in this wyde worlde y-be,[2]
290   And trewe of° love these women were echoon.°   *in / each one*
    Now wheither was that a wonder thing or
    noon,°   *was that not a marvel*
That right anoon° as that they gonne   *immediately*
    espye°   *as soon as they noticed*
This flour, which that I clepe° the dayesye,   *call*
Ful sodeinly° they stinten° alle at ones,°   *suddenly / stopped / once*
295   And kneled doun, as it were for the nones,°   *occasion*
And songen with o° vois, "Hele° and honour   *one / Health, well being*
To trouthe of womanhede, and to this flour
That bereth our alder prys in figuringe!°   *symbolizes the honor of us all*
Hir whyte coroun bereth the
    witnessinge!"°   *crown bears witness, seals the case*
300   And with that word, a compas enviroun,°   *in a circle*
They setten hem ful softly adoun.
First sat the god of Love, and sith° the quene   *next*
With the whyte coroun, clad in grene;
And sithen al the remenaunt, by and by,°   *then all the rest, one by one*
305   As they were of estaat,° ful curteisly;   *according to their rank*

---

2. I did not believe it possible that the whole of mankind, all who had ever existed since the time
that God fashioned Adam of earth, could possibly equal (the number of) a third or a fourth (of
these women). (This statement echoes Dante's *Inferno* 3.55–57.)

Ne nat a word was spoken in the place
The mountaunce of a furlong-wey of space.³
   I kneling by this flour, in good entente°   *good faith*
Abod° to knowen what this peple mente,   *Waited*
310 As stille as any stoon, til at the laste,
This god of Love on me his eyen° caste   *eyes*
And seyde, "Who kneleth ther?" and I answerde
Unto his asking° whan that I it herde   *question*
And seyde, "Sir, it am I," and com him nere°   *came nearer to him*
315 And salued° him. Quod° he, "What   *greeted / Said*
     dostow° here   *are you doing*
So nigh° myn owne flour, so boldely?   *near*
It were better worthy,° trewely,   *would be better*
A worm to neghen neer° my flour than thou." *for a worm to approach*
   "And why, sir," quod I, "and it lyke you?"°   *if you please*
   "For thou," quod he, "art therto nothing
320   able.°   *are completely worthless*
It is my relik, digne and delytable,°   *precious and pleasing*
And thou my fo,° and al my folk werreyest,°   *foe / make war upon*
And of myn olde servaunts thou misseyest°   *slander*
And hindrest hem° with thy translacioun   *harm them*
325 And lettest° folk from hir° devocioun   *hinder / their*
To serve me, and holdest° it folye   *consider*
To serve Love. Thou mayst° it nat denye,   *cannot*
For in pleyn text withouten nede of glose°   *interpretation*
Thou hast translated the Romaunce of the Rose,⁴
330 That is an heresye ageyns my lawe
And makest wyse folk fro me withdrawe.°   *forsake me*
And of Criseyde⁵ thou hast seyd as thee liste,°   *whatever you like*
That maketh men to women lasse
     triste,°   *which makes men trust women less*
That been as trewe as ever was any steel.
335 Of thyn answere avyse thee right weel;°⁶   *Consider your answer carefully*

---

3. For the length of time it takes to travel a furlong (⅛ mile; i.e., a short time).
4. The *Romance of the Rose* was a famous thirteenth-century love vision, composed by two authors, Guillaume de Lorris and Jean de Meun, at least part of which was also translated by Chaucer. Sections of this poem, especially those written by Jean de Meun, can be construed as sharply critical of courtly love. Some excerpts are included here in the Contexts section.
5. In Chaucer's long romance *Troilus and Criseyde*, likely written shortly before the *Legend of Good Women* in the early to mid 1380s. This romance was based on Giovanni Boccaccio's *Il Filostrato*, making it in the most general sense a "translation"; see below, the excuse Chaucer offers at 369–72. For a fuller discussion of the position of the *Legend* in Chaucer's larger poetic career, see my introduction to the poem.
6. In the G-text, the poet adds the following 49 lines (G 267–315), which allude specifically to texts that might have been in Chaucer's library and which for the most part (though critics disagree about the significance of specific texts) would have presented a favorable image of women. The reference to the poet's advancing age in the last line is one of the pieces of evidence used to date the G-text after the F-text.

But natheles° answere me now to this,   *nevertheless*
Why noldest thou as wel han seyd° goodnesse   *didn't you describe the*
Of wemen as° thou hast seyd wikkednesse?   *as much as*
270 Was ther no good matere in thy minde°   *subject matter in your memory*
Ne in alle thy bokes ne coudest thou nat finde
Sum story of wemen that were goode and trewe?
Yis, God wot,° sixty bokes olde and newe   *knows*
Hast thou thyself, alle fulle of stories grete
275 That bothe Romains and eek Grekes trete°   *also Greeks treat, write about*

For, though that thou reneyed hast my lay°   *have renounced my law*
As other wrecches han doon° many a day,   *vile folk have done*
By seynte Venus, that my moder° is,   *mother*
If that thou live, thou shalt repenten this
340 So cruelly, that it shal wel be sene!"°   *seen, made public*
    Tho spak° this lady clothed al in grene   *Then spoke*
And seyde, "God, right of your curtesye,°   *courtesy demands that*
Ye moten herken° if he can replye   *must listen*
Agayns al this that ye han to him meved.°   *accused him of*
345 A god ne sholde nat be thus agreved,°   *aggrieved, resentful*
But of his deitee° he shal be stable°   *in his divinity / constant*
And therto° gracious and merciable.°   *also / merciful*
And if ye nere a god, that knowen al,
Than mighte it be as I yow tellen shal:[7]
350 This man to yow may falsly been accused,
That as by right him oughte been excused,
For in your court is many a losengeour,°   *flatterer*
And many a queynte totelere accusour,°   *cunning slandering tattler*
That tabouren in° your eres° many a soun   *drum into / ears*
355 Right after hir imaginacioun°   *purely imagined (or made up)*

    Of sundry wemen, which lyf that they ladde
And ever an hundred gode ageyn oon° badde   *good women for one (who was)*
This knoweth God and alle clerkes eke°   *scholars also*
That usen swiche materes for to seke.°   *look into such matters.*
280 What seith Valerie,° Titus,° or Claudian?   *Valerius (identity disputed) / prob. Titus Livius*
What seith Jerome ageyns Jovinian?°   *St. Jerome in Against Jovinian*
How clene maydens° and how trewe wyves,°   *pure (are) virgins / true (are) wives*
How stedfast widwes° during al hir lyves,   *steadfast (are) widows / their whole*
Telleth Jerome, and that nat of a fewe
285 But, I dar seyn, an hundred on a rewe°   *in a row*
That it is pitee for to rede and routhe°   *pity*
The wo that they endure for hir trouthe.°   *their fidelity*
For to hir love° were they so trewe   *their lovers*
That, rather than they wolde take a newe,°   *new lover*
290 They chose to be dede° in sundry wyse   *dead*
And deyden° as the story wol devyse,°   *died / describe*
And some were brend,° and some were cut the hals,°   *burned / cut by the throat*
And some dreynt° for they wolden nat° be fals;   *drowned / did not want to*
For alle keped° they hir maydenhed°   *protected / their virginity*
295 Or elles° wedlok or hir widwehed.°   *else / their virtue as widows*
And this thing was nat kept for holinesse,°   *because they had chosen a religious life*
But al for verray° vertu and clennesse°   *true / purity*
And for° men shulde sette° on hem no lak,°   *so that / attribute to them / fault*
And yit they were hethen,° al the pak   *heathen*
300 That were so sore adrad° of alle shame   *sorely afraid*
These olde° wemen kepte so hir name°   *ancient / guarded so their reputations*
That in this world I trow° men shal nat finde   *believe*
A man that coude be so trewe and kinde
As was the leste° woman in that tyde.°   *least important / time*
305 What seith also the epistel of Ovyde°   *the Heroides by Ovid*
Of trewe wyves and of hir labour?°   *their efforts, hardships*
What Vincent in his Estorial Mirour?°   *Vincent of Beauvais in the Speculum Historiale*
Eek° al the world of autours° maystow here,°   *Also / authors / you may listen to*
Cristen and hethen, trete of swich matere;°   *discuss such subject matter*
310 It nedeth nay alday° thus for to endyte.°   *all day / write about it*
But yit I sey, what eyleth° thee to wryte   *ails*
The draf° of stories and forgete the corn?   *dross, waste*
By Seint Venus, of whom that I was born,
Although thou reneyed° hast my lay°   *renounced / law*
315 As othere olde foles° many a day,   *fools*
Thou shalt repente it so that it shal be sene!°   *seen, made public*

7. That is, if you did not already know everything in your omniscience, I might be able to give you some new information (about the narrator, the petitioner).

To have your daliance° and for envye;   *an intimate chat (with you)*
These been the causes, and I shal nat lye.
Envye is lavender° of the court alway,   *laundress (washer of dirty linens)*
For she ne parteth,° neither night ne day,   *departs*
360 Out of the hous of Cesar,°   *i.e., any king, emperor, or political leader*
thus seith Dante;
Whoso that goth, algate she wol nat wante.[8]
And eek paraunter,° for° this man is   *also perhaps / because*
nice,°   *foolish*
He mighte doon it gessing no malice,°   *without malice*
But for he useth thinges for to make;°   *is accustomed to write things*
365 Him rekketh nought° of what matere   *It makes no difference to him*
he take;
Or him was boden maken thilke tweye
Of som persone, and durste it nat withseye,[9]
Or him repenteth utterly of this.
He ne hath nat doon so grevously amis°   *amiss*
370 To translaten that° olde clerkes° wryten,   *what / scholars*
As though that he of malice° wolde endyten°   *maliciously / invent*
Despyt° of love, and had himself it   *Scorn*
wrought.°   *made it up himself*
This shulde a rightwys° lord have in his thought,   *just, fair-minded*
And nat be lyk tiraunts of Lumbardye,
375 That han no reward but at tirannye.[1]
For he that king or lord is naturel,°   *by natural right*
Him oughte nat be tiraunt ne cruel
As is a fermour,° to doon the harm he   *tax collector*
can.°   *can (get away with)*
He moste thinke it is his lige° man   *liege (owing feudal service)*
380 And° is his tresour and his gold in cofre.°   *Who / coffer*
This is the sentence° of the Philosophre:[2]
A king to kepe° his liges in justice;   *maintain*
Withouten doute that is his office.°   *duty*
Al° wole he kepe his lordes hir   *Although*
degree,°   *preserve aristocratic privilege*
385 As it is right and skilful° that they° be   *reasonable / i.e., the lords*
Enhaunced° and honoured and most dere—   *Magnified*
For they been half-goddes in this world here—
Yet mot° he doon bothe right to pore and riche,   *must*
Al° be that hir estat be nat yliche,°   *Although / alike*
390 And han of° pore folk compassioun,   *have on*
For lo, the gentil kind° of the leoun:°   *noble nature / lion*
For whan a flye offendeth him or byteth,
He with his tail awey the flye smyteth°   *swats the fly away*

---

8. Whoever else leaves, she at least (i.e., Envy) will not be absent. (Chaucer is citing Dante, *Inferno* 13.64–65.)
9. Or he was commanded to make those same two poems (the *Romance of the Rose* and *Troilus and Criseyde*) by some person and did not dare refuse.
1. Who grow rich solely as the result of tyranny. (The Visconti of Milan were notorious for their tyrannical rule of Lombardy.)
2. This is the meaning expressed by the Philosopher. (The "Philosopher" here is Aristotle, and Chaucer is likely alluding to his *Politics*, or alternatively the pseudo-Aristotelian *Secretum Secretorum* [*Secret of Secrets*], following John Fisher, *Complete Poetry and Prose*, 628 note.)

Al esily,° for of his genterye°	*gently / noble lineage*
395 Him deyneth° nat to wreke him°	*He does not lower himself / be revenged*
on a flye	
As doth a curre or elles another	
beste.°	*mongrel dog or else another beast*
In noble corage° oughte been areste,°	*spirit / self-restraint*
And weyen° every thing by equitee,°	*weigh / principles of equity*
And ever han reward to° his owen	*regard for, respect for*
degree.°	*honor, rank*
400 For, sir, it is no maystrie° for a lord	*triumph, cause for pride*
To dampne° a man withoute answere of	*condemn*
word,°	*the opportunity to reply*
And for a lord that is ful foul to use.°	*an obnoxious practice*
And if so be he may him nat excuse°	*the accused has no excuse*
But asketh° mercy with a dredful° herte	*asks for / fearful*
405 And profreth him, right in his bare sherte³	
To been right at° your owne jugement,	*to submit to*
Than oughte a god by short avysement°	*without lengthy deliberation*
Considre his owne honour and his trespas.°	*(the nature of) his crime*
For sith° no cause of deeth lyth° in his cas,	*since / lies*
410 Yow oughte been° the lighter merciable;°	*ought to be / more merciful*
Leteth your yre,° and beth somwhat	*Lay aside your anger*
tretable.°	*open to reason*
The man hath served yow of his conning°	*as well as he knew how*
And forthred° wel your lawe in his making.°	*advanced / poetry writing*
Al° be it that he can nat wel endyte,°	*Although / is not a good writer*
415 Yet hath he maked lewed° folk delyte	*ignorant, uneducated*
To serve yow in preysing of your name.	
He made the book that hight° the Hous of Fame,	*is called*
And eek° the Deeth of Blaunche the	*also*
Duchesse,°	*i.e., the Book of the Duchess*
And the Parlement of Foules, as I gesse,	
420 And al the love of Palamon and Arcyte	
Of Thebes,⁴ though the story is knowen lyte,°	*little known*
And many an ympne° for your halydayes,°	*hymn / holy days, holidays*
That highten° balades, roundels, virelayes;⁵	*are called*
And, for to speke of other holynesse,	
425 He hath in° prose translated	*into*
Boece°	*Boethius (the Consolation of Philosophy)*
And mad the lyf° also of Seynt Cecyle;⁶	*saint's legend*
He made also, goon is a grete whyl,°	*a long time ago*
Origenes upon the Maudeleyne;⁷	
Him oughte now to have the lesse peyne;°	*suffer less pain*
430 He hath mad° many a lay and many a	*composed*
thing.°	*song and other poems*
Now as ye been a god and eek° a king,	*also*

---

3. Comes forward dressed in just his plain shirt (i.e., attired simply and humbly).
4. A reference to an early version of the Knight's Tale, the first story in the *Canterbury Tales*.
5. Different short poetic forms in the French style. (For some of Chaucer's experiments in the genres alluded to here, see the Short Poems section of this Norton Critical Edition.)
6. An early version of the Second Nun's Tale in the *Canterbury Tales*.
7. A lost translation of a work believed to have been by Origen, concerning Mary Magdalen.

I, your Alceste, whylom° quene of Trace,[8]   *once*
I aske yow this man,° right of your grace,   *on behalf of this man*
That ye him never hurte in al his lyve,
435   And he shal sweren to yow, and that as blyve,°   *quickly*
He shal no more agilten in this wyse,°   *offend in this manner*
But he shal maken,° as ye wol devyse,°   *make poems / determine*
Of women trewe in loving al hir lyve,°   *their lives*
Wherso ye wol,° of mayden or of wyve,   Whichever (of the two) you wish
440   And forthren° yow as moche as he misseyde°   *promote / misspoke*
Or° in the Rose or elles° in Creseyde."   *Either / else*
     The god of Love answerde hir thus anoon,°   *at once*
"Madame," quod° he, "it is so long agoon°   *said / has been a long time*
That I yow knew° so charitable and trewe,   *I have known you to be*
445   That never yet sin that° the world was newe   *since*
To me ne fond I better noon than ye.°   *no one better than you*
If that I wolde save my degree,°   *preserve my (own) honor*
I may ne wol nat werne° your requeste;   *cannot nor do I wish to refuse*
Al lyth° in yow, doth with him as yow leste.°   *lies / whatever pleases you*
450   I al foryeve° withouten lenger space;°   *forgive everything / delay*
For whoso yeveth a yift° or doth a grace,°   *whoever gives a gift / favor*
Do it by tyme,° his thank is° wel the more;   *promptly / thanks are*
And demeth ye° what he shal do therfore.   *you decide*
Go thanke now my lady here," quod he.
455   I roos and doun I sette me on my knee,
And seyde thus: "Madame, the God above
Foryelde° yow, that ye the god of Love   *Reward*
Han maked me his wrathe to foryive,°   *to give up his anger against me*
And yeve° me grace so long for to live   *give*
460   That I may knowe soothly what ye be°   *truly who you are*
That han me holpe° and put in this   *has helped me*
     degree.°   *given me this honor*
But trewly I wende, as in this cas,
Nought have agilt ne doon to love trespas.
Forwhy a trewe man, withouten drede,
465   Hath nat to parten with a theves dede;[9]
Ne a trewe lover ought me nat to blame°   *should not blame me*
Though that I speke° a fals lover som shame.   *speak about*
They oughte rather with me for to holde°   *join with, support me*
For that° I of Creseyde wroot or tolde   *Because*
470   Or of the Rose. Whatso° myn auctour mente,   *Whatever*
Algate,° God wot,° it was myn entente   *In any event / knows*
To forthren° trouthe in love and it cherice;°   *advance / cherish*
And to be war fro° falsnesse and fro vice   *to warn (others) away from*
By swich ensample;° this was my meninge."   *such examples*

8. Alceste, first named in the F-version of the Prologue here (in G, she is named at 179), was queen of Thessaly rather than Thrace. She is famed for her offer to die in the place of her husband Admetus, and appears as a model of the perfect self-sacrificing woman in various texts by Chaucer and other contemporary writers. See, for example, *Troilus and Criseyde* 5.1527–33. Her story is told more fully in the Prologue, below, 510–15. Although her story is traditional and widely known, the identification of Alceste with the daisy is original to Chaucer.
9. But truly I did not believe, in this situation, that I had committed a crime, or trespassed against love, because an honest man, without a doubt, should not share in the blame of a thief's deed.

475 And she answerde, "Lat be° thyn arguinge, *Leave off*
For Love ne wol nat countrepleted° be *contradicted*
In right ne wrong,° and lerne that of° *Whether right or wrong / from*
me!
Thou hast thy grace,° and hold thee right therto.° *favor / hang onto it*
Now wol I seyn what penance thou shalt do
480 For thy trespas. Understond it here:
Thou shalt whyl that° thou livest, yeer by yere, *as long as*
The moste party° of thy tyme spende *greater portion*
In making° of a glorious legende *the composition*
Of gode women, maydenes and wyves,
485 That weren trewe in lovinge al hir° lyves, *their*
And telle of false men that hem° bitrayen, *them*
That al hir lyf ne doon nat but assayen° *do nothing but attempt (to see)*
How many women they may doon a shame,° *dishonor*
For in your world that is now holde a game.° *considered a sport*
490 And though thee lyke nat a lover be,° *you choose not to be a lover*
Spek wel of love; this penance yive° I thee. *give*
And to the god of Love I shal so preye
That he shal charge° his servants, by any weye *direct*
To forthren° thee and wel thy labour *promote*
quyte.° *repay, reward you for*
495 Go now thy wey, this penance is but lyte.° *quite small*
And whan this book is made,° yive it° the *completed / present it to*
quene
On my behalfe, at Eltham, or at Shene."[1]
The god of Love gan smyle, and than he sayde,
"Wostow,"° quod° he, "wher° this be wyf *Do you know / said / whether*
or mayde,
500 Or quene, or countesse, or of what degree,° *rank*
That hath so litel° penance yiven° thee *such a small / given to*
That hast deserved sorer for to smerte?° *to suffer more painfully*
But pitee renneth sone° in gentil° herte; *flows swiftly / noble*
That maistow° seen. She kytheth° what *may you / shows, reveals*
she is."
505 And I answerde, "Nay, sir, so have I blis, *as I may have bliss*
No more but that° I see wel she is good." *no more than that*
"That is a trewe tale, by myn hood,"° *by my hood (a colloquialism)*
Quod Love, "and that thou knowest wel, pardee,° *by God*
If it be so that thou avyse thee.° *think about it*
510 Hastow nat° in a book, lyth° in thy cheste, *Don't you have / which lies*
The grete goodnesse of the quene Alceste,
That turned was into a dayesye;
She that for° hir housbonde chees° to dye, *in place of / chose*
And eek° to goon to helle rather than he, *also*
And Ercules rescowed hir, pardee,° *rescued her, by God*
515 And broughte hir out of helle agayn° to blis?" *back*
And I answerd ageyn, and seyde, "Yis,
Now knowe I hir! And is this good Alceste

---

1. Eltham and Sheen were royal residences of Richard II outside of London. Reference to them is deleted from the G-version of the Prologue.

The dayesye, and myn owne hertes reste?° — *peace, repose*
520 Now fele° I wel the goodnesse of this wyf, — *feel, perceive*
That bothe after hir deeth and in hir lyf
Hir grete bountee° doubleth hir renoun. — *generosity*
Wel hath she quit me° myn affeccioun — *repaid me for*
That I have to hir flour, the dayesye.
525 No wonder is though° Jove hir — *that*
    stellifye,° — *stellified her (made her a star)*
As telleth Agaton,[2] for hir goodnesse.
Hir whyte coroun bereth of it witnesse,° — *crown bears witness to it*
For also° many vertues hadde she — *just as many*
As smale floures in hir coroun be.
530 In remembraunce of hir and in honour,
Cibella made the dayesy and the flour — *Cybele (a fertility goddess)*
Y-corouned al with whyt, as men may see,
And Mars yaf ° to hir coroun reed,° — *gave / redness (on the petal tips)*
    pardee,° — *by God*
In stede of rubies, set among the whyte."
535   Therwith this quene wex° reed for shame a lyte° — *grew / a little*
Whan she was preysed so in hir presence.
Than seyde Love, "A ful greet necligence
Was it to thee, that ilke tyme° thou made — *the same time when*
'Hyd, Absolon, thy tresses,' in balade,
540 That thou forgate hir in thy song to
    sette,° — *to mention her (Alceste) in your song*
Sin that° thou art so gretly in hir dette° — *Since / debt*
And wost so wel,° that kalender° is she — *You know very well / a model*
To any woman that wol lover be,
For she taught al the craft of fyn lovinge° — *art of courtly love*
545 And namely of wyfhood the livinge° — *proper wifely conduct*
And al the boundes° that she oughte kepe;° — *moral rules / observe*
Thy litel wit was thilke tyme aslepe.° — *asleep at that time*
But now I charge° thee upon thy lyf, — *command*
That in thy legend thou make of this
    wyf° — *compose poetry about this wife*
550 Whan thou hast other smale y-made° — *written about other lesser (women)*
    bifore,
And fare now wel, I charge° thee no more.° — *command / nothing else*
    But er° I go, thus moche I wol thee telle, — *before*
Ne shal no trewe lover come in helle.
These other ladies sitting here arowe° — *in a row*
555 Been in thy balade, if thou canst hem
    knowe,° — *are able to recognize them*
And in thy bookes alle thou shalt hem finde.° — *you will find them all*
Have hem° now in thy legend al in minde, — *them*
I mene of hem° that been in thy knowinge.° — *those / you know about*
For here been twenty thousand mo° sitting — *more*
560 Than thou knowest, and good women alle

2. A possible reference to a character in Plato's *Symposium*, also known as "Agatho's Feast." The *Symposium*, however, does not allude to Alcestis's stellification.

And trewe of love for aught that may
    befalle;° *regardless of what might happen*
Make the metres of hem as thee leste.° *verses about them as you please*
I mot goon° hoom, the sonne draweth *must go*
    weste,° *draws toward the west*
To paradys, with al this companye,
565 And serve alwey the fresshe dayesye.
    At Cleopatre I wol that thou° beginne, *would have you*
And so forth, and my love so shalt thou winne,
For lat see now what man that lover be° *who is a lover*
Wol doon° so strong a peyne for love as she. *Will suffer*
570 I wot° wel that thou mayst nat al it *know*
    ryme,° *cannot record in rhyme all*
That swiche° lovers diden in hir° tyme; *such / their*
It were° too long to reden and to here.° *would take / to read and hear*
Sufficeth me° thou make° in this manere, *It is enough for me / write*
That thou reherce° of al hir lyf the *repeat*
    grete° *the most important parts*
After° these olde auctours listen to *Following what*
575 trete.° *prefer to include*
For whoso° shal so many a story telle, *whoever*
Sey shortly° or he shal too longe dwelle." *must speak briefly*
And with that word my bookes gan° I take *did*
And right thus° on my legend gan I make.[3] *just so / began to write*

The Legend of Cleopatra

Incipit Legenda Cleopatrie, Martiris, Egipti regine.[1]

580   After the deeth of Tholomee the king,[2]
    That al Egipte hadde in his governing,
    Regned° his quene Cleopataras; *Ruled, governed*
    Til° on a tyme befel ther swich a cas,° *Until / it came about*
    That out of Rome was sent a senatour
585   For to conqueren regnes° and honour° *kingdoms / gain honor*
    Unto° the toun of Rome, as was usaunce,° *For / customary*
    To° have the world unto hir *So they might*
        obeisaunce,° *under their control*
    And, sooth to seye, Antonius was his name.
    So fil it, as Fortune him oughte a shame
590   Whan he was fallen in prosperitee,
    Rebel unto the toun of Rome is he.
    And over al this the suster of Cesar,

---

3. In the next to last line of the G-text, the poet awakens.
1. This manuscript heading, known as an "incipit," is Latin for "Here begins the Legend of Cleopatra, martyr, Queen of Egypt." It helps to establish the genre of the collection as saints' lives or "legends."
2. Probably Ptolemy XIII, Cleopatra's brother with whom, according to the custom, she reigned after the death of Ptolemy Auletes, her father, in 51 B.C.E. (though another brother, with whom she later ruled, was also named Ptolemy).

He lafte hir falsly er that she was war[3]
And wolde algates han° another wyf,   *have at any rate*
595 For whiche he took° with Rome and Cesar   *brought down on himself*
        stryf.°   *strife*
    Natheles forsooth° this ilke° senatour   *Nevertheless in truth / same*
    Was a ful worthy gentil werreyour,°   *noble warrior*
    And of° his deeth it was ful greet damage,°   *because of / loss, harm*
    But love had brought this man in swich a rage°   *such madness*
600 And him so narwe° bounden in his las°   *tightly / snare*
    Al for the love of Cleopataras
    That al the world he sette at no value.
    Him thoughte nas to him no thing so due[4]
    As Cleopatras for to love and serve;
605 Him roughte nat° in armes for to sterve° *He didn't care if he / were to die*
    In the defence of hir and of hir right.°   *her legitimacy (i.e., to rule)*
        This noble quene eek° loved so this knight,   *also*
    Thurgh his desert° and for his chivalrye.   *For his merit*
    As certeynly, but if that bookes lye,°   *unless books lie*
610 He was of persone° and of gentilesse°   *body / noble character*
    And of discrecioun° and hardinesse,°   *judgment / bravery*
    Worthy to any wight° that liven may.   *as any person*
    And she was fair as is the rose in May.
    And, for to make shortly° is the beste,   *because to write concisely*
615 She wex° his wyf and hadde him as hir leste.°   *became / as she liked*
        The wedding and the feste to devyse,
    To me, that have y-take swich empryse
    Of so many a story for to make,
    It were too long lest that I sholde slake
620 Of thing that bereth more effect and charge,[5]
    For men may overlade° a ship or barge;   *overload*
    And forthy° to th'effect° than wol I skippe,   *therefore / main point*
    And al the remenant° I wol lete it slippe.   *rest of it, remainder*
        Octovian, that wood° was of this dede,°   *enraged / by this action*
625 Shoop him an ost on° Antony to lede   *Raised an army against*
    Al utterly for his destruccioun,
    With stoute° Romains, cruel as leoun;°   *strong, bold / lions*
    To ship they wente, and thus I let hem saile.
    Antonius was war° and wol nat faile   *aware (of Octavian's plans)*
630 To meten° with these Romains if he may;   *encounter*
    Took eek his reed,° and bothe upon a day   *He took his counsel as well*

3. And truth to tell, Antony was his name. So it happened, as he was prospering, Fortune paid (Antony) his dues in shame, when he rebelled against Rome and betrayed Caesar's sister before she knew it. (Mark Antony ruled Rome with Gaius Octavius [also called "Octavian," Julius Caesar's adopted son] and Marcus Aemilius Lepidus after the death of Julius Caesar in 44 B.C.E., during the Second Triumvirate. To strengthen their alliance, Mark Antony married Octavian's sister Octavia, though he soon deserted her for Cleopatra. Octavian ruled from 31 B.C.E. to 14 C.E., after defeating Antony at the battle of Actium, described below. Fortune is the classical and medieval goddess of chance, who makes a practice of casting down the fortunate at the time of their greatest happiness; see also the *Book of the Duchess* 618 note.)
4. It seemed to him that there was nothing so important.
5. It would take so long for me to describe the wedding and wedding feast, (since I) am burdened with recounting so many stories (i.e., of good women, as assigned by the god of Love in the Prologue), that I might lose the energy to describe things that have more substance and weight.

His wyf and he and al his ost° forth wente   *army*
To shippe anoon,° no lenger they ne stente;°   *at once / did they stay*
And in the see it happed hem to mete°—   *it chanced that they met*
635 Up goth the trompe°—and for to shoute and shete,°   *trumpet / shoot*
And peynen hem to sette on with the sonne.[6]
With grisly° soun out goth the grete gonne,°   *horrible / large guns*
And heterly° they hurtlen al at ones,°   *fiercely / shoot straightway*
And fro° the top doun cometh the grete stones.   *from*
640 In goth the grapenel so ful of crokes;
Among the ropes renne° the shering-hokes.   *run*
In with the polax presseth° he and he;   *shoves forward*
Behind the mast beginneth he to flee,
And out agayn, and dryveth him overborde;[7]
645 He stingeth° him upon° his speres orde;°   *pierces / with / his spear's point*
He rent° the sail with hokes lyke a sythe;°   *rips / scythe*
He bringeth the cuppe and biddeth hem be
   blythe;°   *urges them to be joyful*
He poureth pesen upon the hacches slider;
With pottes ful of lym they goon togider;[8]
650 And thus the longe day in fight they spende
Til, at the laste, as every thing hath ende,
Antony is shent° and put him to the flighte,   *destroyed*
And al his folk to-go, that best go mighte.°   *fled, who are able to get away*
   Fleeth eek° the quene, with al hir purpre° sail;   *Also flees / purple*
655 For strokes,° which that wente as thikke as hail,   *Considering the blows*
No wonder was she mighte it nat endure.
And whan that Antony saw that aventure,°   *occurrence, misadventure*
"Allas," quod° he, "the day that I was born!   *said*
My worshippe° in this day thus have I lorn."°   *honor / lost*
660 And for dispeyr° out of his wit he sterte,°   *despair / lost his mind*
And roof° himself anoon° thurghout the herte   *stabbed / at once*
Er that he ferther went° out of the place.   *Before he went any farther*
His wyf, that coude of Cesar have no grace,°   *mercy*
To Egipte is fled for drede° and for distresse.   *fear*
665   But herkneth ye that speke of kindenesse,°   *constancy, natural affection*
Ye men, that falsly sweren many an ooth
That ye wol dye if that your love be wrooth,°   *gets angry (with you)*
Here may ye seen of women which a trouthe.[9]
This woful Cleopatre hath mad swich routhe°   *such lament*
670 That ther nis° tonge noon that may it telle.   *is not*
But on the morwe° she wold no lenger   *in the morning, at dawn*
   dwelle°   *wait*
But made hir subtil werkmen° make a shryne   *clever craftsmen*

6. They took pains to attack with the sun at their backs.
7. Chaucer uses some specialized vocabulary for weaponry in this passage: The "grapenel" in 640 is
a grappling iron full of hooks or "crokes" (for drawing a vessel alongside of its enemy); in 641,
shearing hooks are used to cut a ship's rigging, and in 642, a polax is a battle-ax. Chaucer's
vagueness with pronouns here reflects the confusion of battle; in these last two lines one sailor
flees to a position behind the mast, then emerges from his protected spot and is driven overboard.
8. Pours out dried peas to make the decks slippery; with pots of quicklime (thrown at an enemy to
blind him), they clashed (in battle).
9. Here you may see what kind of fidelity (women are capable of).

Of alle the rubies and the stones fyne
In al Egipte that she coude espye,°   *discover, find out*
675 And putte ful the shryne of spicerye°   *filled the shrine with spices*
And let the cors embaume,° and forth she   *had the body embalmed*
    fette°   *fetched*
This dede cors° and in the shryne it shette.°   *dead body / shut it up*
And next° the shryne a pit than doth she grave,°   *next to / she has dug*
And alle the serpents that she mighte have,
680 She putte hem in that grave, and thus she seyde:
"Now, love, to whom my sorweful° herte obeyed   *sorrowful*
So ferforthly° that fro° that blisful houre   *completely / from*
That I yow swoor to been al frely youre°—   *completely, unreservedly yours*
I mene° yow, Antonius, my knight—   *mean*
685 That never waking, in the day or night,
Ye nere° out of myn hertes remembraunce   *were not*
For wele or wo, for carole or for daunce;[1]
And in° myself this covenant° made I tho°   *to / promise / then*
That, right swich° as ye felten,° wele°   *such / experienced / prosperity*
    or wo,
690 As ferforth° as it in my power lay,   *Insofar as*
Unreprovable° unto my wyfhood ay,°   *Irreproachable / always*
The same wolde I felen, lyf or deeth.
And thilke covenant whyl me lasteth
    breeth°   *that promise while my breath lasts*
I wol fulfille, and that shal wel be sene,
695 Was never unto hir love a trewer quene."
And with that word, naked, with ful good
    herte,°   *undismayed, with a good spirit*
Among the serpents in the pit she sterte,°   *jumped*
And ther she chees° to have hir buryinge.   *chose*
Anoon the neddres gonne° hir for to stinge,   *Immediately the adders did*
700 And she hir deeth receyveth, with good chere°   *attitude, frame of mind*
For love of Antony, that was hir° so dere:—   *to her*
And this is storial sooth,° it is no fable.   *historical truth*
   Now, er° I finde a man thus trewe and stable,   *until*
And wol° for love his deeth so freely° take,   *who will / readily, generously*
705 I prey God lat our hedes° never ake!°[2]   *heads / ache*
    Amen.

Explicit Legenda Cleopatrie, martiris.[3]

---

1. For good fortune or bad, for song or dance (proverbial expressions).
2. The implication being that the attempt to think of a man as faithful and self-sacrificing as Cleopatra would be so arduous as to cause the seeker's head to ache.
3. The manuscript notation that marks the end of a text is called an "explicit." Translated from the Latin, it means "Here ends the Legend of Cleopatra, martyr."

The Legend of Thisbe

Incipit Legenda Tesbe Babilonie, Martiris.[1]

At Babiloyne° whylom fil it° thus,	Babylon / once it happened
The whiche toun the quene Semiramus	
Let dichen al about, and walles make[2]	
Ful hye° of harde tyles wel y-bake.°	Very high / hard-baked
710 Ther weren dwellinge in this noble toun	
Two lordes, which that were of greet renoun,°	fame, reputation
And woneden so nigh,° upon a grene	lived so near (to each other)
That ther nas° but a stoon-wal hem	was nothing
bitwene,°	between them
As ofte in grete tounes is the wone.°	custom
715 And sooth to seyn,° that o° man hadde a sone,	truth to tell / one
Of al that londe oon° of the lustieste.°	one / most vigorous, lively
That other hadde a doughter, the faireste,	
That estward° in the world was tho° dwellinge.	eastward / then
The name of everich gan° to other springe	each of them did
720 By° women, that were neighebores aboute.	By means of
For in that contree yet, withouten doute,°	to be sure
Maydens been y-kept° for jelosye	were guarded
Ful streite lest° they diden som folye.	very stringently in case
This yonge man was cleped° Piramus,	called
725 Tisbe hight° the mayd, Naso[3] seith thus;	Thisbe was the name of
And thus by report was hir name	
y-shove°	were their names bandied about
That,° as they wexe° in age, wex hir° love;	So that / grew / their
And certeyn,° as by reson of hir age,	truly
Ther mighte have been bitwix hem° mariage	between them
730 But that hir fadres° nolde it nat assente,°	their fathers / would not agree
And bothe in love ylyke sore they brente°	they burned with equal heat
That noon of alle hir° frendes mighte it lette°	their / prevent (their love)
But prively° somtyme yet they mette	secretly
By sleighte° and speken som of hir° desyr;	craftiness / about their
735 As, wry the glede,° and hotter is the fyr,°	cover the burning coal / fire
Forbede° a love, and it is ten so wood.°	Forbid / ten times as crazy
This wal which that bitwix hem° bothe stood	between them
Was cloven a-two,° right fro the cop	split apart
adoun°	from the top down
Of olde tyme of his fundacioun,°	at its foundation
740 But yet this clifte° was so narwe and lyte,°	crack / narrow and little
It nas nat° sene dere ynough a myte.°	was not / in the slightest
But what is that that love can nat espye?°	spy out
Ye lovers two if that I shal nat lye	
Ye founden first this litel narwe clifte,	

---

1. Here begins the Legend of Thisbe of Babylon, martyr.
2. Which town, the Queen Semiramis had encircled with ditches and walls. (Semiramis was the ambitious and lustful mythical queen of Babylon.)
3. Publius Ovidius Naso (Ovid or Naso) tells the story of Pyramus and Thisbe in the *Metamorphoses* 4.55–166.

745 And with a soun° as softe as any shrifte,°   *sound / confession*
They lete hir° wordes thurgh the clifte pace°   *their / pass*
And tolden, whyl that they stood in the place,
Al hir compleynt of love and al hir wo
At every tyme whan they durste so.°   *dared to do so*
750   Upon that o° syde of the wal stood he,   *one*
And on that other syde stood Tisbe,
The swote soun° of other° to receyve,   *sweet sound / the other one*
And thus hir wardeins° wolde they deceyve.   *their guardians*
And every day this wal they wolde threte°   *threaten*
And wisshe to God that it were doun
755   y-bete.°   *beaten down (to the ground)*
Thus wolde they seyn, "Allas, thou wikked wal,
Thurgh thyn envye thou us lettest al!°   *hinder us in all ways*
Why nilt thou cleve° or fallen al a-two?°   *won't you break / to pieces*
Or at the leste, but° thou woldest so,   *at least, unless*
760 Yet woldestow° but ones° lete us mete,   *would you / only once*
Or ones that we mighte kissen swete,°   *sweetly, lovingly*
Than were we covered of° our cares colde.   *would we be recovered from*
But natheles° yet be we to thee holde°   *nevertheless / beholden, obligated*
In as moche as thou suffrest° for to goon   *permit*
765 Our wordes thurgh thy lyme° and eek° thy stoon.   *lime (for mortar) / also*
Yet oughte we with thee been wel apayd."°   *pleased*
And whan these ydel° wordes weren sayd,   *idle, foolish*
The colde wal they wolden kisse of stoon
And take hir leve,° and forth they wolden goon,   *take their leave*
770 And this was gladly in the eventyde°   *evening*
Or wonder erly lest men it espyde;°   *so nobody would see them*
And longe tyme they wrought in this manere°   *behaved in this way*
Til on a day whan Phebus gan to clere°—   *the sun came out*
Aurora° with the stremes° of hir hete°   *The dawn / streams / heat*
775 Had dryed up the dew of herbes wete°—   *from the moist plants*
Unto this clifte, as it was wont to be,°   *was their custom*
Com° Pyramus, and after com Tisbe   *Came*
And plighten trouthe° fully in hir fey°   *made a promise / by their faith*
That ilke same° night to stele awey   *very same*
780 And to begyle° hir wardeins everichoon,°   *deceive / all of them*
And forth out of the citee for to goon;
And, for the feldes° been so brode and wyde,   *because the fields*
For to mete in o place° at o tyde,°   *one (certain) place / time*
They sette mark hir° meting sholde be   *determined that their*
785 Ther° King Ninus⁴ was graven° under a tree,   *Where / buried*
For olde payens° that ydoles heried°   *pagans / worshipped idols*
Useden tho° in feldes to been beried,   *Were accustomed then*
And faste° by this grave was a welle,   *close*
And shortly° of this tale for to telle,   *briefly*
790 This covenant was affermed wonder faste,°   *with great earnestness*
And longe hem thoughte that the sonne laste

_____

4. Semiramis's deceased husband.

That it nere goon under the see adoun.⁵
  This Tisbe hath so greet affeccioun
  And so greet lyking° Piramus to see   *such a strong desire*
795 That, whan she saw hir tyme mighte be,°   *her moment*
  At night she stal awey ful prively°   *secretly*
  With hir face y-wimpled° subtilly;   *veiled*
  For alle hir frendes—for to save hir trouthe°—   *to keep her vow (in love)*
  She hath forsake. Allas, and that is routhe°   *a pity*
800 That ever woman wolde be so trewe
  To trusten man but she the bet him knewe!°   *unless she knew him better*
  And to the tree she goth a ful good pas,°   *goes with good speed*
  For love made hir so hardy° in this cas,   *audacious, fearless*
  And by the welle adoun she gan hir dresse.°   *she sat down*
805 Allas, than comth a wilde leonesse°   *lioness*
  Out of the wode withouten more arest°   *without delay*
  With blody mouthe of strangling of a best,° *from choking (another) beast*
  To drinken of the welle ther as she sat;
  And whan that Tisbe had espyed that
810 She rist hir° up with a ful drery herte,°   *rises / very fearful heart*
  And in a cave with dredful° foot she sterte,°   *frightened / rushed away*
  For by the mone° she saw it wel withalle.°   *moon / indeed*
  And as she ran hir wimpel° lete she falle   *veil, headdress*
  And took noon heed, so sore she was awhaped°   *terrified*
815 And eek° so glad of that she was° escaped;   *also / because she had*
  And thus she sit and darketh wonder
      stille.°   *hides in the dark very quietly*
  Whan that this leonesse hath dronke hir fille
  Aboute° the welle gan she for to winde,   *Around*
  And right anoon° the wimpel gan° she finde,   *very quickly / headdress did*
820 And with hir blody mouth it al torente.°   *tore it all to pieces*
  Whan this was doon, no lenger she ne stente°   *longer did she stop*
  But to the wode hir wey° than hath she   *to the woods her way*
      nome.°   *taken*
  And at the laste this Piramus is come,
  But al too longe, allas, at hoom° was he.   *home*
825 The mone shoon, men mighte wel y-see;°   *see clearly (by moonlight)*
  And in his weye as that he com ful faste
  His eyen to the grounde adoun° he caste,   *down*
  And in the sonde,° as he beheld adoun,   *on the sandy ground*
  He saw the steppes brode° of a leoun,   *broad, large*
830 And in his herte he sodeinly agroos,°   *shuddered with fear*
  And pale he wex,° therwith his heer aroos,°   *grew / hair stood on end*
  And neer° he com and fond the wimpel° torn.   *near / veil, headdress*
  "Allas," quod° he, "the day that I was born!   *said*
  This o° night wol us lovers bothe slee!°   *one / slay*
835 How sholde I axen° mercy of Tisbe   *ask*
  Whan I am he that have yow slayn, allas!
  My bidding° hath yow slayn as in this cas.°   *request, advice / matter*

───

5. It seemed to them that the sun stayed (in the sky) a long time before it would set beneath the sea.

Allas, to bidde a woman goon by nighte
In place ther as peril fallen mighte,°   *might befall (her)*
840   And I so slow! Allas, I ne hadde be
Here in this place a furlong-wey er ye!⁶
Now what° leoun that be in this foreste,   *whatever*
My body mote he rente,° or what beste°   *may he rip apart / beast*
That wilde is, gnawen mote he now myn herte!"
845   And with that worde he to the wimpel sterte,°   *rushed to the veil*
And kiste it ofte and wepe on it ful sore,
And seyde, "Wimpel, allas, ther nis no more°   *there is nothing else (to do)*
But° thou shalt fele as wel the blood of me   *Except*
As thou hast felt the bleding of Tisbe!"
850   And with that worde he smoot him° to the herte.   *smote, stabbed himself*
The blood out of the wounde as brode sterte°   *burst out as widely*
As water whan the conduit° broken is.   *pipe*
          Now Tisbe, which that wiste nat° of this,   *who knew nothing*
But sitting in hir drede,° she thoughte thus,   *terror*
855   "If it so falle that my Piramus
Be comen hider and may° me nat y-finde,   *here and does*
He may me holden fals and eek unkinde."°   *also unnatural, untrue*
And out she comth, and after him gan espyen°   *looked for him*
Bothe with hir hert° and with hir eyen°   *heart / eyes*
860   And thoughte, "I wol him tellen of my drede
Bothe of the leonesse and al my dede."°   *everything I did*
And at the laste hir love than hath she founde
Beting with his heles° on the grounde,   *His heels beating*
Al blody, and therwithal abak she sterte,°   *she hastened backward*
865   And lyke the wawes quappe gan hir herte,
And pale as box she wex, and in a throwe
Avysed hir and gan him wel to knowe,
That it was Piramus, hir herte dere.⁷
Who coude wryte whiche a deedly chere°   *what a grim, deathly face*
870   Hath Tisbe now, and how hir heer she rente°   *she tore at her hair*
And how she gan hirselve to turmente
And how she lyth and swowneth° on the grounde   *collapses and swoons*
And how she wepe of teres ful his
          wounde,°   *tears (enough to fill) his wound*
How medeleth° she his blood with hir compleynte,   *mingles*
875   And with his blood hirselven gan she peynte,°   *painted herself*
How clippeth° she the dede cors,° allas!   *embraces / the dead body*
How doth this woful Tisbe in this cas!
How kisseth she his frosty mouth so cold!
"Who hath doon this, and who hath been so bold
880   To sleen my leef?° O spek, my Piramus!   *dear one*
I am thy Tisbe, that thee calleth thus."
And therwithal she lifteth up his heed.
          This woful man, that was nat fully deed,°   *completely dead*

6. Alas, that I did not arrive here at this place the length of time that it takes to travel a furlong (⅛ mile; i.e., a short time) before you did.
7. And like the waves her heart began to pound, and she grew as pale as the wood of the boxtree, and considering over a certain length of time, she began to understand that it was Pyramus, her dear heart.

Whan that he herde the name of Tisbe cryen,
885 On hir he caste his hevy deedly° eyen   *deathly*
And doun ageyn and yeldeth up the gost.°   *gives up the ghost (i.e., dies)*
   Tisbe rist° up, withouten noise or bost,°   *rises / boast (i.e., meekly)*
And saw hir wimpel and his empty shethe,°   *sheath*
And eek his swerd,° that him hath doon to dethe;   *also his sword*
890 Than spak she thus: "My woful hand," quod° she,   *said*
"Is strong ynough in swich a werk to me,°   *for me to achieve such a deed*
For love shal yeve° me strengthe and hardinesse°   *give / boldness*
To make my wounde large ynough,° I gesse.   *enough*
I wol thee folwen deed,° and I wol be   *follow you in death*
895 Felawe and cause eek° of thy deeth,"   *Both companion and cause of*
   quod she.
"And though that nothing save the° deeth only   *except*
Mighte thee fro° me departe° trewely,   *from / separate*
Thou shalt no more departe now fro me
Than fro the deeth, for I wol go with thee.
900   And now, ye wrecched jelous fadres oure,°   *jealous fathers of ours*
We, that weren whylom children youre,°   *once your children*
We preyen yow, withouten more envye,
That in o grave yfere° we moten° lye,   *together in one grave / may*
Sin° love hath brought us to this pitous°   *Since / piteous, lamentable*
   ende.
905 And rightwis° God to every lover sende,   *(that the) just, righteous*
That loveth trewely, more prosperitee
Than ever hadde Piramus and Tisbe,
And lat no gentil° woman hir assure°   *noble / take the chance*
To putten hir in swich an aventure.°   *in such jeopardy*
910 But God forbede but° a woman can   *forbid except that*
Been as trewe in loving as a man,
And, for my part, I shal anoon it kythe!"°   *demonstrate it at once*
And, with that worde, his swerd she took as swythe°   *immediately*
That warm was of hir loves blood and hoot,°   *hot*
915 And to the herte she hireselven smoot.°   *smote, stabbed*
   And thus are Tisbe and Piramus ago.°   *gone, passed away*
Of trewe men I finde but fewe mo°   *more*
In alle my bookes, save° this Piramus,   *except*
And therfor have I spoken of him thus,
920 For it is deyntee to° us men to finde   *a particular pleasure for*
A man that can in love be trewe and kinde.
Here may ye seen, what lover so he
   be,°   *whatever (kind of) lover he may be*
A woman dar and can as wel° as he.   *will hazard and achieve as much*

Explicit legenda Tesbe.[8]

8. Here ends the Legend of Thisbe.

The Legend of Dido

Incipit Legenda Didonis martiris, Cartaginis regine.[1]

Glory and honour, Virgil Mantoan,[2]
925 Be to thy name, and I shal as I can
Folow thy lantern, as thou gost biforn,°   *travel ahead (of me, in telling)*
How Eneas to Dido was forsworn.
In thyn Eneide° and Naso[3] wol I take   *Aeneid*
The tenour° and the greet effectes° make.   *focus, tone / main events*
930   Whan Troye brought was to destruccioun
By Grekes sleighte,° and namely° by Sinoun   *craft / chiefly*
Feyning° the hors offred unto Minerve,[4]   *Dissembling about*
Thurgh which that many a Troyan moste sterve,°   *Trojan must die*
And Ector[5] had after his deeth appered,°   *appeared*
935 And fyr so wood° it mighte nat be stered°   *fire so wild / controlled*
In al the noble tour of Ilioun,°   *tower of Ilium (Troy)*
That of the citee was the cheef dungeoun,°   *main keep, fortification*
And al the contree was so lowe y-brought,
And Priamus the king fordoon and
    nought,°   *killed and brought to nothing*
940 And Eneas was charged by Venus
To fleen away, he took Ascanius,
That was his sone, in his right hand and fledde;
And on his bak he bar° and with him ledde   *bore*
His olde fader cleped° Anchises,   *named*
945 And by the weye his wyf Creusa[6] he les.°   *lost*
And mochel sorwe° hadde he in his minde   *great sorrow*
Er° that he coude his felawshippe° finde. *Before / (Trojan) comrades*
But at the laste whan he had hem° founde   *them*
He made him redy in a certeyn stounde°   *length of time*
950 And to the see ful faste he gan him hye°   *hurried*
And saileth forth with al his companye
Toward Itaile, as wolde destinee.°   *destiny would (have it be)*
But of his aventures in the see
Nis nat to purpos° for to speke of here,   *Is not part of my plan*
955 For it acordeth nat° to my matere.   *is not relevant to*
But, as I seyde, of him and of Dido
Shal be my tale, til that I have do.°   *until I have finished*
    So longe he sailed in the salte see°   *salty sea*
Til in Libye° unnethe° aryved he   *Libya / with difficulty*
960 With shippes seven and with no more navye,

1. Here begins the Legend of Dido, martyr, Queen of Carthage.
2. Virgil, the author of the *Aeneid*, was from the city of Mantua. Virgil tells the story of Dido and Aeneas in *Aeneid* 1 and 4; relevant sections of his narration, taken from *Aeneid* 4, are included in the Contexts section of this Norton Critical Edition.
3. Ovid tells the story of Dido and Aeneas in the *Heroides* 7, in the form of a letter from Dido to Aeneas, which is included in the Contexts section of this Norton Critical Edition.
4. Sinon was the Greek trickster in the *Aeneid* who persuaded the Trojans that the giant wooden horse, which actually contained Greek warriors, was a gift for Minerva that would bring the Trojans great success in battle if brought within their city.
5. Prince of Troy, oldest son of King Priam.
6. Aeneas's mother was Venus, goddess of Love; his father was the mortal Anchises, his wife Creusa, and his son Ascanius.

And glad was he to londe for to hye,°   *speedily make his way*
So was he with the tempest al toshake.°   *all tossed about by the storm*
And whan that he the haven had y-take
He had a knight was called Achates,
965 And him of al his felawshippe he chees°   *he chose from all his comrades*
To goon with him the contree for
    t'espye;°   *to spy out, explore the country secretly*
He took with him no more companye.
But forth they goon and lafte his shippes ryde,°   *riding at anchor*
His fere° and he withouten any gyde.°   *companion / guide*
970 So longe he walketh in this wildernesse
Til at the laste he mette an hunteresse.
A bowe in honde and arwes° hadde she,   *arrows*
Hir clothes cutted were unto the knee,° *knee-length (to facilitate hunting)*
But she was yet the fairest creature
975 That ever was y-formed by nature,
And Eneas and Achates she grette,°   *greeted*
And thus she to hem spak° whan she hem mette: *spoke*
"Saw ye," quod° she, "as ye han walked wyde,° *said / walked widely about*
Any of my sustren° walke yow besyde   *sisters*
980 With any wilde boor or other beste°   *beast*
That they han hunted to° in this foreste,   *have been hunting*
Y-tukked up, with arwes in hir cas?"[7]
    "Nay, soothly,° lady," quod this Eneas,   *truly*
"But, by thy beautee, as it thinketh me,
985 Thou mightest never erthely womman be,[8]
But Phebus suster° artow,° as I   *Phoebus Apollo's sister (Diana) / you are*
    gesse.
And, if so be that thou be a goddesse,
Have mercy on our labour and our wo."
    "I nam no goddesse, soothly," quod she tho;°   *then*
990 "For maydens walken in this contree here°   *here in this country*
With arwes° and with bowe in this manere.   *arrows*
This is the regne of Libie ther ye bene,°   *where you are*
Of which that Dido lady° is and quene,"   *mistress*
And shortly° tolde him al the occasioun° *briefly / reasons, circumstances*
995 Why Dido com° into that regioun,   *came*
Of which as now me lusteth nat to ryme;
It nedeth nat, it nere but los of tyme.
For this is al and som, it was Venus,
His owne moder, that spak with him thus,[9]
1000 And to Cartage° she bad he sholde him dight° *Carthage / take himself*
And vanished anoon° out of his sight.   *at once*
I coude folwe° word for word, Virgyle,   *follow*
But it wolde lasten al too longe a whyle.°   *time*
    This noble quene that cleped was° Dido,   *was called*
1005 That whylom° was the wyf of Sitheo,[1]   *once*

7. With their skirts tucked up (and) with arrows in their quivers.
8. Judging from your beauty, I believe that you cannot be a mortal (earthly) woman.
9. About which I have no desire now to make rhymes. It's not necessary; it would be a waste of time, for this is the long and short of it: It was Venus, his own mother, who spoke thus with him.
1. Sichaeus, Dido's first husband, at this time deceased.

That fairer was than is the brighte sonne,

This noble toun of Cartage hath begonne,°   *founded*

In which she regneth in so greet honour

That she was holde of alle quenes

    flour°   *the flower (epitome) of all queens*

1010 Of gentilesse,° of freedom,° of beautee,   *nobility / generosity*

That wel° was him that mighte hir ones° see;   *fortunate / once*

Of kinges and of lordes so desyred

That al the world hir beautee hadde y-fyred,

She stood so wel in every wightes grace.[2]

1015   Whan Eneas was come unto that place,

Unto the maister° temple of al the toun   *chief*

Ther° Dido was in hir devocioun,   *where*

Ful prively° his wey than hath he nome.°   *All secretly / taken*

Whan he was in the large temple come—

1020 I can nat seyn if that it be possible,

But Venus hadde him maked invisible,

Thus seith the book, withouten any les°—   *lie*

And whan this Eneas and Achates

Hadden in this temple been overal,°   *gone everywhere*

1025 Than founde they depeynted° on a wal   *painted*

How Troye and al the lond° destroyed was.   *(Trojan) land*

"Allas, that I was born!" quod° Eneas,   *said*

"Thurghout the world our shame is kid so wyde,   *so widely known that*

Now it is peynted upon every side.°   *everywhere*

1030 We that weren in prosperitee

Been now disclaundred,° and in swich   *disgraced*

    degre°   *(held) of such (low) status*

No lenger for to liven I ne kepe!"°   *I do not care*

And with that worde he brast° out for to wepe   *burst*

So tendrely° that routhe° it was to sene.°   *movingly / a pity / to see*

1035 This fresshe° lady, of the citee quene,   *fresh, delightful*

Stood in the temple in hir estat royal,

So richely and eek° so fair withal,   *also*

So yong, so lusty,° with hir eyen glade,°   *lively / smiling eyes*

That if that God that heven and erthe made

1040 Wolde han° a love for beautee and goodnesse   *have*

And womanhede,° trouthe,° and   *femininity / constancy*

    seemlinesse,°   *loveliness*

Whom sholde he loven but this lady swete?

Ther nis no° womman to him half so mete.°   *is no / suitable*

   Fortune, that hath the world in governaunce,°   *rules over the world*

1045 Hath sodeinly° brought in so newe a chaunce,°   *suddenly / occurrence*

That never was ther yet° so fremde a cas,°   *before / strange a circumstance*

For al the companye of Eneas,

Which that he wende han loren° in the see,   *believed had been lost*

Aryved is nat fer fro° that citee,   *Has arrived not far from*

1050 For° which the grettest of his lordes some   *As a result of*

By aventure been° to the citee come,   *By chance are*

---

2. She was so desired by kings and lords that her beauty had ignited the whole world; she stood so highly in the esteem of all.

Unto that same temple for to seke°   *seek*
The quene, and of hir socour to beseke,°   *to beg her help*
Swich renoun° was ther spronge° of hir   *Such fame / there spread about*
    goodnesse.
1055 And, whan they hadden told al hir° distresse   *their*
And al hir tempest° and hir harde cas°   *storm / misfortunes*
Unto the quene appered Eneas
And openly beknew° that it was he.   *made it known*
Who hadde joye than but° his meynee°   *then except / group of men*
1060 That hadden founde hir° lord, hir governour?°   *their / leader*
    The quene saw they dide him swich° honour,   *such*
And had herd ofte of Eneas er tho,°   *before then*
And in hir herte she hadde routhe and wo°   *pity and woe*
That ever swich a noble man as he
1065 Shal been disherited° in swich degree,°   *disinherited / to such extent*
And saw the man, that he was lyk a knight°   *had a knightly appearance*
And suffisaunt of persone° and of might   *capable in body*
And lyk° to been a verray gentil° man,   *likely / a true noble*
And wel his wordes he besette° can,   *arrange*
1070 And had a noble visage° for the nones,°   *face / for the occasion*
And formed wel of braunes° and of bones.   *muscles*
For after° Venus hadde he swich fairnesse°   *taking after / such beauty*
That no man might be half so fair, I gesse,
And wel a lord° he seemed for to be.   *a perfect nobleman*
1075 And, for° he was a straunger, somwhat she   *because*
Lyked him the bet° as, God do bote,°   *better / God help us*
To som folk ofte newe thing is swote.°   *sweet*
Anoon° hir herte hath pitee of his wo,   *At once*
And with that pitee love com in also,
1080 And thus for pitee and for gentilesse°   *noble compassion*
Refresshed° moste he been of his distresse.   *Relieved*
She seyde certes° that she sory was   *certainly*
That he hath had swich peril and swich cas,°   *such (hard) luck*
And in hir frendly speche in this manere
1085 She to him spak and seyde as ye may here:°   *hear*
    "Be ye nat Venus sone and Anchises?°   *(the son of) Anchises*
In good feith, al the worship° and encrees°   *honor / advancement*
That I may goodly° doon yow, ye shul have.   *possibly*
Your shippes and your meynee° shal I save,"°   *men, retainers / protect*
1090 And many a gentil° word she spak him to,   *noble*
And comaunded hir messagers to go
The same day withouten any faile
His shippes for to seke° and hem vitaile.°   *seek / provision with food*
Ful many a beste° she to the shippes sente,   *beast (i.e., livestock for food)*
1095 And with the wyn° she gan hem to presente;°   *wine / presented them*
And to hir royal paleys° she hir spedde,   *palace*
And Eneas alwey with hir she ledde.
What nedeth yow the feste to descryve?°   *to describe the feast to you*
He never beter at ese° was his lyve.°   *more comfortable / life*
1100 Ful was the feste of deyntees° and richesse,°   *delicacies / opulence*
Of instruments, of song, and of gladnesse,

And many an amorous looking° and devys.°   *glance / scheme*
 This Eneas is come to Paradys
Out of the swolow° of helle, and thus in joye   *mouth*
1105 Remembreth him° of his estat° in Troye.   *recalls his / prosperity*
To dauncing chambres ful of parements,°   *decorations, tapestries*
Of riche beddes and of ornaments,
This Eneas is lad after the mete.°   *meal*
And with the quene whan that he had sete,
1110 And spices parted,° and the wyn agoon,°   *removed / taken away*
Unto his chambres was he lad anoon°   *at once*
To take his ese and for to have his reste
With al his folk, to doon what so hem leste.°   *whatever pleased them*
 Ther nas coursere° wel y-brydled   *was no mount*
  noon,°   *none with fine bridle*
1115 Ne stede° for the justing wel to goon,°   *steed / well fitted out for jousting*
Ne large palfrey° esy for the   *riding horse*
  nones,°   *comfortable for the occasion*
Ne juwel fretted° ful of riche stones,   *adorned*
Ne sakkes° ful of gold of large wight,°   *sacks, bags / great weight*
Ne ruby noon° that shynede by° night,   *Nor any ruby / shone by*
1120 Ne gentil hautein faucon heronere,°   *noble, proud, heron-hunting falcon*
Ne hound for hert° or wilde boor or dere,°   *to hunt the hart / deer*
Ne coupe° of gold with florins newe y-bete°   *cup / florins newly minted*
That in the lond of Libie° may be gete°   *Libya / may be acquired*
That Dido ne hath it Eneas y-sent,°   *has not sent it to Aeneas*
1125 And al is payed,° what that° he hath   *everything is paid for / whatever*
  spent.
 Thus can this honourable quene hir gestes calle°   *welcome her guests*
As she that can in freedom passen° alle.   *generosity surpass*
 Eneas soothly eek,° withouten les,°   *truly also / lie*
Hath sent unto° his shippe by° Achates   *a message to / by means of*
1130 After° his sone and after riche thinges,   *To call for*
Both sceptre, clothes, broches, and eek° ringes,   *brooches and also*
Som for to were,° and som for to presente°   *wear / give*
To hir that al these noble thinges him sente,
And bad his sone, how that he sholde make
1135 The presenting° and to the quene it take.   *The presentation (of gifts)*
 Repaired° is this Achates again,   *Returned*
And Eneas ful blisful is and fain°   *glad*
To seen his yonge sone Ascanius.
But natheles,° our auctour° telleth us   *nevertheless / author (Virgil)*
1140 That Cupido, that is the god of love,
At preyere° of his moder hye above   *At the request*
Hadde the lyknes° of the child y-take°   *the likeness, appearance / taken on*
This noble quene enamoured to make°   *to make fall in love*
On° Eneas; but, as of that scripture,°   *With / text*
1145 Be as be may,° I take of it no cure.°   *Be that as it may / heed*
But sooth° is this, the quene hath mad swich   *truth*
  chere°   *such friendly welcome*
Unto this child that wonder is to here;°   *marvelous to hear about*
And of the present° that his fader sente   *gifts*

She thanked him ful ofte° in good entente.° *over and over / in good faith*
1150 Thus is this quene in plesaunce° and in joye, *delight*
With al this newe lusty° folk of Troye. *high-spirited*
And of the dedes° hath she more enquered° *deeds / asked about*
Of Eneas, and al the story lered° *learned*
Of Troye; and al the longe day they tweye° *the two of them*
1155 Entendeden° to speken and to pleye, *made it their purpose*
Of° which ther gan to breden° swich a fyr° *From / to grow / fire*
That sely° Dido hath now swich° desyr *simple, guileless / such*
With Eneas, hir newe gest,° to dele,³ *guest*
That she hath lost hir hew and eek hir hele.° *hue and also her health*
1160 Now to th'effect,° now to the fruit of al *point*
Why I have told this story, and tellen
shal.° *shall continue to tell (more of it)*
Thus I beginne; it fil° upon a night *happened*
Whan that the mone upreysed had hir light,° *had raised up her light*
This noble quene unto hir reste wente.
1165 She syketh sore° and gan hirself *sighs sorely*
turmente;° *tormented herself*
She waketh, walweth,° maketh many a *tosses and turns*
brayde,° *sudden movement*
As doon these loveres, as I have herd sayde.° *heard it said*
And at the last unto hir suster Anne
She made hir moon,° and right thus° spak *moan, complaint / just so*
she thanne.
1170 "Now, dere suster myn,° what may it be *dear sister of mine*
That me agasteth° in my dreme?" quod° she. *terrifies / said*
"This ilke° Troyan is so in my thought *same*
For that me thinketh° he is so wel *Because it seems to me*
y-wrought,° *handsome*
And eek° so lykly for to be a man,° *also / manly*
1175 And therwithal° so mikel° good he can,° *furthermore / much / is able to do*
That al my love and lyf lyth in his cure.° *care*
Have ye nat herd him telle his aventure?° *account of his adventures*
Now certes,° Anne, if that ye rede° me, *certainly / advise*
I wolde fain° to him y-wedded be;° *gladly / be married*
1180 This is th'effect;° what sholde I more seye? *all there is to it*
In him lyth° al, to do me° live or deye."° *lies / make me / die*
Hir suster Anne, as she that coude hir
good,° *knew what was best for her*
Seyde as hir thoughte, and somdel it
withstood.° *argued against (the marriage) somewhat*
But herof° was so long a sermoning° *about this matter / discussion*
1185 It were° too long to make rehersing;° *would take / repeat (it all)*
But fynally it° may nat been withstonde;° *i.e., the wedding / blocked*
Love wol love, for no wight wol it wonde.° *person will restrain it*
The dawening uprist° out of the see;° *dawn rises / sea*
This amorous quene chargeth° hir meynee° *commands / her retinue*

---

3. Have to do with. (The verb "dele," which appears here and elsewhere in the legendary, is somewhat ambiguous in meaning, signifying among other things either general interactions or those with specific sexual content.)

1190 The nettes dresse,° and speres brode° and	*to prepare / broad-headed*
kene;°	*sharp*
An° hunting wol° this lusty fresshe° quene,	*Out / will go / lively vibrant*
So priketh hir° this newe joly wo.°	*spurs her on / jolly woe*
To hors is al hir lusty° folk y-go;°	*lively, vigorous / has gone*
Unto the court° the houndes been y-brought,	*courtyard*
1195 And upon coursers° swift as any thought	*spirited horses*
Hir yonge knightes hoven al aboute,°	*wait around in readiness*
And of hir women eek an huge route.°	*also a large company*
Upon a thikke palfrey,° paper whyte,	*sturdy riding horse*
With sadel rede,° enbrouded with delyte,°	*red / embroidered for delight*
1200 Of gold the barres up enbosed hye,°	*embossed with gold bars*
Sit Dido, al in gold and perre wrye,°	*covered in gold and precious stones*
And she is fair, as is the brighte morwe°	*morning*
That heleth seke° folk of nightes sorwe.°	*heals sick / the night's sorrow*
Upon a courser,° startling° as the fyr°—	*swift horse / leaping about / fire*
1205 Men mighte turne° him with a litel	*guide*
wyr°—	*wire (the horse is so responsive)*
Sit Eneas, lyk Phebus° to devyse;°	*Apollo / describe*
So was he fresshe arayed° in his wyse.°	*charmingly dressed / fashion*
The fomy° brydel with the bit of gold	*foamy*
Governeth° he, right as himself hath wold,°	*Controls / just as he wishes*
1210 And forth this noble quene thus lat I ryde°	*I leave to ride*
On hunting with this Troyan by hir syde.	
The herd of hertes° founden is anoon,°	*harts / is discovered at once*
With "Hay! Go bet! Prik thou! Lat goon, lat goon!	
Why nil the leoun comen or the bere	
1215 That I mighte ones mete him with this spere?"[4]	
Thus seyn these yonge folk, and up they kille	
These wilde hertes and han hem° at hir° wille.	*have them / their*
Among° al this to romblen gan the	*During*
heven,°	*the heavens began to rumble*
The thunder rored with a grisly steven;°	*horrible sound*
1220 Doun com the rain, with hail and sleet so faste,	
With hevenes fyr,° that it so sore agaste°	*i.e., lightning / sorely frightened*
This noble quene and also hir meynee,°	*retinue*
That ech of hem was glad awey to flee.	
And shortly,° fro° the tempest hir to save,°	*soon / from / to save herself*
1225 She fledde hirself into a litel cave,	
And with hir wente this Eneas also—	
I noot° with hem if ther wente any mo,°	*don't know / any others*
The auctour° maketh of it no mencioun—	*author (Virgil)*
And here began the depe affeccioun	
1230 Betwix hem two;° this was the firste	*between the two of them*
morwe°	*dawn, day*
Of hir° gladnesse, and ginning of hir	*their*
sorwe°	*the beginning of their sorrow.*
For ther hath Eneas y-kneled so	

---

4. These are the typical exclamations offered variously by those participating in the hunt: "Hey! Go Faster! Use your spurs! Let (the dogs) go! Let (the dogs) go! Why won't the lion or the bear come so that I can once meet him with this spear?"

And told hir al° his herte, and al his wo,   *everything (that was in)*
And sworn so depe° to hir to be trewe,   *solemnly*
1235 For wele or wo, and chaunge for no newe,[5]
And as a fals lover so wel can pleyne°   *complain, lament*
That sely° Dido rewed° on his peyne,   *simple, guileless / took pity on*
And took him for husbond and becom his wyf
For evermo,° whyl that hem laste lyf.°   *evermore / they both should live*
1240 And after this, whan that the tempest stente,°   *storm ceased*
With mirth out as they comen, hoom they wente.[6]
The wikked fame up roos,° and that anoon,°   *arose / immediately*
How Eneas hath with the quene y-goon
Into the cave; and demed as hem liste;°   *(people) thought as they liked*
1245 And whan the king that Yarbas[7] hight,° it wiste,°   *was called / knew*
As he that had hir loved ever his lyf,°   *loved her his whole life*
And wowed° hir to have hir to° his wyf,   *wooed / as*
Swich sorwe° as he hath maked and swich   *Such sorrow*
chere,°   *such expression (of grief)*
It is a routhe° and pitee for to here.°   *sadness / hear*
1250 But, as in love alday it happeth° so,   *happens*
That oon° shal laughen at anothers wo;   *one*
Now laugheth Eneas and is in joye
And more richesse° than ever he was in Troye.   *wealth, splendor*
O sely° women, ful of innocence,   *simple, guileless*
1255 Ful of pitee, of trouthe,° and conscience,°   *constancy / solicitude*
What maketh yow to° men to trusten so?   *in*
Have ye swich routhe° upon hir feined   *such pity*
wo,°   *their pretended woe*
And han swiche olde ensamples yow biforn?°   *before (your eyes)*
See ye nat alle how they been forsworn?
1260 Wher see ye oon, that he ne hath laft his leef,
Or been unkinde, or doon hir som mischeef,
Or piled hir, or bosted of his dede?
Ye may as wel it seen as ye may rede;[8]
Tak heed now of this grete gentilman,
1265 This Troyan, that so wel hir plesen can,
That feineth him° so trewe and obeising,° *Who pretends to be / obedient*
So gentil° and so privy of his doing,°   *noble / discreet*
And can so wel doon alle his obeisaunces,°   *pay (her) homage*
And waiten° hir at festes° and at daunces   *attend to / banquets*
1270 And whan she goth to temple and hoom ageyn,
And fasten° til he hath his lady seyn,°   *go without food / seen*
And bere in his devyses° for hir sake   *wear in his heraldic devices*
Noot I nat° what; and songes wolde he make,   *I know not*
Justen,° and doon of armes many thinges,°   *Joust / do deeds of arms*
1275 Sende hir lettres, tokens, broches, ringes—

---

5. For better or worse (literally "prosperity or woe"), and never to exchange her for a new love.
6. Just as they came out (at the beginning of the hunt) with mirth, so also do they return home.
7. In Virgil's *Aeneid*, Iarbas is the king of a neighboring land who has courted Dido for a long time without success.
8. Where do you see one who has not left his dear one, or been disloyal, or done some mischief to her, or robbed her, or boasted of his conquest? You may as easily see it (in life) as read about it (in books).

Now herkneth° how he shal his lady serve!° — *listen to / repay*
Theras he was in peril for to sterve° — *perish*
For° hunger and for mischeef in the see,° — *Because of / disaster at*
And desolat,° and fled° from his contree, — *abandoned / escaped*
1280 And al his folk with tempest al todriven,° — *storm driven about*
She hath hir body and eek hir reame° yiven° — *also her kingdom / given*
Into his hond, theras she mighte have been
Of other lond° than of Cartage a queen, — *lands*
And lived in joye ynough;[9] what wolde ye more?
1285   This Eneas, that hath so depe y-swore,° — *sworn (fidelity) so solemnly*
Is wery° of his craft° within a throwe;° — *weary / work / short time*
The hote ernest° is al overblowe.° — *ardent love / blown away*
And prively° he doth his shippes dighte° — *secretly / readies his ships*
And shapeth him° to stele awey by nighte. — *makes his plans*
1290   This Dido hath suspecioun of this
And thoughte wel that it was al amis,° — *all was not well*
For in his bedde he lyth anight and syketh;° — *lies at night and sighs*
She asketh him anoon,° what him mislyketh,° — *at once / is troubling him*
"My dere herte, which that I love most?"° — *whom I love most of all*
1295   "Certes,"° quod° he, "this night my fadres — *Certainly / said*
gost° — *father's spirit*
Hath in my slepe so sore° me tormented, — *grievously*
And eek° Mercurie his message hath presented — *also*
That nedes to the conquest of Itaile
My destinee is sone for to saile,
1300 For which me thinketh brosten is myn herte!"[1]
Therwith his false teres° out they sterte,° — *tears / burst*
And taketh hir within° his armes two. — *(he) takes her in*
"Is that in ernest?"° quod she; "wil ye so?° — *serious / will you do this*
Have ye nat sworn to wyfe me to take,° — *to make me (your) wife*
1305 Allas, what° womman wil ye of me make? — *what kind of*
I am a gentil° woman and a queen; — *noble*
Ye wil nat fro° your wyf thus foule fleen?° — *from / wickedly flee*
That I was born, allas! What shal I do?"
To telle in short,° this noble quene Dido, — *briefly*
1310 She seketh halwes° and doth sacrifyse; — *shrines*
She kneleth, cryeth, that routhe is to devyse,° — *is pitiable to describe*
Conjureth° him and profreth° him to be — *implores / offers*
His thral,° his servant in the leste gree;° — *slave / of the lowest standing*
She falleth him to foote° and swowneth° — *before him at his feet / swoons*
there
1315 Dischevele, with hir brighte gilte here,[2]
And seith, "Have mercy! Let me with yow ryde!
These lordes which that wonen me besyde° — *who live near me*
Wil me destroyen only for your sake.° — *because of you*

---

9. And lived in bounteous joy; what more is there to say? (Chaucer's sarcasm here is followed by the
revelation of Aeneas's failure to live up to his vows of love.)
1. That by necessity it is my destiny to sail soon to conquer Italy, for which reason I feel my heart is
broken! (In the *Aeneid*, Mercury is clearly presented as Jupiter's emissary who brings the message
from the god to Aeneas that he shirks his duty to found a kingdom in Italy for his descendants by
dallying with Dido.)
2. Her bright, golden hair hanging loose.

And so° ye wil me now to wyfe take°   *If / take me as your wife*
1320 As ye han sworn, than wol I yeve yow leve°   *grant you permission*
To sleen me with your swerd now sone at eve,°   *this very evening*
For than yet shal I dyen as your wyf.
I am with childe,° and yeve° my child his lyf.   *with child, pregnant / give*
Mercy, lord, have pitee in your thought!"
But al this thing availeth hir right
1325   nought,°   *does her no good*
For on a night sleping he let hir lye,
And stal° awey unto his companye,   *stole*
And as a traitour forth he gan to saile
Toward the large contree of Itaile.°   *Italy*
1330 Thus hath he laft Dido in wo and pyne;°   *pain*
And wedded ther a lady hight Lavyne.³
A cloth he lafte and eek° his swerd   *also*
      stonding°   *standing (propped) up*
Whan he fro° Dido stal in hir° sleping,   *from / stole as she was*
Right at hir beddes heed,° so gan he hye°   *bed's head / he rushed off*
1335 Whan that he stal awey to his navye,°   *navy, fleet of ships*
Which cloth, whan sely° Dido gan awake,°   *innocent / awakened*
She hath it kist° ful ofte° for his sake;   *kissed it / over and over*
And seyde, "O swete cloth, whyl Jupiter it leste,⁴
Tak now my soule, unbind me of this
      unreste!°   *release me from my troubles*
1340 I have fulfild° of Fortune⁵ al the cours."°   *completed / the entire circuit*
And thus, allas, withouten his socours,°   *comfort, aid*
Twenty tyme y-swowned° hath she thanne.°   *swooned / then*
And whan that she unto hir suster Anne
Compleyned° had, of which I may nat° wryte—   *Lamented / cannot*
1345 So greet a routhe° I have it for t'endyte°— *Such great pity / write about it*
And bad° hir norice° and hir suster goon°   *directed / nurse / to go*
To fecchen fyr° and other thing anoon,°   *To fetch fire / at once*
And seyde that she wolde sacrifye.°   *wished to offer a sacrifice*
And whan she mighte hir tyme wel espye,°   *find an opportunity*
1350 Upon the fyr of sacrifys° she sterte,°   *sacrificial fire / leapt*
And with his swerd she roof hir° to the herte.   *stabbed herself*
      But, as myn auctour° seith,⁶ right thus° she   *author, source / just so*
      seyde,
Er° she was hurt, bifore that she deyde,°   *Before / died*
She wroot a lettre anoon,° that thus began: *at once*
1355 "Right° so," quod° she, "as that the whyte swan   *Just / said*
Ageyns his deeth beginneth for to singe,⁷

---

3. Lavinia is Aeneas's future wife according to the *Aeneid*.
4. As long as it was pleasing to Jupiter (i.e., the cloth was sweet to her as long as the gods permitted her relationship with Aeneas to continue).
5. The reference is to the circling of Fortune's wheel, which casts down what it has previously raised up; see also the *Book of the Duchess* 618 note.
6. The author referred to here is Ovid, who presents the story, as indicated above, from Dido's point of view in his *Heroides* (see 928 note), even though previously in the legend Chaucer had used the term "auctour" for Virgil (see 1139, 1228).
7. At the approach of his death begins to sing. (The idea that the swan sings anticipating its own death is conventional. The image opens Dido's letter to Aeneas in Ovid's *Heroides* 7.1–4; see also "Anelida and Arcite" 346; the *Parliament of Fowls* 342.)

Right so to yow make I my compleyninge.°   *lament*
Nat that I trowe to geten yow again,°   *believe I will win you back*
For wel I wot° that it is al in vain,   *know*
1360 Sin that° the goddes been contraire° to me.   *Since / are opposed*
But sin my name° is lost thurgh yow," quod she,   *Since my reputation*
"I may wel lese° on yow a word or letter,   *may as well lose*
Al be it that° I shal be never the better,   *Even though*
For thilke° wind that blew your ship awey,   *that very*
1365 The same wind hath blowe awey your fey."°   *fidelity*
But who wol° al this letter have in minde   *whoever wishes to*
Rede Ovide,° and in him he shal it   *Read Ovid (i.e., in the* Heroides)
finde.

Explicit Legenda Didonis martiris, Cartaginis regine.[8]

The Legend of Hypsipyle and Medea

Incipt Legenda Ysiphile et Medee, Martirum.[1]

INTRODUCTION

Thou rote° of false lovers, Duk° Jasoun!   *root (source, origin) / Duke*
Thou sly devourer and confusioun°   *complete humiliation*
1370 Of gentil women, tendre creatures,
Thou madest thy reclaiming and thy lures
To ladies of thy statly apparaunce,
And of thy wordes farced with plesaunce,
And of thy feyned trouthe and thy manere,
1375 With thyn obeissaunce and thy humble chere,
And with thy countrefeted peyne and wo.[2]
Ther° other falsen oon,° thou falsest two!   *Where / one*
O, ofte swore thou that thou woldest dye
For love whan thou ne feltest maladye°   *felt no sickness at all*
1380 Save foul delyt,° which that thou callest love.   *Except filthy delight*
If that I live, thy name shal be shove°   *widely known, spread*
In Englissh that thy secte° shal be knowe.°   *sect, cult / known*
Have at thee, Jasoun! Now thyn horn is blowe![3]
But certes,° it is bothe routhe and wo°   *certainly / pitiable and sad*
1385 That love with false loveres werketh so,[4]
For they shal have wel better love and chere°   *reception, hospitality*
Than he that hath abought his love ful dere°   *paid dearly for, suffered for*
Or had in armes° many a blody box,°   *in battles / bloody blow*

---

8. Here ends the Legend of the martyr Dido, Queen of Carthage.
1. Here begins the Legend of Hypsipyle and Medea, martyrs.
2. With the attractive lure of your regal appearance, you captured ("reclaimed"—a metaphor taken from hawking) the ladies, also using your words, stuffed with flattery, your false loyalty, your submissiveness and humble manner, and your counterfeit pain and woe.
3. In these colloquialisms ("Have at thee! Your horn is blown!"), Chaucer indicates that Jason's true nature is being revealed. Editors have variously interpreted the horn allusion as either an echo from Dante's *Inferno* 19.5, where the deeds of criminals are publicly exposed, or an extension of the hunting metaphor; see the *Riverside Chaucer*, Explanatory Note, p. 1069.
4. That this is how love works for false lovers.

For ever as tendre a capoun et the fox
1390 Though he be fals and hath the foul betrayed
As shal the good-man that therfor hath payed.[5]
Al have he° to the capoun   *Although he (the good-man) has*
    skille° and right,   *just claim*
The false fox wol have his part at night.
On° Jasoun this ensample is wel y-sene°   *By / pattern is well illustrated*
1395 By Isiphile° and Medea the quene.   *Hypsipyle*

HYPSIPYLE

In Tessalye, as Guido telleth us,
Ther was a king that highte° Pelleus   *was called*
That had a brother, which that highte Eson,[6]
And, whan for age° he mighte unnethes   *because of old age*
    gon,°   *could scarcely walk*
1400 He yaf° to Pelleus the governing   *He (Eson) gave*
Of al his regne and made him lord and king.
Of which Eson this Jasoun geten° was,   *begotten (i.e., he was his son)*
That° in his tyme in al that lond ther nas°   *Such that / was*
Nat swich° a famous knight of gentilesse,°   *Nowhere such / nobility*
1405 Of freedom,° and of strengthe and lustinesse.°   *generosity / vigor*
After his fadres° deeth he bar him° so   *father's / conducted himself*
That ther was noon that liste been his fo°   *wished to be his foe*
But dide° him al honour and   *(all) paid*
    companye,°   *(sought his) companionship*
Of which this Pelleus hath greet envye,
1410 Imagining that Jasoun mighte be
Enhaunsed° so and put in swich degree°   *Elevated / such status*
With love of lordes of his regioun
That from his regne he may be put
    adoun.°   *he (Pelleus) might be overthrown*
And in his wit a-night compassed° he   *at night plotted*
1415 How Jasoun mighte best destroyed be
Withoute sclaunder of his compassement,°   *the slander of his collusion*
And at the laste he took avisement°   *decided*
To senden him into som fer contree°   *some distant land*
Ther as° this Jasoun may destroyed be.   *Where*
1420 This was his wit,° al° made he to Jasoun   *strategy / although*
Greet chere° of love and of affeccioun   *A great appearance*
For drede° lest his lordes it espyde.°   *fear / spy out, suspect (his deceit)*
So fil it,° so as fame renneth wyde,°   *it happened / spreads about widely*
Ther was swich tyding overal° and swich   *such news everywhere*
    los°   *rumor*
1425 That in an yle° that called was Colcos°   *island / Colchis (in the Black Sea)*

---

5. For, despite being false and having betrayed the bird, the fox eats capons (castrated male chickens) just as tender as those enjoyed by the householder who bought the bird.
6. Chaucer's chief sources for the stories of Hypsipyle and Medea are Guido delle Colonne, referenced in 1396 (*History of the Destruction of Troy* 1–3), and Ovid (*Metamorphoses* 7.1–403 and *Heroides* 6, 12). Chaucer's tale begins in Thessaly and sets up the background by introducing King Eson (more properly Aeson), Jason's father, and rival King Pelleus (Pelias), Jason's jealous uncle.

Beyonde Troye, estward° in the see,°   *eastward / sea*
That therin was a ram that men mighte see
That had a flees° of gold that shoon so brighte   *fleece*
That nowher was ther swich° another sighte;   *such*
1430 But it was kept alwey with° a dragoun,   *always guarded by*
And many othere mervails,° up and doun,   *marvels*
And with° two boles° maked al of bras   *by / bulls*
That spitten fyr,° and moche thing° ther was.   *fire / much else*
But this was eek° the tale, nathelees,°   *also / nevertheless*
1435 That whoso wolde° winne thilke° flees,   *whoever wishes to / this same*
He moste° bothe, er° he it winne mighte,   *must / before*
With the boles and the dragoun fighte;
And King Oetes° lord was of that yle.°   *Aeetes / island*
      This Pelleus bethoughte upon° this wyle,°   *came up with / subterfuge*
1440 That he his nevew° Jasoun wolde enhorte°   *nephew / exhort, encourage*
To sailen to that lond him to disporte,°   *to entertain himself*
And seyde, "Nevew, if it mighte be
That swich a worship° mighte fallen° thee   *such an honor / fall to*
That thou this famous tresor mightest winne
1445 And bringen it my regioun withinne,°   *back to my kingdom*
It were to° me greet plesaunce° and honour;   *would cause / delight*
Than were I holde to quyte° thy labour,   *I would be bound to repay*
And al the cost° I wol myselven make;°   *expense / take care of, pay*
And chees° what folk that thou wilt with thee take.   *(You) choose*
1450 Lat see now, darstow° taken this viage?"°   *do you dare to / expedition*
Jasoun was yong, and lusty of corage,°   *eager at heart*
And undertook to doon this ilke empryse.°   *this same enterprise, task*
      Anoon° Argus his shippes gan devyse;°   *At once / began to make ready*
With Jasoun wente the stronge Ercules°   *Hercules*
1455 And many another that he with him ches.°   *chose to go*
But whoso axeth° who is with him gon,   *whoever asks*
Lat him go reden Argonauticon,[7]
For he wol telle a tale long ynough.°   *enough*
Philotetes anoon° the sail up   *Philoctetes straightway*
      drough,°   *drew up, pulled up*
1460 Whan that the wind was good, and gan him hye°   *hasten*
Out of his contree called Tessalye.°   *Thessaly*
So long he sailed in the salte see°   *salty sea*
Til in the yle of Lemnon[8] aryved° he—   *arrived*
Al be this nat rehersed of Guido,
1465 Yet seith Ovide in his Epistles so[9]—
And of this yle° lady was and quene°   *island / the mistress and queen was*
The faire yonge Isiphilee the shene°   *the bright*
That whylom Thoas doughter was, the king.[1]
Isipilee was goon in hir pleying,°   *for recreation*

---

7. The *Argonautica* by Valerius Flaccus. The builder of Jason's ship was Argus (see 1453), the ship itself was named the "Argo," and its occupants called the "Argonauts." Although Hercules was an Argonaut, his role here in the courtship of Hypsipyle is original to Chaucer. The ship's pilot, Philoctetes (1459), is taken from Guido delle Colonne; see 1398 note.
8. Lemnos is a Greek island in the eastern Aegean Sea.
9. Athough Guido (delle Colonne) does not narrate this part of the story, Ovid tells it in his *Heroides*.
1. Who was the daughter of the former king, Thoas.

1470 And, roming° on the clyves by the see,°   *roaming / cliffs by the sea*
Under a banke anoon espyed° she   *suddenly noticed*
Wher that the ship of Jasoun gan aryve.°   *arrived*
Of hir goodnesse adoun she sendeth
    blyve°   *quickly sends (a messenger) down*
To witen if that any straunge wight
1475 With tempest thider were y-blowe a-night,
To doon him socour, as was hir usaunce
To forthren every wight, and doon plesaunce
Of verray bountee and of curtesye.²
    This messagere adoun him gan to hye,°   *hurried*
1480 And fond° Jasoun and Ercules also   *found*
That in a cogge° to londe were y-go°   *small boat / had come*
Hem° to refresshen and to take the eyr.°   *Themselves / air*
The morwening atempre was° and fair,   *morning was mild, temperate*
And in his wey the messagere hem mette.
1485 Ful cunningly° these lordes two he grette°   *knowledgeably / greeted*
And dide° his message, axing° hem anoon°   *delivered / asking / at once*
If they were broken° or ought wo   *had suffered damage*
    begoon,°   *any distress*
Or hadde nede of lodesmen° or vitaile,°   *pilot / provisions*
For of socour° they shulde nothing faile,   *assistance*
1490 For it was utterly the quenes wille.°   *i.e., that help should be offered*
    Jasoun answerde mekely and stille,°   *meekly and quietly*
"My lady," quod° he, "thanke I hertely°   *said / heartily*
Of hir° goodnesse; us nedeth trewely   *For her*
Nothing as now, but that we wery be°   *except that we are weary*
1495 And come for to pleye° out of the see   *relax*
Til that the wind be better in our
    weye."°   *is more favorable for our journey*
    This lady rometh by the clif to pleye
With hir meynee,° endelong the   *her household*
    stronde,°   *all along the shore*
And fynt° this Jasoun and this other stonde°   *finds / standing*
1500 In spekinge of° this thing, as I yow tolde.   *conversation about*
    This Ercules and Jasoun gan beholde
How that the quene it was, and faire hir grette°   *charmingly greeted her*
Anonright° as they with this lady mette,   *Straightaway*
And she took heed, and knew by hir° manere,   *their*
1505 By hir aray,° by wordes and by chere,°   *their clothing / their demeanor*
That it were gentilmen of greet degree.°   *high status*
And to the castel with hir ledeth she
These straunge° folk and doth hem greet honour,   *unknown, foreign*
And axeth hem of travail° and labour   *asks them about the hardship*
1510 That they han suffred in the salte see;°   *salty sea*
So that, within a day or two or three,
She knew by° folk that in his shippes be   *from*
That it was Jasoun, ful of renomee,°   *Jason, of great renown,*

---

2. To find out if any foreigner had been blown off course there by storm in the night, so that she might give him aid, as it was her custom to further every person, and, motivated by true generosity and courtesy, to give pleasure to all.

And Ercules,° that had the grete los,°   *Hercules / reputation*
1515 That soughten° the aventures of Colcos;   *Who were the ones seeking*
And dide hem honour° more than bifore,   *honored them*
And with hem deled ever lenger the more,
For they been worthy folk, withouten les.³
And namely° most she spak° with Ercules;   *especially / spoke*
1520 To him hir herte bar° he sholde be   *lays bare that*
Sad, wys,° and trewe, of wordes avisee,°   *steadfast, wise / discreet*
Withouten any other affeccioun°   *feeling*
Of love or evil imaginacioun.°   *false fancy*
   This Ercules hath so this Jasoun preysed°   *praised*
1525 That to the sonne° he hath him up areysed,°   *sun / raised up*
That half so trewe a man ther nas of love
Under the cope of heven that is above,⁴
And he was wys, hardy, secree,° and riche—   *brave, trustworthy*
Of° these three pointes° ther nas noon him   *In / qualities*
   liche.°   *to equal him*
1530 Of freedom passed he,° and lustihede,°   *In generosity he surpassed / vigor*
Alle tho° that liven or been dede;°   *those / are dead*
Therto° so greet a gentilman was he   *In addition*
And of Tessalie lykly° king to be.   *Thessaly likely*
Ther nas no lak but° that he was agast°   *flaw except / afraid*
1535 To love, and for to speke shamefast.°   *bashful*
He hadde lever° himself to mordre° and dye   *would rather / murder*
Than that men shulde a lover him espye:°   *discover him to be*
"As wolde God that I hadde y-yive
My blood and flesh, so that I mighte live,
1540 With the nones that he hadde owher a wyf
For his estat; for swich a lusty lyf
She sholde lede with this lusty knight!"⁵
   And al this was compassed° on   *had all been planned (in advance)*
   the night
Betwixe him Jasoun and this Ercules.
1545 Of° these two here was mad a shrewed les°   *By / wicked lie*
To come to hous upon an innocent.⁶
For to bedote° this quene was hir assent.°   *dupe / their agreement*
And Jasoun is as coy as is a mayde;°   *timid, demure as a maiden*
He looketh pitously,° but nought° he sayde,   *looks woeful / nothing*
1550 But frely yaf° he to hir conseileres°   *gave liberally, abundantly / counselors*
Yiftes° greet, and to hir officeres.   *gifts*
As wolde God I leiser hadde° and tyme   *had the leisure*
By proces° al his wowing° for to ryme.   *Step by step / wooing, courtship*
But in this hous° if any fals lover be,   *i.e., among my audience*
1555 Right as himself now doth,° right so dide he,   *Just as he now behaves*

---

3. And she had more and more to do with them, the longer they were together, for they were worthy folk, it is no lie. (For the ambiguity of the verb "dele," see the note to 1158.)
4. (Saying that) there is not half so true a man (as Jason) anywhere under the canopy of heaven above.
5. God willing, I would give my flesh and blood, providing I'd live through the experience, if only he (Jason) could find a wife somewhere suitable to his position; for such a joyful life she would lead with this vigorous knight!
6. In order to seduce an innocent woman.

With feyning° and with every sotil dede.°	*pretense / subtle, crafty deed*
Ye gete no more of me but ye wil rede	
Th'original that telleth al the cas.[7]	
The somme° is this: that Jasoun wedded was	*sum, upshot*
1560	Unto this quene and took of hir substaunce°	*wealth*
What so him liste° unto his	*Whatever he pleased*
purveyaunce,°	*for his own support*
And upon hir begat he children two,	
And drow° his sail and saw hir never	*hoisted up*
mo.°	*never saw her again*
A lettre sente she to him certeyn,°	*certainly*
1565	Which were too long to wryten and to seyn,°	*say*
And him repreveth of° his greet untrouthe,	*reproves him for*
And preyeth him on hir to have som routhe.°	*pity*
And of his children two, she seyde him this:	
That they be lyke of alle thing ywis	
1570	To Jasoun, save they coude nat begyle,[8]	
And preyed God, er it were longe whyle°	*that before long*
That she[9] that had his herte y-raft hir fro°	*stolen from her*
Moste° finden him to hir untrewe also,	*Might*
And that she moste bothe hir children spille,°	*kill*
1575	And alle tho that suffreth° him his wille.	*those who permit him to do*
And trew to Jasoun was she al hir lyf,	
And ever kepte hir chast as for° his wyf;	*chaste as befits*
Ne never had she joye at hir herte,	
But dyed for his love of sorwes smerte.°	*painful sorrow*

MEDEA

1580	To Colcos° comen is this duk° Jasoun,	*Colchis / duke*
That is of love devourer and dragoun.	
As matere appetyteth forme alwey	
And from forme into forme it passen may,	
Or as a welle that were botomlees,[1]	
1585	Right° so can fals Jasoun have no pees°	*Just / peace*
For to desyren thurgh his appetyt	
To doon with gentil women° his delyt;	*To take with noble women*
This is his lust° and his felicitee.°	*desire / absolute happiness*
Jasoun is romed forth to the citee	
1590	That whylom cleped was Jaconitos,°	*once was called Jaconites*
That was the maister toun° of al Colcos,	*principal town*
And hath y-told the cause of° his coming	*reason for*

---

7. You won't get any more (about the wooing) from me, but you can read about it in my source, which gives all the details.
8. And about his two children, she had this to say: that they were similar in all ways to Jason, except in being without guile.
9. I.e., Medea, whose story Chaucer tells next. This is Chaucer's only allusion in the legendary to Medea's murder of her own children as punishment for Jason's infidelity, as Medea's own story breaks off before that event.
1. Just as matter always desires form, and may pass from form to form, or like a bottomless well. (I.e., Fickle Jason's object of desire is constantly changing, and his lust has no end. The technical comparison of sexual desire to matter's appetite for form is taken from Chaucer's source, Guido delle Colonne [see above, 1398 note]; in Guido, however, the gender roles are reversed, making matter female.)

Unto Oetes,° of that contree king, *Aeetes*
Preying him that he moste doon his assay° *might make an attempt*
1595 To gete the flees° of gold if that he may, *fleece*
Of which the king assenteth to his bone° *request*
And doth him honour, as it is to done,° *is customary*
So ferforth° that his doughter and his eyr,° *To such an extent / heir*
Medea, which that° was so wys° and fair *who / clever, knowledgeable*
1600 That fairer saw ther never man with eye,
He made hir doon to° Jasoun companye *caused her to keep*
At mete,° and sitte by him in the halle.° *dinner / (dining) hall*
  Now was Jasoun a semely man withalle,° *very handsome man*
And lyk a lord,° and had a greet renoun,° *lordly / famous*
1605 And of his look as real as a leoun,° *regal as a lion*
And goodly° of his speche, and famulere,° *gracious / friendly*
And coude° of love al craft and art plenere° *knew / completely*
Withoute book, with everich observaunce.° *down to every fine point*
And as Fortune hir oughte a foul mischaunce,[2]
1610 She wex enamoured upon° this man *fell in love with*
"Jasoun," quod she, "for ought I see or can
As of this thing the which ye been aboute,
Ye han yourself y-put in moche doute.[3]
For whoso wol° this aventure acheve, *whoever will*
1615 He may nat wel asterten,° as I leve,° *escape / believe*
Withouten deeth but I his helpe be.° *unless I am his helper*
But natheles° it is my wille," quod° she, *nonetheless / said*
"To forthren° yow so that ye shul nat dye, *assist*
But turnen sound hoom° to your Tessalye."° *turn home safely / Thessaly*
1620 "My righte° lady," quod this Jasoun tho,° *own true / then*
"That ye han° of my deeth or of my wo *have*
Any reward,° and doon me this honour, *regard*
I wot wel that° my might ne my labour *know well that neither*
May nat deserve it in my lyves day;° *throughout my life*
1625 God thanke yow ther I ne can ne may.[4]
Your man am I, and lowly° yow beseche *humbly*
To been my help withoute more speche;
But certes for my deeth shal I nat spare."[5]
  Tho gan° this Medea to him declare *Then began*
1630 The peril of this cas fro° point to point, *from*
And of his bataile and in what disjoint
He mote stonde, of which no creature,
Save only she, ne mighte his lyf assure.[6]
And shortly° to the point right° for to go, *quickly / straight*
1635 They been acorded ful° betwix hem two° *fully agreed / the two of them*
That Jasoun shal hir wedde as trewe knight,

2. And as Fortune owed her a piece of bad luck. (For this idiom, cp. above, 589 and note.)
3. "Jason," said she, "for all that I can see and know concerning this enterprise that you have undertaken, you have put yourself in great jeopardy."
4. I. e., God give you the thanks you deserve which is beyond what I can offer.
5. But certainly even to the death, I shall not hold back (in this adventure).
6. And of his battle and what difficulties he must face, from which no other being could save his life, except only for her.

And term y-set to come sone at night[7]
Unto hir chambre and make ther his ooth°   oath
Upon the goddes that he for leef ne looth°   for better or worse
1640 Ne sholde hir never falsen° night ne day,   would never betray her
To been hir husbond whyl he liven may
As she that from this deeth him saved here.
And hereupon° at night they mette yfere,°   to this end / together
And doth his ooth,° and goth with hir to bedde.   he makes his oath
1645 And on the morwe° upward he him spedde,   morning
For she hath taught him how he shal nat faile
The flees° to winne and stinten his bataile,°   fleece / end his battle
And gat him name° right as a conquerour   earned him a reputation
1650 Right thurgh the sleight° of hir enchantment.   subtlety
     Now hath Jasoun the flees,° and hoom is went° fleece / has gone home
With Medea and tresor ful greet woon.°   great abundance of treasure
But unwist° of hir fader is she goon   unknown
To Tessaly with Duk Jasoun hir leef,°   dear one
1655 That afterward hath brought hir to mischeef.°   misfortune
For as a traitour he is from hir go,°   gone
And with hir lafte° his yonge children two,   left
And falsly hath betrayed hir, allas!
And ever in love a cheef° traitour he was,   preeminent, the worst
1660 And wedded yet the thridde° wyf anon°   a third / quite soon
That was the doughter of the king Creon.[8]
     This is the meed of° loving and guerdon°   payment for / the reward
That Medea receyved of° Jasoun   from
Right° for hir trouthe and for hir kindenesse,   Just so (an intensifier)
1665 That° loved him better than hirself, I gesse,   She who
And lafte hir fader and hir heritage.°   inheritance
And of Jasoun this is the vassalage°   noble distinction
That in his dayes nas ther° noon   there was not
     y-founde°   anywhere found
So fals a lover going on the grounde°   i.e., alive
1670 And therfor in hir lettre thus she seyde
First, whan she of his falsnesse him umbreyde:°   reproached
"Why lyked me° thy yelow heer to see   did it please me
More than the boundes° of myn honestee,°   restraints / chastity
Why lyked° me thy youthe and thy fairnesse   pleased
1675 And of thy tonge° the infinit graciousnesse?°   speech / endless allure
O, haddest thou in thy conquest deed y-be,
Ful mikel untrouthe had ther dyed with thee!"[9]
     Wel can Ovide hir lettre in vers endyte,°   compose
Which were° as now too long for me to wryte.   would be

Explicit Legenda Ysiphile et Medee, Martirum.[1]

---

7. And they appointed a specific time (for him) to come in the early night.
8. Jason's third wife was Creon's daughter Creusa, according to Ovid's *Heroides* 12, Chaucer's chief source for the last twenty-five lines of this legend.
9. Oh, if only you had been killed (instead of winning) battle-victory, a great deal of falseness would have died there with you.
1. Here ends the Legend of Hypsipyle and Medea, martyrs.

The Legend of Lucrece

Incipit Legenda Lucrecie Rome, martiris.[1]

1680	Now mot I seyn° the exiling of kinges	*must I speak about*
	Of Rome, for hir horrible doinges,°	*their horrible deeds*
	And of the laste king Tarquinius,	
	As seyth Ovyde and Titus Livius.[2]	
	But for that cause° telle I nat this storye,	*reason*
1685	But for to preise and drawen to memorye°	*commemorate*
	The verray° wyf, the verray trewe° Lucresse,	*faithful / absolutely faithful*
	That for hir wyfhood and hir stedfastnesse	
	Nat only that these payens hir comende°	*pagans praised her*
	But he, that cleped is in our legende	
1690	The greet Austin, hath greet compassioun	
	Of this Lucresse that starf at Rome toun;[3]	
	And in what wyse° I wol but shortly° trete,	*manner (she died) / briefly*
	And of this thing I touche but the grete.°	*touch only on the main (events)*
	Whan Ardea beseged was aboute	
1695	With Romains that ful sterne were and stoute,[4]	
	Ful longe lay the sege and litel wroughte,°	*accomplished little*
	So that they were half ydel as hem thoughte;°	*idle as it seemed to them*
	And in his pley Tarquinius the yonge[5]	
	Gan for to jape,° for he was light of	*joke around*
	tonge,°	*foolish in speaking*
1700	And seyde that "it was an ydel lyf;	
	No man did ther no more° than his wyf;	*there accomplished any more*
	And lat us speke of wyves, that is best;	
	Praise every man his owne as him lest,°	*pleases him*
	And with our speche lat us ese our	
	herte."°	*ease our hearts, raise our spirits*
1705	A knight that highte° Colatyne up sterte°	*was named / jumped*
	And seyde thus: "Nay, sir, it is no nede°	*not necessary*
	To trowen° on the word but on the dede.°	*trust / deed*
	I have a wyf," quod° he, "that, as I trowe,°	*said / believe*
	Is holden good of alle that ever hir knowe; [6]	
1710	Go we° tonight to Rome, and we shal see."	*Let's go*
	Tarquinius answerde, "That lyketh° me."	*pleases*
	To Rome be they come and faste hem dighte°	*quickly made their way*

1. Here begins the Legend of Lucretia of Rome, martyr.
2. While Chaucer cites two sources for his legend of Lucrece, Titus Livius's *Ab urbe condita* (i.e., Livy's *History of Rome*) and Ovid (from the *Fasti* 2.685–852), there are few signs that he actually used Livy in this tale; details not taken from Ovid could have come from other sources, such as the *Romance of the Rose*. Sextus Tarquinius, also mentioned here, was the son of the last Roman king, Tarquinius Superbus, and the cousin of Lucrece's husband, Colatyn (L. Collatinus), introduced later in 1705.
3. But he, who is called the great Augustine in our saints' lives has great compassion for this Lucrece who died in Rome. (Saint Augustine discusses the case of Lucretia in *The City of God* 1.19, where he indeed displays enormous sympathy for her plight but ultimately condemns her as a suicide.)
4. When Ardea was entirely besieged by Romans, who were very fierce and bold. (Ardea was a wealthy city south of Rome under the control of the Rutulians.)
5. The appellation "the young" distinguishes this Tarquinius from his father Tarquinius Superbus, the king.
6. Is considered virtuous by all who have ever known her.

To Colatynes hous and doun they lighte,° *dismounted*
Tarquinius and eek° this Colatyne. *also*
1715 The husbond knew the estres° wel and *layout of the house*
fyne,° *perfectly*
And prively° into the hous they goon;° *secretly / go*
Nor at the gate porter was ther noon,° *was there any porter*
And at the chambre-dore° they abyde.° *chamber (bedroom) door / wait*
This noble wyf sat by hir beddes syde
1720 Dischevele, for no malice she ne thoughte.
And softe wolle our book seith that she wroughte[7]
To kepen hir fro slouthe° and ydelnesse, *from sloth*
And bad° hir servants doon hir *requested*
besynesse° *attend to their tasks*
And axeth hem,° "What tydings° heren ye? *asks them / news*
1725 How seith men of° the sege, how shal it be? *What are men saying about*
God wolde° the walles weren° falle adoun; *I wish to God / would*
Myn husbond is so longe out of this toun
For which the drede doth me so to smerte;
Right as a swerd it stingeth to myn herte
1730 Whan I think on the sege or of that place;
God save my lord, I preye him for his grace!" [8]
And therwithal ful tenderly° she wepe, *sorrowfully*
And of° hir werk she took no more kepe,° *to / paid no more attention*
But mekely she lete hir eyen falle,
1735 And thilke semblant° sat hir wel withalle.° *that same appearace / indeed*
And eek° hir teres ful of honestee° *also / purity*
Embelisshed hir wyfly chastitee;
Hir countenaunce° is to hir herte digne,° *outer bearing / befits her heart*
For they acorde° bothe in dede and signe.° *agree / gesture*
1740 And with that word hir husbond Colatyn,
Er° she of him was war,° com sterting° in *Before / aware / bounding*
And seyde, "Drede° thee nought, for I am here!" *Fear*
And she anoon up roos° with blisful chere° *rose up at once / expression*
And kiste him as of wyves is the wone.° *the way of wives*
1745 Tarquinius, this proude kinges sone,
Conceived° hath hir beautee and hir chere, *Observed*
Her yelow heer, hir shap,° and manere, *figure*
Her hew,° hir wordes that she hath compleyned, *complexion*
And by no crafte hir beautee nas nat feyned;
1750 And caughte to this lady swich desyr
That in his herte brende as any fyr
So woodly, that his wit was al forgeten.[9]
For wel, thoughte he, she wolde nat be geten.° *won*
And ay the more° that he was in dispair° *the more and more / despair*

7. This noble wife sat at the side of her bed with hair unbound, for she expected no wickedness (to be done to her), and our book (i.e., Chaucer's source) says that she spun soft wool.
8. My husband has been so long out of town, and therefore fear brings me such pain that it is as if a sword were piercing my heart when I think about the siege or about that place (i.e., Ardea); I pray God of his grace (that he might) save my lord (i.e., Colatyn).
9. And her beauty was not improved by art (e.g., cosmetics). And he was taken by such desire for this lady that in his heart something like a fire burned so madly that he forgot all reason.

1755 The more he coveteth and thoughte hir fair.
His blinde lust was al his covetinge.[1]
   A-morwe,° whan the brid began to singe,   *In the morning*
Unto the sege° he comth ful prively,°   *siege / very discreetly*
And by himself he walketh soberly,°   *solemnly*
1760 Th'image of hir recording alwey newe:[2]
"Thus lay hir heer, and thus fressh was hir hewe;°   *complexion*
Thus sat,° thus spak, thus span; this was hir   *Thus she sat*
   chere,°   *her expression*
Thus fair she was, and this was hir manere."
Al this conceit° his herte hath now y-take.°   *notion / taken*
1765 And as the see with tempest al toshake,°   *storm tossed, agitated*
That after° whan the storm is al ago,°   *So that afterwards / gone*
Yet wol° the water quappe° a day or two,   *Still will / pound, heave*
Right so though that° hir forme wer absent   *Just so even though*
The plesaunce° of hir forme was present.   *pleasure*
1770 But natheles° nat plesaunce but delyt,° *nonetheless / sensuous delight*
Or an unrightful talent with despyt—
"For, maugre hir, she shal my lemman be;
Hap helpeth hardy man alday," quod° he;   *said*
"What ende that I make, it shal be so;"[3]
1775 And girt° him with his swerde and gan to go,° *he girded, fastened / went*
And forth he rit til° he to Rome is come,   *rides until*
And al aloon his wey than hath he nome.°   *taken*
Unto the hous of Colatyn ful right.°   *straightaway*
Doun was the sonne, and day hath lost his light,
1780 And in he com unto a privy halke,°   *secluded corner*
And in the night ful theefly gan he stalke° *he stalked stealthily*
Whan every wight° was to his reste brought, *living creature, person*
Ne no wight had° of tresoun swich° a *Nor did anyone have / such*
   thought
Were it by window or by other gin,°   *contrivance*
1785 With swerde y-drawe shortly° he comth in *sword drawn quickly*
Ther as° she lay, this noble wyf Lucresse.   *Where*
And, as she wook,° hir bed she felte presse.° *woke / being pressed*
"What beste° is that," quod she, "that weyeth° *beast / weighs*
   thus?"
"I am the kinges sone, Tarquinius,"
1790 Quod he, "but and° thou crye, or noise make,   *and if*
Or if thou any creature awake,
By thilke° God that formed man on lyve,° *that same / gave man life*
This swerd thurghout thyn herte shal I ryve."°   *stab*
And therwithal° unto hir throte he sterte° *with that / seized her throat*
1795 And sette the point al sharp upon hir herte.
No word she spak,° she hath no might° therto. *spoke / strength*
What shal she sayn? Hir wit° is al ago.° *presence of mind / gone*

---

1. I.e., his coveting of Lucrece is entirely motivated by and converted into blind lust.
2. Remembering her image over and over.
3. Or an unlawful desire motivated by malice. "For whatever she wishes, she shall be my lover; luck always helps the bold man," said he. "Whatever the result of my act, it shall be so." (The last sentence, though the pronoun "it" is ambiguous, shows Tarquin's resolve to go forward regardless of the consequences.)

Right as a wolf that fynt a lomb aloon,° *finds a lamb alone*
To whom shal she compleyne or make moon?° *accusation*
1800 What, shal she fighte° with an hardy° *struggle / (such a) powerful*
knight?
Wel wot° men that a woman hath no might. *know*
What, shal she crye,° or how shal she asterte° *cry out / escape*
That hath hir° by the throte with swerde at *From one who has her*
herte?
She axeth grace° and seith° al that she can. *asks for mercy / says*
1805 "Ne wolt thou nat," quod he, this cruel man,
"As wisly Jupiter my soule save,[4]
As I shal in the stable slee thy knave,° *slay your stableboy, servant*
And leye him in thy bed and loude crye° *cry out*
That I thee finde in swich avouterye;° *such adultery*
1810 And thus thou shalt be deed° and also lese° *dead / lose*
Thy name,° for thou shalt noon other *reputation*
chese."° *have no other choice*
These Romain wyves loveden so hir name
At thilke° tyme and dredden° so the shame *that / feared*
That, what for fere of sclaunder° and drede of deeth, *fear of slander*
1815 She loste bothe at ones wit° and breeth,° *at once consciousness / breath*
And in a swough° she lay and wex so deed° *swoon / grew so death-like*
Men mighte smyten of° hir arm or heed;° *strike off / head*
She feleth nothing, neither foul ne fair.
Tarquinius that art a kinges eyr° *heir*
1820 And sholdest as by linage° and by right° *lineage, ancestry / uprightness*
Doon as a lord and as a verray° knight, *true*
Why hastow doon dispyt° to chivalrye? *have you done (an) outrage*
Why hastow doon this lady vilanye?° *dishonor*
Allas, of thee this was a vileins dede!° *disgraceful deed*
1825 But now to purpos:° in the story I rede, *the main point*
Whan he was goon and this mischaunce is
falle,° *misfortune has befallen*
This lady sente after hir frendes alle,
Fader, moder,° husbond, al yfere;° *Father, mother / together*
And al dischevele with hir heres clere
1830 In habit swich as women used tho
Unto the burying of hir frendes go,[5]
She sit in halle with a sorweful sighte.° *sorrowful, despairing look*
Hir frendes axen° what hir ailen mighte° *ask / is troubling her*
And who was deed?° And she sit ay° wepinge, *dead / always*
1835 A word for shame ne may she forth out bringe,
Ne upon hem she durste nat beholde.
But atte laste of Tarquiny she hem tolde,[6]

---

4. "No, you will not (have that mercy)," said he, this cruel man, "as surely as Jupiter may save my soul." (Such oaths to pagan gods are common in Chaucer and help him set the scene before Christianity, even as he may allude to a monotheistic Christian God as well in the same text [e.g., 1792 above].)
5. And with her bright hair all unbound, in such attire as women then wore to go to the burials of their friends.
6. For shame, she cannot bring forth a word, nor dared she (even) to look at them, but at last, she told them about Tarquin.

This rewful° cas and al this thing horrible. — *pitiable*
The wo to tellen° it were impossible, — *To recount the woe*
1840 That she and alle hir frendes made atones.° — *together*
Al° hadde folkes hertes been of stones, — *Although*
It mighte have maked hem upon hir rewe,° — *them take pity on her*
Hir herte was so wyfly and so trewe.
She seyde that, for hir gilt ne for hir blame,
1845 Hir husbond sholde nat have the foule name,
That wolde she nat suffre by no wey.[7]
And they answerden alle° upon hir fey° — *all answered / their faith*
That they foryeve it° hir, for it was right;° — *forgave / only just*
It was no gilt,° it lay nat in hir might,° — *guilt / power*
1850 And seyden hir ensamples° many oon.° — *gave her precedents / many a one*
But al for nought; for thus she seyde anoon:° — *right back*
"Be as be may," quod she, "of forgiving;
I wol nat have no forgift for nothing."[8]
But prively° she caughte° forth a knyf, — *secretly / brought*
1855 And therwithal° she rafte hirself° hir lyf. — *with it / deprived herself of*
And as she fel adoun,° she caste hir look,° — *fell down / glance*
And of hir clothes yet she heed took;° — *took heed*
For in hir falling yet she hadde care° — *took care*
Lest that hir feet or swiche° thing lay bare, — *such*
1860 So wel she loved clennesse° and eek° trouthe. — *purity / also*
Of hir had al the toun of Rome routhe,° — *pity*
And Brutus by hir chaste blood hath swore
That Tarquin sholde y-banisshed be therfore
And al his kin; and let the peple calle° — *convened the people*
1865 And openly the tale he tolde hem alle
And openly let carie hir on a bere[9]
Thurgh al the toun, that° men may see and here° — *so that / hear*
The horrible deed of hir oppressioun.° — *i.e., rape*
Ne never was ther king in Rome toun
1870 Sin thilke° day; and she was holden° there — *that same / considered*
A seynt, and ever hir day y-halwed dere° — *solemnly celebrated as holy*
As in hir° lawe. And thus endeth Lucresse, — *their*
The noble wyf, as Titus° bereth witnesse. — *Livy*
I tell it for° she was of love so trewe, — *because*
1875 Ne in hir wille she chaunged for no newe.[1]
And for the stable herte, sad,° and kinde,° — *constant / true*
That in these women men may alday° finde; — *always*
Ther as they caste hir herte,° ther it dwelleth. — *their hearts*
For wel I wot° that Crist himselve telleth — *know*
1880 That in Israel, as wyd as is the lond,
That so greet feith in al that he ne fond° — *in no one did he find*
As in a woman,[2] and this is no lye.° — *lie*

---

7. Her heart had such wifely virtue and (was) so true. She said that her husband should not have a filthy reputation due to her guilt or offense; she would not allow that on any account.
8. "Be that as it may," said she, "as to forgiving; I will not have any forgiveness, no matter what."
9. And had her carried forth on a bier (for all to see).
1. Nor did any new (interest cause her to) waver in her will.
2. Probably a blending of biblical passages derived respectively from the miracles of the Syro-Phoenician woman and of the centurion (Matthew 15:28, Matthew 8:10, and Luke 7:9). In fact,

And as of men, looketh which° tirannye   *see what*
They doon alday; assay hem whoso liste,°   *whoever wishes to test them*
1885 The trewest is ful brotel° for to triste.°   *too brittle, flimsy / trust*

Explicit Legenda Lucrecie Rome, Martiris.[3]

The Legend of Ariadne

Incipit Legenda Adriane de Athenes.[1]

Juge Infernal, Minos, of Crete king,
Now cometh thy lot, now comestow on the ring.[2]
Nat for thy sake only wryte I this storye
But for to clepe° ageyn unto memorye   *call*
1890 Of Theseus the greet untrouthe of love,[3]
For which the goddes of the heven above
Been wrooth° and wreche han take° for   *angry / vengeance have taken*
thy sinne.
Be reed° for shame! Now I thy lyf° beginne.   *Blush / legend*
Minos, that was the mighty king of Crete,
1895 That hadde° an hundred citees stronge and grete,   *ruled*
To scole° hath sent his sone Androgeus,   *school*
To Athenes; of the° whiche it happed° thus   *from / came about*
That he was slayn, lerning° philosphye   *studying*
Right in that citee nat but° for envye.   *only*
1900 The grete Minos, of the whiche° I speke,   *of whom*
His sones deeth is comen for to wreke;°   *revenge*
Alcathoe[4] he bisegeth harde and longe,
But natheles° the walles be so stronge,   *nonetheless*
And Nisus, that was king of that citee,
1905 So chivalrous° that litel dredeth° he.   *valiant / little fears*
Of Minos or his ost° took he no cure°   *host, army / had no concern*
Til on a day befel an aventure,°   *by chance it happened*
That Nisus doughter[5] stood upon the wal
And of the sege° saw the maner al;   *siege*
1910 So happed it° that at a scarmishing°   *it happened / skirmish*
She caste hir herte upon° Minos the king   *gave her heart to*
For his beautee and for his chivalrye

---

the Bible does not specifically make the claim about the faith of women as Chaucer presents it
here.
3. Here ends the Legend of Lucretia of Rome, martyr.
1. Here begins the Legend of Ariadne of Athens.
2. Judge of the Underworld, Minos, King of Crete, now comes your turn; now you come into the
arena. (The background for Chaucer's story is taken largely from Ovid's *Metamorphoses* 7.456–
58, 8.6–182, and *Heroides* 10. King Minos's wife Pasiphae lusted for a bull and, from this union,
gave birth to the Minotaur, a monster half bull and half man. Minos's father [also called Minos],
or alternatively his grandfather, was the son of Jupiter and Europa and traditionally judge of the
Underworld.)
3. Theseus's great falsity in love.
4. A citadel in Megara, a city near Athens.
5. In the *Metamorphoses*, Nisus's daughter, Scylla, falls hopelessly in love with Minos and cuts off
her father's magical lock of purple hair that protects king and kingdom.

	So sore° that she wende for to dye.°	*intently / thought she would die*
	And shortly of this proces for to pace⁶	
1915	She made Minos winnen thilke° place	*that same*
	So that the citee was al at his wille°	*under his control*
	To saven whom him list° or elles spille.°	*whom he wished / else to kill*
	But wikkedly he quitte° hir kindenesse	*repaid*
	And let hir drenche° in sorwe° and distresse	*drown / sorrow*
1920	Nere that the goddes hadde of hir pitee,	
	But that tale were too long as now for me.⁷	
	Athenes wan° this king Minos also,	*won*
	And Alcathoe and other tounes mo;°	*more other towns*
	And this th'effect,° that Minos hath so driven°	*result / overpowered*
	Hem° of Athenes, that they mote him	*i.e., the people*
1925	yiven°	*must give him*
	Fro° yere to yere hir° owne children dere	*From / their*
	For to be slayn° as ye shul after here.°	*To be killed / hear*
	This Minos hath a monstre, a wikked beste,⁸	
	That was so cruel that without areste°	*delay*
1930	Whan that a man was brought in his presence	
	He wolde him ete,° ther helpeth no defence.°	*eat / resistance*
	And every thridde yeer° withouten doute°	*third year / without fail*
	They casten lot,° and as it com aboute,	*cast or draw lots*
	On riche, on pore,° he moste° his sone take,	*poor / must*
1935	And of his child he moste present make°	*make an offering*
	Unto Minos, to save him or to spille,°	*kill*
	Or lete his beste° devoure him at his wille.	*beast*
	And this hath Minos doon right in despyt;°	*for sheer resentment*
	To wreke° his sone was set al his delyt°	*avenge / delight*
1940	And maken hem° of Athenes his thral°	*them / slaves*
	Fro° yere to yere whyl that° he liven shal;	*From / as long as*
	And hoom° he saileth whan this toun is wonne.	*home*
	This wikked custom is so longe y-ronne°	*has continued so long*
	Til that of Athenes King Egeus	
1945	Mot sende his owne sone, Theseus,	
	Sith that the lot is fallen him upon	
	To be devoured, for grace is ther non.⁹	
	And forth is lad° this woful yonge knight	*led*
	Unto the court of king Minos ful right,°	*directly*
1950	And in a prison fetered° cast is he	*fettered, shackled*
	Til thilke° tyme he sholde y-freten° be.	*Until that / eaten*
	Wel maistow wepe,° O woful Theseus,	*Well may you*
	That art a kinges sone and dampned° thus.	*condemned*
	Me thinketh this, that thou were depe y-holde	
1955	To whom that saved thee fro cares colde!¹	

---

6. In order to move through this narrative more quickly (i.e., in short).
7. Except that the gods took pity on her, but (to tell) that tale now would take me too long. (Chaucer omits the Ovidian metamorphosis, in which Scylla is transformed into a lark.)
8. This Minos has a monster, a wicked beast (i.e., the Minotaur; see above, note to 1887).
9. Until King Egeus of Athens must send his own son, Theseus, since the lot has fallen upon him to be devoured, for there is no mercy.
1. It seems to me that you would be deeply beholden to whoever saved you from (such) chilling distress.

And if now any woman helpe thee,
Wel oughtestow° hir servant for to be,   *ought you*
And been hir trewe lover yeer by yere.
But now to come ageyn to my matere.°   *back to my main subject*
1960   The tour theras° this Theseus is throwe°   *dungeon where / thrown*
Doun in the botom derke and wonder lowe°   *deep down*
Was joyning° in the walle to a foreyne,[2]   *adjoining*
And it was longing° to the doughtren tweyne°   *belonged / two daughters*
Of King Minos, that in hir chambres grete°   *their spacious chambers*
1965   Dwelten above toward the maister strete,°   *facing the main street*
In mochel° mirthe, in joye and in solas.°   *great / happiness*
Noot I nat° how, it happed ther per cas°   *I don't know / by chance*
As Theseus compleyned him by nighte,
The kinges doughter, Adrian that highte,
1970   And eek hir suster Phedra, herden al[3]
His compleyning as they stood on the wal
And lokeden° upon the brighte mone.°   *looked, gazed / moon*
Hem leste nat° to go to bedde sone,   *They did not wish*
And of° his wo they had compassioun.   *for*
1975   A kinges sone to been in swich° prisoun   *such a*
And be devoured, thoughte hem° greet pitee.   *it seemed to them a*
     Than Adrian spak° to hir suster free°   *spoke / her noble sister*
And seyde, "Phedra, leve° suster dere,   *beloved*
This woful lordes sone may ye nat here,
1980   How pitously compleyneth he his kin
And eek his pore estat that he is in[4]
And gilteles?° Now certes it is routhe!°   *guiltless / pitiable*
And if ye wol assenten,° by my trouthe,°   *agree / on my honor*
He shal be holpen,° how so that we do!"° *helped / however we can*
1985   Phedra answerde, "Ywis, me is as wo°   *Truly, I am as sorry*
For him as ever I was for any man;
And to his help the beste reed I can
Is that we doon the gayler privily
To come and speke with us hastily,
1990   And doon this woful man with him to come.[5]
For if he may this monstre overcome,°   *defeat this monster*
Than were he quit;° ther is noon other   *would he be released*
          bote.°   *remedy*
Lat us wel taste° him at his herte-rote,°   *test / heart's depths*
That if so be that he a wepen° have   *weapon*
1995   Wher that he dar,° his lyf to kepe° and   *Whether he would dare / protect*
          save,
Fighten with this feend° and him° defende.   *fiend, monster / himself*
For in the prison ther° he shal descende,   *where*

---

2. A privy (i.e., toilet) attached to or built into the outer wall of a structure.
3. As Theseus bewailed his fate at night, the king's daughter, who was named Adrian (Ariadne), as
well as her sister Phedra (Phaedra) heard all.
4. Can you not hear how heartrendingly this woeful lord's son laments (what has become of) his
kindred and also the lowly state to which he's fallen?
5. And to assist him, the best advice I can offer is that we secretly summon the jailer to come in
haste to speak with us, and bring this woeful man with him.

Ye wite° wel that the beste° is in a place   *know / beast*
That nis nat° derk and hath roum eek° and space   *is not / has room also*
2000 To welde° an ax or swerd or staf or knyf,   *wield, handle*
So that, me thinketh,° he sholde save his lyf;   *I believe*
If that he be a man, he shal do so.
And we shal make him balles eek also
Of wexe and towe, that whan he gapeth faste
2005 Into the bestes throte he shal hem caste
To slake his hunger and encombre his teeth;⁶
And right anoon,° whan that Theseus seeth°   *straightaway / sees*
The beste achoked,° he shal on him lepe°   *choking / leap*
To sleen° him er° they comen more to-hepe.°   *slay / before / together*
2010 This wepen shal the gayler° er that tyde°   *jailer / beforehand*
Ful prively° within the prison hyde;   *Very secretly*
And for the hous is crinkled to and fro
And hath so queynte weyes for to go—
For it is shapen as the mase is wrought⁷—
2015 Therto° have I a remedie in my thought,°   *For this / solution in mind*
That by a clewe of twyne° as he hath goon,°   *clew of twine / gone*
The same wey he may returne anoon,°   *forthwith, shortly*
Folwing alwey° the threed as he hath come.   *Always following*
And whan that he this beste° hath overcome,°   *beast / defeated*
2020 Than may he fleen° awey out of this drede,°   *flee / danger*
And eek° the gayler° may he with him lede°   *also / jailer / lead out*
And him avaunce° at hoom° in his contree°   *promote / home / country*
Sin that° so greet a lordes sone is he.   *Since*
This is my reed° if that he dar° it take."   *advice / dares to*
2025   What sholde I lenger sermoun° of it make?   *a longer discourse*
The gayler cometh and with him Theseus.
Whan these thinges been acorded° thus,   *had been agreed upon*
Adoun sit° Theseus upon his knee: *Down sits*
"The righte° lady of my lyf," quod° he,   *rightful / said*
2030 "I, sorweful° man, y-dampned° to the deeth,   *sorrowful / condemned*
Fro° yow, whyl that me lasteth° lyf or breeth,   *From / I possess*
I wol nat twinne° after this aventure,   *depart*
But in your servise thus I wol endure°   *remain, persist*
That, as a wrecche unknowe,° I wol yow serve   *an unknown wretch*
2035 For evermo til that myn herte sterve.°   *heart fails*
Forsake I wol at hoom myn heritage°   *inheritance*
And, as I seyde, been of your court° a page *in your entourage, household*
If that ye vouche-sauf° that in this place°   *consent / i.e., here in Crete*
Ye graunte me to han° so greet a grace°   *bestow upon me / great a favor*
2040 That I may han nat but° my mete° and drinke;   *nothing but / food*
And for my sustenance yet wol I swinke°   *labor*
Right° as yow list,° that Minos ne no wight—   *Just / wish*
Sin that he saw me never with eyen sight—

---

6. And we shall also make balls of wax and tow (flax or hemp fiber) for him, so that when (the Minotaur) opens wide his mouth, (Theseus) will cast (the balls) into the beast's throat to allay his hunger and get stuck on his teeth.

7. And because the house (i.e., the Labyrinth, where the Minotaur is kept) is full of winding passages (that go) to and fro, and because it has such intricate passageways to go through—for it is shaped just as a maze is constructed—.

Ne no man elles, shal me conne espye;[8]
2045 So slyly and so wel I shal me gye°   *conduct myself*
And me so wel disfigure° and so lowe°   *disguise / humbly*
That in this world ther shal no man me knowe,
To han° my lyf and for to han presence°   *save / be in the presence*
Of yow that doon° to me this excellence.°   *do / act of kindness*
2050 And to my fader shal I senden here
This worthy man that is now your gaylere°   *jailer*
And him to guerdon that° he shal wel be   *to reward him so that*
Oon° of the grettest men of° my contree.   *One / in*
And if I durste seyn,° my lady bright,   *dare say*
2055 I am a kinges sone and eek° a knight.   *also*
As wolde God,° if that it mighte be   *God willing*
Ye weren in my contree, alle three,
And I with yow to bere° yow companye,   *keep*
Than shulde ye seen if that I therof lye.°   *am lying about this*
2060 And if I profre° yow in low° manere   *offer / humble*
To been your page° and serven yow right here,   *be your personal servant*
But I yow serve as lowly in that place,
I prey to Mars to yeve me swich a grace
That shames deeth on me ther mote falle
2065 And deeth and povert to my frendes alle;[9]
And that my spirit by nighte mote go°   *may wander*
After my deeth and walke to and fro;
That I mote° of a traitour have a name°   *may / the reputation*
For which° my spirit go° to do me shame.   *Causing / to walk*
2070 And if I ever claime other degree°   *(higher) status (than page)*
But° if ye vouche-sauf to yeve° it me,   *Unless / deign to give*
As I have seyd, of shames° deeth I deye!°   *a shameful / may I die*
And mercy, lady! I can nat elles° seye."   *more*
A seemly° knight was Theseus to see   *handsome*
2075 And yong, but of a twenty yeer and three;°   *only twenty-three*
But whoso° hadde y-seyn° his   *whoever / seen*
    countenaunce,°   *expression*
He wolde have wept for routhe° of his   *from pity*
    penaunce;°   *for his suffering*
For which this Adriane in this manere
Answerd him° to his profre° and to his   *Responded / offer*
    chere:°   *appearance*
2080 "A kinges sone and eek a knight," quod she,
"To been my servant in so low degree,
God shilde it for the shame of women alle,
And leve me never swich a cas befalle![1]
But sende yow grace of hert° and sleight° also   *heart / skill*
2085 Yow to defende and knightly sleen° your fo,°   *bravely to slay / foe*

---

8. (I promise) that nobody, not Minos—since he has never seen me with (his own) eyes—nor any
    other man, will be able to recognize me.
9. If I don't serve you as humbly in that place (i.e., Athens), I pray to Mars that he give me such
    fortune that a shameful death may befall me, and (also) death and poverty (befall) all of my friends.
1. "(For) a king's son as well as a knight," she said, "to be my servant (and) of such a lowly station,
    God forbid that (such a thing should happen) for the shame (it would bring to) all women! And
    (may God) never permit such a fate to befall me!"

And leve herafter° that I may yow finde   *let it be afterwards*
To me and to my suster here so kinde
That I repente nat to yeve yow° lyf.   *for saving your*
Yet were it° better that I were your wyf°   *it would be / wife*
2090 Sin that° ye been as gentil° born as I   *Since / nobly*
And have a reaume,° nat but faste by,°   *kingdom / near at hand*
Than that I suffred° giltles yow to sterve°   *allowed / to die*
Or that I let yow as a page serve.
It is no profer as unto° your kinrede;°   *offer that befits / high birth*
2095 But what is° that that man nil° do for drede?°   *is it / won't / from fear*
And to my suster,° sin that° it is so   *as for my sister / since*
That she mot goon° with me, if that I go,   *must go*
Or elles suffre deeth as wel as I,
That ye unto your sone as trewely
2100 Doon hir be wedded at your hoom-coming.[2]
This is the fynal ende° of al this thing.   *conclusion, resolution*
Ye swere it heer° on al that may be sworn."   *Swear to it here*
     "Ye,° lady myn," quod° he, "or elles torn°   *Yes / said / else torn apart*
Mote° I be with° the Minotaur tomorwe!°   *May / by / tomorrow*
2105 And haveth hereof my herte-blood to borwe°   *heart's blood as a pledge*
If that ye wile;° if I had knyf or spere,   *wish it*
I wolde it leten out° and theron swere,   *i.e., draw my own blood*
For than at erst° I wot° ye wol me leve.°   *more readily / know / believe*
By Mars, that is the cheef of my bileve,°   *supreme (god) in my religion*
2110 So that° I mighte liven and nat faile   *Provided that*
Tomorwe for t'acheve my bataile°   *to win my battle*
I nolde never fro° this place flee   *would never from*
Til that ye shuld the verray preve° see.   *actual proof, evidence*
For now, if that the sooth° I shal yow say,   *truth*
2115 I have y-loved yow ful many a day
Though ye ne wiste it nat,° in my contree,   *did not know it*
And aldermost° desyred yow to see   *most of all*
Of any erthly° living creature.   *earthly*
Upon my trouthe° I swere and yow assure°   *honor / guarantee*
2120 These seven yeer° I have your servant be.°   *years / been*
Now have I yow, and also have ye me,
My dere herte, of Athenes duchesse!"
     This lady smyleth at his stedfastnesse
And at his hertly° wordes and his chere,°   *sincere / show (of emotion)*
2125 And to hir suster seyde in this manere
Al softely, "Now, suster myn," quod she,
"Now be we duchesses, bothe I and ye,
And sikered° to the regals° of Athenes,   *pledged / royal family*
And bothe hereafter lykly to be° quenes,   *are likely to become*
2130 And saved fro° his deeth a kinges sone,   *(we have) rescued from*
As ever of gentil° women is the wone°   *noble / custom*
To save a gentil man emforth hir° might   *to the utmost of their*

2. (I ask that) you marry her to your son as truly (as we are married) when you return home. (There
seems to be some inconsistency in the time scheme here, for Theseus at age twenty-three [see
2075], hardly seems old enough to be the father of a son suitable for marriage to Phaedra. More-
over, his son, Hippolytus, is the product of his marriage to the Amazon queen Hippolyta, an event
that, according to the Knight's Tale [see *Canterbury Tales* 1.980] has not yet taken place.)

In honest cause and namely° in his right.° *especially / just cause*
Me thinketh no wight° oughte hereof us   *person*
 blame°   *blame us for this*
2135 Ne beren° us therefor an evel name."° *lay upon / reputation*
  And shortly° of this matere° for to make, *briefly / subject matter*
 This Theseus of hir hath leve y-take,°   *taken (his) leave*
 And every point performed was in dede°   *in deeds*
 As ye have in this covenant° herd me rede.° *pact, agreement / narrate*
2140 His wepen,° his clew,° his thing° that I *weapon / i.e., of twine / thing(s)*
  have said
 Was by the gayler° in the hous y-laid°   *jailer / laid out*
 Ther as° this Minotaur hath his dwelling   *Where*
 Right faste by° the dore at his entring.   *Just next to*
 And Theseus is lad° unto his deeth,   *led*
2145 And forth unto this Minotaur he geeth,°   *goes*
 And by° the teching of this Adriane   *by following*
 He overcom this beste° and was his bane,° *beast / slayer*
 And out he cometh by the clewe again
 Ful prively° whan he this beste hath slain; *stealthily*
2150 And by the gayler° geten hath a barge° *from the jailer / boat*
 And of° his wyves tresor° gan it charge° *with / wife's treasure / loaded it*
 And took his wyf and eek° hir suster free° *also / noble*
 And eek the gayler, and with hem° alle three *them*
 Is stole° awey out of the lond by nighte   *has stolen*
2155 And to the contree of Ennopye him dighte
 Ther as he had a frend of his knowinge.[3]
 Ther festen they,° ther dauncen they and singe, *they feast*
 And in his armes hath° this Adriane   *he has*
 That of the beste° hath kept him from his *from the beast*
  bane,°   *destruction*
2160 And gat° him ther a newe barge° anoon° *he got / boat / soon*
 And of his contree-folk° a ful greet   *countrymen*
  woon,°   *very large number*
 And taketh his leve,° and hoomward saileth he. *leave*
 And in an yle amid the wilde see[4]
 Ther as° ther dwelte creature noon°   *Where / none*
2165 Save wilde bestes° and that ful many oon,° *beasts / a one*
 He made his ship a-londe° for to sette;   *ashore*
 And in that yle° half a day he lette°   *island / delayed*
 And seyde, that on the lond he moste° him reste;° *must / rest up*
 His mariners han doon right as him leste.° *did just as he wished*
2170 And for to tellen shortly° in this cas°   *briefly / case*
 Whan Adriane his wyf aslepe was,
 For that° hir suster fairer was than she   *Because*
 He taketh hir in his° hond, and forth goth he *by the*
 To shippe, and as a traitour stal his way° *stole away*
2175 Whyl that° this Adriane aslepe lay,   *While*
 And to his contree-ward° he saileth blyve°— *toward his country / rapidly*

---

3. And he made his way to the country of Oenopia (former name of the island Aegina) where he had
 a friend and confidant (?).
4. And on an island, in a remote, uncharted sea.

A twenty devil wey the wind him dryve!—
And fond his fader drenched in the see.[5]
     Me list no° more to speke of him pardee.°   *I do not wish / by God*
2180 These false lovers, poison be hir bane!°   *their destruction*
But I wol turne ageyn to Adriane
That is with slepe for werinesse atake.°   *taken*
Ful sorwefully hir herte° may awake.   *heart*
Allas, for thee my herte hath now pitee!°   *pity, compassion*
2185 Right in the dawening° awaketh she   *Just at dawn*
And gropeth° in the bedde and fond right   *feels around*
     nought.°   *found nothing*
"Allas!" quod° she, "that ever I was wrought!°   *said / born*
I am betrayed!" And hir heer torente°   *she tore at her hair*
And to the stronde° barefoot faste she wente   *shore*
2190 And cryed, "Theseus, myn herte swete!
Wher be ye,° that I may nat with yow mete,°   *are you / find you*
And mighte° thus with bestes° been y-slain?"   *you might / by beasts have*
     The holwe° rokkes answerde hir again.°   *hollow / back*
No man she saw, and yet shyned the mone,°   *the moon shone still*
2195 And hye° upon a rokke she wente sone°   *high / soon*
And saw his barge° sailing in the see.   *boat*
Cold wex° hir herte, and right thus° seyde she: *grew / just so*
"Meker° than ye finde I the bestes wilde!"   *Meeker*
Hadde° he nat sinne that hir thus begylde?°   *Did / beguiled*
2200 She cryed, "O turne again° for routhe° and sinne!   *back / pity*
Thy barge hath nat al his meynee inne!"°   *company, crew*
Hir kerchef° on a pole up stikked° she   *head cloth / hoisted*
Ascaunce that he sholde it wel y-see[6]
And him remembre° that she was° behinde   *recall / was left*
2205 And turne again,° and on the stronde° hir finde;   *back / shore*
But al for nought;° his wey he is y-goon.°   *nothing / gone*
And doun she fil a-swown° upon a stoon°   *in a faint / stone*
And up she rist° and kiste° in al hir care°   *rises / kissed / anguish*
The steppes° of his feet ther° he hath fare,°   *footprints / where / walked*
2210 And to hir bedde right thus she speketh tho:°   *then*
"Thou bed," quod she, "that hast receyved two,
Thou shalt answere of two and nat of oon!
Wher is thy gretter part away y-goon?
Allas, wher shal I, wrecched wight, become?[7]
2215 For, though so be that° ship or boot heer come,   *Even if*
Hoom to my contree dar I nat° for drede;°   *I dare not go / fear*
I can myselven in this cas nat rede."°   *not advise*
     What° shal I telle more hir compleining?   *Why*

---

5. May the wind drive him the way of twenty devils! (a conventional oath; see *Canterbury Tales* 1.3713, 1.4257, 8.782). And he found his father drowned in the sea. (According to the Ovidian legend, Theseus's father, Aegeus, drowned when Theseus returned to Athens because Theseus failed to hoist white sails to signal his father that he was alive and well.)
6. As if (it might be possible) that he would see it. (Ariadne's hope is ironic on several counts, since Theseus is neither near enough nor in a frame of mind to return.)
7. "You bed," said she, "that has received two, you ought to answer for two and not for one! Where has the greater part gone away? Alas, what shall become of me, wretched creature?"

It is so long, it were an hevy° thing.   *would be a depressing*
2220 In hir epistle Naso telleth al;⁸
But shortly° to the ende I telle shal.   *quickly*
The goddes have hir holpen° for pitee,   *helped*
And in the signe of Taurus men may see
The stones of hir coroun shyne clere.⁹
2225 I wol no more speke of this matere,
But thus this false lover can begyle°   *beguile, trick*
His trewe love. The devil quyte him his whyle!°   *repay him for his time*

*Explicit Legenda Adriane de Athenes.*¹

The Legend of Philomela

Incipit Legenda Philomene.

*Deus dator formarum.*¹

Thou yever° of the formes, that hast wrought°   *giver / made*
The faire world and bare it in thy thought²
2230 Eternally, er° thou thy werk began,   *before*
Why madest thou unto the sclaunder° of man   *for the slander, shame*
Or—al be that it was nat thy doing,
As for that fyn to make swich a thing—
Why suffrest thou that Tereus was bore,³
2235 That is in love so fals and so forswore,°   *forsworn*
That fro° this world up to the firste° hevene   *from / highest sphere of*
Corrumpeth,° whan that folk his name   *spreads contamination*
    nevene?°   *mention*
And, as to° me, so grisly was his dede°   *for / deed*
That, whan that I his foule story rede,
2240 Myn eyen wexen° foule and sore also;   *eyes grow, become*
Yet last° the venim° of so longe ago   *So long lasts / venom*
That it enfecteth him° that wol beholde°   *infects anyone / will look upon*
The story of Tereus, of which° I tolde.   *about whom*
Of Trace° was he lord and kin to Marte,°   *Thrace / Mars*
2245 The cruel god that stant° with blody darte;°   *stands / bloody spear*
And wedded had he with a blisful chere°   *happy mien, expression*
King Pandiones faire doughter dere
That highte Progne, flour of hir contree,

---

8. In her letter, Ovid (Publius Ovidius Naso) tells it all. (See *Heroides* 10; also above 1887 note.)
9. And in the astrological sign of Taurus men can see the stones of her crown (i.e., stars) shine brightly. (In fact, Ariadne's constellation (the "Northern Crown") is opposite to the sign of Taurus, and the *Riverside Chaucer* [Explanatory Notes, p. 1072] therefore suggests that Chaucer means here that the constellation is visible when the sun is in Taurus.)
1. Here ends the Legend of Ariadne of Athens.
1. Here begins the Legend of Philomela. God (is) the giver of forms. (The exact source of this widely known Platonic phrase is unidentified.)
2. Had the prototype in your mind.
3. Or—if it was not your intention for that purpose to make such a thing—why did you allow Tereus to be born? (Tereus was a Thracian king, descended from Mars. Chaucer takes the story chiefly from Ovid's *Metamorphoses* 6.424–674.)

Though Juno list nat at the feste be,
2250 Ne Ymeneus that god of wedding is;[4]
But at the feste° redy been ywis°   *feast / are surely*
The Furies three with alle hir mortal brond.[5]
The owle al night aboute the balkes wond,°   *wound about the roofbeams*
That prophet is of wo and of mischaunce.°   *misfortune*
2255 This revel° ful of songe and ful of daunce   *party, celebration*
Last a fourtenight° or litel lasse.°   *two weeks / a little less*
But shortly of° this story for to passe,   *briefly over*
For I am wery° of him for to telle,   *weary*
Five yeer° his wyf and he togeder dwelle°   *years / live together*
2260 Til on a day she gan so sore longe°   *began to yearn so intensely*
To seen hir suster, that she saw nat longe,[6]
That for° desyr she niste° what to seye.   *because of / did not know*
But to hir husband gan she for to preye
For Goddes love that she moste ones goon°   *might go once*
2265 Her suster for to seen and come anoon,°   *return in a little while*
Or elles, but she moste to hir wende,
She preyde him that he wolde after hir sende.[7]
And this was day by day al° hir preyere   *i.e., unceasingly*
With al humblesse of wyfhood, word, and chere.°   *expression*
2270   This Tereus let make his shippes yare°   *made ready his ships*
And into Grece° himself is forth y-fare°   *Greece / has traveled*
Unto his fader-in-lawe and gan him preye°   *requested*
To vouche-sauf° that for a month or tweye°   *grant / two*
That Philomene, his wyves° suster, mighte   *wife's*
2275 On Progne his wyf but ones° have a sighte—   *just once*
"And she shal come to yow ageyn anoon.°   *very soon*
Myself with hir° wol bothe come and goon,°   *accompanying her / go*
And as myn hertes lyf I wol hir kepe."°   *protect her*
    This olde Pandion, this king, gan wepe°   *began to weep*
2280 For tendernesse of herte for to leve°   *allow*
His doughter goon,° and for to yive° hir leve;°   *to go / give / leave*
Of° al this world he lovede nothing so.°   *In / so much*
But at the laste leve hath she to go,
For Philomene with salte teres eke°   *salty tears also*
2285 Gan of hir fader grace to beseke°   *besought, entreated*
To seen hir suster, that hir longeth° so,   *for whom she yearns*
And him embraceth with hir armes two.
And therwithal° so yong and fair was she   *on top of that*
That,° whan that Tereus saw hir beautee,   *So that*
2290 And of aray° that ther was noon hir liche°   *clothing / none her equal*
And yet of beautee was she two so° riche,   *twice as*

---

4. King Pandion's beloved (and) beautiful daughter who was named Procne, the flower of her land, though Juno did not wish to attend the (marriage) feast, nor (did) Hymeneus, who is the god of weddings. (Pandion was King of Athens. The absence of Juno and Hymeneus [also known simply as Hymen] from the wedding bodes ill, for Juno is the goddess of married women and Hymeneus the god of marriage.)
5. The three Furies with all their deadly torches (able to kindle passions).
6. To see her sister, whom she had not seen for a long time.
7. Or else, if she might not go to (her sister Philomela), she begged him that he would send after her (to come to Athens).

He caste his fyry herte° upon hir so   *fixed his burning heart*
That he wol have° hir how so that it go,°   *will possess / come what may*
And with his wyles° kneled and so preyde   *wiliness, craftiness*
2295 Til at the laste Pandion thus seyde:
      "Now, sone," quod° he, "that art to me so dere,   *said*
I thee betake° my yonge doughter here   *entrust*
That bereth° the key of° al my hertes lyf.   *Who carries / to*
And grete° wel my doughter and thy wyf   *(ask that you) greet*
2300 And yive hir leve° somtyme for to pleye°   *give her leave / take time off*
That she may seen me ones er I deye."°   *once more before I die*
And soothly° he hath mad him riche feste,°   *truly / (a) sumptuous feast*
And to° his folk, the moste and eek the   *for*
      leste°   *from most to least high*
That with him com; and yaf him yiftes° grete,   *gave him gifts*
2305 And him conveyeth° through the maister strete°   *escorts / main street*
Of Athenes, and to the see him broughte,
And turneth hoom; no malice° he ne thoughte.°   *evil / expected*
      The ores° pulleth forth the vessel faste   *oars*
And into Thrace arriveth° at the laste,   *(Tereus) arrives*
2310 And up into a forest he hir ledde,
And to a cave prively° him spedde;°   *secretly / hastened*
And in this derke cave if hir leste°   *she wanted*
Or leste noughte,° he bad hir° for to reste;   *did not / ordered*
Of° whiche hir herte agroos,° and seyde° thus, *For / shuddered / she said*
2315 "Wher is my suster, brother Tereus?"
And therwithal° she wepte tenderly,   *with that*
And quook° for fere pale and pitously°   *trembled / pitifully*
Right as° the lamb that of° the wolf is byten,°   *Just like / by / bitten*
Or as the colver° that of the egle is smyten°   *dove / seized*
2320 And is out of his clawes forth escaped,
Yet it is afered° and awhaped°   *terrified / stunned*
Lest it be hent eft-sones,° so sat she.   *captured another time*
But utterly it may noon other be.[8]
By force hath he, this traitour, doon a dede,°   *deed*
2325 That he hath reft hir of hir maydenhede°   *taken her virginity*
Maugree hir heed, by strengthe and by his might.
Lo, here a dede of men and that a right![9]
She cryeth "Suster!"° with ful loude stevene,°   *Sister / very loud voice*
And "Fader dere!"° and "Help me, God in hevene!"   *Father dear*
2330 Al helpeth nat;° and yet this false theef   *Nothing does any good*
Hath doon this lady yet a more mischeef°   *a still greater wrong*
For fere° lest she sholde his shame crye,°   *fear / cry aloud*
And doon him openly° a vilanye,   *accuse him publicly of*
And with his swerd hir tong of kerveth° he   *cuts out her tongue*
2335 And in a castel made hir for to be°   *put her away*
Ful prively° in prison evermore,   *Quite secretly*

8. I.e., there is absolutely no turning back: "it may be no other way."
9. Despite anything that she could do, by strength and force. Lo, here is the righteous act of (a typical) man! ("Maugree hir heed" [literally "in spite of her head"] is a conventional expression for "by force"; see *Canterbury Tales* 1.1169, 3.887, 7.3412.)

And kepte hir to his usage and his store,
So that she mighte him nevermore asterte.[1]
O sely° Philomene, wo is thyn herte;   *innocent, helpless*
2340 God wreke thee, and sende thee thy bone![2]
Now is it tyme I make an ende° sone.   *i.e., to this story*
     This Tereus is to his wyf y-come,
And in his armes hath his wyf y-nome,°   *taken*
And pitously he wepe and shook his heed
2345 And swoor° hir that he fond hir suster deed;°   *swore to / dead*
For which this sely° Progne hath swich wo°   *innocent / such woe*
That nigh° hir sorweful herte brak a-two;°   *almost / broke in two*
And thus in teres° lete I Progne dwelle,   *tears*
And of hir suster forth I wol yow telle.
2350   This woful lady lerned had in youthe
So that she werken and enbrouden couthe
And weven in hir stole the radevore
As it of women hath be woned yore.[3]
And soothly° for to seyn she had hir fille°   *truly / was well provided*
2355 Of mete° and drink and clothing at hir wille,   *With food*
And coude eek rede° and wel ynough   *also read*
     endyte,°   *compose (a text)*
But with a penne coude she nat wryte;
But lettres can she weven to and fro[4]
So that, by that° the yeer was al ago,°   *by the time / had passed*
2360 She had y-woven in a stamin large°   *on a large woolen cloth*
How she was brought from Athenes in a barge,°   *on a boat*
And in a cave how that she was brought;
And al the thing that Tereus hath wrought,°   *done*
She waf° it wel and wroot the story above,   *wove*
2365 How she was served for hir suster° love;   *sister's*
And to a knave° a ring she yaf anoon°   *serving boy / gave then*
And preyed him, by signes° for to goon   *gestures*
Unto the quene and beren hir° that clooth,   *carry to*
And by signes swoor him many an ooth
2370 She sholde him yeve what° she geten mighte.   *give whatever (reward)*
     This knave anoon° unto the quene him   *quickly*
     dighte°   *made his way*
And took it hir, and al the maner tolde.°   *told (her) all the circumstances*
And, whan that Progne hath this thing° beholde,   *i.e., the tapestry*
No word she spak,° for sorwe° and eek° for rage,   *spoke / sorrow / also*
2375 But feyned hir° to goon on pilgrimage   *pretended*
To Bachus temple; and, in a litel stounde°   *little while*
Hir dombe suster° sitting hath she founde,   *mute sister*
Weping in the castel her aloon.°   *alone there*
Allas, the wo, the compleint, and the moon°   *moaning*

1. And he retained her for his use and as his property, so that she might not ever be able to escape from him.
2. God avenge you, and send you an answer to your prayers!
3. So that she knew how to work with fabrics and to embroider and weave a tapestry on a frame as women were accustomed to do long ago.
4. She can weave letters (by passing the shuttle) back and forth (through the threads of the warp of the cloth).

2380	That Progne upon hir° dombe suster maketh!	*for the sake of her*
	In armes everich of hem other taketh,⁵	
	And thus I lete hem in hir sorwe° dwelle.	*their sorrow*
	The remenant is no charge for to telle,	
	For this is al and som: Thus was she served	
2385	That never harm agilte ne deserved	
	Unto this cruel man, that she of wiste.⁶	
	Ye may be war° of men if that yow liste.°	*beware / if you please*
	For al be that° he wole nat for shame	*although*
	Doon so as Tereus to lese his name,°	*sacrifice his reputation*
2390	Ne serve yow as a mordrour° or a knave,°	*murderer / rogue*
	Ful litel whyle shul ye trewe° him have—	*faithful*
	That wol I seyn al° were he now my brother—	*say although*
	But° it so be that he may have noon other.	*Unless*

*Explicit Legenda Philomene.*⁷

The Legend of Phyllis

*Incipit Legenda Phillis.*¹

	By preve° as wel as by auctoritee,°	*evidence / on (good) authority*
2395	That wikked fruit cometh of a wikked tree,	
	That may ye finde if that it lyketh yow.°	*if you please*
	But for this ende° I speke this as now:	*purpose*
	To telle yow of false Demophon.	
	In love a falser herde° I never non,°	*heard / of none*
2400	But if° it were his fader° Theseus.	*Unless / father*
	"God, for his grace, fro swich oon kepe° us!"	*from such a one protect*
	Thus may these women preyen that it here.°	*hear*
	Now to th'effect° turne I of my matere.°	*main events / subject matter*
	Destroyed is of Troye the citee;°	*the city of Troy*
2405	This Demophon² com° sailing in the see	*comes*
	Toward Athenes, to his paleys° large;	*palace*
	With him com many a ship and many a barge°	*boat*
	Ful of his folk, of which ful many oon°	*many a one*
	Is wounded sore, and sek,° and wo begoon.°	*sick / woebegone, miserable*
2410	And thay han° at the sege° longe y-lain.°	*have / siege / encamped*
	Behinde him com a wind and eek° a rain	*also*
	That shoof so sore,° his sail ne mighte stonde;°	*drove so hard / stay up*
	Him were lever° than al the world a-londe,°	*He would rather / make land*
	So hunteth° him the tempest° to and fro.	*chases, tosses / storm*

5. Each of them takes the other in her arms.
6. The rest (of the story) is of no importance to tell, for this is the long and short of it: Thus was she served who never was guilty or, as she was aware, deserved harm from this cruel man. (Of all the abbreviations in his sources, the one Chaucer makes here is perhaps the most notable. In the story as Ovid tells it [see 2234 note], Procne and Philomela take their revenge on Tereus by killing Itys, the young son of Procne and Tereus, and serving him up to his father in a grisly supper, at the conclusion of which Procne and Philomela are transformed respectively into the swallow and the nightingale, and Tereus into the hoopoe.
7. Here ends the Legend of Philomela.
1. Here begins the Legend of Phyllis.
2. Demophon is the son of Theseus and Phaedra. Chaucer's main source is Ovid's *Heroides* 2.

2415 So derk it was, he coude nowher go;°   *not navigate*
And with a wawe° brosten° was his stere.°   *wave / broken / rudder*
His ship was rent so lowe° in swich° manere   *so broken down / such*
That carpenter ne coude it nat amende.°   *could not fix it*
The see by nighte as any torche brende°   *burned*
2420 For wood,° and posseth° him now up now doun   *madly / tosses*
Til Neptune hath of him compassioun,
And Thetis, Thorus, Triton, and they alle,
And maden him upon a lond to falle
Wherof that Phillis lady was and quene,
2425 Ligurgus doughter, fairer on to sene
Than is the flour ageyn the brighte sonne.[3]
Unnethe° is Demophon to londe y-wonne,°   *Scarcely / landed*
Wayk° and eek wery,° and his folk forpyned° *Weak / also weary / wasted*
Of° werinesse and also enfamyned;°   *From / famished*
2430 And to the deeth he almost was y-driven.
His wyse folk to conseil° han him yiven°   *counsel / given*
To seken help and socour of° the queen,   *relief, comfort from*
And looken° what his grace° mighte been,   *to see / good fortune*
And maken in that lond som chevisaunce°   *arrangement, provision*
2435 To kepen him fro wo and fro mischaunce,°   *misfortune*
For sek° was he and almost at the deeth;   *sick*
Unnethe° mighte he speke or drawe his breeth,   *Scarcely*
And lyth° in Rodopeya[4] him for to reste.   *he lies, stays*
Whan he may° walke, him thoughte° it was   *could / it seemed to him*
the beste
2440 Unto the court to seken for socour.°   *to seek aid*
Men knewe him wel and diden him honour,
For of Athenes duk° and lord was he,   *duke*
As Theseus his fader hadde y-be°   *been*
That in his tyme was of greet renoun,°   *had great fame*
2445 No man so greet in al his regioun,
And lyk° his fader of face and of stature°   *like / physical form*
And fals of love; it com him of° nature.   *came to him by*
As doth the fox Renard, the foxes sone
Of kinde he coude his olde faders wone
2450 Withoute lore, as can a drake swimme
Whan it is caught and caried to the brimme.[5]
This honourable Phillis doth him chere,°   *shows him hospitality*
Hir lyketh wel his port° and his manere.   *bearing, appearance*
But for I am agroted herbiforn
2455 To wryte of hem that been in love forsworn,
And eek to haste me in my legende—

3. Until Neptune takes mercy on him, as do Thetis, Thorus, Triton, and all (such gods), and caused him to make landfall where Phillis, Licurgus's daughter, was mistress and queen (and) more fair than the flower facing the bright sun. (Neptune is the chief god of the sea. Thetis is a sea nymph, daughter of the sea god Nereus and mother of Achilles. Triton is Neptune's son and a sea god in his own right. Thorus remains unidentified but is presumably a sea or wind god. Phillis's land is Thrace.)
4. The region near Rhodope, a mountain range in Thrace.
5. As Renard the fox does, (so) the fox's son takes up by nature his old father's inclinations without lessons, as a drake knows how to swim when it is raised in captivity and (then) carried to the water.

Which to performe God me grace sende—
Therfor I passe shortly in this wyse.[6]
Ye han wel herd of Theseus devyse°　　　　　　　*Theseus's scheme*
2460　In the betraysing° of fair Adriane°　　　　　　*betrayal / Ariadne*
That of hir pitee kepte him from his bane.°　　　　　*destruction*
At shorte wordes,° right° so Demophon　　　　　　*In short / just*
The same wey, the same path hath gon°　　　　　*gone, traveled*
That° dide his false fader Theseus.　　　　　　　*On which*
2465　For unto Phillis hath he sworen thus,
To wedden hir, and hir his trouthe plighte,°　　*pledged his fidelity*
And piked of° hir al the good° he mighte,　*stolen from / (worldly) goods*
Whan he was hool and sound° and hadde his reste;　*healthy and well*
And doth with Phillis what so that him leste;°　*whatever he pleased*
2470　And wel coude I if that me leste so°　　　　　*it pleased me*
Tellen al his doing to and fro.
　　He seyde unto his contree moste° he saile,　*homeland must*
For ther he wolde hir wedding apparaile°　　　*prepare for*
As fil° to hir honour and his also.　　　　*fitting, appropriate*
2475　And openly he took his leve tho°　　　　　　*then*
And hath hir sworn he wolde nat sojorne,°　　　*delay*
But in a month he wolde ageyn retorne.
And in that lond° let make his　　　　　　　*i.e., Thrace*
　　ordinaunce°　　　　　　　　　　　*issued commands*
As verray lord,° and took the obeisaunce°　*like a true lord / homage*
2480　Wel and hoomly,° and let his shippes　　　　*familiarly*
　　dighte,°　　　　　　　　　　　　*readied his ships*
And hoom he goth the nexte wey° he mighte;　*earliest opportunity*
For unto Phillis yet ne com° he nought.　　　*returned*
And that hath she so harde and sore abought,°　*keenly suffered for*
Allas, that as the stories us recorde
2485　She was° hir owne deeth right with a　　　　*brought about*
　　corde°　　　　　　　　　　　　*a (hangman's) rope*
Whan that she saw that Demophon hir trayed.°　　*betrayed*
　　But to him first she wroot° and faste° him prayed　*wrote / earnestly*
He wolde come and hir deliver of° peyne,　　　*from*
As I reherse° shal a word or tweyne.°　　　　*repeat / two*
2490　Me list nat vouche-sauf on him to swinke,
Ne spende on him a penne ful of inke,[7]
For fals in love was he right as his syre.°　　*just like his father*
The devil sette hir° soules both a-fyre!°　　*their / on fire*
But of the lettre of Phillis wol I wryte
2495　A word or tweyne,° although it be but lyte.°　*two / only a little*
　　"Thyn hostesse," quod° she, "O Demophon,　*said*
Thy Phillis, which that is so wo begon,°　*sorrowful, woebegone*
Of Rodopeye,° upon yow mot° compleyne,　*(see line 2438) / must*
Over the terme° set betwix us tweyne,°　　*date, time limit / two*
2500　That ye ne holden forward° as ye seyde.　　*kept your promise*

6. But because I am already glutted with writing about those who are forsworn in love, and also in
order to hasten forward in my legendary—which God send me the grace to finish—therefore I'll
speak briefly on this matter.
7. It's not my preference to bestow on him my labor, nor to expend on him a pen full of ink.

Your anker,° which ye in our haven° leyde,   *anchor / harbor*
Highte° us that ye wolde comen out of° doute *Held out hope / without a*
Er that° the mone ones wente° aboute.   *Before / moon once cycled*
But tymes foure° the mone hath hid hir face   *four times*
2505 Sin thilke° day ye wente fro° this place,   *Since that / from*
And foure tymes light the world again.
But for al that, if I shal soothly sain,°   *speak truthfully*
Yet hath the streem of Sitho nat y-brought
From Athenes the ship; yet comth it nought.[8]
2510 And if that ye the terme rekne° wolde *calculate the stipulated time*
As I or other trewe lovers sholde,
I pleyne° not, God wot,° biforn my day."° *complain / knows / due date*
But al hir lettre° wryten I ne may   *her entire letter*
By ordre,° for it were to me a charge,° *point by point / burden*
2515 Hir lettre was right° long and therto large;° *very long / also unreserved*
But here and there in ryme I have it laid°   *set down*
Ther as me thoughte° that she wel hath said,— *Where it seemed to me*
She seyde, "Thy sailes comen nat ageyn,°   *do not return*
Ne to thy word ther nis no fey certeyn,° *is assuredly no faith*
2520 But I wot° why ye come nat," quod° she;   *know / said*
"For° I was of my love to yow so free.°   *Because / generous*
And of the goddes that ye han forswore,
If that hir vengeance falle on yow therfore,
Ye be nat suffisaunt to bere the peyne.[9]
2525 To moche° trusted I, wel may I pleyne,°   *Too much / complain*
Upon your linage° and your faire tonge,° *(noble) ancestry / tongue*
And on your teres° falsly out y-wronge.°   *tears / wrung out*
How coude ye wepe so by craft?"° quod she;   *trickery*
"May ther swiche° teres feyned° be? *such / counterfeit*
2530 Now certes,° if ye wolde have in memorie,° *certainly / think back*
It oughte be to yow but litel glorie
To have a sely° mayde thus betrayed!   *innocent*
To God," quod she, "preye I, and ofte have prayed,
That it be now the grettest prys° of alle   *prize, reward*
2535 And moste honour that ever thee shal befalle!
And whan thyne olde auncestres peynted be,
In which men may hir worthinesse see,
Than preye I God thou peynted be also,
That folk may reden forby as they go,[1]
2540 'Lo, this is he that with his flaterye
Betrayed hath and doon hir vilanye° *abused, disgraced her*
That° was his trewe love in thoughte and dede!'   *She who*
But soothly,° of o° point yet may they rede,° *truly / one / perceive*
That ye been lyk° your fader as in this,   *like*

---

8. Still the stream of Sitho (i.e., the Thracian sea) has not brought (your) ship from Athens; still it does not come.
9. And if the vengeance of the gods that you have forsworn falls on you for this, you will not be strong enough to bear the pain.
1. And when your forbears of old times are painted so that men may see their worthiness, then I pray to God that you will also be painted, so that people may understand. (The reward alluded to in 2534 seems to refer back to the "glorie" mentioned in 2531 and also forward to this imagined portrait that will shame Theseus.)

2545	For he begyled° Adriane ywis°	*beguiled, deceived / indeed*
	With swich° an art and with swich sotelte°	*such / subtlety*
	As thou thyselven° hast begyled me.	*you yourself*
	As in that point although it be nat fayr°	*just*
	Thou folwest him certeyn° and art his eyr.°	*certainly take after him / heir*
2550	But sin° thus sinfully ye me begyle,	*since*
	My body mote ye seen° within a whyle	*you will see*
	Right in the haven° of Athenes fletinge°	*harbor / floating*
	Withouten sepulture and buryinge,°	*tomb or burial rites*
	Though ye been harder than is any stoon."°	*stone*
2555	And whan this lettre was forth sent anoon,°	*at once, quickly*
	And knew° how brotel° and how fals he was,	*(she) knew / fickle*
	She for dispeyr° fordid hirself,° allas!	*in despair / killed herself*
	Swich sorwe° hath she, for she besette hir° so.	*sorrow / placed her trust*
	Be war,° ye women, of your sotil° fo,	*Beware / subtle, cunning*
2560	Sin yet this day men may ensample see;	
	And trusteth, as in love, no man but me.[2]	

Explicit Legenda Phillis.[3]

The Legend of Hypermnestra

Incipit Legenda Ypermistre.[1]

In Grece whylom weren brethren two,
Of whiche that oon was called Danao,
That many a sone hath of his body wonne
2565 As swiche false lovers ofte conne.
Among his sones alle ther was oon
That aldermost he lovede of everichoon.
And whan this child was born, this Danao
Shoop him a name and called him Lino.
2570 That other brother called was Egiste,
That was of love as fals as ever him liste,
And many a doughter gat he in his lyfe;
Of which he gat upon his righte wyfe
A doughter dere, and dide hir for to calle
2575 Ypermistra, yongest of hem alle;[2]

2. Since even to this day, people can find examples (of such false men). And (so) trust no man in love except for me. (This is a complex and extraordinary admission on the part of the narrator, both obviously humorous and also seriously related to the themes of the poem. By declaring his own self-interest in the narrative outcome at the same time that he disingenuously solicits the reader's trust, Chaucer paradoxically undermines the masculine narrative authority that the entire poem claims to shore up—and indeed he weakens the authority of books that the poem, from its opening lines, had at least pretended to seek to strengthen.)
3. Here ends the Legend of Phyllis.
1. Here begins the Legend of Hypermnestra.
2. There were once two brothers in Greece, one of whom was named Danao, who had sired many sons with his body, as such false lovers are often able to do. Of all his sons there was one he loved more than all the others. And when this child was born, this Danao gave him a name and called him Lino. The other brother was named Egistus, who was as false in love as ever he pleased, and sired many a daughter in his life, (and one) begotten upon his lawful wife (was) a darling daughter, youngest of them all, (whom) he called Hypermnestra. (Chaucer takes the story of Danaus and his brother Aegyptus [called by Chaucer Egiste or Egistus] from Ovid's *Heroides* 14. In the Ovidian

The whiche child of° hir nativitee	*at*
To alle gode thewes° born was she,	*personal qualities*
As lyked° to the goddes er° she was born	*was pleasing / before*
That of the shefe° she sholde be the corn;	*sheaf*
2580 The Wirdes,° that we clepen° Destinee,	*Fates / call*
Hath shapen hir that she mot° nedes be	*so that she must*
Pitouse,° sadde, wyse, and trewe as steel.	*Compassionate*
And to this woman it acordeth weel;	
For though that Venus yaf hir greet beautee,	
2585 With Jupiter compouned so was she	
That conscience, trouthe, and drede of shame,	
And of hir wyfhood for to kepe hir name,	
This, thoughte hir, was felicitee as here.	
And rede Mars was that tyme of the yere	
2590 So feble that his malice is him raft;	
Repressed hath Venus his cruel craft.	
What with Venus and other oppressioun	
Of houses, Mars his venim is adoun	
That Ypermistra dar nat handle a knyf	
2595 In malice, though she sholde lese hir lyf.	
But natheles as heven gan tho turne	
To badde, aspectes hath she of Saturne	
That made hir for to deyen in prisoun,[3]	
As I shal after° make mencioun.	*later*
2600 To Danao and Egistes also,	
Although so be that they were brethren° two—	*brothers*
For thilke° tyme nas spared° no linage°—	*at that / avoided / consanguinity*
It lyked hem° to maken mariage	*pleased*
Betwix Ypermistra and him Lino,	
2605 And casten swich° a day it shal be so,	*they planned such*
And ful acorded° was it utterly;	*fully agreed upon*
The aray is wrought,° the tyme is faste by.	*arrangements are made*
And thus Lino hath of his fadres brother°	*i.e., his uncle's*
The doughter wedded, and eche of hem° hath	*each of them*
other.°	*the other*
2610 The torches brennen° and the lampes brighte,	*burn*
The sacrifices been ful redy dighte;°	*fully prepared*
Th'encens° out of the fyre reketh sote,°	*The incense / smokes sweetly*
The flour, the leef is rent up by the rote°	*torn up by the root*
To maken garlandes and crounes hye;°	*large crowns*
2615 Ful is the place of soun° of minstralcye,	*the sounds*

---

story, all fifty sons and daughters marry, with only Hypermnestra resisting the command to kill
her husband Lino [in Ovid, Lynceus].)

3. And in this woman (these virtues) are harmonious. For though Venus gave her great beauty, she
was so tempered (by the influence of) Jupiter that conscience, fidelity, fear of shame, and (a desire)
to maintain her reputation of wifely virtue, (these) seemed to her his supreme earthly happiness. And
red Mars was at that time of the year so feeble that his evil influence was taken from him; Venus
(in her planetary position) repressed his cruel craft. Under the influence of Venus and other
astrological houses (i.e., planetary positions), the venom of Mars is so weakened that Hyperm-
nestra dares not handle a knife in malice, though she would (for that) lose her life. But nonetheless
as the heavens then turned to the bad, she received aspects of Saturn that made her die in prison.
(This elaborate horoscope severely limits Hypermnestra's freedom, making it impossible for her
to wield a knife as her father commands and insuring that she will die in prison.)

Of songes amorous of° mariage   *about*
As thilke° tyme was the pleyn usage.°   *at that / widespread custom*
And this was in the paleys of Egiste,
That in his hous was lord right as him liste,°   *just as he wished*
2620 And thus the day they dryven° to an ende;   *pass*
The frendes taken leve,° and hoom they wende.°   *leave / go*
The night is come, the bryd° shal go to bedde;   *bride*
Egiste to his chambre° faste him spedde,   *chamber, bedroom*
And prively° he let° his doughter calle.°   *secretly / had / summoned*
2625 Whan that the hous was voided of hem alle,°   *cleared of them all*
He looked on his doughter with glad chere,°   *a benign expression*
And to hir spak° as ye shul after here:°   *spoke / hear*
      "My righte° doughter, tresor° of myn herte,   *own / treasure*
Sin first that day that shapen was my sherte,
2630 Or by the fatal sustren had my dom,[4]
So nigh° myn herte never thing ne com   *near to*
As thou, myn Ypermistra, doughter dere!
Tak heed what I thy fader sey thee here,
And werk after thy wyser evermo.[5]
2635 For alderfirste,° doughter, I love thee so   *first of all*
That al the world to me nis° half so leef;°   *is not / dear*
Ne I nolde rede° thee to thy mischeef°   *would not advise / harm*
For al the gode° under the colde mone.   *goods, wealth*
And what I mene, it shal be seyd right sone°   *revealed quite soon*
2640 With protestacioun,° as in this wyse:°   *the condition / manner*
That but° thou do as I shal thee devyse°   *unless / advise, command*
Thou shalt be deed,° by him that al hath   *dead*
      wrought!°   *made everything*
At shorte wordes,° thou ne scapest nought°   *In short / will not escape*
Out of my paleys or that thou be deed°   *i.e., you won't get out alive*
But° thou consente and werke after my   *Unless*
2645   reed;°   *follow my instructions*
Tak this to thee for ful conclusioun."°   *(my) final word*
      This Ypermistra caste hir eyen° doun   *eyes*
And quook° as dooth the leef of aspe° grene;   *trembled / aspen leaf*
Deed wex hir hewe and lyk as ash to sene,[6]
2650 And seyde,° "Lord and fader, al your wille   *(she) said*
After my mighte, God wot,° I shal fulfille   *knows*
So° it to me be no confusioun."°   *As long as / debasement*
      "I nil,"° quod° he, "have noon excepcioun,"°   *won't / said / reservation*
And out he caughte° a knyf as rasour kene.°   *whipped out / razor-sharp*
2655 "Hyd° this," quod he, "that it be nat y-sene;°   *Hide / seen, visible*
And whan thyn husbond is to bed y-go,°   *has gone*
Whyl that he slepeth, cut his throte a-two.°   *slit his throat*
For in my dremes° it is warned° me   *dreams / forewarned*
How that my nevew° shal my bane° be,   *nephew / murderer*

---

4. Since the day my first shirt was made, or (from that day I) took my destiny from the fatal sisters (i.e., the three Fates Clotho, Lachesis, and Atropos, imagined in ancient myth as spinners). (Chaucer is drawing on a conventional medieval idea that a person's destiny is woven before the weaving of his first shirt.)
5. And always follow the advice of one wiser than you.
6. Deathly pale grew her complexion and, to look upon, like the ash tree.

2660	But whiche I noot, wherfor I wol be siker.	
	If thou sey nay, we two shal have a biker,	
	As I have seyd by him that I have sworn."[7]	
	This Ypermistra hath nigh hir wit forlon;°	*nearly lost her wits*
	And for to passen harmles of° that place,	*leave unharmed from*
2665	She graunted° him; ther was noon other grace.°	*gave in to / mercy*
	And therwithal a costrel° taketh he	*flask*
	And seyde, "Herof a draught° or two or three	*drink*
	Yif° him to drinke whan he goth to reste,°	*Give / goes to bed*
	And he shal slepe as longe as ever thee leste,°	*you wish*
2670	The narcotiks and opies° been so stronge:	*narcotics and opiates*
	And go thy wey lest that him thinke longe."[8]	
	Out comth the bryd,° and with ful sober	*bride*
	chere°	*solemn expression*
	As is of maydens ofte the manere	
	To chambre° is brought with revel and with	*the chamber, bedroom*
	songe,	
2675	And shortly,° lest this tale be too longe,	*briefly*
	This Lino and she been sone° brought to bedde,	*soon*
	And every wight° out at the dore° him spedde.	*person / door*
	The night is wasted,° and he fel aslepe.	*spent, worn away*
	Ful tenderly beginneth she to wepe;°	*weep*
2680	She rist hir up,° and dredfully° she quaketh°	*arises / fearfully / trembles*
	As doth the braunche that Zephirus° shaketh,	*i.e., the west wind*
	And husht were alle in Argon that citee.°	*the city of Argos*
	As cold as any frost now wexeth she,°	*she grows*
	For pitee by the herte hir streyneth° so,	*grips*
2685	And drede° of deeth doth hir so moche wo,°	*fear / gives her such misery*
	That thryes° doun she fil in swich a were.°	*thrice / such an anxious state*
	She rist hir up and stakereth her° and there,	*staggers here*
	And on hir handes faste looketh° she.	*looks intently*
	"Allas, and shal myn handes blody° be?	*bloody*
2690	I am a mayd,° and as by my nature	*maiden*
	And by my semblant° and by my vesture°	*physical form / attire*
	Myn handes been nat shapen° for a knyf	*are not made*
	As for to reve° no man fro° his lyf.	*take / from*
	What devil° have I with the knyf to do?	*the devil*
2695	And shal I have my throte corve a-two?	
	Than shal I blede, allas, and me beshende![9]	
	And nedes cost° this thing mot° have an ende:	*Of necessity / must*
	Or° he or I mot nedes lese° our lyf.	*Either / must necessarily lose*
	Now certes,"° quod° she, "sin° I am his wyf,	*certainly / said / since*
2700	And hath my feith, yet is it bet for me[1]	
	For to be deed° in wyfly honestee	*dead*

---

7. But which (nephew) I do not know, and so I want to be certain. If you say no, we two (you and I) will have a conflict, as I have (already) said and sworn to. (In these lines, Chaucer obliquely alludes to the story in Ovid, where Danaus is arranging for the murder of all fifty of his nephews.)
8. And (now) go your way (i.e., leave me) lest that it seem to him (i.e., your husband) that (you are taking) a long time.
9. And (on the other hand, i.e., if I resist my father's command) shall I have my (own) throat slit? Then I shall bleed, alas, and be ruined!
1. (Since) he has my pledge of faith, it is better for me.

Than be a traitour° living in my shame.   *betrayer*
Be as be may, for ernest or for game,°   *i.e., whatever happens*
He shal awake and ryse and go his way
2705 Out at this goter² er that° it be day"—   *before*
And wepe° ful tenderly upon his face,   *(she) weeps*
And in hir armes gan him to embrace,°   *embraced him*
And him she roggeth° and awaketh softe.°   *shakes / gently*
And at a window leep° he fro the lofte°   *leapt / from the upstairs room*
2710 Whan she hath warned him and doon him bote.°   *done him good*
    This Lino swifte was and light of fote,°   *foot*
And from his wyf he ran a ful good pas.°   *at great speed*
This sely° woman is so wayk,° allas,   *innocent / weak*
And helples so, that er° that she fer° wente   *before / far*
2715 Hir cruel fader dide hir for to hente.°   *had her seized*
Allas, Lino, why art thou so unkinde?°   *untrue*
Why ne haddest thou remembred° in thy minde   *did you not remember*
To taken hir, and lad° hir forth with thee?   *bring*
For whan she saw that goon awey was he,
2720 And that she mighte nat so faste go
Ne folwen° him, she sette hir doun right tho,°   *i.e., keep up with / then*
Til she was caught and fetered° in prisoun.   *fettered, shackled*
    This tale is seyd for this conclusioun. . . .

[UNFINISHED]

---

2. Window leading to the drain or gutter of a roof.

Anelida and Arcite

Highly experimental, though largely unsuccessful, Chaucer's "Anelida and Arcite" occupies a mysterious position in his canon. Its fragmentary condition and the poet's lack of mastery over form and subject matter have caused many critics to place it early in Chaucer's career, but the verse form and subject matter themselves suggest that he more likely wrote it in the mid to late 1380s, after translating Boethius's *Consolation of Philosophy* and during the period when he was working the story of Thebes into other poems. These poems would have included "Palamon and Arcite," listed in the *Legend of Good Women* (420), probably an early version of the Knight's Tale, which also concerns the Theban knight Arcite and the Athenian lord Duke Theseus. The *Legend of Good Women* (dated in the late 1380s) itself explores the theme of betrayal that lies at the heart of "Anelida," a topic that is also central to *Troilus and Criseyde*, probably completed not long before the *Legend*. Moreover, recent work on "the matter of Armenia" in the court of Richard II suggests that a visit to Richard's court by the deposed Armenian king, Levon VI, in 1385–86, may have informed Chaucer's characterization of the Armenian queen Anelida,[1] again suggesting a date after 1385. Such a date also makes sense of the fact that most of the poem is written in rhyme royal, seven-line stanzas of iambic pentameter (rhyming ababbcc), the same verse form Chaucer uses in the *Parliament of Fowls* (1380–82) and in *Troilus and Criseyde*.

Yet "Anelida and Arcite," though it contains some of Chaucer's finest individual lines of verse, does not measure up to the sustained achievement of his other poems written during this time period. To be sure, there is much to admire here. C. S. Lewis famously praised line 18 ("singest with vois memorial in the shade") as embodying "within itself the germ of the whole central tradition of high poetical language in English."[2] But long stretches of the poem lumber along in what another reader refers to as a "level drone,"[3] uncertain about how to reconcile the style of the courtly French poets Guillaume de Machaut and Jean Froissart[4] with the epic machinery of Statius and Chaucer's Italian contemporary Giovanni Boccaccio. Chaucer also borrows from Ovid's *Heroides*, a classical collection of epistolary laments of famous women jilted by their lovers. Especially notable is the relationship between the Ovidian Dido and Anelida, since both heroines deploy the image of the swan singing in anticipation of its own death. Ovid's Dido begins her complaint with this image just at the point where Anelida breaks off (346–47; compare the *Legend of Good Women* 1355–56).[5] Critics remain unsure of how to evaluate the resulting

1. Carolyn P. Collette and Vincent J. DiMarco, "The Matter of Armenia in the Age of Chaucer," *Studies in the Age of Chaucer* 23 (2001): 317–58.
2. C. S. Lewis, *The Allegory of Love: A Study in Medieval Tradition* (London: Oxford University Press, 1936), 201.
3. Stephen Knight, *Rymyng Craftily: Meaning in Chaucer's Poetry* (Sydney: Angus and Robertson, 1973), 12.
4. For a fuller discussion of the poem's debt to the *dits amoureux* of Machaut and Froissart, see James I. Wimsatt, "*Anelida and Arcite*: A Narrative of Complaint and Comfort," *The Chaucer Review* 5 (1970): 1–8.
5. The entire Ovidian epistle of Dido is included in the Contexts section of this Norton Critical Edition.

literary crossbreed that is "Anelida and Arcite": Is it vapid and artificial? Or is it an audacious poetic experiment that manages to keep powerful sentiment this side of bathos by the discipline of poetic form?

At the heart of the problem lies the poem's structure, at once ambitious and forced. Divided into seventy-line sections, it begins with an epic invocation to the gods and muses, shifting after three stanzas to a description of the Athenian duke Theseus's victorious return from his wars against the Amazons and the civil war in Thebes between the two sons of Oedipus; this is narrative material borrowed mostly from Boccaccio's *Il Teseide* (*The Book of Theseus*), which Chaucer would use again in the Knight's Tale to far better effect. In the second seventy-line section, the poet awkwardly turns away from such bellicose topics to the lovely Armenian queen Anelida whose love for the false Arcite is only marginally less motivated than her presence in Thebes in the first place. Although already characterized as "double" and "false" (e.g., lines 11, 49, 87, 97), Arcite begins as an attentive, if jealous, lover, at least for the requisite seventy lines. At line 141, the Theban knight predictably betrays his tender Armenian mistress with a new love whose chief recommendation is that she plays hard to get, thus plunging Anelida into the depths of despair, again for seventy lines.

Chaucer now lurches abruptly from narrative to lyric, as Anelida accuses Arcite of faithlessness in a complaint whose 140 lines (again divided into two seventy-line segments) occupy virtually all of what remains of the poem. The surprise now, however, is the confidence and grace Chaucer brings to this lyric set piece. Here the poet shows what he is capable of achieving when he turns his hand to a complex metrical form in the French style. As W. W. Skeat helpfully sets out the complaint (using rubrics followed by this edition as well), it is composed of a "Proem," nine lines of rhyming pentameter (aabaabbab), which introduces the "Strophe,"[6] led off by four more nine-line stanzas with the same meter and rhyme scheme. The fifth stanza of the "Strophe" is made up of sixteen lines of tetrameter, which include two quatrains of the rhyming pattern aaab followed by two quatrains of the rhyming pattern bbba. The "Strophe" finishes with a final nine-line stanza, pentameter once more, that adds to each line an internal rhyme. Beginning at the precise center of the poem, the "Antistrophe" exactly repeats the rhyme scheme and pattern of the "Strophe": four nine-line stanzas of pentameter, one sixteen-line stanza of tetrameter, followed by a nine-line stanza with the meter, rhyme scheme, and internal rhyme of its counterpart in the "Strophe." A concluding stanza balances the Proem. Elaborately circular, the complaint begins and ends with the same line, which means that the a-rhyme of the Proem has become the b-rhyme of the Conclusion. The complaint is also rife with *rimes riches* (rhymes on homonyms), and even includes one stanza of monorhyme (a stanza based on a single rhyme; stanza three of the "Antistrophe").

Anelida's complaint is, in short, a metrical *tour de force*, similar in form to the medieval *virelay*, popular in fourteenth-century France; in the *virelay*, a sequence of tercets (rhyming aab) form stanzas that are themselves linked in a chain of rhymes (when the rhyme of the last line of one stanza is repeated in the first line of the next). The *virelay*, a musical form, however, generally adopts two-, three-, or four-beat lines; consequently, in "Anelida," the two tetrameter sixteen-line stanzas and the two stanzas with internal rhyme most closely recall the rapid accumulation of rhymes that characterizes this lavish form. The chain rhymes of the *virelay* also remind one of the care Chaucer takes to link his stanzas formally and to tie the end of the complaint to the

---

6. "Strophe" and "Antistrophe" are terms taken from ancient Greek literature, and refer to a grouping of lines that are answered by another grouping of metrically corresponding lines.

beginning.[7] In its rich complexity and formal control, Anelida's complaint has also been compared to the Middle English *Pearl*.

Most remarkably, here in the most ornate and highly structured part of the poem, Chaucer achieves an affecting naturalness. The form of the poem is psychologically expressive in many ways. The rapid turns of thought in Anelida's lament dramatically represent her grief and distraction; rhetorical questions become real ones, demonstrating Chaucer's ability to sweep shifts of mood and perspective into swift, economical clauses: "And shal I preye, and weyve womanhede? / Nay, rather deeth than do so foul a dede, / And axe mercy, gilteles! What nede?" (299–301). The monorhyme in this stanza, where Anelida briefly recognizes the emotional trap in which she has fallen, reflects her inability to emerge from the maze of her own subjectivity. Some of the most ornate poetic language in the complaint has an evocative beauty, perhaps no line or image more so than the sword of sorrow which, sharpened by treacherous pleasure, pierces Anelida's heart with its cruel edge: "So thirleth [pierces] with the point of remembraunce / the swerd of sorowe, y-whet with fals plesaunce, / Myn herte" (211–13). Chaucer here also shows how deeply he has internalized his sources, transforming Dante's "puntura de la rimembranza" ("prick of memory"; *Purgatorio* 12.20), an image of the penance of the prideful, to the service of disappointed love. That poetic alchemy also conveys some of the psychological and philosophical complexity of this poem, for, while Anelida is not herself blameworthy or prideful, her riotous indulgence in grief and recrimination suggests a disordered soul in tension with her claim to "plainness" or constancy. As Lee Patterson has written, "If Anelida is betrayed by Arcite, she is also self-betrayed."[8]

"Anelida and Arcite" is thus more than a simple love poem. Like his other "Theban writings" (Patterson's phrase), it investigates the self-betrayals of language and poetry themselves. Several patterns of imagery unify the poem, for example its frequent references to colors (see lines 1, 146, 180, 289, 353). But Anelida's luxuriant use of the "colors of rhetoric" (the standard medieval term for rhetorical embellishment) is in tension with her claim to transparency. Although the speaker insists that her color is "asshen" (173), the vividness of her grief makes her almost radiant. Are such contradictions inadvertent, or has Chaucer deliberately set out in "Anelida" to follow what he calls the "slye weye" (48), as he self-consciously explores the topic of division? Does he have an explicit interest here in the structural and thematic relationship between the wounds of war and of love? Some readers, like Patterson, who calls the poem's "reduplicative structure . . . thematically expressive,"[9] see in the gap between the poet's epic and romantic subject matter the signs of an exciting poetic experiment. Or as W. A. Davenport notes, just as Theseus and Creon subjugate Scythia and Thebes, so Anelida is devastated by Arcite, a pattern that we know will be repeated again in the history of Thebes when, in time to come, the conquering hero Theseus lays waste to the city of Creon in which Anelida resides: "Anelida's story is thus suspended between one bloody conflict and another."[1] Rather than a flaw in its fabric, the interweaving of such public and private threads may be appreciated as a part of the poem's texture.

If the underlying structure of the poem is seen as contrast or antithesis rather than continuous narration, the contrasts are also with other works in the Chaucerian canon.[2] Not only does the Theban story connect "Anelida and Arcite"

7. For the relationship of Anelida's complaint to the virelay, see Wimsatt, *Chaucer and His French Contemporaries: Natural Music in the Fourteenth Century* (Toronto: U of Toronto P, 1991), 27–28.
8. Lee Patterson, *Chaucer and the Subject of History* (Madison: U of Wisconsin P, 1991), 66.
9. Ibid. 62.
1. W. A. Davenport, *Chaucer: Complaint and Narrative* (Cambridge: D. S. Brewer, 1988), 27.
2. For example, see Alfred David, "Recycling *Anelida and Arcite*: Chaucer as a Source for Chaucer,"

to the Knight's Tale (and less directly to *Troilus and Criseyde*), but the plight of woman betrayed ties it to the *Legend of Good Women* and to the Squire's Tale, where the lament of a female falcon against the gross deceptions of her avian suitor ("under hewe of trouthe . . . / So depe in greyn he dyed his col- oures" [So fully he disguised his true color]; 5.508, 511) echoes many of the specific images and themes of Anelida's complaint against Arcite, including the inevitability of male infidelity, traced back to Lamech, the original bigamist (compare "Anelida" 150–54 to *Canterbury Tales* 5.550–51). Motifs in "Ane- lida" also suggest gifts that are presented in the similarly unfinished Squire's tale: the ring (131), the horse (157, 183–84), and the sword (211–12, 270– 71).[3]

But not all such intertextual references are so neatly aligned. The Arcite of Boccaccio's *Il Teseide* or of the Knight's Tale is known for his courtly passion and fidelity to his mistress Emelye. To see him play such a different and dis- reputable role here, as he abandons Anelida, is a shock, causing some readers to conclude that Chaucer himself then turned away from "Anelida" in frustra- tion or distaste. But perhaps Arcite's behavior is not entirely incompatible with his role elsewhere. In the Knight's Tale, Arcite had already hinted at a darker side as he posed the somewhat opportunistic question to his cousin Palamon, "Who shal yeve (give) a lovere any lawe?" (1.1164), essentially arguing the case for "all's fair in love and war." Just as Chaucer was fascinated by the existence of opposing perspectives on figures like Aeneas, blamed by Ovid but praised by Virgil, or Theseus, the great Athenian ruler from the Knight's Tale who deserted the maiden Ariadne after she had helped him defeat the Minotaur (see the *Legend of Good Women* 1886–2227), so also he may have wished to show us two sides of Arcite. Nothing in this poem prevents the fair Emelye herself from being the Theban knight's new lady, thus making "Anelida and Arcite" a fascinating prequel (earlier in narrative time, not necessarily in bio- graphical time) to the poet's other Theban narratives and, like them, exploring themes of doubleness in love, language, and literary tradition.

But such elaborate interpretations of the poem's thematic and structural divisions depend on unprovable assumptions about its textual status. While the existence of "Anelida" in twelve manuscripts is testimony to its popularity in the fifteenth century (the *Book of the Duchess* and the *House of Fame* each survive only in three), the manuscripts also reflect the confusion of the early scribes as to the poem's form, even as to which parts were really by Chaucer. Fewer than half of the manuscripts print the poem in the standard order (in most the first 210 lines of narrative either follow the complaint or are missing altogether). And only four manuscripts include the final stanza (351–57), which follows Anelida's complaint with a promise to narrate her sacrifice in the Temple of Mars. The critical consensus is that these final lines are in fact spurious. These textual problems have led one scholar to suggest that the only part of the poem actually written by Chaucer is the complaint itself, and that the first 210 lines were originally part of an entirely different poem by a dif- ferent poet.[4]

Clearly many conclusions about "Anelida" must be regarded as tentative, since they rest on a more unitary and stable text than the manuscripts have left us. For example, various readers over the years have speculated about how Chaucer might have intended to complete the poem: Might he have been plan- ning for Arcite to return to Anelida with a message of comfort, on the model

Studies in the Age of Chaucer, Proceedings 1, ed. Paul Strohm and Thomas J. Heffernan (Knoxville, TN: New Chaucer Society, 1984): 105–15.
3. Collette and DiMarco, 331.
4. A. S. G. Edwards, "The Unity and Authenticity of *Anelida and Arcite*: The Evidence of the Man- uscripts," *Studies in Bibliography* 41 (1988): 178–88.

of the French *dits amoureux*, or might he have meant for Anelida's despair to be addressed in the form of a dream-vision?[5] Or is the poem more pessimistic: Is Anelida perhaps, like her prototype Dido, preparing to kill herself? Without the final stanza, though, we have no proof that the poem as we have it (lines 1–350) is not indeed "finished." Reflecting its own formal circularity, in the end "Anelida and Arcite" remains something of a Chaucerian mystery, as haunting as its enigmatic and anachronistic heroine.

The text here is based chiefly on the version found in the Fairfax manuscript (Fairfax 16, Bodleian Library).

Anelida and Arcite

Thou ferse° god of armes, Mars the rede,°	*fierce / red, ruddy*
That in the frosty contree called Trace,°	*Thrace*
Within thy grisly° temple ful of drede°	*horrible / fearful, dreadful*
Honoured art as patroun of that place,	
5 With thy Bellona, Pallas, ful of grace,	
Be present and my song continue° and gye;°	*sustain / guide*
At my beginning thus to thee I crye.[1]	

For it ful depe is sonken° in my minde	*penetrated deeply*
With pitous° hert in Englyssh to	*compassionate*
endyte°	*(that I should) compose*
10 This olde storie, in Latin which I finde,	
Of quene Anelida and fals Arcite,[2]	
That elde,° which that al can frete° and bite,	*which age / devour*
As it hath freten mony a noble storie,	
Hath nigh° devoured out of oure memorie.	*nearly*

15 Be favorable eek, thou Polymya,	
On Parnaso that with thy sustres glade,	
By Elycon nat fer from Cirrea,	
Singest with vois memorial in the shade,	
Under the laurer which that may not fade,[3]	

---

5. Wimsatt, *"Anelida and Arcite,"* 7–8; Michael D. Cherniss, "Chaucer's *Anelida and Arcite*: Some Conjectures," *The Chaucer Review* 5 (1970): 9–21.
1. Chaucer bases his opening invocation to Mars on 1.1–3 of Giovanni's Boccaccio's *Il Teseide (The Book of Theseus)*, though Chaucer reverses the order of Boccaccio's stanzas. The references to Bellona, goddess of war, and Pallas (Athena), goddess of wisdom, are taken from Chaucer's avowed source, Statius's *Thebaid* (see line 21), where the two are distinct; they are, however, often confused (as here) in medieval glosses on the *Thebaid* and other poems.
2. The name Anelida is most likely derived ultimately from an Italian translation of Laudine, Yvain's wife in Chrétien de Troyes' romance *The Knight of the Lion*, but the derivation does not explain her character, her history, or her connection with Armenia (see line 72). Arcite is taken from Boccaccio's *Il Teseide*, where his role as faithful lover of the fair Emilia, which Chaucer would explore in the Knight's Tale, differs sharply from his behavior here.
3. Favor (me) also, you Polymnia, who along with your joyful sisters sing with memorable voice in the shade under the laurel tree, which does not wither. (Polymnia was one of the nine muses [her "sisters" here], associated with sacred song and with memory; the traditional dwelling of the muses was on Mount Helicon in the mountain range of the Parnassus, but Chaucer treats Helicon as a well sacred to the Muses; see the *House of Fame* 521–22. Cirra was a Greek port city, erroneously located by Chaucer and other medieval writers near Mount Parnaso; the laurel was the favorite tree of Apollo, god of poetry [see *House of Fame* 1107–08] and a traditional prize for athletes, heroes, and poets.)

20 And do° that I my ship to haven° winne.   *bring about / harbor*
    First folowe I Stace, and after him Corinne.[4]

The Story

    Iamque domos patrias Cithice post aspera gentiis
    Prelia luarigero subeunte Thesea curru
    Letifici plausus missusque ad sidera vulgi. . . .[5]

    Whan Theseus with werres° longe and grete   *wars*
    The aspre° folk of Cithe[6] had overcome,   *harsh, cruel*
    With laurer° corouned in his char gold-bete,°   *laurel / gold-plated chariot*
25 Hom to his contree-houses° is he come,   *houses of his country*
    For which the peple, blisful al and some,
    So cryden that to the sterres° it wente,   *stars*
    And him to honouren dide al hir entente.°   *did all they could*

    Biforn° this duk,° in signe of victorie,   *In front of / duke*
30 The trompes° come, and in° his baner large   *trumpets / on*
    The image of Mars, and in token of glorie
    Men myghten seen of tresour many a charge,°   *many loads of treasure*
    Many a bright helm,° and many a spere and targe,°   *helmet / shield*
    Many a fresh° knight, and many a blisful route,°   *lively / group, retinue*
35 On hors, on fote,° in al the felde aboute.°   *foot / field around*

    Ipolita° his wyf, the hardy° quene   *Hippolyta / valiant*
    Of Cithia,° that he conquered hadde,   *Scythia*
    With Emelye hir yonge suster shene,°   *beautiful, luminous*
    Faire in a char° of gold he with him ladde,°   *chariot / led*
40 That al the ground about° hir char she spradde°   *around / spread*
    With brightnesse of the beautee in hir face,
    Fulfilled of largesse° and of alle grace.   *with generosity*

    With his triumphe and laurer-crouned° thus,   *crowned with laurel*
    In al the floure° of Fortunes yevynge,°   *flower (i.e., peak) / bounty*
45 Lete° I this noble prince Theseus   *Leave*
    Toward Athenes in his wey rydinge,
    And founde° I wol in shortly° for to bringe   *attempt / briefly*
    The slye° wey of that I gan° to write,   *deceitful / about which I began*
    Of quene Anelida and fals Arcite.

---

4. Despite Chaucer's claim that he follows Statius, there is no known source for the main theme and action of *Anelida*; the poem borrows more from Boccaccio than from Statius, though here as elsewhere Chaucer does not use Boccaccio's name. Corinna may refer to a Theban poetess (mentioned by Statius) who won a poetry-writing contest; other possibilities include Ovid's mistress in the *Amores*, Corinna, whose name was sometimes confused with the title or author of parts of that work, or Corinnus, author of a lost account of the Trojan War. The shift from Statius to Corinna is roughly aligned with the shift in the poem's subject matter from epic to romance.

5. And now, after harsh wars against the Scythians, Theseus approached his native land in a chariot decked with laurel, and the applause of the joyous crowd rang to the stars. (The lines are quoted from Statius's *Thebaid* 12.519–21; the stanza that follows provides a close translation of the Latin into Middle English.)

6. Scythia, a region to the north/northeast of the Black Sea, home to the mythical Amazons, against whom Theseus has been fighting, and whose queen Hippolyta (see below, 36) he brings back as his bride.

50 Mars, which that thurgh his furious course of ire,
    The olde wrathe of Juno to fulfille,[7]
    Hath set the peples hertes° bothe on fyre   *hearts*
    Of Thebes and Grece, everich other to kille°   *each to kill the other*
    With blody speres, ne rested never stille°   *nor did (either side) desist*
55 But throng° now her, now ther, among hem°   *forced (their way) / them*
        bothe,
    That everich other slough,° so wer they   *slew*
        wrothe.°   *enraged were they*

    For whan Amphiorax and Tydeus,
    Ipomedon, Parthonopee also
    Were dede, and slayn proude Campaneus,
60 And whan the wrecched Thebans, bretheren two,
    Were slayn, and Kyng Adrastus hoom ago,[8]
    So desolat° stood Thebes and so bare°   *devastated / vulnerable*
    That no wight° coude remedie of his fare.°   *person / its plight, condition*

    And whan the olde Creon[9] gan espye°   *perceived*
65 How that the blood roial was brought adoun,°   *destroyed*
    He held° the citee by his tyrannye   *controlled*
    And did the gentils° of that regioun   *caused the nobility*
    To been his frendes and dwellen in the toun.
    So, what for love of him and what for awe,°   *fear*
70 The noble folk wer to the toun y-drawe.°   *brought back*

    Among al these Anelida, the quene
    Of Ermony,[1] was in that toun dwellinge,   *Armenia*
    That fairer was than is the sonne shene;   *shining sun*
    Thurghout the world so gan hir name
        springe,°   *did her reputation spread*
75 That hir to seen had every wyght lykinge,°   *person the desire*
    For, as of trouthe,° is ther noon hir liche°   *fidelity / no one like her*
    Of al the women in this worlde riche.°   *splendid*

    Yong was this quene, of twenty yeer of elde,°   *age*
    Of midel stature,° and of swich fairenesse°   *average size / such beauty*

7. Mars, who following the furious course of his rage, (sought) to gratify the ancient wrath of Juno.
   (Juno hated the Thebans because of the adulteries committed by her husband, Jove, with Theban
   women.)
8. Departed to (his) home. (Adrastus, King of Argos, led the campaign of the "seven against Thebes"
   who were pursuing Polynices' claim for the throne against his brother Eteocles; Campaneus and
   Hippomedon were two of the seven chieftains; Amphiarus, a seer, and Tydeus also took their side
   in the battle.)
9. Ruler of Thebes and uncle of the claimants to the throne.
1. Armenia. (The appearance of the Armenian queen in ancient Thebes is clearly unhistorical, leading
   some critics to suggest a confusion with Queen Harmonia, recipient of the ill-fated "brooch of
   Thebes," mentioned by Chaucer in the "Complaint of Mars" (246–62) and in the Wife of Bath's
   Tale (*Canterbury Tales* 3.743). But the reference is almost certainly to medieval Lesser Armenia,
   which played an important role in fourteenth-century European politics as an outpost in the
   struggle of European Christians against the Muslims. The deposed Armenian king, Levon VI,
   visited England in 1385–86, and Chaucer most likely played a role the following year in secret
   negotiations for an alliance with France prompted by Levon's interests. Armenia was often rep-
   resented in contemporary literature as doomed and/or betrayed. See Carolyn Collette and Vincent
   DiMarco, "The Matter of Armenia in the Age of Chaucer," *Studies in the Age of Chaucer* 23
   [2001]: 317–58.)

80 That Nature had a joye hir to behelde,°   *look upon her*
And for to speken of hir stedfastnesse°   *constancy, faithfulness*
She passed hath Penelope and Lucresse,²
And shortly, if she shal be comprehended,°   *summed up in words*
In hir might nothing been amended.°   *improved upon*

85 This Theban knight [Arcite] eek,° sooth to seyn,°   *also / truth to tell*
Was yong and therwithal a lusty° knight,   *in addition a vigorous*
But he was double° in love and nothing pleyn,°   *duplicitous / sincere*
And subtil in that crafte over any wight,°   *beyond any (other) person*
And with his cunning wan° this lady bright,   *won (in love)*
90 For so ferforth° he gan hir trouthe assure,°   *completely / pledged his faith*
That she him trusted over° any creature.   *beyond*

What shuld I seyn? She loved Arcite so
That whan that he was absent any throwe°   *short space of time*
Anoon° hir thoughte hir herte brast   *Immediately*
     a-two,°   *(would) burst in two*
95 For in hir sight to hir he bar him lowe,°   *behaved humbly*
So that she wende° have al his hert y-knowe;°   *believed / (that she) knew*
But he was fals; it nas but feyned chere,°   *was only pretense*
As nedeth nat to men swich craft to lere.³

But nevertheles ful mikel besynesse°   *much work*
100 Had he er that° he mighte his lady winne,   *Did he have before*
And swoor° he wolde dyen for distresse,   *he swore that*
Or from his wit he seyde he wolde twinne.°   *depart (i.e., lose his mind)*
Allas the while, for it was routhe° and sinne,°   *pitiable / sinful*
That° she upon his sorowes wolde rewe,°   *Done so that / have compassion*
105 But nothing thinketh the fals as doth the trewe.

Hir fredom fond Arcite in swich manere,
That al was his that she hath, moche or lite,⁴
Ne to no creature made she chere°   *was she friendly*
Ferther° then that it lyked° to Arcite.   *To a greater degree / was pleasing*
110 Ther nas no lak° with which he mighte her wite,°   *was no fault / blame*
She was so ferforth yeven hym to plese°   *devoted to pleasing him*
That al that lyked him° it did hir ese.°   *pleased him / made her happy*

Ther nas° to hir no maner lettre° y-sent   *was not / any kind of letter*
That touched° love, from any maner wight,°   *mentioned / person*
That she ne shewed it° him er° it was   *concealed from / before*
115   brent;°   *burnt*
So pleyn° she was and did hir fulle might   *straightforward, sincere*

2. She surpassed Penelope and Lucretia. (Penelope was the faithful wife of Odysseus; Lucretia, another faithful wife whose story Chaucer tells in the *Legend of Good Women* [1680–1885], committed suicide after being raped.)
3. Such craft as men do not need to study (for it comes to them naturally).
4. But the way that false people think is in no way similar to the thinking of true people. Such manner of generosity Arcite found (in her) that everything that she possessed was his, large or small.

That she nil hyden nothing° from hir knight   *will conceal nothing*
Lest he of any untrouthe° hir upbreyde;°   *infidelity / reproach*
Withoute bode his heste she obeyde.[5]

120 And eek° he made him° jelous over here,°   *also / acted / her*
That° what that any man had to hir sayd   *So that*
Anoon° he wolde preyen° hir to swere   *At once / ask*
What was that word, or make him evel apayd.°   *act displeased*
Than wende° she out of hir wit have   *thought*
    brayd;°   *might lose her mind*
125 But al this nas but sleight° and flaterye,   *was nothing but deceit*
Withoute love he feyned° jelosye.   *feigned, pretended*

And al this took she so debonerly°   *graciously, courteously*
That al his wille, hir thoughte it skilful thing,°   *seemed reasonable to her*
And ever the lenger° she loved him tenderly   *the more*
130 And did him honour as° he were a king.   *as if*
Hir herte was to him wedded with a ring;[6]
So ferforth° upon trouthe is hir entente°   *completely / set her purpose*
That wher° he goth, hir herte with him wente.   *wherever*

Whan she shal ete,° on him is so hir thought   *i.e., sits down to a meal*
135 That wel unnethe° of mete° took she kepe,°   *scarcely / food / heed*
And whan that she was to hir reste brought,°   *i.e., goes to bed*
On him she thoughte alwey til that she slepe;
Whan he was absent, prively° she wepe;   *in private, alone*
Thus liveth faire Anelida the quene
140 For fals Arcite, that did hir al this tene.°   *suffering, sorrow*

This fals Arcite, of° his newfanglenesse,°   *in / fickleness*
For° she to him so lowly° was and trewe,   *Because / humble, submissive*
Took lesse deyntee for° hir stedfastnesse°   *delight in / constancy*
And saw another lady, proud and newe,
145 And right anoon he cladde him in hir hewe[7]—
Wot I not° whether in whyte, rede, or grene—   *I don't know*
And falsed° fair Anelida the quene.   *was false to*

But nevertheles, greet wonder was it noon
Though he were fals, for it is kinde of man
150 Sith Lamek was, that is so longe agoon,
To been in love as fals as ever he can;
He was the firste fader that began
To loven two, and was in bigamye;
And he found tentes first, but if men lye.[8]

---

5. Without being asked, she obeyed his (every) command (i.e., his word was her command).
6. That is, he promised his faith to her by giving her a ring, an act that had a quasi-legal significance during the Middle Ages.
7. And all at once he dressed himself in her colors. (Note that blue, the color of fidelity, is not one of those mentioned here.)
8. But nevertheless, it was little wonder that he was false, for such is the nature of man, since the time of Lamech so long ago, to be as false in love as he can. He was the very first who undertook

155 This fals Arcite, somwhat moste he feyne,°   *feign, fake it*
    Whan he wex° fals, to covere his traitorye,°   *grew / conceal his treachery*
    Right as° an hors that can both byte and   *Just like*
        pleyne,°   *whinny (in pain)*
    For he bar hir on honde° of trecherye   *accused her*
    And swoor he coude hir doublenesse espye,°   *perceive her falseness*
160 And al was falsness that she to him mente.[9]
    Thus swoor this theef, and forth his wey he wente.

    Allas, what herte might enduren it,
    For routhe° and wo, hir sorow for to telle?°   *pity / describe*
    Or what man hath the cunning° or the wit?   *skill, ability*
165 Or what man might within the chambre dwelle,°   *remain in the room*
    If I to him rehersen shal° the helle,   *were to narrate*
    That suffreth fair Anelida the quene
    For fals Arcite, that did hir al this tene?°   *this great injury*

    She wepeth, waileth, swowneth pitously,°   *swoons pitifully*
170 To grounde deed° she falleth as a stoon;   *as if dead*
    Craumpissheth° hir limes° crookedly;   *Cramps, contracts / limbs*
    She speketh as° hir wit were al agoon;°   *as if / had departed*
    Other colour than asshen° hath she noon,   *that of ashes (i.e., pallor)*
    Noon other word speketh she, moche or lite,°   *more or less*
175 But "Mercy, cruel herte myn, Arcite!"

    And thus endureth° til that she was so mate°   *(she) carries on / worn out*
    That she ne hath foot on which she may sustene,°   *remain standing*
    But forth languisshing° ever in this estate,°   *growing weaker / condition*
    Of° which Arcite hath nother routhe ne   *For*
        tene;°   *neither pity nor distress*
180 His herte was elleswhere, newe and grene,
    That on hir wo ne deyneth him nat to thinke;
    Him rekketh never wher she flete or sinke.[1]

    His newe lady holdeth him so narowe
    Up by the bridel, at the staves ende,[2]
185 That° every word he dredeth as° an arowe;   *So that / fears like*
    Hir daunger[3] made him bothe bowe and bende,°   *stoop and kneel*
    And as hir liste,° made him turne or wende°   *she pleases / come or go*

---

to love two (women), the father of bigamy, and he invented tents, if sources don't lie. (See Genesis 4:19–24; in addition to having two wives, Lamech was a descendant of Cain, a self-confessed killer in vengeance, a fact that may have significance in the Theban context of this poem. It was his son Jabal who, in the biblical phrase, "was the father of those who dwell in tents"; see 154.)

9. And that her intentions toward him were entirely false.

1. So that he does not condescend to imagine her woe; it does not matter at all to him whether she floats or sinks.

2. His new lady holds him so tightly (by the reins, pulling him) up by the bridle (but holding him at a distance) with a staff (probably the shaft of a cart; i.e., she maintains control over him while keeping him from getting too close to her).

3. "Daunger" is the traditional standoffishness a lady shows her suitor as part of the courtly game of love, often expecting that it will merely increase his ardor.

For she ne graunted him in hir livinge°   *during her life*
No grace, why that he hath lust° to singe;   *any reason to want to*

190 But drof him forth, unnethe liste hir knowe
That he was servaunt to hir ladyshippe,[4]
But lest that he were proud, she helde him lowe;
Thus serveth he, withoute fee or shippe;°   *wages*
She sent him now to londe, now to shippe,
195 And for she yaf° him daunger al his fille,°   *gave / his fill of disdain*
Therfor she had him at hir owne wille.°   *entirely in her power*

Ensample of° this, ye thrifty° women alle,   *A lesson from / worthy*
Take here of Anelida and fals Arcite,
That for hir liste him "dere herte" calle
200 And was so meke, therfor he loved hir lite;[5]
The kinde° of mannes herte is to delite   *nature*
In thing that straunge° is, also° God me save,   *unfamiliar, novel / as*
For what he may not gete, that wolde he have.[6]

Now turne we to Anelida ageyn,
205 That pyneth° day by day in languisshing;°   *Who pines / depression*
But whan she saw that hir ne gat no geyn,°   *she was achieving nothing*
Upon a day, ful sorowfully wepinge,
She caste hir for to make° a   *set about to compose*
compleynynge,°   *complaint*
And with hir owne hond she gan it write,°   *wrote it*
210 And sente it to hir Theban knight Arcite.

The compleynt of Anelida the quene upon fals Arcite[7]

PROEM

So thirleth with the point of remembraunce
The swerd of sorowe, y-whet with fals plesaunce,
Myn herte, bare of blis and blak of hewe,[8]
That° turned is in quaking° al my daunce,   *So that / into trembling*
215 My suretee° in awhaped° countenaunce,   *peace of mind / bewildered*
Sith it availeth nat° for to been trewe;   *Since it does no good*
For whoso° trewest is, it shal hir rewe,°   *whoever / make her sorry*
That° serveth love and doth hir observaunce°   *She who / service*
Alwey to oon,° and chaungeth° for no newe.   *one / alters*

4. But she drove him forth, scarcely troubling herself to acknowledge that he was her ladyship's servant.
5. That because it pleased her to call him "dear heart" and because she was so meek, therefore he loved her little.
6. Proverbial: He wants what he cannot have.
7. The heading is taken from the Fairfax manuscript. The numberings and subheadings, "Proem," "Strophe," etc., are from Skeat's edition (*Complete Works*, vol. 1, pp. 373–78), retained to help organize the verse formally. For further discussion of the complex poetic form of Anelida's complaint, see my introduction.
8. The sword of sorrow, sharpened with deceptive pleasure, pierces my heart, stripped of happiness and black in color, with the knifepoint of memory. (An echo of Dante's "la puntura de la rimembranza" [the prick of memory] from *Purgatorio* 12.20.)

STROPHE

220 1. I wot° myself as wel as any wight,°   *know / creature, person*
     For I loved oon° with al my herte and might   *one*
     More than myself an hundred thousand sythe,°   *times*
     And called him my hertes lyf, my knight,
     And was al his, as fer as it was right;°   *proper, seemly*
225 And whan that he was glad, than was I blythe,°   *happy*
     And his disese was my deeth as swythe;°   *quickly*
     And he ageyn° his trouthe° hath me plight°   *in return / fidelity / promised*
     For evermore, his lady me to kythe.°   *acknowledge*

     2. Now is he fals, allas, and causeles,°   *without cause, reason*
230 And of my wo he is so routheles°   *without pity*
     That with a worde him list nat ones deyne⁹
     To bringe ageyn my sorowful herte in pes,°   *peace*
     For he is caught up in another les.°   *lie*
     Right as him list,° he laugheth at my peyne,   *Just as he likes*
235 And I ne can myn herte not restreyne°   *cannot stop my heart*
     For to love him alwey neveretheles;
     And of al this I not° to whom me   *don't know*
        pleyne.°   *I (should) complain*

     3. And shal I pleyne—allas, the harde
        stounde!°—   *painful circumstance*
     Unto my fo that yaf ° myn herte a wounde   *foe who gave*
240 And yet desyreth° that myn harm be more?   *still desires*
     Nay, certes, ferther wol I never founde
     Noon other helpe, my sores for to sounde.¹
     My destinee hath shapen it so ful yore;°   *a long time ago*
     I wil noon° other medicyne ne lore;°   *do not wish for / advice*
245 I wil been ay ther° I was ones° bounde,   *always there where / once*
     That° I have seyd, be° seyd for evermore!   *That which / let it be*

     4. Allas, wher is become° your   *where has it gone*
        gentilesse,°   *graciousness*
     Your wordes ful of plesaunce° and humblesse,°   *charm, delight / humility*
     Youre observaunces° in so low° manere   *services / lowly, meek*
250 And your awaiting° and your besynesse°   *attentiveness / devotion, solicitude*
     Upon° me, that ye calden° your maistresse,   *To / whom you called*
     Your sovereyn lady in this worlde here?
     Allas, is ther now nother° word ne chere°   *neither / gesture, expression*
     Ye vouche-sauf° upon myn hevinesse?°   *(might) grant / grief*
255 Allas, youre love, I bye it al to dere.°   *pay too much for it*

     5. Now, certes, swete,° though that ye   *certainly, sweetheart*
     Thus causeles the cause be
     Of my deedly adversitee,

9. That with a (single) word, it did not please him to deign (condescend).
1. No, indeed, I will not look elsewhere for a helper to heal my wounds (of love). (I.e., despite Arcite's
   falseness, Anelida resolves to remain true to him.)

Your manly reson oughte it to respite
260 To sleen your frend,[2] and namely° me,   *especially*
That never yet in no degree°   *to any extent*
Offended yow, as wisly He
That al wot, out of wo my soule quite.[3]
But for I shewed° yow, Arcite,   *because I showed*
265 Al that men wolde to me write,
And was so besy yow to delite°—   *devoted to pleasing you*
Myn honour save°—meke, kinde, and free,°   *preserving / generous*
Therfor ye put on me this wite,°   *blame*
And of me rekke not a mite,°   *care not a bit*
270 Though that the swerd of sorow bite°   *pierces*
My woful herte thurgh your crueltee.

6. My swete fo,° why do ye so, for shame?   *foe*
And thinke ye that furthered be° your name,   *will be magnified*
To love a newe and been untrewe? Nay!
275 And putte yow in sclaunder° now and blame,   *bring slander upon you*
And do to me adversitee° and grame,°   *injury / harm, humiliation*
That love yow most—God, wel thou wost°—alway   *you know*
Yet come ageyn,° and be al pleyn° som day,   *back / sincere*
And than shal this, that now is mis,° be game,°   *amiss / joy, festivity*
280 And al foryive,° whyle that I live may.   *(will be) forgiven*

1. Lo, herte myn, al this is for to seyne,°   *to say (i.e., ask)*
As whether shal I preye or elles pleyne?[4]
Whiche is the wey to doon° yow to be trewe?   *cause*
For either mot° I have yow in my cheyne°   *must / bond (of love)*
285 Or with the deeth ye mot departe us tweyne;°   *drive us two apart*
Ther been noon other mene weyes newe,°   *no new ways out*
For God so wisly° on my soule rewe,°   *surely / take pity*
As verrayly° ye sleen° me with the peyne;   *truly / slay*
That may ye see unfeyned of° myn hewe.°[5]   *unfeigned from / hue*

290 2. For thus ferforth° have I my dethe sought;   *completely*
Myself I mordre° with my privy° thought;   *murder / private, inner*
For sorow and routhe of° your unkindenesse   *grief from*
I wepe, I wake, I faste; al helpeth nought;°   *nothing helps*
I weyve joye that is to speke of ought;[6]
295 I voide° companye, I flee gladnesse;   *avoid, shun*

2. Although, without reason, you are the cause of my deadly misfortune, your manly rationality ought
   to restrain you from killing your friend. (The lines have the flavor of philosophical paradox; like a
   god, Arcite is the uncaused cause, his rationality put into the service of love.)
3. A kind of general asseveration; loosely translated, "as surely as I hope to be saved from woe by
   God who knows everything."
4. Which shall I do—plead or complain? (While "preye" is often used in a religious context, "pleyne"
   has a legal connotation, similar to the verb "accuse.")
5. A second possible meaning for this line is suggested by John Fisher, *The Complete Poetry and
   Prose of Geoffrey Chaucer*, 681 note: "without coloring of pretense." One might take Fisher's
   reading further, for the poem's color imagery links literal color with the "colors" of rhetorical
   embellishment. Anelida's pallor thus signifies her lack of linguistic pretense, somewhat ironic in
   that she delivers this line in a highly stylized section of the poem.
6. I.e., I abandon the joy that comes from normal conversation.

Who may avaunte hir bet of hevinesse°   *boast of more sadness*
Than I? And to this plyte° have ye me brought,   *plight, state*
Withoute gilt;° me nedeth no witnesse.   *(my) guilt*

3. And shal I preye, and weyve womanhede?°[7]
300 Nay, rather deeth than do so foul a dede,
And axe° mercy, gilteles! What nede?   *ask for*
And if I pleyne° what lyf that I lede,   *complain about*
Yow rekketh nat;° that knowe I, out of drede;°   *don't care / without doubt*
And if I unto yow myne othes bede°   *offer oaths, promises (of love)*
305 For myn excuse,° a scorn shal be my mede.°   *plea / reward*
Your chere floureth, but it wol not sede;°[8]
Ful longe agoon I oughte have taken hede.°   *been on guard*

4. For though I hadde yow tomorowe ageyn,°   *back again*
I might as wel holde° Aprill fro reyn,°   *stop / from raining*
310 As holde yow, to make yow be stedfast.°   *faithful*
Almighty God, of trouthe sovereyn,°   *lord, ruler*
Wher is the trouthe of man? Who hath it sleyn?°   *slain, destroyed*
Who° that hem° loveth, she shal hem finde   *Whoever / them (i.e., men)*
as fast°   *firm*
As in a tempest° is a roten mast.°   *storm / i.e., of a ship*
315 Is that a tame best that is ay feyn
To renne away, whan he is lest agast?°[9]

5. Now mercy, swete, if I misseye!°   *say something wrong*
Have I seyd ought amis,° I preye?   *anything amiss*
I not;° my wit is al aweye.   *don't know*
320 I fare as doth the song of Chaunte-pleure[1]
For now I pleyne, and now I pleye;
I am so mased° that I deye;°   *distraught / die*
Arcite hath born° awey the keye   *carried*
Of al my worlde, and my good aventure.°   *fortune*
325 For in this world nis° creature   *there is not a*
Waknge in more discomfiture°   *dejection*
Than I, ne° more sorow endure.°   *nor who / undergoes, suffers*
And if I slepe a furlong wey or tweye,°[2]
Than thinketh me° that your figure   *it seems to me*
330 Bifore me stant,° clad in asure,°   *stands / blue (the color of fidelity)*
To profren eft° and newe assure°   *offer again / promise anew*
For to be trewe, and mercy me to preye.°   *entreat from me*

---

7. And shall I beg and turn my back on womanhood? (In courtly love, the man, not the woman, should be the suitor. In this verse, built up from a single rhyme, Anelida arrives at a kind of moment of truth or objectivity about her situation, framed by entreaties to Arcite for mercy and promises of forgiveness. Here, briefly, she recovers her dignity as she acknowledges and takes some responsibility for the futility of her situation.)
8. Your expression blooms with flowers, but (they) will not take root. (I.e., you act agreeably, but you don't mean what you say.)
9. Is that a well-tamed beast who is always glad to run away, when he is least afraid?
1. A proverbial expression—"to sing-to weep"—adapted from the title of a thirteenth-century French poem. In its original context, the joys of this world were contrasted with the sorrows of the next, but over time it came to describe any alternation of joy and grief.
2. The length of time it takes to travel a furlong (⅛ of a mile) or two (i.e., a short time).

6. The longe night this wonder° sight I drye,°   *extraordinary / experience*
And on the day for this afray° I dye,   *fear*
335 And of al this right nought, ywis, ye recche.°   *truly you care not a bit*
Ne never mo myn eyen° two be drye,   *more will my eyes*
And to your routhe° and to your trouthe I crye.   *pity*
But welawey,° to fer° be they to fecche!°   *alas / too far away / fetch*
Thus holdeth me my destinee a wrecche.
340 But me to rede out of this drede, or gye,
Ne may my wit, so weyk is it, nat strecche.[3]

Conclusion

Than ende I thus, sith° I may do no more.   *since*
I yeve° it up for now and evermore,   *give*
For I shal never eft° putten in balaunce°   *again / jeopardy*
345 My sekernes,° ne lerne of love the lore.°   *peace of mind / the teachings*
But as the swan, I have herd seyd ful yore,°   *long ago*
Ageyns his deth shal singen his penaunce,[4]
So singe I here my destinee or chaunce,
How that Arcite Anelida so sore
350 Hath thirled with the point of remembraunce![5]

The Story continued[6]

Whan that Anelida this woful quene
Hath of hir hand writen in this wyse,°   *manner*
With face deed,° betwixe pale and grene,   *deathly*
She fel a-swowe;° and sith° she gan° to ryse,   *in a swoon / then / began*
355 And unto Mars avoweth° sacrifise   *vows, promises*
Within the temple, with a sorowful chere°   *expression*
That shapen was° as ye shal after here.°   *came to pass / hear as follows*

[UNFINISHED]

---

3. Thus I consider my fate to be misery. Nor is my understanding, weak as it is, able to extend to giving advice or guidance out of this peril.
4. At the approach of his death shall the swan sing a confession of his sins. (The idea that the swan anticipates death with a song was conventional; see the *Parliament of Fowls* 342; also, the *Legend of Good Women* 1356, and Ovid's *Heroides* 7.1–4, where Dido introduces her similar complaint against Aeneas with this comparison; see the selection from the *Heroides* in the Contexts section of this Norton Critical Edition.)
5. How Arcite has so painfully pierced Anelida with the knifepoint of memory. (Repeats the first line of the "Strophe"; see 211.)
6. Several of the best manuscripts omit this stanza, causing many readers to question its authenticity.

Short Poems

Chaucer is known today chiefly for his skill as a writer of narrative poetry. But by his contemporaries and for years after his death, he was clearly also revered as a writer of short, often occasional verse on various topics. In one such poem he is witty and satiric, in another straightforwardly romantic, and elsewhere again deeply religious. Ten of these poems, approximately half of those that survive, are printed here. These represent some of the best known of Chaucer's shorter poems, though space constraints have prevented me from including the astrological allegories "The Complaint of Mars" and "The Complaint of Venus." "Anelida and Arcite," presented in a separate section, illustrates Chaucer's lifelong fondness for and skill in the mode of complaint. "An ABC" is a straightforward devotional or religious poem; "Merciless Beauty" and "To Rosemounde" are poems of courtly love; "Lack of Steadfastness," "Truth," and "Gentilesse," known as Chaucer's "Boethian ballads," explore principles of moral virtue from a philosophical perspective;[1] "Words to Adam," the Envoys to Scogan and Bukton, and Chaucer's final poem, his "Complaint to His Purse," are what I call "poems of personal address," which establish a conversational and sometimes petitionary relationship with a recipient who is addressed by name. These categories, however, are complicated by the complex and often ironic way that Chaucer has of mixing topics and genres, of swerving from a conventional treatment of love or a serious philosophical complaint to a playful pecuniary petition (as he does respectively in the "Complaint to His Purse" and "Envoy to Scogan") or to a moment of earnest religious devotion (as in "Truth").

A modern reader who brings to these poems the post-Romantic expectation that a lyric poem should express immediate and seemingly genuine personal feeling may come away feeling disappointed by the artificiality and detachment of Chaucer's short lyrics. Even professional medievalists disagree about their quality, one critic calling them "occasional, ephemeral, run-of-the-mill . . . technically adequate platitudes, written for the moment and circulated among a few friends at court."[2] These poems, however, can be appreciated for their wit, their sophisticated shifts of topic and mode of address, their subtle blending of literary and naturalistic tones—that is, for what another reader has defined as their "urbane manner."[3] Because they are free of narrative embedding and speak directly and conversationally to real people in Chaucer's world, they encourage biographical speculation by supplementing the sparse details we have about the poet's actual life. At the same time, paradoxically, they are almost impossible to date securely, and their flashes of humor make it difficult to discover from them much, if anything, about the real Chaucer and his feelings about the events of his life and times.

Although probably autobiographical in the largest sense, these poems are far from confessional. They are deeply social, politically involved, many of them

1. Chaucer's other two "Boethian ballads," not printed here, are "The Former Age" and "Fortune."
2. Rossell Hope Robbins, "The Lyrics," *Companion to Chaucer Studies*, ed. Beryl Rowland, rev. ed. (New York: Oxford UP, 1979), 396.
3. P. M. Kean, *Chaucer and the Making of English Poetry*, vol. 1, *Love Vision and Debate* (London: Routledge and Kegan Paul, 1972), 31–45.

specifically addressed to what R. T. Lenaghan has identified as a "circle of gentlemen and clerks" in the civil service of King Richard II and Henry IV.[4] They often read like tantalizing puzzles, which one must solve by looking voyeuristically over the shoulders of those fourteenth-century courtiers, long dead but still cryptically addressing each other by name as they negotiate the precarious political environment of late fourteenth-century England. Such poems of personal address frequently survive in relatively few manuscripts ("Words to Adam" in only two, the Envoys to Scogan and Bukton each in only three, as against fourteen manuscripts of the more abstract "Lack of Steadfastness" or twenty-three manuscripts of "Truth"). As more is known about the Age of Chaucer and his specific milieu, new features of these little verses sometimes shift suddenly into view. For instance, Chaucer's "Words to Adam" has recently taken on additional meaning and importance with the identification of the scribe addressed there as the historical Adam Pinkhurst. Another theory—that Chaucer may have been murdered for his political allegiances or religious views—uses evidence from the short poems "An ABC" and "The Complaint of Chaucer to His Purse" for support.[5] Testimony for and against such theories, still the subject of lively debate, comes from the short poems.

   Chaucer himself alludes to his short poems in several places. In the *House of Fame*, the eagle that ravishes Geoffrey into the heavens informs him that his vision is a reward from Jupiter for serving Love by composing "bookes, songes, dytees, / In ryme or elles in cadence" (622–23). In the *Legend of Good Women*, the lady Alceste asks the God of Love to take mercy on the poet-narrator because of the many "hymns" he has written for Love's holy days and other such poems "[t]hat highten [are called] balades, roundels, virelayes" (F 423); in his Retraction following the *Canterbury Tales*, "many a song and many a lecherous lay" are among the writings that Chaucer felt called upon to revoke. His contemporaries and the writers who followed him in the next generation also praised his ability as a versifier, which they found in abundance in his short lyrics. His fifteenth-century imitator and admirer John Lydgate, for example, claims that he "compiled ful many a fressh dite (ditty or short poem), / Compleyntis, baladis, roundelis, virelaies" (verse forms discussed in more detail below). And in one version of the *Lover's Confession*, Chaucer's friend and contemporary John Gower observes that "the lond fulfild is overal" with "ditees" and "songes glade" composed by Chaucer in his "youthe."[6]

   Comments like this one from Gower are somewhat surprising given that only about twenty of Chaucer's short poems survive (perhaps one or two more depending on what disputed poems are admitted to the canon), and few can be firmly dated to his early career. In fact, several of the shorter poems are linked to events that took place near the end of Chaucer's life, and others sound a Boethian tone of weariness and sardonic resignation to the follies of mankind far from the lively note of youth that Gower seems to be describing. In the "Envoy to Bukton," for example, Chaucer cites his own Wife of Bath and hard personal experience to warn a friend against marriage; this poem was almost certainly written in the last decade of Chaucer's life. Likewise in the "Envoy to Scogan," Chaucer describes his head as gray, his shape as round, and his muse, which he paraded forth in youth, as now a rusty sword better off sheathed. Other poems, like "Lack of Steadfastness," seem appropriate for the hard years of the late 1380s when Richard II was fighting for royal power

---

4. The article, R. T. Lenaghan's "Chaucer's Circle of Gentlemen and Clerks," *The Chaucer Review* 18 (1983): 155–60, is included in the Criticism section of this Norton Critical Edition.
5. The first discovery is reported by Linne Mooney in "Chaucer's Scribe," *Speculum* 81 (2006): 97–138; the second theory is advanced in Terry Jones, *Who Murdered Chaucer? A Medieval Mystery* (New York: St. Martins Press, 2003), esp. 177–82, 337–43.
6. John Lydgate, *Fall of Princes*, ed. Henry Bergen, EETS OS 121 (London: Oxford UP, 1924), 1.Prol.352–53, p. 10; John Gower, *Confessio Amantis*, ed. Russell A. Peck (New York: Holt, Rinehart and Winston, 1968), 522.

against the Lords Appellant in the Merciless Parliament of 1388. Setbacks for Richard in those years also affected the royalist Chaucer, who retired to the country after 1386, many think to avoid the kind of political persecution that ended in the brutal beheading of another fourteenth-century courtier and writer, Thomas Usk, in 1388.

Many of the short poems seem late not only on the basis of subject matter; they also are among the most metrically complex of Chaucer's writings. In his narrative poems, Chaucer seems to have begun his career using a four-beat line, which he employed in the *Book of the Duchess* (1368–72) and the *House of Fame* (usually dated before 1380). But this early line does not appear in his short lyrics, which consistently use the five-beat line of his later verse and which also engage in many other metrical experiments. Metrical form argues against an early date even for "An ABC," traditionally placed early in Chaucer's career because of the remark of an editor in 1602 that it was written for Blanche of Lancaster, who died in 1368. The verse form of "An ABC," however, is the "Monk's stanza" (so-called because of its use in the Monk's Tale), a challenging eight-line stanza of iambic pentameter lines rhyming ababbcbc. "An ABC" is an accomplished translation of a prayer taken from Guillaume de Deguilleville's *Pilgrimage of the Life of Man*, which skillfully juxtaposes the insecurity and desperation of the sinful narrator with the infinite patience and stability of the Virgin Mother. Its appearance in sixteen manuscripts attests to the admiration that its medieval readers had for it, and its religious theme would have been equally appropriate for the poet in either his younger or older years. While other short poems like the "Complaint to Pity" (not printed here) or "Merciless Beauty"—both love poems—might have been written in Chaucer's youth, there is finally not much evidence for a significant body of love ditties from the poet's early career. What seems more certain is that he enjoyed writing short poems of an occasional nature late into his poetic career. His very last poem, written in 1399–1400, "The Complaint of Chaucer to His Purse," is just such a short occasional petition. The poems are loosely organized here according to theme and traditional date; additional information about dating and historical context is provided in the footnotes.

Various theories have been advanced to account for the paucity of surviving lyrics, and especially the youthful hymns and ditties to love that both Chaucer and Gower describe our poet as having composed. Perhaps these should include the lyrics or lyrical interludes embedded in longer works; there are seven such interludes in *Troilus and Criseyde* alone, and lyric interpolations also appear in other poems like the *Book of the Duchess*, the *Parliament of Fowls*, the *Legend of Good Women*, and even the *Canterbury Tales*.[7] Another theory is that Chaucer began writing in French, which was the standard language of courtly poetry, and that his lost lyrics were perhaps poems like the fifteen lyrics written in French by a mysterious "Ch" (perhaps Chaucer himself) and probably composed at the English court during the years of Chaucer's youth.[8] Such a beginning in the French tradition is consistent with the influence of French poetry on Chaucer, which was strong and lasting. Despite the fact that early twentieth-century critics liked to divide Chaucer's career into French, Italian, and English periods, following Chaucer's various travels onto the continent, Chaucer's habits of poetic borrowing were more elastic and consistently eclectic than such a rigid schema allows. As James I. Wimsatt has pointed out, "Chaucer's 'French period' was lifelong."[9]

The French lyric form that most deeply influenced Chaucer in his short

---

7. Arthur K. Moore, "Chaucer's Lost Songs," *Journal of English and Germanic Philology* 48 (1949): 196–208.
8. Although he does not make the case that they are by Chaucer, James I. Wimsatt allows that this might be the case in his edition and translation of these poems, *Chaucer and the Poems of 'Ch' in University of Pennsylvania MS French 15* (Cambridge: D. S. Brewer, 1982).
9. Wimsatt, "Guillaume de Machaut and Chaucer's Love Lyrics," *Medium Aevum* 47 (1978): 85.

poems was the *ballade*. The classic French *ballade* was made up of three stanzas each closed by a repeating refrain; by Chaucer's time, some poets were also adding to this format an envoy, which is a dedicatory stanza that sends the poem forth, most typically to a prince. The three stanzas of the *ballade* can take a variety of metrical forms, but Chaucer limits his to two, both imitated from the French: the rhyme royal stanza (seven lines rhyming ababbcc) or the "Monk's stanza" (described above). Often the envoy takes a different, shorter form than the rest of the poem. "The Complaint of Chaucer to His Purse" follows the *ballade* form exactly; the envoy of this poem breaks into the poem's playful, mock-courtly complaint to the poet's empty purse with a rather serious appeal to the "verray king" (24), the newly crowned Henry IV. Other typical *ballades* are "Truth" (also called the "Balade de bon conseyl"), "Lack of Stead-fastness," and the "Envoy to Bukton." Chaucer also wrote *ballades* like "To Rosemounde" and "Gentilesse" that lack an envoy, and the "Envoy to Scogan" which incorporates an envoy but is not a *ballade* in other respects. The *ballade* form served Chaucer well because of its flexibility and because it allows for shifts of tone and address.

But the influence of French "fixed forms" on Chaucer was not limited to the *ballade*. "Merciless Beauty," which most scholars believe was written by Chaucer despite a lack of attribution in the one manuscript where it is found, is a delicious, lightly humorous poem written in the demanding French *rondeau* form; as Chaucer deployed this form, it consisted of thirteen lines on two rhymes, repeating lines 1–2 in the middle of the poem and the first three lines at the end (ABBabABbabbABB). Some readers have also noted the influence of the "virelay" on parts of "Anelida and Arcite" (especially 256–71 and 317–32). A *ballade* (without the envoy) can also be found in the Prologue to the *Legend of Good Women* (F 249–69) and a *rondeau* at the end of the *Parliament of Fowls* (680–92). While the French poems on which Chaucer modeled his lyric practice were often set to music, the only short poem that Chaucer clearly intended for a musical setting was this *rondeau* in the *Parliament* (for, as he tells us in line 677 of that poem, "the note, I trowe, maked was in Fraunce"). The interpolation of a shorter lyric poem into a longer narrative is also a feature Chaucer borrowed from his medieval French sources. The *Fountain of Love*, by Guillaume de Machaut, a highly influential French poet from the generation before Chaucer, like the *Parliament of Fowls*, included a rondeau close to the end of the poem.[1]

Chaucer was ever a devotee of ancient and continental traditions in prefer-ence to the native English sources he would have had at hand; his use of lyric was no exception to this rule. As well as drawing on French and Italian forms in his lyrics, he reached back to classical sources like Boethius's *Consolation of Philosophy*, where lyric and narrative were combined long before this would be the case in medieval poetry, and Ovid's *Heroides*, the *locus classicus* of the lover's complaint. When he included English lyrics in the *Canterbury Tales*, it was with tongue in cheek—as when the rooster in the Nun's Priest's Tale sings the popular English song "My lief is faren in londe" (7.2879). He seems to have been more embarrassed than admiring of the poetry of his countrymen. Despite his preference for this broad, continental tradition, however, Chaucer's Englishness was impossible for him to repress entirely. He did choose finally to write in English, though he was highly conscious of the ways in which the shortage of rhyme in his native language restricted his ability to move comfort-ably within the French forms he was adapting to the English tradition ("sith rym in Englissh hath swich skarsete" ["since rhymes in English are so scarse"]; "Complaint of Venus" 80).

Even beyond such compromises, however, Chaucer inevitably made the

---

1. An English translation/summary of this poem is included in the Contexts section of this Norton Critical Edition.

skepticism and irony of his native tradition into a unique strength. His discomfort with the excesses of courtly poetry are expressed humorously in these short poems, as he describes himself as fish rolled in jellied sauce ("To Rosemounde" 17) or declares that he doesn't give a bean for love ("Merciless Beauty"). Whatever the milieu, Chaucer spins the delicate irony of French courtly poetry in a charmingly natural, even material direction. His individuality as a poet thus emerges in these short verses no less than it does in his longer narrative poems; their exacting ear for bathos sets them apart from other contemporary lyrics, whether one views them as practice poems or as private coterie performances perhaps not intended for wider publication. Although small pieces, they are not inconsiderable.

The text here of "An ABC," is taken from Ff 5.30 Cambridge University Library; that of "Chaucer's Words to Adam," from R.3.20, Trinity College, Cambridge; that of "Merciless Beauty" from Pepys 2006, Magdalene College, Cambridge; of "To Rosemounde," from MS Rawlinson Poetry 163, Bodleian Library; of "Truth," from the Ellesmere MS, corrected against Additional 10340, British Library; of "Gentillesse," from Caxton's printed edition, corrected against Cotton Cleopatra D.VII, British Library; of "Lack of Steadfastness," from Cotton Cleopatra D.VII, British Library; of the "Envoy to Scogan," the "Envoy to Bukton," and "The Complaint of Chaucer to His Purse," from Fairfax 16, Bodleian Library.

An ABC

Or "Prier a Nostre Dame"[1]

Almighty and al merciable° quene,	*merciful*
To whom that al this world fleeth for sucour,°	*flees for succor, aid*
To have relees of° sinne, of sorwe,° and	*relief from / sorrow*
tene,°	*suffering*
Glorious virgine, of alle floures flour,°	*the flower of all flowers*
5 To thee[3] I flee, confounded in° errour!	*overwhelmed by*
Help and releve,° thou mighty debonaire,°	*give comfort / meek one*
Have mercy on my perilous langour!°	*affliction*
Venquisshed° me hath my cruel	*Defeated*
adversaire.°	*opponent (i.e., Satan)*
Bountee so fix hath in thyn herte his tente,[2]	
10 That wel I wot thou wolt my socour be,	
Thou canst nat werne him that,° with good	*refuse anyone who*
entente,°	*intention*

1. The subtitle, "Prayer to Our Lady" (the Virgin Mary), from the French, is taken from one of the manuscripts. The more common title, given the poem by John Lydgate in the fifteenth century, refers to its abecedarian form: Each of the eight-line stanzas is introduced by a letter of the alphabet, starting with A, proceeding to Z, but omitting J and U (as not distinguished from I and V) and W, and substituting the Greek "chi," written X for that letter. "An ABC" is a loose but highly skilled translation of an original taken from Guillaume of Deguilleville's *The Pilgrimage of the Life of Man*, written around 1330. Thomas Speght, in his 1602 edition of Chaucer's poetry, claimed that Chaucer wrote this poem for Blanche of Lancaster, which would give it a date before Blanche's death in 1368, placing it very early in Chaucer's career. Noting the poem's five-beat line and its poetic skill, however, other readers argue for a later date.
2. Benevolence has so raised his pavilion in your heart.
3. In Middle English, "thou," "thy(n)," and "thee" are the familiar forms of the pronoun; throughout the poem, note the suggestive mixture of the familiar "thou" and the formal "you" in the petitioner's address to the Virgin Mary.

Axeth° thyn help, thyn herte is ay so free;°   *Asks for / always so generous*
Thou art largesse° of pleyn felicitee,°   *munificence / perfect delight*
Haven of refut,° of quiete, and of reste.   *refuge*
15 Lo, how that theves sevene chacen me!⁴
Help, lady bright, er that° my ship tobreste!°   *before / breaks apart*

Comfort is noon,° but in yow, lady dere,   *(there) is none*
For lo, my sinne and my confusioun,
Which oughten nat in thy presence appere,
20 Han take on me a grevous accioun
Of verray right and desperacioun,⁵
And as by right they mighten wel sustene°   *maintain*
That I were worthy my dampnacioun,°   *damnation*
Nere° mercy of yow, blissful° hevene quene.   *If it were not for / blessed*

25 Doute is ther noon, thou quene of misericorde,°   *mercy, compassion*
That thou n'art° cause of grace and mercy here;   *are the*
God vouched-sauf° thurgh thee with us   *granted*
    t'acorde.°   *be reconciled*
For certes,° Cristes blisful moder° dere,   *certainly / mother*
Were now the bowe bent in swich manere
30 As it was first, of justice and of yre,⁶
The rightful° God nolde of no° mercy here,°   *just / would not of / hear*
But thurgh thee han° we grace as we desyre.   *have*

Evere hath myn hope of refut° been in thee,   *refuge*
For herbiforn ful ofte° in many a wyse°   *often before now / many ways*
35 Hast thou to misericorde° receyved me.   *mercy*
But mercy, lady, at the great
    assyse°   *session of court (i.e., the Last Judgment)*
Whan we shul come bifore the hye justyse.°   *high judge*
So litel fruit shal thanne in me be founde,
That, but thou er that day correcte me,
40 Of verray right my werk me wol confounde.⁷

Fleeing, I flee for sucour to thy tente,
Me for to hyde from tempest,° ful of drede,°   *storm / fear*
Biseching yow that ye yow nat absente°   *withdraw*

4. Behold, how seven thieves (i.e., the seven deadly sins) pursue me!
5. For behold, my sin and (moral) confusion, which ought not to appear in your presence, have taken against me a grievous legal action of perfect justice and despair. (Chaucer personifies his sin as an adversary in a court case, using legal and penitential terminology that unifies several themes and sections of the poem. This imagery is conventional and taken in large part from the prayer he is translating.)
6. If the bow of justice and anger were bent back (i.e., the arrows aimed) as it was first (i.e., before the birth of Christ).
7. That, unless before that day you correct me, by legal rights my acts will condemn me. (The verb "correct" can have a range of meanings: to make corrections, to admonish, to punish. Line 39 is problematic because it violates the ababbcbc rhyme scheme by slipping in an "a" rhyme at the penultimate line. Several of the best manuscripts respond with various emendations ["me chastise," "correct my folise," etc.], none of which seems authorial. Following the suggestion that "correct me" could be a misreading of medieval handwriting for "correct vice," the *Riverside Chaucer* so alters the line, but this is not a version found in any of the manuscripts, most of which read as here: "correcte me." It is suggestive that the error in prosody occurs just at the moment the speaker asks Mary for correction; the formal error is perhaps intended to reflect the imperfection of the petitioner's spiritual state.)

Though I be wikke.° O help yet at this   *am wicked*
    nede!°   *moment of need*
45 Al° have I been a beste° in wil and dede,°   *Although / beast / deed*
Yet, lady, thou me clothe with thy grace.
Thyn enemy and myn—lady, tak hede—
Unto my deth in point is me to chace.[8]

Glorious mayde° and moder,° which that nevere   *maiden, virgin / mother*
50 Were bitter, neither in erthe° nor in see,°   *earth / sea*
But ful of swetnesse and of mercy evere,
Help that my Fader° be nat wroth° with me!   *Father / angry*
Spek° thou, for I ne dar nat him y-see.°   *Speak / dare not look upon*
So have I done in erthe, allas the whyle,°   *time*
55 That certes but if° thou my sucour be,   *truly unless*
To stink eterne° he wole my gost° exyle.   *i.e., to hell / spirit*

He vouched-sauf,° telle him, as was his wille,   *granted*
Becomen° a man to have our alliaunce,°   *To become / a bond with us*
And with his precious blood he wroot the bille°   *legal document*
60 Upon the crois,° as general acquitaunce°   *cross / release, aquittal*
To every penitent in ful creaunce;°   *who has full faith*
And therfor, lady bright, thou for us preye.
Thanne shalt thou bothe stinte al his grevaunce,[9]
And make oure fo to failen of° his preye.   *foe fail (to capture)*

65 I wot° it wel, thou wolt been oure sucour,   *know*
Thou art so ful of bountee,° in certeyn,   *goodness, generosity*
For, whan a soule falleth in errour,
Thy pitee goth and haleth him ageyn.°   *pulls him back*
Than makest thou his pees° with his sovereyn,   *peace*
70 And bringest him out of the crooked strete.
Whoso thee loveth° he shal nat love in veyn,   *Whoever loves you*
That shal he finde as he the lyf shal lete.°   *leave behind (i.e., die)*

Kalenderes enlumined been they
That in this world been lighted with thy name,[1]
75 And whoso° goth to yow the righte° wey,   *whoever / nearest, also proper*
Him thar nat drede° in soule to be lame.   *need not fear*
Now, quene of comfort, sith thou art° that same   *since you are*
To whom I seche° for my medicyne,   *seek*
Lat nat my fo no more my wounde entame,°   *reopen*
80 Myn hele° into thyn hand al I resyne.°   *health / entrust*

Lady, thy sorwe° can I nat portreye°   *sorrow / describe*
Under that crois,° ne his grevous penaunce.°   *cross / penance, suffering*
But, for your bothes peynes, I yow preye,

8. Take heed, lady: Your enemy and mine (i.e., Satan) is prepared to pursue me unto the point of my death.
9. Then shall the two of you (Mary and her son Jesus) together put a stop to His grievance (against me).
1. Medieval liturgical calendars decorated Church feasts with illuminated letters; the letters of Mary's name would have "lighted" or illuminated the days of her feasts.

Lat nat our alder fo° make his bobaunce,°   *all our enemy / boast*
85   That he hath in his listes of mischaunce
Convict that ye bothe have bought so dere.²
As I seyde erst,° thou ground° of oure   *before / foundation*
     substaunce,°   *being*
Continue on us thy pitous eyen clere!³

Moises, that° saw the bussh with flaumes rede°   *Moses who / red flames*
90   Brennninge,° of which ther never a stikke   *Burning*
     brende,°   *twig burned*
Was signe of thyn unwemmed maidenhede.°   *immaculate virginity*
Thou art the bussh on which ther gan descende
The Holy Gost, the which that Moises wende°   *believed*
Had been a-fyr;° and this was in figure.⁴   *on fire*
95   Now, lady, from the fyr thou us defende
Which that in helle eternally shal dure.°   *last*

Noble princesse, that never haddest pere,°   *equal*
Certes,° if any comfort in° us be,   *Certainly / for*
That cometh of° thee, thou Cristes moder° dere,   *from / mother*
100 We han° non other melodye or glee°   *have / entertainment*
Us to rejoise° in our adversitee,   *delight, gladden*
Ne advocat noon° that wol and dar° so preye   *Nor any advocate / dare*
For us, and that for litel hyre° as ye,   *payment*
That helpen for an Ave-Marie or tweye.⁵

105 O verray° light of eyen° that been blinde,   *true / for eyes*
O verray lust of° labour and distresse,   *joy in*
O tresorere of bountee° to mankinde,   *disburser of benevolence*
Thee whom God chees to° moder for   *chose as*
     humblesse!°   *(her) humility*
From his ancille° he made thee maistresse°   *maidservant / mistress*
110 Of hevene and erthe, our bille° up for to bede.° *petition / offer, present*
This world awaiteth evere on° thy goodnesse,   *always watches for, expects*
For thou ne failest nevere wight at° nede.   *(any) person in*

Purpos° I have som tyme for t'enquere°   *(The) intention, desire / learn*
Wherfore and why the Holy Ghost thee soughte,
115 Whan Gabrielles vois cam to thyn ere.⁶
He nat to werre° us swich° a wonder wroughte,   *make war upon / such*

---

2. That he has, in his arena of misfortune, vanquished (by trial by combat) those for whom you have both paid so dearly. (The metaphor of trial by combat is combined here with the understanding of Christ's death as payment in blood for the human soul.)
3. Keep on us the focus of your bright, compassionate eyes.
4. Medieval typological or "figural" interpretation of the Bible linked Old Testament events to their New Testament fulfillments. The M-verse, with its obvious Marian associations, marks the mid-point of the poem, and links the Old Testament story of the burning bush (Exodus 3:2–3) to the miracle of Mary's ever fertile virginity, a paradox Chaucer also explores in the Prologue to the Prioress' Tale in the *Canterbury Tales* 7.467–73.
5. Who (will) help in exchange for an Ave-Maria or two. (An "Ave-Maria" is a prayer to the Virgin Mary, in English "Hail, Mary.")
6. Wherefore and why (i.e., the whole story behind how) the Holy Ghost sought you out, when the voice of (the angel) Gabriel came to your ear. (The reference is to the Annunciation; see Luke 1: 26–38).

But for to save us that he sithen
   boughte.°   *afterwards bought (with his blood)*
Thanne nedeth us no wepen° us for to save,   *weapon*
But only ther° we dide nat, as us oughte,   *(in cases) where*
120 Do penitence and mercy axe and have.°   *ask for and receive*

Quene of comfort, yet whan I me bithinke°   *consider*
That I agilt have° bothe him and thee,   *wronged, offended*
And that my soule is worthy for to sinke,
Allas, I, caitif,° whider° may I flee?   *wretch / whither, where*
125 Who shal unto thy sone my mene° be?   *mediator, intercessor*
Who, but thyself, that art of pitee welle?°   *wellspring*
Thou hast more routhe° on oure adversitee   *pity*
Than in this world mighte any tonge° telle.   *tongue*

Redresse° me, moder, and me chastyse,°   *Reform, correct / reprove*
130 For certeynly my Fadres° chastisinge,   *Father's*
That dar I nought abyden° in no wyse,   *withstand*
So hidous° is his rightful° rekeninge.   *dreadful / just*
Moder, of° whom oure mercy gan to springe,   *from*
Beth ye my juge, and eek° my soules leche;°   *also / physician*
135 For ever in yow is pitee haboundinge°   *abounding*
To ech° that wol of pitee yow biseche.   *each (person)*

Sooth is,° that God ne graunteth no pitee   *It is true*
Withoute thee; for God of his goodnesse
Foryiveth noon, but it lyke unto thee.°   *unless it pleases you*
140 He hath thee maked vicaire° and maistresse   *(his) deputy*
Of al the world, and eek gouvernouresse°   *also ruler, guardian*
Of hevene, and he represseth° his justyse   *restrains*
After° thy wil, and therefore in witnesse°   *To conform to / evidence*
He hath thee corouned in so real wyse.°   *royal (a) fashion*

145 Temple devout, ther° God hath his woninge,°   *where / dwelling*
Fro° which these misbileved depryved   *From*
   been,°   *unbelievers are excluded*
To yow my soule penitent I bringe.
Receyve me, I can no ferther fleen!°   *flee*
With thornes venimous,° o hevene queen,   *poisonous*
150 For° which the erthe acursed was ful yore,°   *By / for a long time*
I am so wounded as ye may wel seen,
That I am lost almost, it smert so sore.°   *hurts so sorely*

Virgine, that art so noble of apparaile,°   *bearing (including dress)*
And ledest us into the hye tour°   *high tower*
155 Of Paradys, thou me wisse and counsaile°   *instruct and counsel*
How I may have thy grace and thy sucour,
Al° have I been in filthe and in errour.   *Although*
Lady, unto that court thou me ajourne,°   *appoint a day (for me)*
That cleped° is thy bench,° o fresshe flour,   *is called / law court*
160 Ther as that° mercy evere shal sojourne.°   *Where / reside*

Xristus,[7] thy sone, that in° this world alighte°   to / came down
Upon the crois° to suffre his passioun,°   cross / martyrdom
And eek that Longius his herte pighte
And made his herte blood to renne adoun,[8]
165 And al was this for my salvacioun;
And I to him am fals and eek unkinde,°   also ungrateful, unnatural
And yet he wole nat° my dampnacioun—   does not wish for
This° thanke I yow, sucour of all mankinde!   For this

Ysaac was figure of his deeth,[9] certeyn,
170 That so ferforth° his fader° wolde obeye   completely / father
That him ne roughte nothing to be sleyn;[1]
Right° so thy Sone list° as a lamb to deye.°   Just / was pleased / die
Now lady, ful of mercy, I yow preye,
Sith° he his mercy mesured so large,°   Since / out so generously
175 Be ye nat skant,° for alle we singe and seye   sparing, stingy
That ye been from vengeaunce ay our targe.°   always our shield

Zacharie yow clepeth the opene welle
To wasshe sinful soule out of his gilt.[2]
Therfore this lessoun out I wel° to telle   (do) well
180 That, nere° thy tender herte, we weren spilt.°   were it not for / destroyed
Now lady brighte, sith° thou canst and wilt   since
Been to the seed of Adam merciable,°   merciful to Adam's descendants
Bring us to that palais° that is bilt°   palace / built
To° penitents that been to mercy able.° Amen.   for / fit, prepared

Chaucer's Words to Adam, His Own Scribe

Adam, scriveyn,° if ever it thee befalle   scrivener, copyist
Boece or Troilus[1] for to wryten newe,°   again
Under thy long lokkes° thou most have the scalle[2]   locks (of hair)
But after my making thou wryte more trewe.[3]
5 So ofte adaye° I mot° thy werk renewe,°   each day / must / revise

7. Christ (construing the Greek symbol for "chi" as the letter X).
8. And also Longinus pierced his heart and made his heart's blood flow down. (The story of Longinus,
    the blind Roman soldier forced to pierce Christ's heart with his spear—and then cured of his
    blindness by Christ's blood—was widely known from biblical apocrypha, collections of saints'
    legends, and the medieval drama.)
9. Isaac was a prefiguration of his death. (For the use of "figure," see 94 note. For the story of Isaac,
    who was almost sacrificed by his father at God's command, see Genesis 22, Hebrews 11:17–19.)
1. He did not care at all (even if he were) to be slain.
2. Zechariah (the biblical prophet) calls you the open well, (which) washes the guilt from the sinful
    soul. (See Zechariah 13:1.)
1. Chaucer's scribe has recently been identified as Adam Pinkhurst, who also produced a manuscript
    of Chaucer's *Boece* (his translation of Boethius's *Consolation of Philosophy*) and *Troilus and Cri-
    seyde*; he is also the scribe of the two best manuscripts of the *Canterbury Tales* (the Hengwrt and
    Ellesmere manuscripts). "Chaucer's Words to Adam" was probably composed during the mid (to
    late) 1380s, when the poet was still drafting or had recently completed *Troilus* and *Boece*, and is
    significant for showing the close working relationship between the poet and his scribe; see Linne
    Mooney, "Chaucer's Scribe," *Speculum* 81 (2006): 102. "To Adam" is a deceptively simple stanza.
    The poem's personalized tone is enriched by the symbolic resonance of the biblical fall and that
    other imperfect Adam, and the metrical sophistication of its rhyme royal form (seven-line stanza
    rhyming ababbcc) is belied by the raggedness of its own pentameter.
2. A scabby disease of the scalp.
3. Unless your copy conforms more accurately to what I have written.

It to correcte and eek to rubbe and scrape;⁴
And al is thurgh° thy negligence and rape.°   *because of / haste*

Merciless Beauty¹

Your eyen two wol slee° me sodeinly;   *will slay*
I may the beautee of hem° nat sustene°   *them / bear, endure*
So woundeth it thurghout my herte kene.°   *grievously, painfully*

And but° your word wol helen° hastily   *unless / heal*
5 My hertes wounde whyl that it is grene,°   *green (i.e., fresh)*
     Your eyen two wol slee me sodeinly;
     I may the beautee of hem nat sustene.

Upon my trouth° I sey you feithfully   *honor*
That ye been° of my lyf and deeth the quene,   *are*
10 For with my deeth the trouthe shal be sene:°   *seen, revealed*
     Your eyen two wol slee me sodeinly;
     I may the beautee of hem nat sustene,
     So woundeth it thurghout my herte kene.

So hath your beautee fro° your herte chaced°   *from / chased (out)*
15 Pitee that me n'availeth nat to pleyne,²
     For Daunger³ halt° your mercy in his cheyne.°   *holds / chain*

Giltles my deeth thus han ye me purchaced.⁴
I sey yow sooth,° me nedeth nat to feyne,°   *(the) truth / feign, pretend*
     So hath your beautee fro your herte chaced
20   Pitee that me n'availeth nat to pleyne.

Allas, that nature hath in yow compaced°   *contained*
So° grete beautee that no man may atteyne°   *Such / attain, achieve*
To mercy though he sterve° for the peyne,   *die*
     So hath your beautee fro your herte chaced
25   Pitee that me n'availeth nat to pleyne,
     For Daunger halt your mercy in his cheyne.

Sin I fro Love escaped am so fat,⁵
I never think° to been in his prison lene;°   *plan (again) / lean, skinny*

4. Also to rub and scrape (the parchment, thus erasing the error).
1. Although "Merciless Beauty" appears in manuscript with other poems by Chaucer, it is not spe-
    cifically attributed to him, so some editors have doubted its authenticity; most, however, agree
    that it is by Chaucer. The poem is in the form of a rondel (or *rondeau*), a French "fixed form" on
    two rhymes that recycles the opening stanza as a refrain in subsequent stanzas. Skeat presents the
    poem in three sections, the first (lines 1–13) entitled "Captivity," the second (14–26) "Rejection,"
    and the third (27–39) "Escape" (*Complete Works*, vol. 1, pp. 387–88). Because Chaucer's poem
    falls out in three parts, each a separate rondel, it is also known as a "triple rondel." A lovely example
    of a thoroughly conventional form, "Merciless Beauty" offers few hints that would suggest a spe-
    cific date for the poem.
2. Pity, so that it does me no good to complain.
3. The conventional haughtiness or aloofness shown by a courtly lady to her wooer.
4. (Although I am) guiltless, you have thus sought my death.
5. Since I have escaped from Love (and am still) so fat.

Sin° I am free, I counte him nat a   *Since*
bene.°   *don't give a bean for him*

30 He° may answere and seye this and that;   *I.e., Love*
I do no fors,° I speke right° as I mene.   *don't care / just*
Sin I fro Love escaped am so fat,
I never think to been in his prison lene.

Love hath my name y-strike out of his sclat,°   *removed from / slate (list)*
35 And he is strike out of° my bookes clene°   *deleted from / fully*
For evermo; ther is noon other mene.°   *way, course of action*
Sin I fro Love escaped am so fat,
I never think to been in his prison lene;
Sin I am free, I counte him nat a bene.

To Rosemounde[1]

Madame, ye been° of al beautee shryne°   *are / shrine, reliquary*
As fer as cercled° is the mapamounde;[2]   *encircled*
For as the cristal glorious ye shyne,
And lyke ruby been your chekes rounde.
5 Therwith ye been so mery and so jocounde°   *joyful*
That at a revel° whan that I see yow daunce,   *party, feast*
It is an oynement unto° my wounde,   *salve for*
Though ye to me ne do no daliaunce.[3]

For though I wepe of teres ful a tyne,°   *a whole tubful*
10 Yet may that wo myn herte nat confounde;°   *destroy*
Your semy° vois that ye so small out twyne°   *small / delicately spin out*
Maketh my thought in joye and blis habounde.°   *abound*
So curteisly I go, with° love bounde,   *by*
That to myself I sey, in my penaunce,
15 Suffyseth me° to love you, Rosemounde,   *It is sufficient for me*
Though ye to me ne do no daliaunce.

Nas never pyk walwed in galauntyne[4]
As I in love am walwed and y-wounde,°   *stirred up*
For which ful ofte I of° myself devyne°   *about / divine, believe*
20 That I am trewe Tristam[5] the secounde.
My love may nat refreyde° nor affounde;°   *grow cold / fail*

1. The identity of "Rosemounde" (if she is other than a literary fiction) is uncertain, though some readers find the playful tone appropriate for a poem addressed to a child (with round cheeks and a small voice, see lines 4 and 11); one theory holds that she is Richard II's child-bride, the French princess Isabelle, who was seven years old when he married her in 1396, suggesting a possible date for the poem.
2. I.e., throughout the entire globe. The medieval "mappamundi" (from the Latin "map of the world") depicted the known lands of the world encircled by the sea; also, note the word play on Rosemounde, "rose of the world."
3. Although you do not engage me in friendly conversation (in a courtly context, flirtatious intimate talk).
4. Pike rolled in galantine (a jellied sauce).
5. Tristan, famous lover of Isolde in medieval legend.

I brenne ay° in an amorous plesaunce.°   *burn forever / pleasure*
Do what yow list,° I wil your thral° be founde,   *please / slave*
Though ye to me ne do no daliaunce.

Truth

Or "Balade de bon conseyl"[1]

Flee fro the prees,° and dwelle with   *crowd*
    soothfastnesse,°   *truthfulness*
Suffyse unto thy thing,[2] though it be smal;
For hord hath hate, and climbing tikelnesse,[3]
Prees hath envye, and wele blent° overal;   *prosperity blinds*
5   Savour no more than thee bihove shal;°   *is good for you*
Rule wel thyself, that other folk canst rede;°   *advise*
And trouthe shal delivere,° it is no drede.°   *set (you) free / fear*

Tempest thee° nought al crooked to   *Trouble yourself*
    redresse,°   *put to rights*
In trust of hir that turneth as a bal.[4]
10   Moche wele stant° in litel besynesse;°   *Great well-being rests / activity*
Bewar therfore to sporne° ageyns an al;°   *kick / an awl (a pointed tool)*
Stryve nat, as doth the crokke° with the   *piece of (breakable) crockery*
    wal.
Daunte° thyself, that dauntest otheres   *Control*
    dede;°   *the deeds of others*
And trouthe shal delivere, it is no drede.

15   That thee° is sent, receyve in buxumnesse,°   *That which to you / humility*
The wrastling for this world axeth° a fal.   *asks for*
Here is noon hoom,° here nis° but   *not (your) home / is nothing*
    wildernesse.
Forth, pilgrim, forth! Forth, beste,° out of thy stal!   *beast*
Know thy contree, look up, thank God of al;°   *for everything*
20   Hold the hye° wey, and lat thy gost° thee lede,   *high, main / spirit*
And trouthe shal delivere, it is no drede.

---

1. "Ballad of good counsel," a title in many of the manuscripts. As one of Chaucer's "Boethian ballads," "Truth" may cautiously be dated in the period 1382–90.
2. Let your own possessions be enough for you. (This was a literary and philosophical commonplace.)
3. For hoarding (greed) brings about hate, and advancement (social and professional ambition causes) insecurity.
4. In trust of her who turns like a sphere. (The allusion is to the goddess Fortune and her revolving wheel.)

Envoy[5]

Therfore, thou Vache,[6] leve° thyn old wrecchednesse;°   *cease / misery*
Unto the world leve now to be thral;°   *slave*
Crye him mercy,° that of his hye   *for mercy from him (i.e., God)*
   goodnesse
25 Made thee of nought,° and in especial   *from nothing*
Draw unto him, and prey in general
For thee, and eek for other,° hevenlich   *also for others*
   mede;°   *heavenly reward*
And trouthe shal delivere, it is no drede.

Gentilesse[1]

The firste stok, fader° of gentilesse—   *original ancestor, father*
What° man desireth gentil° for to be,   *Whatever / noble*
Must folowe his trace,° and alle his wittes dresse°   *footsteps / apply*
Vertu to love and vices for to flee.
5 For unto vertu longeth dignitee,°   *pertains worth*
And nought the revers, saufly° dar I deme,°   *confidently / judge*
Al were he myter, croune, or diademe.[2]

The firste stok was ful of rightwisnesse,°   *righteousness*
Trewe of his word, sobre, pitous,° and free,°   *compassionate / generous*
10 Clene of his gost,° and loved besynesse,°   *Pure in spirit / diligence, activity*
Ageynst the vice of slouthe,° in honestee;°   *sloth / honor, virtue*
And but° his heir love vertu as did he,   *unless*
He is nought gentil though he riche seme,
Al were he myter, croune, or diademe.

15 Vice may wel be heir to old richesse;°   *wealth (old money)*
But ther may no man, as men may wel see,
Bequethe his heir his vertuous noblesse;°   *innate nobility*
That is appropred unto no degree,
But to the firste fader in magestee,[3]

---

5. The "envoy" (in French, "a thing sent," i.e., a letter) is a coda to the poem that traditionally sends it off to a prince (see "The Complaint of Chaucer to His Purse," "Lack of Steadfastness"), or alternatively to a lady. In addressing "Truth" more personally to a friend (see 22), Chaucer lightens the poem's courtly and philosophical tone; this is a manipulation of convention of which Chaucer was fond (see, below, "Envoy to Bukton," "Envoy to Scogan"). The "envoy" in "Truth" is found in only a single manuscript and would therefore not have been known by most early readers.
6. Sir Philip de la Vache was a friend and associate of Chaucer's who was temporarily out of favor during the late 1380s, at the time Chaucer may have written a version of this poem; the word "vache" also means "cow" in French, linking the envoy to the pattern of reference in line 18.
1. As the definitions in the *Middle English Dictionary* indicate, the word "gentilesse" can be loosely translated as "nobility." Nobility, however, could be either spiritual or material, an oppposition Chaucer explores here and elsewhere in his poetry, for example in the so-called "gentilesse speech" given by the Wife of Bath (see *Canterbury Tales* 3.1109–1212). The poem is often dated in the 1380s, with other ballads on Boethian themes.
2. Whether he wear miter, crown, or diadem (signifying three distinct forms of earthly power—respectively, the bishop's liturgical headdress, the crown of a king, and the emperor's diadem).
3. That (i.e., true nobility) is the property of no (specific) social class, but belongs to the original ancester in his majesty (his sovereign power and greatness). (Some readers take this "ancestor" literally, but the reference here is likely to God or Christ.)

20 That maketh his heires hem° that can him queme,°   *those / please*
    Al were he myter, croune, or diademe.

Lack of Steadfastness[1]

  Somtyme° this world was so stedfast° and   *Once, formerly / constant*
      stable
  That mannes° word was obligacioun,°   *a man's / a binding pledge*
  And now it is so fals and deceivable,°   *deceptive*
5 That word and deed, as in conclusioun,
  Ben nothing lyk,° for turned up so   *Bear no resemblance (to each other)*
      doun
  Is al this world for mede° and   *profit, bribery*
      wilfulnesse,°   *obstinacy, selfishness*
  That° al is lost for lak° of stedfastnesse.   *So that / the lack*

  What maketh this world to be so variable°   *unstable*
  But lust° that folk have in dissensioun?°   *the pleasure / disagreement*
10 Among us now a man is holde unable,°   *incompetent, without merit*
  But° if he can, by som collusioun,°   *Unless / trickery, conspiracy*
  Don his neighbour wrong or oppressioun.°   *injury*
  What causeth this, but wilful wrecchednesse,°   *vileness, baseness*
  That al is lost, for lak of stedfastnesse?

15 Trouthe° is put doun, resoun is holden   *Honesty, Integrity*
      fable;°   *falsehood*
  Vertu hath now no dominacioun,
  Pitee exyled, no man is merciable.°   *merciful*
  Thurgh covetyse° is blent discrecioun;°   *greed / moral judgment is blinded*
  The world hath made a permutacioun°   *an exchange*
20 Fro° right to wrong, fro trouthe to fikelnesse,°   *From / fickleness, deceit*
  That al is lost, for lak of stedfastnesse.

Envoy [to King Richard][2]

  O prince, desyre to be honourable,
  Cherish thy folk° and hate extorcioun!   *your people (your subjects)*
  Suffre° nothing that may be reprevable°   *Permit / blameworthy*
25 To thyn estate,° don° in thy regioun.   *high office / to be done*

---

1. As one of Chaucer's "Boethian ballads," "Lack of Steadfastness" may cautiously be dated in the period 1382–90.
2. For the function of the "envoy" here at the poem's close, see above, "Truth," note 5. The words "to King Richard" appear in only a single manuscript, but another related manuscript also includes the information that the poem was written for Richard II in its title, and most scholars accept the relevance of the advice given here to Richard, especially during the difficult political years of 1386–90, leading up to and following the so-called "Merciless Parliament" in 1388, when the Lords Appellant convicted many of Richard's favorites of treason, dealing a serious blow to the young king's sovereignty. Chaucer's plea that Richard should exercise his royal power is paradoxically less a chastisement of Richard than a defense of his right to rule. It has been read as basically flattering to the king, whose favor Chaucer continued to depend upon for his livelihood.

Shew forth thy swerd of castigacioun,°   *sword of punishment, correction*
Dred° God, do° law, love trouthe and worthinesse,   *Fear / enforce*
And wed° thy folk ageyn to stedfastnesse.   *marry*

Envoy to Scogan[1]

Tobroken° been the statuts hye° in   *Shattered, smashed / laws high*
    hevene
That creat° were eternally to dure,°   *created / endure*
Sith that° I see the brighte goddes sevene°   *Since / i.e., the planets*
Mow° wepe and waile, and passioun endure,   *May*
5 As may in° erthe a mortal creature.   *on*
Allas, fro whennes may this thing procede,
Of which errour I deye almost for drede?[2]

By worde eterne whylom° was it shape°   *eternal once / ordained*
That fro the fifte cercle,[3] in no manere,
10 Ne mighte a drope of teres doun° escape,   *tears downward*
But now so wepeth Venus in hir spere°   *sphere*
That with hir teres she wol drenche° us here.   *will drown*
Allas, Scogan, this is for thyn offence,
Thou causest this deluge of pestilence.°   *foul, ruinous deluge*

15 Hast thou nat seyd, in blaspheme of the
    goddes,°   *blasphemy against the planets*
Thurgh pryde or thurgh thy grete rakelnesse°   *rashness*
Swich thing° as in the lawe of love forbode° is?   *Such a thing / forbidden*
That, for° thy lady saw nat thy distresse,   *because*
Therfor thou yave° hir up at Michelmesse?[4]   *gave*
20 Allas, Scogan, of° olde folk ne yonge°   *by / nor young*
Was never erst° Scogan blamed for his tonge.°   *previously / tongue*

Thou drowe° in scorn Cupyde eek to record°   *called / also to witness*
Of thilke° rebel word that thou hast spoken,   *that same*
For which he wol no lenger° be thy lord.   *will no longer*
25 And, Scogan, though his bowe be nat broken,[5]
He wol nat with his arwes been y-wroken°   *arrows be revenged*

---

1. Henry Scogan, a friend and admirer of Chaucer's, was a civil servant in the courts of Richard II and Henry IV. He wrote a ballad (printed by W.W. Skeat, *Chaucerian and Other Pieces*, 237–44) in which he quotes the poem "Gentilesse," written by "my maister Chaucer," to his own students, the sons of Henry IV.
2. Alas, whence may this thing proceed, (this) aberration (that causes) me almost to die from fear? (Chaucer refers to the weeping and wailing of the planets—i.e., to an unusually heavy rain, sometimes used to date the poem late in the year 1393, which was marked by storms in September and October.)
3. That from the fifth circle (i.e., sphere—the planetary sphere of Venus).
4. Michaelmas, the feast of St. Michael the Archangel, celebrated September 29.
5. Compare the lines in *Troilus and Criseyde*, where Cupid specifically shows the young renegade to love, Troilus, that his bow is *not* broken by causing him to fall in love with Criseyde (*Troilus and Criseyde* 1.208).

On thee, ne me, ne noon of our figure;[6]
We shul of° him have neither hurt ne   *shall from*
   cure.°   *restoration to health*

Now certes,° frend, I drede of° thyn   *certainly / fear for*
   unhap,°   *misfortune*
30 Lest for thy gilt the wreche° of Love procede   *vengeance*
On alle hem° that been hore° and rounde   *all those / gray/white-haired*
   of shap,
That been so lykly folk in love to spede,[7]
Than shul we for our labour han no mede,°   *reward*
But wel I wot° thou wilt answere and seye,   *know*
35 "Lo, olde Grisel list to ryme and pleye!"[8]

Nay, Scogan, sey nat so, for I m'excuse;[9]
God help me so, in no rym,° doutelees,°   *rhyme / surely, indubitably*
Ne thinke I never of slepe to wak° my muse,   *from sleep to awaken*
That rusteth in my shethe° stille in pees.°   *sheath, scabbard / peace*
40 Whyle I was yong, I putte it forth in prees,[1]
But al shal passe that men prose° or ryme;   *write in prose*
Tak every man his turn, as for his tyme.

Envoy[2]

Scogan, that knelest at the stremes hede
Of grace, of alle honour and worthinesse,
In th'ende of which streme I am dul as dede,
45 Forgete in solitarie wildernesse;[3]
Yet, Scogan, thinke on Tullius[4] kindenesse,
Minne° thy frend there it may fructifye;°   *Remember / bring profit*
Farwel, and look thou never eft Love diffye!°   *again defy Love*

---

6. With figures like ours. (Chaucer was fond of mocking his rotundity; see, for example, his self-presentation in the Prologue to the Tale of Sir Thopas, *Canterbury Tales* 7.700.)
7. Who are such promising candidates to prosper in love. (Chaucer is being ironic here; Scogan's specific crime against Love and its relationship to the poem's other themes remain obscure, finessed by ironic shifts of tone such as this one.)
8. "Behold, the old gray horse likes to rhyme and play!"
9. Excuse myself (i.e., let me bow out; clearly ironic, as the poem itself violates the promise to stop writing).
1. When I was young, I brought it (i.e., his muse) forth in public. (Literally, the muse should be feminine, but the two best manuscripts read "it" here, probably because the metaphor of the muse as a sword rusting in its scabbard intervenes.)
2. For the function of the "envoy" here at the poem's close, see above, "Truth," note 5.
3. Scogan, who kneels at the stream's source of grace, of all honor and worthiness, at the end of which stream am I as benumbed (dejected) as a dead person, forgotten in a solitary wilderness. (While the stream may have metaphorical resonance, early scribal glosses sugguest that it literally refers to the Thames, locating Scogan at court in Windsor and Chaucer at Greenwich. Chaucer's distance from and Scogan's proximity to the seat of power lead most readers to take this envoy as a request for Scogan's help at court; perhaps such help was forthcoming, as Chaucer's annuity was renewed in February, 1394.)
4. Marcus Tullius Cicero, whose writings on friendship were widely known in the Middle Ages.

Envoy to Bukton[1]

My maister° Bukton, whan of Criste our   *master (a general honorific)*
    king
Was axed,° "What is trouthe or soothfastnesse?"°   *It was asked / honesty*
He nat a word answerde to that axing,°   *question*
As who° seyth, "No man is al° trewe," I gesse.   *one who / entirely*
5   And therfor, though I highte° to expresse   *promised*
The sorwe and wo° that is in mariage,   *sorrow and woe*
I dar nat wryte of it no° wikkednesse   *any*
Lest I myself falle eft in swich dotage.°   *again into such foolishness*

I wol nat seyn how that it° is the cheyne   *i.e., marriage*
10   Of Sathanas,° on which he gnaweth evere,   *Satan*
But I dar seyn, were he out of° his peyne,   *escaped from*
As by his wille, he wolde be bounde nevere.[2]
But thilke doted° fool that eft hath   *that befuddled*
    levere°   *prefers again to*
Y-cheyned be than° out of prisoun crepe,   *rather than*
15   God lete him never fro his wo dissevere,°   *be free of his woe*
Ne no man him bewaile though he wepe.[3]

But yet, lest thou do worse, take a wyf;
Bet is to wedde than brenne in worse wyse.
But thou shalt have sorwe on thy flesh thy lyf,[4]
20   And been thy wyves thral,° as seyn these wyse,°   *wife's slave / wise men*
And if that holy writ may nat suffyse,°   *i.e., to make my point*
Experience shal thee teche, so may happe,°   *it may happen*
That thee were lever to be take in Fryse[5]
Than eft° falle of wedding in the trappe.   *again*

Envoy[6]

25   This litel writ, proverbes,° or figure°   *set of proverbs / poetic illustration*
I sende yow, take kepe° of it, I rede:°   *heed / advise*
Unwys is he that can no wele endure.°   *not tolerate good fortune*

---

1. Bukton is likely Sir Peter Bukton of Holderness, Yorkshire, a steward to Richard II, Henry IV, and Henry's son Thomas; alternatively Sir Robert Bukton of Goosewold, Suffolk, who served King Richard II and Queen Anne, and was for many years a member of Parliament. Both were members of the class of educated civil servants and courtiers that composed a core audience for Chaucer's poetry, as can be seen in line 29, where the poet assumes Bukton's familiarity with the Wife of Bath, from some version or circulated draft of that tale from the *Canterbury Tales.*
2. He (Satan) would not be willingly bound (chained up) ever again. (The image of Satan chained in hell is a medieval convention, with ultimate sources in biblical apocrypha.)
3. Nor should any (other) man cry for him, (even if) he (the remarried man himself) weeps.
4. It is better to wed than to burn in a worse fashion. But you shall experience physical pain throughout your life. (In line 18, Chaucer alludes to 1 Corinthians 7:9—"It is better to marry than to burn"—a passage also quoted by the Wife of Bath, *Canterbury Tales* 3.52.)
5. That you would rather be captured in Frisia. (The Frisians were notoriously merciless fighters; the expedition of William of Hainault against Friesland in 1396 is sometimes used to date the poem to this period or the years just preceding.)
6. For the function of the "envoy" here at the poem's close, see above, "Truth," note 5.

If thou be siker,° put thee nat in drede.°   *would be safe / danger*
The Wyf of Bathe I prey yow that ye rede
30 Of this matere that we have on honde.[7]
God graunte yow your lyf frely to lede
In fredom, for ful hard is° to be bonde.°   *it is / bound, fettered*

The Complaint of Chaucer to His Purse[1]

To yow, my purse, and to noon other wight°   *person, being*
Complaine I, for ye be° my lady dere.   *you are*
I am so sory now that ye be light,
For certes but if ye make me hevy chere,[2]
5 Me were as leef° be leyd upon my bere,°   *I'd just as soon / bier*
For which unto your mercy thus I crye
Beth hevy° ageyn or elles mot° I dye.   *weighty / else must*

Now voucheth-sauf° this day er it be° night   *grant, agree / before it is*
That I of° yow the blisful soun° may here,   *from / happy sound*
10 Or see your colour lyke the sonne bright[3]
That of yelownesse hadde never pere.°   *equal*
Ye be my lyf, ye be myn hertes stere°   *rudder*
Quene of comfort and of good companye,
Beth hevy ageyn or elles mot I dye.

15 Now purse that been to me my lyves light°   *the light of my life*
And saveour° as doun in this worlde here   *(earthly) savior*
Out of this toune[4] help me thurgh your might
Sin that° ye wole nat been my tresorere°   *Since / treasurer (giver of funds)*
For I am shave as nye as any frere;[5]
20 But yet I prey unto your curtesye
Beth hevy ageyn or elles mot I dye.

7. I ask that you read the Wife of Bath concerning this matter that we are discussing. (There are many similarities between the poet's attitudes here and the Wife of Bath's observations on marriage as a power struggle in the Prologue to her Canterbury tale, although she praises wedlock as an arena for the exercise of female power.)
1. Chaucer here adapts the genre of love complaint to that of begging poem; for historical circumstances, see below, esp. note 6.
2. I am so sorry now that you are merry, for truly unless you present me with a serious demeanor. (In these playful lines, Chaucer draws upon multiple meaning of the words "light" and "hevy": "light" could describe literal weight, or it could mean light in character [i.e., cheerful, happy, or even frivolous or fickle]; "hevy" likewise could signify weight, or alternatively the quality of being sober, doleful, or even angry. In the context of the poem, the complex juxtaposition of these different meanings becomes humorously paradoxical.)
3. Extending the word play, Chaucer now alludes to the conventional golden color of a courtly maiden's hair as well as, on the poem's literal level, to gold coins, which make a happy clinking sound in one's purse.
4. Literally "town," probably Westminster, where Chaucer had taken refuge (perhaps from his creditors) in a house on the abbey grounds.
5. For I am shaven as closely as any friar. (I.e., I have as little money as a tonsured friar has hair; also, possibly an allusion to Chaucer's residence at Westminster Abbey.)

Lenvoy de Chaucer[6]

O conquerour of Brutes Albyoun[7]
Which that by line° and free eleccioun   *lineage, descent*
Been verray° king, this song to yow I sende,   *Are the true*
25 And ye that mowen° alle oure harmes amende   *may*
Have minde upon° my supplicacioun.   *Keep in mind, remember*

6. For the function of an "envoy" here at the poem's close, see above, "Truth," note 5. The patron to whom Chaucer sends his poem is the newly crowned Henry IV, who after the deposition of Richard II in 1399 would have been responsible for renewing the life annuity granted to Chaucer by his predecessor. The address to Henry IV enables us to date the poem between Henry's accession to the throne in October, 1399, and February, 1400 (when Henry did in fact renew Chaucer's annuity), making it very likely the last poem that Chaucer wrote before his death later in 1400. This section of the poem (not found in all manuscripts) is referred to by various titles; the rubric "Lenvoy de Chaucer" is taken from the best and most complete manuscript.
7. The Albion of Brutus. (Albion was another name for Britain itself. According to tradition, the island was named after Brutus, the grandson of Aeneas, founder of Rome. Here and in the lines that follow Chaucer pays prudent homage to Henry IV, affirming his right to the throne by conquest, descent, and the election of the people; for a similar breakdown of Henry's right to the throne, see John Gower, *The Tripartite Chronicle*, in *The Major Latin Works of John Gower*, trans. Eric W. Stockton (Seattle: U of Washington P, 1962), 321.)

CONTEXTS

CONTEXTS

RUTH EVANS

From Chaucer in Cyberspace: Medieval Technologies of Memory and the *House of Fame*†

[In the opening paragraphs of Ruth Evans's provocative essay on the *House of Fame*, she provides a striking image of the universe of texts in Chaucer's time period. This image can perhaps help modern readers to organize and appreciate the relevance to Chaucer of the various "Contexts" printed here.]

Let us imagine Chaucer sitting at his desk in his house over Aldgate in front of his PC. It is 1379. On the screen is the poem he is currently working on, *The House of Fame* (1379–80).[1] Behind this he has opened a number of windows, on which are copies of Latin, French, and Italian texts he has downloaded from the Internet, texts he intends to use as sources: Macrobius's discussion of dream classification in his commentary on the *Somnium Scipionis*, Virgil's *Aeneid*, Dante's *Divine Comedy*, and Ovid's *Heroides*, *Metamorphoses*, and *Ars amatoria*. On Chaucer's hard disk are yet more sources: commentaries on Ovid (the *Ovide moralisé*; Pierre Bersuire's commentary); collections of quotations from the Bible; French love poetry by Machaut and Froissart; most of the *Roman de la rose*. Also on his hard disk are copies of texts in Middle English—though Chaucer chooses not to own up to using them.[2] *Piers Plowman* (B-version, ca. 1379)[3] and the famous Auchinleck manuscript (National Library of Scotland, Advocates' MS 19.2.1, ca. 1330–40), containing vernacular romances and religious verse.[4] He has bookmarks to his favorite Web sites, including an archive of Lollard material with information on the Wycliffite translation project. And he can also access the virtual libraries constituted by manuscript anthologies produced in London, such as Auchinleck or Cambridge University Library MS Ii.iii.21, which contains Boethius's text of the *Consolation of Philosophy*, together with its Latin commentaries and his own English translation of the work.[5] As the articulation of a vast memory, the computer is the latest in a procession of mnemonic aids and archival technologies that, I will argue, can be traced back to the future. The computer analogy is helpful in understanding *The House of Fame* because it is itself a poem that is obsessed by late medieval technologies of memory and archiving. Part comic, part anxious, it projects a series of powerful imaginative visions of types of recording apparatus and their nightmarish others: the engravings in Venus's temple, the ice-rock foundation, Fame's

† From *Studies in the Age of Chaucer* 23 (2001): 43–46. Reprinted by permission of the author. The author's notes have been renumbered.
1. All citations of Chaucer's work are from Larry D. Benson, gen. ed., *The Riverside Chaucer*, 3d ed. (Boston: Houghton Mifflin, 1987). Line numbers are cited parenthetically in the text.
2. See Nicholas Watson, "The Politics of Middle English Writing," in Jocelyn Wogan-Browne, Nicholas Watson, Andrew Taylor, Ruth Evans, eds., *The Idea of the Vernacular: An Anthology of Middle English Literary Theory, 1280–1520* (University Park: Pennsylvania State University Press, 1999), p. 346. For Chaucer's debt to English vernacular writing, see W. A. Davenport, *Chaucer and His English Contemporaries* (New York: St. Martin's Press, 1998).
3. Frank Grady, "Chaucer Reading Langland: *The House of Fame*," SAC 18 (1996): 3–23.
4. Derek Pearsall, *The Life of Geoffrey Chaucer: A Critical Biography* (Oxford and Cambridge, Mass.: Blackwell, 1992), pp. 73–77; Wogan-Browne et al., eds., *Idea of the Vernacular*, pp. 354–56.
5. Pearsall, *Life*, p. 164.

rumbling House, the fantastic whirling twiggy structure that stands below it. And it probes the interrelations between these memorial and recording technologies and Chaucer's own production as an embodied subject: a man of letters haunted by *auctorite*.[6]

Chaucer did not, of course, have access to electronic writing machines, databases, or search engines. The existence of numerous medieval artificial memory systems signals that Chaucer's access to knowledge is different from our own, since Chaucer, like many other medieval writers, tends to *remember* his quotations rather than check them accurately against standardized texts, a practice that is expected of modern authors in an age of copyright and authorial responsibility. And despite the claims that are sometimes made that computer technologies represent a return to medieval production, insofar as they are not bound by the linear structure of the printed book, such claims are quite simply anachronistic. The proliferation of knowledge and information among today's most highly developed computer-age societies has brought about a rift in knowledge legitimation that would not have been recognized by late medieval societies. Yet many of the tools and systems of modern cybernetics, microcomputing, and informatics were initially developed by the schoolmen of the twelfth century. As Michael Clanchy has amply documented, this period saw the rise of sophisticated systems of information storage, display, and retrieval: library catalogues, encyclopedias and compendia, *glossae* and *summae* (p. 106), *florilegia* (p. 107), rubrics, headings, and paragraphs (p. 133), marginal hands with outstretched index fingers to mark a particular item in a document, capital letters, running titles, introductory paragraph flourishes (p. 172), marginal abbreviations and symbols, and the use of a clear and orderly layout on the page.[7] Richard and Mary Rouse have very precisely dated the emergence of indexing tools to the second decade of the thirteenth century[8] and have studied thirteenth-century collections of biblical *distinctiones* (alphabetical compendia for preachers).[9] The principle of using the alphabet to classify words for reference goes back to antiquity but came into widespread use in the thirteenth century under the impulse of the friars, who brought in the demand for immediate information.[1]

Additionally, the elaborate systems of artificial memory outlined in the rhetorical treatises of the later Middle Ages offer significant parallels to modern techniques of scanning in that they override the spatiotemporal

---

6. In a paper presented at the Twelfth Biennial Congress of the New Chaucer Society (London, July 2000), Caroline Barron argued that Chaucer's predominant social affiliation was to the academy of letters.
7. Michael Clanchy, *From Memory to Written Record, England 1066–1397*, 2d ed. Oxford: Clarendon Press, 1993). For a back-to-the-future approach to information storage and retrieval in the early modern period, see Neil Rhodes and Jonathan Sawday, eds., *The Renaissance Computer: Knowledge Technology in the First Age of Print* (London and New York: Routledge, 2000).
8. Richard H. Rouse and Mary A. Rouse, *Preachers, Florilegia and Sermons* (Toronto: Pontifical Institute, 1979), p. 4, and "*Statim invenire*: Schools, Preachers, and New Attitudes towards the Page," in Robert L. Benson and Giles Constable, eds., *Renaissance and Renewal in the Twelfth Century* (Oxford: Clarendon Press, 1985).
9. *Distinctiones* originally referred to the distinguishing of multiple spiritual meanings for terms in a text, later furnishing divisions on a theme that could provide the basis for sermon structure; see Richard H. Rouse and Mary A. Rouse, "Biblical Distinctions in the Thirteenth Century," *Archives d'histoire doctrinale et littéraire du Moyen Age* 41 (1974): 27–37, at p. 37.
1. Clanchy, *From Memory*, pp. 180 and 182; H. G. Pfander, "The Mediæval Friars and Some Alphabetical Reference-Books for Sermons," *MÆ* 20 (1934): 19–29; Mary Carruthers, *The Book of Memory: A Study of Memory in Medieval Culture* (Cambridge: Cambridge University Press, 1999), p. 101.

organization of the written text and of reading itself, allowing the reader to locate material anywhere in a work: forwards, backwards, or non-sequentially. The ability to perform dazzling mnemonic feats such as reciting a text backwards as well as forwards was highly esteemed by both ancient and medieval writers. The twelfth-century cleric Hugh of St. Victor, for example, recommends just such a mental scrolling of the psalter in his treatise *De tribus maximis circumstantiis gestorum*: "And then I imprint the result of my mental effort by the vigilant concentration of my heart so that, when asked, without hesitation I may answer, either in forward order, or by skipping one or several, or in reverse order and recited backwards according to my completely mastered scheme of places, what is first, what second, what indeed 27th, 48th, or whatever psalm it should be."[2] Let us imagine how Chaucer in cyberspace might—ironically—be able to access the writings of Thomas Bradwardine, the archbishop of Canterbury (d. 1349), mentioned in *The Nun's Priest's Tale* (line 3242), a man who compiled a treatise on how to operate a similar virtual filing system.[3]

The point of indulging in this retrospective science fiction, however, is not to make us wonder at the modernity of the Middle Ages or at the belatedness of the postmodern present. Nor is it to provoke anxieties about anachronism, as experienced by those readers of Umberto Eco's *The Name of the Rose* who found some characters' utterances in the novel "too modern," although in every instance Eco was quoting fourteenth-century texts.[4] There is certainly a question here about what we recognize as "historical" as well as what we recognize as "modern." Anachronism is an important issue: I began this essay with my fantasy of Chaucer at his computer in order to jolt the reader out of the all-too-frequent fetishizing of the Middle Ages as a preelectronic era, irreconcilably other to our own. * * *

* * *

PUBLIUS VIRGILIUS MARO ("VIRGIL")

From the Aeneid†

[The most significant work by Virgil (70–19 B.C.E.) is the famous epic of the founding of Rome, the *Aeneid*, which strongly influenced Chaucer and other poets of the Middle Ages. For example, Virgil was Dante's guide through Hell and Purgatory in the *Divine Comedy*. In addition to being praised as poetry, the *Aeneid* was subject to allegorical interpretation by medieval Christian writers, which increased its popularity.

---

2. Carruthers, *Book of Memory*, pp. 262–63. On the proliferation and dominance of these mnemonic systems in the Middle Ages, see Mary Carruthers, *The Craft of Thought: Meditation, Rhetoric, and the Making of Images, 400–1200* (Cambridge: Cambridge University Press, 1998). See also Jocelyn Penny Small, *Wax Tablets of the Mind: Cognitive Studies of Memory and Literacy in Classical Antiquity* (London and New York: Routledge, 1997).
3. For a translation of Bradwardine's *De memoria artificiali* (ca. 1325–35), see Carruthers, *Book of Memory*, pp. 281–88.
4. Umberto Eco, *Postscript to* The Name of the Rose (San Diego, New York, and London: Harcourt Brace Jovanovich, 1984), p. 76.
† From *The Aeneid*, translated with an introduction by David West (London: Penguin Books, 1990), 80–103. Reprinted by permission of Penguin Books Ltd.

Written in Latin, the *Aeneid* made the Matter of Troy accessible to medieval audiences. Chaucer alludes to the story of Troy in numerous poems, including the *Book of the Duchess*, the *House of Fame*, and in his own epic romance, *Troilus and Criseyde*. He includes the tale of Aeneas' affair with Dido, queen of Carthage, in the *House of Fame* and in the *Legend of Good Women*. Along with Ovid's *Heroides*, Book 4 of the *Aeneid*, excerpted below, was one of Chaucer's chief sources for the story of Aeneas's wooing and ultimate desertion of the Carthaginian queen.]

But the queen had long since been suffering from love's deadly wound, feeding it with her blood and being consumed by its hidden fire. Again and again there rushed into her mind thoughts of the great valour of the man and the high glories of his line. His features and the words he had spoken had pierced her heart and love gave her body no peace or rest. The next day's dawn was beginning to traverse the earth with the lamp of Phoebus' sunlight and had moved the dank shadow of night from the sky when she spoke these words from the depths of her affliction to her loved and loving sister: 'O Anna, what fearful dreams I have as I lie there between sleeping and waking! What a man is this who has just come as a stranger into our house! What a look   10
on his face! What courage in his heart! What a warrior! I do believe, and I am sure it is true, he is descended from the gods. If there is any baseness in a man, it shows as cowardice. Oh how cruelly he has been hounded by the Fates! And did you hear him tell what a bitter cup of war he has had to drain? If my mind had not been set and immovably fixed against joining any man in the bonds of marriage ever since death cheated me of my first love, if I were not so utterly opposed to the marriage torch and bed, this is the one temptation to which I could possibly have succumbed. I will admit it, Anna, ever since the death of my poor husband Sychaeus, since my own brother spilt his blood   20
and polluted the gods of our home, this is the only man who has stirred my feelings and moved my mind to waver: I sense the return of the old fires. But I would pray that the earth open to its depths and swallow me or that the All-powerful Father of the Gods blast me with his thunderbolt and hurl me down to the pale shades of Erebus and its bottomless night before I go against my conscience and rescind its laws. The man who first joined himself to me has carried away all my love. He shall keep it for himself, safe in his grave.'

The tears came when she had finished speaking, and streamed down upon her breast. But Anna replied: 'O sister, dearer to me than the   30
light of life, are you going to waste away, living alone and in mourning all the days of your youth, without knowing the delight of children and the rewards of love? Do you believe this is what the dead care about when they are buried in the grave? Since your great sadness you have paid no heed to any man in Libya, or before that in Tyre. You have rejected Iarbas and other chiefs bred in Africa, this rich home of triumphant warriors. Will you now resist even a love your heart accepts? Have you forgotten what sort of people these are in whose land you have settled? On the one side you are beset by invincible Gaetulians, by Numidians, a race not partial to the bridle, and the   40

inhospitable Syrtes; on the other, waterless desert and fierce raiders from Barca. I do not need to tell you about the war being raised against you in Tyre and your brother's threats. I for my part believe that it is with the blessing of the gods and the favour of Juno that the Trojan ships have held course here through the winds. Just think, O my sister, what a city and what a kingdom you will see rising here if you are married to such a man! To what a pinnacle of glory will Carthage be raised if Trojans are marching at our side! You need only ask the blessing of the gods and prevail upon them with sacrifices. Indulge   50
your guest. Stitch together some reasons to keep him here while stormy seas and the downpours of Orion are exhausting their fury, while his ships are in pieces and it is no sky to sail under.'

With these words Anna lit a fire of wild love in her sister's breast. Where there had been doubt she gave hope and Dido's conscience was overcome. * * * [Dido and Anna visit the shrines of various gods in order to make sacrifices on Dido's behalf. Despite these offerings, Dido remains distracted by her passion for Aeneas.] Dido was on fire with love and wandered all over the city in her misery and madness like a wounded deer which a shepherd hunting in the woods of Crete   70
has caught off guard, striking her from long range with steel-tipped shaft; the arrow flies and is left in her body without his knowing it; she runs away over all the wooded slopes of Mount Dicte, and sticking in her side is the arrow that will bring her death.

Sometimes she would take Aeneas through the middle of Carthage, showing him the wealth of Sidon and the city waiting for him, and she would be on the point of speaking her mind to him but checked the words on her lips. Sometimes, as the day was ending, she would call for more feasting and ask in her infatuation to hear once more about the sufferings of Troy and once more she would hang on his lips as he told the story. Then, after they had parted, when the fading   80
moon was dimming her light and the setting stars seemed to speak of sleep, alone and wretched in her empty house she would cling to the couch Aeneas had left. There she would lie long after he had gone and she would see him and hear him when he was not there for her to see or hear. Or she would keep back Ascanius and take him on her knee, overcome by the likeness to his father, trying to beguile the love she could not declare. The towers she was building ceased to rise. Her men gave up the exercise of war and were no longer busy at the harbours and fortifications making them safe from attack. All the work that had been started, the threatening ramparts of the great walls and the cranes soaring to the sky, all stood idle.

As soon as Saturnian Juno, the dear wife of Jupiter, realized that   90
Dido was infected by this sickness and that passion was sweeping away all thought for her reputation, she went and spoke to Venus: * * * 'I do not fail to see that you have long been afraid of our walls and looked askance at the homes of lofty Carthage. But how is this going to end? Where is all this rivalry going to lead us now? Why do we not instead agree to arrange a marriage and live at peace for ever? You have achieved what you have set your whole heart on: Dido is passionately   100
in love and the madness is working through her bones. So let us make

one people of them and share authority equally over them. Let us allow her to become the slave of a Phrygian husband and to hand over her Tyrians to you as a dowry!'

* * *

* * * [Although she suspects Juno's motives, Venus admits to Juno that it would be simpler to let the Tyrians and Trojans join as one kingdom, but she does not know if Jupiter would look favorably upon the union. She craftily suggests that Juno approach her husband with the plan, and Juno responds,]

* * * 'Aeneas and poor Dido are preparing to go hunting together in the forest as soon as tomorrow's sun first rises and the rays of the Titan unveil the world. When the beaters are scurrying about and putting nets round copses, I shall pour down a dark storm of rain and hail on them and shake the whole sky with thunder. Their companions will run away and be lost to sight in a pall of darkness. Dido and the leader of the Trojans will both take refuge in the same cave. I shall be there, and if your settled will is with me in this, I shall join them in lasting marriage and make her his. This will be their wedding.' This was what Juno asked and Venus of Cythera did not refuse her but nodded in assent. She saw through the deception and laughed.

Meanwhile Aurora rose from the ocean and when her light came up into the sky, a picked band of men left the gates of Carthage carrying nets, wide-meshed and fine-meshed, and broad-bladed hunting spears, and with them came Massylian horsemen at the gallop and packs of keen-scented hounds. The queen was lingering in her chamber and the Carthaginian leaders waited at her door. There, resplendent in its purple and gold, stood her loud-hoofed, high-mettled horse champing its foaming bit. She came at last with a great entourage thronging round her. She was wearing a Sidonian cloak with an embroidered hem. Her quiver was of gold. Gold was the clasp that gathered up her hair and her purple tunic was fastened with a golden brooch. Nor was the Trojan company slow to move forward, Ascanius with them in high glee. Aeneas himself marched at their head, the most splendid of them all, as he brought his men to join the queen's. He was like Apollo leaving his winter home in Lycia and the waters of the river Xanthus to visit his mother at Delos, there to start the dancing again, while all around the altars gather noisy throngs of Cretans and Dryopes and painted Agathyrsians; the god himself strides the ridges of Mount Cynthus, his streaming hair caught up and shaped into a soft garland of green and twined round a band of gold, and the arrows sound on his shoulders— with no less vigour moved Aeneas and his face shone with equal radiance and grace. When they had climbed high into the mountains above the tracks of men where the animals make their lairs, suddenly some wild goats were disturbed on the top of a crag and came running down from the ridge. Then on the other side there were deer running across the open plain. They had gathered into a herd and were raising the dust as they left the high ground far behind them. Down in the middle of the valley young Ascanius was riding a lively horse and revelling in it, galloping past the deer and the goats and praying that among these

flocks of feeble creatures he could come across a foaming boar or that
a tawny lion would come down from the mountains.

While all this was happening a great rumble of thunder began to stir 160
in the sky. Down came the rain and the hail, and Tyrian huntsmen,
men of Troy and Ascanius of the line of Dardanus and grandson of
Venus, scattered in fright all over the fields, making for shelter as rivers
of water came rushing down the mountains. Dido and the leader of the
Trojans took refuge together in the same cave. The sign was first given
by Earth and by Juno as matron of honour. Fires flashed and the heav-
ens were witness to the marriage while nymphs wailed on the mountain
tops. This day was the beginning of her death, the first cause of all her 170
sufferings. From now on Dido gave no thought to appearance or her
good name and no longer kept her love as a secret in her own heart,
but called it marriage, using the word to cover her guilt.

Rumour did not take long to go through the great cities of Libya. Of
all the ills there are, Rumour is the swiftest. She thrives on movement
and gathers strength as she goes. From small and timorous beginnings
she soon lifts herself up into the air, her feet still on the ground and
her head hidden in the clouds. They say she is the last daughter of
Mother Earth who bore her in rage against the gods, a sister for Coeus 180
and Enceladus whom Jupiter had killed. Rumour is quick of foot and
swift on the wing, a huge and horrible monster, and under every feather
of her body, strange to tell, there lies an eye that never sleeps, a mouth
and a tongue that are never silent and an ear always pricked. By night
she flies between earth and sky, squawking through the darkness, and
never lowers her eyelids in sweet sleep. By day she keeps watch perched
on the tops of gables or on high towers and causes fear in great cities,
holding fast to her lies and distortions as often as she tells the truth. At
that time she was taking delight in plying the tribes with all manner of 190
stories, fact and fiction mixed in equal parts: how Aeneas the Trojan
had come to Carthage and the lovely Dido had thought fit to take him
as her husband; how they were even now indulging themselves and
keeping each other warm the whole winter through, forgetting about
their kingdoms and becoming the slaves of lust. When the foul goddess
had spread this gossip all around on the lips of men, she then steered
her course to king Iarbas to set his mind alight and fuel his anger.

* * * Iarbas, they say, was driven out of his mind with anger when he 203
heard this bitter news. Coming into the presence of the gods before
their altars in a passion of rage, he offered up prayer upon prayer to
Jupiter, raising his hands palms upward in supplication: * * * 'This
woman was wandering about our land and we allowed her at a price to
found her little city. We gave her a piece of shore to plough and laid
down the laws of the place for her and she has spurned our offer of
marriage and taken Aeneas into her kingdom as lord and master, and
now this second Paris, with eunuchs in attendance and hair dripping
with perfume and Maeonian bonnet tied under his chin, is enjoying
what he has stolen while we bring gifts to temples we think are yours
and keep warm with our worship the reputation of a useless god.'

As Iarbas prayed these prayers with his hand on the altar, the All-
powerful god heard him and turned his eyes towards the royal city and 220

the lovers who had lost all recollection of their good name. Then he
spoke to Mercury and gave him these instructions: 'Up with you, my
son. Call for the Zephyrs, glide down on your wings and speak to the
Trojan leader who now lingers in Tyrian Carthage without a thought
for the cities granted him by the Fates. Take these words of mine down
to him through the swift winds and tell him that this is not the man
promised us by his mother, the loveliest of the goddesses. It was not for
this that she twice rescued him from the swords of the Greeks. She told
us he would be the man to rule an Italy pregnant with empire and   230
clamouring for war, passing the high blood of Teucer down to his
descendants and subduing the whole world under his laws. If the glory
of such a destiny does not fire his heart, if he does not strive to win
fame for himself, ask him if he grudges the citadel of Rome to his son
Ascanius. What does he have in mind? What does he hope to achieve
dallying among a hostile people and sparing not a thought for the Lav-
inian fields and his descendants yet to be born in Ausonia? He must
sail. That is all there is to say. Let that be our message.'

Jupiter had finished speaking and Mercury prepared to obey the com-
mand of his mighty father. First of all he fastened on his feet the golden
sandals whose wings carry him high above land and sea as swiftly as the   240
wind. Then, taking the rod which summons pale spirits out of Orcus or
sends them down to gloomy Tartarus, which gives sleep and takes it
away and opens the eyes of men in death, he drove the winds before
him and floated through the turbulent clouds till in his flight he saw
the crest and steep flanks of Atlas whose rocky head props up the sky.
This is the Atlas whose head, covered in pine trees and beaten by wind
and rain, never loses its dark cap of cloud. The snow falls upon his
shoulders and lies there, then rivers of water roll down the old man's   250
chin and his bristling beard is stiff with ice. This is where Mercury the
god of Mount Cyllene first landed, fanning out his wings to check his
flight. From here he let his weight take him plummeting to the wave
tops, like a bird skimming the sea as it flies along the shore, among the
rocks where it finds the fish. So flew the Cyllenian god between earth
and sky to the sandy beaches of Libya, cleaving the winds as he swooped
down from the mountain that had fathered his own mother, Maia.

As soon as his winged feet touched the roof of a Carthaginian hut,
he caught sight of Aeneas laying the foundations of the citadel and   260
putting up buildings. His sword was studded with yellow stars of jasper,
and glowing with Tyrian purple there hung from his shoulders a rich
cloak given him by Dido into which she had woven a fine cross-thread
of gold. Mercury wasted no time: 'So now you are laying foundations
for the high towers of Carthage and building a splendid city to please
your wife? Have you entirely forgotten your own kingdom and your own
destiny? The ruler of the gods himself, by whose divine will the heavens
and the earth revolve, sends me down from bright Olympus and bids
me bring these commands to you through the swift winds. What do you   270
have in mind? What do you hope to achieve by idling your time away
in the land of Libya? If the glory of such a destiny does not fire your
heart, spare a thought for Ascanius as he grows to manhood, for the
hopes of this Iulus who is your heir. You owe him the land of Rome
and the kingdom of Italy.'

No sooner had these words passed the lips of the Cyllenian god than he disappeared from mortal view and faded far into the insubstantial air. But the sight of him left Aeneas dumb and senseless. His hair stood on end with horror and the voice stuck in his throat. He longed to be away and leave behind him this land he had found so sweet. The warning, the command from the gods, had struck him like a thunderbolt. But what, oh what, was he to do? What words dare he use to approach the queen in all her passion? How could he begin to speak to her? His thoughts moved swiftly now here, now there, darting in every possible direction and turning to every possible event, and as he pondered, this seemed to him a better course of action: he called Mnestheus, Sergestus and brave Serestus and ordered them to fit out the fleet and tell no one, to muster the men on the shore with their equipment at the ready, and keep secret the reason for the change of plan. In the meantime, since the good queen knew nothing and the last thing she expected was the shattering of such a great love, he himself would try to make approaches to her and find the kindest time to speak and the best way to handle the matter. They were delighted to receive their orders and carried them out immediately.

But the queen—who can deceive a lover?—knew in advance some scheme was afoot. Afraid where there was nothing to fear, she was the first to catch wind of their plans to leave, and while she was already in a frenzy, that same wicked Rumour brought word that the Trojans were fitting out their fleet and preparing to sail away. Driven to distraction and burning with passion, she raged and raved round the whole city like a Bacchant stirred by the shaking of the sacred emblems and roused to frenzy when she hears the name of Bacchus at the biennial orgy and the shouting on Mount Cithaeron calls to her in the night. At last she went to Aeneas, and before he could speak, she cried: 'You traitor, did you imagine you could do this and keep it secret? Did you think you could slip away from this land of mine and say nothing? Does our love have no claim on you? Or the pledge your right hand once gave me? Or the prospect of Dido dying a cruel death? Why must you move your fleet in these winter storms and rush across the high seas into the teeth of the north wind? You are heartless. Even if it were not other people's fields and some home unknown you were going to, if old Troy were still standing, would any fleet set sail even for Troy in such stormy seas? Is it me you are running away from? I beg you, by these tears, by the pledge you gave me with your own right hand—I have nothing else left me now in my misery—I beg you by our union, by the marriage we have begun—if I have deserved any kindness from you, if you have ever loved anything about me, pity my house that is falling around me, and I implore you, if it is not too late for prayers, give up this plan of yours. I am hated because of you by the peoples of Libya and the Numidian kings. My own Tyrians are against me. Because of you I have lost all conscience and self-respect and have thrown away the good name I once had, my only hope of reaching the stars. My guest is leaving me to my fate and I shall die. "Guest" is the only name I can now give the man who used to be my husband. What am I waiting for? For my brother Pygmalion to come and raze my city to the ground? For the Gaetulian Iarbas to drag me off in chains? Oh if only you had given me a child

before you abandoned me! If only there were a little Aeneas to play in
my palace! In spite of everything his face would remind me of yours and
I would not feel utterly betrayed and desolate.'   33

She had finished speaking. Remembering the warnings of Jupiter,
Aeneas did not move his eyes and struggled to fight down the anguish in
his heart. At last he spoke these few words: 'I know, O queen, you can
list a multitude of kindnesses you have done me. I shall never deny them
and never be sorry to remember Dido while I remember myself, while
my spirit still governs this body. Much could be said. I shall say only a
little. It never was my intention to be deceitful or run away without your
knowing, and do not pretend that it was. Nor have I ever offered you
marriage or entered into that contract with you. If the Fates were leav-   34
ing me free to live my own life and settle all my cares according to my
own wishes, my first concern would be to tend the city of Troy and my
dear ones who are still alive. The lofty palace of Priam would still be
standing and with my own hands I would have built a new citadel at Per-
gamum for those who have been defeated. But now Apollo of Gryneum
has commanded me to claim the great land of Italy and "Italy" is the
word on the lots cast at his Lycian oracle. That is my love, and that is my
homeland. You are a Phoenician from Asia and you care for the citadel
of Carthage and love the very sight of this city in Libya; what objection
can there be to Trojans settling in the land of Ausonia? How can it be a   35
sin if we too look for distant kingdoms. Every night when the earth is
covered in mist and darkness, every time the burning stars rise in the
sky, I see in my dreams the troubled spirit of my father Anchises coming
to me with warnings and I am afraid. I see my son Ascanius and think of
the wrong I am doing him, cheating him of his kingdom in Hesperia and
the lands the Fates have decreed for him. And now even the messenger
of the gods has come down through the swift winds—I swear it by the
lives of both of us—and brought commands from Jupiter himself. With
my own eyes I have seen the god in the clear light of day coming within
the walls of your city. With my own ears I have listened to his voice. Do
not go on causing distress to yourself and to me by these complaints. It   36
is not by my own will that I still search for Italy.'

All the time he had been speaking she was turned away from him,
but looking at him, speechless and rolling her eyes, taking in every part
of him. At last she replied on a blaze of passion: 'You are a traitor. You
are not the son of a goddess and Dardanus was not the first founder of
your family. It was the Caucasus that fathered you on its hard rocks
and Hyrcanian tigers offered you their udders. Why should I keep up a
pretence? Why should I keep myself in check in order to endure greater
suffering in the future? He did not sigh when he saw me weep. He did
not even turn to look at me. Was he overcome and brought to tears?   37
Had he any pity for the woman who loves him? Where can I begin when
there is so much to say? Now, after all this, can mighty Juno and the
son of Saturn, the father of all, can they now look at this with the eyes
of justice? Is there nothing we can trust in this life? He was thrown
helpless on my shores and I took him in and like a fool settled him as
partner in my kingdom. He had lost his fleet and I found it and brought
his companions back from the dead. It drives me to madness to think
of it. And now we hear about the augur Apollo and lots cast in Lycia

and now to crown all the messenger of the gods is bringing terrifying commands down through the winds from Jupiter himself, as though that is work for the gods in heaven, as though that is an anxiety that disturbs their tranquillity. I do not hold you or bandy words with you. 380 Away you go. Keep on searching for your Italy with the winds to help you. Look for your kingdom over the waves. But my hope is that if the just gods have any power, you will drain a bitter cup among the ocean rocks, calling the name of Dido again and again, and I shall follow you not in the flesh but in the black fires of death and when its cold hand takes the breath from my body, my shade shall be with you wherever you may be. You will receive the punishment you deserve, and the news of it will reach me deep among the dead.'

At these words she broke off and rushed indoors in utter despair, leaving Aeneas with much to say and much to fear. Her attendants 390 caught her as she fainted and carried her to her bed in her marble chamber. But Aeneas was faithful to his duty. Much as he longed to soothe her and console her sorrow, to talk to her and take away her pain, with many a groan and with a heart shaken by his great love, he nevertheless carried out the commands of the gods and went back to his ships.

By then the Trojans were hard at work. All along the shore they were hauling the tall ships down to the sea. They set the well-caulked hulls afloat and in their eagerness to be away they were carrying down from the woods unworked timber and green branches for oars. You could see 400 them pouring out of every part of the city, like ants plundering a huge heap of wheat and storing it away in their home against the winter, and their black column advances over the plain as they gather in their booty along a narrow path through the grass, some putting their shoulders to huge grains and pushing them along, others keeping the column together and whipping in the stragglers, and the whole track seethes with activity. What were your feelings, Dido, as you looked at this? Did you not moan as you gazed out from the top of your citadel and saw the 410 broad shore seething before your eyes and confusion and shouting all over the sea? Love is a cruel master. There are no lengths to which it does not force the human heart. Once again she had recourse to tears, once again she was driven to try to move his heart with prayers, becoming a suppliant and making her pride submit to her love, in case she should die in vain, leaving some avenue unexplored. 'You see, Anna, the bustle all over the shore. They are all gathered there, the canvas is calling for the winds, the sailors are delighted and have set garlands on the ships' sterns. I was able to imagine that this grief might come; I 420 shall be able to endure it. But Anna, do this one service for your poor sister. You are the only one the traitor respected. To you he entrusted his very deepest feelings. You are the only one who knew the right time to approach him and the right words to use. Go to him, sister. Kneel before our proud enemy and tell him I was not at Aulis and made no compact with the Greeks to wipe out the people of Troy. I sent no fleet to Pergamum. I did not tear up the ashes of his dead father Anchises. Why are his cruel ears closed to what I am saying? Where is he rushing away to? Ask him to do this last favour to the unhappy woman who loves him and wait till there is a following wind and his escape is easy. 430

I am no longer begging for the marriage which we once had and which he has now betrayed. I am not pleading with him to do without his precious Latium and abandon his kingdom. What I am asking for is some time, nothing more, an interval, a respite for my anguish, so that fortune can teach me to grieve and to endure defeat. This is the last favour I shall beg. O Anna, pity your sister. I shall repay it in good measure at my death.'

These were Dido's pleas. These were the griefs her unhappy sister brought and brought again. But no griefs moved Aeneas. He heard but did not heed her words. The Fates forbade it and God blocked his ears 440 to all appeals. Just as the north winds off the Alps vie with one another to uproot the mighty oak whose timber has hardened over long years of life, blowing upon it from this side and from that and howling through it; the trunk feels the shock and the foliage from its head covers the ground, but it holds on to the rocks with roots plunged as deep into the world below as its crown soars towards the winds of heaven—just so the hero Aeneas was buffeted by all this pleading on this side and on that, and felt the pain deep in his mighty heart but his mind remained unmoved and the tears rolled in vain.

Then it was that unhappy Dido prayed for death. She had seen her 450 destiny and was afraid. She could bear no longer to look up to the bowl of heaven, and her resolve to leave the light was strengthened when she was laying offerings on the incense-breathing altars and saw to her horror the consecrated milk go black and the wine, as she poured it, turn to filthy gore. No one else saw it and she did not tell even her sister. There was more. She had in her palace a marble shrine dedicated to Sychaeus, who had been her husband. This she used to honour above all things, hanging it with white fleeces and sacred branches. When the darkness of night covered the earth, she thought she heard, coming from this shrine, the voice of her husband and the words he uttered as 460 he called to her, and all the while the lonely owl kept up its long dirge upon the roof, drawing out its doleful song of death. And there was more. She kept remembering the predictions of ancient prophets that terrified her with their dreadful warnings, and as she slept Aeneas himself would drive her relentlessly in her madness, and she was always alone and desolate, always going on a long road without companions, looking for her Tyrians in an empty land. She would be like Pentheus in his frenzy when he was seeing columns of Furies and a double sun and two cities of Thebes; or like Orestes, son of Agamemnon, driven in 470 flight across the stage by his own mother armed with her torches and black snakes, while the avenging Furies sat at the door.

And so Dido was overwhelmed by grief and possessed by madness. She decided to die and planned in her mind the time and the means. She went and spoke to her sorrowing sister with her face composed to conceal her plan and her brow bright with hope. * * * [Dido tells Anna of her plan to consult a Massylian priestess who is skilled in the arts of necromancy and curses. She declares her intent to resort to magic to preserve Aeneas's love or to release her from her own.] 'Go now, telling 494 no one, and build up a pyre under the open sky in the inner courtyard of the palace and lay on it the armour this traitor has left hanging on the walls of my room, everything there is of his remaining, and the marriage bed on which I was destroyed. I want to wipe out everything that can remind me of such a man and that is what the priestess advises.'

She spoke, and spoke no more. Her face grew pale, but Anna did not understand that these strange rites were a pretence and that her sister 500 meant to die. She had no inkling that such madness had seized Dido, no reason to fear that she would suffer more than she had at the death of Sychaeus. She did what she was asked.

But the queen knew what the future held. As soon as the pine torches and the holm-oak were hewn and the huge pyre raised under the open sky in the very heart of the palace, she hung the place with garlands and crowned the pyre with funeral branches. Then she laid on a bed an effigy of Aeneas with his sword and everything of his he had left behind. There were altars all around and the priestess with hair stream- ing called with a voice of thunder upon three hundred gods, Erebus, 510 Chaos, triple Hecate and virgin Diana of the three faces. She had also sprinkled water to represent the spring of Lake Avernus. She also sought out potent herbs with a milk of black poison in their rich stems and harvested them by moonlight with a bronze sickle. She found, too, a love charm, torn from the forehead of a new-born foal before the mare could bite it off. Dido herself took meal in her hands and worshipped, standing by the altars with one foot freed from all fastenings and her dress unbound, calling before she died to gods and stars to be witnesses to her fate and praying to whatever just and mindful power there is that 520 watches over lovers who have been betrayed.

It was night and weary living things were peacefully taking their rest upon the earth. The woods and wild waves of ocean had been stilled. The stars were rolling on in mid-course. Silence reigned over field and flock and all the gaily coloured birds were laid to sleep in the quiet of night, those that haunt broad lakes and those that crowd the thickets dotted over the countryside. But not Dido. Her heart was broken and she found no relief in sleep. Her eyes and mind would not accept the 530 night, but her torment redoubled and her raging love came again and again in great surging tides of anger. These are the thoughts she dwelt upon, this is what she kept turning over in her heart: 'So then, what am I to do? Shall I go back to those who once wooed me and see if they will have me? I would be a laughing stock. Shall I beg a husband from the Numidians after I have so often scorned their offers of marriage? Shall I then go with the Trojan fleet and do whatever the Trojans ask? I suppose they would be delighted to take me after all the help I have given them! They are sure to remember what I have done and be prop- erly grateful! No: even if I were willing to go with them, they will never 540 allow a woman they hate to come aboard their proud ships. There is nothing left for you, Dido. Do you not know, have you not yet noticed, the treacheries of the race of Laomedon? But if they did agree to take me, what then? Shall I go alone into exile with a fleet of jubilant sailors? Or shall I go in force with all my Tyrian bands crowding at my side? It was not easy for me to uproot them from their homes in the city of Sidon. How can I make them take to the sea again and order them to hoist sail into the winds? No, you must die. That is what you have deserved. Let the sword be the cure for your suffering. You could not bear, Anna, to see your sister weeping. When the madness was taking

me, you were the first to lay this load upon my back and put me at the
mercy of my enemy. I was not allowed to live my life without marriage,   55
in innocence, like a wild creature, and be untouched by such anguish
as this—I have not kept faith with the ashes of Sychaeus.'

While these words of grief were bursting from Dido's heart, Aeneas
was now resolved to leave and was taking his rest on the high stern of
his ship with everything ready for sailing. There, as he slept, appeared
before him the shape of the god, coming to him with the same features
as before and once again giving advice, in every way like Mercury, the
voice, the radiance, the golden hair, the youthful beauty of his body:
'Son of the goddess, how can you lie there sleeping at a time like this?   56
Do you not see danger all around you at this moment? Have you lost
your wits? Do you not hear the west wind blowing off the shore? Having
decided to die, she is turning her schemes over in her mind and plan-
ning some desperate act, stirring up the storm tides of her anger. Why
do you not go now with all speed while speed you may? If morning
comes and finds you loitering here, you will soon see her ships churning
the sea and deadly torches blazing and the shore seething with flames.
Come on then! No more delay! Women are unstable creatures, always
changing.'

When he had spoken he melted into the blackness of night and   57
Aeneas was immediately awake, terrified by the sudden apparition.
There was no more rest for his men, as he roused them to instant action:
'Wake up and sit to your benches,' he shouted. 'Let out the sails and
quick about it. A god has been sent down again from the heights of
heaven—I have just seen him—spurring us on to cut our plaited ropes
and run from here. We are following you, O blessed god, whoever you
are. Once again we obey your commands and rejoice. Stand beside us
and graciously help us. Put favouring stars in the sky for us.'

As he spoke he drew his sword from its scabbard like a flash of light-
ning and struck the mooring cables with the naked steel. In that instant   580
they were all seized by the same ardour and set to, hauling and hustling.
The shore was emptied. The sea could not be seen for ships. Bending to
the oars they whipped up the foam and swept the blue surface of the
sea.

Aurora was soon leaving the saffron bed of Tithonus and beginning
to sprinkle new light upon the earth. The queen saw from her high
tower the first light whitening and the fleet moving out to sea with its
sails square to the following winds. She saw the deserted shore and
harbour and not an oarsman in sight. Three times and more she beat
her lovely breasts and tore her golden hair, crying 'O Jupiter! Will this   59
intruder just go, and make a mockery of our kingdom? Why are they
not running to arms and coming from all over the city to pursue him?
And others should be rushing ships out of the docks. Move! Bring fire
and quick about it! Give out the weapons! Heave on the oars!—What
am I saying? Where am I? What madness is this that changes my
resolve? Poor Dido, you have done wrong and it is only now coming
home to you. You should have thought of this when you were offering
him your sceptre. So much for his right hand! So much for his pledge,
the man who is supposed to be carrying with him the gods of his native
land and to have lifted his weary old father up on to his shoulders! Could

I not have taken him and torn him limb from limb and scattered the   600
pieces in the sea? Could I not have put his men to the sword, and
Ascanius, too, and served his flesh at his father's table? I know the
outcome of a battle would have been in doubt. So it would have been
in doubt! Was I, who am about to die, afraid of anyone? I would have
taken torches to his camp and filled the decks of his ships with fire,
destroying the son and the father and the whole Trojan people before
throwing myself on the flames. O heavenly Sun whose fires pass in
review all the works of this earth, and you, Juno, who have been witness
and party to all the anguish of this love, and Hecate whose name is
heard in nightly howling at crossroads all over our cities, and the aveng-   610
ing Furies and you, the gods of dying Dido, listen to these words, give
a hearing to my sufferings, for they are great, and heed my prayers. If
that monster of wickedness must reach harbour, if he must come to
shore and that is what the Fates of Jupiter demand, if the boundary
stone is set and may not be moved, then let him be harried in war by a
people bold in arms; may he be driven from his own land and torn from
the embrace of Iulus; may he have to beg for help and see his innocent
people dying. Then, after he has submitted to the terms of an unjust
peace, let him not enjoy the kingdom he longs for or the life he longs
to lead, but let him fall before his time and lie unburied on the broad   620
sand. This is my prayer. With these last words I pour out my life's blood.
As for you, my Tyrians, you must pursue with hatred the whole line of
his descendants in time to come. Make that your offering to my shade.
Let there be no love between our peoples and no treaties. Arise from
my dead bones, O my unknown avenger, and harry the race of Dardanus
with fire and sword wherever they may settle, now and in the future,
whenever our strength allows it. I pray that we may stand opposed,
shore against shore, sea against sea and sword against sword. Let there
be war between the nations and between their sons for ever.'

Even as she spoke Dido was casting about in her mind how she could   630
most quickly put an end to the life she hated. She then addressed these
few words to Sychaeus' nurse, Barce, for the black ashes of her own
now lay far away in her ancient homeland: 'My dear nurse, send my
sister Anna quickly to me, telling her to sprinkle her body with river
water and take with her the animals and the other offerings as
instructed. That is how she is to come, and your own forehead must be
veiled with a sacred ribbon. I have prepared with due care offerings to
Jupiter of the Styx and I am now of a mind to complete them and put
an end to the pain of love by giving the pyre of this Trojan to the flames.'   640

The old woman bustled away leaving Dido full of wild fears at the
thought of what she was about to do. Her cheeks trembling and flecked
with red, her bloodshot eyes rolling, she was pale with the pallor of
approaching death. Rushing through the door into the inner courtyard,
she climbed the high pyre in a frenzy and unsheathed the Trojan sword
for which she had asked—though not for this purpose. Then her eyes
lit on the Trojan clothes and the bed she knew so well, and pausing for
a moment to weep and to remember, she lay down on the bed and spoke
these last words: 'These are the possessions of Aeneas which I so loved   650
while God and the Fates allowed it. Let them receive my spirit and free
me from this anguish. I have lived my life and completed the course

that Fortune has set before me, and now my great spirit will go beneath the earth. I have founded a glorious city and lived to see the building of my own walls. I have avenged my husband and punished his enemy who was my brother. I would have been happy, more than happy, if only Trojan keels had never grounded on our shores.' She then buried her face for a moment in the bed and cried: 'We shall die unavenged. But let us die. This, this, is how it pleases me to go down among the shades. Let the Trojan who knows no pity gaze his fill upon this fire from the high seas and take with him the omen of my death.'   66

So she spoke and while speaking fell upon the sword. Her attendants saw her fall. They saw the blood foaming on the blade and staining her hands, and filled the high walls of the palace with their screaming. Rumour ran raving like a Bacchant through the stricken city. The palace rang with lamentation and groaning and the wailing of women and the heavens gave back the sound of mourning. It was as though the enemy were within the gates and the whole of Carthage or old Tyre were falling   67 with flames raging and rolling over the roofs of men and gods. Anna heard and was beside herself. She came rushing in terror through the middle of the crowd, tearing her face and beating her breast, calling out her sister's name as she lay dying: 'So this is what it meant? It was all to deceive your sister! This was the purpose of the pyre and the flames and the altars! You have abandoned me. I do not know how to begin to reproach you. Did you not want your sister's company when you were dying? You could have called me to share your fate and we would both have died in the same moment of the same grief. To think it was my   68 hands that built the pyre, and my voice that called upon the gods of our fathers, so that you could be so cruel as to lay yourself down here to die without me. It is not only yourself you have destroyed, but also your sister and your people, their leaders who came with you from Sidon and the city you have built. Give me water. I shall wash her wounds and catch any last lingering breath with my lips.'

Saying these words, she had climbed to the top of the pyre and was now holding her dying sister to her breast and cherishing her, sobbing as she dried the dark blood with her own dress. Once more Dido tried to raise her heavy eyes, but failed. The wound hissed round the sword beneath her breast. Three times she raised herself on her elbow. Three   69 times she fell back on the bed. With wavering eyes she looked for light in the heights of heaven and groaned when she found it.

All-powerful Juno then took pity on her long anguish and difficult death and sent Iris down from Olympus to free her struggling spirit and loosen the fastenings of her limbs. For since she was dying not by the decree of Fate or by her own deserts but pitiably and before her time, in a sudden blaze of madness, Proserpina had not yet taken a lock of her golden hair or consigned her to Stygian Orcus. So Iris, bathed in dew, flew down on her saffron wings, trailing all her colours across the   70 sky opposite the sun, and hovered over Dido's head to say: 'I am commanded to take this lock of hair as a solemn offering to Dis, and now I free you from your body.'

With these words she raised her hand and cut the hair, and as she cut, all warmth went out of Dido's body and her life passed into the winds.

PUBLIUS OVIDIUS NASO
("OVID")

From the *Heroides*†

[Ovid (43 B.C.E.–17 C.E.) was widely admired and imitated throughout the Middle Ages, his popularity at times rivaling that of Virgil. Although best known for the *Metamorphoses*, a catalogue of myths united by the theme of change, his satiric poems on love and seduction (e.g., the *Amores*, the *Ars amatoria*, and the *Remedia amoris*) also influenced medieval writers. Ovid's writings on romantic love were a source for the thirteenth-century *Romance of the Rose*, a love vision that was one of the most important literary influences on Chaucer's work.

Ovid's *Heroides* ("Heroines") presents a series of letters written from the perspective of famous mythological women, to the husbands and lovers who have deserted them. Each letter, or monologue, poignantly explores its writer's character, allowing Ovid to retell the most famous classical myths from a new, female perspective.

The *Heroides*' influence on Chaucer is most apparent in the first book of the *House of Fame* and in the *Legend of Good Women*. In the latter work, Chaucer bases many of his stories of abandoned women on the laments invented by Ovid, though he takes pleasure as well in showing places where Ovid's versions are in tension with other literary treatments. For example, Chaucer's account of the Carthaginian queen Dido, forsaken by Aeneas, owes much to Ovid's characterization, but also allows for a Virgilian point of view on the heroine's tragedy.]

Dido to Aeneas

[In *Heroides* 7, Dido addresses Aeneas, acknowledging his inevitable abandonment of her, yet pleading for him to remain with her in Carthage. She prays to Venus and to Love to have pity on her, and proceeds to warn Aeneas of the dangers of the sea, especially to those who have been unfaithful in love.]

> And so, at fate's call, the white swan lets himself
>   down in the water-soaked grasses by
> the Meander's shoreline to sing his last song;
>   but I will not hope to move your heart
> 5 with my prayer because the god opposes me.
>   After the loss of all that is mine,
> good name, chastity of both body and soul,
>   a loss of words is not important.
> But I ask again: are you still determined
> 10   to abandon me to misery
> and permit both your ships and your promises
>   to sail from this shore on the same wind?
> Aeneas, are you still determined to leave
>   both your mooring and your solemn pledge

† From the *Heroides*, translated by Harold Isbell (London: Penguin Books, 1990), 57–65. Reprinted by permission of Penguin Books Ltd. The translator's notes have been omitted.

15   to seek a kingdom in remote Italy,
          a place whose shores you have never seen?
      Aren't you impressed by the new walls of Carthage
          and the sceptre I've placed in your hand?
      You have rejected what is done and insist
20   on pursuing some unfinished work.
      I have given you a kingdom; still you seek,
          through all the world, a land of your own.
      Let us suppose you find the country you seek:
          who would give it to you? Is there one
25   man who would trust a foreigner in his fields?
          You must win another Dido's love,
      you must give pledges to some other woman
          and I know you will again be false.
      How do you hope to found another city
30   like this so that you in a tower
      can observe a people that belongs to you?
          If all your wishes were granted now,
      without any further delay, could you find
          a wife who will love you as I have loved you?
35   Like devout incense thrown on smoking altars,
          like wax torches tipped with sulphur, I
      am burning with love: all day long and all night,
          I desire nothing but Aeneas.
      But Aeneas is not grateful; he rejects
40   my care for him. If I had no love
      for him he could go and I would be willing.
          But no matter how bad he might think
      I am, I can never say that I hate him
          but I will complain: he is unfaithful.
45   When my complaint has been said, I love him more.
          Venus spare me, let me be his wife;
      Brother, Love, change the hard heart of your brother
          that he will do service in your camp.
      If this cannot be, I who was first to love—
50   I say this without the slightest shame—
      can supply the love that will kindle the fuel
          for loving that he has within him.
      But this is all delusions and lies, the dream
          that hovers before me is not true;
55   his mother's heart does not beat in Aeneas.
          You were conceived by rocks and mountains,
      born of oaks on the high cliffs, of the savage
          beasts, or of raging seas, such a sea
      of hostile tides as now you can observe, tossed
60   by the winds, on which you will soon sail.
      Where do you flee? The rising storm will stop you,
          indeed, it will be my gift to you.
      Look now, how the wind tosses the rolling waves.
          What I had wanted to owe to you
65   I will owe to the winds of the storm because

winds and waves are more than just your soul.
My worth is not great enough for you to die
    in fleeing from me on the high seas—
why can I not place a wrong value on you—
70   if you are able to risk dying
to be free of me, then you have paid too much
    for this hatred you are indulging.
The winds must soon cease, and over the smooth waves
    old Triton will drive his sky-born team.
75 Oh that you too might be so easily changed;
    and so you shall be changed, unless you
are harder than the oak. Why does one who knows
    the sea like you so trust the waters
whose power you have felt? When you have cast off
80   your mooring because the sea is good,
there will still remain much to fear from the sea.
    It is right that this should be, for it
was from the sea, near Cythera, it is said,
    that the naked mother of the Loves
85 came, and so one who has been unfaithful should
    not tempt the waves that flow in that place.
I am doomed, but I fear that I will ruin
    him who ruined me, that I will harm
him who harmed me, I fear my foe will be wrecked
90   at sea and be drowned. Aeneas live,
I pray it, for by living you will be hurt
    more than you could be hurt by dying.
You will be well-known as the cause of my fate.
    Imagine—may this be no omen—
95 that the storm has swept you up, what will you think?
    You will think of me and your false tongue;
you will think of Dido forced to die because
    one from Phrygia was unfaithful;
you will see the tears of your abandoned bride,
100   her shoulders bent in grief, hair undone,
all stained with blood. What is it that you gain now
    to pay you enough that you can say,
'This was I justly owed, the gods forgive me,'
    as the thunderbolts are hurled at you?
105 Wait a little, for your meanness and the sea's
    to calm, for your safe voyage will be
your reward for waiting. Perhaps you
    can ignore such things, still you must let
young Iulus live. You alone will have enough
110   if it is known that you caused my death.
What is Ascanius' guilt, or your Penates'
    that they be worthy of such a fate?
Have they been saved from a burning city so
    that now they can be lost in the sea?
115 But you are false. All this talk of your father
    and the gods, all borne on your shoulders

to escape the flames, is still more of your lies.
    I was not first nor will I be last
to feel the heavy burden of your deceit.
120   Do they ask about your son's mother?
She was left dead and abandoned by her lord.
    You told me that, and I should have known
that you were only giving me fair notice.
    Now, let me be burned as she was burned
125 for such a punishment is very much less
    than the pain my crime should win for me.
And I am certain that your gods are angry
    for this is now the seventh winter
that you have been tormented by the harsh winds.
130   The sea washed you up on my shore and
I welcomed you to a safe refuge; hardly
    knowing your name, I gave you my throne.
I wish these gifts had been all, that everything
    else could be buried and forgotten.
135 That awful day, when a sudden storm came out
    of the blue sky and we took shelter
in a high-ceilinged cave, was my doom. I heard
    a voice, I thought it was a nymph's song
but it was the Eumenides shouting out
140   a warning of the fate that was mine.
Virtue lost, you may exact the penalty
    which I owe to Sychaeus, I go
in shame and misery to seek forgiveness.
    His statue stands in a marble shrine
145 among green branches and ribbons of white wool.
    From that sacred place four times I heard
a voice that I remember quite well faintly
    calling out to me, 'Elissa, come.'
He calls me to his bed because I am his.
150   I am late because I have confessed
my awful crime, I come in shame, forgive me.
    He who caused my fall was worthy and
he makes my sin less hateful. It was my hope
    that his divine mother and the weight
155 of his old father would make a faithful son
    become for me a faithful husband.
If I have failed, my fault has a worthy cause;
    if he be true, I have no regret.
Now, near the end of life, my fate is unchanged
160   and it will follow me to the end.
My husband's blood washed the altars of his house,
    my brother reaped the fruits of that crime.
I was driven out of Tyre into exile
    leaving both his ashes and my land.
165 My enemy pursued me along hard paths;
    I reached this coast, having escaped both
my brother and the sea, and I bought these shores,

the land that I gave you, faithless man.
I founded my city, I laid foundations
170   on which huge walls would rise, exciting
the jealous fears of the neighbouring kingdoms.
    A stranger and a woman, I found
myself soon threatened by war. Quickly, I raised
    gates and prepared a hasty defence.
175 I have a thousand suitors, each one eyeing
    me with fondness and all complaining
because I prefer a foreigner. Tie me,
    give me to Iarbas of Gaetulia;
I would permit it. My brother might sprinkle
180   his profane hand with my blood as it
was sprinkled once with the blood of my husband.
    Set aside your gods and holy things,
your hand profanes them. An unholy right hand
    should never worship a deity.
185 If it was decreed that you worship
    these gods who escaped a city's flames,
it might well be that these same gods now regret
    the fate that let them escape those flames.
But perhaps it is Dido, swollen with child,
190   whom you abandon with part of you.
To the mother's fate must be added the child's,
    you will cause your unborn child to die.
Iulus' brother will soon die with his mother,
    one fate will take us both together.
195 'But the god has ordered this!' It is my wish
    he had prevented your coming here,
that Trojan foot never had touched Punic soil.
    Could this be the same god who led you
to spend so many years on the harsh seas, tossed
200   and tormented by the hostile winds?
Surely, you could more easily return straight
    to Pergamum, if it but remained
thriving as it did when Hector was alive.
    But the Simois of your fathers
205 is not what you seek, it is the Tiber's stream.
    You will land in that place a stranger
while the land you seek is so hidden from sight,
    so draws back from the keels of your ships,
that you will never be able to approach
210   until you have become an old man.
Stop this wandering! Choose me and my dowry—
    the riches of Pygmalion and
the people I brought to this place. Move Ilion
    to this safer Tyrian city,
215 take pleasure in a king's estate and divine
    rights that belong to a king's sceptre.
If it is war for which you thirst, if Iulus
    must have battlefields to prove his strength

we shall find enemies for him to conquer.
220   Nothing will be lacking because we
shall have here a place for both the laws of peace
and a place for the display of arms.
I ask only this and by your mother pray,
and by your brother's arrows and by
225   your divine companions, gods of Dardanus,
may those Trojans you saved survive fate,
may that awful war be your last misfortune,
may Ascanius find joy at last
and may the bones of old Anchises find rest
230   here in a peaceful grave. Only spare
this house that has been given into your hands
without condition. I ask no more.
You can accuse me of nothing more than love.
I do not come from Phthia nor
235   and I a daughter of Mycenae; neither
husband nor father ever fought you.
If some scruple prevents your calling me wife,
then let me be merely your hostess.
Whatever you require of Dido, she will
240   gladly do so long as she is yours.
Believe me, Aeneas, I know how the waves
can break against these African shores.
They will let you sail or keep you here in port
according to the times they decide.
245   When the wind is right you will raise the white sails,
but then the seaweed may keep you here.
Trust me to watch the skies and guess the weather;
I will see that you get underway.
Even if it were your desire to stay, then
250   I myself will not let you remain.
Your sailors need rest and your fleet needs repair:
shattered by storms, it is not ready.
By your former kindness to me, by that debt
which I will owe you after marriage,
255   give me just a little time until the sea
and my love for you have both grown calm,
while with time and courage I acquire the strength
to bear up bravely in my sadness.
But if you will not listen to me, then with
260   my own hands I will pour my life out.
You have been so cruel and are cruel to me now;
Soon, I will be able to escape.
You should see my face while I write this letter:
a Trojan knife nestles in my lap;
265   tears fall from my cheeks on its hammered steel blade
and soon it will be stained with my blood.
How fitting that this knife was your gift to me,
for death will not diminish my wealth.
My heart has already been torn by your love,

270   another wound will hardly matter.
       Anna, my sister; you, my sister, wretched
         with the knowledge of my shameful guilt:
       too soon, you must give my ashes their last grace.
       When I have been consumed by the flames,
275   do not write, 'Elissa, wife of Sychaeus',
         but in the marble of my tomb, carve:
       'From Aeneas came a knife and the cause of death,
       from Dido herself came the blow that left her dead.'

PUBLIUS OVIDIUS NASO
("OVID")

From the Metamorphoses†

[Ovid is best remembered for the *Metamorphoses*, a collection of the greatest
tales in Greco-Roman mythology, linked by the common theme of transfor-
mation. The *Metamorphoses* was used as a source of classical mythology from
Late Antiquity through the Middle Ages. In the *Book of the Duchess*, Chaucer
retells the story of Ceyx and Alcyone. As well as introducing Morpheus, the
god of sleep to whom Chaucer's narrator prays for rest, Ovid's tale of a mourn-
ing spouse sets the tone for Chaucer's vision of a Knight grieving over the loss
of his lady.]

[The Story of Ceyx and Alcyone]

[In Book 11 of the *Metamorphoses*, King Ceyx decides to sail to Apollo's temple
at Claros to consult the oracle. Fearing that he will drown, his wife, Queen
Alcyone, begs him not to go; she tells him that, even though she is the daughter
of Aeolus, god of the winds, this connection will not save him from danger.
Despite her misgivings, Ceyx sets sail. His ship is soon caught in a violent
storm and breaks apart.]

       A whirlwind breaking in destroys the mast
       and wrecks the rudder too; now the last wave,
790   like a conqueror rejoicing in his spoils,
       rears up and looks down on the lesser waves,
       and no more lightly than if one could tear
       Mount Athos and Mount Pindus from their seats
       and haul them both into the open sea,
       that wave came crashing down upon the ship,
       and by its weight and overwhelming force,
       plunged it right to the bottom; with it went

† From the *Metamorphoses*, translated by Charles Martin (New York: Norton, 2004), 393–401, 408–
09. Reprinted by permission of W. W. Norton & Company, Inc. The translator's notes have been
omitted.

most of its men, sucked down into that vortex,
and fated not to breathe the air again.
800   But some still hang on pieces of the ship
that floated to the surface; here the hand
that used to hold the scepter clings to flotsam.
Ceyx calls upon his father and upon
the father of his wife—in vain, alas,
but now the name most often on his lips
is that of Alcyone, repeatedly
recalled to mind and called to, as he swam:
he prayed that he might float where she would find him,
and that his lifeless corpse could be entombed
810   by her devoted hands. And while he swam,
as often as the waves allowed him breath,
he murmured Alcyone's name to them
and to himself.
               But look now: towering
over the lesser swells, a giant bow
of blackest water breaks upon him now
and buries him beneath the shattered surface.
     That morning you would not have recognized
great Lucifer in his obscurity,
for even though he could not leave the sky,
820   he hid his face within the densest clouds.
     But Alcyone, meanwhile, unaware
of this disaster, counting down the nights,
makes haste now as she finishes the robes
that he will wear when he returns to her,
and those that she will wear herself as well,
at the homecoming that will never be.
     Devoutly, she sends clouds of incense up
to all the gods, but most of all to Juno,
before whose altar she prays on behalf
830   of her poor spouse, no longer in existence,
that he would be kept safe and would return
and would not find another woman—this
alone of all her prayers would find an answer.
But Juno could no longer bear to be
petitioned for someone already dead,
and wished to keep her altar from the touch
of hands that were unwittingly profaned;
"Iris," she said, "most faithful messenger,
go to the soporific halls of Sleep
840   as swiftly as you can, and order him
to send a likeness of extinguished Ceyx
to Alcyone, sleeping, so that she
might learn the truth about her situation."
     The goddess spoke. Her messenger put on
a cloak dyed in a thousand varied colors,
and crossed the sky upon a rainbow's arc,
and sought, as ordered, the abode of Sleep,

concealed beneath a panoply of clouds.
There is a hollow mountain near the land
850 of the Cimmerians, and deep within
there is a cave where idle Sleep resides,
his special place, forbidden to the Sun
at any hour from the dawn to dusk;
the earth around it breathes out clouds of fog
through dim, crepuscular light.
                No wakeful cock
summons Aurora with his crowing song,
no restless watchdog interrupts the stillness,
nor goose, more keenly vigilant than dogs:
no wild and no domesticated beasts,
860 not even branches, rustling in the wind,
and certainly no agitated clamor
of men in conversation.
                Here mute repose
abides, and from the bottom of the cave,
the waters of the sleep-inducing Lethe
flow murmuring across their bed of pebbles.
    Outside, in front, the fruitful poppies bloom,
and countless herbs as well, that dewy night
collects and processes, extracting Sleep,
which it distributes to the darkened earth.
870 Doors are forbidden here, lest hinges creak,
no guardian is found upon the threshold;
but on a dais in the middle of the cave
a downy bed of blackest ebony
is set with a coverlet of muted hue;
upon it lies the god himself, at peace,
his knotted limbs in languorous release;
around him on all sides are empty shapes
of dreams that imitate so many forms,
as many as the fields have ears of wheat,
880 or trees have leaves, or seashore grains of sand.
    The maiden brushed aside these obstacles
before her as she entered; the god's home
was lit up by the splendor of her garments.
    But Sleep could scarcely lift his eyelids, weighed
down by his idleness: time after time
they slid back down again, and his chin bumped
against his breastbone as he nodded, till
he finally awakened from himself,
and hoisted himself up upon one elbow,
890 and recognizing Iris, asked her what
she had come there for.
                The messenger replied,
"O Sleep, that gives your peace to everything,
most tranquil, Sleep, of all the deities,
the foe of care, the spirit's gentle balm
that soothes us after difficult employment,

restoring our powers for the morrow;
O Sleep, whose forms are equal to the real,
order an image in the shape of Ceyx
to go to Alcyone in her chamber
900 and represent the shipwreck that destroyed him.
Juno commands this."
                        Having carried out
her orders, Iris took her leave at once,
unable any longer to resist
the slumber she felt stealing through her limbs;
and so she fled, and swiftly journeyed back
upon that rainbow she had lately crossed.

But from the nation of his thousand sons,
old Father Sleep arouses Morpheus,
skillful at simulating human form:
910 there wasn't any other of his children
as capable of copying the ways
men walked, or looked, or sounded when they spoke;
he did their clothing, too, and knew what words
they would most often use. He specialized
in human beings only: someone else
impersonated beasts and birds and serpents;
the gods refer to him as Icelon,
but human beings call him Phobetor.
A third, Phantasas, has another skill:
920 he imitates the soil and rocks and waves
and tree trunks, anything without a mind;
these show themselves at night to kings and leaders,
while others wander among common folk.

The father passed these by and chose from all
his offspring Morpheus to do the task
Iris had ordered; having done so, he
repaired immediately to his couch
and closed his eyes; his chin fell to his breast:
time for old Sleep to get a little rest.
930 Morpheus, meanwhile, flies on silently
through darkness, coming in no time at all
to the city of Haemonia, where he
removes his wings, assumes the face and form
of Ceyx, and turns up, pale as death and naked,
in the bedchamber of his wretched wife,
with his beard soaked, and matted, streaming hair.

And then, profusely weeping, he leans over
their bed and says, "Do you not recognize
your Ceyx, my wholly pitiable spouse,
940 or have my features been so changed with death?
Another look—you'll recognize me then,
and find no husband but your husband's shade!
Your prayers, my Alcyone, went unanswered!
I am now dead! Don't hope for my return!
The cloud-gathering south wind seized my ship

on the Aegean, tossed it in high winds
until it broke apart; yours was the name
upon my lips, in vain, until I drowned.
      "No doubtful messenger announces this,
950 you hear no unreliable account:
but I myself am uttering these words,
the shipwrecked man who stands before you now!
      "Arise then, stir yourself, go shed your tears
and put on garments suitable for mourning:
do not let me go off to Tartarus,
that place of emptiness, without lament."
      Morpheus told her these things in a voice
that she could easily believe was his,
and seemed to be sincerely weeping too,
960 and gestured with his hands as Ceyx would do.
Weeping, Alcyone groans and moves her arms
in sleep: attempting to embrace his form,
she grasps the air instead, and cries out,
                                        "Stay!
We'll go as one where you are hastening!"
      Awakened by the sound of her own voice
and by her husband's image, she attempts
to verify if it was really him
whom she has just observed; roused by her cries,
the servants had brought in a lamp, and she,
970 unable now to find him anywhere,
began to strike herself about the face,
and tearing at the robes upon her breast,
struck it as well, and without bothering
to let her hair down, started tearing it.
      And answered, when they asked what caused her grief,
"Alcyone is no one any more:
she died with Ceyx! No consolation, please!
He perished in a shipwreck: this I know,
for I have seen and recognized my man,
980 and stretched my hands to hold him as he fled!
      "He was a ghost—but even as a ghost,
he clearly was my husband. Nonetheless,
if you should ask, he did not *quite* appear
as normally he did, nor did his face
glow as it usually used to do.
      "I saw the doomed man standing pale as death
and naked with his hair still dripping wet:
look where he just now stood, right over here!"
      She searched to see if footprints still remained.
990 "And it was this which my divining mind
led me to fear when I implored him not
to leave, entrusting himself to the winds.
      "But even though we both would now be dead,
I'd rather you had taken me along,
for going would have been more to the purpose:

I would not have to spend my life alone,
and we would not have separately died.
      "A part of me is dead; apart from it
I perish, tossed upon those very waves
1000 that parted us! The sea does not have me?
In having him, the sea has me as well!
      "My mind would be more cruel than the sea
if I should struggle to prolong my life,
attempt to overcome such wretchedness!
I will not fight against it, nor surrender
you, my beloved, whom I must lament!
      "But rather I will come as your companion,
and if the same urn may not hold us both,
the letters carved in stone will let us mingle:
1010 if not our bones, at least our names will touch!"
      Grief forbade speaking further; weeping spoke
in place of words, beyond what words could say,
and groans that rose up from her broken heart.
      It was now dawn: she left her palace and
once again sought that sad place on the shore
where she had stood and witnessed his departure,
and as she lingered there and told herself,
"He was right there when he released the cable,
and over here was where we kissed good-bye—"
1020 while thinking of what had happened in that place
and looking out to sea, she noticed, at a distance,
something that bobbed and floated on the water,
something resembling a human corpse;
at first she didn't know what it could be,
but after a while the waves drove it toward shore,
and even though it was some distance off,
it was apparently a body—whose?
      She could not tell yet; nonetheless, because
it clearly was the victim of a shipwreck,
1030 an omen stirred within her, and she cried,
weeping as though for one unknown to her,
"Alas, poor man, whoever you might be,
and—if you have one—for your wife!"
                              The waves
prodded the body nearer, and the more
she looked at it, the less composed she was,
and now it had come close enough to shore
for her to recognize it, and she knew
it was her husband!
                    "It is he," she cries,
and tears her hair, and tears her face and garments,
1040 and reaches out with trembling hands to ask,
"O dearest husband, now so pitiful,
is this the homecoming you promised me?"
      There was a breakwater along the shore

on which the anger of the sea was spent
and which it would exhaust itself attacking.
She leapt from it—a miracle she could!
And suddenly, Alcyone was flying;
beating the air with unexpected wings,
the saddened bird lightly skimmed the whitecaps,
1050 and as she flew, her long and narrow beak
gave out hoarse cries, as though of one grief-laden,
and when she reached his silent, bloodless corpse
with her new wings, embraced his cherished limbs
and gave him a cold kiss with her hard beak.
Now, whether Ceyx could really feel that kiss
or simply had his head raised by the current
was a matter of some popular debate;
no: he *did* feel it; and at length the gods
showed mercy and transformed them both; as birds,
1060 their love and conjugal vows remain in force:
they mate and rear their young; for seven days,
halcyon days, in winter, Alcyone
broods on a nest that floats upon the waves,
which at that time are still: Aeolus guards
the winds and keeps them in his custody,
when, for his grandsons' sakes, he calms the sea.

* * *

[*Ovid's House of Fame or Rumor*]

[In Book 12 of the *Metamorphoses*, the Greeks, preparing to attack Troy, are waylaid in their ships by stormy winds. The sight of a serpent devouring fledgling birds is interpreted as a sign of the Greeks' ultimate victory over the Trojans. After their sacrifice to Diana causes the sea's wrath to subside, the Greeks sail to the shores of Troy. Fame or Rumor (one word in Latin, *Fama*, suffices for both) spreads the news among the Trojans that the Greek fleet is on its way. This passage provides a source for Chaucer's description of the houses of Fame and Rumor in the *House of Fame*.]

At the world's center is a place between
the land and seas and the celestial regions
60 where the tripartite universe is joined;
from this point everything that's anywhere
(no matter how far off) can be observed,
and every voice goes right into its ears.
Rumor lives here; she chose this house herself,
well situated on a mountaintop,
and added on some features of her own;
it has innumerable entrances
and a thousand apertures—but not one door:
by day and night it lies completely open.

70   It is constructed of resounding brass
        that murmurs constantly and carries back
        all that it hears, which it reiterates;
        there is no quiet anywhere within,
        and not a part of it is free from noise;
        no clamor here, just whispered murmurings,
        as of the ocean heard from far away,
        or like the rumbling of thunder when
        great Jupiter has made the dark clouds speak.
        Crowds fill the entryway, a fickle mob
80   that comes and goes; and rumors everywhere,
        thousands of fabrications mixed with fact,
        wander the premises, while false reports
        flit all about. Some fill their idle ears
        with others' words, and some go bearing tales
        elsewhere, while everywhere the fictions grow,
        as everyone adds on to what he's heard.
        Here are Credulity and Heedless Error,
        with Empty Joy and Fearful Consternation;
        and here, with Unexpected Treachery,
90   are Whispers of Uncertain Origin;
        nothing that happens, whether here on earth
        or in the heavens or the seas below,
        is missed by Rumor as she sweeps the world.

                    *   *   *

MARCUS TULLIUS CICERO

From Scipio's Dream†

[Cicero was a Roman orator and prominent statesman (106–43 B.C.E.), who is widely considered one of the greatest Latin writers and rhetoricians. He composed many arguments and essays on behalf of both friends and contemporaries, and made a number of influential political speeches. Originally, *Scipio's Dream* was part of the sixth book of Cicero's *De re publica*.

In the *Parliament of Fowls*, Chaucer's narrator falls asleep reading *Scipio's Dream* and is visited by a vision of Affrican, Scipio's adopted grandfather. Affrican (Publius Cornelius Scipio Africanus the Elder) acts as a guide figure both for Scipio in *Scipio's Dream* and for Chaucer's narrator as he journeys to an imagined ideal garden. Chaucer also mentions Scipio briefly as an important visionary in the *House of Fame* and in the *Book of the Duchess*.]

---

† From *Commentary on the Dream of Scipio*, translated by William Harris Stahl (New York: Columbia University Press, 1952), 87–92. Reprinted by permission of Columbia UP. The translators' notes have been abbreviated and renumbered.

CHAPTER I[1]

[1] When I arrived in Africa in the consulship of Manius Manilius[2] (I was military tribune in the fourth legion, as you know), the intention that was uppermost in my mind was to meet King Masinissa,[3] who for very good reasons was most friendly to my family. [2] When I came before him, the old man embraced me with tears in his eyes and, after a pause, gazing heavenward, said: "To you, O Sun on high, and to you other celestial beings, my thanks are due for the privilege, before I pass from this life, of seeing in my kingdom and beneath this very roof Publius Cornelius Scipio, at the mere mention of whose name I am refreshed; for the memory of that excellent and invincible leader never leaves my mind."[4]

Then we questioned each other, I about his kingdom and he about our commonwealth, and in the ensuing conversation we spent the whole day. [3] Moreover, enjoying the regal splendor of our surroundings, we prolonged our conversation far into the night; the aged king could talk of nothing but Scipio Africanus, recollecting all his words as well as his deeds.

After we parted for the night, I fell into a deep slumber, sounder than usual because of my long journey and the late hour of retirement. [4] I dreamt that Africanus was standing before me—I believe our discussion was responsible for this, for it frequently happens that our thoughts and conversations react upon us in dreams somewhat in the manner of Ennius' reported experiences about Homer,[5] of whom he used to think and speak very often in his waking hours. My grandfather's appearance was better known to me from his portrait-mask than from my memories of him.[6] Upon recognizing him I shuddered, but he reproved my fears and bade me pay close attention to his words.

CHAPTER II

[1] "Do you see that city which I compelled to be obedient to the Roman people but which is now renewing earlier strife and is unable to remain at peace?" (From our lofty perch, dazzling and glorious, set among the radiant stars, he pointed out Carthage.) "To storm it you have now come, ranking not much higher than a private soldier. Two years hence as consul[7] you will conquer it, thus winning for yourself the cognomen which until now you have had as an inheritance from me.[8] After destroying Carthage and celebrating your triumph, you will hold the office of censor;[9] you will go

---

1. *Scipio's Dream* was originally the closing portion of the sixth book of Cicero's *De re publica*. This translation is based upon the interpretation that Macrobius gave to Cicero's words. It will consequently deviate on a few occasions from Cicero's intended meaning. A careful rendition of the Ciceronian meaning may be found in C. W. Keyes's translation of the *De re publica* and *De legibus* in The Loeb Classical Library (London and New York, 1928), pp. 261–83.
2. 149 B.C.E.
3. An ally of Rome in the Second Punic War, he materially assisted Scipio the Elder in defeating Hannibal in 202 B.C.E.
4. The elder Publius Cornelius Scipio Africanus, conqueror of Hannibal in 202 B.C.E. and adoptive grandfather of the narrator of this dream, Publius Cornelius Scipio Africanus the Younger.
5. Cf. Lucretius *De rerum natura* 1.123–25; Cicero *Academica* 11.51; Persius *Satirae* vi.10–11.
6. The descendants of a Roman who held one of the higher magistracies were accorded the privilege of displaying a wax mask of him in their atrium. Cicero (*De senectute* xix) places the death of the elder Scipio and the birth of the younger Scipio in 185 B.C.E. Polybius (Livy *Ab urbe condita* xxxix. 52) gives the date of the elder Scipio's death as 183.
7. Elected consul in 147 B.C.E., Scipio was proconsul when he destroyed Carthage in 146.
8. The cognomen Africanus.
9. In 142 B.C.E.

as legate to Egypt, Syria, Asia, and Greece;[1] you will be chosen consul a second time in your absence, and you will bring to a close a great war, destroying Numantia.[2] [2] Arriving at the Capitol in a chariot, you will find the commonwealth gravely disturbed because of the policies of my grandson.[3] Then, Scipio, it will behoove you to display to your people the brilliance of your intellect, talents, and experience.

"But at that point I see the course of your life wavering between two destinies, as it were. When your age has completed seven times eight recurring circuits of the sun, and the product of these two numbers, each of which is considered full for a different reason, has rounded out your destiny, the whole state will take refuge in you and your name; the Senate, all good citizens, the Allies, and the Latins will look to you; upon you alone will the safety of the state depend; and, to be brief, as dictator you must needs set the state in order, if only you escape death at the hands of your wicked kinsmen."

[3] Hereupon Laelius[4] let out a cry, and the others groaned deeply; but Scipio said with a smiling expression: Hush! please; don't awaken me from my sleep; hear the rest of the dream.

CHAPTER III

[1] "But that you may be more zealous in safeguarding the commonwealth, Scipio, be persuaded of this: all those who have saved, aided, or enlarged the commonwealth have a definite place marked off in the heavens where they may enjoy a blessed existence forever. Nothing that occurs on earth, indeed, is more gratifying to that supreme God who rules the whole universe than the establishment of associations and federations of men bound together by principles of justice, which are called commonwealths. The governors and protectors of these proceed from here and return hither after death."

[2] At this point, though I was greatly dismayed, not at the fear of dying but rather at the thought of being betrayed by relatives, I nevertheless asked whether he and my father Aemilius Paulus[5] and the others whom we think of as dead were really still living.

"Of course these men are alive," he said, "who have flown from the bonds of their bodies as from a prison; indeed, that life of yours, as it is called, is really death. Just look up and see your father Paulus approaching you."

[3] When I saw him, I wept profusely, but he embraced and kissed me and forbade me to weep. As soon as I could check my tears and speak out, I said: "I pray you, most revered and best of fathers, since this is truly life, as I hear Africanus tell, why do I linger on earth? Why do I not hasten hither to you?"

[4] "You are mistaken," he replied, "for until that God who rules all the region of the sky at which you are now looking has freed you from the fetters of your body, you cannot gain admission here. Men were created with the understanding that they were to look after that sphere called

---

1. Cicero (*Academica* 11.5) places the date of the embassy before that of the censorship.
2. Again chosen consul in 134 B.C.E., he destroyed Numantia in 133 after a siege of fifteen months.
3. Tiberius Gracchus.
4. A very dear friend of the younger Scipio and one of the speakers in Cicero's dialogue *De amicitia.* Here Cicero interrupts Scipio's narrative, which is resumed in the following chapter.
5. Became one of Rome's greatest heroes by his defeat of Perseus, king of Macedonia, in 168 B.C.E. He had his son (the dreaming Scipio) adopted by the son of the elder Scipio Africanus.

Earth, which you see in the middle of the temple. Minds have been given to them out of the eternal fires you call fixed stars and planets, those spherical solids which, quickened with divine minds, journey through their circuits and orbits with amazing speed. [5] Wherefore, Scipio, you and all other dutiful men must keep your souls in the custody of your bodies and must not leave this life of men except at the command of that One who gave it to you, that you may not appear to have deserted the office assigned you. But, Scipio, cherish justice and your obligations to duty, as your grandfather here, and I, your father, have done; this is important where parents and relatives are concerned, but is of utmost importance in matters concerning the commonwealth. [6] This sort of life is your passport into the sky, to a union with those who have finished their lives on earth and who, upon being released from their bodies, inhabit that place at which you are now looking" (it was a circle of surpassing brilliance gleaming out amidst the blazing stars), "which takes its name, the Milky Way, from the Greek word."

[7] As I looked out from this spot, everything appeared splendid and wonderful. Some stars were visible which we never see from this region, and all were of a magnitude far greater than we had imagined. Of these the smallest was the one farthest from the sky and nearest the earth, which shone forth with borrowed light. And, indeed, the starry spheres easily surpassed the earth in size. From here the earth appeared so small that I was ashamed of our empire which is, so to speak, but a point on its surface.

CHAPTER IV

[1] As I gazed rather intently at the earth my grandfather said: "How long will your thoughts continue to dwell upon the earth? Do you not behold the regions to which you have come? The whole universe is comprised of nine circles, or rather spheres. The outermost of these is the celestial sphere, embracing all the rest, itself the supreme god, confining and containing all the other spheres. In it are fixed the eternally revolving movements of the stars. [2] Beneath it are the seven underlying spheres, which revolve in an opposite direction to that of the celestial sphere. One of these spheres belongs to that planet which on earth is called Saturn. Below it is that brilliant orb, propitious and helpful to the human race, called Jupiter. Next comes the ruddy one, which you call Mars, dreaded on earth. Next, and occupying almost the middle region, comes the sun, leader, chief, and regulator of the other lights, mind and moderator of the universe, of such magnitude that it fills all with its radiance. The sun's companions, so to speak, each in its own sphere, follow—the one Venus, the other Mercury— and in the lowest sphere the moon, kindled by the rays of the sun, revolves. [3] Below the moon all is mortal and transitory, with the exception of the souls bestowed upon the human race by the benevolence of the gods. Above the moon all things are eternal. Now in the center, the ninth of the spheres, is the earth, never moving and at the bottom. Towards it all bodies gravitate by their own inclination."

CHAPTER V

[1] I stood dumbfounded at these sights, and when I recovered my senses I inquired: "What is this great and pleasing sound that fills my ears?"

"That," replied my grandfather, "is a concord of tones separated by un-equal but nevertheless carefully proportioned intervals, caused by the rapid motion of the spheres themselves. The high and low tones blended together produce different harmonies. Of course such swift motions could not be accomplished in silence and, as nature requires, the spheres at one extreme produce the low tones and at the other extreme the high tones. [2] Consequently the outermost sphere, the star-bearer, with its swifter motion gives forth a higher-pitched tone, whereas the lunar sphere, the lowest, has the deepest tone. Of course the earth, the ninth and stationary sphere, always clings to the same position in the middle of the universe. The other eight spheres, two of which move at the same speed, produce seven different tones, this number being, one might almost say, the key to the universe. Gifted men, imitating this harmony on stringed instruments and in singing, have gained for themselves a return to this region, as have those who have devoted their exceptional abilities to a search for divine truths. [3] The ears of mortals are filled with this sound, but they are unable to hear it. Indeed, hearing is the dullest of the senses: consider the people who dwell in the region about the Great Cataract, where the Nile comes rushing down from lofty mountains; they have lost their sense of hearing because of the loud roar. But the sound coming from the heavenly spheres revolving at very swift speeds is of course so great that human ears cannot catch it; you might as well try to stare directly at the sun, whose rays are much too strong for your eyes."

I was amazed at these wonders, but nevertheless I kept turning my eyes back to earth.

CHAPTER VI

[1] My grandfather then continued: "Again I see you gazing at the region and abode of mortals. If it seems as small to you as it really is, why not fix your attention upon the heavens and contemn what is mortal? Can you expect any fame from these men, or glory that is worth seeking? You see, Scipio, that the inhabited portions on earth are widely separated and nar-row, and that vast wastes lie between these inhabited spots, as we might call them; the earth's inhabitants are so cut off that there can be no com-munication among different groups; moreover, some nations stand obliquely, some transversely to you, and some even stand directly opposite you; from these, of course, you can expect no fame. [2] You can also dis-cern certain belts that appear to encircle the earth; you observe that the two which are farthest apart and lie under the poles of the heavens are stiff with cold, whereas the belt in the middle, the greatest one, is scorched with the heat of the sun. [3] The two remaining belts are habitable; one, the southern, is inhabited by men who plant their feet in the opposite direction to yours and have nothing to do with your people; the other, the northern, is inhabited by the Romans. But look closely, see how small is the portion allotted to you! The whole of the portion that you inhabit is narrow at the top and broad at the sides and is in truth a small island encircled by that sea which you call the Atlantic, the Great Sea, or Ocean. But you can see how small it is despite its name! [4] Has your name or that of any Roman been able to pass beyond the Caucasus, which you see over here, or to cross the Ganges over yonder? And these are civilized lands

in the known quarter of the globe. But who will ever hear of your name in the remaining portions of the globe? With these excluded, you surely see what narrow confines bound your ambitions. And how long will those who praise us now continue to do so?"

CHAPTER VII

[1] "Not even if the children of future generations should wish to hand down to their posterity the exploits of each one of us as they heard them from their fathers, would it be possible for us to achieve fame for a long time, not to mention permanent fame, owing to the floods and conflagrations that inevitably overwhelm the earth at definite intervals. [2] What difference does it make whether you will be remembered by those who came after you when there was no mention made of you by men before your time? They were just as numerous and were certainly better men. Indeed, among those who can possibly hear of the name of Rome, there is not one who is able to gain a reputation that will endure a single year. [3] Men commonly reckon a year solely by the return of the sun, which is just one star; but in truth when all the stars have returned to the same places from which they started out and have restored the same configurations over the great distances of the whole sky, then alone can the returning cycle truly be called a year; how many generations of men are contained in a great year I scarcely dare say. [4] As, long ago, the sun seemed to be failing and going out when Romulus' soul reached these very regions, so at the time when it will be eclipsed again in the very same quarter, and at the same season, and when all constellations and planets have been returned to their former positions, then you may consider the year complete; indeed, you may be sure that not a twentieth part of that year has yet elapsed.

[5] "Therefore, if you despair of ever returning to this region in which great and eminent men have their complete reward, how insignificant will be that human glory which can scarcely endure for a fraction of a year? But if you will look upwards and contemplate this eternal goal and abode, you will no longer give heed to the gossip of the common herd, nor look for your reward in human things. Let Virtue, as is fitting, draw you with her own attractions to the true glory; and let others say what they please about you, for they will talk in any event. All their gossip is confined to the narrow bounds of the small area at which you are gazing, and is never enduring; it is overwhelmed with the passing of men and is lost in the oblivion of posterity."

CHAPTER VIII

[1] After he said these words, I interrupted: "If, as you say, Africanus, a man who has served his country steadfastly finds a passage to the sky, so to speak, then, though I have walked in your steps and those of my father from boyhood and have never forsaken your brilliant example, I shall now strive much more zealously, with the promise of such a reward before me." [2] "Do you then make that effort," he said, "and regard not yourself but only this body as mortal; the outward form does not reveal the man but rather the mind of each individual is his true self, not the figure that one designates by pointing a finger. Know, therefore, that you are a god if,

indeed, a god is that which quickens, feels, remembers, foresees, and in the same manner rules, restrains, and impels the body of which it has charge as the supreme God rules the universe; and as the eternal God moves a universe that is mortal in part, so an everlasting mind moves your frail body.

[3] "For that which is always self-moved is eternal, but when that which conveys motion to another body and which is itself moved from the outside no longer continues in motion, it must of course cease to be alive. Therefore, only that which is self-moved never ceases to be moved, since it never abandons itself; rather, it is the source and beginning of motion for all other things that move. [4] Now a beginning has no origin: all things originate in a beginning, but a beginning itself cannot be born from something else, since it would not be a beginning if it originated elsewhere. But if it has no beginning, then indeed, it has no ending: for if a beginning were destroyed it could not be reborn from anything else; nor could it create anything else from itself if, indeed, everything has to come from a beginning. [5] Thus it happens that the beginning of motion, that which is self-moved, originates in itself; moreover, it cannot experience birth or death; otherwise the whole heavens and all nature would have to collapse and come to a standstill and would find no force to stir them to motion again."

CHAPTER IX

[1] "Therefore, since it is clear that that which is self-moved is eternal, is there anyone who would deny that this is the essence possessed by souls? Everything that is set in motion by an outside force is inanimate, but that which has soul is moved by its own inward motion, for this is the peculiar function and property of soul. If the soul is unique in being self-moved, surely it is without birth and without death.

[2] "Exercise it in the best achievements. The noblest efforts are in behalf of your native country; a soul thus stimulated and engaged will speed hither to its destination and abode without delay; and this flight will be even swifter if the soul, while it is still shut up in the body, will rise above it, and in contemplation of what is beyond, detach itself as much as possible from the body. [3] Indeed, the souls of those who have surrendered themselves to bodily pleasures, becoming their slaves, and who in response to sensual passions have flouted the laws of gods and of men, slip out of their bodies at death and hover close to the earth, and return to this region only after long ages of torment."

He departed, and I awoke from sleep.

MACROBIUS AMBROSIUS THEODOSIUS

From the *Commentary on Scipio's Dream*†

[Macrobius was a Roman grammarian and philosopher (flourished ca. 399–422 C.E.). His commentary on the *Somnium Scipionis* (the Dream of Scipio) gained popularity in the Middle Ages for its discourse on the nature of different dream-types. It is generally accepted that Macrobius's commentary is responsible for both the preservation and elevation of this portion of Cicero's work.

Chaucer refers to Macrobius's commentary on *Scipio's Dream* in both the *Book of the Duchess* and the *Parliament of Fowls*; in the former he mistakenly attributes the dream itself to Macrobius, though he correctly ascribes it to Cicero in the *Parliament of Fowls*. Additionally, Macrobius's writings on dream-types relate to the beginning of Chaucer's *House of Fame*, in which the narrator describes the varied forms dreams may take and the reasons for their appearance.

Macrobius's commentary opens with a discussion of the relationship between Plato's and Cicero's discussions of life after death. Rather than convey his message via a man returned from the dead as Plato did in the *Republic*, Cicero's visionary is one newly awakened from a dream. Chapter 2 concludes with a discussion of two types of fables (those that are purely imaginative and those whose fictions are based on a firm foundation of truth), preferring only the second in philosophical writings. Just as some fictions are preferable to others, so also some kinds of visions also are more likely to yield truth. In the section that follows, Macrobius proceeds to a brief exposition of dream theory, including the five categories of dream outlined below.]

CHAPTER III

[1] After these prefatory remarks, there remains another matter to be considered before taking up the text of *Scipio's Dream*. We must first describe the many varieties of dreams recorded by the ancients, who have classified and defined the various types that have appeared to men in their sleep, wherever they might be. Then we shall be able to decide to which type the dream we are discussing belongs.

[2] All dreams may be classified under five main types.[1] there is the enigmatic dream, in Greek *oneiros*, in Latin *somnium*; second, there is the prophetic vision, in Greek *horama*, in Latin *visio*; third, there is the oracular dream, in Greek *chrematismos*, in Latin *oraculum*; fourth, there is the nightmare, in Greek *enypnion*, in Latin *insomnium*; and last, the apparition, in Greek *phantasma*, which Cicero, when he has occasion to use the word, calls *visum*.

[3] The last two, the nightmare and the apparition, are not worth inter-

---

† From *Commentary on the Dream of Scipio*, translated by William Harris Stahl (New York: Columbia University Press, 1952), 87–92. Reprinted by permission of Columbia UP. The translators' notes have been abbreviated and renumbered.

1. The elaborate classification and description of dreams forming this chapter was one of the most popular sections of the *Commentary* and caused the author to be regarded as one of the leading authorities on dreams during the Middle Ages. The classification is of course not original; the bulk of it bears striking resemblances to the classification given by Artemidorus at the opening of his *Onirocriticon*.

preting since they have no prophetic significance. [4] Nightmares may be caused by mental or physical distress, or anxiety about the future: the patient experiences in dreams vexations similar to those that disturb him during the day. As examples of the mental variety, we might mention the lover who dreams of possessing his sweetheart or of losing her, or the man who fears the plots or might of an enemy and is confronted with him in his dream or seems to be fleeing him. The physical variety might be illustrated by one who has overindulged in eating or drinking and dreams that he is either choking with food or unburdening himself, or by one who has been suffering from hunger or thirst and dreams that he is craving and searching for food or drink or has found it. Anxiety about the future would cause a man to dream that he is gaining a prominent position or office as he hoped or that he is being deprived of it as he feared.

[5] Since these dreams and others like them arise from some condition or circumstance that irritates a man during the day and consequently disturbs him when he falls asleep, they flee when he awakes and vanish into thin air.[2] Thus the name *insomnium* was given, not because such dreams occur "in sleep"—in this respect nightmares are like other types—but because they are noteworthy only during their course and afterwards have no importance or meaning.

[6] Virgil, too, considers nightmares deceitful: "False[3] are the dreams (*insomnia*) sent by departed spirits to their sky." He used the word "sky" with reference to our mortal realm because the earth bears the same relation to the regions of the dead as the heavens bear to the earth. Again, in describing the passion of love, whose concerns are always accompanied by nightmares, he says: "Oft to her heart rushes back the chief's valour, oft his glorious stock; his looks and words cling fast within her bosom, and the pang withholds calm rest from her limbs."[4] And a moment later: "Anna, my sister, what dreams (*insomnia*) thrill me with fears?"[5]

[7] The apparition (*phantasma* or *visum*) comes upon one in the moment between wakefulness and slumber, in the so-called "first cloud of sleep." In this drowsy condition he thinks he is still fully awake and imagines he sees specters rushing at him or wandering vaguely about, differing from natural creatures in size and shape, and hosts of diverse things, either delightful or disturbing. To this class belongs the incubus, which, according to popular belief, rushes upon people in sleep and presses them with a weight which they can feel. [8] The two types just described are of no assistance in foretelling the future; but by means of the other three we are gifted with the powers of divination.

We call a dream oracular in which a parent, or a pious or revered man, or a priest, or even a god clearly reveals what will or will not transpire, and what action to take or to avoid.[9] We call a dream a prophetic vision if it actually comes true. For example, a man dreams of the return of a friend who has been staying in a foreign land, thoughts of whom never enter his

---

2. Cf. Artemidorus 1.1, iv.
3. *Aeneid* vi.896. For the Virgilian passages use has been made of the excellent translation of H. R. Fairclough in the Loeb Classical Library (New York, 1930). On a few occasions, as here, Macrobius has succumbed to his exegetical penchant and has distorted the obvious Virgilian meaning to suit his purpose. On such occasions it has been necessary to adapt Professor Fairclough's translation. Macrobius' other major work, the *Saturñalia*, deals largely with Virgil's poetry.
4. *Ibid.* iv.3–5.
5. *Ibid.* 9.

mind. He goes out and presently meets his friend and embraces him. Or in his dream he agrees to accept a deposit, and early the next day a man runs anxiously to him, charging him with the safekeeping of his money and committing secrets to his trust. [10] By an enigmatic dream we mean one that conceals with strange shapes and veils with ambiguity the true meaning of the information being offered, and requires an interpretation for its understanding. We need not explain further the nature of this dream since everyone knows from experience what it is. There are five varieties of it: personal, alien, social, public, and universal. [11] It is called personal when one dreams that he himself is doing or experiencing something; alien, when he dreams this about someone else; social, when his dream involves others and himself; public, when he dreams that some misfortune or benefit has befallen the city, forum, theater, public walls, or other public enterprise; universal, when he dreams that some change has taken place in the sun, moon, planets, sky, or regions of the earth.)

[12] The dream which Scipio reports that he saw embraces the three reliable types mentioned above, and also has to do with all five varieties of the enigmatic dream. It is oracular since the two men who appeared before him and revealed his future, Aemilius Paulus and Scipio the Elder, were both his father;[6] both were pious and revered men, and both were affiliated with the priesthood. It is a prophetic vision since Scipio saw the regions of his abode after death and his future condition. It is an enigmatic dream because the truths revealed to him were couched in words that hid their profound meaning and could not be comprehended without skillful interpretation.

It also embraces the five varieties of the last type. [13] It is personal since Scipio himself was conducted to the regions above and learned of his future. It is alien since he observed the estates to which the souls of others were destined. It is social since he learned that for men with merits similar to his the same places were being prepared as for himself. It is public since he foresaw the victory of Rome and the destruction of Carthage, his triumph on the Capitoline, and the coming civil strife. And it is universal since by gazing up and down he was initiated into the wonders of the heavens, the great celestial circles, and the harmony of the revolving spheres, things strange and unknown to mortals before this; in addition he witnessed the movements of the stars and planets and was able to survey the whole earth.

[14] It is incorrect to maintain that Scipio was not the proper person to have a dream that was both public and universal inasmuch as he had not yet attained the highest office but, as he himself admitted, was still ranked "not much higher than a private soldier."[7] The critics say that dreams concerning the welfare of the state are not to be considered significant unless military or civil officers dream them, or unless many plebeians have the same dream. [15] They cite the incident in Homer[8] when, before the assembled Greeks, Agamemnon disclosed a dream that he had had about a forthcoming battle. Nestor, who helped the army quite as much with his prudence as all the youth with their might, by way of instilling confidence in the dream said that in matters of general welfare they had to confide in

6. One his father by nature, the other his grandfather by adoption.
7. *Scipio's Dream* ii.1.
8. *Iliad* ii.56–83.

the dream of a king, whereas they would repudiate the dream of anyone else. [16] However, the point in Scipio's favor was that although he had not yet held the consulship or a military command, he—who himself was destined to lead that campaign—was dreaming about the coming destruction of Carthage, was witnessing the public triumph in his honor, and was even learning of the secrets of nature; for he excelled as much in philosophy as in deeds of courage.

[17] Because, in citing Virgil above as an authority for the unreliability of nightmares, we excerpted a verse from his description of the twin portals of dreams, someone may take the occasion to inquire why false dreams are allotted to the gate of ivory and trustworthy ones to the gate of horn. He should avail himself of the help of Porphyry, who, in his *Commentaries*, makes the following remarks on a passage in Homer[9] presenting the same distinction between gates: "All truth is concealed. [18] Nevertheless, the soul, when it is partially disengaged from bodily functions during sleep, at times gazes and at times peers intently at the truth, but does not apprehend it; and when it gazes it does not see with clear and direct vision, but rather with a dark obstructing veil interposed."[19] Virgil attests that this is natural in the following lines: "Behold—for all the cloud, which now, drawn over thy sight, dulls thy mortal vision and with dank pall enshrouds thee, I will tear away."[1] If, during sleep, this veil permits the vision of the attentive soul to perceive the truth, it is thought to be made of horn, the nature of which is such that, when thinned, it becomes transparent. When the veil dulls the vision and prevents its reaching the truth, it is thought to be made of ivory, the composition of which is so dense that no matter how thin a layer of it may be, it remains opaque.

ANICIUS MANLIUS SEVERINUS BOETHIUS

From the *Consolation of Philosophy*†

[The late Roman Christian philosopher Boethius (480–524 C.E.) was the author of treatises on music and mathematics and the translator of works of ancient philosophy by Aristotle and other writers. While the head of government services under Theodoric the Great, he was unjustly accused of treason, for which he was ultimately executed. During his imprisonment, he wrote his most widely recognized work, the *Consolation of Philosophy*, in which he supports the idea of a Platonic goodness that orders the universe. The belief that virtue is its own reward was solace for the wrongful charges leveled against him.

Chaucer, who wrote a translation of the *Consolation* himself, drew upon many of its themes in his work. For example, the eponymous goddess of the *House of Fame*, shares her mutable stature with Boethius's Lady Philosophy, and the image of a mind carried by wings above the clouds is a source for "Geffrey's" celestial journey in that poem. Boethius was also an important source for the fickle goddess Fortune. Additionally, the *Consolation* provided

---

9. Odyssey xix.562–67. Cf. Virgil Aeneid vi.893–96.
1. *Aeneid* ii.604–6.
† From *The Consolation of Philosophy*, translated with an introduction and notes by Richard Green (Indianapolis: Bobbs-Merrill, 1962), 3–7, 21, 60, 76. The translator's notes have been abbreviated and renumbered.

the underlying structure of many medieval dream visions, which typically present an allegorical figure guiding a troubled narrator to a resolution of his problems. Chaucer was fond of experimenting with this form, for instance in the *Book of the Duchess*, where he includes a distressed narrator but omits the guide figure, or in the *Parliament of Fowls*, where the guide abruptly abandons the dreamer to his own resources. The *Consolation* was also a major influence on many of Chaucer's shorter lyrics.]

Book I

POEM I

I who once wrote songs with keen delight am now by sorrow driven to take up melancholy measures. Wounded Muses tell me what I must write, and elegiac verses bathe my face with real tears. Not even terror could drive from me these faithful companions of my long journey. Poetry, which was once the glory of my happy and flourishing youth, is still my comfort in this misery of my old age.

Old age has come too soon with its evils, and sorrow has commanded me to enter the age which is hers. My hair is prematurely gray, and slack skin shakes on my exhausted body. Death, happy to men when she does not intrude in the sweet years, but comes when often called in sorrow, turns a deaf ear to the wretched and cruelly refuses to close weeping eyes.

The sad hour that has nearly drowned me came just at the time that faithless Fortune favored me with her worthless gifts. Now that she has clouded her deceitful face, my accursed life seems to go on endlessly. My friends, why did you so often think me happy? Any man who has fallen never stood securely.

PROSE I

Lady Philosophy appears to him and drives away the Muses of poetry.

While I silently pondered these things, and decided to write down my wretched complaint, there appeared standing above me a woman of majestic countenance whose flashing eyes seemed wise beyond the ordinary wisdom of men. Her color was bright, suggesting boundless vigor, and yet she seemed so old that she could not be thought of as belonging to our age. Her height seemed to vary: sometimes she seemed of ordinary human stature, then again her head seemed to touch the top of the heavens. And when she raised herself to her full height she penetrated heaven itself, beyond the vision of human eyes. Her clothing was made of the most delicate threads, and by the most exquisite workmanship; it had—as she afterwards told me—been woven by her own hands into an everlasting fabric. Her clothes had been darkened in color somewhat by neglect and the passage of time, as happens to pictures exposed to smoke. At the lower edge of her robe was woven a Greek Π, at the top the letter Θ, and between them were seen clearly marked stages, like stairs, ascending from the lowest level to the highest.[1] This robe had been torn, however, by the hands of violent men, who had ripped away what they could. In her right hand, the woman held certain books; in her left hand, a scepter.

---

1. Π and Θ are the first letters of the Greek words for the two divisions of philosophy, theoretical and practical.

When she saw the Muses of poetry standing beside my bed and consoling me with their words, she was momentarily upset and glared at them with burning eyes. "Who let these whores from the theater come to the bedside of this sick man?" she said. "They cannot offer medicine for his sorrows; they will nourish him only with their sweet poison. They kill the fruitful harvest of reason with the sterile thorns of the passions; they do not liberate the minds of men from disease, but merely accustom them to it. I would find it easier to bear if your flattery had, as it usually does, seduced some ordinary dull-witted man; in that case, it would have been no concern of mine. But this man has been educated in the philosophical schools of the Eleatics and the Academy.[2] Get out, you Sirens; your sweetness leads to death. Leave him to be cured and made strong by my Muses."

And so the defeated Muses, shamefaced and with downcast eyes, went sadly away. My sight was so dimmed by tears that I could not tell who this woman of imperious authority might be, and I lay there astonished, my eyes staring at the earth, silently waiting to see what she would do. She came nearer and sat at the foot of my bed. * * *

* * *

PROSE 2

Seeing his desperate condition, Philosophy speaks more gently and promises to cure him.

* * * "Don't you recognize me? Why don't you speak? Is it shame or astonishment that makes you silent? I'd rather it were shame, but I see that you are overcome by shock." When she saw that I was not only silent but struck dumb, she gently laid her hand on my breast and said: "There is no danger. You are suffering merely from lethargy, the common illness of deceived minds. You have forgotten yourself a little, but you will quickly be yourself again when you recognize me. To bring you to your senses, I shall quickly wipe the dark cloud of mortal things from your eyes." Then, she dried my tear-filled eyes with a fold of her robe.

* * *

PROSE 3

Boethius recognizes Lady Philosophy. She promises to help him as she has always helped those who love and serve her.

* * * [W]hen the clouds of my sorrow were swept away[,] I recovered my judgment and recognized the face of my physician. When I looked at her closely, I saw that she was Philosophy, my nurse, in whose house I had lived from my youth. "Mistress of all virtues," I said, "why have you come, leaving the arc of heaven, to this lonely desert of our exile? Are you a prisoner, too, charged as I am with false accusations?"

She answered, "How could I desert my child, and not share with you the burden of sorrow you carry, a burden caused by hatred of my name? Philosophy has never thought it right to leave the innocent man alone on

---

2. The Eleatics represent a school of Greek philosophy at Elia in Italy. Zeno, one of its members in the fifth century B.C.E., was thought to be the inventor of dialectic, the art of reasoning about matters of opinion. The Academy is the traditional name for Plato's school of philosophy.

his journey. Should I fear to face my accusers, as though their enmity were something new? Do you suppose that this is the first time wisdom has been attacked and endangered by wicked men? We fought against such rashness and folly long ago, even before the time of our disciple Plato. And in Plato's own time, his master Socrates, with my help, merited the victory of an unjust *death.*"[3] * * * [Boethius tells Philosophy the reasons for his imprisonment, describing how his dedication to justice as a public servant earned him many powerful enemies. He laments that God could have allowed evil to overcome virtue, and prays for Fortune to give up its capricious influence on the lives of men. Philosophy responds that grief has clouded Boethius's judgment, and that he has not lost his integrity or anything of true value.]

Book II

PROSE I

Philosophy reminds Boethius of the nature and habits of the goddess Fortune.

Philosophy was silent for a while; then, regaining my attention by her modest reserve, she said: "If I understand the causes of your diseased condition, you are suffering from the absence of your former good fortune. What you regard as a change has greatly upset you. I am well acquainted with the many deceptions of that monster, Fortune. She pretends to be friendly to those she intends to cheat, and disappoints those she unexpectedly leaves with intolerable sorrow. If you will recall her nature and habits, you will be convinced that you had nothing of much value when she was with you and you have not lost anything now that she is gone. But I do not suppose that I have to labor this point with you.

"When Fortune smiled on you, you manfully scorned her and attacked her with principles drawn from my deepest wisdom. But every sudden change of fortune brings with it a certain disquiet in the soul; and this is what has caused you to lose your peace of mind. * * *

* * * You are wrong if you think that Fortune has changed toward you. This is her nature, the way she always behaves. She is changeable, and so in her relations with you she has merely done what she always does." * * * [Philosophy describes Fortune's continuously turning wheel, which brings both joy and misery to men. She tells Boethius that Fortune's happiness is not true happiness, because it is changeable and easily lost. She even maintains that misfortune is more valuable than good fortune, because good fortune deceives, while misfortune teaches. She informs Boethius that riches, honor, power, fame, and worldly pleasure provide no real satisfaction, and that true happiness is that which makes one self-sufficient and worthy of reverence. Philosophy sings the following song to invoke the Creator's help in finding the source of such happiness.]

3. For a description of the death scene of Socrates, see Plato, *Phaedo* 115a–118.

Book Three

POEM 9

"Oh God, Maker of heaven and earth, Who govern the world with eternal reason, at your command time passes from the beginning. You place all things in motion, though You are yourself without change. No external causes impelled You to make this work from chaotic matter. Rather it was the form of the highest good, existing within You without envy, which caused You to fashion all things according to the eternal exemplar. You who are most beautiful produce the beautiful world from your divine mind and, forming it in your image, You order the perfect parts in a perfect whole.

"You bind the elements in harmony so that cold and heat, dry and wet are joined, and the purer fire does not fly up through the air, nor the earth sink beneath the weight of water." * * *

Book Four

PROSE 1

[Philosophy teaches Boethius that perfect goodness and true happiness are found in a divine Creator, who is the ultimate goal of all things. Even so, Boethius wonders how there can be evil in the world and how wickedness can go unpunished. Philosophy replies that this is not the case; she declares that the good will always be powerful, and vice will be met with weakness and futility. She likens the steps of her argument to an ascent through the heavens.]

* * * "[S]ince under my guidance you have understood the essence of true happiness, and have found out where it resides, I shall now run through the steps in my explanation which I think necessary and show you the path which will take you home. And I shall give wings to your mind which can carry you aloft, so that, without further anxiety, you may return safely to your own country under my direction, along my path, and by my means.

POEM 1

"My wings are swift, able to soar beyond the heavens. The quick mind which wears them scorns the hateful earth and climbs above the globe of the immense sky, leaving the clouds below. It soars beyond the point of fire caused by the swift motion of the upper air until it reaches the house of stars. There it joins Phoebus in his path, or rides with cold, old Saturn, companion of that flashing sphere, running along the starry circle where sparkling night is made. When it has seen enough, it flies beyond the farthest sphere to mount the top of the swift heaven and share the holy light."

* * *

ALAIN DE LILLE

From the *Complaint of Nature*†

[Alain de Lille (flourished late twelfth century C.E.) was a French theologian and academic who taught in the schools of Paris, later moving to Montpelier and eventually withdrawing to Citeaux, where he joined the Cistercian Order. His finest works include the *Anticlaudianus*, an allegory on the creation of the perfect human soul, and *The Complaint of Nature* (*De planctu naturae*), which places Neoplatonist ideas in a Christian context. The *Complaint of Nature* resembles Boethius's *Consolation of Philosophy*, with the allegorical Philosophy recast as Nature.

Chaucer refers to the *Complaint of Nature*, or "Pleynt of Kinde," in line 316 of the *Parliament of Fowls*. As the narrator specifically tells us there, he borrows his portrait of the goddess directly from "Aleyn," who depicted Nature with all of creation represented on her beautiful gown—save for humanity, whose section of the garment is badly torn. An excerpt from the description of her gown, arrayed with numerous species of birds, is presented below.]

* * *

A garment, woven from silky wool and covered with many colors, was as the virgin's robe of state. Its appearance perpetually changed with many a different color and manifold hue. At first it startled the sight with the white radiance of the lily. Next, as if its simplicity had been thrown aside and it were striving for something better, it glowed with rosy life. Then, reaching the height of perfection, it gladdened the sight with the greenness of the emerald. Moreover, spun exceedingly fine, so as to escape the scrutiny of the eye, it was so delicate of substance that you would think it and the air of the same nature. On it, as a picture fancied to the sight, was being held a parliament of the living creation. There the eagle, first assuming youth, then age, and finally returning to the first, changed from Nestor to Adonis. There the hawk, chief of the realm of the air, demanded tribute from its subjects with violent tyranny. The kite assumed the character of hunter, and in its stealthy preying seemed like the ghost of the hawk. The falcon stirred up civil war against the heron, though this was not divided with equal balance, for that should not be thought of by the name of war where you strike, but I only am struck. The ostrich, disregarding a worldly life for a lonely, dwelt like a hermit in solitudes of desert places. The swan, herald of its own death, foretold with its honey-sweet lyre of music the stopping of its life. There on the peacock Nature had rained so great a treasure-store of beauty that you would think she afterwards would have gone begging. The phoenix died in its real self, but, by some miracle of nature, revived in another, and in its death aroused itself from the dead. The bird of concord paid tribute to Nature by decimating its brood. There lived sparrows, shrunk to low, pygmean atoms; while the crane opposite went to the excess of gigantic size. The pheasant, after it had endured the

† From *The Complaint of Nature*, translated by Douglas M. Moffat (New York: Henry Holt and Company, 1908), 11–13, 15. The translator's notes have been omitted.

confinement of its natal island, flew into our worlds, destined to become the delight of princes. The cock, like a popular astrologer, told with its voice's clock the divisions of the hours. But the wild cock derided its domestic idleness, and roamed abroad, wandering through the woody regions. The horned owl, prophet of misery, sang psalms of future deep sorrowing. The night owl was so gross with the dregs of ugliness that you would think that Nature had dozed at its making. The crow predicted things to come in the excitement of vain chatter. The dubiously colored magpie kept up a sleepless attention to argument. The jackdaw treasured trifles of its commendable thieving, showing the signs of inborn avarice. The dove, drunk with the sweet Dionean evil, labored at the sport of Cypris. The raven, hating the shame of rivalry, did not confess for its brood its own offspring, until the sign of dark color was disclosed, whereupon, as if disputing with itself it acknowledged the fact. The partridge shunned now the attacks of the powers of the air, now the traps of hunters, now the warning barks of dogs. The duck and the goose wintered, according to the same law of living, in their native land of streams. The turtle-dove, widowed of its mate, scorned to return to love, and refused the consolation of marrying again. The parrot on the anvil of its throat fashioned the coin of human speech. There the trick of a false voice beguiled the quail, ignorant of the deceit of the serpent's figure. The woodpecker, architect of its own small house, with its beak's pick made a little retreat in an oak. The hedge-sparrow, putting aside the role of step-mother, with the maternal breast of devotion adopted as its child the alien offspring of the cuckoo; but the offspring, though the subject of so great a boon, yet knew itself not as own son, but as stepchild. The swallow returned from its wandering, and made with mud under a beam its nest and home. The nightingale, renewing the complaint of its ravishment, and making music of harmonious sweetness, gave excuse for the fall of its chastity. The lark, like a high-souled musician, offered the lyre of its throat, not with the artfulness of study but with the mastery of nature, as one most skilled in the lore of melody; and refining its tones into finer, separated these little notes into inseparable chains. The bat, bird of double sex, held the rank of cipher among small birds. These living things, although as it were in allegory moving there, seemed to exist actually.

Fine linen, with its white shaded into green, which the maiden, as she herself shortly afterward said, had woven without a seam, and which was not of common material, but rejoiced in a skilled workmanship, served for her mantle. Its many intricate folds showed the color of water, and on it a graphic picture told of the nature of the watery creation, as divided into numerous species.* * *

A damask tunic, also, pictured with embroidered work, concealed the maiden's body. This was starred with many colors, and massed into a thicker material approaching the appearance of the terrestrial element. In its principal part man laid aside the idleness of sensuality, and by the direct guidance of reason penetrated the secrets of the heavens. Here the tunic had undergone a rending of its parts, and showed abuses and injuries. But elsewhere its parts were united in unbroken elegance, and suffered no discord nor division. On these the magic of a picture gave life to the animals of the earth.* * *

GUILLAUME DE LORRIS AND JEAN DE MEUN

From the *Romance of the Rose*†

[The *Romance of the Rose* was one of the most influential poems of the later Middle Ages. An allegory of courtly love, it was widely read in both France and in England. The two sections of the poem, the second much longer than the first, were probably written about forty to fifty years apart. The author of the first section, Guillaume de Lorris (flourished ca. 1230 C.E.), began composing his 4058 lines around 1225–1230. Later Jean de Meun (ca. 1225-40–1305 C.E.), in his 17,721-line continuation, explains in a witty speech given by the God of Love that Guillaume died before he was able to complete the poem. The God of Love then predicts that "Jean Chopinel . . . born at Meung-sur-Loire" will finish the work "without avarice or envy . . . if time and place can be found" (10565–10586). While both Guillaume and Jean were born near Orléans, Jean later moved to Paris, where he was associated with the city's university.

Guillaume de Lorris's section of the poem draws upon, and in large part helps to define, traditional courtly love. Jean de Meun continues this theme, though he portrays the ideals of courtly love with considerable irony, providing a humorous, sometimes sharply critical, scholastic survey of love in all its manifestations. The two authors' different approaches to the topic of love, plus the subtle ways in which Jean de Meun draws upon Guillaume's writing, still inspire debate about the poem's overall unity.

The *Romance of the Rose* is one of Chaucer's principal literary influences. He wrote a translation of at least part of it himself. In one way or another, the thirteenth-century poem informed all of Chaucer's dream visions, but especially the *Book of the Duchess*, where "text and glose" (333) of the *Rose* decorate the windows of the dreamer's bedchamber, and the Prologue to the *Legend of Good Women*, where the God of Love specifically condemns the narrator for translating the work. The excerpt below begins in Guillaume de Lorris's part of the text, with the beginning of the poem, and extends, with some omissions, to line 1732; it then picks up again with a discussion of Fortune that appears early in Jean de Meun's section.]

Many men say that there is nothing in dreams but fables and lies, but one may have dreams which are not deceitful, whose import becomes quite clear afterward. We may take as witness an author named Macrobius, who did not take dreams as trifles, for he wrote of the vision which came to King Scipio. Whoever thinks or says that to believe in a dream's coming true is folly and stupidity may, if he wishes, think me a fool; but, for my part, I am convinced that a dream signifies the good and evil that come to men, for most men at night dream many things in a hidden way which may afterward be seen openly.

In the twentieth year of my life, at the time when Love exacts his   21
tribute from young people, I lay down one night, as usual, and slept
very soundly. During my sleep I saw a very beautiful and pleasing
dream; but in this dream was nothing which did not happen almost
as the dream told it. Now I wish to tell this dream in rhyme, the more
to make your hearts rejoice, since Love both begs and commands me
to do so. And if anyone asks what I wish the romance to be called,
which I begin here, it is the Romance of the Rose, in which the whole
art of love is contained. Its matter is good and new; and God grant
that she for whom I have undertaken it may receive it with grace. It
is she who is so precious and so worthy to be loved that she should
be called Rose.

I became aware that it was May, five years or more ago; I dreamed   45
that I was filled with joy in May, the amorous month, when everything
rejoices, when one sees no bush or hedge that does not wish to adorn
itself with new leaves. The woods, dry during the winter, recover their
verdure, and the very earth glories in the dews which water it and
forgets the poverty in which the winter was passed. Then the earth
becomes so proud that it wants a new robe; and it knows how to make
a robe so ornate that there are a hundred pairs of colors in it. I mean,
of course, the robe of grass and flowers, blue, white, and many other
colors, by which the earth enriches itself. The birds, silent while they
were cold and the weather hard and bitter, become so gay in May, in
the serene weather, that their hearts are filled with joy until they must
sing or burst. It is then that the nightingale is constrained to sing and
make his noise; that both parrot and lark enjoy themselves and take
their pleasure; and that young men must become gay and amorous in
the sweet, lovely weather. He has a very hard heart who does not love
in May, when he hears the birds on the branches, singing their heart-
sweet songs. And so I dreamed one night that I was in that delicious
season when everything is stirred by love, and as I slept I became aware
that it was full morning. I got up from bed straightway, put on my
stockings and washed my hands. Then I drew a silver needle from a
dainty little needlecase and threaded it. I had a desire to go out of the
town to hear the sound of birds who, in that new season, were singing
among the trees. I stitched up my sleeves in zigzag lacing and set out,
quite alone, to enjoy myself listening to the birds who were straining
themselves to sing because the gardens were bursting into bloom.

Happy, light-hearted, and full of joy, I turned toward a river that I   103
heard murmuring nearby, for I knew no place more beautiful to enjoy
myself than by that river, whose water gushed deep and swift from a
nearby hill. It was as clear and cold as that from a well or fountain,
and it was but little smaller than the Seine, but was spread out wider.
I had never seen a stream so attractively situated, and I was pleased
and happy to look upon that charming place. As I washed my face and
refreshed myself with the clear, shining water, I saw that the bottom
of the stream was all covered and paved with gravel. The wide, beau-
tiful meadow came right to the edge of the water. The mild morning
air was clear, pure, and beautiful. Then I walked out away through
the meadow, enjoying myself as I kept to the river bank in descending
the stream.

When I had gone ahead thus for a little, I saw a large and roomy 129 garden, entirely enclosed by a high crenelated wall, sculptured outside and laid out with many fine inscriptions. I willingly admired the images and paintings, and I shall recount to you and tell you the appearance of these images as they occur to my memory.

In the middle I saw Hatred, who certainly seemed to be the one 139 who incites anger and strife. In appearance the image was choleric, quarrelsome, and full of malice; it was not pleasing, but looked like a woman crazy with rage. Her face was sullen and wrinkled, with a pug nose; she was hideous and covered with filth and repulsively wrapped up in a towel.

Beside her, to the left, was another image of the same size. I read 152 her name, Felony, beneath her head.

I looked back to the right and saw another image named Villainy, 156 who was of the same nature and workmanship as the other two. She seemed a creature of evil, an insolent and unbridled scandal-monger. He who could produce an image of such a truly contemptible creature knew how to paint and portray; she seemed full of all sorts of defamation, a woman who knew little of how to honor what she should.

* * *

[The dreamer continues his account of the paintings on the wall of the garden, describing the images of Covetousness, Avarice, and Envy.]

Next, quite close to Envy, Sorrow was painted on the wall. Her color 291 seemed to show that she had some great sorrow in her heart. She looked as though she had jaundice, and Avarice was nothing like as pale and gaunt as she. The dismay, the distress, the burdens and troubles that she suffered, day and night, had made her grow yellow and lean and pale. Nothing in the world ever lived in such martyrdom nor was ever so greatly enraged as it seemed that she was; I believe that no one ever knew how to do anything for her that could please her. She did not even want to be consoled at any price nor to let go of the sorrow she had in her heart; she had angered her heart too much, and her grief was too deep-rooted. She seemed to sorrow immeasurably, 313 for she had not been slow to scratch her whole face, and she had torn her dress in many places, until it was practically worthless, as though she had been in a violent rage. Her hair, which she had torn out in bad temper and anger, was all unplaited and lay straggling down her neck. And know truly that she sobbed most profoundly. There was no one so hardhearted who, seeing her, would not have felt great pity as she tore and beat herself and struck her fists together. The grief-stricken wretch was completely occupied in creating woe. She took no interest in enjoyment, in embraces and kisses, for whoever has a sorrowful heart—know it as the truth—has no talent for dancing or caroling. No one who grieved could ever bring himself to have a good time, for joy and sorrow are two contraries.

* * *

[After that of Sorrow, the dreamer describes the portrayals of Old Age, Time, Joy, and Diversion, accompanied by his sweetheart, Joy.]

On the other side the God of Love stayed near to her [Joy]. It is he   865
who apportions the gifts of love according to his desire, who governs
lovers, and who humbles the pride of men, making sergeants of seig-
neurs and servants of ladies, when he finds them too haughty. In his
bearing the God of Love did not resemble a boy. His beauty, indeed,
was greatly to be valued. But I fear that I should be grievously bur-
dened in describing his dress, since it was not of silk but of tiny flowers
made by delicate loves. The gown was covered in every part with
images of losenges, little shields, birds, lion cubs, leopards, and other
animals, and it was worked with flowers in a variety of colors. There
were flowers of many sorts, placed with great skill. No flower born in
the summertime was missing from it, not even the flower of the broom,
the violet, the periwinkle, or any yellow, indigo, or white flower. Inter-
mingled in places there were large, wide rose leaves. On his head he
wore a chaplet of roses; but the nightingales that fluttered around his
head kept knocking them down to the earth. He was completely cov-
ered with birds, with parrots, nightingales, calender-larks, and titmice.
It seemed that he was an angel come straight from heaven. He had a
young man, called Sweet Looks, whom he kept there beside him.

* * *

[The dreamer names the arrows held by Sweet Looks, the first five of
which are Beauty, Simplicity, Openness, Company, and Fair Seeming.
He details the appearance and function of each, then lists the other
five arrows, their dark counterparts: Pride, Villainy, Shame, Despair,
and New Thought. The dreamer observes the revels being held by all
of the individuals he has seen.]
 * * * Straightway the God of Love began to follow me, bow in hand,
from a distance. Now may God protect me from a mortal wound if he
goes so far as to shoot at me! Knowing nothing of all this, always
enjoying myself, I went along quite freely through the garden, while
the God of Love set his intent on following me; but he did not stop
me in any place until I had been everywhere.

The garden was a completely straight, regular square, as long as it   1323
was wide. Except for some trees which would have been too ugly, there
was no tree which might bear fruit of which there were not one or
two, or perhaps more, in the garden. There were apple trees, I well
remember, that bore pomegranates, an excellent food for the sick.
There was a great abundance of nut trees that in their season bore
such fruit as nutmegs, which are neither bitter nor insipid. There were
almond trees, and many fig and date trees were planted in the garden.
He who needed to could find many a good spice there, cloves, licorice,
fresh grains of paradise, zedoary, anise, cinnamon, and many a delight-
ful spice good to eat after meals.

There were the domestic garden fruit trees, bearing quinces,   1347
peaches, nuts, chestnuts, apples and pears, medlars, white and black
plums, fresh red cherries, sorb-apples, service-berries, and hazelnuts.
In addition, the whole garden was thronged with large laurels and tall
pines, with olive trees and cypresses, of which there are scarcely any
here. There were enormous branching elms and, along with them,
hornbeams and beech trees, straight hazels, aspen and ash, maples,

tall firs, and oaks. Why should I stop here? There were so many different trees that one would be heavily burdened before he had numbered them. Know too that these trees were spaced out as they should be; one was placed at a distance of more than five or six fathoms from another. The branches were long and high and, to keep the place from heat, were so thick above that the sun could not shine on the earth or harm the tender grass for even one hour.

There were fallow-deer and roe-deer in the garden, and a great 1375 plenty of squirrels, who climbed among the trees. There were rabbits, who came forth out of their burrows for the whole day and in more than thirty ways went scampering around one another on the fresh green grass. In places there were clear fountains, without water insects or frogs and shaded by the trees, but I couldn't tell you the number of them. In little brooks, which Diversion had had made there as channels, the water ran along down, making a sweet and pleasing murmur. Along the brooks and the banks of the clear, lively fountains, sprang the thick, short grass. There one could couch his mistress as though on a feather bed, for the earth was sweet and moist on account of the fountains, since as much grass as possible grew there.

But the thing that most improved the place was the appearance that, 1399 winter and summer, there was always an abundance of flowers. There were very beautiful violets, fresh, young periwinkles; there were white and red flowers, and wonderful yellow ones. The earth was very artfully decorated and painted with flowers of various colors and sweetest perfumes.

I won't offer you a long fable about this pleasant, delectable place, 1411 and it is now time for me to stop, for I could not recall all of the beauty and great delight of the garden.* * *

* * *

[The dreamer continues his wanderings in the garden, unaware of the God of Love's pursuit. He comes upon the Fountain of Love, where Narcissus met his fate, and becomes engrossed in studying his reflection. In the "mirror," he sees also the reflection of rosebushes heavy with flower, which distract him away.]

* * *There were great heaps of roses; none under heaven were as beautiful. There were small, tight buds, some a little larger, and some of another size that were approaching their season and were ready to open. The little ones are not to be despised; the broad, open ones are gone in a day, but the buds remain quite fresh at least two or three days. These buds pleased me greatly. I did not believe that there were such beautiful ones anywhere. Whoever might grasp one should hold it a precious thing. If I could have a chaplet of them, I would love no possession as much.

Among these buds I singled out one that was so very beautiful that, 1655 after I had examined it carefully, I thought that none of the others was worth anything beside it; it glowed with a color as red and as pure as the best that Nature can produce, and she had placed around it four pairs of leaves, with great skill, one after the other. The stem was straight as a sapling, and the bud sat on the top, neither bent nor inclined. Its odor spread all around; the sweet perfume that rose from it filled the entire area. And when I smelled its exhalation, I had no power to withdraw, but would have approached to take it if I had dared stretch out my hand to it. But the sharp and piercing thorns that grew from it kept me at a distance. Cutting, sharp spikes, nettles, and barbed thorns allowed me no way to advance, for I was afraid of hurting myself.

The God of Love, who had maintained his constant watch over me 1681 and had followed me with drawn bow, stopped near a fig tree, and when he saw that I had singled out the bud that pleased me more than did any of the others, he immediately took an arrow and, when the string was in the nock, drew the bow—a wondrously strong one—up to his ear and shot at me in such a way that with great force he sent the point through the eye and into my heart. Then a chill seized me, one from which I have, since that time, felt many a shiver, even beneath a warm fur-lined tunic. Pierced thus by the arrow, I fell straightway to the earth. My heart failed; it played me false. For a long time I lay there in swoon, and when I came out of it and had my senses and reason, I was very weak and thought that I had shed a great quantity of blood. But the point that pierced me drew no blood whatever; the wound was quite dry. I took the arrow in my two hands and began to pull hard at it, sighing as I pulled. I pulled so hard that I drew out the feathered shaft, but the barbed point called Beauty was so fixed inside my heart that it could not be withdrawn. It remains within; I still feel it, and yet no blood has ever come from there.

I was in great pain and anguish because of my doubled danger: I 1721 didn't know what to do, what to say, or where to find a physician for my wound, since I expected no remedy for it, either of herbs or roots. But my heart drew me toward the rosebud, for it longed for no other place. If I had had it in my power, it would have restored my life. Even the sight and scent alone were very soothing for my sorrows. * * *

[Pierced by the arrow of Beauty, the dreamer finds himself drawn even nearer to the single rose that has captured his delight above all the others. While he is distracted, Love continues to shoot the other arrows that excite love, until the dreamer is pierced by the last one, Fair Seeming. This last arrow has been treated with a healing ointment, so that it will not hurt the dreamer overly much. Love finally shows himself, and the dreamer swears to be his servant.] * * *

* * *

[Later, in Jean de Meun's section of the poem, the allegorical figure of Reason warns the dreamer not to put faith in the false promises of Fortune.]

"Allow me to be your servant and you my loyal friend. You will leave 5842 the god who has put you in this plight and will not value at one prune the whole wheel of Fortune. You will be like Socrates, who was so strong and stable that he was neither happy in prosperity nor sad in adversity. He put everything in one balance, good happenings and mishaps, and made them of equal weight, neither enjoying luck nor being weighed down by misfortune. Whatever might come to pass, he was neither joyous nor heavy because of things. He was the one, says

Solinus, who, according to Apollo's answer, was judged the wisest man in the world. He was the one whose face always wore the same expression no matter what happened. He was never found changed even by those who killed him with hemlock because he denied the existence of many gods and believed in a single god, and preached that others should avoid swearing by many gods.

"Heraclitus and Diogenes[1] were also of such heart that, even in 5869 poverty and distress, they never were saddened. Firmly fixed in their resolutions, they underwent all the misfortunes which came to them. Do you the same, nor ever serve me in any other way. Do not let Fortune overcome you, however she torments or strikes you. He is neither a good nor strong fighter who cannot contend against Fortune when she makes her efforts and wishes to discomfit and vanquish him. One must not let himself be taken but must defend himself vigorously. She knows so little of fighting that everyone who fights against her, whether in palace or dunghill, can overcome her in the first round. He who fears her at all is not brave, for no man who knew all her strength, and understood himself without doubt, could be tripped up by her as long as he didn't voluntarily throw himself to earth. It is still 5894 a great pity to see men who can defend themselves let themselves be led out to hang. He who wanted to complain of such a situation would be wrong, since there is no greater laziness. Take care then never to take anything from her, neither honors nor services. Let her turn her wheel, which she turns constantly without stopping, while, like a blind person, she remains at the center. Some she blinds with riches, honors, and dignities, while she gives poverty to others; and when it pleases her, she rakes everything back. He who allows himself to be upset by events or who takes pleasure in anything is a great fool, since he can protect himself; he can certainly do so, but only if he wishes to. Apart from this, there remains one thing certain: you are making a goddess of Fortune and elevating her to the heavens. You should not do so, since it is neither right nor reasonable that she have her dwelling in paradise. She is not so very fortunate; instead, she has a very perilous house.

"There is a rock placed in the depths of the sea, in its center, pro- 5921 jecting on high above it, against which the sea growls and argues. The waves, continually struggling with it, beat against it, worry it, and many times dash against it so strongly that it is entirely engulfed; again it sheds the water which has drenched it, the waves draw back, and it rises again into the air and breathes. It does not keep any one shape, but is always changing, always re-forming, appearing in a new shape and transforming itself."* * *

---

1. The references to Socrates, Heraclitus, and Diogenes come from the *Collection of Wondrous Things* (*Collectanea Rerum Mirabilium*) by the third-century author Julius Solinus [*Editor*].

DANTE ALIGHIERI

From the *Divine Comedy*†

[The great Italian writer Dante Alighieri (1265–1321 C.E.) was both poet and philosopher—at once politically passionate, culturally progressive, and deeply traditional in his Christian theology. Like Chaucer, he chose to write in the vernacular. Chaucer followed him as well in integrating love poetry with philosophical themes, a hallmark of the *dolce stil nuovo* ("sweet new style"), which Dante perfected. Among his achievements, the *Divine Comedy*, a Christian vision of man's journey through Hell, Purgatory, and Paradise, remains his undisputed masterpiece. Due to his political allegiances, Dante was exiled from his native Florence around 1301, never to return. It was during his exile that he composed the *Comedy*.

In his dream visions, Chaucer's debt to Dante is widespread. He cites him by name in the *Legend of Good Women* (360), while in the *Parliament of Fowls*, the inscription over the gate to the garden of Nature quietly echoes the writing over the entrance to Hell described in the *Inferno*. The *House of Fame* in particular is closely related to the *Divine Comedy*, not least in its tripartite structure; here, Chaucer also closely follows two of the *Comedy's* invocations, and his eagle-guide is taken from the eagle that carries Dante in Canto 9 of the *Purgatorio*. Throughout his poetic career, Chaucer was profoundly influenced by Dante but was known to poke a wee bit of fun at him as well.]

Inferno

CANTO III

[In one of the most famous of all moments in the *Divine Comedy*, just before entering Hell, Dante encounters a forbidding inscription over the gate. He asks his guide Virgil to gloss it for him.]

THROUGH ME THE WAY INTO THE SUFFERING CITY,
THROUGH ME THE WAY TO THE ETERNAL PAIN,
THROUGH ME THE WAY THAT RUNS AMONG THE LOST.

4   JUSTICE URGED ON MY HIGH ARTIFICER;
MY MAKER WAS DIVINE AUTHORITY,
THE HIGHEST WISDOM, AND THE PRIMAL LOVE.

7   BEFORE ME NOTHING BUT ETERNAL THINGS
WERE MADE, AND I ENDURE ETERNALLY.
ABANDON EVERY HOPE, WHO ENTER HERE.

10   These words—their aspect was obscure—I read
inscribed above a gateway, and I said:
"Master, their meaning is difficult for me."

13   And he to me, as one who comprehends:
"Here one must leave behind all hesitation;
here every cowardice must meet its death.

16   For we have reached the place of which I spoke,
where you will see the miserable people,

---

† From *The Divine Comedy*, translated by Allen Mandelbaum (London: Alfred A. Knopf, 1995), 68, 254–55, 379–80. Reprinted by permission of Everyman's Library. The translator's notes have been abbreviated.

those who have lost the good of the intellect."

19   And when, with gladness in his face, he placed
his hand upon my own, to comfort me,
he drew me in among the hidden things.

22   Here sighs and lamentations and loud cries
were echoing across the starless air,
so that, as soon as I set out, I wept.

*   *   *

Purgatorio

CANTO IX

[In the early morning hours before his entrance into Purgatory proper,
Dante dreams of a magnificent eagle.]

*   *   *

13   At that hour close to morning when the swallow
begins her melancholy songs, perhaps
in memory of her ancient sufferings,

16   when, free to wander farther from the flesh
and less held fast by cares, our intellect's
envisionings become almost divine—

19   in dream I seemed to see an eagle poised,
with golden pinions, in the sky: its wings
were open; it was ready to swoop down.

22   And I seemed to be there where Ganymede
deserted his own family when he
was snatched up for the high consistory.

25   Within myself I thought: "This eagle may
be used to hunting only here; its claws
refuse to carry upward any prey

28   found elsewhere." Then it seemed to me that, wheeling
slightly and terrible as lightning, it
swooped, snatching me up to the fire's orbit.

31   And there it seemed that he and I were burning;
and this imagined conflagration scorched
me so—I was compelled to break my sleep.

*   *   *

Paradiso

CANTO I

[Dante's invocation to Apollo, the source for Chaucer's invocation to Book
3 of the *House of Fame*]

*   *   *

13   O good Apollo, for this final task
make me the vessel of your excellence,
what you, to merit your loved laurel, ask.

16   Until this point, one of Parnassus' peaks
      sufficed for me; but now I face the test,
      the agon that is left; I need both crests.

19   Enter into my breast; within me breathe
      the very power you made manifest
      when you drew Marsyas[1] out from his limbs'
             sheath.

22   O godly force, if you so lend yourself
      to me, that I might show the shadow of
      the blessed realm inscribed within my mind,

25   then you would see me underneath the tree
      you love; there I shall take as crown the leaves
      of which my theme and you shall make me worthy.

                    *   *   *

GUILLAUME DE MACHAUT

From the *Fountain of Love*†

[Guillaume de Machaut (ca. 1300–1377 C.E.) was a French poet and composer
of music admired throughout Europe for his technically innovative poems on
courtly love. He was a major influence on Chaucer, whom he may have met
during one of Chaucer's various travels to France, though this is uncertain.
His impact on Chaucer's work is seen especially in the *Book of the Duchess*,
the *Legend of Good Women* (which is closely related to Machaut's *Judgment
of the King of Navarre*), and in his shorter lyric and narrative poems (e.g.,
"Anelida and Arcite"). Not only did Chaucer borrow verse forms from Machaut;
he also learned from him how to use his art to negotiate the delicate relation-
ship between poet and powerful patron. Like Chaucer's dream poems,
Machaut's love visions (also called in French *dits amoureux*) feature a semi-
autobiographical narrator, often himself an aspiring lover, though Chaucer
would move this narrator further toward overt comedy.

The *Fountain of Love* (*Fonteinne Amoureuse*) supplied a model for the *Book
of the Duchess*. Machaut composed the work for the famous French patron of
the arts, Jean, Duke de Berry, as he was about to be sent to England as a
hostage in 1360. In the poem, the Duke confesses his love and sorrow to his
new wife, Jeanne d'Armagnac, from whom he must be separated. In the Duke's
complaint, Machaut, like Chaucer, uses Ovid's story of Ceyx and Alcyone as a
point of comparison.

The poem as translated below is substantially complete, with all significant
omissions summarized by the translator.]

In order to give delight and consolation to myself, and to bind my thoughts
to the true love that holds me in those bonds where I shall never tire of
being, nor ever say 'alas!', I wish cheerfully to begin something in honour

---

1. Marsyas: a satyr who challenged Apollo to a musical contest, lost, and was punished by being
   skinned alive * * *

† From *The Fountain of Love* (*Le Dit de la Fonteinne Amoureuse*), in *Chaucer's Dream Poetry: Sources
and Analogues*, edited and translated by Barry Windeatt (Woodbridge, Suffolk: D.S. Brewer, 1982),
26–40. Reprinted by permission of the translator. The translator's notes have been omitted.

of my lovely lady, which will be gladly received, and delightfully written out of the delightful experience of that true heart which is devoted to her. Now I beg those who read this to pick out the good from the bad while reading, if there is any good in it. For when a thing is well chosen then people rightly enjoy it more, and ladies and gentlemen who read it must take more pleasure in it and feel among the chosen few. But I don't want to include anything ugly, for when there is rumbling thunder and menacing clouds the weather is dark and gloomy. For this reason I wish to renounce everything base. And I will begin without delay when I have named him for whom I am composing this book, and my own name as well, for there is certainly no reason why that should be left out, as I am constrained to this more than anybody—Fine Loving commands me to do it, and Pleasure wishes that I attend to it, and Pleasure does not desire anything that is trifling. My heart is pledged and my body is a hostage until it is done. Now I will tell you what you should do to discover our names. [*Here in an anagram the author identifies himself and Jean, duc de Berry.*] Now see if I am lying! For truly, if I were lying I should be most perplexed and ashamed.

[55] Now I want to begin on my theme and tell everything that happened, which at first was obscure and frightening to me, but in the end turned out happily for me. Not long ago I was in bed somewhere but not sleeping, like somebody who is asleep yet still awake. I was just dozing on and off, because it was rather difficult for me to get to sleep when melancholy attached itself to my thoughts. But when nature was just about to take its rest in me, I heard somebody lamenting very bitterly, and I could well see that he was not pretending, because he was complaining and groaning so deeply that I felt a shiver of horror and fear at it. And I heard this two or three times, at which I was very distressed. Then I listened carefully to find out what it could be, for I was not very familiar with that room or place. But as I listened, I imagined in my heart that it was some spirit by which I might be murdered. Then I was extremely frightened and shrank back into my bed—you would have thought I had a fever, for I am more cowardly than a hare, and I trembled and sweated for fear. I lay there in such a bad way, that if anybody had taken my doublet, my belt or my shirt, I would not have stopped him at all! No, indeed, by God! anybody who had taken my body would not have seen me stir. And if anybody says this is cowardice or melancholy I would not care two apples for his opinion, for I have seen braver men than one might ever see or name, whether in this country or overseas, who would not lie in a room on their own for the price of Rheims or Paris. And when they are armed indeed, by God, they fear nothing but dishonour. Because of this I wish to be excused.

Nevertheless I would still like to say—because it has to do with my theme—that if I were armed on the field of battle and saw the enemy advancing to deal his blows, and if I could either leave or stay in the thick of battle, by the faith I owe my creator, I know which I would do! Think of it what you will, but it is not pleasant to be driven out of one's wits, and it is often much better to go after the good things than to die or flee. For I would like to bear witness and say that a cowardly knight, and a clerk who wants to be brave, are not worth a handful of straw in deeds of arms or in battle, for each is acting contrary to what is right. If they do well, it's just luck. And although I am an ignorant, silly, impertinent clerk, I have been, by my two faiths, sometime in such place with the good King of

Bohemia (whose soul may God have in His company!) that I was brave in spite of myself, for there was no way I knew how to escape, so I had to be brave. For the country was wild and unknown to me, I didn't know the language, and I was certainly safer if I stayed at his side than far away from him, for I didn't dare go anywhere else in case I was taken for a spy. And if it is thought to be boasting, such praise is very fitting to those brave in arms. When battle plans are made, it is wise to put one's lord in the best and safest place to avoid ill fortune. Whoever keeps close to his lord cannot be dishonoured, and if there are chickens, capons or any other delicacies he has some crumb or part of what is left. For if the lord makes his departure, there is less unworthiness in accompanying one's lord, for to fly can win grace; he makes an honourable pursuit who wins grace through honour, without flattery or deceit, without pillaging and stealing. I speak altogether in general terms without saying anything specific. . . .

[189] But I am putting off too long what I first wanted to talk about, and I now wish to take up my subject again and go on. I listened so long and so hard to this person whom I heard talking in his misery, and I was fortunate in this, for his speech—which I half-heard—gave me very great pleasure. He said in a loud voice, 'Farewell, my lady, I am going away. I am not arranging anything, except that I am leaving you my heart, so that I am going away without a heart. And I do not know where I am going, nor do I have a fixed date to return. I entrust myself to God, to Love and to you, dear lady, whom I love a hundred times more than myself, by my soul. But my lady, before I go far away from you—which saddens me greatly—I shall compose a sad complaint in that severe sorrow which burns my heart, and makes me grow pale and marks my face. And if God gives me the grace not to make a mistake or do wrong in this complaint, and it is to your liking, I shall be in the seventh heaven, and I shall live so much more happily because of it, for you will know of my feelings.'

Then I immediately felt myself out of my depression, got myself dressed and tidied myself up and lit the candle. But all the time I was listening towards the right of the fireplace, where there was a window through which I could hear his words, for I was near to the window. I took my writing-desk, which is inlaid with ivory, and all my writing implements, in order to write down the complaint which he wished to make. Then he began it very piteously on his part, and for my own part I transcribed it very happily.

The Complaint of the Lover

[235] 'Sweet lady, may it please you to hear my lament, as I go away sighing—sad, sorrowful and overwhelmed with grief—nor can I tell the year or the month of my return. Alas! in this I am losing the gracious company of your sweet eyes, which many times through their sweetness have very sweetly sweetened my sorrow, joyfully turned my tears into joy and given me back my wits and my strength—for of these I was completely deprived when I saw your splendour, which surpasses all others in grace and worth.

'That sweet look was all my comfort: it maintained my spirit within my body, for—if it had not been for that—I would long ago have been dead, because it sustained me against all desolation. Alas, it was the delight of my love, and the true haven of my life and health. It was worth a great deal to me, for when the spirit of refusal came into my lady, this sweet look immediately contradicted it, and sweetly kept me, so that my spirit was reassured and not frightened anymore. Thus my heart always took all its comfort from that sweet look.

'And when I lose the solace and joy of that very sweet look that I used to have, if I lament and sigh and weep I cannot do anything else, for in this world I have a single wish, and I do not wish for anything but that. I was always happy in thinking of that look. Alas! now I do not know if I will ever see the sweet lightnings of her look, through which I was pierced to the heart and set to bearing the sweet enterprise of love, for I must go far away from her. But I will preserve her honour wherever I am.

[283] 'There is something else which is even harder for me, for I am going away, and there is nobody who can mention my sorrow to my pure lady, because nobody knows what I endure. She herself does not know the wound that my heart feels through her sweet face, and that I cannot see, imagine, think, nor conceive how I can have happiness, for I serve and love her without any deceit or baseness. Alas! now I am leaving with very little hope, and perhaps somebody else is begging her for her love who— if she loves him—truly kills my heart.

'And if it should be, my sweet lady, that I am not loved or called lover by you, or if (God preserve me from this) your pure heart is given in love to another, I should be so mortally wounded that sooner or later I should die or go mad because of it. For in that I am borne up by your sweet look— such that I don't care about anything else—and my heart is enamoured by your glance, then if I had a quarter share of your love, as God may keep me, there never was a lover anywhere so highly honoured.

[315] 'And when with a quarter of your love I could be taken out of hell and put into the earthly paradise, if I do not have it I must suffer every pain, for that would be to lose everything in honour and way of life, in heavenly and earthly happiness. For despair, which leads a creature to death in hell eternally, will be within me—be sure of that. But unless you are my sovereign lady, there will be nothing left of me sooner than an empty valley is covered with broom.

'And when my life, my death, and my health lies in you, sweet and lovely lady, if you would deign to be on my side, I am cured. And if it should be that you do not love me at all, or prefer another, or are hostile to my feelings, I am humiliated. It is up to you, and at your pleasure. But when I have been taken prisoner and surrender myself as a captive into your keeping, submissive and true, you ought not to hurt me, I think, when without impropriety I love and esteem you more than Paris ever did the beautiful Helen.

'I do not know how, nor can, nor wish to defend myself, and thus I must wait upon your mercy. Because I do not wish to offend you or Love, I will wait until pity for me gives rise in you to grace and mercy, and until your tender face deigns to turn towards me its sweet look. But I do not know when that will be, which much distresses me, for I am too far away from your pretty body, which will force my true heart to split in two if I do not have mercy—I who have never loved, nor wish to love, nor ever will love another. And, by my faith! I will die, without any mistaking.

[363] 'Alas! wretched me! what is the value of this waiting? And what is it worth that I have put all my hopes in you, when I do not know, my sweet, noble lady, if you recall how desire for your love possesses me? how it

burns me, and assails and torments me? how I live in wretched melancholy when it has to be that your beauty, from which all joy springs, and your goodness—which bears up all honour, and which my heart serves, loves, obeys and fears—are absent from me? or when I do not see your noble body, in which there is nothing that is not perfect and which is always pretty and delightful? It is this which puts me and holds me on the path of death.

'This is why I have tasted sadness; this is what slays all my joys; this is what so pierces and kills my heart, and so hurts me that I see nothing that can comfort me. I can think of nothing but of desolation, in which my longing overcomes my hope, and joy does not know the way to my heart, but sadness knows the right way there very well. It is her keep, her principal stronghold, her chief resort: there she lives and reigns as queen and mistress, there she holds my heart in mortal distress, and with great largesse distributes the jewels of death.

'Alas! there is nothing which is not against me, and I see nothing that can make any difference in my situation, so I must suffer my woes in silence. And I am a hostage, and thus can do very little through my honour, for I am young and to be of more worthiness I ought to frequent places where worthiness and valour dwell. Now I am in a cage, which is to say that I am in captivity, where I can perform very few deeds of service, and this will do my name great harm, which I must lament. Thus I am losing my youth, my time, my lady, and my fresh spirits. It would be more honourable for me to be in Carthage or in Cairo.

[411] 'And if I lose your love, my lady—you who control my love and my heart from afar, because you have possession of my life—I certainly believe that this will be because I am worth very little and have won very little honour. But now I cannot seek other labour or other battle, nor can I do anything that is worthwhile, for I have taken the straw and left behind the grain—that is you, my lady, in whom there is nothing lacking—and thus I fall from high to low. Thus it must be that desire continually assails me, and because of this I say that the hope which love gives me is worth nothing.

'And if I thus have little hope, nobody should be surprised at it, to be sure, for I am poor in honour, worth, and goodness, while you are the flower, the very best of all good qualities—as I know by true experience—root and branch of honour, of prudence and of honesty. If you quickly and rightly refused me, and gave your love to someone better, yet you could still soon set me right through your power, for I am rich in good will, and well furnished with love and loyalty, and desire to do your will only.

'And so I wish to praise and complain on love. I wish to praise love in that without relenting it makes my true heart remain on such a lady in whom all good dwells. But I complain on love because from fearing, serving, loving and desiring unfeignedly I cannot do anything through which I might expect mercy or that she would love me. Alas, unhappy me! this is what constrains my heart, what stains my face and is always changing its colours; this is what is extinguishing both my hope and my strength. For this my heart groans, weeps, and goes on doing so. But my lady cannot hear the complaint of my heart.

[459] 'And even if I am put into confinement, all my hope is not lost, but indeed it is much diminished. Yet Love, from which Hope comes, will soon augment it when she pleases, for all hearts soon change where Love

is. And if my lady takes pleasure in my pain, or if—in order to injure me—Standoffishness, who hates and despises me, urges her to kill me, or if grace is always forbidden to me in love, which saves many a lover from death, then everything will soon be destroyed, taken, and overcome.

'I have no other hope, and so I sigh and weep, although I well know that love can in a very little time cure a heart which is working towards death. But I have no hope that mercy will come from beyond the sea, or seek to cure me from my woe, nor that love will help me at all from such a great distance, nor that her heart would take my part and be advocate for me, when my heart must always stay in her bonds and never be free of love. Alas! this kills me and makes me say "alas!" This is why I am sorrowful, sad and afflicted.

'Dear gods, how can I last in such a state, how can I endure such evils? Where do these evils come from? They come from beyond the sea and will slay me, for there is nothing on this side of the sea that can cure them, and I have to go there, while my lady would not think of coming there too. It is not fitting. And when she launched the dart of love which wounded me in the heart, to be sure, I believe she did not think to make me fall in love. And thus I believe that my sorrowing heart will never be cured of the wound it has, unless Love sets Pity to work, which has never helped me.

[507] 'Now let us suppose that Love wished to help me, and that Pity wished to soften and change the honest heart of my lady. How can this be? It is not fitting for her to send to me, or show herself friendly towards me, before I humbly beg to have her grace. She loves honour more than a valley full of gold, and well knows how to preserve it everywhere, and she is so wise that she does nothing and will do nothing that harms her honour. And I am far away from her sweet, noble face, and so do not see that Pity will cure me very easily.

'And if I send to my dear lady to say that she has pierced my heart, and that love of her burns it without fire and martyrs it without flame, and that desire more and more enflames it, she will say that I am causing her dishonour, and that I should not tell my pain to man or woman. And if I were to write to her, I do not know if she would read my letter. And from so far away I would not be able to tell her that she is starving me of the very sweet, good things of love, so that I would not know how to pick out the worst of my griefs, for in my predicament I cannot see anything which, by my soul, does not grow worse all the time.

'So I must find some other way, if I wish to know how I can advance this love that I want to keep up, and which quite destroys me. When Fortune caused King Ceyx to perish in the sea, he had to die. But Alcyone, who was his queen, could never enquire enough, or enough consult soothsayers, that she knew the truth of what had happened. And so she had him searched for on the sea; for in truth, she loved him more than anything, with a most pure love. She tore her hair and beat her breast, and because of her love for him she could not sleep.

[555] 'Alcyone's heart was so afflicted by the sorrow she had for her husband, who perished at sea through Fortune, that she said weeping to Juno several times: "I beg you, powerful goddess, hear my sad plea." She offered her many sacrifices and gifts for her beloved, and to know where, and how, and when he died. She was always begging for this very much, so that the goddess Juno had such great pity for her that Alcyone saw Ceyx

in her sleep. I will now tell you how it happened: the God of Sleep did it through his command and caused her to fall asleep.

'Juno, who saw and heard Alcyone's prayer, which came from a devoted, humble and true heart, said to her loyal messenger Iris, "Listen to me. I well know that you are prompt and light of foot. Go now to the god who hates noise and light, who loves all manner of sleeping and hates disturbance. Tell him that I send you to him, and tell him of the grief and suffering of Alcyone. Instruct him to show her King Ceyx, and the manner in which he died, and how and why." Iris replied, "I understand you, my lady. I will very gladly take this message, by my faith."

'Iris is immediately ready for her journey: she takes her wings and flies through the air hidden in a cloud. She goes on until she arrives in a large valley surrounded by two great mountains, and with a stream which murmured through the landscape. There was a house there which was marvellously beautiful, and within is the god who sleeps and slumbers so much that there is nothing that can properly wake him. Iris comes into the house, but is greatly amazed that there is neither man or woman awake inside. She herself feels ready for sleep, and is frightened.

[603] 'In the chamber where the God of Sleep is asleep, there is an extremely rich bed. There he lies, lost to the world, in such an attitude that his chin touches his breast. He does not move his mouth, nor a hand or foot. In that place no cock is heard, nor the clucking of hens, nor the barking of dogs. No doctor is needed, nor any special means, in order to sleep well, for there is nobody in that place who coughs or blows his nose. Iris said to him, "Sleeping god of Sleep, I come to you from Juno, goddess of all good." In short, she delivered her message irreproachably well.

'Iris did not wait until it grew light, but came away without leave, for she would not willingly stay there. That place made her weak, sleepy and depressed. She only wanted to get back to the gods, and so she fled away. But the gentle god, who had thousands of his offspring round about him, dreams and fantasies of all sorts, of good and bad, of joys and sorrows, turned in his bed. That noble lord opened one of his eyes just a little and, as best he could, set himself to doing what Iris asked.

'The thousand sons, and the thousand daughters too, who were round about him, transformed themselves at will, for they took on the forms of creatures, so that they showed themselves very diversely in sleep through dreams. By this means people dreamed, and in dreaming saw many things, both sweet and bitter: some are painful, some are hard; one is clear, others are obscure; they know how to speak all languages; they take the shape of water, of fire, of iron, of wood. They have no other occupation, no other concern, and they go everywhere.

[651] 'The God of Sleep calls one of his sons—it is Morpheus—and tells him the news that Iris had brought him from Juno the beautiful: which is that Alcyone's beloved lies dead upon the ocean sand. "Go and show her, so that she sees the death of Ceyx and the loss of his ship." Then Morpheus took the naked shape of Ceyx, much drenched and filled with water, and with matted, dishevelled hair. He comes into the chamber of Alcyone, discoloured, pale, and desolate, and reveals to her everything of the disaster he suffered.

'The God of Sleep through his power caused Alcyone to be sleeping in her bed. Morpheus was before her and said to her, "Dear wife, here is

Ceyx, for whom you have so lost all joy and pleasure that nothing pleases you. I have no colour, joy or spirit within me. Look upon me, and remember me. Do not think, fair one, that I am lamenting without cause: see my hair, see my wild beard, see my clothes, which show you a true token of my death." This woman woke up so that she might hold him, but he—who had no power to remain any longer—vanished away.

'In this way, the beautiful Alcyone clearly saw King Ceyx, and knew without doubt the manner of his passing. But she lamented and wept for him so long, with such great, deep sighs, that Juno, because of her complaints, so contrived that their human bodies changed into two birds that fly over the sea night and day. They are called kingfishers; for truly, when sailors are in difficulty at sea and see these birds nearby, they often cause them to have good fortune or storms.

[699] 'Now I must come to my point and say what I want to say: it is certain that in my bed I neither rest nor sleep, and that I have neither happiness nor repose. And this makes me very much afraid, if I may say so, that I shall be called a fool when I am unable to sleep in this way, which makes people amazed, and indeed, amazes me myself. For this reason, I want to beg the God of Sleep that Morpheus so act that in a few words my noble lady beyond compare may know my heart, my sadness, my grief—and that with kindly good will it is kept quite secret.

'If Morpheus transports himself before her five or six times, and pleads with her in my form, which is half-dead, I cannot believe, if he really tells her how much distressed I am, and that I do not take any pleasure in anything, that my lady would be so hard and unbending that Pity will not open the door of her frank heart to Dous Penser—that heart which is empty of all evils, stream and well of all good, the sweet fruit of sense, grace and honour. And Dous Penser is so well instructed, that he will tell her how I am both day and night, and of the mortal anguish that I bear for her.

'In this way, she will be able to know how much I love her, and how her eyes have taken away the spirit from my heart through her look, which is neither haughty nor unworthy. This will be if the God of Sleep wishes it, and Morpheus, who will make her heart completely sure of mine, and will tell her fully how I lament every day for her love, and that I must die for her love—it cannot be otherwise because of the sorrow that possesses me—unless through Pity Love moves her to give help to my worthless heart, which suffers great misfortune and very sorrowful thoughts. Alas, Morpheus! I see how it must be. To you I make my complaint about it.

[747] 'I cannot find nor know any other way, for a messenger, ink and parchment, myself or anybody else, cannot be used. But I imagine that she would see while sleeping that I do not cease to love and serve her with a pure heart, and that in this service I am afflicted and my strength is undermined. If she is hostile, what good will this thing do me? But if she keeps Morpheus's speech secretly in her heart and, in the morning when she wakes, she remembers it and interprets each word for herself, then I believe indeed that my affair will be going well.

'And if Pity wishes to have pity on me, and gracious Love by amorous thoughts reminds her of my sorrowful sorrow, I do not doubt for a moment that she will be more gracious towards me, and more anxious to know how I am getting on. And if all is well, she will be very happy about all this.

And if Love, Desire, and Dous Penser unite, and this desire is implanted in the heart, and Morpheus reminds her, she would not be so cruel as not to think of the dream, and the thought would be delightful to her.

'This would be something very advantageous to me, if she thought while in bed and at table, and everywhere that thinking is possible—for indeed, often-thinking should not be something fanciful, but rather it should be something substantial, if there is no changeableness or unreliability. Also, she will see the pains that she causes me if Morpheus justly imitates me; that I love her with a whole, true heart, constant and steady; and that she has pierced me through the heart by the laughing appeal of her sweet eyes—but that bow and arrow are not made of yew or maple!

[795] 'I hope then that the carefree god would not fail me in this moment of need. If he helps me then I shall indeed be in such a state that I shall think quite worthless all that woe of mine that I fear too much, for I shall never have happiness without regaining my lost hope. Nor will I care at all about the onset and assault of desire which pierces and assails me, whether near or distant. And because of that, I promise and give a cap and a soft feather-bed to the god who is so knowing and worthy, in order that he sleeps better.

'I also wish to pray to the God of Love that he hear my pitiful complaints; and that he so act through his subtle means that Morpheus's speech, when he tells of my tears, my great unhappiness, and my hard sorrows, shall be as clear as day to my beloved rather than a parable; and that he should be pleased to tell my beloved—who is not at all silly or foolish—how she drives me to distraction, and that my heart flies to her from beyond the sea to seek for help. Indeed, I cannot go, for I am in prison, where I have enough leisure to put myself to school again, but whatever I see, except what I am speaking of, is hateful to me.

'It is my lady who holds my true heart in her prison—it became hers once despite itself. It is right that it should be obedient, and be so attentive that it will never be ransomed; and that it should die there or have a reward that will cure it, that it will be loved or dead, before it comes out of that prison. Now may it please God that no thought so foolish be in my heart that it thinks any malice or treachery, for it cannot have any better role, and if it serves her loyally and without sin, it will indeed be able to have the gift of her love for service.

'And however much I am troubled and frightened by the amorous wound that she gave me through her gay manner, which desolates me completely, I have no will to retreat, for it seems to me that my hope springs, and my loving heart is not to be despised. This is why. The gods are too clever; my lady has a frank and noble heart; and I love her inordinately. This is a true thing. And though I am now in exile, not everything that lies in danger is utterly dead; and also, I do not know if it is myself that Love is testing.

[859] 'And when my lady has several times seen in her dream the great unhappiness that I have suffered for her, and that there is no pretence in me, nor the pains I have undergone—if her heart is a little moved by that, I do not know how this will be known by me. But now I consider: in Morpheus there is such generosity that he will tell me of her manner and attitude, if she has already been requested in love. For she is so well-bred, she loves honour so much and so hates dishonour, that if she is enkindled with love, this would never be known through her.

'And so I must make my offering to the God of Sleep, and above all worship the God of Love, and humbly give them praise for the good hope that grows in my heart, and beg Morpheus that he set himself to help me, if the God of Sleep commands him. I must also not offend Good Hope and Sweet Thought, because I must be of their company. For truly, whoever falls out with those two, however much he loves, is throwing himself into the mire, and he who upsets or changes them must pay for the damage.

'This is to say, that he must rightly pay for it who does not have Good Hope as his true father, and Sweet Thought too as his dear mother. For whoever makes despair and melancholy his associates, even if he is a king, will live in misery and ensure that he loses honour, generosity and every happiness. But when the lover serves in hope, Sweet Thought makes him attractive and apt, and his love is not reluctant to give him a green hat of happiness. But he who lives in sadness may have his head covered with sad and bitter care.

[907] 'So I wish to forget the evil of madness, for it ill suits me. It goes away on foot, but it comes on horseback, and this saddens me very much, for it has sought me out everywhere and neglected nothing, but has always found my heart loyal, and encouraged by Sweet Thought, and also by courteous Hope. In this way I wish to behave in this trouble, and wisely seek in my heart if I can through Sweet Thought gain joy and delight, and then hold on to them tightly through Hope who secures Sweet Thought in the lover's heart, while waiting for Morpheus who soon comes and goes by night. And if he takes away from me the pain that so torments that it would have destroyed me if it had not been for Sweet Thought and Hope, then I think that no lover ever had such honour anywhere. For I will have such glory that I would not trade my position for the fine gold crowns of France and of England.

'By God, not all the wealth which abounds in heaven, in earth, and in the deep sea, gems, honours, the future life, all the gold and silver that is mined—all this I do not prize at a stone, compared with the love of the beautiful, blonde-haired lady. Dear lord God, when I think of her beauty I feel in my heart so delightful a wound, that I think she will still be the source of my tears, and Morpheus will say to me as I sleep: "Never regret your sadness, for you have conquered the richest treasure that there is in the world."

[955] 'If this is so, I feel my affair is assured, and truly I assure myself enough about it, for the gods will not be so cruel to me if they remember the pains that I endure for my lady. And they know very well that I love her with a pure heart; and if I say I love her, or swear it, I ought to be believed. Pygmalion made the ivory image, to which he made many imploring petitions and loved without relenting, but he did not have so very noble a victory nor such joy as I shall have if Morpheus makes true that which I think will be true. Because of this, I don't think my unhappiness is worth a rotten pear.

'I wish to be a joyful lover and no longer miserable, and taste the sweet delights that Hope and Sweet Thought give me, which make me happy, for I always have these two as companions. And it often happens when I am alone that somebody speaks to me, but I am so preoccupied that I do not utter a word, for I am thinking too intently of that fair good creature who is the sum of all good qualities—and this makes me embarrassed. But my heart is so fixed in thinking of her that it sees no other lady that is of any value to me, however beautiful, or even if a queen. . . .

[1003] 'My sweet lady!—whose picture I carry impressed in my heart, painted there by pure love with the brush of memory and surrounded by loyalty, so that nobody else will be painted there because of her beauty— through memory, I quickly answer the call of my earthly god. Without ever changing, I shall die here, for her eyes which are neither proud nor wicked have given me so many joys—I often utter and often repeat this complaint.

'Do not be offended, lady, if I do not rhyme any further, for any spring could be exhausted. I have put one hundred rhymes into this complaint, whoever cares to count them. I was inspired to them by your beauty, which keeps me awake from the evening through to early the next day. But in a thousand years I will not tell the tenth part of your beauty. It surpasses everything. Everybody says so: duke, king and count. Now may it please God that I never so shame myself in service as to have an unworthy thought, for this quite wears away, stains and overcomes beauty. Nothing is to be compared, for through her all ills are overcome.'

[1035] He stayed there for a very long time without saying anything, and I really listened in case he wanted to say any more, but there was nothing further, so I left off writing. Then I half-opened a window to see what hour it could be, but it was almost day-break. I did not delay very long, but dressed and got myself ready. I fastened my cloak at my neck, and put my hat upon my head. Then I read all the way through the complaint that I had written, to see if he had repeated any rhymes, but I did not find one, and I very thoroughly examined it, and marvelled that there were one hundred different rhymes. This done, I got up from there, blessed myself, washed my hands, and then I went out without waiting to ask and learn who he was that I had heard. I went straight towards the chamber where he lay, and I well remember that there was a young lord awakened by a bird. And as it was truly day by now he saluted me first in French and not in Latin, and I responded politely that God give him good fortune, and that he had had great trouble to stay awake all night in this way. But he said to me, 'Nothing troubles me, but on the contrary it is a joy and a pleasure to me, and also in true trust my lord has commanded me to do it.' And he named him by his right name.

[1075] I asked him where he lay and he told me, 'Here truly is the chamber where he lies, so privately that of all his household he only has one knight there whom he very much trusts. You will very soon see him come, if you would like to stay beside me and if it will not trouble you, because I am certain that he is getting up.' And I said I would wait. I looked through the place, which was very splendid and spotless, to where there was a great company of knights and retinue in groups, all waiting to go and divert themselves. But I did not wait very long, for on several sides I heard both great and small saying: 'Here is my lord!'

[1097] Then I turned a little and set my eyes and my wits to examining his manner, his body, his state and expression. But never in any day of my life did I see a more handsome manner in man or woman, and physically he was perfect, for he was tall and straight, well-built in every way, noble, handsome, young and graceful. I well believe that his heart was pierced and wounded by the arrows of love, and that he knew all the necessary points of the life of a lover. He had a very gracious, pleasant, cheerful,

simple and gentle face, but it was a little pale because he had stayed awake
and suffered all night long. And normally he had a good colour, if he was
not weary from staying up. On his head he had a chaplet, and on his finger
a ring which he looked at anxiously. But the chaplet truly suited him very
well—I don't know where it came from. And indeed, I thought when I had
considered his face, his body and his manner, that he bore himself nobly
and that he prized honour and good renown more than mere material gain.
For suddenly he made this gesture, which certainly did not displease me:

    One of his neighbours sent him a very fine horse, a good mount and
finely saddled; also a very fine sparrow-hawk, well-trained for hunting; and
also a little dog—I never saw such a good one. He prized the gift very
highly and received it politely, saying, 'Here is a splendid gift: it is indeed
worthy of a reward.' And to the servant who brought it he gave fifteen of
his florins. But the present did not stay very long in his place, for very soon
the dog, the bird and the horse were all sent and presented by a servant
to a lady whose honour and spirit God preserve, for I hear her very well
spoken of, and everybody also said, 'My lord, you could not make better
use of them, or send them to a better mistress.' And also, briefly, he was
so splendidly attired that he seemed to be a king's son, or born the sov-
ereign lord of all the land.

    [1161] But such a person may be rich in beauty and poor in loyalty, and
such a person is strong like Renard, who is recreant and cowardly; and
such a person is rich who is poor in the goods of this worldly life; and such
a person often thinks himself wise and has no better knowledge than a
page. I am saying all this for great men: they cannot govern well if they
are not true and valiant men, brave, and also generous like Alexander in
distributing their great wealth, and wise too in seeing and foreseeing their
great affairs, without any games of dice or drinking. They should take up
arms gladly because it is their true calling, for the prince who arms himself
will win valour for himself. They should uphold justice and guard the
church, orphans and widows. Alas! it is nowadays a great reproach to them
that justice is uncertain and in flight, and the church is quite destroyed.
Widows and orphans do not have their property, their houses and mills—
alas! for they have lost everything. If He who is prince and lord of kings,
of kingdoms and empires, did not in His great compassion remember such
people, I think they would fare very badly. But He is always merciful and
compassionate to both body and soul. Now I wish to leave this subject and
return to my original theme, for sometimes one makes things worse to talk
of good and truth.

    [1205] With the other people I followed him; but truly, I did not know
anybody there, and I would gladly have spoken to him a little longer by
ourselves. Yet I thought I would go on, and so went forward, and did not
go too far from him, but knelt down a little way away. And when he saw
me like this, in his goodness he did not hesitate at all, but left his company,
quickly came towards me, took me by the right hand and reproved me
because I was kneeling. I said that I ought to do this. Then he drew me to
his side away from the others after he had raised me up from my knees.
So he led me along while talking for a long time, and as we went along he
asked me where I came from, and wanted to know everything about how
and why I had come to his house. And when I had heard his speech,
without pretending to be clever, I replied to him in this way:

'My lord, as God give me joy, I wished to see you more than any lord in this world, because of the good that abounds in you. I heard tell of it so much every day, that reason drew my will to love and obey you and gladly see you. But the guest who brings nothing with him and knocks at the door acts madly or presumptuously if he is not well known there. My lord, I have acted in this way and you will correct my mistake, for I have come without being asked, in order to commend myself to you. But I have been told that you love me and often call me, and it is this which moved me to come when I knew of it. And certainly, I should never have dared to come like this if it did not please you. But I love you a great deal, such as a poor man can love, even if the love of a poor man is worth little or nothing. But whether or not it is worth little, I wholly deliver up to you my heart and body to your bidding. Now give your commands boldly, for if I prized any gift most dearly I would most willingly give it to you.'

[1271] He replied very sweetly, 'Sweet friend, by my troth, you are very welcome. You have held yourself back for a long time from visiting and seeing me. But since you are in my power—by the faith I owe to Saint Mary—you will not escape me before you tell me your news, for I well believe and think that it will be courteous and delightful, fine, gentle and honourable. But I thank you five hundred times when you wish to love me so, that you give yourself wholly and abandon yourself freely to me in this way. And by my faith! if I can, I will very willingly deserve it, for I value this gift more highly than two thousand silver marks.' And so we went hand in hand until we found ourselves at the entrance of a very lovely park. A knight brought him a very beautiful bow, but he did not wish to draw it and said, 'Go in joy, for this place delights me very much.' He led me by the hand across lush grass to a very beautiful fountain which fell, sweet, clear and pure, into a bowl of dark marble. But no sheep, dog, deer, or other animal drank at all at this fountain because the story of Narcissus was set up there on a pillar of ivory, and so subtly inlaid and enamelled that, by my faith, I thought when I saw it that he was alive.

[1313] On the marble of the fountain were carved Venus, Paris and Helen, and all aspects of their affair, and how she was abducted and taken off to Troy by ship. Paris made his suit to her; Venus was the bawd, and so kindled Lady Helen with the brand that burns without smoke that she did not know what to do to defend herself. Helen's weeping was so well depicted that it seemed very lifelike. The battle was also included, how Achilles fought against Hector in the combat, but could not win at all nor withstand his mortal blows; and the marvellous archer killed so many people that it was a marvel. Troilus, too, was depicted, suffering greatly for his Briseyda, the daughter of Calchas of Troy. What should I tell you? I never in any day of my life saw so accomplished a piece of work. In the middle was set a golden serpent with twelve heads, through which by means of machinery and conduits the fountain spouted ceaselessly day and night. There were beautiful meadows very well set out all around the marble fountain, and the trees were planted with such masterly skill that the sun had no dominion there and everything was instead beautifully shaded and green. But I never heard such singing, nor such great melody, as from the birds that were there, for they so strove to sing that the whole place, the woods and meadows, echoed with their songs. Every fruit, every flower, every plant that one could name, whether from this country or from overseas, was there in great abundance. I do not know who planted them. For this reason I firmly believe and declare, that in the whole world there is no place, no earthly paradise, that could be more beautiful or more noble.

[1371] The lord sat down and made me sit, to see and listen to the fountain, which was the very antithesis of everything rude and base, and also the surrounding area, which was properly set out. And then he started to ask me if there was anything that could be bettered. I said, 'By my soul, nothing at all, my lord.' And then he told me that this was formerly the haunt of Cupid, the god of love, and that Jupiter and Venus came there many times to take pleasure, to embrace and kiss, to have that pleasure that nature took most pains over, and to have more than enough joy and solace, for sometimes one is plagued, as with rain after fine weather. Jupiter set up the garden and contributed the golden serpent, and truly, Venus had the marble and ivory carved by Pygmalion, who works with great skill and accomplished all this work. Cupid made the rest, which is beautiful and pleasant, and the nymphs and fairies held their assemblies there, and still often came there to hold their gatherings, their games, festivities, and dances, and also their schools of love. It is also ordained that if any mortal creature drinks of this fountain he must become inclined to love. 'Its fame is current in many places, and for this reason it is everywhere called the Amorous Fountain, which has made many a lady joyful and caused many lovers to complain and weep, when for all their service and adoration they cannot win mercy. And it makes them love so much that some have died a pitiful death without any help. Now I have told you the whole truth about the delightful fountain, and I beg you, my friend, to get up and drink of it.'

[1425] I replied that I would not, and that I was already so much inclined to love that the fountain and its power could not put more love in my heart than was there, and that Venus knew this very well, who is lady, queen, and mistress of lovers, and their goddess. But I told him that, if he pleased, he should rise and drink from it. He replied that he would not, and that he would never drink of it, for he had drunk so much of it that he thought himself deceived.

And then he said to me, 'Sweet friend, since chance has brought us together it is fitting that whoever has something worthy to say should say it. I will tell you of the sickness that pierces my heart and soul: I love a lady so marvellously good and beautiful that she has no equal in the world. But I cannot speak to her, and I have to go far away from her and have no set time to return. Because of this, I do not know what is going to happen, for she does not know the suffering that martyrs and slays me for her. And truly, it is not fitting that there should be any approach made or message sent to her. For by my soul! I would not dare, nor reveal this love to anybody, for it would displease her, I suppose. For this reason, I have lost hope, and live in such great misery that nothing in the world can comfort me. For this reason I do not expect to live much longer, and I have been in this state for a long time. And I have to go away into captivity and leave my true inheritance. In captivity?—rather, into exile, which completely desolates me. That beautiful creature will soon have forgotten me, who will never forget her. Forgotten me! Lord! will she remember that I love her more than a hundred thousand others? I believe yes; but indeed, no. I know and see that she does not remember me at all, and I must die for her. And so I have no comfort. For truly, if she was aware of it she would have some compassion. Was there ever any fate so sorrowful and cruel? And I cannot go back, for I cannot do it. It could not happen, it is just impossible. For I will love her always with my whole heart, and afterwards, when I am dead, I believe that my spirit will not die with my body, but rather will pray for my lady when my body is in its grave, that God preserve her and her honour, and always have her in His protection.

[1501] 'For this reason, my friend, I want to beg you to be so kind as to set yourself to making for me a lay or complaint about my love and my sorrow. For I know very well that you know all the theory and practice of true love in all its aspects, and its fierce assaults and onsets have given you many pangs sharper than the skin of a hedgehog.'

I was very happy indeed when I heard him speak in this way, for I knew very well that he was the self-same man with the very subtle intelligence, whom I had heard making complaint in his bed, and sorrowing and lamenting. I put my hand into my wallet, took out his whole complaint and said, 'Receive, my lord, your request: here it is, all ready.' He took it and read it all through. He never stopped or hesitated over what was written, word for word as he had composed it for me. And when he had finished reading it, he began to laugh very graciously, blessed himself with amazement, and said, 'My heart is greatly amazed and troubled by this thing, for I kept it so secret that I cannot think or understand how any man alive can know of it. Tell me, friend, how you came across this, for I truly need to know it.' I briefly related to him the truth of the matter: how I heard him from my bed; the fear I had of it in my bed where I lay. I did not conceal the truth of what I have recited above, and he was greatly amazed at it. He rested his head and arms on me, and very gently went directly to sleep in my lap. I looked all round, but there was nobody about. And so I started to think of my lady, and as I was in this sweet and joyful thought, I bent my head. And because I had not slept enough, and because there were only the two of us there, I also went to sleep. But first I covered him with my cloak, because of the breeze which was blowing, for the morning was very dewy, and the stream from the fountain, full of joy and sadness, made the air and the green grass more dewy and fresh. And when I had completely fallen asleep and left my thoughts, I dreamed a dream while sleeping, that I do not think at all false. Rather I consider it truthful and good [1568].

[The poet now has a lengthy dream. Two beautiful ladies appear, one with a golden crown and carrying a golden apple with the inscription: 'To be given to the most beautiful.' She reproves the knight sleeping in the poet's lap—she will ordain that he will have his wish. Then she undertakes to explain the golden apple to the poet. She now tells the story of Peleus's wedding to Thetis, attended by all the gods, including Pallas, Juno, and herself—she identifies herself as Venus. Discord—offended at not being invited—comes and throws down before the three goddesses the golden apple with its inscription. The three goddesses each lay claim to the apple. Jupiter will not risk displeasing any of them by giving judgement, and allots that task to Paris, the Shepherd of Troy.

Mercury conducts the three goddesses to where Paris is all alone as a shepherd. Mercury tells him he is not really a shepherd, but the son of Priam and Hecuba. When pregnant with Paris, Hecuba dreamed that the child would be the undoing of Troy, and Priam ordered that the child be killed at birth, but Hecuba, when she saw the beauty of the baby, arranged for it to be brought up secretly. Paris then determines the judgement and awards the apple to Venus.

Venus now complains that the sleeping duke has no trust in her, nor does he make any sacrifice to her of bull or heifer. She brings his lady to him to comfort him, who takes him by the hand and calls him her lover.

Now follows *Le Comfort de l'Amant et de la Dame* (2207–2494): the lady comforts the lord with declarations of love. He will take her image with him in his heart into exile. Hope will keep her well. By thought she will be near to him. She reproaches depression and self-pity. Venus's help should be relied on: she helped in the love of Danaë and Jupiter. He should trust Venus rather than Fortune. He should not worry about being unable to do knightly deeds, for she would rather have him in good health. He should think of his return, love firmly, take heart and comfort, and he will soon be in the haven of peace and joy. He should not think her coming to him improper, for Venus caused her to come to him.

His lady kisses him more than a hundred times and exchanges her ruby ring for his diamond one. Then Venus and the lady depart. The two men awake, to find to their amazement that they have had the same dream, and to find the ruby ring on the lord's finger.

They rise and wash in a stream from the fountain. The lord praises and thanks Venus, and says he will sacrifice to her in a temple that he will build to her, together with a temple to the god of sleep. The lord recalls his lady. The poet recalls the 'Istoire des Romains', where one hundred senators have the same dream. The lord is comforted by his dream.

One of the lord's knights approaches and reminds him that his meal is getting spoiled, for they have been there half a day. They go to the duke's castle and dine. After dinner the duke asks the poet to accompany him as far as the coast. When the duke boards his ship he sings a rondel, and afterwards gives the poet a gift of jewels, which the poet declares were more than was really proper for him. The duke sails away over the sea, not forgetting his ruby ring, and armed against desire, sighs and tears. 'Thus he departed. I took my leave. Now tell me, was this well dreamed?' (2848)].

GIOVANNI BOCCACCIO

From the *Book of Theseus* (*Il Teseide*)†

[Although Chaucer never refers to Boccaccio (1313–1375 c.e.) by name, the Italian writer is commonly acknowledged to be his greatest influence. Many critics believe he is the mysterious "Lollius" mentioned three times in Chaucer's work, twice as his source in *Troilus and Criseyde* and once in the *House of Fame* as a notable authority on Troy. Chronologically, Boccaccio's career overlapped with Chaucer's, though he was some thirty years Chaucer's senior.

† From *The Book of Theseus* (*Teseida delle nozze d'Emilia*), translated by Bernadette Marie McCoy (New York: Medieval Text Association, 1974), 176–79. Reprinted by permission of the translator. The notes have been abbreviated.

Like Chaucer, he experimented with literary form and narrative voice, and was in his early years a frank humorist who at the same time helped elevate the vernacular to literary status.

Boccaccio's *Il Teseide* or the *Book of Theseus* tells the story of the competition between the royal kinsmen and prisoners of war, the knights Palaemon and Arcites, for the same woman. It is the direct source for Chaucer's Knight's Tale in the *Canterbury Tales* and provides the Theban setting of "Anelida and Arcite." Chaucer's *Troilus and Criseyde* has its origins in Boccaccio's *Il Filostrato*, and the *Decameron*, Boccaccio's masterpiece, is a collection of stories in the spirit of the *Canterbury Tales*, though whether Chaucer knew the *Decameron* remains uncertain. It is also unknown if Chaucer and Boccaccio ever met, though Chaucer did make a trip to Italy in 1372–73, where he could have encountered Boccaccio and also the great poet Francesco Petrarch (1304–1374 C.E.).

The passage below describes the ascent of Palaemon's prayer to win the fair Emilia's hand in marriage as it travels through the Temple of Venus. Here we see the inspiration for Chaucer's own account of Venus's shrine in the *Parliament of Fowls*. Also included is an excerpt from a gloss or note, traditionally attributed to Boccaccio himself, instructing the reader on how to interpret the Temple. As the glossator indicates, there are two Venuses—one lawful and one lewd—and it is the second that he depicts.]

50

As the Prayer of Arcites sought out Mars, so the Prayer of Palaemon[1] went to merciful Venus on Mount Cithaeron where the temple of Cytherea, and her dwelling place, rests somewhat shaded among very tall pines. As the Prayer approached it, Yearning was the first one that she saw on that eminence.

51

As she went along farther with Yearning, she saw that which is sweet and pleasant to every sight, in the guise of a leafy and beautiful garden full

1. The reason why the author gives a certain form to the Prayer is shown above, and so I do not care to repeat it. Just as he described the house of Mars earlier, so here he intends to describe that of Venus. Since he does not care to describe the kind of place where the house is located and the things that belong to the said house, in order and succession, still they can be considered in order by anyone who wants. The kind of place where the said house is, who they are who dwell in that house, what forms and functions they have, how the house is constructed, and what the adornments of this house are can be readily determined.

First therefore, the kind of place will be seen. The author says that it is on Mount Cithaeron, among pines, etc., as appears in the text. To clarify this matter it must be realized that just as Mars, as was said above, consists in the irascible appetite, so Venus consists in the concupiscible. This Venus is twofold, since one can be understood as every chaste and licit desire, as is the desire to have a wife in order to have children, and such like. This Venus is not discussed here. The second Venus is that through which all lewdness is desired, commonly called the goddess of love. Here the author describes the temple of this goddess, and the other things that belong to it, as appears in the text. So the author describes this temple of Venus as being on Mount Cithaeron, for two reasons. One, because it was, in fact, there, since Mount Cithaeron is near Thebes and the Thebans celebrated a solemn feast thereon in certain seasons of the year, and they offered many sacrifices to the honor of Venus. The second thing is because of the quality of the place, which is very appropriate to Venus, because it is a temperate region as regards the heat and the cold. This is seen very clearly by anyone who considers it carefully, since those parts of Greece in which Mount Cithaeron is located are not too far north nor too far south, but almost between the one and the other.

* * *

of very green plants, of fresh grasses, and of every new flower, and she saw clear fountains springing there, and it seemed to her that among the other shrubs the myrtle flourished most.

52

She heard birds of almost every kind singing through the branches. She watched them with delight, too, as they made their nests. She also saw rabbits darting about here and there through the young grass, and timid little deer, and roe buck and a great variety of many other little animals.

53

She seemed to hear, besides, delightful singing and every musical instrument. As she passed along with a quick step, somewhat rapt out of herself and gazing about, she saw that every corner of the lofty and beautifully adorned place was filled with spirits who flew about here and there and returned to their places. As she watched them,

54

among the shrubs on the side of a fountain she saw Cupid with his bow placed at his feet, making arrows. Those which his daughter Voluptuousness selected she tempered in the waters; and the Prayer saw Idleness seated beside them; and she saw that with Memory he barbed the shafts which she first tempered.

55

She also saw Comeliness strolling with Elegance and Affability while Courtesy was in their midst entirely concealed. She saw the Arts that have the power to force others to commit follies, and these were very different in their appearance from our idea of them. And she saw Vain Delight standing alone with Nobility.

56

Next she saw Beauty pass near by, without any adornment and gazing at herself. And she saw Charm walking with her, and each one was praising the other. Then she saw lithe and lovely Youth standing near them, making merry. On the other side she saw mad Boldness, Flattery, and Pandering walking together.

57

In the center she saw a temple with tall copper columns, and she saw youths and ladies dancing before it; the latter were either beautiful in their persons or comely because of their attire. They were ungirded and barefoot, with hair and gowns flowing, and they passed the whole day in this way. Then she saw many sparrows and doves flying about and nesting on top of the temple.

58

And she saw Madonna Peace sitting quietly near the entrance to the temple with one hand holding a curtain lightly before the portals. Patience sat discreetly near her, very wretched in appearance and pale of countenance. And she saw Promises and Arts everywhere around.

59

When she entered the temple, she heard a storm of Sighs bursting into flame with hot Desires. This fire enkindled all the altars with new flames born of Martyrdoms, and each of these flames shed tears caused by a cruel and wicked lady called Jealousy whom she saw there.

60

And she saw that Priapus held the highest place there, in such a garb that anyone who wanted to see him at night could do so, as when, with its braying, the most slothful of animals aroused Vesta whom Priapus desired not a little and toward whom he was advancing. She also saw garlands of many different flowers throughout the great temple.

61

She saw there the bows of many of Diana's devotees hung up and broken. Among these was that of Callisto who was transformed into the northern Bear. And there were the apples of disdainful Atalanta who excelled in running, and the weapons, also, of that other haughty one who gave birth to comely Parthenopaeus, grandson of the Calydonian Oeneus.

62

She saw stories painted everywhere, and among these, traced with consummate skill, she saw all the works of the bride of Ninus made clear. She saw Pyramus and Thisbe and the mulberries, already stained, at the foot of the wall. She saw the great Hercules on the lap of Iole among them, and sorrowful Byblis piteously on her way to entreat Caunus.

63

When she did not see Venus, she was told—she did not know by whom—"She takes her delight in the most secret part of the temple. If you want her, enter through that quiet door." So without any other regard, for she was humbly garbed, the Prayer drew near to enter there to fulfill the mission entrusted to her.

64

When she first approached, she found Opulence guarding the door, at which she marveled greatly. When she was permitted by Opulence to enter, she saw that the place was dark when she first went in. As she remained there, however, she found that there was a little light, and she saw Her reclining naked on a huge bed that was very beautiful to see.

65

She had golden curls, unbraided and bound about her head. Her countenance was such that those who have been most praised have no beauty to compare with hers. Her arms and her bosom and her elevated breasts were completely visible, and the rest of her body was covered by a robe so flimsy that it scarcely concealed anything.

66

The place was scented with a thousand perfumes. Bacchus sat on one side of her, and Ceres with her delicacies on the other. She held Lust by the hand, and she also held the apple which she had won in the Idaean vale when she was chosen over her sisters. And when the Prayer had seen this, she submitted the petition, which was granted without demur.

* * *

CRITICISM

CHARLES MUSCATINE

From Chaucer's Early Poems†

The *Book of the Duchess*, the *House of Fame* and the *Parliament of Fowls*, Chaucer's earliest important poems, are generally believed to have been written in that order.[1] Traditional criticism has made much of the progressive technical accomplishment and the widening sphere of interest, nourished by reading and observation, that they display. We may safely accept these and focus our attention on a third factor, the development of Chaucer's feeling for the adjustment between style and meaning. In this light the first poem is in a class by itself. It is the least accomplished technically and the narrowest in scope, but it is in a sense the most finished. It is the most homogeneous in style and the clearest in meaning. Perhaps only hindsight enables us to see in it already the beginning of that flamboyance of style which erupts in the *House of Fame* and is just brought under control in the *Parliament*. Seen thus, the early poems show no smooth progression, but rather ambitious experiment and even artistic failure, before the control felt in the *Parliament* is brought to the mastery of the *Troilus and Criseyde*.

The two great ponderables of this experimental stage are the two styles of the French tradition, fertilized by reading in Latin and Italian and by writing in English, but still retaining their distinct, contrasting characters of a conventional style and a naturalistic one. The experiments are in the harnessing of the two, not in the "revolt" from or submergence of the former. The *Book of the Duchess* has been shown to be a combination of borrowings from six or seven French courtly works of the fourteenth century.[2] It signalizes well enough Chaucer's initial dependence on the courtly tradition. Unfortunately, however, it tends to focus the attention on transient models of style, and to mask his deeper, perennial relationship to this tradition; for while Chaucer soon gives up the wholesale borrowing of themes and passages from Guillaume de Machaut and his followers, he does not give up the tradition of conventionalism that he, like them, inherits from the twelfth and thirteenth centuries. Even in this earliest poem we can see him reaching back, beyond the allegorical prettiness of his immediate models, to a feeling for the original potency of the style.

Machaut and his school write in the style of Guillaume de Lorris. But they lose, or perhaps never seek, that technique of organizing the allegory

---

† From *Chaucer and the French Tradition: A Study in Style and Meaning* (Berkeley: University of California Press, 1957), 98–123, 260–61. Reprinted by permission of the author. The author's notes have been renumbered, and some citations from Chaucer's text have been abbreviated or deleted; in all such cases, inclusive lines quoted are indicated before the citation.

1. The best account of the literary characteristics and historical significance of the early poems is that of Wolfgang Clemen, *Der junge Chaucer: Grundlagen und Entwicklung seiner Dichtung*, Kölner Anglistische Arbeiten, XXXIII (Bochum-Langendreer, 1938). The most appreciative criticism of the poems is in the articles of Bertrand H. Bronson, "The *Book of the Duchess* Re-opened," *PMLA*, LXVII (1952), 863–881; "Chaucer's Hous of Fame: Another Hypothesis," Univ. of California Publications in English, III, No. 4 (1934), 171–192; "In Appreciation of Chaucer's Parlement of Foules," Univ. Calif. Publ. English, III, No. 5 (1935), 193–223; "The Parlement of Foules Revisited," *ELH*, XV (1948), 247–260. For the chronology see R. D. French, *Chaucer Handbook*, p. 392. New reasons for putting *HF* before *PF* are adduced by Robert A. Pratt, "Chaucer Borrowing from Himself," *MLQ*, VII (1946), 262–264.
2. See G. L. Kittredge, "Guillaume de Machaut and *The Book of the Duchess*," *PMLA*, XXX (1915), 1–24.

307

around a consecutive psychic experience which gives the *Roman de la Rose* so much of its authority. Nor do they characteristically present a narrative that compares with older romance in its representation of a consequential, if imaginative, action. Machaut inherits and brings to easy fluency the whole idiom and machinery of love allegory—the dream, the lovely setting, the richly described personifications, and the refined diction,—using them to debate a question of love, to pay a compliment to a duke or king or lady, to provide a vehicle for a collection of lyrics or a tale or two taken from Ovid. This general diminution of theme leaves him with a style too rich to be functional. The poetry thus too often converts device to ornament, making of its materials something trivial and banal. This result is aggravated, if anything, by the poet's self-conscious virtuosity of technique.

But critics, particularly Chaucerians, are wrong when they deduce from the artificiality of Machaut either the poet's constitutional blindness to "life" or the style's inherent incapacity to support meaning.[3] The defect is neither of these. In fact, there is a strain of topicality, of contemporary realism, in Machaut. The *Remede de Fortune* has a notably detailed description of a day in a fourteenth-century château, down to the servants brushing the dirt from their masters' clothes. Contemporary persons appear in the poems: Jean de Luxembourg, Charles the Bad, Jean, Duke of Berry, and most prominently, Guillaume de Machaut himself, poet and intimate (as he was) of these dukes and kings. The poems are generally sprinkled with touches of a shrewd and mundane sort.[4]

Critics have a habit of picking out these touches in Machaut, like raisins from pastry, and attributing to them much of his virtue. Machaut's editor is at some pains to describe this realism as a means of giving to the allegorical fiction an air of verity.[5] Actually it does the reverse. In making himself the narrator of his vision poems, Machaut no doubt obtained some audience interest, and his sophisticated observations of the world around him have their own value. But he loses in this representation of a familiar, knowing self that fine air of receptivity to the wonders of the dream world that Guillaume de Lorris had created with his boyish narrator. When the latter mentions a silver needle, or a basin, little candles, or a ladder for climbing an imaginary wall, it is as if he knew no difference between sensory and imaginative experience. Machaut brings in the familiar, even his own foibles, with a knowing smile—as if to show that he does know the difference. The earlier poet creates in us an astonished belief; the later, with his wink and his knowledge, his little *aperçus*, creates knowing make-believe. The "artificiality" of this poetry, then, is of the poet's, not the style's making. It depends, indeed, partly on his peculiar linkage of convention and realism.

Nothing could better make this plain than Machaut's *Jugement dou Roy de Navarre,* a love debate and compliment to that noble. It opens with a long diatribe on the times, followed by a graphic description of the Black

---

3. This is, for instance, the implication of John Livingston Lowes, *Geoffrey Chaucer and the Development of His Genius* (Boston: Houghton Mifflin, 1934), pp. 84–93; cf. George Lyman Kittredge, *Chaucer and His Poetry* (Harvard Univ. Press, 1915), p. 54, where "contemporary French fashions of allegory and symbolism and pretty visions" are contrasted with "the language of the heart."
4. *Œuvres de Guillaume de Machaut,* ed. Ernest Hoepffner, 3 vols., SATF (Paris, 1908–1921), as follows: *Remede de Fortune,* vv. 3889–4012; *Jugement dou Roy de Behaingne* 1185–1123; *Fonteinne Amoureuse* 89–188; *Dit dou Lyon* 1537–78; and *Voir Dit,* ed. P. Paris (Paris, 1875), *passim.*
5. Hoepffner ed., *Œuvres de Machaut,* I, lvii–lix; II, x–xi; III, xxxix.

Death of 1349. Machaut describes the terrible rampage of Death over the world, the corruption of the very air that spread the infection. He seals himself in his house, in terror, and is only called to the window, when the danger has passed, by the celebrant survivors' music. He then emerges, goes riding in the fields, and into the visionary, courtly debate that is the body of the poem.[6]

From the same plague had fled a year earlier the band of ladies and youths who tell the stories of the *Decameron*. In both works the somber introduction serves something of a frank escapism. The terror and the survival of it are equal notabilities, and we can impute to Machaut's design what Boccaccio professes, that the plague scenery will set off the beauty of the palaces and pleasances to come. Yet in Boccaccio there is no ultimate escapism. The successive gardens, the happy choiceness of the members of the *brigata*, serve to fix his point of view with the cultured, the leisured, and the sensitive, and to claim a basis of unchallengeable refinement for his philosophy of sex and nature.[7] From this point of vantage we turn in the tales to a whole world of shrewd, often malicious, observation. Then the *brigata*, for reasons impishly adduced, returns to plague-ridden Florence. In Boccaccio there is thus a certain deep and subtle play with the values of his diverse materials. Machaut lacks this depth. One searches in vain the body and ending of his poem for some hint of a relationship to its beginning. Apart from the elementarily simple contrast, they are merely both there: the plague and the courtly diversion. In juxtaposition the one is horribly, historically real; it makes of the other, with its pretty Lady, and twelve allegorical maidens and (historically real) King of Navarre, a flimsy confection.

The burgeoning vein of realism in Chaucer's early poems, then, is not so much a revolt from the sphere of Machaut as a divergent response to a common endowment of convention and experience—common, too, to Deschamps and Boccaccio and to the whole secular literature of the late Middle Ages. The problematical ambivalence of this endowment is that first fully articulated by Jean de Meun. It is recorded by each of these later writers in his own way. Boccaccio makes the easiest and most graceful compromise, giving up neither phenomenon nor dream, raising the one to polite literature, lowering the other to the edge of profaneness. His is a homogeneous, middle style. The vast, various production of Deschamps reflects the capacity of this fourteenth-century ambivalence to become a chaos; he has all the material—*pièces historiques, amoureuses, badines et burlesques, grivoises et grossières, satiriques, didactiques, relatives aux mœurs et aux usages,* as his editor classifies it,[8]—but there is no ordering, no comprehensive grasp and control. The poet in him is second to the journalist. Machaut, as we have seen, sidesteps the problem. Chaucer's English contemporary, William Langland, wrestles endlessly with it. For him the pull between an apostolically pure moral idealism and a sickeningly vivid sense of the facts of life was too great to control. His style produces a hallucinatory effect, in which the distinctions between abstract and concrete,

---

6. *Navarre* 37–540.
7. Cf. Erich Auerbach, *Mimesis: The Representation of Reality in Western Literature,* trans Willard R. Trask (Princeton, 1953), p. 216; Edith G. Kern, "The Gardens in the *Decameron* Cornice," *PMLA,* LXVI (1951), pp. 522–523.
8. Gaston Raynaud ed., *Oeuvres complètes de Eustache Deschamps,* IX, SATF (Paris, 1894), 378.

moral and physical, have all but been lost. But Chaucer's early poems record his discovery, confrontation, and beginning mastery of the problem.

I. THE "BOOK OF THE DUCHESS"

The *Book of the Duchess* is an elegy on the death of Blanche, Duchess of Lancaster. It resembles the *dits* of Machaut in its topicality, in its limitation of theme, in its predominant conventionalism of style, and in a modest tincture of realism. It produces the effect of refinement and restraint of feeling of its models at their best, but except for a few touches of rhetorical exhibitionism it is without the French overelaborateness. The center of the poem is an idealized description of the lady, with a narrative, likewise idealized, of the winning of her by her lover. The part of telling the story and making the description is given to a Man in Black, that is, to her bereaved husband and Chaucer's patron, John of Gaunt. His recitation is in turn framed in a dream of the Narrator, wherein the latter, wandering away from a hunt, accidentally overhears the Man in Black's complaint, but tactfully and sympathetically pretends ignorance of the lady's death so that the other may find relief in pouring out his sorrow. The dream is introduced by a prologue in which the sleepless Narrator relates his reading of the story of Ceyx and Alcyone, and his discovery of the God of Sleep.

The poem's success, as I have said, is partly owing to a conservatism of style, which, in the using of little more than the theme requires, approximates the functionalism of the style of Guillaume de Lorris. Though personification inheres in the diction, no personifications appear as characters in the action. The poem has as its end neither psychic analysis nor moral philosophy, and there is thus an initial wisdom in barring out the conventional figures which, short of some such end, could only be decorative. Chaucer, on the other hand, uses the device of the dream, conventionally and functionally, to exclude those reminders of common life, of business, war, and politics, that would cling to a realistic representation of his subject and thus smudge the purity of feeling proper to the occasion. It opens to him the ideal landscape that is his setting, the exemplarily polite conversation, the high-courtly narrative, the brilliant and elaborate portraiture, and the lyrical utterances that form the body of the poem.

I am loath to attribute the success of this frame to what has often been called Chaucer's "flawless" dream psychology, if by this is meant a kind of factualism.[9] It is difficult to distinguish the surface incoherence of dream sequence from the incoherence of plot sequence that is characteristic of conventional narrative of this kind. Where plot is of the slimmest significance and the essence of the poetry is in action of a nonrepresentational kind, neither poet nor audience will pay much attention to ordinary probability. Thus we never quite learn the fate of the blind man in the *Man of Law's Tale*, though the restoration of his sight is a miracle of much importance; and what becomes of the dwarf in Chrétien's *Lancelot?*[1] Though not in dreams, they both melt into thin air, like the Dreamer's horse in the *Book of the Duchess* and the guide in the *Parliament of Fowls*. Chaucer's problem is not to make his dream coincide with the facts of dreaming (whatever he may have thought them to be), but rather to inweave it with

9. See, for instance, Kittredge, *Chaucer*, pp. 66–68; Lowes, *Chaucer*, pp. 122–123.
1. See *MLT* 554–74; Chrétien de Troyes, *Lancelot*, ed. Wendelin Forester (Halle, 1899), 447–48.

poetic relevance to his theme; in short, to unite the device with a meaning that it can support.

We have excellent appreciation of the poem on this level; we have been shown the exquisite relevance of the Ceyx-Alcyone story to the main body of the dream, the identification and sympathy between the Dreamer and the Man in Black, the believable charm of Blanche's portrait, the sense of well-being that this dreaming of sorrow happily leaves us with.[2] There is a fine, anticipatory fitness in the early steps of the dream, in the ringing chorale of the birds, in the colorful bedchamber with decorations that suggest momentous events yet to come, in the call of the hunting horn through the brilliant, cloudless air. There is a quiet eulogy in the choice of a hunt itself. It leads, for the Dreamer, to unsuspected game; he, with his untrained whelp, finds far more than the Emperor Octavian can with all his skilled retinue. We are led, in this sequence, through progressively wonderful events to a place quite remote from the ordinary course of affairs, but of richly realized idealization, where the elegy may begin.

The realism in the *Book of the Duchess* is comparatively faint, yet in this context it already becomes a source of difficulty. By realism, of course, I do not refer to the fine concreteness of specification in the descriptions. Guillaume de Lorris has it; it is the common property of good poets. When the Narrator remarks of the singing birds that awaken him.

[298]   they sate among
        Upon my chambre roof wythoute,
        Upon the tyles . . .

we recognize that the description is more Chaucerian, more particular and sensuous, than its models,[3] but it is no less enchanting. It has something of the same deeply ingrained feeling for the materials of house and land that is a constant in Chaucer's English, natural to him. We recognize it in the language of the gentle narrator of the *Knight's Tale:*

[886]   I have, God woot, a large feeld to ere,
        And wayke been the oxen in my plough.

In neither poem does this strain of imagery by itself work against the idealistic temper of its context.

But the characterization of the Narrator in the *Book of the Duchess* has a realism of attitude about it; it introduces a mild note of comic irony, which is doubtless owing to the poet's position *vis-à-vis* his patron and his audience. The Narrator has a kinship with the Man in Black—they are both disappointed lovers,—but his characterization is such that we cannot take his affairs so seriously. The rhetorical elaboration and formal lyricism of the Man in Black's complaints are designed to evoke the highest reaches of seriousness. The Narrator's opening remarks on his own romantic insomnia, couched in a neutral, conversational style despite the conventional hyperbole of statement, seem in the shadow of the other's grief almost comically unequal. Chaucer was to develop this inadequacy of his Narrator as lover—or as anything else—in poem after poem. Here the first movement toward this pose serves to define the distance between poet and

2. Bronson, "Book of the Duchess," esp. pp. 871–872, 879–881.
3. For this important commonplace of Chaucer criticism see Clemen, *Der junge Chaucer*, pp. 49, 155–156, 178–183.

patron, between the Narrator and the elevated objects of his narration. At the same time it creates a discrepancy between the known sophistication of the poet and the obtuseness of the part he has made for himself. In this perspective the characterization of the Narrator becomes overtly humorous. He is naïvely ignorant of the classical gods: "For I ne knew never god but oon" (237); more naïvely, he misses the main point of the Ceyx story— its tale of bereavement—to fasten on its possible offer of a cure for his insomnia. To "thilke Morpheus" he makes a comically literal offer of a featherbed, then throws into the bargain an array of bedroom finery that would do credit to a mercer's apprentice; for sleep he will pay Juno too.[4] Here are the makings of him who rimed the tale of Sir Thopas.

The Narrator's prosaism of outlook is most at odds with the dominant tone of the poem in the Ceyx episode itself. It can be felt tentatively in the command of Juno to her messenger: "Now understand wel, and tak kep!" (138), an accent that is later given to the goose in the *Parliament of Fowls* (563). It may be suggested in an awkward literalism in the description of Morpheus and his crew, "That slep and dide noon other werk" (169). It is astonishingly clear in the awakening of Morpheus. In Ovid, Statius, and the *Ovide moralisé*, the effect of the scene turns on the contrast between the dark, deadly somnolence of the cave of Sleep and the fragile brilliance of Juno's messenger. Iris awakens the sleepy god with the gleaming of her garments, and delivers her message in measured, rhetorical tones.[5] Less is made of the poetry of the scene in Machaut's *Fonteinne amoureuse* (543– 698), but nothing in the tradition of the passage remotely anticipates the realism of Chaucer's version [178–88]:

> [178] This messager com fleynge faste
> And cried, "O, ho! awake anoon!"
> Hit was for noght; there herde hym non.
> "Awake!" quod he, "whoo ys lyth there?"
> And blew his horn ryght in here eere,
> And cried "Awaketh!" wonder hyë.
> This god of slep with hys oon yë
> Cast up, axed, "Who clepeth ther?"
> "Hyt am I," quod this messager.

The metamorphosis of Iris into a male is only less startling than the scene's violence of sound and action, which transports us instantly from the mythical cave to an army camp. The mind behind the narrative tears so bluntly through the finery of the traditional rendering that we need hardly know the tradition to feel the shock of the passage in its context. It is a moment of intense, comic practicality in the midst of conventionalism. Its single-minded insistence on the sleepiness of Morpheus suggests a linkage with the prosaic offer of a feather-bed, and with the further posed obtuseness

4. *BD* 240–69. In fairness to the Narrator, we must note that he says he made this offer "in my game" (238), jokingly, and yet seriously: "And yet me lyst ryght evel to pleye—" (239).

5. *Ovid, Metamorphoses* XI, 592–632; Statius, *Thebaid* X, 84–136; *Ovide moralisé* XI, 3431–3515, ed. C. de Boer, 5 vols. (Amsterdam, 1915–1938), Vol. IV (Verhandelingen der Koninklijke Akademie van Wetenschappen te Amsterdam, Afdeeling Letterkunde, Nieuwe Reeks, XXXVII), pp. 201–203. John Gower's version, later than Chaucer's, has little color; see *Confessio Amantis* IV, 2927–3123, in his *Works*, ed. G. C. Macaulay, 4 vols. (Oxford, 1899–1901), II, 380–385. Froissart does not tell the story of Ceyx and Alcyone, and gives only an insignificant account of the awakening of Morpheus; see *Paradys d'Amour* 23–28 in his *Œuvres: Poésies*, ed. A. Scheler, 3 vols. (Brussels, 1870–1872), I. 2.

of the claim (270 ff.) that neither Joseph nor Macrobius could rightly interpret the "wonderful" dream that follows.

In the early steps of the dream, our guide to the dream world has an open, willing, receptive, and sympathetic character that reminds us of the Narrator of the *Roman de la Rose*. His attention is easily led from the bird song to the decorated chamber windows, thence to the hunt, finally to the whelp and the Man in Black. We are led with him unsuspiciously, for this facet of his character harmonizes well with the suggestions of ignorance and simplicity that we have already seen in him. Our mildly ironical superiority over him does not hinder, in the dream, a common receptiveness toward the elevated matters to come. Nor are we surprised by his exemplary tact in the handling of the Man in Black. It is a situation that calls for the finest behavior [514–38]:

> [514] But at the last, to sayn ryght soth,
> He was war of me, how y stood
> Before hym, and did of myn hood,
> And had ygret hym, as I best koude;
> Debonayrly, and nothyng lowde,
> He sayde, "I prey the, be not wroth.
> I herde the not, to seyn the soth,
> Ne I sawgh the not, syr, trewely."

But Chaucer's further development of this motif takes a quasi-dramatic form. The narrative of the bereaved lover is periodically interrupted by short, colloquial interchanges that are designed to motivate its continuation. Though the Narrator has overheard in the other's lament that the lady is dead, he tactfully feigns ignorance, and the lover betrays an answering eagerness to tell his story [742–58, 1135–44]:

test hypothesis in reading.

> [750] "I telle the upon a condicioun
> That thou shalt hooly, with al thy wyt,
> Doo thyn entent to herkene hit."
> "Yis, syr." "Swere thy trouthe therto."
> "Gladly." "Do thanne holde hereto!"
> "I shal ryght blythely, so God me save,
> Hooly, with al the wit I have,
> Here yow, as wel as I kan."
> "A Goddes half!" quod he, and began . . .

> [1135] "And telleth me eke what ye have lore,
> I herde yow telle herebefore."
> "Yee!" seyde he, "thow nost what thow menest;
> I have lost more than thou wenest."

The passages like these create the one difficulty of interpretation. Set in a dream, beside the conventionally rhetorical utterances of the Man in Black, their air of realism is surprising and awkward. The interposition of a realistic perspective produces a confusion in our view of the Narrator; for there is an unfortunate similarity between his feigned ignorance in this colloquy and his comic obtuseness in the prologue to the dream. His having clearly overheard the Man in Black's complaint aggravates this similarity, and many readers, lured by the periodically realistic perspective, have found in both prologue and dream a fatal consistency of characterization. They thus see the Narrator as slow-witted to the point of stupidity; for some, he brings into the most serious part of the poem a tasteless vein of humor, if not a blatantly impossible self.[6]

This interpretation of the Narrator's position in the dream would not have much support were it not, as I have indicated, for the corroborative tone of such passages as the awakening of Morpheus. Whether one takes the characterization to be accident or design, then, there is a basis for it in the materials of the poem. Chaucer inherits a modest device from the French tradition (whether his Narrator is the naïve one of Lorris or the knowingly courteous one of Machaut, or both), and develops it with such verve that it exceeds its function as an instrument of perspective. The characterization calls a shade too much attention to itself, as if the poet were not yet aware of the full power of the device, or could not yet manage his realism with precise control of its effect.

The style of the *Book of the Duchess,* then, shows two concurrent movements in the light of French tradition: one toward a functional use of courtly convention, the other toward a realism that suggests comic disenchantment. The latter movement is, I admit, comparatively faint, and I may have given it more attention here than a balanced reading of the poem would justify. But my object has been rather to trace the emergence of Chaucer's central stylistic problem: this strain of realism in the midst of conventional elevation, with the attendant problem of their mutual adjustment, is the only clue in this competent courtly elegy that such poems as the *House of Fame* and the *Parliament of Fowls* will follow.

2. THE "HOUSE OF FAME"

I have said that only hindsight could see in the *Book of the Duchess* a suggestion of the style of the *House of Fame.* Now, looking at the latter, one still marvels at the violence with which the suggestion was taken up. The minor problem of stylistic management in the earlier poem has here grown to what has been called "nearly a major disaster."[7] Not for nothing did Manly consider the *House of Fame* a prologue to a collection. Technically, it is full of choice and widely prized accomplishments. Structurally, it is most charitably seen as an experiment, wherein the poet's energy and imagination by far outrun his sense of form.

The rhetorical preliminaries exhibit the playful, exuberant inconstancy that informs the whole. The epic machinery of proem and invocation at the opening is undercut at once with the syntactic breathlessness of that fifty-line sentence on the causes of dreams (all to demonstrate the ignorance of the Narrator) and again in the curious self-consciousness of

---

6. This situation has generated a whole spectrum of interpretations. For adverse comment see C. S. Lewis, *The Allegory of Love,* (Oxford University Press, 1936), p. 170; J. S. P. Tatlock, *The Mind and Art of Chaucer* (Syracuse, 1950), p. 30. Favorable comment sometimes sees the Narrator as consistently naïve: Lowes, *Chaucer,* pp. 124–125; Howard Rollin Patch, *On Rereading Chaucer* (Cambridge, Mass., 1939), p. 33. Sometimes it straddles the issue, making contradictory statements: Kittredge, *Chaucer,* pp. 48–53, 70; Clemen, *Der junge Chaucer,* pp. 57–59. And sometimes, starting with the Narrator's tact within the dream, it sees him as consistently mature and sophisticated, even in the prologue: Bronson, "Book of the Duchess," pp. 863–864, 869–877; James R. Kreuzer, "The Dreamer in the *Book of the Duchess,*" PMLA, LXVI (1951), 543–547. An intermediate reading, which sees the Narrator as more awestruck than either stupid or sophisticated, is offered by Donald C. Baker, "The Dreamer Again in *The Book of the Duchess,*" PMLA, LXX (1955), 279–282.

7. Raymond Preston, *Chaucer* (London and New York, Sheed & Ward, 1952), p. 39.

[66]   But at my gynnynge, trusteth wel,
       I wol make invocacion . . .

The invocation is oddly mixed; there is a reminiscence of the opening of
Dante's *Paradiso:*

[81]   And he that mover ys of al
       That is and was and ever shal . . .

but, like so much of the Dantean material in this poem, the incipient
seriousness of it is swallowed up in the parody of the anathema that fol-
lows, introduced with its scrap of nursery rhyme, "dreme he barefot, dreme
he shod" (98). The proem to Book II begins with a popular swing to the
verse:

[509] Now herkeneth every maner man
       That Englissh understonde kan,
       And listeneth of my drem to lere.
       For now at erste shul ye here
       So sely an avisyon . . .

Then it turns, inexplicably, to invoking Venus and the Muses in the high
style of the Italians. Only the invocation to Book III is "straight," taken
from the *Paradiso.* With regard to the amount of actual play in the poem,
one wonders how seriously this and the other reminiscences of the *Divine
Comedy* are to be read.

The "story" is of the same motley texture. The main characteristic of the
Dido episode is the usual medieval reduction of classical tale to something
more mundane and compendious and, withal, more moralized. On the side
of mundanity Clemen notes the glimpse of the angry goddess Juno, run-
ning and crying "as [she] were wood" (202), and of Venus "my lady dere,
/ Wepynge with ful woful chere" (213–214). The bluntness of the narrative
gives it, as Clemen says, the aura of an ordinary, everyday betrayal. He
notes, too, that it falls now and then into the idiom of popular balladry,
with its fillers and tags, as "Lord and lady, grom and wenche" (206), and
". . . he made hir a ful fals jape" (414).[8] But alongside this popular strain
one should note the extreme and awkward conventionalism of the com-
plaints of Dido, in which the formality of speech actually incorporates the
logic and diction of scholasticism:

[305] "As thus: of oon he wolde have fame
       In magnyfyinge of hys name;
       Another for frendshippe, seyth he;
       And yet ther shal the thridde be
       That shal be take for delyt,
       Loo, or for synguler profit."

[334] "Now see I wel, and telle kan,
       We wrechched wymmen konne noon art;
       For certeyn, for the more part,
       Thus we be served everychone.
       How sore that ye men konne groone,
       Anoon as we have yow receyved,

8. *Der junge Chaucer,* pp. 106–108.

> Certaynly we ben deceyvyd!
> For, though your love laste a seson,
> Wayte upon the conclusyon,
> And eke how that ye determynen,
> And for the more part diffynen."

The poverty of the versification and the improbability of the diction should not blind us to the fact that Chaucer will elsewhere use the conventional machinery of philosophical monologue with good effect. What is confusing is the essential pointlessness of the device here, where the amplification stands in such grotesque stylistic disharmony with its narrative context.

The moralization of the episode, of which these speeches are a part, is likewise unsteady. Dido is presented first as an exemplary victim of man's duplicity. Then, as if Chaucer were here first discovering the theme of his poem, she becomes rather a victim of Fame [349–57]:

> [353]   "Eke, though I myghte duren ever,
> That I have don, rekever I never,
> That I ne shal be seyd, allas,
> Yshamed be thourgh Eneas,
> And that I shal thus juged be . . ."

But then there follow some seven exempla of "untrouthe." We might be surer that this was to be the primary significance of the episode were it not that Eneas is then fully excused of his "grete trespas" (428) and the Narrator leads us out of the temple of Venus, into a desert the meaning of which has not yet been plumbed.

Book II replaces the antique matters of Venus and Dido with Chaucerian autobiography, popular science, and pure comedy. The vehicle for most of this is the golden Eagle, who first appears to the Narrator at the end of Book I. Flown out of the *Purgatorio*, he now descends to earth, to be plucked of his allegorical significance and to serve as the Narrator's conveyance to the house of Fame. The Narrator is "Geffrey" Chaucer, his obtuseness of the *Book of the Duchess* filled out with some of the most personal details the poet has left us. He is already fat, henpecked, and with the labor of his studies and his reckonings (as Controller of Customs) he lives the life of a hermit. The trip, says the Eagle, is Jove's reward for faithful literary service to Love.

But the Eagle is much more than the conventional guide of the love visions. His first word is reminiscent of the awakening of Morpheus:

> [554]   Thus I longe in hys clawes lay,
> Til at the laste he to me spak
> In mannes vois, and seyde, "Awak!
> And be not agast so, for shame!"
> And called me tho by my name,
> And, for I shulde the bet abreyde,
> Me mette, "Awak," to me he seyde,
> Ryght in the same vois and stevene
> That useth oon I koude nevene . . .

Nothing in the poem is more impressive and surprising than the consistently naturalistic perspective in which this character is seen. Even his famous exposition of the theory of sound is subsumed by it [853–74].

[853] "Telle me this now feythfully,
Have y not preved thus symply,
Withoute any subtilite
Of speche, or gret prolixite
Of termes of philosophie,
Of figures of poetrie,
Or colours of rethorike?
Pardee, hit oughte the to lyke!
For hard langage and hard matere
Ys encombrous for to here
Attones; wost thou not wel this?"

That the exposition has indeed been a model of clarity is achievement enough. Convention would have admitted it to the poem on a nondramatic level, as necessary indoctrination. Thus Lancelot and Lavinia, Troilus, Anelida and Dorigen, or any of the characters of conventional narrative, can go on at length without the suggestion that they are either learned or fluent. We have seen Jean de Meun, indeed, give such learned material to characters who are otherwise specifically nonlearned. But here, with no exigency of realism at all apparent, Chaucer makes the talent for exposition a trait of the speaker himself. The Eagle is a study for Pandarus. Conceived naturalistically, he cannot deliver a lecture without directing attention to it himself. He is a character: an anxious, learned tourist guide and pedagogue. Much of his lecturing has a structural value in the information it conveys to the reader. Thus the speech on sound is a conceivably relevant introduction to the description of the house of Fame in Book III. Yet the information is ultimately swallowed up in the characterization, and there is at least one exchange which seems to have no other function but local satire. At the end of the Book, the Narrator falls into one of his fantasies, thinking of Boethius on philosophic flight, of Martianus Capella and Alain de Lille on the heavenly bodies. The Eagle, incidentally a mind reader, leaps to the pedagogical opportunity:

[992] "Lat be," quod he, "thy fantasye!
Wilt thou lere of sterres aught?"

The Narrator's reply is comically perverse:

"Nay, certeynly," quod y, "ryght naught."

The Lecturer is hardly to be daunted, but his formerly docile pupil is firm [995–1018]:

[995] "And why?" "For y am now to old."
"Elles I wolde the have told,"
Quod he, "the sterres names, lo,
And al the hevenes sygnes therto,
And which they ben." "No fors," quod y.

Chaucer is here in command of an idiom that is only dimly seen in the *Book of the Duchess;* this comic dialogue is one of the great technical accomplishments of the poem.

The deliciousness of the characterization, however, should not blind us to the fact that it has no describable function beyond its intrinsic humor. It is not part of a pattern. The Eagle hardly reappears in Book III, nor does the ironic revelation of his weakness stand in meaningful relationship to either the material he presents or the conventional functions he fulfills. It is a free-floating, gratuitous display of talent and of humor, thoroughly Chaucerian in its quality, but not yet bent to the magisterial control of the mature narrative artist.

The third Book shares the antique, bookish flavor of the first, and its unsteadiness. The description is extremely profuse, as if the poet were pouring out all his lore. There is an artistic economy in its creating the sense of overwhelming richness of sight and sound that we should expect in Fame's house. The many-eared, many-eyed goddess is described as changing wondrously in height as she sits gorgeously and permanently enthroned, surrounded by the Muses and bearing on her shoulders the fame of Alexander and Hercules. Down from the dais runs a double row of metal columns; atop them stand "folk of digne reverence," historians and poets of the great deeds of the world. The patterned management of Fame's nine sets of suitors, displayed with a minimum of commentary, is Chaucer's best piece of self-expressive allegory. But set amidst this splendor and formalism, Fame herself periodically shrinks to the dimensions of a fishwife [1776–88]:

> [1776]   "Fy on yow," quod she, "everychon!
> Ye masty swyn, ye ydel wrechches,
> Ful of roten, slowe techches!"

This is the idiom suited to the peasant Dangier, rampaging in the Lady's mind to snub presumptuous suitors; it is not intrinsically unsuitable for allegory, nor even for representing the graceless whims of Fame. Yet the mixture of styles is so violent that one wonders, even when the poet makes explicit his modest carelessness of fame later on, whether this naturalization of Fame in so conventional and "high" a context is not caprice rather than irony.

Chaucer at least seems not yet to have got his material into focus. He works at each episode with gusto, then leaves it behind as if forgotten. Eight hundred verses of "this lytel laste bok" are passed when we learn that the house of Fame is, after all, not the place that he has been brought here to see. Then follows the remarkable description of the house of Rumor, and as finally the narrative seems to gather itself to the revelation of some vital piece of news, the poem breaks off unfinished.

In the absence of an ending, there is no possibility of a secure interpretation of any poem; for this poem the matter is worse. It is hard to conceive of any ending at all that could consistently follow from what we have. Perhaps this is why, like the overblown *Anelida and Arcite* of the same period, the poem was left unfinished. The first and third Books are reasonably close in theme and style. They share an otherwordly locus, rich, symbolical description, and an irony touching on pessimism. Bronson's hypothesis, that the poem was to raise someone to bad eminence in a matter of love,[9] is perhaps as close as we shall come to relating these Books. But whoever succeeds in harmonizing them with the second Book will deserve the niche of Colle tregetour himself. The oscillations of perspective that we see in the local progress of the narrative are magnified in the

9. "Hous of Fame," pp. 184–187.

larger sequence of the Books. A strain of irony, largely the product of this oscillation, runs through the poem. But the question here is one of direction. How does the irony cut? The effect of the Eagle's characterization is to break through the curtain of dream and allegory, to reduce the journey to commonplace naturalistic terms. But to what end?

It would be worse than churlishness to comb this fascinating poem for incoherencies, were it not that incoherency is the central fact of its character. In view of its range of subject matter, and its technical facility from passage to passage, we must agree with Kittredge that the poem "is composed, in small and great, with astonishing virtuosity. It is full of spirit and originality, and instinct throughout with conscious power."[1] Yet the virtuosity and the consciousness of power outstrip the artistic judgment. The *House of Fame* is Chaucer's most flamboyant poem, the one most characteristically late Gothic, colorful, varied to extremes, undigested. In this direction it more truly reveals the nature of Chaucer's artistic problem than the *Book of the Duchess* does. Or rather, it does not give the false impression that he is simply trying to find his way out of the conservative embrace of conventionalism. He constructs the Eagle and the fabulous edifice of Fame with equal gusto. He is himself embracing as much as his arms can strain of the cultural and stylistic endowment of the times. But he does not yet know what to do with it. What we find in the later works is not progressively more naturalism, but more control, the subordination of technique to method, the management of these diverse materials in the interest of a coherent pattern of meaning.

3. THE "PARLIAMENT OF FOWLS"

We have, before the *Troilus,* a dramatic instance of the growth of Chaucer's feeling for this management in the second half of the *Parliament of Fowls.* It is a prelude to his maturity, not only in general artistic soundness, but also in the particular configuration which the various elements of his thought and style take. Although like the *House of Fame* it shows Chaucer far afield from French sources and exclusively French traits of style, the "unlikely and disparate materials"[2] of the poem have been variously drawn toward a meaningful polarity of relationship, the idealist-realist, conventional-naturalistic polarity of the French tradition.

The first half of the poem is charmingly and exasperatingly variegated, in the manner of the *House of Fame.* Chaucer, writing now in an athletically flexible rime-royal stanza, again adopts the dream vision as a frame. His Narrator is again an outsider to love but an enthusiastic reader, and he begins his tale with an account of a book he has recently read. It is Cicero's *Somnium Scipionis.* The brief but earnest résumé of the book, with the moral and other-worldly exhortations of Africanus that end it, constitutes the chief variance from conventional love-vision material in this part of the poem, and the chief point of critical difficulty. From here we are introduced to the Narrator's dream, in which, at first guided by the moral Africanus, he comes upon a courtly pleasance, a temple of Venus, and finally to Nature's presidency over a parliament of birds on St. Valentine's Day.

1. *Chaucer,* p. 74.
2. Bronson, "Parlement . . . Revisited," p. 260.

Bronson has well traced the playful oddments of tone that give the first section a lightly ironic flavor: the status of the Narrator as a noncombatant on the field of love; the puzzling invocation to Venus "north-north-west"; the curiously comic adaptation of Dante's legend on the gate of Hell for the gate to this garden of Love; the ambiguous treatment of Venus herself; the mixture, in the garden description, of conventional inhabitants of love gardens with such questionable figures as Flaterye, Messagerye, and Meede.[3] All these, and many smaller touches, suggest that the love vision is not being taken with perfect seriousness. Yet the general presence of irony is not enough to establish a unifying theme. Here, as in the *House of Fame*, there is some doubt concerning how the irony cuts, and some grounds for feeling that all is not under control. The heavy influence of Boccaccio in the description was both for good and for ill. It produces stanzas of unparalleled brilliance,[4] and some of careless and mechanical amplification. It leads the poet into the hothouse closeness of the description of Venus, which, missing the full sensuality of the Italian, hits on a voyeurism that is unique in Chaucer. The whole section, with its exuberant cataloguing of trees and personifications and traditional lovers, has somewhat less relationship to what follows than one would like. If Chaucer had at this point visualized ending his poem with a parliament of birds, would he have been content with the passing description of birds in verses 190–192? With the appearance of Nature (298) the poem seems to begin anew, and if there is an irony in the rejection of Venus for Nature as the goddess presiding over these matters of love, it does not strike us as premeditated, but rather as the happy result of the poet's escape from a set of materials that were too fancy and Italian for his present use. From Boccaccio he turns to the more medieval inspiration of Alain de Lille.

The parliament proper redeems the earlier part, casting something of a retrospective coherence over it, and it draws the *Dream of Scipio* into an orbit related obliquely to its own. Its movement is sequential, if not plotlike. The long catalogue of birds at its beginning is securely related to the action in subject and theme. The personified Nature behaves as she ought, that is, functionally and not decoratively. The poem proceeds to its conclusion with a newly acquired thematic coherence. Perhaps some contemporary event, faded now beyond recognition, gave the poet his original focus here, or perhaps it was simply the St. Valentine's idea itself, which appears suddenly in verse 309. One may guess that here, as with the *Book of the Duchess*, the "occasional" status of the poem has helped the poet to hold his materials together. But both these possible foci have been transcended for a more general theme. I have no hesitancy in following Clemen's and Bronson's lead in identifying it as the comic, contradictory variety of men's attitudes toward love.[5] The bare theme as thus stated has some significance for Chaucer's art. It is Jean de Meun's theme; it is also one of the possible themes of the *House of Fame*. The handling of it is, however, incomparably more significant, for it shows the poet for the first time boldly aligning his style in the pattern of his attitudes, and with his characteristic ironic effect.

3. "Appreciation," pp. 198, 203–211.
4. *PF* 183–210.
5. Clemen, *Der junge Chaucer*, pp. 190, 200–201; Bronson, "Appreciation," pp. 216–219. Cf. Gardiner Stillwell, "Unity and Comedy in Chaucer's *Parlement of Foules,"JEGP*, XLIX (1950), 473.

The parliament begins when Nature, with the beautiful female eagle on her hand, calls on the birds to choose their mates. The tercel eagle, as the highest in rank and most worthy, speaks first. His is a courtly posture, and his speech is in the high-courtly idiom [414–41]:

[414] With hed enclyned and with ful humble cheere
This royal tersel spak, and tariede noght:—
"Unto my soverayn lady, and not my fere,
I chese, and chese with wil, and herte, and thought,
The formel on youre hond, so wel iwrought,
Whos I am al, and evere wol hire serve,
Do what hire lest, to do me lyve or sterve."

The female responds with a handsome blush of modesty, and then two other tercels "of lower kynde" in turn make claim to her hand. One claims greater length of service, and the other greater depth of devotion. Their speeches are naturally less courtly than the first, but nothing at this point mars the effect of genteel, ceremonial order in the procession of their pleas. Chaucer draws out this effect finely by implicating the Narrator [484–90]:

[484] Of al my lyf, syn that day I was born,
So gentil ple in love or other thyng
Ne herde nevere no man me beforn,
Who that hadde leyser and connyng
For to reherse hire chere and hire spekyng.

Then, with an audacity equaled only by its thumping success, Chaucer introduces the opposite note, full blast [491–501]:

[491] The noyse of foules for to ben delyvered
So loude rong, "Have don, and lat us wende!"
That wel wende I the wode hadde al toshyvered.
"Com of!" they criede, "allas, ye wol us shende!
Whan shal youre cursede pletynge have an ende?"

The famous, hugely naturalistic squabble among the lesser fowl follows. It quickly boils over the issue of the tercels into the question of love itself. The goose is for no nonsense: "But she wol love hym, lat hym love another!" She is seconded by the duck, but not before the turtledove has spoken [582–95]:

[586] "Forsothe, I preyse nat the goses red,
For, though she deyede, I wolde non other make;
I wol ben hires, til that the deth me take."

"Wel bourded," quod the doke, "by myn hat!
That men shulde loven alwey causeles,
Who can a resoun fynde or wit in that?"

The "gentil tercelet" abuses this vulgar ignorance of love, then the cuckoo's even deeper pragmatism is criticized by the merlin. Nature brings the squabble to a close with both issues unresolved. The female eagle, given her choice, asks a year's respite. The other birds choose their mates, and the narrative closes in an atmosphere of communal felicity [666–72]:

[666] And whan this werk al brought was to an ende,
       To every foul Nature yaf his make
       By evene acord, and on here wey they wende.

After singing an exquisite roundel welcoming summer, the birds fly away
and the Narrator awakens to his books again.

The "contending lovers" and the "court of love" are the commonly rec-
ognized traditional motifs which the parliament is based on, but neither
retains much importance under Chaucer's hand. The debate is peppered
with scholastic and legal terminology, *ple, juge, parti, preve, verdit, diffyne,
termine, argumentes,* for realistic, parliamentary flavor, and not to outline
a genuine debate for the audience. The irony of the case, rather than the
issues, is the prime consideration. The very inconclusiveness of the out-
come shows that the pointed contrast of courtly and bourgeois attitudes
is designedly balanced. It produces a comic reflection of one attitude on
the other; each is partly admirable, partly foolish. The ending leaves us
with no hard feelings.

The parliament scene, with its realism, is the part of the poem most
often praised, and one may justly savor for its own sake the deliciousness
with which Chaucer can now handle colloquial rhythm and diction. Yet if
anything is true of the art of the scene, it is that the realism does not
achieve half its effect without the carefully measured stanzas of the courtly
idiom that it breaks in upon. The ironic reflection of views is paralleled by
an ironic reflection of styles, in which each component is essential to the
total effect. The freely given, insular comic realism of the *House of Fame*
is here used for a purpose larger than itself, subordinated to a larger com-
plex of style and meaning. The courtly idiom has equivalent status; as we
have seen, it is managed with equivalent circumspection. The passage seen
large, then, shows Chaucer in a new command of his diverse materials.
He is done, here, with the random and nebulous effects of the *House of
Fame* and of the first part of this poem. While we shall watch him extend,
refine, and modulate this balanced, ironic position to the end of the *Can-
terbury Tales,* and make a poetry infinitely complex out of it, it will never
again be a complexity that borders on confusion, nor an irony that suggests
chance.

The clarity and precision of the art of the parliament scene implies a
similar quality in the vision of the poet; the scene forecasts in an early and
simple form the character of Chaucer's ultimate response to the ambiva-
lence that earthly love and life present so strongly to the late medieval
mind. He sees the courtly and bourgeois modes, idealism and practicality,
in ironic juxtaposition. He holds them in balance, sympathetically and crit-
ically, exploring each for its own essence and for the light it casts on the
other. In this he is more tolerant than Boccaccio, more serious than
Machaut, and much more in control of his material than Deschamps. He
makes, more than any of his European contemporaries, a capacious, com-
prehensible order out of his legacy of style and meaning from the French
tradition. Most of his writing that deals with secular values, then, can be
understood in terms of the character of the parliament scene. It forecasts
particularly the nature of the local comedy in the *Troilus.*

The parliament scene is not the whole of the poem, however. I am less
sure of the meaning of the envelope. The introduction of the Narrator and

the long, static description of the *locus amoenus* before the action begins are in the pattern of the *Roman de la Rose,* and very deeply embedded in Chaucer's own sense of structure. Bronson has said perhaps all that can be said for the relevance of the place description to the parliament when he describes the latter as a gathering into sharper focus and precision of the irony which plays intermittently about the poem from its very commencement.[6] The problem of the Narrator and his summary of the *Somnium Scipionis* presses for more attention. The last stanza of the poem adverts to this beginning with a suggestion of coherence that is hard to ignore. Furthermore, the content of the *Somnium* seems to create with the parliament scene a second and larger issue in the thought of the poem: that between heavenly and earthly love. If so, it gives the poem the larger philosophical pattern, if not the dimensions, of the *Troilus* and the *Canterbury Tales.*

The poem ends thus [693–99]:

> [695] I wok, and othere bokes tok me to
> To reede upon, and yit I rede alwey.
> I hope, ywis, to rede so som day
> That I shal mete som thyng for to fare
> The bet, and thus to rede I nyl nat spare.

These lines hark back to two early stanzas; the first introduces the *Somnium Scipionis* and the second introduces the Narrator's dream [15–21, 85–91]. The picture [there] of the Narrator in search of "a certeyn thing to lerne" has prompted interpretations of the poem as serious philosophy, as if Chaucer were in some way trying to reconcile the morality of Cicero's book with the mundane concerns represented by the birds, and by his being himself a love poet. Africanus' command to work for the common weal (74–75) suggests a contrast with the inability of the birds to do so. The dictum that lecherous folk shall be punished in the hereafter (79–81) may refer to the lovers within the garden. The generally otherworldly orientation of the book, recommending heavenly love or true felicity, seems pointedly antithetical to the earthly love and "false felicity" dealt with later.[7] There is tonal support for this in the irony of the description, extending even to the catalogue of birds. Here the vices of secular life are recorded in surprisingly full measure for a valentine [358–62]:

> [360] The drake, stroyere of his owene kynde;
> The stork, the wrekere of avouterye;
> The hote cormeraunt of glotenye . . .

There is no doubt that a serious view is involved with the poem, but the poem cannot support the theory that makes of it a sober philosophical tract. The most that can be said here is that the philosophical issue, if raised, is not pursued. The felicity of the birds is not made to feel false, and the best poetry of the poem celebrates sensuous life with undiluted enthusiasm. To bring seriously to bear the idea that this life is a kind of

---

6. "Appreciation," p. 219.
7. See R. E. Goffin, "Heaven and Earth in the 'Parlement of Foules,' " *MLR,* XXXI (1936), 493–499; R. M. Lumiansky, "Chaucer's *Parlement of Foules:* A Philosophical Interpretation," *RES,* XXXIV (1948), 81–89. Cf. Stillwell, "Unity and Comedy," pp. 473–474, 478; Bronson, "Appreciation," p. 201.

death (54), to bring it to bear on that lively, feathered crowd assembled by Nature on St. Valentine's Day, is too crushing a notion for the poetry to sustain. Granting that the tone must remain ambiguous, I favor a less ambitious reading, on the side that sees the irreconcilability of Africanus and the birds as a comic antithesis, a joke at the expense of the Narrator, for his bookishness.

The *House of Fame* gives us a precedent. Its Narrator is a bookish recluse, divorced from life [652–59]. There is a comic fitness in Jove's sending, as guide for this character, the mercilessly pedagogical Eagle; we have seen it dramatized at the end of Book II. The Narrator of the *Parliament* is in a similar state.[8] An indefatigable bookworm, with a touching faith in the power of books to solve problems, he sits absorbedly down to what we are to take to be his usual fare, a moral work in Latin on heaven and hell:

> [27]   To rede forth hit gan me so delite,
> That al that day me thoughte but a lyte.

His perfectly serious summary of its somber content is in character. Who will relish more this *contemptus mundi* than a preoccupied scholar? Each man to his own. The night, that takes animals from their "besynesse," takes him from his book. And if he is to dream, naturally his guide will not be a lady with blonde tresses, but the moral Africanus himself. The stanza on the content of dreams underlines this comic fitness of things, and all goes smoothly, with the possible exception of his awkward invocation to Venus, until the scholar is betrayed by his own guide. Africanus, with some pointed comment on his incapacities, literally shoves him into a garden of love. Thus does this recluse come to be writing of earthly love; and when his dream is done he goes back, nothing daunted, to his books, still pursuing the profit in them, almost unaware of his betrayal, and of the comic insight into earthly "besynesse" that he has left us with.

This is a gracious and humorous way for a poet with some reputation for seriousness and scholarship to write a valentine. Without complete certainty of its success, one can still see important relationships between this method and that of the *Troilus*. It shows, beneath the perennial joke between the Narrator and his audience, a movement toward bringing the handling of the former into deep involvement with the total effect of the poem. I refer not only to the use of the Narrator's naïve personality to promote imaginative surrender to the dream world, a device that is a constant in the early poems, learned from Guillaume de Lorris; I refer also to the Narrator's vein of *sentence* and doctrine, which in a bolder way now begins to have the kind of relevance to the action that we shall find in the *Troilus*.

A comic treatment of the poem's moralizing does not prevent its prefig-

---

8. No poem will prove anything about another, but in the absence of better explanation, the comparison will have to do. At any rate, I lean no more heavily on *HF* here than Chaucer does. Much of the same reading was running through his head when he composed the two poems. Each contains, for instance, a temple of Venus. Pratt, "Chaucer Borrowing," pp. 262–263, shows that the invocation to Venus in *PF* is probably adapted from *HF*. More germane to the issue, the motif of the guided journey in recompense for the Narrator's labors is common to both. The promise of love tidings, made by the Eagle in *HF*, is fulfilled by Africanus in *PF* (112, 168). The Ciceronian view of the littleness of the earth as seen from above is strikingly secularized in *HF*, into travelogue material (907; cf. Clemen, *Der junge Chaucer*, p. 124). I suggest, then (*post*), that its seriousness in *PF* does not yet extend beyond the characterization of the Narrator.

uring the larger philosophical pattern of the *Troilus*. The epilogue of the *Troilus* embodies the same moral as the opening of the *Parliament*, and in each this moral is set against the main body of the poem.[9] In both, the local problem of the modes of earthly love is related to the larger problem of earth and heaven. Other things being equal, the materials of both poems are strikingly similar. Yet their ultimate tones differ much. The difference between them, between a comic and a tragic expression of the same problem, is thus much a matter of structure. Not for nothing does the palinode in the *Parliament* come first. The birds break in on its bookish, *a priori* morality with a vivacious assertion of life. In the *Troilus*, experience is examined first, and out of its ironic contradictions the serious moral inevitably grows.

A. C. SPEARING

[*The Parliament of Fowls* as Dream-Poetry]†

Chaucer's third dream-poem was *The Parliament of Fowls*, which probably dates from 1382. In style, it is considerably more settled and composed than the two earlier dream-poems. Italian influences, which had affected only the content of the *House*, have now been absorbed stylistically too, and it is written not in the octosyllabic couplets of the two earlier poems, but in rime royal stanzas. The effect is less of rapid movement, whether gay or nervous, than in the earlier poems, and more of 'a grave sweetness and a poised serenity',[1] though colloquial touches are by no means excluded, and indeed stand out more sharply in this more dignified setting. Here more than ever Chaucer shows his awareness of the long and complex tradition of visionary writing, but it is now as much a matter of deft and pervasive allusion as of explicit reference. In structure, however, Chaucer remains very close to *The Book of the Duchess*. Indeed, one might guess that, after *The House of Fame*, where, under the impact of insoluble personal problems, he had pushed the use of dream-methods for literary creation so far as to make the poem unfinishable, he now decided to follow more exactly the causal sequence that had proved so successful in his first dream-poem. As in the *Book* there is a long introductory section, in which the narrator is still awake and reads a book about a dream, which then provides motivation for his own dream. As in the *House*, the narrator is a devotee of love but only in books, not through experience:

> For al be that I knowe nat Love in dede,
> Ne wot how that he quiteth folk here hyre,
> Yit happeth me ful ofte in bokes rede
> Of his myrakles, and his crewel yre. (8–11)

But, in laying its emphasis on the narrator as would-be lover rather than poet of love, the *Parliament* is nearer to the *Book* than it is to the *House*.

9. Cf. Bronson, "Appreciation," pp. 199–202; Goffin, "Heaven and Earth," pp. 497–499.
† From *Medieval Dream-Poetry* (Cambridge: Cambridge UP, 1976), 89–101, 223–24. Reprinted with the permission of Cambridge University Press. The author's notes have been renumbered.
1. J. L. Lowes, *Geoffrey Chaucer* (Oxford, 1934), p. 117.

However, the distinction is not very clear-cut; there are one or two explicit references to the narrator as poet, and there is also a pervasive suggestion that love and poetry can be seen in the same terms, as creative experiences, which are highly desirable and yet difficult of achievement.[2] It is significant that the narrator invokes Venus not only as the cause of his dream, but also for help 'to ryme and ek t'endyte' (119) when he comes to set it down.

The narrator is introduced as reading one particular book, 'a certeyn thing to lerne' (20). What that thing is, we are never explicitly told, and at the end of the poem he resumes his search in 'othere bokes' (695); but here perhaps the poem is truly dreamlike, in that it solves the Dreamer's problems (at least for us) in the very act of reflecting them. The thing sought is surely found in the dream itself, without the Dreamer being aware of it, though if asked to define it one could only say that it is the meaning of the whole poem, which cannot properly be expressed in other terms. To put it more crudely than the poem does, what the narrator is seeking is presumably the meaning of that love which is the major subject of medieval courtly poetry, but which he sees chiefly as a cause of suffering; what he finds in the dream is a subtle placing of love in the larger context of the social order and of the relationship between the natural and the human, nature and culture. But to put it like that *is* to put it crudely, for the poem itself is deliberately enigmatic; it holds back from direct statements and conceptual formulations, and prefers to explore and order experience in the way dreams actually do, through images. Perhaps it would be better to say, through symbols, using 'symbol' in its Jungian sense as 'the expression of an intuitive perception which can as yet, neither be apprehended better, nor expressed differently'.[3]

The book the narrator of the *Parliament* is reading is the *Somnium Scipionis* itself, 'Tullyus of the drem of Scipioun' (31), of which he proceeds to give a compact summary. It is seen as a threefold vision of judgment, according to the traditional formula embodied in the *Divine Comedy*, except that earth takes the place of purgatory between heaven and hell:

> Chapiteris sevene it hadde, of hevene and helle
> And erthe, and soules that therinne dwelle. (32–3)

In the summary the emphasis is on heaven, that 'blysful place' which is the reward of the good; and the word 'blysse' is repeated three times, and the phrase 'blysful place' twice, in this brief passage. Another repeated phrase is 'commune profit': heavenly bliss is the reward above all of those who have pursued the welfare of the community rather than private profit or even personal salvation. Finally the narrator, as it gets dark, puts the book down, dissatisfied with its teaching,

> For both I hadde thyng which that I nolde,
> And eke I nadde that thyng that I wolde. (90–1)

That is enigmatic indeed, but similar statements are made elsewhere in Chaucer's poems, for example in *The Complaint unto Pity* and *The Com-*

---

2. In this Chaucer is continuing a tradition that goes far back in medieval courtly poetry, though it rarely achieved conscious realization. Cf. E. I. Condren, 'The Troubadour and his Labor of Love', *Mediaeval Studies*, vol. xxxiv (1972), pp. 174–95: 'Many troubadour lyrics seem indeed to speak about a new and rarefied concept of love—about *fin' amors*. But several of them also use the language of love to describe the poet's search for poetry. Similarly, the poet's anguish and frustration in love are frequently co-subjects with his inability to create songs' (p. 175).
3. *Contributions to Analytical Psychology* (London, 1928), p. 232.

plaint to his Lady, and they always refer to the situation of the unrequited lover, who has the suffering that he does not wish but lacks his lady's mercy, which he does desire.[4] So in one way these lines probably refer to what we already know, the narrator's role as one who has had no success in love. But a similar phrase is also used by Philosophy in the *De Consolatione*, to refer to the general state of man, who seeks mistaken means to arrive at that ultimate good which is his goal, and therefore suffers from a perpetual anxiety, because 'the lakkide somewhat that thow woldest nat han lakkid, or elles thou haddest that thow noldest nat han had' (III, pr. 3. 33–6). Thinking of *The House of Fame*, we might feel inclined to see the dissatisfaction as that of the medieval courtly poet, conscious of lacking the 'love-tidings' he needs if he is to produce the expected kind of poetry, and finding in the *Somnium Scipionis* a philosophical doctrine which seems to be of no use to him, because it contains nothing about love (except, significantly, in the phrase 'that lovede commune profyt' (47)). The dream will reconcile these contradictions, and will provide the poet with 'mater of to wryte' (168); but in its immediate context the statement is mysterious, used to express a state in which the mind is dissatisfied for an undefinable cause, weary as night falls, but still seeking for a truth that will answer its longings.

The narrator falls asleep, and dreams that Scipio Africanus stands at his bedside, just as Scipio the younger saw him in the book he has been reading. As in the two earlier dream-poems, there is an ambiguity concerning the status of the dream, which implies an ambiguity in the status of the poem itself, and by extension of imaginative fiction in general. The only theory about the causation of dreams which is stated in this poem occurs in a stanza I have mentioned before, which sees all dreams as reflecting states of body or mind: the hunter dreams of hunting, the sick man of drinking, the lover of success in love, and so on. And the narrator seems to assume the truth of this theory at the very end of the poem, where, after his awakening, he goes on reading more books in the hope that they will so affect his mind that one day he will have a dream that will do him good:

> I hope, ywis, to rede so som day
> That I shal mete som thyng for to fare
> The bet, and thus to rede I nyl nat spare. (697–9)

(Indeed I hope [or expect] some day to read in such a way that I shall dream some thing that will bring me greater success, and thus I will not refrain from reading.)

But he has already expressed doubt—

> Can I not seyn if that the cause were
> For I hadde red of Affrican byforn,
> That made me to mete that he stod there (106–8)

—and, as we have seen, he goes on to say that it was Venus who made him dream as he did. Taken literally, this would imply that the dream was a *somnium coeleste*, inspired by the goddess of love in her planetary form; taken metaphorically, it would indicate that it was a *somnium animale*, inspired by the narrator's waking thoughts of love. Then again, a dream

4. Noted by D. S. Brewer, ed., *The Parlement of Foulys* (London, 1960), p. 103.

which introduces a venerable figure such as Scipio Africanus the elder would count, according to Macrobius, as an *oraculum*, like the younger Scipio's own dream. If this were true, then the *Parliament* would be the kind of vision that *The House of Fame* stopped short of being; on the other hand, as J. A. W. Bennett has remarked, Chaucer 'reduces to a minimum Africanus' oracular function: the latter becomes a benevolent compère rather than the embodiment of divine wisdom'.[5] Are we to see the dream which follows as offering supernatural guidance, or as a fantasy woven by the Dreamer's mind out of his waking preoccupations and his reading? Chaucer does not commit himself to any answer to this question, nor to the question which by implication follows from it: are we to see a poem like this as a mere deceptive fiction, or does it offer access, through imagination, to truth?

Like the waking section, the dream in the *Parliament* follows closely the pattern of *The Book of the Duchess*. A preliminary section describes the dream-place (forest or garden), and then comes what appears to be the real subject of the poem (meeting with Black Knight or gathering of birds). We shall find in the *Parliament* as much as in the *Book* that what may seem merely a preliminary diversion is in fact related to the main subject through the kind of linkage that belongs to dreams. Africanus leads the Dreamer to the gate of a walled park, reminiscent of the walled garden of the *Roman de la Rose*. Over it are written two inscriptions 'of ful gret difference' (125), one at each side. These derive from the single inscription over the mouth of hell in Dante's *Inferno*, which promises grief and despair to all who enter. But Chaucer's inscriptions are, characteristically, more ambiguous. One promises:

> Thorgh me men gon into that blysful place
> Of hertes hele and dedly woundes cure;
> Thorgh me men gon unto the welle of grace,
> There grene and lusty May shal evere endure.
> This is the wey to al good aventure.
> Be glad, thow redere, and thy sorwe of-caste;
> Al open am I—passe in, and sped thee faste! (127–33)

Then the other:

> 'Thorgh me men gon,' than spak that other side,
> 'Unto the mortal strokes of the spere
> Of which Disdayn and Daunger is the gyde,
> Ther nevere tre shal fruyt ne leves bere.
> This strem yow ledeth to the sorweful were
> There as the fish in prysoun is al drye;
> Th'eschewing is only the remedye!' (134–40)

The Dreamer is paralysed by the contradiction between the two inscriptions, but Africanus tells him that they are meant to refer only to one who is 'Loves servaunt' (159), and therefore not to him. And so he 'shof' (shoved) the Dreamer in through the gate, telling him that he can only be an onlooker, not a participant, but that he will at least gain material for his poetry.

5. *The Parlement of Foules: An Interpretation* (Oxford, 1957), p. 54.

What is behind the gate is evidently a garden of love, like that in the *Roman de la Rose* and its successors, and the inscriptions are saying that love is both heaven and hell. It is the 'blysful place' promised to the good in the *Somnium Scipionis*, with imagery of health, flowing water, and greenness; it is also a place of dryness, sterility and death, which can be avoided only by never entering the garden in the first place. The dream of a heaven and a hell is explicable psychologically through the influence of the vision of judgment read about in the *Somnium Scipionis*; but now the heaven and the hell are the same place—an original variant on the traditional pattern of visions. So far as the dream is to be thought of as providing material for poetry, one might also suggest that two contrary states of the imagination are indicated by the double inscription. The imagery of dryness and sterility recalls the desert outside the temple of Venus in book I of *The House of Fame*, which I suggested was a symbol, among other things, of the failure of inspiration; the imagery of growth and flowing water, on the other hand, suggests a renewal of creativity. Love, as the subject for poetry, can provide either or both of these.

The Dreamer enters the garden, and it proves to be a typical paradise-landscape, with a meadow and a river, a temperate climate, leaves that are always green, day that lasts for ever, birds singing like angels, and harmonious music sweeter than was ever heard by God 'that makere is of al and lord' (199). It contains the whole variety of natural species, instanced by lists of trees and of animals. But it soon becomes clear that this seeming paradise, as in the *Roman de la Rose*, is really a pseudo-paradise of idealized desire. In it 'Cupide, oure lord' (212) sharpens his arrows, 'Some for to sle, and some to wounde and kerve' (217), and his bow lies ready at his feet. The Dreamer sees personifications of pleasing qualities such as Pleasure, Courtesy and Beauty, but also others less pleasing, such as Foolhardiness, Flattery and Bribery, and, most forcefully described, with a real shudder in the rhythm of the last line, Cunning:

> . . . the Craft that can and hath the myght
> To don by force a wyght to don folye—
> Disfigurat was she, I nyl nat lye. (220–2)

Now he presses further into the garden, and comes upon a temple of brass, the atmosphere of which is at once exotic and sinister. It may have Patience and Peace sitting at the door, but inside the air is hot with lovers' sighs, which make the altar flames burn more fiercely, and which he sees are incited by 'the bittere goddesse Jelosye' (252). The description of this temple is based on that of the temple of Venus in Boccaccio's *Teseida*; but in the *Parliament*, unlike book I of *The House of Fame*, we are not told to whom the temple is dedicated. Chaucer tells us that the 'sovereyn place' in it is held by Priapus, and leaves us to guess that it is his temple rather than Venus's. Priapus is the god of the phallus as well as of gardens, and a recent scholar has suggested that 'Chaucer's direct reference to the story in Ovid's *Fasti* of Priapus' thwarted attempt to make love to the nymph Lotis clearly marks the temple as a place of sexual frustration'.[6] Moreover, the Dreamer tells us that

---

6. G. D. Economou, *The Goddess Natura in Medieval Literature* (Cambridge, Mass., 1972), p. 136.

> Ful besyly men gonne assaye and fonde
> Upon his hed to sette, of sondry hewe,
> Garlondes ful of freshe floures newe. (257–9)

(People were eagerly attempting and endeavouring to set on his head garlands full of fresh new flowers, of various colours.)

The emphasis on *attempting* to do this is not in Boccaccio, who says merely that there were garlands of flowers about the temple; and, though the modern reader may think of a notorious incident in chapter 15 of *Lady Chatterley's Lover*, the suggestion Chaucer intends is probably that the cult of sexuality cannot be so easily prettified, however 'besyly men gonne assaye and fonde'. In a dim corner, the Dreamer finds Venus performing a kind of striptease act, which draws an approving snigger from him. The temple is hung with broken bows, symbolizing the lost virginities of those who 'here tymes waste. In hyre servyse' (283–4), and it is decorated with paintings of famous figures from myth and legend who died for love.

From this hothouse atmosphere, the Dreamer re-emerges into the garden 'that was so sote [sweet] and grene' (296), and walks about to recover from his insight into obsessive sexuality. There he sees another goddess, contrasting with Venus. This is Nature,

> . . . a queene,
> That, as of lyght the somer sonne shene
> Passeth the sterre, right so over mesure
> She fayrer was than any creature. (298–301)

Chaucer does not describe her in detail, but, with another of the poem's allusions to the visionary tradition, simply says that she looked just as Alanus described her in the *De Planctu Naturae*. Now, however, the birds of different species, which in Alanus were pictured on her garments, have come alive, and they are all crowded round her, awaiting her judgment. The day, we learn, is that of St Valentine, when the birds choose their mates; and it is likely that the *Parliament* was composed to form part of the St Valentine's day celebrations in Richard II's court. 1382 was the year of Richard's marriage, at the age of fifteen, to Anne of Bohemia. Nature is later described as God's deputy, 'vicaire of the almighty Lord' (379), but there is little emphasis on her subordination to some higher realm of values. By contrast with the *Roman de la Rose*, this poem lays its stress not on the limitation of Nature's realm but on its extensiveness, though it is also concerned with the intricate relationships between the natural and the human. Nature is so surrounded with birds, the Dreamer says, that 'unethe was there space / For me to stonde, so ful was al the place' (314–15); and indeed, from this point on, the Dreamer drops almost completely out of sight, as if the birds had squeezed him out of the poem; and so does Africanus, his guide. This is one way in which the *Parliament* is very different from both of Chaucer's earlier dream-poems: the subject-matter of the dream itself becomes so solid and energetic that it elbows the Dreamer aside, and instead of a contrast of points of view between Dreamer and guide there is a contrast *within* what the Dreamer sees. There may be a connection between this disappearance of the Dreamer's point of view and the poem's lack of emphasis on the Dreamer as poet; here it is what is seen that is important, not the role of the person who sees it.

The first things seen are all the species of birds, described in five stanzas, each bird with its own epithet or attribute, which serves to humanize it or to align it with some aspect of human life—the noble falcon, the meek-eyed dove, the thieving crow, the gluttonous cormorant, the wise raven, and so on. These are traditional epithets, evidence of the longstanding human tendency to think of birds as constituting a society parallel to human society. We may compare this list with the earlier list of trees in the garden. Both are concerned not simply with description of the natural world, but with the interaction of the natural and the human. The epithets in the list of trees call attention to the usefulness of the different species to men: the oak for building, the box for making pipes, the fir for ships' masts, the yew for bows, and so on. The list of birds, on the other hand, presents them as independent of human beings but parallel to them. The anthropologist Claude Lévi-Strauss has suggested some reasons for this attitude towards birds, which

> can be permitted to resemble men for the very reason that they are so different. They are feathered, winged, oviparous and they are also physically separated from human society by the element in which it is their privilege to move. As a result of this fact, they form a community which is independent of our own but, precisely because of this independence, appears to us like another society, homologous to that in which we live: birds love freedom; they build themselves homes in which they live a family life and nurture their young; they often engage in social relations with other members of their species; and they communicate with them by acoustic means recalling articulated language. Consequently everything objective conspires to make us think of the bird world as a metaphorical human society: is it not after all literally parallel to it on another level? There are countless examples in mythology and folklore to indicate the frequency of this mode of representation.[7]

There are also countless examples in medieval literature, among them Clanvowe's *Cuckoo and the Nightingale* * * * and the earlier English poem *The Owl and the Nightingale*, in which the two birds are used to articulate a whole range of binary contrasts among human attitudes.

In *The Parliament of Fowls*, under Nature's arbitration, the birds are choosing their mates. Like men in medieval society, they are divided into several broad classes: the birds of prey, those that live on worms, those that live on seeds, and water-fowl. Fittingly, in terms of the human hierarchy of the Middle Ages, Nature begins with the noblest, the birds of prey, and among these with the highest, the royal eagle. But here there is a difficulty, for there are three candidates for the hand—or wing—of the beautiful female eagle, the formel, whom Nature herself is holding on her hand. They are, naturally, three male eagles, or tercels. Each speaks in turn to stake his claim to her: the first rests his claim essentially on the total humility of his devotion, the second on the length of his service as her admirer, the third on his exclusive loyalty. The statement of these claims, in a style of appropriately courtly amplitude, occupies some time, but meanwhile the other classes of birds are anxious to express their own

7. *The Savage Mind* (London, 1966), p. 204.

views. Their attitudes are often less courtly than those of the aristocratic
birds, and the poem echoes with cries of 'kokkow' and 'quek quek'; indeed,
our last reminder of the Dreamer's presence as an observer occurs just
here, when he complains that 'thourgh myne eres the noyse wente tho'
(500). Nature determines that each class of birds shall select its own
spokesman to offer a solution to the dilemma. The falcon, for the birds of
prey, says that there is no further possibility of discussion, and the three
tercels must fight to the death, unless the formel can choose among them
herself. The goose, for water-fowl, offers the simple solution that any of
the tercels who is not loved by the formel should choose another female
as his mate—an uncourtly view, which is treated with ridicule by the spar-
rowhawk and the other 'gentil foules alle' (575). The turtledove, on behalf
of the seed-fowl, claims that each of the tercels must show his loyalty to
the formel by loving no-one else until he dies, even if she should die first—
a *reductio ad absurdum* of courtly claims for the transcendent value of
personal emotion, in which we are perhaps intended to see a touch of
bourgeois sentimentality. The duck agrees with the goose: there are other
fish in the sea, other stars in the sky:

> 'Ye quek!' yit seyde the doke, ful wel and fayre,
> 'There been mo sterres, God wot, than a payre!' (594–5)

The last verdict is that of the cuckoo, for the lowly worm-fowl, the *vylayns*
of bird-society: since the eagles cannot agree, let them remain solitary all
their lives. Another *gentil* bird, the small falcon called a merlin, protests
against this in most *ungentil* language, calling the cuckoo 'wormes corup-
cioun' (614); but at this point Nature intervenes again.

In the paralleling of different types of bird with the attitudes supposed
to be appropriate to different social classes, there is a close resemblance
to the way in which primitive men use the categories built into nature as
means of thinking about their own lives as part of human culture. In many
areas of life such habits of thought have been retained by civilized societies
too, so that, as Lévi-Strauss puts it, 'The differences between animals,
which man can extract from nature and transfer to culture, . . . are adopted
as emblems by groups of men in order to do away with their own resem-
blances'.[8] In the *Parliament* the poet of a highly civilized society to some
extent reverses the original process: the already existing human groupings,
and the attitudes which accompany them, are transferred to the realm of
the birds, a realm which remains under the dominion of Nature. There
are objectively and permanently different species of birds; but they are only
birds, after all. One consequence of this is that we can think about their
differences of attitude, even towards so central a subject as love, with
amused tolerance. The irreducible birdlikeness of the eagle in *The House
of Fame* had a similar function, in preventing us from being able to take
him too seriously as a figure of authority. This part of the poem, the actual
parliament of the birds, is very funny, not least as a parody of the unruly
parliament of Chaucer's own time. Its amusing aspects, indeed, have per-
haps tended to overshadow the rest of the poem. A second consequence
of the way in which the birds remain birds is that Nature, the mother of
them all, can call them to order, if necessary somewhat sharply: 'Holde

8. Ibid. p. 107.

youre tonges there!' (521) or ' "Now pes!" quod Nature, "I commaunde here!' " (617). Their different degrees of *worthinesse* are not conceived as a merely historical phenomenon, but are ratified as part of Nature's 'ryhtful ordenaunce' (390). And she is in a position to insist that their mating must be by mutual agreement, by *eleccioun* (621) rather than by the force that the earlier temple of brass seemed to imply.

Finally, towards the end of the dream, a provisional solution to the dilemma of who shall mate with the formel is achieved by moving out of the realm of birds and back into that of men and women. Nature allows the formel to make her own choice—which was what the falcon had originally urged. Nature herself, it appears, is on the side of the *gentil*, even though she 'alwey hadde an ere / To murmur of the lewednesse [coarseness] behynde' (519–20). She advises the formel, saying that were she not Nature but Reason she would counsel her to choose the first of the tercels; but the actual choice she leaves to the bird herself. The formel, however, declines to choose; she does not yet wish to serve Venus or Cupid, and she needs more time to make up her mind. This too Nature grants. She allows her until the next St Valentine's day to make her choice, and meantime the three tercels have a year to prove their devotion to her. With this problem removed for the time being, all the other birds can now choose their mates. They choose immediately, and before their departure they sing a roundel in honour of Nature, the exquisite lyric 'Now welcome, somer, with thy sonne softe' (680). The noise of the birds' 'shoutyng' when the song is finished awakens the Dreamer from his sleep, and the poem ends with him reading still more books, in the hope of one day having a dream that will do him good.

There is a striking contrast between the evident dissatisfaction of the Dreamer with his dream, which he thinks has not given him what he was seeking in his books, and the satisfying completeness which most readers find in the poem that contains the dream. The difference is that between the conscious mind, always seeking for rational solutions to life's problems on the 'bookish' level of philosophy, and the unconscious mind, which achieves mastery over problems by enacting them in the form of concrete images rather than through rational analysis. One scholar writes of all Chaucer's dream-poems that 'The great originality of these poems is in their attempt to exploit the possibilities of *dispositio*—over-all structural arrangement—in ways more complex and meaningful than anything the [rhetorical] manuals suggest in their perfunctory treatments of it.'[9] This is particularly true of *The Parliament of Fowls*: the meaning of the poem is conveyed through certain contrasts embodied rather than stated in the dream-experience, and it was surely his sensitive understanding of dreams that enabled Chaucer to go beyond the inadequate treatment of *dispositio* in the *artes poeticae*. There is, for example, the contrast between the temple of Priapus and Venus and the garden of Nature, between love conceived as enslaving obsession and love conceived as natural impulse, operating within the orderly hierarchy of Nature; then there is the further contrast, within the natural order, now seen as mirroring the human order, between different attitudes towards love. We *feel* the contrast between the enclosure of Venus and Priapus and the freedom of Nature (and we may note

9. R. O. Payne, *The Key of Remembrance* (New Haven, 1963), p. 145.

that the temple is set within Nature's garden: Nature is more inclusive than sexuality). This freedom, always combined with order, is enacted in the parliament, where every attitude is allowed freedom of expression. This is how the 'commune profit' of the *Somnium Scipionis* is achieved in Nature's realm, which in one way encloses and in another way is homologous with the realm of human society. The cuckoo even uses the phrase 'comune spede' (507), which means the same as 'commune profit'. And the freedom of speech and choice includes a freedom not to choose, or at least to defer choosing. The poem ends unexpectedly, so far as the suitors are concerned: this mating season for them brings not the achievement of love but its deferment. This has the advantage of finally transferring the freedom of discussion to the poem's audience. As some scholars have suggested, *The Parliament of Fowls* leads up to a *demande d'amour*, a love-question to be settled by the courtly listeners as *they* think fit. Whom should the formel choose next St Valentine's day? It is for us to decide. Moreover, the deferment of the choice implies a richer civilization than merely seasonal activities might lead us to expect. Human love, the poem implies, involves not merely the gods of sex and their temple of illicit passions, but the possibility of resisting Nature, or at least of gaining a certain margin of freedom within which to choose the time and manner of one's submission. No doubt, as Jean de Meun's La Vielle puts it, quoting Horace,

> qui voudroit une forche prandre
> por soi de Nature deffandre
> et la bouteroit hors de sai,
> revandroit ele, bien le sai (13991–4)

(if anyone wanted to take up a pitchfork to protect himself against Nature and shove her out of himself, she would come back, I know well).

But human beings, though they may not be able to overcome Nature completely, at least are not like birds in being so absolutely dominated by natural impulse that they cannot resist the mating season. The subject of the poem, as I have argued, is that central subject of anthropological study, the relation between nature and culture. The dream, then, though it does not satisfy the Dreamer, does weave the thoughts that had been preoccupying him, both from books and from life, into a new and more richly significant pattern. Love, heaven, hell, the 'commune profit': all these appear, transmuted, in the dream, which offers, like myth, an imaginative mastery over the problems of human life.

The mastery is only imaginative, of course, and that is one meaning of the poem's dream-framework. Once the dream is over, the Dreamer may still be troubled by problems so fundamental to human nature that they cannot be abolished. Moreover, the poem in its texture, its 'feel', is genuinely like a dream. It may make use of conceptual thought, but it does so in the most tentative way, with conceptual oppositions largely replaced by concrete contrasts, and one contrast merging dreamlike into another. Such a delicate structure could not have been created by a poet who was truly in the dreamlike state in which he represents himself. A superb intelligence is at work in *The Parliament of Fowls*, and some words written about a great poet of the twentieth century would apply equally well to this poem of Chaucer's:

The poet's magnificent intelligence is devoted to keeping as close as possible to the concrete of sensation, emotion and perception. Though this poetry is plainly metaphysical in preoccupation, it belongs as purely to the realm of sensibility, and has in it as little of the abstract and general of discursive prose, as any poetry that was ever written.[1]

R. T. LENAGHAN

From Chaucer's Circle of Gentlemen and Clerks†

Identifying Chaucer's audience, indeed any poet's audience, is a chancy business. Even the most benevolent skepticism will dissolve much of the evidence. Yet the attempt deserves to be made for Chaucer because he is an ironist, and irony is so much a social phenomenon, so much a matter of intellectual harmony between writer and audience. And there is, after all, some evidence about his audience which can withstand the skeptical wash.

He does address poems to identifiable people. Trying to determine Chaucer's circle, I have asserted elsewhere that the royal households are the institutional location for his circle, and although a circle is not the same as an audience, the same names and identifications are still central: Bukton, Scogan, and Vache.[1] Since royal rank does not present the problems for determining an audience that it does for determining a circle, we can add the two kings, Richard II and Henry IV. It seems then that no matter how skeptical we are inclined to be about the evidence, no matter how much we would restrict its implications, we can identify a special audience or a small part of a more general audience and place it in the royal households.

The latter point is convenient because it invites the application of the work of the historians who have studied British administrative institutions. Tout, of course, is the primary name and of particular interest for his occasional comments on Chaucer's career as one of a number of lay administrators, who, taken as a group, would develop into a civil service.[2] McFarlane in his work on the Lollard knights describes the balance of responsibilities and rewards that directed and motivated the careers of men whose work was essentially the operation of the English government in the late fourteenth century.[3] The lay administrator for the crown was a clearly established presence in Chaucer's time.

Administrative and social historians show us a nascent civil service. The old style religious clerk, writing the king's letters and keeping his books, had created his departments and, by Chaucer's day in the king's household, was sharing the work of administration with laymen. The result was some-

---

1. F. R. Leavis, 'T. S. Eliot's Later Poetry', in *Education and the University*, 2nd edn (London, 1948), p. 88.
† From "Chaucer's Circle of Gentlemen and Clerks," in *The Chaucer Review* 18.2 (1983): 155–60. Copyright © 1983 by The Pennsylvania State University. Reprinted by permission of the publisher. The author's notes have been abbreviated.
1. "Chaucer's Circle," a paper read at the meeting of The New Chaucer Society, April 1980.
2. T. F. Tout, *Chapters in the Administrative History of Medieval England* (Manchester: The University Press, 1923–1935), 111, 201–02.
3. K. B. McFarlane, *Lancastrian Kings and Lollard Knights* (Oxford: The Clarendon Press, 1972).

what paradoxical—a lay clerk—and the rewards—land and marriages—
were those suited to lay status. Richard Green in *Poets and Princepleasers*
has added a good deal to our knowledge of the king's household.[4] It was
an overtly vertical organization. The king was at the top, and his officers
and agents were grouped in hierarchies beneath him. Green makes force-
fully explicit a point that dovetails with a stress implicit in Tout and explicit
in McFarlane. Green shows that household appointments for poets were
not likely to have been sinecures intended to subsidize their poetry. Tout
and McFarlane make it clear that an appointment was an appointment to
do a job in the government. Institutions were functional agencies; they had
work to do. It follows then that a poet in the household of a prince would
have administrative responsibilities and that they would take precedence
over his poetry. He was a civil servant first and a poet second, although,
in the rather special blend of social club and administrative agency that
the households seem to have been, achievement as a poet could well have
advanced a career as a civil servant.

So much for the relatively settled world of administrative history, doc-
uments, and records, of appointments, responsibilities, and rewards. I
should now like to venture an inference drawn from the elusive or uncer-
tain distinction between king and crown. To begin with what seems safe:
Richard II must have had a clear awareness of the limits and difficulties
of royal power. A larger part of the history of his reign is the account of
struggles to control the government, the struggles of the king for the crown.
The departments of government were the working parts of the prize; the
contestants wanted to assume control of a regular, efficient apparatus. It
follows that administrative experience and expertise were valuable and,
what is more important, would have been defined and assessed within the
institutions, at least at the lower levels. This is the way of bureaucracies.
In short, institutional duties and functions conferred standing. I am not
claiming a modern, independent civil service. I am simply asserting the
plausibility of institutional identification for government administrators,
even in so personal an agency as the household, and then the consequent
plausibility of a lateral allegiance among those who share that identifica-
tion. The agencies of the crown, even the household, had social substance
in their own right, something not strictly derived from the King.

This inference is plausible: it is also conjectural. But it is a useful con-
jecture because it is consistent with the testimony of some of the poems
in which Chaucer names his addressees and thus specifies his audience,
inviting us to link the implied audience with the intended. Bukton and
Scogan were men whose standing and careers were like Chaucer's, and
the envoys to them, full of ironic raillery, read like exchanges between
equals. They give literary substance to the lateral allegiance I was just
suggesting. Henry Scogan was a squire in the king's household, and the
letter to him reads like just that, an ordinary letter.[5] It starts with the
weather, goes on to what Chaucer has heard about Scogan's personal life,
admonishes him, and anticipates his rebuttal that the admonition is just
another one of Chaucer's jokes. Then he says that he isn't writing com-
petitively any more and seems to conclude with a platitude. But that isn't

---

4. Richard Firth Green, *Poets and Princepleasers: Literature and the English Court in the Late Middle
   Ages* (Toronto: Univ. of Toronto Press, 1980), p. 12.
5. "Chaucer's *Envoy to Scogan*: The Uses of Literary Conventions," *ChauR*, 10 (1975), 46–61.

the end. He talks about his own situation, which is unhappy, forgotten and remote, and asks Scogan to remember him where it will do some good. That content could be contemporary, but what stamps it in its time and place is the pervasive reference to the conventions of love poetry, the pantheon and code of Love. The conceit gracefully shapes the content of the letter. It also reminds Scogan that he and Chaucer are friends, alike as literary men and civil servants—two styles of clerk. They are gentlemen. The letter to Bukton is similar. Old Grisel is rhyming and playing, joking about marriage, marshalling clichés and citing the Wife of Bath, perhaps against Bukton's impending marriage. The two poems, then, are joking exchanges between identifiable equals and serve in a sort of pitch pipe function for what I have been calling a "lateral" reading.

The poems addressed to Richard II and Henry IV, "Lak of Stedfastnesse" and "Purse," are far less likely texts for such a reading, and indeed I do not claim such testimony for them. Nevertheless, they bear interestingly on the question of Chaucer's audience because each has a lateral dimension. They are addressed to kings, and so there is no question that a social inferior is speaking to his social superior. Within that hierarchical pattern, however, the particular roles assumed and styles asserted are noteworthy. In "Steadfastness" the speaker's role is clearly defined. He is a moralist, an instructor of a prince. The purpose is straightforward edification; the prince should be just. What is not altogether straightforward about this traditional address is the somewhat paradoxical relation it creates between the moralist and the prince. On the one hand the moralist is, however discreetly, flattering the prince by attributing to him moral principles and a sense of responsibility. No matter how discreet, flattery of a prince subordinates the flatterer, but, paradoxically, the effectiveness of the flattery depends on the independence of the flatterer. The implicit proposition that the prince is moral is more credible if its proponent has his own authority for asserting it. The simple traditional authority would have been ecclesiastical. A chaplain or confessor could lecture a prince because he was in holy orders and the homily directly discharged his duty as a clerk. While any layman, basing his authority on probity and learning, might do the same, a poet's claim to learning would give him a special title as a sort of lay clerk, and experience in the household would make him aware of the realities of governmental administration and of values and attitudes in the community of administrators. His roles as poet and civil servant combine to give him some independent standing. That his independence could not have matched a churchman's does not mean that he had none. His institutional standing made him significant, at least collectively; his household experience made him sensitive to the attitudes and convictions of the prince and those around him; and the learning associated with the poet's craft dignified his treatment of these attitudes and convictions. A household poet could claim by virtue of his position an authority that entitled him to educate a prince. However fragile it may have been in the realities of political power, the speaker's role in "Steadfastness" assumes a subtle, ethical independence.

The second of these poems, "Purse," is more relaxed in tone, and my interest is more in the addressee's role than in the speaker's. Again the function of the poem is clear; it is a petition for relief, for money. As before, the speaker is clearly subordinate; he proclaims his dependence (and a specific allegiance, which was presumably necessary because of Henry's recent accession). The envoy is absolutely clear about the relative positions of the petitioner-speaker and his addressee. The poem itself, however, is something else again. In it Chaucer works the basic joke of addressing his purse as his lady and lamenting that she is light. The conceit invites the extravagance of praise and lament conventional in love poetry, and its ironic application to his personal finances implies some modest sophistication on the part of his addressee, who will see that lightness is as regrettable in a purse as in a lady. Irony depends on shared knowledge and attitudes, and it has a levelling effect, which is, of course, what I find important here. The deference of the envoy is balanced by the familiarity of the joke. Chaucer wanted money (presumably his pension) from the king. The envoy provides a clear statement of his petition and his petitioner's role, while the poem does a playful turn on two forms of lightness, asserting in the process a stylistic bond with the king. Both men, the king and the poet-civil servant, are amused by the same thing.

"Steadfastness" and "Purse" are petitions, one general and ethical and the other personal and financial. The references clearly identify the addressees/audiences, and the dramatic situations are hierarchical. Yet, when you consider the assumptions made about the kings, the full roles assigned to them—in short, when you treat the intended audience as an implied audience—then the hierarchical relation seems more complicated. The king is not only a ruler; he is also a gentleman, ethical, good natured, attuned to the forms and conventions of ordinary cultivation. This can hardly be surprising since kings like other men live in their cultures, but the role projected for Richard and Henry does have a levelling effect. The king is approved for being like lesser men; the poem enters him into their fellowship.

✳ ✳ ✳

What I have stressed here in the paper is of course an undertone. The slightest assertion of rank and power would render it inaudible. Yet it has a considerable force. It gives voice to aspirations plausible among the gentleman-clerks of the early civil service, and just as importantly it asserts an ideal sufficiently attractive to a prince as to invite some suspension of the claims of rank and power.

RICHARD FIRTH GREEN

Chaucer's Victimized Women†

When Arlyn Diamond writes of Chaucer that, "unwilling to abandon the values and hierarchies he inherits, unable to reconcile them with what he has observed of human emotion and social realities, he accepts uneasily the medieval view of women as either better or worse than men, but never

† From *Studies in the Age of Chaucer* 10 (1988): 3–21. Reprinted by permission of the author. The author's notes have been renumbered.

quite the same,"[1] she is employing a critical tool which Simone de Beauvoir's formulation of *l'altérité de la femme* first made widely available to feminists.[2] Diamond is being scrupulously fair here; no author, however enlightened, could have responded with more than a sense of unease to so fundamental a social equation ("Il est le Sujet, il est l'Absolu: elle est l'Autre"), before its implications had even begun to be articulated. But if this central equation has remained depressingly intact down the ages, the terms used to express it have varied over time, and one task for any reader of earlier literature who accepts the burden of historical responsibility must be to try to reformulate them in ways which minimize the inevitable anachronism of so quixotic a venture. In what follows I should like to explore one distinctive manifestation of such *altérité* among Chaucer's contemporaries, and by examining the way it is reflected in the treatment of a number of his female characters try to bring the sense of unease Diamond speaks of into sharper focus.

The particular group of Chaucerian heroines I wish to discuss is one which lay outside Diamond's brief and appears, at first glance, to offer unpromising material for sympathetic feminist analysis. It comprises Dido (in both *The House of Fame* and *The Legend of Good Women*), several of her fellow martyrs (Medea, Hypsipyle, Ariadne, and Phyllis), Anelida, and Canacee's Falcon—all, of course, cynically seduced and heartlessly betrayed, the innocent victims of masculine duplicity. Perhaps because, as Elizabeth Hardwick has suggested, we live in an age where the devaluation of innocence has made seduction an impossibility, we now find it difficult to approach this subject with any degree of seriousness: "The seducer at his work is essentially comic,"[3] and his victim, even when treated with sympathy, unappealing—her essential otherness magnified by masculine sentimentality. No doubt many modern readers will concur with R. W. Frank's view of *The Legend of Dido* as a curious combination of "an almost tragic Dido, [and] an almost comic Aeneas"[4] or prefer the bookish ironies of John Fyler's reading of her story to the melodramatic implications of taking it at face value.[5] In claiming that Chaucer treats seriously the plight of Dido and her fellow victims, I am, however, very far from suggesting that his primary interest is to exploit the pathos of their victimization—that he merely continues a tradition (at least as old as the *Heroides*) of sentimentalizing female defenselessness; what his treatment does reveal, I will argue, is that in one important respect his view of women is in marked contrast to the "values and hierarchies he inherits," at least from the French tradition.

Sexual morality in Chaucer, as D. S. Brewer has so clearly demonstrated, is inseparable from the concept of honor. While dishonor may await the knight who offends against "trouthe" by breaking his word to his lady,

1. Arlyn Diamond, "Chaucer's Women and Women's Chaucer," in Arlyn Diamond and Lee R. Edwards, eds., *The Authority of Experience: Essays in Feminist Criticism* (Amherst: University of Massachusetts Press, 1977), p. 82.
2. Simone de Beauvoir, *Le Deuxième sexe*, 2 vols. (Paris: Gallimard, 1949), 1:13–21.
3. Elizabeth Hardwick, *Seduction and Betrayal: Women and Literature* (New York: Random House, 1974), p. 208.
4. Robert Worth Frank, Jr., *Chaucer and* The Legend of Good Women (Cambridge, Mass.: Harvard University Press, 1972), p. 78.
5. John M. Fyler, *Chaucer and Ovid* (New Haven, Conn.: Yale University Press, 1979), pp. 110–13.

it cannot be said that it is *generally* accepted in Chaucer's poetry, any more than in the western tradition as a whole, that to debauch and destroy a woman is regarded as dishonourable. Honour here diverges from virtue and justice and of course from the teachings of Christianity, and perhaps the most that can be said is that Chaucer more nearly associates honour with virtue in this respect than do Continental writers.[6]

I am not sure, however, that this characterization of the gulf between Chaucer and his Continental contemporaries goes quite far enough, for I will argue that the relatively greater emphasis placed on virtue in the Chaucerian code of honor depended upon his far deeper respect for the fundamental quality of "trouthe" in sexual matters. So familiar is this ideal to readers of Chaucer and his English contemporaries that we should perhaps remind ourselves that it was by no means universally accepted. A few French instances may help illustrate the distinction.

The Knight of the Tower, writing (ca. 1373) for the edification of his daughters, cites the first Marshal Boucicault, one of the French heroes of the early part of the Hundred Years' War, as a contemporary instance of the dangers of conversing with smooth-tongued courtiers. Even if his story of a paragon of chivalry who felt himself under no obligation to extend his "trouthe" to include women is apocryphal, the attitude it exposes was apparently commonplace.[7] Boucicault, confronted by three ladies with their discovery that he has protested undivided devotion to each of them, is quite unrepentant:

> "How, my ladyes!" said Boussicault. "Knowe ye that I haue done ony deceyte or tromperye?"
>
> "Yes," said that one. "For ye haue desired my faire cosyns that ben here, & also so haue ye me, and ye haue sworen to eche of vs that ye louyd eche best aboue al creatures. This is a grete lesyng, & it is not trouthe, for ye be not worthy ne of valewe to haue thre; and therfore ye ben fals and deceyuable, and ye ought not to be putt in the nombre ne in th'acounte of good and trewe knyghtes."
>
> "Now, my ladyes, haue ye al said. Ye haue grete vnright & I shall tell yow wherfore. For at the tyme that I said so, to eche of yow I had thenne my plesaunce, and thought so at that tyme. And therfore ye doo wronge to holde me for a deceyuer."[8]

So shameless an admission of duplicity is rare after the middle of the fourteenth century (the historical Boucicault died in 1368), perhaps because it was felt to be in bad taste; with "increasing insincerity"[9] erotic fashion must henceforth pay tribute to the crowning virtue of loyalty.

In 1389 four French noblemen (one of them was Boucicault's son) sought distraction from the tedium of a long sea voyage as they returned from the Holy Land by composing a debate in verse on the respective advantages of loyalty and fickleness in love. The result, the *Cent ballades*,

---

6. D. S. Brewer, "Honour in Chaucer," *E&S*, n.s., 26 (1973):7.
7. The apocryphal nature of the story is suggested by the fact that a somewhat similar exchange occurs in an early fourteenth-century collection of *demandes d'amour*, Alexander Klein, *Die Altfranzösischen Minnefragen* (Marburg: Ebel, 1911), pp. 96–99.
8. *The Book of the Knight of the Tower*, trans. William Caxton, ed. M. Y. Offord, EETS, e.s., vol. 2 (London: Oxford University Press, 1971), p. 42 [my punctuation].
9. Raymond L. Kilgour, *The Decline of Chivalry* (Cambridge, Mass.: Harvard University Press, 1937), p. 128.

is of no great literary value, nor is its outcome, a unanimous verdict for loyalty, a matter of much surprise, but what is of interest for our present purpose is its appendix: the *Cent ballades* concludes with an invitation to "tous les amoureux" to contribute their own opinions on the subject,[1] and thirteen seem to have been moved to do so—not perhaps what Gallup might regard as a statistically significant sample, but revealing nonetheless. Seven of the respondents (3–6, 9, 11, and 12) come out strongly in favor of loyalty, but surprisingly enough there are three (1, 2, and 7) who support fickleness, and three don't-knows. In view of a complete absence of evidence in the English tradition for any contrary viewpoint, this handful of dissenters is all the more valuable. The supporters of fickleness, all members of the older generation, include no less a person than the king's uncle, the duc de Berri, who writes that one should have not just one mistress but three or four pair of them, and that to all "on peut l'un dire, et l'autre doit on faire" ("you may say one thing, but you should do the opposite"; 7.27–30.) The don't-knows comprise one who cannot say (8), one who will not say (10), and one who cynically suggests that whatever lovers say is just so much empty rhetoric: "Ainsi dist on, mais il n'en sera riens" ("That's what they say, but nothing will come of it"; 13.28).

To see whether such cynicism was justified, let us look for a moment at one of the *Cent ballades'* defenders of loyalty in love, the king's brother, the duc de Touraine. One could scarcely ask for a clearer instance of amatory hypocrisy. About the time the duke was writing, "Il est bien vray que j'ay servy / De cuer, de corps tresloiaument / Une dame que j'ayme sy" ("It is quite true that I have most loyally served with heart and body one lady, whom I love so much"; 3.1–3), he was involved in a notorious court scandal, his wife, Valentina Visconti, having discovered that he had tried to bribe a young Parisian girl with the enormous sum of a thousand gold crowns to get her to go to bed with him. Froissart, who tells the story, seems quite complacent about the duke's sexual adventures: "[Il] estoit jeune et amoureux, et voulentiers veoit dames et damoiselles et se jouoit et esbatoit entre elles" ("[He] was an amorous youth, who much enjoyed the sight of ladies and young women and happily entertained himself among them").[2] A chorus of witnesses suggests that this entertainment did not lessen as he grew older: "Il n'y estoit si grande que il ne volsist dechevoir" ("There was no lady, however great, whom he did not seek to betray"), says one;[3] another calls him "nimis in carnalibus lubricus" ("overeager for the pleasures of the flesh");[4] yet a third, less complimentary, remarks, "Ad omnem ferme speciosam mulierem, velud equus aliquis emissarius, adhiniebat" ("[He] would whinny like a studhorse after just about any attractive woman").[5]

One of this duke's *chambellans*, the poet Jean de Garencières, may well have been thinking of his master when he wrote of the way love was commonly regarded among the aristocracy: "N'il ne leur chault s'ilz sont amez

1. *Les Cent Ballades: poème du XIVe siècle*, ed. Gaston Raynaud, SATF (Paris: Firmin-Didot, 1905), p. 199.
2. Jean Froissart, *Oeuvres*, ed. Kervyn de Lettenhove, 25 vols. (Brussels: Devaux, 1867–77), 14:318.
3. *Chronique anonyme du règne de Charles VI*, in *La Chronique d'Enguerran de Monstrelet*, vol. 6, ed. L. Douët-d'Arcq, SHF (Paris: Renouard, 1862), p. 196.
4. Nicolas de Baye, *Journal, 1400–1417*, ed. A. Tuetey, 2 vols., SHF (Paris: Renouard, 1888), 2:294.
5. Thomas Basin, *Histoire de Charles VII*, ed. Charles Samaran, 2 vols. (Paris: Belles Lettres, 1933), 1:13. Further contemporary evidence of the duke's lubricity is to be found in Émile Collas, *Valentine de Milan, Duchesse d'Orléans* (Paris: Plon, 1911), pp. 297–302.

ou non, / Mais qu'on die qu'ilz soient bien des belles" ("They don't care
whether they're loved or not, as long as they're thought good with
women").[6] At any rate, the amours of the duke's son did not escape Gar-
encières's attention: he calls him *Le Prince de Bien Mentir*, "un enfant
malicieux, / Ou nul ne doit avoir fiance, / Car il en a ja plus de deux /
Deceues, ou païs de France" ("a wicked boy whom no one can trust for he
has already betrayed more than two [women] in this land of France"; p. 52,
lines 11–14); far from offending the young man (who was about twenty
when they were written), these lines seem to have flattered his vanity, for
many years later he copied them into his own manuscript. After seeing
how the libertine father could advertise himself a loyal servant of love at
the end of the *Cent ballades*, we should not be surprised to learn the iden-
tity of the son: he was none other than that master of courtly decorum
and refined erotic sensibility, the poet-prisoner Charles d'Orléans.

By 1400 the cynical attitude toward women I have been attempting to
characterize already had a long literary history in France.[7] Whether one
believes that Jean de Meun had consciously helped foster it will depend
on how much sympathy one has for Christine de Pizan's view of the second
part of the *Roman de la Rose* as "dottrine plaine de decevance, voye de
dampnacion" ("a lesson filled with deceit, a pathyway to hell").[8] Whatever
justice there may be in John Fleming's reading of its hero as a benighted
sensualist who "rejects Reason and embraces false courtesy, hypocrisy, and
wicked counsel in order to achieve the sordid 'heroism' of a seduction,"[9]
there can be little doubt that Christine was not alone among later medieval
readers in her failure to appreciate that "the *Roman de la Rose* is ironic,"
or in her readiness to trace its pedigree back to Ovid rather than Augus-
tine.[1] In many ways Christine de Pizan's remarkable attack upon Jean de
Meun in the debate over the *Roman de la Rose* was a reaction to the studied
hypocrisy of men like the duc de Touraine, whom she saw as de Meun's
disciples;[2] it was a reaction, I would argue, that Chaucer anticipated,
though his distaste for this particular brand of erotic duplicity—which
Gower significantly regarded as one of the "peccata Gallica" ("French
sins")—took a somewhat different form.[3]

No doubt there was, as Gower implies, a certain difference in national
attitudes here, and Chaucer's position was not wholly idiosyncratic. As

6. Jean de Garencières, *Les Poésies complètes de Jean de Garencières*, ed. Y. A. Neal (Paris: Université
   de Paris, 1952–3), p. 70 (lines 143–44). Cf. the sixth and seventh companies in *The House of
   Fame*, whose members are concerned with their reputation for being great lovers: "Lat us to the
   peple seme / Suche as the world may of us deme / That wommen loven us for wod" (lines 1745–47);
   Geoffrey Chaucer, *The Riverside Chaucer*, ed. Larry D. Benson et al., 3d ed. (Boston: Houghton
   Mifflin, 1987), p. 368.
7. Philippe Ménard, *Le Rire et le sourire dans la roman courtois en France au Moyen Âge* (Geneva:
   Droz, 1969), pp. 228–34.
8. Christine de Pizan et al., *Le Débat sur le Roman de la Rose*, ed. Eric Hicks (Paris: Champion,
   1977), p. 26.
9. John V. Fleming, *The Roman de la Rose: A Study in Allegory and Iconography* (Princeton, N.J.:
   Princeton University Press, 1969), p. 50.
1. Fleming's casual dismissal of the thorough survey of fourteenth-century attitudes toward the
   Roman in Pierre-Yves Badel, *Le Roman de la Rose au XIVe siécle* (Geneva: Droz, 1980), does the
   book less than justice; John V. Fleming, *Reason and the Lover* (Princeton, N.J.: Princeton Uni-
   versity Press, 1984), p. 139.
2. Christine's actual opinion of the duke himself, of course, is quite another matter. He was, after
   all, a powerful man whose displeasure she could ill afford to provoke, and she seems in fact to
   have tried unsuccessfully to secure his patronage; Charity Cannon Willard, *Christine de Pizan:
   Her Life and Works* (New York: Persea, 1984), p. 169.
3. John Gower, *Vox clamantis*, in *The Complete Works of John Gower: The Latin Works*, ed. G. C.
   Macaulay (Oxford: Clarendon Press, 1902), 7:157.

early as *The Owl and the Nightingale* we can find expressions of sympathy for betrayed women (1433–48),[4] and one of the Harley lyrics deplores the fact that their faith in lovers' promises was often misplaced (12.19–24):

> Lut in londe are to leue,
> þah me hem trewe trouþe ʒeue,
> for tricherie to ʒere;
> when trichour haþ is trouþe yplyght,
> byswyken he haþ þat suete wyht,
> þah he hire oþes swere.[5]

Such expressions of moral indignation often appear more marked in English secular verse than in French; in *Ywain and Gawain*, for example, the English translator expands Chrétien de Troyes's disparagement of those who falsely claim to be lovers into a pointed diatribe against masculine faithlessness (lines 33–40):

> þai tald of more trewth þam bitw[e]ne
> þan now omang men here es sene,
> For trowth and luf es al bylaft;
> Men uses now anoþer craft.
> With worde men makes it trew and stabil,
> Bot in þaire faith es noght bot fabil;
> With þe mowth men makes it hale,
> Bot trew trowth es nane in þe tale.[6]

We might expect Chaucer with his wider horizons to treat this native tradition somewhat lightly, yet I hope to show that he shares Gower's distaste for the cynicism of prevailing French court fashion, exceeding even the most critical of his Continental contemporaries in his uncompromising attitude toward erotic duplicity: as Douglas Kelly says, "Only in Chaucer and Gower do we perceive any serious questioning of courtly love as such in a context like Jean de Meun's."[7] In this regard Chaucer's influence might, indeed, be claimed to have contributed much to the quite distinct character of the later English courtly tradition. Over a hundred years after his death, as Marguerite de Navarre's story of an ostentatiously faithful "millort" proves, for a lover to "vivre à l'angloise" meant paying over-scrupulous attention to female honor.[8]

To gauge the gap between Chaucer and Jean de Meun on this issue, let us look at the French poet's treatment of the most celebrated of all the abandoned heroines of antiquity, Dido. That Chaucer knew the account of Dido in the *Roman de la Rose* is obvious: hers is the first in a sequence

---

4. *The Owl and the Nightingale*, ed. E. G. Stanley (London: Nelson, 1960), pp. 90–91.
5. *The Harley Lyrics: The Middle English Lyrics of MS. Harley 2253*, ed. G. L. Brook, 3d ed. (Manchester: Manchester University Press, 1964), p. 45; cf. the trusting lady in the pastorelle "The Meeting in the Wood": "Betre is make forwardes faste / þen afterward to mene ant mynne" (8.19–20).
6. *Ywain and Gawain*, ed. A. B. Friedman and N. T. Harrington, EETS, vol. 254 (London: Oxford University Press, 1964), p. 2. Cf. lines 24–28: "Ore est amors tornee a fable / Por ce que cil, que rien n'an santent, / Dïent qu'il aimment, mes il mantent, / Et cil fable et mançonge an font, / Qui s'an vantent et droit n'ont"; Chrétien de Troyes, *Yvain*, ed. T. B. W. Reid (Manchester: Manchester University Press, 1942), p. 1.
7. Douglas Kelly, *Medieval Imagination: Rhetoric and the Poetry of Courtly Love* (Madison: University of Wisconsin Press, 1978), p. 178.
8. Marguerite de Navarre, *L'Heptaméron*, ed. Michel François (Paris: Garnier, 1967), pp. 353–56. It is to be noted that Parlamente, who tells the story, seems less willing than her male listeners to ridicule this attitude.

of stories of betrayed heroines (they include Phyllis, Oenone, and Medea) which may well have influenced his choice of images for the temple in *The House of Fame* and of Cupid's martyrs for *The Legend of Good Women*. However, in de Meun's treatment of Dido the coloring imparted by the narrator's persona is far more prominent; his heroine, no less than Chaucer's, is betrayed by a calculating perjurer, but we learn her story from the point of view of a woman, La Vieille, who is herself a faithless player in the game of love and who regards her heroine as more dupe than victim (lines 13187–94):

> Et cis [si] l'en asseüra
> Et li promist et li jura
> Siens seroit toutz jors et sera
> Ne jamés ne la lessera;
> Mes cele gaires n'en joÿ,
> Car li traïtres s'en foÿ,
> Sanz congié, par mer, a navie.
> Dont la bele perdi la vie.

[And so he reassured her and promised and swore to her that he was and ever would be hers and that never would he leave her; but she didn't have much joy of it, for the traitor decamped without leave over the sea by ship, through which the fair one lost her life.][9]

If the dismissive tone of these lines were not alone sufficient to alert us to their cynicism, their context would make it unmistakable. In a passage heavily indebted to Ovid's *Ars amatoria*, La Vieille prefaces her story with a discussion of the insubstantiality of lovers' vows, "Jupiter et li dieu rioient / Quant li amant se parjuroient" ("Jupiter and the gods laugh when lovers perjure themselves"; lines 13127–28), and the folly of placing any faith in them, "Mes mout est fox, se Diex m'ament, / Qui por jurer croist nul amant" ("God love me, anyone who believes in a lover's oath is quite crazy!" lines 13139–40). The moral with which La Vieille ends her story is echoed, interestingly enough, by the due de Berri in his cynical contribution to the *Cent ballades*—a contribution which Chaucer may well have known;[1] she concludes that the woman "les doit l'en aussi trichier, / Non pas son cuer a un fichier" ("ought to deceive them too and not fix her heart in one place"; lines 13267–68). This is itself a variation on Reason's earlier advice to the Lover (advice which was to infuriate Christine de Pizan), "car il vient miex adés, biau mestre, / Decevoir que deceüs estre" ("for it's far better, fair sir, to deceive than be deceived"; lines 4399–400), and also a witty reversal of Ovid's exhortation to male seducers, "Fallite fallentes" ("Deceive the deceivers!" line 645).[2]

Jean de Meun is very close to Ovid in this scene, but Chaucer, who in

---

9. Guillaume de Lorris and Jean de Meun, *Le Roman de la Rose*, ed. Daniel Poirion (Paris: Garnier-Flammarion, 1974), p. 362.

1. W. L. Renwick, "Chaucer's Triple Roundel, 'Merciles Beaute,' " *MLR* 16 (1921): 322–23.

2. Ovid, *Ars amatoria* ed. E. J. Kenney (Oxford: Clarendon Press, 1961), p. 137. In this vein the twelfth-century romance *Eneas* seeks to explain away the embarrassment of Aeneas's perfidious desertion by making it appear just punishment for Dido's own infidelity to the memory of her dead husband, Sychaeus (cf. *Aeneid* 4.552): "Por coi tresspassai ge la foi / que ge plevi a mon seignor? / Ja me venqui ansi amor?" ("Why did I break the faith I plighted to my lord? Love has destroyed me for it"); *Eneas: Roman du XIIe siècle*, ed. J.-J. Salverda de Grave, 2 vols. CFMA (Paris: Champion, 1925–29), lines 1988–90.

other respects owes so much to these two poets, cannot bring himself to accept such an art of love without reservation. While Chaucer's Dido is certainly Ovidian in the sense that his accounts echo what Fyler calls Ovid's "Alexandrian inversion of heroic pretense" (p. 33) by seeing Aeneas's flight from Carthage through the queen's eyes and by suppressing almost entirely the obligation to keep faith with a higher destiny which mitigates the perfidy of Virgil's hero, his portraits are nevertheless only partly affected by the elegant sentimentality of the *Heroides* and not at all by its complimentary pose, the casual cynicism of the *Ars amatoria*. Indeed, except when he is portraying himself as an amatory outsider, Chaucer almost always uses the word "craft" (his normal equivalent of Latin *ars*) pejoratively when he is writing of love.[3] It is difficult not to believe that he is thinking of the *Ars amatoria* when he writes with evident distaste of Aeneas's "craft" (*LGW* 1285–87):

> This Eneas, that hath so depe yswore,
> Is wery of his craft withinne a throwe;
> The hote ernest is al overblowe.

This impression is even stronger with his description of the doubly false Jason, who "coulde of love al craft and art pleyner / Withoute bok, with everych observaunce" (*LGW* 1607–1608), or in these lines on Arcite: "But he was fals; hit nas but feyned chere,— / As nedeth not to men such craft to lere" (*Anel* 97–98). We should not be surprised, then, to find Diomede, who "koude more than the crede / In swich a craft" (*TC* 5.89–90), recalling a lesson from the *Ars amatoria* as he prepares his approach to Criseyde.[4]

The argument that what disturbed Chaucer about Ovid and Jean de Meun (not to mention some of his Continental contemporaries) was their cavalier attitude to "trouthe," lays one open, of course, to the charge of misreading his irony. Fyler, whose emphasis on the spiritual kinship of Chaucer and Ovid cannot in general be faulted, seeks to explain the way *The Legend of Good Women* distorts and omits details from the *Heroides*, not as symptomatic of Chaucer's uneasiness about some of the implications of his source but as an ironic manipulation of literary allusion intended to amuse those who knew their classics. But though he can treat serious subjects playfully—consider, for example, that knowing little aside at the end of *The Legend of Phyllis*: "and trusteth, as in love, no man but me" (*LGW* 2561)—Chaucer nowhere shows unequivocal approval for this particular aspect of Ovidianism.[5] There is, of course, nothing new in the suggestion that Chaucer's treatment of abandoned heroines contains a strain of moral earnestness: Clemen writes of the Dido episode in *The House of Fame*, "Chaucer has a light touch and knows how to entertain and amuse; but that does not mean that there is not any graver intention present beneath the surface."[6] Nor, of course, has the prominence given

---

3. A good example of such pejorative use is *PF*, 220–22: ". . . the Craft that can and hath the myght / To don by force a wyght to don folye— / Disfigurat was she, I nyl nat lye"; on these lines see J. A. W. Bennett, *The Parlement of Foules* (Oxford: Clarendon Press, 1957), p. 88. Cf. John Gower, *Confessio amantis*, in *The English Works of John Gower*, ed. G. C. Macaulay, EETs, e.s., vols. 81–82 (Oxford: Clarendon Press, 1990–1901), 4:916–78.

4. See the note on *TC* 5.790–91 (*Riverside Chaucer*, ed. Benson, p. 1052).

5. On the problem of ironic readings of Chaucer in general, see Derek Pearsall, "Epidemic Irony in Modern Approaches to the *Canterbury Tales*," in Piero Boitani and Anna Torti, eds., *Medieval and Pseudo-Medieval Literature* (Tübingen: Narr, 1984), pp. 79–89.

6. Wolfgang Clemen, *Chaucer's Early Poetry*, trans. C. A. M. Sym (1963; London: Methuen, 1968), p. 87.

to *trouthe* either here or in Chaucer's work in general escaped attention: Clemen himself argues that "['trouthe'] occupies a high place in his hierarchy of values," and George Kane would put it even more strongly: the imperfect realization of "the idea of the wholeness of excellence, with truth as its central principle . . . [became] the principal formative concern of Chaucer's mature writing."[7] The implications of the way Chaucer handles the idea in this particular context, however, have yet to be fully explored.

We are concerned here with the legacy of the word "trouthe" in one of its earliest senses: the quality of standing by one's given word. It is difficult for us, as members of a literate society, to appreciate the importance accorded to such *aðwyrðe* in a world where written evidence could not be depended on; our ancestors, however, had no doubts about its primacy.[8] The very first of King Alfred's laws reads, "We læreð þæt mæst ðearfe is, þæt æghwelc mon his að 7 his wed wærlice healde" ("We direct what is most necessary, that each man keep carefully his oath and his pledge"),[9] and as Alfred's grandson Athelstan, in banishing a group of malefactors for breaking their oaths, explains, "We nytan nanum oþrum þingum to getruwianne, butan hit ðis sy" ("We know of no other things to trust in unless it be this").[1] The Bayeux tapestry graphically illustrates how Harold's failure to keep his oath to William cost him the Battle of Hastings,[2] and the *Peterborough Chronicle* attributes the anarchy of Stephen's reign to the perjury of his vassals: "Hi hadden him manred maked and athes suoren, ac hi nan treuthe ne heolden. Alle he wæron forsworen and here treothes forloren."[3] If Chaucer's world seems far closer to that lost age than to that of his French contemporaries, it is perhaps because English customary law had preserved its oral legacy far more tenaciously than the civil law of the Continent, but at all event "trouthe" for Chaucer, as for the *Gawain* poet, retains something of the primitive force it had for Alfred and Athelstan—the prime moral obligation of civilized society.

The simple demonstration that elsewhere Chaucer shows an unequivocal horror of "untrouthe" will not, in itself, be enough for us to argue that he finds the kind of perjury committed by Aeneas and his fellows impossible to excuse. A double standard in these matters was not unknown. Though the duc de Touraine apparently thought nothing of betraying women at the highest levels of society, the treachery of Richard II's deposition filled him with such righteous indignation that he challenged Henry IV to trial by battle; his own good faith, of course, he knew to be above suspicion: "Quant a moy je me sens sans reprouche, la Dieu-mercy, et ay tousjours fait ce que loial preudomme doit faire envers Dieu, comme envers monseigneur et son royaume" ("For myself, I feel I am blameless, thank god, and I have always done what a true man of honor ought to do

7. George Kane, *The Liberating Truth: The Concept of Integrity in Chaucer's Writings*, 1979 John Coffin Memorial Lecture (London: Athlone Press, 1980), p. 12.
8. See M. T. Clanchy, *From Memory to Written Record* (Cambridge, Mass.: Harvard University Press, 1979).
9. Dorothy Whitelock et al., eds., *Councils and Synods with Other Documents Relating to the English Church, 871–1204*, 2 vols. (Oxford: Clarendon Press, 1981), 1:21.
1. Felix Liebermann, ed., *Die Gesetze der Angelsachsen*, 3 vols. (Halle: Niemeyer, 1903), 1:166.
2. This point is still being made in the early fifteenth century; see *Dives and Pauper*, ed. Priscilla Barnum, 2 vols., EETS, vols. 275, 280 (London: Oxford University Press, 1976–80), 1:257.
3. J. A. W. Bennett and G. V. Smithers, eds., *Early Middle English Verse and Prose* (Oxford: Clarendon Press, 1966), p. 207.

before God, as before my sovereign and his realm").[4] Even Clemen sees no reason to suppose that Chaucer took the fashionable controversy about loyalty in love seriously (p. 86), and only a closer look at the terms in which the fate of Dido and the other heroines is described will show how gravely Chaucer regards their betrayal.

In the first place, he goes out of his way to emphasise that the perfidious lovers swear quite specific oaths of fidelity to their ladies. The troth plighting of Jason and Medea is the most elaborately described (*LGW* 1635– 44):

> They been acorded ful bytwixe hem two
> That Jason shal hire wedde, as trewe knyght;
> And terme set, to come sone at nyght
> Unto hire chamber and make there his oth
> Upon the goddes, that he for lef or loth
> Ne sholde nevere hire false, nyght ne day,
> To ben hire husbonde whil he lyve may,
> As she that from his deth hym saved here.
> And hereupon at nyght they mette in-feere,
> And doth his oth, and goth with hire to bedde.

It can, however, be paralleled in other cases: Theseus's oath to Ariadne is given verbatim in the *Legend* (lines 2119–22) and reported in *The House of Fame* (lines 421–24); both poems make it clear that Demophon is forsworn when he deserts Phyllis (*LGW* 2455 and *HF*389), though only the *Legend* specifies the terms of his oath (lines 2465–66); Canacee's falcon grants the tercelet her love "upon his othes and his seuretee" (*SqT* 528), and so on. Aeneas, who "swore so depe to hire to be trewe / For wel or wo, and chaunge hire for no newe" (*LGW* 1234–35), is no exception to this list of oath breakers. Lest we be in any doubt about the seriousness of such oaths, we should recall that fourteenth-century canon lawyers would probably have seen them as quite sufficient to constitute legal matrimony even without ecclesiastical blessing; certainly, a medieval Medea could legitimately have felt that Jason's *verba de futuro* followed by physical consummation made her his wife, and the canonists would probably have interpreted Theseus's swearing "now have I yow . . . of Athenes duchesse" (*LGW* 2121–22) as the *verba de presenti* which were all that would have been needed to bind him to Ariadne.[5] In fact, it seems clear that all the heroines we are considering might properly have regarded themselves as married to the men who betray them.[6]

A further indication of the underlying seriousness with which Chaucer treats these heroines is his readiness to call their betrayers "traitors"—a heavily loaded term in the feudal vocabulary. Even Fame, for all her boasted fickleness, cannot bring herself to smile on those who have "ydoon

---

4. *La Chronique d'Enguerran de Monstrelet*, ed. L. Douët-d'Arcq. SHF (Paris: Renouard, 1857), 1: 56.
5. R. H. Helmholz, *Marriage Litigation in Medieval England* (Cambridge: Cambridge University Press, 1974), pp. 25–73.
6. For Dido, Hypsipyle, Medea, and Ariadne as "wives," see *LGW* 1238, 1577, 1660, 2171, and *HF* 424; and for Dido, Hypsipyle, Medea, and Phyllis as "wedded," see *HF* 244, *LGW* 1559, 1636, 2466, 2473; Anelida's case is less clear, though her heart is said to be "wedded" to Arcite "with a ring" (*Anel* 131). See also Henry Ansgar Kelly, *Love and Marriage in the Age of Chaucer* (Ithaca, N.Y.: Cornell University Press, 1975), pp. 202–16.

the trayterye" (*HF* 1811–22). Clearly, to break one's oath to another man was to lay oneself open to the charge of treason (*KnT* 1129–32):

> "It nere," quod he, "to thee no greet honour
> For to be fals, ne for to be traitour
> To me, that am thy cosyn and thy brother
> Ysworn ful depe, and ech of us til oother";

but whether all Chaucer's contemporaries would have felt equally happy about applying the term to those who broke their word to women is far less clear. Chaucer's use, however, is unequivocal. In both Virgil and Ovid, Aeneas is described as *perfidus*, though only by Dido, and in the *Roman de la Rose* the force of the epithet *traïres* is somewhat weakened by the fact that it is La Vieille who uses it; in Chaucer there is no such mediation (*HF* 265–67):

> Allas! what harm doth apparence,
> Whan hit is fals in existence!
> For he to hir a traytour was;

and (*LGW* 1326–28),

> For on a nyght, slepynge, he let hire lye,
> And stal awey unto his companye,
> And as a traytour forth he gan to sayle.

The epithet is also applied to Jason—"as evere in love a chef traytour he was" (*LGW* 1659)—and to Theseus (*LGW* 2174); others, moreover, suffer the imputation of treason: "This fals Arcite, sumwhat moste he feyne, / When he wex fals, to covere his traitorie" (*Anel* 155–56).

If the full force of such an imputation is easily missed by the modern reader, it would not have escaped a contemporary. Christine de Pizan, incensed by the cynical advice of Reason in the *Roman de la Rose* that it is better to deceive than to be deceived, demands of Jean de Meun's defender Pierre Col: "Quel differance mettras tu entre Traïson et Decevance? Je n'y en say point, mais que l'ung sonne pis que l'autre" ("What distinction can you make between treason and deception? I know of none, except that one sounds worse than the other"; *Débat* 128),[7] and a little later, after drily reminding him of Reason's notorious taste for plain language, she dissects this particular euphemism: "La condition du deseveur est: menteur, parjure, faulz samblant, flateur, traitre" ("The nature of the 'deceiver' is that of a liar, perjurer, hypocrite, flatterer, traitor"; p. 130). A hundred years later we can still find Castiglione's courtiers quibbling over just this distinction as Bernardo argues that Gasparo's use of the term *burla* ("trick") to apply to the seducer's stratagems is really a euphemism for *tradimento* ("treason").[8]

In the English tradition, and arguably under Chaucer's influence, the term "treason" is regularly and deliberately applied to the falsehood of lovers. Thus Chaucer's use of the word seems to have made an impression

---

7. A similar distinction is drawn by Chaucer's contemporary Honoré Bonet (or Bouvet), though the context here is a discussion of military tactics: "Ce que les droits apellent traison on le nomme presentement subtilté et cautele" ("What the laws call treason is nowadays called cleverness and trickery"); Honoré Bonet, *L'Arbre des batailles*, ed. Ernest Nys (Brussels: Muquardt, 1883), p. 213.

8. "Queste burle, che forse più tosto tradimenti che burle chiamar si poriano" ("These 'tricks,' which perhaps might sooner be called 'treasons' than 'tricks' "; 2.94); Baldassar Castiglione, *Il Libro del Cortegiano*, ed. A. Quondam (Milan: Garzanti, 1981), p. 250.

on Thomas Usk, who writes of hypocritical seducers, in a passage that is heavily indebted to the Dido story in the *House of Fame*:

> Anon as filled is your lust, many of you be so trewe, that litel hede take ye of suche kyndnesse; but with traysoun anon ye thinke hem bigyle. . . . Whan a woman is closed in your nette, than wol ye causes fynden, and bere unkyndenesse her on hande, or falsetè upon her putte, your owne malicious trayson with such thinge to excuse.[9]

This usage may well have struck Chaucer's pupil Thomas Hoccleve too, for in his translation of Christine de Pizan's *Epistre de Cupide* he writes of "the traitour Eneas" (line 309) at a point where his original gives him no warrant for the epithet—that he was thinking of *The Legend of Good Women* here is strongly suggested by his allusion to "our legende of martirs" in the next stanza.[1] Perhaps the most striking evidence for the independence of this Chaucerian tradition, however, comes from the B fragment of the translation of the *Roman de la Rose* (lines 4833–42):

> They falsen ladies traitoursly,
> And swern hem othes utterly.
>
> . . . .
>
> Wymmen, the harm they bien full sore;
> But men this thenken evermore,
> That lasse harm is, so mote I the,
> Deceyve them than deceyved be.

Not only does the Chaucerian translator introduce the adverb "traitoursly" without any warrant from his original, he waters down the troublesome passage which follows by substituting "lasse harm" for *miex* and representing it not as the cynical advice (ironic or otherwise) of Reason herself but as the disreputable rationalization of libertines.

The characterization of Chaucer as "all womanis frend" by Gavin Douglas (in the prologue to the first book of his translation of the *Aeneid*) has been cited by Arlyn Diamond and others to prove that his sympathy for the sufferings of women was remarkable enough to excite comment in one of his followers. A glance at Douglas's remark in context, however, will show that it implies far more than simply indulgent amusement at Chaucer's unusual tenderheartedness. What really disturbed the Scots bishop was Chaucer's accusing Aeneas of perjury and in particular his calling him "traytour" (1.410–49):

> My mastir Chauser gretly Virgill offendit.
> All thoch I be tobald hym to repreif,
> He was fer baldar, certis, by hys leif,
> Sayand he followit Virgillis lantern toforn,
> Quhou Eneas to Dydo was forsworn.
> Was he forsworn? Than Eneas was fals—
> That he admittis and callys hym traytour als.
> Thus wenyng allane Ene to haue reprevit,
> He hass gretly the prynce of poetis grevit,

---

9. Thomas Usk, *The Testament of Love*, in W. W. Skeat, ed., *Chaucerian and Other Pieces* (London: Oxford University Press, 1897), pp. 54–55.
1. Thomas Hoccleve, *Lepistre de Cupide*, in *Hoccleve's Works: the Minor Poems*, ed. F. J. Furnivall and I. Gollancz, rev. J. Mitchell and A. I. Doyle, EETS, e.s., vols. 61, 73 (reprinted in 1 vol.; London: Oxford University Press, 1970), p. 303 (cf. also lines 57–63).

. . . .
But sikkyrly of resson me behufis
Excuss Chauser fra all maner repruffis;
In lovyng of thir ladeis lylly quhite
He set on Virgill and Eneas this wyte,
For he was evir (God wait) all womanis frend.[2]

One early reader of this passage was quite clear about what was at issue: in the margin of the Trinity College Cambridge manuscript of the poem someone has written beside Douglas's main defense of Virgil (the standard one, that Aeneas was only acting on orders from above), "This argument excusis nocht the tratory of Eneas na his maysweryng . . . He falit than gretly to the sueit Dydo"; and where Douglas goes on to claim that "Ene maid nevir aith," the same reader adds pointedly, "Heir he argouis better than befoir."

If Chaucer really deserves to be called "all womanis frend," it is clearly not for any mere sentimentalization of defenseless womanhood; still less is it for his "lovyng of thir ladeis lylly quhite" (praising lily-white ladies was a skill he shared with the duc de Touraine). It is for his recognition of the double standard by which the sworn word between man and man might be regarded as absolutely binding, whereas in affairs of the heart it became merely an expedient device to gain one's end. This double standard is at least as old as Ovid—"Ludite, si sapitis, solas impune puellas" ("If you are wise, deceive only women with impunity"; *Ars* 1.643)—and there can be no doubt that it is founded upon the presumption of female *altérité*. Women can be denied access to the code of honor which binds together civilized society because they are not regarded as members of that society. Such a denial of women's essential humanity finds telling expression in one of Ovid's favorite metaphors, that of love as a hunt and woman as prey—a metaphor which, as Marcelle Thiébaux has shown, the Middle Ages were to exploit over and over again.[3]

Christine de Pizan at least is under no illusions about Ovid's fundamental antifeminism, for when she sets out to prepare, with Reason's help, the *champ des escriptures* on which her *Cité des dames* is to be built, he is the first obstacle to be cleared away.[4] Earlier, the debate over *Roman de la Rose* had moved her, in a passage whose impassioned rhetoric rings down the centuries, to castigate the *Ars amatoria* for dehumanizing womankind (*Débat* 138–39):

> Ha! livre mal nommé L'Art d'amours! Car d'amours n'est il mie! mais art de faulse malicieuse industrie de decevoir fanmes puet il bien estre appellés. C'est belle doctrine! Est ce dont tout gaaingnié que de bien decevoir ces fames? Qui sont fames? Qui sont elles? Sont ce serpens, loups, lyons, dragons, guievres ou bestes ravissables devourans et ennemies a nature humainne, qu'il conviengne fere art a les decevoir et prandre? Lisez donc l'Art: aprenés a fere engins! Prenés les fort! Decevés les! Vituperés les! Assallés ce chastel! Gardés que nulles n'eschappent entre vous, hommes, et que tout soit livré a honte!

---

2. Gavin Douglas, *Virgil's* Aeneid, *Translated into Scottish Verse*, ed. D. F. C. Caldwell, STS, 4 vols. (Edinburgh: Blackwood, 1957–64), 2:14–16.
3. Marcelle Thiébaux, *The Stag of Love* (Ithaca, N.Y.: Cornell University Press, 1974).
4. Christine de Pizan, "The *Livre de la cité des dames* of Christine de Pisan: A Critical Edition," ed. M. C. Curnow (Ph.D. diss., Vanderbilt University, 1975; Ann Arbor: UMI, 76–96), pp. 647–48.

Et par Dieu, si sont elles vos meres, vos suers, vos filles, vos fammes et vos amies; elles sont vous mesmes et vous mesmes elles. Or les decevés assés, car "il vaut trop mieulx, biau maistre," etc.

[Huh! the *Art of Love*—what a poor title! It isn't about love at all! It might better have been called the art of nasty tricks for deceiving women. What a fine lesson! Is it then such a great prize to deceive these women? Who are women? Who are they? Are they serpents, wolves, lions, dragons, vipers, or ravening, devouring beasts, enemies to the human race, that it should be necessary to have an art to deceive and capture them? Read then this art! Learn to make traps! Hold them close! Deceive them! Abuse them! Assault the fortress! Take care, oh men, that none of them escape you, and that all are delivered over to shame! And yet, by God, they are your mothers, your sisters, your daughters, your wives, and your friends. They are yourselves, and you are them. Now go and deceive them, for "it is much better, fine sir (to deceive than be deceived)."]

She returns to this theme in a quieter vein when she introduces the story of Dido in her *Cité des dames* (p. 928):

Et n'est mie doubte que les femmes sont aussi bien ou nombre du pueple de Dieu et de creature humaine que sont les hommes, et non mie une autre espece ne de dessemblable generacion par quoy elles doyent estre forcloses des enseignemens motaux.

[There is not the slightest doubt that women are as much to be numbered among God's people and the human race as are men; they are certainly not some other species, nor a separate breed which should be denied access to civilized instruction.]

If Chaucer can hardly be expected to match Christine's acuity in recognizing that at the root of the problem lay the dehumanization of women, I have tried to suggest that he would at least have understood her attitude toward the *Ars amatoria*, for he too was disturbed by the way it had fostered the hypocritical assumption that lovers' vows alone need not conform to the universal convention of the inviolability of oaths—in other words, by the masculine conspiracy to exclude women from the social contract woven into the very fabric of feudalism.[5] This aspect of Chaucer's work will, I believe, bear further investigation, though when Donald Howard writes, "We may find that women's studies will help us understand something about Chaucer as yet ignored, his unusual interest in and empathy with women, especially victimized women,"[6] he seems to me to direct attention to just that aspect of it which, I fear, feminists will find least congenial: the late-medieval cult of womanly "pitee" which Chaucer certainly helped promulgate. Like a comparable cult exploited by Samuel Richardson, however, its benefits were illusory; in Terry Eagleton's words, "The 'exaltation' of women, while undoubtedly a partial advance in itself, also serves to shore up the very system which oppresses them."[7] Sharing

5. Working from the opposite perspective (that is, women who keep faith rather than men who break it), Daniel Murtaugh comes to a similar conclusion: "Arveragus pays his wife and himself the highest possible compliment when he makes them both subject to the same moral law, which has *trouthe* as its highest value and the breaking of faith as its worst sin"; "Women and Geoffrey Chaucer," *ELH* 38 (1971): 491.

6. Donald Howard, "Chaucer: The Life and Its Work," *Chaucer Newsletter* 5, no. 1 (1983): 1.

7. Terry Eagleton, *The Rape of Clarissa* (Oxford: Blackwell, 1982), p. 15.

their heartbreak," as one recent critic expresses it, is hardly enough.[8] Arlyn Diamond is, of course, right to stress the limits, from women's perspective, to Chaucer's friendship, but I hope I have been able to show that he could at least go a little further than well-meaning sympathy—that, however imperfectly, he was indeed aware of a disturbing inequity within "the very system."[9]

ELAINE TUTTLE HANSEN

The Feminization of Men in Chaucer's
Legend of Good Women†

> "No, I don't want to destroy you, any more than I want to save you. There has been far too much talk about you, and I want to leave you alone altogether. My interest is in my own sex; yours evidently can look after itself. That's what I want to save."
>
> Verena saw that he was more serious now than he had been before, that he was not piling it up satirically, but saying really and a trifle wearily, as if suddenly he were tired of much talk, what he meant. "To save it from what?" she asked.
>
> "From the most damnable feminization!"
>
> —HENRY JAMES, *The Bostonians*[1]

Basil Ransom's confession of interest in his own sex corresponds felicitously to what I will argue are the motives and concerns of a literary character imagined more than five hundred years earlier, the narrator of Chaucer's *Legend of Good Women*. While the latter never stops "piling it up satirically," he speaks, like Basil Ransom, "a trifle wearily" about the whole subject of women, and both male characters are in fact obsessed with redeeming themselves and their sex from the "damnable feminization" that this tired talk can serve at once to foster and to obscure. As readers acquainted with both texts may recognize, the correspondence between the modern novel and the medieval poem might be pursued a bit further; I invoke it here, however, only to anchor my use of the term "feminization" in a familiar literary scene and language, and to acknowledge from the outset what probably goes without saying to any reader of this volume. In reading Chaucer, I seek in part to appropriate a historical masterwork into a twentieth-century context, making the old text a field on which currently interesting battles can be waged (and where a number of live mines, to extend a borrowed metaphor, can be expected to blow up[2]). While this

8. George Sanderlin, "Chaucer's *Legend of Dido*—A Feminist Exemplum," *ChauR* 20 (1986): 337.
9. I should like to express here my gratitude to Sheila Delany, whose invitation to contribute to a session on "Sex and Gender in Chaucer's Work" at the New Chaucer Society meeting in York in 1984 first set me thinking about this subject; to Alan Gaylord, whose pointed comments on the paper that resulted made me rethink it; and to my colleagues Louise Forsyth, Minnette Grunmann-Gaudet, and Elizabeth Harvey for their patient whetting of my dull feminist sensibilities.
† This essay first appeared in *Seeking the Woman in Late Medieval and Renaissance Writings*, ed. by Sheila Fisher and Janet E. Halley. Copyright © 1989 by The University of Tennessee Press. Reprinted by permission of The University of Tennessee Press. The author's notes have been renumbered.
1. Henry James, *The Bostonians* (New York: Modern Library, 1956), 342–43.
2. The allusion is to Annette Kolodny's "Dancing Through the Minefield: Some Observations on the Theory, Practice, and Politics of a Feminist Literary Criticism," *Feminist Studies* 6 (1980): 1–25; apropos of my point here, see the first of Kolodny's "three crucial propositions" to which a feminist approach gives rise: "Literary history (and, with that, the historicity of literature) is a fiction" (8).

approach breaks the rules of one familiar variety of historicism, it is sanctioned by the recent pronouncements of eminent theorists of another kind of literary history. Hans Robert Jauss, for example, affirms that "the tradition of art presupposes a dialogue between the present and the past, according to which a past work cannot answer and speak to us until a present observer has posed the question which returns it from its retirement."[3] The *Legend of Good Women* is the text among Chaucer's poetic works that has been comparatively in retirement for centuries. The question that brings it most dramatically out of its relative seclusion is the one that feminist observers of canonical authors, at once steeped in a historical tradition of male writing beginning long before Chaucer and continuing long after James and yet vitally engaged in the contemporary investigation into the concepts of "woman" and "gender," are obliged to pose.

In an earlier consideration of this poem's tone and its author's gender politics, I have already taken up this question once, the question of how a contemporary feminist scholar might approach one of the least interpreted and—on the question of "woman"—most interesting of Chaucer's masterworks.[4] In this second assay, I want first to develop what I noted in passing in my original focus on Chaucer's treatment of his traditional heroines: the narrator's equally problematic treatment of his traditional heroes, his consistent debunking of men, and his increasingly harsh attacks on "fals lovers," which I read as both mask and symptom of the narrator's overriding interest in his own sex. Specifically I want to argue now that this concern is directed toward precisely the kind of feminization that Basil Ransom deplores, the feminization of men who indulge in heterosexual adventures, and who talk with and about women. In the second part of this essay, I want to take issue with the notion, implied by my earlier reading, that we can redeem that putative historical subject we call "Chaucer" as either a feminist or a humanist; and to underscore briefly why in looking both at the Chaucerian canon and at "woman" in history and in literature, we should bring the *Legend of Good Women* out of retirement to play a more central part in the current conversation between the present and the past.

In arguing for the relevance of a modern usage of a term like "feminization" to our study of a fourteenth-century poem, I do of course lay my argument open to the charge that it ignores historical differences. To avoid this, I might have begun not with Henry James, but with some discussion of the ways in which medieval authorities viewed the problem. A well-known passage in Orderic Vitalis' *Historia Ecclesiastica* might have made a better epigraph; here, Orderic deplores the unmanly and impious behavior of the younger generation in the late eleventh-century court of King Rufus, noting in particular the tight shirts and long, womanly hair of these *effeminati* and *catamitae*:

> Tunc effeminati passim in orbe dominabantur indisciplinate debachabantur sodomiticisque spurciciis foedi catamitae flammis urendi turpiter abutebantur. Ritus heroum abiciebant, hortamenta sacerdotum deridebant, barbaricumque morem in habitu et uita tenebant.

---

3. "Literary History as a Challenge to Literary Theory," in *New Directions in Literary History*, ed. Ralph Cohen (Baltimore: Johns Hopkins Univ. Press, 1974), 27.
4. "Irony and the Antifeminist Narrator in Chaucer's *Legend of Good Women*," *Journal of English and Germanic Philology* 82 (1983): 11–31.

Nam capillos a uertice in frontem discriminabant, longos crines ueluti mulieres nutriebant, et summopere comebant, prolixisque nimiumque strictis camisiis indui tunicisque gaudebant.

[At that time effeminates set the fashion in many parts of the world: foul catamites, doomed to eternal fire, unrestrainedly pursued their revels and shamelessly gave themselves up to the filth of sodomy. They rejected the traditions of honest men, ridiculed the counsel of priests, and persisted in their barbarous way of life and style of dress. They parted their hair from the crown of the head to the forehead, grew long and luxurious locks like women, and loved to deck themselves in long, over-tight shirts and tunics.][5]

Germane to my discussion of feminization in Chaucer's world, too, is Orderic's conflation of charges of homosexuality *and* excessive heterosexual interest; a few sentences later in this same passage, for example, he adds:

Femineam mollitiem petulans iuuentus amplectitur, feminisque uiri curiales in omni lasciuia summopere adulantur.

[Our wanton youth is sunk in effeminacy, and courtiers, fawning, seek the favours of women with every kind of lewdness.][6]

Or I might have begun by surveying the recent work of certain literary critics and historians, broadly interested in sociopolitical approaches to literature, who have begun to supply a medieval context in which to speak of the issues involved in the study of what we now call feminization. Toril Moi, for instance, building on Marc Bloch's earlier observations concerning the influence of noblewomen on aristocratic males of the *courtoisie*, explains the feminization of the knightly classes from the twelfth-century on as strategic to the naturalization of class differences:

Signalling their cultural superiority, the "effeminisation" of the aristocracy paradoxically enough comes to signify their "natural" right to power. It is precisely in its insistence on the "natural" differences between rulers and ruled that courtly ideology achieved its legitimising function, a function which operates long after the feudal aristocracy has lost its central position in society.[7]

Without explicitly speaking of feminization, Eugene Vance similarly reads the twelfth-century romance as serving the interests of a new class and ideology. Most interesting for the purposes of my argument, Vance considers the identification of one poet with his fictional female characters, the silk workers in the Pesme Avanture episode of Chretien's *Yvain*, and suggests that it reveals the male author's anxiety that the worker of texts,

5. Both Latin text and translation are taken from Marjorie Chibnall, ed. and trans., *The Ecclesiastical History of Orderic Vitalis*, vol. 4, bks. 7 and 8 (Oxford: Clarendon Press, 1973), 188–89. Two recent discussions brought this passage to my attention: Sharon Farmer, "Persuasive Voices: Clerical Images of Medieval Wives," *Speculum* 61 (1986): 517–43; and Brian Stock, *The Implications of Literacy* (Princeton, N.J.: Princeton Univ. Press, 1983), 481–82.
6. Ibid. In *Christianity, Social Tolerance, and Homosexuality* (Chicago: Univ. of Chicago Press, 1980), John Boswell repeatedly points out that homosexuality and effeminacy were not necessarily connected in classical or medieval thinking. "The use of femininity as a measure of undesirability or weakness more properly belongs in a study of misogyny," he notes (24 n. 43).
7. Toril Moi, "Desire in Language: Andreas Capellanus and the Controversy of Courtly Love," in *Medieval Literature: Criticism, Ideology and History*, ed. David Aers (New York: St. Martin's, 1986), 19.

like the weaver of textiles, will be exploited by the new ideology.[8] R. Howard Bloch has also made a persuasive case for the association in authoritative medieval discourse of the mutability of gender and improper sexual differentiation with the indeterminacy of meaning and improper writing attributed to poetic discourse.[9] And R. F. Green, without raising the question of gender himself, describes the situation of the fourteenth-century court poet in ways that might enable us to understand a part at least of his feminization: like woman, he is a marginalized figure at court, who must be careful not to offend those of higher rank and authority; he seeks, like a wife or daughter, to please and entertain those who have power over him.[1]

Both the historical evidence and the richness of such recent scholarly investigations are more complicated, however, than the preceding paragraphs can even begin to suggest, or than I can pursue in this brief essay. Its working assumption, then, is that what I call "feminization"—the occupation of a position associated with what is conventionally identified as feminine in a given social world—is a long-lived problem with specific historical contours extending throughout the centuries of western culture. In studying this problem, we need to analyze both continuities and disjunctions between its manifestations at particular historical moments and in particular texts. In this essay, I undertake only a small part of this analysis, which is in turn only one aspect of a broad investigation into the cultural interaction of class and gender. My limited aim is to show in some detail, first, how one text embodies and turns on the problem of feminization and then to sketch out much more briefly how this problem resonates throughout the later Chaucerian canon and speaks to certain pressing concerns of late twentieth-century feminist literary criticism.

Despite its title, what drives the *Legend of Good Women* from its opening dream vision to its arguably strategic incompletion is not the subject of women, good or otherwise, but the subject of two kinds of men: legendary heroes who become involved with women, and male authors who traffic in stories about women. As I have argued elsewhere, the narrator of this poem is writing both for and against a male audience, at once defending himself and his poetry against the criticism of a male tyrant, the God of Love, while identifying with masculine interests and privilege.[2] To borrow some useful nomenclature from a recent study of similar issues in (again) later texts, we can say, in other words, that the subject of the *Legend of Good Women* is "male homosocial desire." In *Between Men: English Literature and Male Homosocial Desire*, Eve Sedgwick recasts the work of twentieth-century theorists like Lévi-Strauss and Girard from a feminist perspective to shed light on the literary representation of a wide continuum of male bonds, ranging from the homophobic to the homoerotic, and pays particular attention to "triangular transactions" between men in which women figure not as subjects but as objects of exchange.[3] With a consistent

8. Eugene Vance, "Chretien's *Yvain* and the Ideologies of Change and Exchange," *Yale French Studies* 70 (1986): 42–62.
9. R. Howard Bloch, "Silence and Holes: the *Roman du Silence* and the Art of the Trouvère," *Yale French Studies* 70 (1986): 81–99.
1. Richard F. Green, *Poets and Princepleasers* (Toronto: Univ. of Toronto Press, 1980), 99–134.
2. "Irony and the Antifeminist Narrator," especially 26ff.
3. *Between Men* (New York: Columbia Univ. Press, 1985).

awareness of the socioeconomic and political contexts in which homoso-
cial desire takes literary shape, Sedgwick reminds us that the texts she
examines come from a specific place and culture and were written over a
relatively short span of time; she also suggests, however, that her insights
have wider application. She does not "delineate a separate male homoso-
cial literary canon," Sedgwick argues, because "the European canon as it
exists is already such a canon, and most so when it is most heterosexual."[4]
Chaucer's entire *oeuvre*, I would suggest, provides early support for this
large claim, and a closer examination of the classical tales of heterosexual
adventure retold in the *Legend of Good Women* is crucial to our under-
standing of how this is so. In this poem, heterosexual union is clearly
presented not as a good or even attainable end, but as a serious and even
insuperable problem, a necessary yet perilous part of the quest for stable
masculine identity and homosocial bonds between men. And what is most
dangerous about heterosexual desire, according to the Legends, is the more
or less feminine position—vulnerable, submissive, subservient and self-
sacrificing, on the one hand; crafty and duplicitous, on the other—that
men in love or lust for a woman seem forced to assume.

The actual centrality of men in a poem ostensibly devoted to women's
stories is made possible in part by the agenda set out in the Prologue, where
the first-person speaker of the poem, self-dramatized as a poet of love but
not (much of) a lover, recounts a dream-vision in which he meets Cupid,
here a grown-up God of Love, accompanied by Queen Alceste and a large
band of literary ladies all "trewe of love" (G. 193).[5] The God of Love cas-
tigates the dumbstruck poet at length as a heretic who has encouraged
people to transgress the laws of Love, in particular by telling stories of
wicked women like Criseyde instead of celebrating the countless hordes
of faithful heroines. After rebuking the God for his overly hasty and tyran-
nical judgment, the good Alceste prescribes a specific literary penance for
these alleged sins against women: the poet is ordered to tell stories both
"Of goode wymmen, maydenes and wyves, / That weren trewe in lovyng
al hire lyves" and "of false men that hem bytraien, / That al hir lyf do nat
but assayen / How many women they may doon a shame" (F. 484–88).
The God of Love commands the poet to begin with the story of Cleopatra,
and again reminds him that his charge is to contrast the heroic sufferings
of women with the failings of men in love: "For lat see now what man that
lover be, / Wol doon so strong a peyne for love as she" (F. 568–69).

But in fact, neither of the first two legends, of Cleopatra and then of
Thisbe, quite fits the bill, for each features a leading man, Antony or Pir-
amus, who proves his "truth" in love by committing suicide even before
the heroine has a chance to do so. This fact may retrospectively undermine
the God of Love's judgment in calling for the story of Cleopatra to begin
with, and thus unwittingly permitting the narrator to show us a "true" man,
by Love's standards. The narrator's commentary at the end of *Thisbe* calls
even more explicit attention to the subversive and "male-identified" stance
he will continue to take throughout the rest of the poem:

> And thus are Tisbe and Piramus ygo.
> Of trewe men I fynde but fewe mo

4. Ibid., 17.
5. All Chaucer quotations are from *The Works of Geoffrey Chaucer*, 2nd ed., ed. F. N. Robinson
(Boston: Houghton Mifflin, 1957).

> In alle my bokes, save this Piramus,
> And therfore have I spoken of hym thus.
> For it is deynte to us men to fynde
> A man that can in love been trewe and kynde.
> Here may ye se, what lovere so he be,
> A woman dar and can as wel as he.
>
> (916–23)

The narrator's primary concern, as suggested by his telling of the first two legends and confirmed by this passage, is to be pleased as a man, to please other men, and hence to make clear his own gender identity, his right to the first-person plural pronoun of line 920. In the last two lines here the ostensive motive of the poem, the celebration of women, is added—as I believe it indeed is related to the poem as a whole—as an afterthought, and virtually a nonsequitur.

But if the narrator wants to identify and bond with "us men," why does he go on to debunk the truly "false" heroes of the next seven legends? Why does he make most of them even more despicable than traditional story demands, and why does he claim to respond with increasingly strong, personal disgust—actually weeping, for instance, as he heaps invective on Tereus, brother-in-law and rapist of Philomela—to their well-known betrayal of his increasingly passive, shallow heroines? Perhaps, after some initial show of resistance, he is simply trying to acquit himself as quickly as possible in the God of Love's (and Alceste's) eyes. But a more interesting possibility emerges if we consider Antony and Piramus as early object lessons in the fate of men who give themselves wholeheartedly to a heterosexual passion, or to the idea of one. In different ways, both are utterly unmanned by their submission to the service of Love. For the love of Cleopatra, Antony loses his reason, his freedom, and his public position: "love hadde brought this man in swich a rage, / And hym so narwe bounden in his las . . . That al the world he sette at no value" (599–602). The defeat at Actium inevitably follows, and the narrator clearly implies that Antony's motive in killing himself is not so much the loss of Cleopatra as it is the loss of manly honor, prowess, and rationality that he has suffered on account of love: " 'My worshipe in this day thus have I lorn,' " he says; and in the very next line the narrator adds, "And for dispeyr out of his wit he sterte, / And rof hymself anon thourghout the herte" (660–61).

Piramus is presented as a less tragic figure, in that he has less manly worship to lose in the first place. He is an adolescent about whom we are told very little; he seems to fall in love because Thisbe lives next door, and because his father and hers forbid the affair. From his unexplained tardiness in arriving at Nynus' tomb, we can only infer that he is not so bold or appetitive or eager as Thisbe, not so able and willing to leave the domestic sphere—"al to longe, allas! at hom was he" (824). Revealing his own fear of women and heterosexuality, he misreads Thisbe's bloody veil as a sign of her death; it more accurately represents, in this version of the story, her confrontation with the feminine aggression and appetite figured in the lioness, forces that the nubile maiden also hides from but is not undone by. In his only speech in the legend, Piramus is less concerned with the loss of Thisbe than with his own failure as a man to protect her (833–41), and his immediate response, when faced with this blow to manly pride, is, like Antony's, suicide.

For both Antony and Piramus, unbearable flaws in their masculine identity—as warrior/ruler in Antony's case, as sexually mature and independent adult male and defender of helpless women in Piramus'—appear to have been caused or at least exposed by their honest efforts to establish and maintain a heterosexual relationship. They consequently choose suicide not because they cannot live without the women they love, but because they cannot live with themselves in the emasculated state to which they have been reduced. But ironically, of course, their suicides simply confirm that they have been feminized by love. Suicide is after all defined by the poem and the larger traditions it draws on[6] as the ultimate act a woman can have recourse to when she is raped or abandoned or otherwise troubled by the vagaries of heterosexual relations, or when like Alceste she can sacrifice herself for her husband. The fate of the only two "good" men the narrator can think of thus signals from the outset the pervasive problem that the *Legend of Good Women* examines: the incompatibility of the roles of adult male and true lover in a world where the latter is by definition feminized in one way or other. Antony and Piramus further introduce the real agenda of the Legends by representing the danger to men in love at either end of the masculine life cycle: Antony is the mature hero lamentably feminized by ungoverned (and of course adulterous) heterosexual desire, Piramus the boy who does not make it to manhood because he rushes (admittedly not quite fast enough) into the dangerous path of love before he is equipped to negotiate the perils along the way, and notably without his father's guidance, let alone approval.

If the first two Legends suggest that manhood is thus difficult both to attain and to maintain, the remaining stories extend the problem of feminization for the fourteenth-century aristocratic male from those men who try to serve Love to a number of men who are not so naively loyal to women or to the God of Love's ostensively woman-centered code. Most of the remaining heroes, older than Piramus and wiser than Antony, seem to know that heterosexual union is sometimes a pleasant or necessary diversion—it confirms one element of their manhood, and often saves their lives—but a dangerous state to settle down in, a place in which the manhood they are supposedly proving is in fact deeply threatened. Unlike Antony or Piramus, the rest survive the mortal dangers of Love by betraying women, but the problem of feminization is not so easily solved. For the very strategies these men use to escape any permanent heterosexual bond are in turn ironically feminizing ones, almost as characteristically so as suicide. In fact femininity, pervasively associated in medieval culture with passivity, weakness, irrationality, self-indulgence, and deceitfulness, seems to be an almost inescapable condition for all the men in the world of the poem, something either inherent in the "human" condition or in the social organization into which all are born.

All of the remaining heroes are in the first place presented as characters

---

6. St. Augustine, for example, links the discussion of whether a man's lust can pollute a Christian woman (i.e., if she is raped) with the discussion of suicide, with much consideration of Lucrece, whom he pronounces guilty. In carefully explaining, in his version of the story, that Lucrece fainted *before* she was raped, Chaucer seems to be vindicating her of the suspicion Augustine raises, the suspicion held against all raped women: what if she enjoyed it? "Quid si enim (quod ipsa tantummodo nosse poterat), quamvis juveni violenter irruenti, etiam sua libidine; illecta consensit, idque in se puniens ita doluit, ut morte putaret expiandum?" (*De Civitate Dei*, I. xix, *Patrologia Latina* 41, p. 33).

caught up—like women—in the plots of other men, constrained by forces beyond their control and unable to rule their own destinies. Theseus is literally imprisoned (in a story about sons who, like daughters in most stories, are objects of exchange between noble fathers); Eneas (another son of an incapacitated father) is defeated, exiled, and lost to boot; Demophon is shipwrecked; Jason and Lyno are conspired against (like Theseus) in the dynastic struggles of elder male relatives. Those few males who are circumstantially freer, apparently more in control of their lives, are actually even more inescapably in bondage to the irrational effect of what is characterized as innate, gratuitous male lust. Tereus rapes Philomela because of an unexplained, unmotivated, perhaps involuntary and brutalizing desire; Tarquinius rapes Lucrece on account of a somewhat more explicable passion, as male competition routed through women (who has the most faithful wife?) fuels the fires of his lust and violence. The male characters' status as victims and pawns—like women, again—of external and/ or internal forces beyond their rational control is also emphasized and aggravated by the frequent reversal of roles anticipated in the story of Piramus and Thisbe, where Thisbe is, as we have seen, more aggressive, eager, even "manly" than her lover—or at least as capable of taking care of herself in the woods. Although the narrator sometimes downplays the unfeminine characteristics of his heroines in order to make them fit the model of "good woman" he is constructing here, we still see that most of them (Dido, Ariadne and Phaedra, Medea, Phyllis, Hypermnestra) are or could be in positions of power over their lovers. The sexual anxiety this circumstance generates in men is brought into the open in the plot of the last story, the legend of Hypermnestra, when Hypermnestra's father gives her a knife on her wedding night and commands her to kill her husband (who is also his nephew) in their nuptial bed. But like Hypermnestra, who is said to be congenitally unable to wield a blade, all the women of the narrator's tradition and devising are uninterested in using their power except to rescue men from life-threatening situations, usually in the hopes of marrying them afterwards.

Although the heroes who come after Antony and Piramus are completely uninterested in stable domestic relationships, the Legends go on to demonstrate that men are always entrapped by heterosexual relations—if not in the lady's arms, then in a vicious circle of feminization. When he has been feminized by circumstances, fate, or innate weakness in the first place, the strategies a hero can subsequently use to escape this status in fact only confirm it. To secure a more powerful woman's assistance, for instance, a hero is often forced, like any victim, to play up his weakness: Eneas weeps and threatens suicide, Theseus begs and bribes and makes false promises; Jason is as "coy as is a mayde" (1548), while his friend Hercules, in Chaucer's version of the story, serves as his pimp. Tarquinius and Lucrece's husband Colatyne leave their post in the Roman camp to steal into the "estres" (1715), the inner spaces, of Lucrece's chamber; in that feminine enclosure Tarquinius' proper masculine reason and honor are defenseless against "his blynde lust" (1756). Tereus, enflamed by the vulnerable beauty of Philomela, uses his "wiles" (2294) to take her from her father's protection; and again the feminizing quality of his lust is imaged by the underscored interiority of the space where the rape occurs, in a "derke cave" within a forest (2310–12). After prostituting himself to win (with little effort) the lady's undying affection, or removing himself to a feminine place where he can indulge in his lust, the hero must then attempt to recover his masculine position—his independence, nobility, and devotion to more important issues—by eschewing the heterosexual union in which he is dependent on a woman. And yet the process of abandoning a woman, like the earlier process of seducing one, is emasculating in one way or another, as men's infidelities and betrayal of women in this poem always involve them once again in lies and storytelling, wiliness and other feminine duplicities, ignoble escapes out the window, and the complete failure of chivalric obligations to protect the lady herself.

By the end of the poem we might well conclude that feminization in this world is hard to avoid because the rules of patriarchy are incompatible with the rules of courtly love, and that men are caught in the consequent contradiction as they try to establish stable gender identity. Whereas patriarchy devalues the culturally feminine and insists on the difference between men and women as well as the power of the former over the latter, the heterosexual union idealized by the laws of Cupid values traits associated with femininity such as irrationality, self-sacrifice, submission, and service, and thus diminishes in theory both the difference and the power differential between male and female. The problematic lack of difference that such a conception of love entails is made clear in various ways: for example, the women in the poem who give themselves utterly to men are in fact all attracted not by otherness and virility, but by the male's temporary or apparent sameness, his passivity, coyness, vulnerability, and dependence (and even, in the case of Jason, his looks)—those very characteristics that also signal the heroes' feminization. In the cases where women are raped, there is no suggestion of their sexual interest or complicity—or even, in the case of Lucrece, of their consciousness. What might be construed as the women's unconscious desire, like the men's, to bond with their own sex cannot be gratified for long by the hero, who for his part must necessarily be unfaithful if he is to demonstrate his manhood, his independence and freedom and difference. And the actual loss of gender differentiation that a successful heterosexual union might bring about, if two actually became one, is perhaps hinted at in the essential similarity of the most innocent and "true" lovers in the poem: Piramus and Thisbe, who speak in one voice, both "wex pale" and are separated only by the cold wall their fathers have built (apparently in vain) to keep them apart.

But if the poem suggests, as so many readers with otherwise different interpretations agree, that there is something wrong with the laws of Love,[7] it also reveals a serious problem in the rule of the fathers. Fathers are in theory at least men who have negotiated that treacherous path of heterosexual desire, and the institution of patriarchal rule should facilitate the next generation's passage to adulthood: hence a father must at once protect his daughters and pass proper standards of manliness on to his sons. But the contradiction in this charge is brought out in the Legends by the fact that all the men of the fathers' generation fail in one way or another to see their offspring to sexual maturity, either through absence, incapacity, or malevolence. Cleopatra's story, as told by this narrator, tellingly begins

---

7. For an earlier and important discussion of Chaucer's critique as a "bourgeois poet" of the literary conventions of Love poetry in the Legends and elsewhere, for instance, see Dorothy Bethurum, "Chaucer's Point of View as Narrator in the Love Poems," *PMLA* 74 (1959): 511–20.

"After the deth of Tholome the Kyng" (580), and so too we are reminded early in the linked stories of Medea and Ysiphile that Eson, the father of their common seducer, Jason, is dead. Living fathers are in some instances too weak (like Anchises and Pandeon) to protect their sons and daughters; or as is more often the case, they cause active harm, intentionally or not, to the next generation. Thisbe's and Piramus' fathers inexplicably prohibit love, and so indirectly cause their childrens' deaths. Oetes, by contrast, unwittingly seals his daughter Medea's doom when he bids her to sit at the table with Jason. Theseus passes on his good looks and his false ways with women to his son Demophon, while Jason and Lyno are both schemed against by jealous uncles. In the latter story, we also see a strong suggestion of incest in Egiste's bizarre speech to his daughter Hypermnestra: in the same breath the father vows his love and threatens to kill the girl if she doesn't murder her bridegroom-cousin Lyno, and it is difficult to avoid the conclusion that this is the story of a Lear-like father who cannot let his daughter grow up and sleep with another man. The public, institutional consequences of such unresolved Oedipal situations—of the patriarchal failure to help sons become men—reaches epic proportions in the legend of Lucrece, where the narrator frames his story with reminders that Tarquinius' irrational lust brings an end to the whole line of Roman kings (1680–84, 1862–64).

I have thus far been arguing from the evidence of the Legends alone that this is a poem for and about men and their anxieties about sex and gender: each alleged heroine's story is embedded in a plot and told in a way that underscores the greater interest and value of masculine affairs; in this world heterosexual love is always emasculating (if not lethal), and the generation of the fathers fails to provide whatever young males might need to escape the pervasive threat of feminization. I want to return briefly now to the figure of the dreamer/poet himself as it is characterized in the Prologue, for there in retrospect we find arguably sufficient explanation for the narrator's only partially concealed antipathy toward women and his complex anxieties about the infectious feminization of the Court of Cupid and its literary servants.

The narrator of the *Legend of Good Women* presents himself in the well-known opening lines (F. 1–209, G. 1–103), before the dream-vision, as a bookworm who is drawn from his fanatic devotion to reading by only one "game": the cult of the marguerite. This emphasizes both the literary man's prior disinterest in actual heterosexual love and his professional obligation to take part in an elaborate courtly word-game, in which the explicit substitution of the daisy for the loved one at once covers over and underscores the unimportance or irrelevance of women.[8] The dream that follows suggests the multiple anxieties of the court poet in such a situation, including his fear of a tyrannical male ruler who (perhaps to demonstrate his own superior sensitivity and potency) blames his servant for writing antifeminist poetry and also calls attention to that servant's emasculated status: "Thow . . . art therto nothyng able," the God of Love says (F. 320, G. 246). Like so many of the heroes of the Legends, the poet is further feminized by the

---

8. On the displacement of the actual lady as object of medieval love poetry, see Green, *Poets and Princepleasers*, 99–134. As noted earlier, Green's discussion of the relative lack of social importance of the court poet informs my argument about the poet's anxieties and strategies in the *Legend of Good Women*.

intervention of a powerful, aristocratic woman who speaks the kind of rational words he for some unexplained (but psychologically and historically plausible[9]) reason cannot. The poet's disinterest in real women can perhaps turn to active antipathy when he is, in effect, treated like a woman himself, not recognized as a man by the male ruler and blocked from proving his manhood either by loving an actual female or by ignoring the subject of women altogether. Again, as in the case of the heroes of the Legends, the only strategy the poet can use to subvert the censure and embarrassment revealed in the dream actually requires behavior widely viewed as feminine—wiliness and duplicity—as he apparently submits and then subtly betrays Cupid's purposes and writes to his own end. Perhaps as part of this subversion, moreover, the poet already suggests through his recounting of the dream that feminization in the Court of Cupid is a corruption spreading right to the top. The God of Love himself, dressed in embroidered robes with a garland of rose leaves on his head (F. 226–28, G. 158–61), also stands corrected for his irrational anger (motivated by what he sees of himself in the daisy worshipper?) by the words of an articulate, rational woman, who admonishes him to act in a more manly, less willful and self-indulgent way.

The question that "retrieves" the *Legend of Good Women* from its "retirement" and brings to light a coherent and interesting reading of the Prologue and the Legends together is, then, the broad question of what "woman" or women—both absent and present, as characters, images, metaphors, as readers and as critics—have to do with this text, written like most other masterworks by and for men. In the belief that this question also raises others that I cannot address in detail in the present essay, I want to turn now to a more general discussion of two ramifications of my argument that suggest how the *Legend of Good Women* can be fruitfully brought more directly to the center of attention of certain current critical investigations as well as of contemporary approaches to Chaucer's more well-known poems.

Pursuing as I have done the import of the narrator's obsession with the feminization of men who try to love or to write first provides a necessary caution to the modern critic's own obsession, brought into the open in the last decade or two, with determining the sexual politics of Chaucer or any other canonical male author. In my own earlier reading of the Legends, I stressed the inherent and extensive antifeminism of both the narrator and the God of Love he is forced to serve, an antifeminism noted by earlier critics, more or less repressed for obvious reasons, and then made manifest again by the question that feminist scholarship asks of any text. So marked is this antifeminism, I argued, that it cannot be attributed to the implied author, Chaucer, first because his "subtle intelligence," displayed in his work as a whole, could not conceivably produce a text that reduced so easily to conventional satire, and second because any discussion of the

---

9. Omitted from my argument here but worthy of fuller consideration as part of the historical context of the poem is the notion thoroughly explored in early twentieth-century scholarship that the *Legend of Good Women* was an occasional poem commissioned by (or presented to) a royal female patron—either Queen Anne, or possibly Joan of Kent, wife of the Black Prince and mother of Richard II. For an overview and bibliography of the historical argument, see John H. Fisher's review in *Companion to Chaucer Studies*, rev. ed., ed. Beryl Rowland (New York and Oxford: Oxford Univ. Press, 1979), 464–76.

antifeminism of the poem also reveals its simultaneous critique of men and the masculinist bias of the God of Love, the court, and the poet who serves both. Without retracting the conclusion that this poem is not trying to perform conventional antifeminist satire or that it does criticize less subtle forms of misogyny, I do want to challenge the naive assumption on my part that a critique of the "socio-gender system" and its constraining effects on male identity and freedom amounts to a "pro-woman" position, and hence to take back the implicit support my earlier views offer to current attempts to reconstruct a Chaucer who is either a feminist or—more perniciously, perhaps—a humanist who transcends through art the constraints of a gendered voice and point of view.[1]

It is easy to understand why critics of varying persuasions might want to construct either kind of Chaucer; the apparently unavoidable drive to divine the author's (or the text's) sexual politics, or to go one step further and reclaim the author's (or the text's) greatness on the grounds that he (or it) has no sexual politics, reveals less about the ostensive end of such projects—"meaning" and "intention" disclosed—than about the constitutive force of our own needs and desires. Fifteen years ago, in an essay entitled "Crocodilian Humor: A Discussion of Chaucer's Wife of Bath," David Reid broached what has since been an untenable critical position: he suggested that Chaucer's brand of humanism involved "baiting women and the middle classes," and that since times have changed—"we are middle class . . . and women are not to be baited really, for their place has changed"—now we cover our "embarrassment" at Chaucer's unacceptable views and practices with an "elaborate misunderstanding" of the Wife and her significance.[2] My rereading of the *Legend of Good Women* might suggest that this poem and its critical reception can offer as much or more support for Reid's view of Chaucer's antifeminist humor and our willful misunderstanding of it as does the Wife's *Prologue* and *Tale*. The *Legend's* rich representation of the feminization of men, although surely a critique of the arbitrariness of gender stereotypes and of crude antifeminism, nevertheless offers nothing "for" women: it does not revalue the feminine, which is even more clearly a pathological condition, nor celebrate woman as a sign or subject; its author does not refuse to traffic in stories about women, but simply insists on doing so on his own terms.

But Chaucer's attitude remains finally inaccessible and irrelevant, and Reid's claim becomes more interesting and even urgent if for a moment at least we pursue not the differences but the similarities between Chaucer's times and our own. I would argue that there may be more real and crucial continuity between the humanism of the *Canterbury Tales* and of our day than Reid wants to believe, more actual commonality between "curmudgeonly and old-fashioned" jokes about women like the Wife of Bath or Cleopatra and the fundamental position of modern criticism. Recent feminist and other broadly speaking "deconstructive" critiques clearly suggest that criticism as we have learned it is as threatened by their challenges to claims of universality, objectivity, certainty, and humanity (or humaneness) as Chaucer's representative fourteenth-century man of letters, the Clerk, say,

---

1. It would be impractical to annotate here the many attempts to discover Chaucer's "attitude toward women" in the past decade or two; for a fair sampling of the major efforts, see my "Irony and the Antifeminist Narrator in Chaucer's *Legend of Good Women*," 11, nn. 1, 2.
2. *Chaucer Review* 4 (1970): 73.

is threatened by the Wife of Bath "and al hir secte"—or as the men of the *Legend of Good Women*, narrator and characters alike, are threatened by the kind of feminization they experience. Such feminization involves, as this text teaches us, both the real presence and the heightened consciousness of external and internal limits; the paralyzing, even fatal recognition that the position represented by ideals of adult male power, courtly or patriarchal, is unattainable by the most heroic of men; as well as the further, more frightening and barely visible perception that such power is itself, like clear gender distinctions, unstable, even illusory, at the same time that both the constraints and uncertainties of sex roles are inescapable. The primal fear of feminization, it might be said, is the fear that men might be women. Akin to this, I submit, is the fear that all criticism might in fact be or become feminist. Criticism might have to become aware, that is, that the gender of reader, author, and critic always matters, affects interpretation, and establishes what gets read by whom in ways we will never fully understand but must no longer ignore; that textuality and sexuality are * * * related with an unsettling complexity that insists on the continued relevance of questions about the silencing, displacement, and impersonation of women's voices, past and present, in male-authored texts; that the myth of the great poet's (or the great text's) androgyny or transcendence *is* a myth.

Implicit in the broad claims of the preceding argument is the more specific point that the *Legend of Good Women* is central to our understanding of Chaucer's other works. Here I can only sketch out what amounts to a prolegomenon to a certain kind of reading of the *Canterbury Tales* that privileges the question of gender and the problem of feminization. Other critics have read the Legends as a kind of apprenticeship in storytelling, a prototype of the framed narrative that comes to fruition in the later, more well-known work, or a failed or flawed experiment that turns out better next time.[3] Situating my reading of the Legends in a similar position, I would stress less its failure or its experimental nature, more its key role in identifying and accounting for the Tales' collective exploration of the complex relation of gender and voice, or again of sexuality and textuality.

Viewed through the perspective foregrounded by the Legends, the pilgrims and the characters they create in their narratives repeatedly reveal the same feminine pathology diagnosed and dissected in the stories of "good" women. All are self-conscious and constrained by the felt and real limits of sex roles, and they notably present us with unmistakable images of divided, illusory, and absent selves. From the beginning of the poem, although all speakers are later seen to be anxious to attain "maistrie" over women (and/or the "woman" in themselves) by one route or another, all also desire to submit to a dominant, more powerful, and markedly masculine judgment: namely, the rule of the Host, Harry Bailley, who "of manhod . . . lakkede right naught" (I. 756). Promising them the power of a

---

3. See, for example: R. M. Garrett, "Cleopatra the Martyr and Hir Sisters," *Journal of English and Germanic Philology* 22 (1923): 64–74; Robert M. Estrich, "Chaucer's Maturing Art in the *Legend of Good Women*," *Journal of English and Germanic Philology* 36 (1937): 326–37; Eleanor Leach, "The Sources and Rhetoric of Chaucer's 'Legend of Good Women' and Ovid's 'Heroides,' " Ph.D. diss., Yale University, 1963; Mary P. Smagola, " 'Spek Wel of Love': The Role of Women in Chaucer's *Legend of Good Women*," Ph.D. diss., Case Western Reserve University, 1972; R. W. Frank, *Chaucer and the Legend of Good Women* (Cambridge: Harvard Univ. Press, 1972); Robert O. Payne, "Making His Own Myth," *Chaucer Review* 9 (1975): 197–211.

voice, the freedom and pleasure of speaking ("confort ne myrthe is noon / To ride by the weye doumb as a stoon," I. 773–74), he ironically enforces their silence, when he wants it, from the beginning: "Hoold up youre hondes, withouten moore speche" (I. 783), he commands, and within three lines they consent. The Host continues to define his position openly as that of the tyrant, just like Cupid: he censures the pilgrims' tales and their critical responses to them beforehand by announcing that he will be the sole judge of their merit; they not only assent but beg him to do as he has decreed (I. 810–14).

The Host's subsequent and sustained concern with the masculinity of his subjects (and hence by implication of himself) and the antifeminism of his literary taste is well documented in the linking matter, and a brief catalogue may suggest those tales in which the problematic feminization of men in love or lust is most markedly at issue. The *Knight's Tale*: Palamon and Arcite, imprisoned cousins, barely conceal their frustrated desire to compete with each other by falling in love with the same vision of woman seen from their prison window; in different ways each proceeds to suffer equal loss of identity; their competition is finally given a much-celebrated public forum, and the winner in battle must die while the final winner in love must give up claims of prowess. The *Miller's Tale*: three men—silly and presumably impotent old John, effeminate Absalon, and wily Nicholas—are further unmanned in their pursuit of Alison (and a similar trio, busy trading corn, women, and even a cradle, appears in the matching *Reeve's Tale*). The *Man of Law's Tale*: evil maternal figures easily trick their ineffectual sons, and Constance (like Alison) is passed from one man who can't hold onto and protect her to another. And so forth: The *Wife of Bath's Tale* stars the knight-rapist who is saved first by the Queen and then by the preachy old Hag; the *Clerk's Tale* actually rewrites the *Legend of Good Women* in complex and misunderstood ways;[4] the *Merchant's Tale* returns to the scene of the old man who fails at all levels to play an adult male role in his belated marriage. The ending of the *Franklin's Tale* transforms the story into a competition, again, among three men, routed through the innocent Dorigen; the *Physician's Tale* centers on the father who cannot protect his daughter from the Tarquinius-like judge, Apius, whose irrational lust destroys him as well as its object; and all this is followed by the complex self-presentation of the "feminoid" Pardoner and the nun-pecked Nun's Priest and his Chauntecleer. Desired, satirized, impersonated, displaced, and damned, the feminine, in the *Canterbury Tales*, turns out to be more or less the human norm, and hence the central source of instability for the narrative as well as for the culture it represents.

---

4. A point I develop in "The Powers of Silence: The Case of the Clerk's Griselda," in *Women and Power in Medieval and Early Modern Europe*, ed. Mary Erler and Maryanne Kowaleski (Athens: Univ. of Georgia Press, 1988), 230–49.

STEVEN KRUGER

From Medical and Moral Authority in the Late Medieval Dream†

The Medical Transformation of Medieval Dream Theory

In the later Middle Ages, the dream was a locus where[***] a merging or crossing of medical and moral discourses was especially apt to occur, and the conflation of the two was facilitated by certain important changes in ideas about dreaming, by what I will call the 'somatizing' of dream theory. Although, throughout the medieval period, somatic causes of dreams were recognized, the twelfth- and thirteenth-century introduction of new medical and scientific texts to the Latin West gave the body and bodily process a new prominence in European dream theory. Thus, the notion that dream images reflect humoral complexion became more and more common as medical texts exerted their influence on medieval culture.[1] This notion was found in Rasis's *Liber ad Almansorem* and Avicenna's *Canon* (both translated into Latin in the second half of the twelfth century),[2] as well as in such newly available non-medical writers as Algazali and Averroes.[3] Avicenna presented the idea in a particularly prominent place, in the first book of the *Canon* as part of a general discussion of the medical signs that indicate which of the humours is dominant.[4] Here, Avicenna discusses as a group a whole range of somatic 'signa' for sanguine, phlegmatic, choleric, and melancholic temperaments: the patient's general physique; skin colour; hairiness; the state of the mouth, tongue, nostrils, pulse, urine, faeces; muscle tone; the presence of abnormal phenomena like vomiting or headache; and the quality of dreams. The rule of sanguine humour is signified 'when a man sees in [his] dreams red things, or much blood coming out of his own body, or [sees] himself swimming in blood, and the like.' A phlegmatic temperament is demonstrated by 'dreams in which waters and rivers and snows and rains and cold are seen.' Red or yellow choler is signified when one dreams of 'fires and yellow banners', 'burning or the heat of a bath or of the sun', or when one sees 'things which are not yellow [as] yellow.' And finally, 'the dreams [that signify the rule of black bile] create terror out of shadows and torture and black things and terrors.'[5]

† From "Medical and Moral Authority in the Late Medieval Dream," in *Reading Dreams: The Interpretation of Dreams from Chaucer to Shakespeare*, edited by Peter Brown, with an introduction by A. C. Spearing (Oxford: Oxford University Press, 1999), 55–83. Reprinted by permission of Oxford University Press. The author's notes have been abbreviated and renumbered, and Latin and French quotations are presented only in English translation. In some cases, citations from Chaucer have been abbreviated; in all such cases, inclusive lines quoted are indicated before the citation.
1. See M. Fattori, 'Sogni e temperamenti' in T. Gregory, *I sogni nel medioevo*, Seminario Internazionale, Rome, 2–4 Oct. 1983 (Rome, 1985), G. Fioravanti, 'La "scientia somnialis" di Boezio di Dacia', *Atti della Accademia delle Scienze di Torino*, ii: *Classe di scienze morali, storiche e filogiche*, 101 (1966–7), 329–69: 347–50.
2. D. Jacquart and C. Thomasset, *Sexuality and Medicine in the Middle Ages*, trans. M. Adamson (Princeton, 1988), 22.
3. For the humoral material in Algazali, see *Algazel's Metaphysics: A Mediaeval Translation*, ed. J. T. Muckle (Toronto, 1933), pars II³, tractatus V. 6 (pp. 190–1). On Averroes use of the humoral topos, see Fioravanti, ' "Scientia somnialis" ', 348.
4. Avicenna, *Liber canonis* (Venice, 1507; repr. Hildesheim, 1964), bk. I, *fen* 2, doctrine 3, ch. 7 (fo. 42ᵛ). See also O. C. Gruner, *A Treatise on the Canon of Medicine of Avicenna, Incorporating a Translation of the First Book* (London, 1930; repr. New York, 1973), 277.
5. Avicenna, *Liber canonis*, bk. I, *fen* 2, doctrine 3, ch. 7 (fos. 42ᵛ–43ʳ). See also Gruner, *Treatise on the Canon*, 277.

Such humoral material quickly became widespread in Latin dream theory, appearing in the twelfth century, for instance, in Pascalis Romanus' *Liber thesauri occulti* (c.1165)[6] and the Cistercian *De spiritu et anima*,[7] and then, during the thirteenth and fourteenth centuries, in writers as diverse as Michael Scot,[8] Albertus Magnus,[9] Vincent of Beauvais,[1] Boethius of Dacia,[2] Arnald of Villanova,[3] William of Aragon,[4] Robert Holkot,[5] and Geoffrey Chaucer.[6]

The dependence of dreams upon the humours may, as Chaucer's Pertelote suggests, provide a useful key for reading dream images, but the importance of medical treatments of dreaming goes beyond their introduction of a 'colour-coded' system for interpreting dreams. The connection between dreams and the humours, along with other newly introduced medical material, is most important as it indicates a new way of looking at dreams, an intensified concern with dream process, with how precisely dreams and their images come into being. We see this in Avicenna's inclusion of dream material within his more general treatment of bodily functions and the Galenic humours. We also see it in more and more elaborate attempts, influenced by both medical writings and the newly rediscovered Aristotelian corpus, to explain the presentation of dreams in relation to the most basic of bodily processes—heating, cooling, dissipation and gathering of energies, digestion, the movement of vapours and spirits among the organs and faculties of the body. To quote briefly from one extensive treatment of this sort, by Vincent of Beauvais:

> The movement [of images in a dream] descends from the locus of the fantasy, and touches the common sense, and returns to the fantasy. Truly, when there is evaporation from the place of digestion to the brain, a thin blood is elevated, and descends to the interior of the animal head [i.e. the head as locus of the animal spirit], upon which

6. Pascalis' work probably predates the Latin translation of Avicenna and Rasis, but since Pascalis is himself a translator, at least from the Greek (see C. H. Haskins, *Studies in Mediaeval Culture* (Oxford, 1929), 169), he probably had access to certain as yet untranslated Galenic works. See S. Collin-Roset, 'Le *Liber thesauri occulti* de Pascalis Romanus (un traité d'interprétation des songes du XIIᵉ siécle)', *AHDLMA* 30 (1963), 111–98: 126. For the humoral material see, in Collin-Roset's edition, bk. 1, ch. 1 (pp. 143–4).
7. The *De spiritu et anima* was often wrongly ascribed to Augustine. For the humoral material, see *De spiritu et anima*, PL 40, ch. 25, trans. E. Leiva and B. Ward in *Three Treatises on Man: A Cistercian Anthropology*, ed. B. McGinn (Kalamazoo, Mich.), 1977), 179–288: 221.
8. Michael Scot flourished in the first half of the 13th cent.
9. Albertus Magnus lived c. 1193–1280. For the humoral material, see the *Summa de creaturis*, in *Opera omnia*, ed. A. Borgnet, 38 vols. (Paris, 1890–9), vol. xxxv, question 50, article 1 (pp. 435–6).
1. Vincent of Beauvais wrote in the mid-13th cent. For the humoral material, see the *Speculum naturale*, bk. 26, ch. 54, cols. 1872–3, borrowed from Albertus Magnus, *Summa de creaturis*. P. Aiken, 'Vincent of Beauvais and Dame Pertelote's Knowledge of Medicine', *Speculum*, 10 (1935), 281–7, sees Vincent as an important source for Chaucer's medically informed view of dreaming in NPT [the Nun's Priest's Tale in the *Canterbury Tales*—Editor].
2. Boethius of Dacia flourished in Paris in the 1270s. For the humoral material, see Boethius of Dacia, *De somniis*, in *Opera*, vol. vi, pt. 2, ed. N. G. Green-Pederson, Corpus Philosophorum Danicorum Medii Aevi (Copenhagen, 1976), 388–90, trans. J. F. Wippel in *On the Supreme Good, On the Eternity of the World, On Dreams* (Toronto, 1987), 74–6.
3. Arnald of Villanova died c.1311. In his discussion of humoral material in the *Praxis medicinalis*, he cites e.g. Avicenna: see Fattori's discussion in 'Sogní e temperamenti', 102–4.
4. William of Aragon flourished c.1330. For the humoral material, see R. A. Pack, 'De pronosticatione sompniorum libellus Guillelmo de Aragonia adscriptus', *AHDLMA* 33 (1966), 237–92: 268–9.
5. Holkot wrote the *Lectiones* on the Book of Wisdom c.1334–6. For the humoral material, see R. Holkot, *In librum sapientiae regis Salomonis praelectiones CCXIII* (Basle, 1586), lectio 103 (p. 350), and *lectio* 202 (p. 666). R. A. Pratt, 'Some Latin Sources of the Nonnes Preest on Dreams', *Speculum*, 52 (1977), 538–70, proposes that Holkot was an important source for the dream-lore of NPT.
6. See Chaucer, NPT 2923–69.

the animal spirit goes forth, carrying images from the locus of the fantasy to the organ of the common sense. When these [images] move the common sense, a dream arises, and the form brought down from the fantasy to the common sense seems to be perceived.[7]

We say moreover that dreams appear more frequently at the end of sleep . . . because . . . at its beginning, the digestive heat is strengthened, and one finds the food mixed up, the pure with the impure. And therefore it brings a disturbed evaporation up into the head, in which images cannot well result. But at the end [of sleep], when the more impure blood sinks downward, and only the thin [blood] rises upward, then the animal spirit is purified, and images begin to result in dreams.[8]

Where an early dream theorist like Gregory the Great (d. 604) asserts that dreams arise 'from the fullness or emptiness of the stomach',[9] but without explaining the processes leading from stomach to dream, or where Macrobius (fourth to fifth century) asserts a connection between the *insomnium* and 'eating or drinking', 'hunger or thirst',[1] but again without giving any more detailed description of internal process, a twelfth-century, medically aware writer like Pascalis Romanus, adapting and elaborating Macrobius, explicates the *insomnium* and *visum* by means of an elaborate psychosomatics. Thus, to counter the 'common opinion' that the *incubus* (a sub-species of Macrobius' *visum*) 'is a small being in the likeness of a satyr and that it presses sleepers at night in such a way that it almost kills them by suffocation', Pascalis deploys a complex medical explanation:

there is a certain blood in the human body that does not run about through the veins nor through any other fixed routes, but is in the heart or around the heart. And when one sleeps lying on the left side or even supine,[2] this blood, by a certain abundance of humours, runs down to that same part and chokes the heart; and it [the heart] is so close to the left side that it cannot [then] be opened or closed [i.e. beat]. For the heart, since it is always the seat of the spirit, is naturally in motion nor does it wish to be obstructed. When, however, the heart is so choked by blood and humours that it cannot freely open and close itself nor be in its natural motion, the humours become heavy in the sleeper, so that he thinks that he is holding up a whole house or some other mass.[3]

As I have suggested elsewhere, such late medieval shifts in dream theory did not reconstruct dreaming as a simply somatic phenomenon: the mainstream of medieval dream theory never reached the position of Aristotle's

7. Vincent of Beauvais, *Speculum naturale* (Douai, 1624; repr. Graz, 1964), bk. 26, ch. 34, cols. 1861–2. Vincent here depends upon Albertus Magnus, *Summa de creaturis*, question 46 (p. 421).
8. Vincent of Beauvais, *Speculum naturale*, bk. 26, ch. 47, col. 1868. Vincent here depends upon Albertus Magnus, *Summa de creaturis*, question 47 (p. 427).
9. Gregory the Great, *Dialogues*, bk. IV, ch. 50, sect. 2, and *Moralia in Job*, bk. VIII, ch. 24, sect. 42. For English versions, see *Dialogues*, trans. O. J. Zimmerman, The Fathers of the Church: A New Translation 39 (New York, 1959); *Morals on the Book of Job*, 3 vols., A Library of Fathers of the Holy Catholic Church, translated by members of the English church (Oxford, 1844–50).
1. Macrobius, *Commentary on the Dream of Scipio*, trans. William Harris Stahl (New York, 1952), 1. 3. 4 (p. 88)
2. Medical writers often consider the position of the body during sleep to influence the digestive process, and hence potentially the quality of dreams. See e.g. Avicenna, *The Poem on Medicine* trans. H. C. Krueger (Springfield, Ill., 1963), 57.
3. Collin-Roset, 'Liber thesauri occulti', bk. I, ch. 10 (pp. 158–9). I quote my own translation of the passage from *Dreaming in the Middle Ages* (Cambridge, 1992), 71, with slight modifications.

Parva naturalia, where the dream would be wholly confined to the realm of the physical.[4] Writers like Vincent, Pascalis, and Albertus Magnus embraced the possibility of both mundane and transcendent dreams: dreams naturally arise from our bodies, but that does not mean that they cannot also be caused or shaped from outside the body—by the planets, by angels and demons, even directly by God. Later medieval dream theorists tended to preserve the complexity of dream types that, from late antiquity on, consistently characterized European dream theory. But with the new medical emphasis on dream process came an essentially new way of regarding that complexity. Rather than assume that each distinct dream type involves a distinct mechanism of action—meaningless dreams arising from within the dreamer, meaningful dreams from outer, transcendent forces (as in Gregory the Great)—at least some late medieval dream theorists began to treat all dreams as involving similar internal processes. This is a possibility anticipated in Augustine's comments on dreaming in both the *De Genesi ad litteram* and *De cura pro mortuis gerenda* (fourth to fifth century), but not there explored in any detail in terms of the psychosomatics of the dream.[5] Writers like Albert and Vincent, however, began in elaborate ways to suggest that common processes unite all dream experience. Thus, Albert, in explaining how heavenly movements might cause dreams that predict the future, developed a complex system that brought internal and external forces together on the common ground of the dream. In part the clarity and truth-value of dreams depend upon the strength of the light (*lumen*), motion (*motus*), or form (*forma*) being transmitted from the heavens; but human process also plays a crucial role in producing these dreams, even those that most clearly reveal some celestial truth:

> the celestial forms sent to us, touching our bodies, move them strongly, and imprint their virtue [on them]. . . . The imaginative soul receives this movement according to the mode which is possible for it, and this [mode] is according to the forms of the imagination [that is, the soul receives the celestial movement in images].[6]

Similarly, both Albert and Vincent feel called upon to explain the mechanism by which angels, given a nature essentially different from the human, might nonetheless communicate with human beings through dreams:

> Truly all dreams exist in corporeal similitudes. . . . Therefore no dreams arise from such pure and simple intellects as belong to angels. We, however, say that, although in the angels forms may be simple, nevertheless, since an angel and [its] intelligence are substances working on human souls, as the philosophers say: those forms are simple in them [the angels], but are received by the soul or souls as

4. Kruger, *Dreaming in the Middle Ages,* 83–122.
5. See Augustine, *De Genesi ad litteram libri duodecim,* ed. J. Zycha, Corpus Scriptorum Ecclesiasticorum Latinorum, vol. 28, sect. 3; pt. I (Prague, 1894), bk. 12, trans. J. H. Taylor as *The Literal Meaning of Genesis,* 2 vols., Ancient Christian Writers: The Works of the Fathers in Translation 42 (New York, 1982), and *De cura pro mortuis gerenda,* PL 40, cols. 591–610, trans. H. Browne as *On Care to Be Had for the Dead,* A Select Library of the Nicene and Post-Nicene Fathers of the Christian Church 3 (Buffalo, 1887), 537–51.
6. Albertus Magnus, Commentary on Aristotle's *De divinatione per somnum,* in *Opera omnia,* ix, 190. Gregory, 'I sogni e gli astri', 121–33, discusses Albert's system. Using Albert's theory as a base, William of Aragon elaborated a similar treatment of dreaming; see Pack, 'De pronosticatione sompniorum'.

particular and corporeal, and this is the solution of Alpharabius. It may also be said that intelligence pours into [the human being] a simple thought, for which thought, certainly, the imagination [then] forms images.[7]

Albert and Vincent are not satisfied simply with asserting that angels have the power to send dreams to human beings; they also want to understand how such dreams might operate given what they know about angels and about the workings of the dream process in the faculty of imagination.

In my view, then, the most important consequence of the new somatic treatment of dreaming is in the ways it enables a bringing together of different kinds of dream—internally and externally motivated, celestial and mundane, angelic, demonic, and human—on the common ground of one unitary dream process involving certain universal psychosomatic elements. This later medieval somatic unification of dreaming might, I think, have significant implications for our reading of late medieval dream narrative. Recognizing the somatic possibilities of the dream may move us away from the simple allegorizing and spiritualizing tendencies of much dream-vision criticism. The dreamer has a body that plays an important part in determining the content and form of his or her dreams, and the progress of the dream may productively be read not just as an itinerary of spiritual ascent but as the effect and record of certain physiological and psychosomatic processes.

In my previous work on the implications of medieval dream theory for reading dream narrative, I have proposed that ideas of the dream's 'doubleness' and 'middleness'—its consistent connection to and navigation between a transcendent realm of spirit and an earthly realm of body—enabled the development of the 'middle vision', a literary genre balancing the mundane and the celestial: 'Poems of this tradition simultaneously evoke opposed ideas about the nature of dreaming, and, by doing so, situate themselves to explore areas of betweenness—the realms that lie between the divine and the mundane, the true and the false, the good and the bad.'[8] As Spearing has recognized, in the complexity of late medieval dream types lies the possibility of a simultaneous deployment of opposed types that will create a consistent, self-conscious ambivalence:

> The dream in *The Book of the Duchess*, then, could be classified as a *somnium naturale*, a *somnium animale*, or a *somnium coeleste*. . . . Seen in one way, the dream is a heavenly vision, conveying the truth in a symbolic form. . . . At the same time, the merely psychological explanation of the dream would provide suggestions for the organization of the dream-poem as an intricate late-medieval work of art. In later dream-poems Chaucer will make these issues explicit and generalize them, so that the uncertainty about the status of dreams can be used as a way of discussing the status of the poem as such.[9]

7. Vincent of Beauvais, *Speculum naturale*, bk. 26, ch. 57, col. 1874; Vincent borrows here from Albertus Magnus, *Summa de creaturis*, question 51 (pp. 442–3).
8. Kruger, *Dreaming in the Middle Ages*, 129. See also p. 135, where I suggest that Chaucer's *BD* in particular participates in the 'sustained ambiguity of the middle vision'; my current consideration of *BD* represents a partial rethinking of that suggestion. See also Kruger, 'Mirrors and the Trajectory of Vision'; id., 'Imagination and the Complex Movement of Chaucer's House of Fame', ChauR 28 (1993–4), 117–34, for readings that emphasize the ambivalence of the dream vision's movement.
9. Spearing, *Medieval Dream-Poetry* (Cambridge, 1976), 61.

And as Lynch suggests, 'the substitution of one mode of knowing for another' in the later Middle Ages enabled, in Chaucer's poetry at least, a 'dialogism' that Lynch would deny to the earlier 'high medieval dream vision': 'The dream vision genre would become, in Bakhtin's terms, "novelized" . . . as generic conventions would come to reflect a significantly different set of assumptions, ones that allowed for a more real pluralism, that permitted, even demanded, multiple expressions of a truth whose unity was difficult or impossible of apprehension.'[1]

While I do not wish here to take back my earlier formulation, or to deny the power of readings of dream poetry like Spearing's and Lynch's that emphasize ambiguity and plurality, I do wish to rethink such positions in the light of what I am here proposing about the 'somatizing' of later medieval dream theory. Given the late medieval focus on a certain unitary process through which mundane and transcendent dream causes would both operate, one might see the dream's doubleness working not so much via a tension or balance of higher and lower terms as through an addition or superimposition of them. * * * Perhaps the dream that Chaucer includes in the frame of his *Book of the Duchess*, Alcyone's dream of her dead husband Ceyx, dramatizes just such a bringing together of somatic and spiritual power. Brought on through her prayer to the gods and through their responding action—that is, brought on by forces that transcend the dreamer's body—Alcyone's dream is nonetheless most striking for its strong physicality: Ceyx's actual body, not some simulacrum, is caught up into the dream, appearing to Alcyone in the flesh.

The Movement of Correction in Chaucer's Book of the Duchess

Chaucer's *Book of the Duchess* evokes bodily illness in a variety of ways.[2] As an elegy, it concerns itself repeatedly, if often obliquely, with death: the real death of Blanche, Duchess of Lancaster, during the plague of 1368;[3] the death of 'White', Blanche's fictional counterpart; the deaths of Ceyx and Alcyone in the Ovidian story Chaucer reshapes by metamorphosing metamorphosis into death; and the deaths from 'sorrowful' illness feared for both the poem's narrator and the knight of his dream:

> For nature wolde nat suffyse
> To noon erthly creature
> Nat longe tyme to endure
> Withoute slep and be in sorwe.
> And I ne may; ne nyght ne morwe,

---

1. K. L. Lynch, 'The *Book of the Duchess* as a Philosophical Vision', *Genre*, 21 (1988), 279–305: 282–3. For Lynch's treatment of the earlier dream-vision tradition, see her *High Medieval Dream Vision* (Stanford, 1988).
2. I am concerned here to pursue a reading of *BD* that, in foregrounding the body, resists the critical tendency noted by L. O. Fradenburg, ' "Voice Memorial": Loss and Reparation in Chaucer's Poetry', *Exemplaria*, 2 (1990), 169–202, to abandon the particular and embodied, often identified with the 'female' or 'feminine', 'in favor of some form of transcendence' (185), a move that replicates the elegiac impulse to pass beyond grief for the individual and to assert a transcendent authority that makes loss make sense.
3. For the argument that Blanche's death occurred in 1368 rather than 1369, as previously believed, see J. J. N. Palmer, 'The Historical Context of the *Book of the Duchess*: A Revision', *ChauR* 8 (1973–4), 253–61; S. Ferris, 'John Stow and the Tomb of Blanche the Duchess', *ChauR* 18 (1983–4), 92–3.

Slepe; and thus melancoyle
And drede I have for to dye.
(18–24)

Hit was gret wonder that Nature
Myght suffre any creature
To have such sorwe and be not ded.
(467–69)

Although Chaucer suppresses 'any reference to plague . . . in favour of a more generalized and abstract allusion to death', as Butterfield has recently argued, the *Book of the Duchess* may nonetheless be productively read in relation to the 'politics of plague'.[4] And the poem explicitly and insistently concerns itself with melancholic illness occasioned by love and by loss. The poem's tripartite structure—focused first on the narrator, then on Alcyone, and finally on the knight—depends upon a triple reiteration of melancholia.[5]

The narrator, while he denies knowledge of the cause of the 'sicknesse' (36) that he has 'suffred this eight yeer' (37)—'Myselven can not telle why / The sothe' (34–5)—presents a remarkably detailed symptomatology, anatomizing in particular the physiological dysfunction of the brain under the influence of sleeplessness. Both the imaginative and estimative faculties are disturbed,[6] with *imaginatio* working overtime (14–15) to present 'Suche fantasies' (28) that the narrator, his *aestimatio* confounded, is unable to judge 'what is best to doo' (29), unable even to distinguish 'Joye' from 'sorowe' [4–15]:

Al is ylyche good to me—
Joye or sorowe, wherso hyt be—
For I have felynge in nothyng,
But as yt were a mased thyng,
Alway in poynt to falle a-doun;
For sorwful ymagynacioun
Ys alway hooly in my mynde.
(9–15)

Despite his estimative disturbance, the narrator is able to recognize the 'sorrowful' nature of his own situation (14, 21) and to identify his sleeplessness as unnatural, 'agaynes kynde' (16), and, therefore, perilous; but awareness of his endangered position does not help him escape from malaise. Rather, it leads, in a kind of vicious circle, to further 'melancolye'

4. A. Butterfield, 'Pastoral and the Politics of Plague', *SAC* 16 (1994), 3–27: 22. P. P. Buckler, 'Love and Death in Chaucer's *The Book of the Duchess*', in J. S. Mink and J. D. Ward (eds.), *Joinings and Disjoinings: The Significance of Marital Status in Literature* (Bowling Green, Oh., 1991), 6–18, also places BD in the context of the Black Death.
5. The importance of the 'triptych' structure of the poem has been emphasized, for instance, in D. C. Baker, 'Imagery and Structure in Chaucer's *Book of the Duchess*', *SN* 30 (1958), 17–26, and H. Phillips, 'Structure and Consolation in the *Book of the Duchess*', *ChauR* 16 (1981–2), 107–18.
6. On *imaginatio* and *aestimatio* and their interrelation, see E. R. Harvey, *The Inward Wits* (London, 1975), esp. pp. 44–6; M. W. Bundy, *The Theory of Imagination in Classical and Mediaeval Thought*, University of Illinois Studies in Language and Literature 12/2–3 (Urbana, Ill., 1927); V. A. Kolve, *Chaucer and the Imagery of Narrative: The First Five Canterbury Tales* (Stanford, 1984), esp. pp. 20–4. Imagination, working with the *sensus communis*, receives and retains images from the five senses; estimation judges the *intentiones* that inhere in images, and it informs the perceiver about the hostility or harmlessness of the things perceived.
   On what he calls the 'psychology of perception and cognition' in BD, see D. Burnley, 'Some Terminology of Perception in the *Book of the Duchess*', *ELN* 23 (1986), 15–22; J. S. Neaman, 'Brain Physiology and Poetics in *The Book of the Duchess*', *RPL* 3 (1980), 101–13; Lynch, '*Book of the Duchess*', 288.

(23) and 'drede' (24), to a 'hevynesse' that, combined with 'Defaute of slep' (25), robs his 'spirit' of 'quyknesse' (26). He lives devoid of vitality: 'I have lost al lustyhede' (27).

The symptoms that the narrator thus describes, and their circular reinforcement, are clearly associated, in medieval medical works, with a superabundance of melancholic humour.[7] As Klibansky, Panofsky, and Saxl point out, Constantinus Africanus, translating Isḥâq ben ʿAmrân, portrays melancholy illness 'as "motions disturbed by black bile with fear, anxiety, and nervousness", that is to say, as a physically conditioned sickness of the soul which could attack all three "virtutes ordinativae"—imagination, reason, and memory—and thence, reacting on the body, cause sleeplessness, loss of weight, and disorder of all the natural functions'.[8] Melancholy, as the cold and dry humour, is particularly conducive to the formation of strong impressions in the imagination, impressions that, as in lovesickness, might then be obsessively considered and reconsidered.[9] The narrator's obsessive depiction of his own obsessive illness fits just such a pattern. And the larger movement of the *Book of the Duchess* can be described as a repeated, circular return to the question of melancholy.[1]

Thus the story of Ceyx and Alcyone, read by the narrator for diversion as he lies sleepless in bed, directly echoes his melancholic illness. Alcyone responds to the disappearance of Ceyx with 'wonder' (78; compare line 1); she is sorrowful (85, 95, 98, 100, 104, 202, 203, 210, 213; compare lines 10, 14, 21); her physical and mental capacities are disturbed—she swoons (103, 123, 215), refuses to eat (92), is 'forwaked' (126), 'wery' (127), 'ful nygh wood' (104). Just as the narrator suggests that 'there is phisicien but oon / That may me hele' (39–40), so Alcyone 'Ne . . . koude no reed but oon' (105). And as though recognizing the points of contact between his own situation and Alcyone's, the narrator responds to her story strongly and sympathetically, feeling 'such pittee and such rowthe' that he 'ferde the worse al the morwe / Aftir to thenken on hir sorwe' (97, 99–100). Indeed, the outcome of Alcyone's illness, her sudden death, presents a limit, the worst-case scenario, for the narrator's own illness, enacting the death he fears for himself.

Significantly, of course, Alcyone's illness, like the narrator's, eventuates in a dream linked to both body and divinity, a dream that reveals the truth but at the same time is closely connected to Alcyone's psychosomatic distress.[2] Here, the somatic connections of the dream are emphasized not

---

7. On melancholy in *BD*, see esp. J. M. Hill, 'The *Book of the Duchess*, Melancholy, and that Eight-Year Sickness', *ChauR* 9 (1974–5), 35–50; C. F. Heffernan, 'That Dog Again: *Melancholia Canina* and Chaucer's *Book of the Duchess*', *MP* 84 (1986), 185–90.

8. R. Klibansky, E. Panofsky, and F. Saxl, *Saturn and Melancholy: Studies in the History of Natural Philosophy, Religion, and Art* (London, 1964), 83. See also p. 92, where Klibansky *et al.* suggest that, in scholastic works, melancholy's effects often were—as in Chaucer—associated specifically with imaginative and estimative dysfunction. The reported symptoms of melancholy remain quite stable at least into the Renaissance: see R. Burton, *The Anatomy of Melancholy*, ed. H. Jackson (New York, 1977), First Partition, 382–429, and the 'synopsis' on pp. 128–9.

9. See e.g. the opening of Gerard of Berry's *Glosses on the Viaticum*, in M. F. Wack, *Lovesickness in the Middle Ages: The Viaticum and its Commentaries* (Philadelphia, 1990), 198–9.

1. M. B. Herzog, 'The *Book of the Duchess*: The Vision of the Artist as a Young Dreamer', *ChauR* 22 (1987–8), 269–81: 270–1.

2. The truthful nature of the dream is perhaps emphasized by the time at which it occurs—'Ryght even a quarter before day' (198). Dreams arising not long before dawn were thought to be more likely to reveal the truth since, by that time, digestion was largely complete. See the passage cited from Vincent of Beauvais, *Speculum naturale*, bk. 26, ch. 47, col. 1868, above. See also Kruger, *Dreaming in the Middle Ages*, 72, 99, 106; C. Speroni, 'Dante's Prophetic Morning-Dreams', *SP* 45 (1948), 50–9.

only by the literal bringing of Ceyx's body to Alcyone's bedside but also by certain clearly melancholic features of the dream situation. Although it is Juno and her 'messager' (133) who respond most directly to Alcyone's prayer for 'grace to slepe and mete / In my slep som certeyn sweven / Wherthourgh that I may knowen even / Whether my lord be quyk or ded' (118–21), the divinity immediately responsible for the dream is Morpheus, the ruler of a 'derke' (155), barren (155–9), chthonic realm, 'ygrave . . . wonder depe' (164–5), pervaded by a 'dedly slepynge soun' (162), 'as derk / As helle-pit overal aboute' (170–1). This dark underworld, from which Alcyone's revelatory dream arises, is inhabited by creatures (potential dreams) who, frozen in lethargy, echo in their attitudes Alcyone's own despondent poses: 'Somme henge her chyn upon hir brest' (174; compare 'she heng doun the hed', 122); 'And somme lay naked in her bed' (176; compare 'And broghten hir in bed al naked', 125).

The narrator's own dream stands in a similarly intimate connection to his illness, and particularly to the state of melancholy. As Heffernan has suggested, Chaucer's depiction of the fawning 'whelp' (389) in the dream may evoke medical accounts of 'melancholia canina' or 'lycanthropia'.[3] It is this whelp which guides the dreamer through a bright landscape to a wood of melancholic dream images—'things tinted with a dark color',[4] 'hit was shadewe overal under' (426)—where the dreamer discovers the knight 'clothed al in blak' (457) lamenting his lost love 'White'.

The knight of course suffers from an illness similar to that of both the narrator and Alcyone: 'he heng hys hed adoun' (461) repeats the gesture of Alcyone and of the inhabitants of the land of Sleep; and his 'compleynte' (464), with its 'dedly sorwful soun' (462), echoes the 'dedly slepynge soun' (162) of Morpheus' cave. Like the narrator's illness, the knight's is here anatomized in some physiological detail [487–99]:

> Whan he had mad thus his complaynte,
> Hys sorwful hert gan faste faynte
> And his spirites wexen dede;
> The blood was fled for pure drede
> Doun to hys herte, to make hym warm—
> (487–91)[5]

Although here the focus is on disturbances of the heart rather than the head, a mental fixation like the narrator's is also detailed [503–13]:

> he spak noght,
> But argued with his owne thoght,
> And in hys wyt disputed faste
> Why and how hys lyf myght laste;
> Hym thoughte hys sorwes were so smerte
> And lay so colde upon hys herte.
> (503–08)

In their ensuing conversation, both the narrator and the knight explicitly note the knight's ailment:

3. Heffernan, 'That Dog Again'.
4. G. Hoffmeister, 'Rasis' Traumlehre: Traumbücher des Spätimittelalters', AK 51 (1969), 150.
5. Cf. J. E. Grennen, 'Hert-Huntyng in the Book of the Duchess', MLQ 25 (1964), 131–9: 139.

> by my trouthe, to make yow hool
> I wol do al my power hool.
> And telleth me of your sorwes smerte;
> Paraunter hyt may ese youre herte,
> That semeth ful sek under your syde.
>
> (553–7)

> May noght make my sorwes slyde,
> Nought al the remedyes of Ovyde,
> Ne Orpheus, god of melodye,
> Ne Dedalus with his playes slye;
> Ne hele me may no phisicien,
> Noght Ypocras ne Galyen.
>
> (567–72)

The *Book of the Duchess* thus focuses attention unremittingly upon the realm of body and bodily illness, but to what end?* * *

Here * * * the dream promises, at least in part, to provide a remedy for illness. Although the narrator, having gestured towards the only 'phisicien' that might heal him (39–40), denies that any remedy is near at hand— 'That wil not be mot nede be left' (42)—the movement to reading, and from reading to sleep, is, as Olson has pointed out, a therapeutic one.[6] The primary symptom of the narrator's illness, his insomnia, is, after all, relieved, and we might reasonably expect the dream that ensues to continue a therapeutic movement. Moreover, as I will suggest, the dream of the *Book of the Duchess* is not simply somatic but rather an intervention in bodily illness supported by the moral force of the dream's traditional transcendent connections. * * * Chaucer's dream moves towards a correction of physical illness that depends, in its notion of somatic health, upon certain moral imperatives.

Alcyone's dream may here be taken as at least a partial model for the narrator's. The Ovidian dream as Chaucer retells it works towards a cure of Alcyone by demanding that she moderate her 'excessive' reaction to Ceyx's absence: 'Let be your sorwful lyf, / For in your sorwe there lyth no red' (202–3). The dream operates through the body of Ceyx, and its primary goal is a relief of Alcyone's bodily and psychological distress. At the same time, all that is somatic in the dream depends upon the action of the gods, and its argument, intended to return Alcyone to bodily health, is directed towards spiritual correction, demanding a detachment from body, a recognition of the limitations of earthly happiness: 'I am but ded' (204); 'To lytel while oure blysse lasteth!' (211). The return to somatic health depends somewhat paradoxically upon a rejection of body, a reordering of spirit that will allow Alcyone to resume an ordered life in the world. While the correction needed for the narrator's return to health is even more complex, it too ultimately involves a simultaneous movement towards reordering the body and letting it go.

Of course, Alcyone's dream fails to achieve its therapeutic goal: rather than move her out of illness, the confirmation of Ceyx's death intensifies 'sorwe' (213) and leads to a swift death. Still, the dream does attempt a

---

6. G. Olson, *Literature as Recreation in the Later Middle Ages* (Ithaca, NY, 1982), 85–9.

certain simultaneously somatic and spiritual correction. And while it fails to cure Alcyone, it does participate in a larger therapeutic trajectory for the narrator. The decision 'To rede and drive the night away' (49) is the narrator's first step out of a circular obsession with his own illness, and the thoughts and actions that the account of Alcyone's dream puts into motion—the playful prayer to Morpheus or Juno 'Or som wight elles' (242–4)—lead immediately to a falling asleep that doubtless represents a first step in the cure of insomniac illness: 'I had be dolven everydel / And ded, ryght thurgh defaute of slep, / Yif I ne had red and take kep / Of this tale next before' (222–5).

With the Alcyone story, then, a forward movement begins for the narrator, countering the poem's initial, melancholic circularities. While those circularities are reiterated in a variety of ways—melancholic illness reappears in the dream; the hunt, broken off, returns at the dream's conclusion; the knight's self-revelation proceeds by fits and starts, structured by a triple reiteration of its refrain, 'Thou wost ful lytel what thou menest, / I have lost more than thow wenest' (743–4, 1137–8, 1305–6); the awakened dreamer promises 'to put this sweven in ryme' (1332) and thus, as the poem ends, recalls its beginning—they are now complicated by a linear movement that strongly promises escape from repetitive, obsessive illness. The sleepless narrator has, after all, finally fallen asleep to dream his 'wonderful', 'ynly swete . . . sweven' (276–7).

The description of the dream as 'ynly swete' neatly evokes, as does the narrator's reference to Macrobius (284), the dream's traditional doubleness. On the one hand, 'ynly swete' might allude to an understanding of dreams as allegorically significant, composed of the *chaf* of images and the enclosed ('ynly'), nourishing ('swete') *fruyt* of hidden significance, containing, like meaningful fictions, an instructive core beneath an entertaining surface.[7] At the same time, given the narrator's warnings about the difficulty of 'reading' this particular dream (277–89), we might be steered away from searching for hidden significance and instead be tempted to see 'ynly swete' as pointing towards the dream's somatic connections: in so far as it is medically therapeutic, working against the internal disturbances of melancholy, the dream is 'inwardly sweet'. My point here is that the poem does not demand from us a decision that the dream should fit either one or the other of these possibilities; rather, it might function both as (morally or spiritually) instructive and as (somatically) corrective.

That the dream stands in some sense counter to its frame—both the narrator's self-description and the account of Alcyone and her own, not successfully therapeutic, dream—is clear from its opening moments. To enter this dream is to move from darkness to light and from passivity to activity, from a night of sleeplessness to a morning awakening.[8] The scenes

---

7. J. I. Wimsatt, 'The Book of the Duchess: Secular Elegy or Religious Vision?', in J. P. Hermann and J. J. Burke, Jr. (eds.), Signs and Symbols in Chaucer's Poetry (University, Ala., 1981), 113–29, makes a similar suggestion at p. 118.

8. On the contrast of night and day in the poem, see Baker, 'Imagery and Structure'. On the contrast between activity and passivity, see L. J. Kiser, 'Sleep, Dreams, and Poetry in Chaucer's Book of the Duchess', PLL 19 (1983), 3–12. On the changes that occur in moving into the dream—including changes in the narrator himself—see e.g. B. H. Bronson, 'The Book of the Duchess Reopened', PMLA 67 (1952), 863–81: 870–1; W. H. Clemen, Chaucer's Early Poetry, trans. C. A. M. Sym (London, 1963), 39; B. F. Huppé and D. W. Robertson, Jr., Fruyt and Chaf: Studies in Chaucer's Allegories (Princeton, 1963), 44–5; J. B. Severs, 'Chaucer's Self-Portrait in the Book of the Duchess', PQ 43 (1964), 27–39: 34–5; R. A. Peck, 'Theme and Number in Chaucer's Book of the Duchess', in A. Fowler (ed.), Silent Poetry: Essays in Numerological Analysis (London, 1970), 73–

of the preamble—the undescribed bedchambers of the narrator and Alcyone, the briefly sketched tempest in which Ceyx perishes, and the sterile realm of Sleep—are replaced by a brightly decorated bedroom and flourishing springtime landscape.[9] The passive, almost paralysed, narrator remains enclosed within his chamber during the poem's preamble, but in the dream he quickly abandons his room, moving out into the world to participate in its activities. Where, before the dream, the narrator's encounter with 'kynde' or 'nature' occurs only in the adversarial experience of illness ('agaynes kynde / Hyt were to lyven in thys wyse', 16–17), and in reading stories meant 'to be in minde, / While men loved the lawe of kinde' (55–6), the dream dramatizes a movement into greater and greater proximity with the natural. Beginning in the enclosed bedchamber where birdsong and sunlight and clear air can be experienced only indirectly, filtered through elaborately decorated windows and walls, the narrator moves first into the social, ritual, and still adversarial encounter with nature that the hunt represents and then, led by the whelp, more directly into the natural landscape.[1]

> And I hym folwed, and hyt forth wente
> Doun by a floury grene wente
> Ful thikke of gras, ful softe and swete,
> With floures fele, faire under fete,
> And litel used; hyt semed thus,
> For both Flora and Zephirus,
> They two that make floures growe,
> Had mad her dwellynge ther, I trowe . . .
> (397–404)

The movement that the dream thus institutes can be consistently read in somatic terms. Initiated in a momentary escape from melancholy when, stimulated by the account of Alcyone's dream, the narrator playfully prays for sleep, the dream itself opens in a landscape far from melancholic. But the dream does not represent simply a reversal or denial of illness. Rather, the bright opening of the dream leads into a movement of discovery whose goal is a return to melancholy that will not be simply circular but will, rather, move the narrator towards an understanding, and correction, of his illness. The dreamer moves out of his bedchamber, into the hunt for a 'hert' that, on the literal level, may fail, but that succeeds in returning the narrator to the 'hert' of his own distress. Led back into a landscape of melancholy ('hit was shadewe overal under', 426) that is simultaneously the landscape of natural phenomena, the narrator discovers first abundant 'herts' that have eluded the literal hunt (427) and then the knight and his grieving 'hert' (488).[2] Although this forward movement leads circularly

115: 78–9 and 93; R. R. Edwards, 'The *Book of the Duchess* and the Beginnings of Chaucer's Narrative, *NLH* 13 (1982), 189–204: 194–5; M. Stevens, 'Narrative Focus in *The Book of the Duchess*: A Critical Revaluation', *AM* 7 (1966), 16–32: 18–19, however, denies that the dreamer undergoes any real change in the course of the poem.

9. See Baker, 'Imagery and Structure'; D. Walker, 'Narrative Inconclusiveness and Consolatory Dialectic in the *Book of the Duchess*', *ChauR* 18 (1983–4), 1–17.

1. Several critics have emphasized the thematic importance of 'kynde' for the poem. See R. M. Lumiansky, 'The Bereaved Narrator in Chaucer's *Book of the Duchess*', *TSE* 9 (1959), 5–17; L. Eldredge, 'The Structure of the *Book of the Duchess*', *RUO* 39 (1969), 132–51; J. M. Flyer, 'Irony and the Age of Gold in the *Book of the Duchess*,' *Speculum*, 52 (1977), 314–28.

2. On the complex wordplay around the *hert*, and for various readings of the significance of literal and figurative hunts in the poem, see M. A. Carson, 'Easing of the "Hert" in the *Book of the*

back to a dark landscape at the centre of which is the lamenting knight, the figure who arrives at that landscape stands in a position very different from that which he occupies at the poem's opening. In the person of his dreaming self, the narrator now stands separate from himself as the subject of illness.[3] Rather than experience the psychic confusions of melancholia from the inside—as at the beginning of the poem—he is now able to project his obsessive involvement in illness outward, on to the (imagined) person of the knight, and to assess this objectification of his illness 'objectively'. Thus, in observing the knight, the narrator moves to delineate, in addition to the symptoms of mental disturbance experienced from within and described at the poem's opening, the illness's full observable effects on body and heart. In the fiction that the dream presents, the narrator is no longer the passive sufferer of melancholy but rather a figure who, like Boethius' Lady Philosophy or like the *confabulator* of medical tradition,[4] may actively lead the knight to expose the causes of his illness and thus pursue its cure (547–57). The dialogue between the narrator and the knight indeed plots out a trajectory of discovery: the knight's initial lyric and allegorical expositions (and avoidances) of his situation give way to a more and more literal, historical account of loss.[5]

Moreover, the dream, especially in its emphasis on a movement from passivity to activity and from the 'agaynes kynde' to the 'natural', is not purely somatic, but also has a certain ideological, moralizing force. The narrator's illness is meaningful not just because it affects one individual's body and threatens his death but also because it potentially disrupts larger social structures thought to be both naturally and divinely instituted. More particularly, the narrator's melancholic illness disturbs his participation in 'properly' gendered and sexualized behaviour, and the dream operates not just to calm somatic disturbance but also to correct the narrator's gender and sexual identifications. That correction gains particular force from the dream's double positioning as an experience able to heighten both somatic and spiritual awareness. On the one hand, because of the dream's transcendent associations, the movement of somatic realignment can take on moral significance; on the other, the moralizing understanding of what is proper to the male body is underpinned by the dream's privileged access to the realm of nature. The corrective movement instituted by the dream, in so far as this is moral in its thrust, gains the force of what is understood

Duchess', ChauR 1 (1966–7), 157–60; D. Luisi, 'The Hunt Motif in *The Book of the Duchess*', *ES* 52 (1971), 309–11; M. Thiébaux, *The Stag of Love: The Chase in Medieval Literature* (Ithaca, NY, 1974), 115–27; R. A. Shoaf, 'Stalking the Sorrowful H(e)art: Penitential Lore and the Hunt Scene in Chaucer's *The Book of the Duchess*', *JEGP* 78 (1979), 313–24; D. Scott-Macnab, 'A Reexamination of Octovyen's Hunt in *The Book of the Duchess*', *MÆ* 56 (1987), 183–99.

3. Readings that posit the knight as the dreamer's surrogate largely follow Bronson, 'Book of the Duchess Re-opened'. For one recent elaboration of such a reading, see R. W. Hanning, 'Chaucer's First Ovid: Metamorphosis and Poetic Tradition in *The Book of the Duchess* and *The House of Fame*', in L. A. Arrathoon (ed.), *Chaucer and the Craft of Fiction* (Rochester, Mich., 1986), 121–63: 122–41.

4. For Boethian readings of BD, see D. W. Robertson, Jr., 'The Historical Setting of Chaucer's *Book of the Duchess*', in J. Mahoney and J. E. Keller (eds.), *Mediaeval Studies in Honor of Urban Tigner Holmes, Jr.*, University of North Carolina Studies in the Romance Languages and Literatures 56 (Chapel Hill, NC, 1965), 169–95; C. P. R. Tisdale, 'Boethian "Hert-Huntyng": The Elegiac Pattern of *The Book of the Duchess*', *ABR* 24 (1973), 365–80; M. D. Cherniss, *Boethian Apocalypse: Studies in Middle English Vision Poetry* (Norman, Okla., 1987), 169–91. See Olson, *Literature as Recreation*, 88, on the narrator as the Black Knight's *confabulator*.

5. On the interplay of the literal and the figurative in the poem, see A. C. Spearing, 'Literal and Figurative in *The Book of the Duchess*', *SAC: Proceedings*, 1 (1984), 165–71, in part a response to D. Aers, 'Chaucer's *Book of the Duchess*: An Art to Consume Art', *DUJ* NS 38 (1977), 201–5.

to be natural to the human body and, in so far as it is somatic, that move-
ment is supported by the dream's supposed access to moral truth.

One of the most striking qualities of the narrator's opening description
of his illness is its absence of explicit references to gender and sexuality.
In the poem's first forty-three lines, the speaker could equally well be male
or female. When the narrator refers to a male attendant reaching him a
book ('he it me tok', 48), we may conclude that the narrator is himself a
man, but we should consider, in a poet who would later consistently imper-
sonate feminine voices, the possibility that, at the poem's outset, a certain
gender undefinedness or ambiguity is intended. Indeed, melancholic ill-
ness, in its challenges to the correct 'estimative' functioning of the mind
and in the danger it therefore poses that an unworthy object might be
elevated to a place of prominence in the subject's (obsessive) thinking and
desire, always threatens a certain overthrowing of mental hierarchy figured
as gender hierarchy, the dominance of (masculine) reason over (feminine)
impulse. In other words, melancholic illness, for the male subject, threat-
ens feminization. As Wack has suggested for lovesickness, in a formulation
that can, I believe, be extended more generally to melancholia:

> The patient considers [the beloved woman] better, more noble, and
> more desirable than other women, even though this may not objec-
> tively be the case. The overestimation of her desirability immobilizes
> the lover's mental faculties in meditation on her mental image . . .
> there is a loss of inner control and governance in the noble subject,
> a degradation of the mental faculties expressed in the infantilization
> or feminization of the lover's body and behaviour.[6]

The narrator's passivity, his inability to overcome the 'fantastic' operations
of his mind, despite his awareness of the dangers these pose for him, cou-
pled with Chaucer's initial reticence about the narrator's gender, contrib-
ute to an opening portrait in which proper masculinity, at least by its
absence, is an issue.[7]

The poem's opening is similarly, indeed more strikingly, reticent when
it comes to the narrator's positioning as a romantic or sexual subject. Of
course, critics beginning with Sypherd have often, and rightly, taken the
details of the eight years' sickness (36–7) and 'phisicien but oon' (39) as
conventions of love poetry that might point towards the narrator's impli-
cation in melancholic *love*sickness.[8] What seems to me most striking about
such details, however, is not their resonance with the poetry of courtly love
but rather their failure to specify for themselves any precise field of ref-
erence. Certainly, they allow for Sypherd's reading but, as a whole series
of opposing critical readings would suggest, they also leave themselves
open to non-romantic—Boethian or theological—interpretations. Here,
the narrator is not lovesick but bereaved, and perhaps spiritually endan-

6. Wack, *Lovesickness*, 72.
7. Cf. E. T. Hansen, *Chaucer and the Fictions of Gender* (Berkeley and Los Angeles, 1992), 61; G. Margherita, *The Romance of Origins: Language and Sexual Difference in Middle English Literature* (Philadelphia, 1994), 94–9.
8. W. O. Sypherd, 'Chaucer's Eight Years' Sickness', *MLN* 20 (1905), 240–3. Those who, with Syph-erd, assess the narrator's predicament as that of a lover include G. L. Kittredge, *Chaucer and his Poetry* (1915; Cambridge, Mass., 1967), 39–40; R. S. Loomis, 'Chaucer's Eight Years' Sickness', *MLN* 59 (1944), 178–80; M. Galway, 'Chaucer's Hopeless Love', *MLN* 60 (1945), 431–9; Bron-son, '*Book of the Duchess* Re-opened', 869; D. Bethurum, 'Chaucer's Point of View as Narrator in the Love Poems', *PMLA* 74 (1959), 511–20: 513; Fyler, 'Irony and the Age of Gold', 315; A. Butterfield, 'Lyric and Elegy in *The Book of the Duchess*', *MÆ* 60 (1991), 33–60: 48–9.

gered.[9] One might, indeed, point out that, in Chaucer's own corpus of writing, the figure of the 'phisicien' refers not only to the beloved woman of romance traditions (as when, in the Book of the Duchess itself, the knight refers to White as 'my lyves leche' (920) or when Criseyde is depicted as Troilus' 'leche', TC II. 571, 1066, 1582), but also to Lady Philosophy ('fisycien', Bo I. prosa 3. 4, and 'leche', Bo I. prosa 4. 5; IV. prosa 2. 129), the Virgin Mary ('my soules leche', ABC 133–4), Christ ('oure soules leche', PardT 916), and God ('oure lyves leche', SumT 1892).

Chaucer seems in fact purposely to have excluded from the poem's opening passage any explicit reference to love or lovesickness. The opening lines of the Book of the Duchess are strongly indebted to the opening of Froissart's Paradys d'Amours:[1]

> I can only be amazed that I am still alive, when I am lying awake so much. And one cannot find a sleepless person more tormented than myself, for as you well know, whilst I am lying awake sad thoughts and melancholy often come to torment me. They bind my heart so tightly, and I cannot loosen them, for I do not want to forget the fair one, for love of whom I entered into this torment and suffer such sleeplessness.[2]

The opening of Froissart's poem operates by first sketching the narrator's melancholic illness and then, in lines 10–12, defining the cause of that illness—love for a beautiful woman ('la belle'). In Chaucer, the account of illness is maintained and elaborated, but its (hetero)sexual cause is never specified.[3] And beyond the non-specification of the narrator's illness as the feminizing but still heterosexual malady of lovesickness, the narrator's language also perhaps implies connections to a certain non-normative, non-procreative, 'perverse' sexuality. His illness is explicitly associated with what is 'agaynes kynde', and while this phrase might have a broad range of implications, like the 'phisicien but oon' pointing in several different directions at once, one of its strong and specific resonances would be with moralizing discourses directed at sexual behaviour 'contra naturam'.[4] Indeed, the knight of the narrator's dream will later speculate that his devotion to (heterosexual) love (see line 774) came to him 'kyndely' (778).

In part the Alcyone episode serves to specify, and heterosexualize, what is unspecified, and even potentially 'queer', in the narrator's initial (non-) sexual stance. Alcyone's situation brings together both the romantic and metaphysical (Boethian/theological) possibilities hinted at, but not specified, in the description of the narrator's illness: Alcyone is both lover, long-

9. See D. W. Robertson, Jr., A Preface to Chaucer (Princeton, 1962), 464; id., 'Historical Setting', 189; Huppé and Robertson, Fruyt and Chaf, 33; Cherniss, Boethian Apocalypse, 171; Wimsatt, Secular Elegy or Religious Vision?', 113–14.

1. For a general discussion of the French sources of BD see J. Wimsatt, Chaucer and the French Love Poets: The Literary Background of the Book of the Duchess (Chapel Hill, NC, 1968).

2. Trans. B. A. Windeatt, Chaucer's Dream Poetry: Sources and Analogues (Woodbridge, Suffolk, 1982), 41.

3. Cf. B. Nolan, 'Art of Expropriation: Chaucer's Narrator in The Book of the Duchess', in D. M. Rose (ed.), New Perspectives in Chaucer Criticism (Norman, Okla., 1981), 205.

4. The phrase goes back, in the Christian tradition, to the New Testament (Romans I: 26–7). It is used in the Middle Ages by such writers as Peter Damian. The fullest literary development of the implications of 'unnatural' sexuality occurs in Alain de Lille's dream vision, De planctu naturae, trans. J. J. Sheridan as The Plaint of Nature (Toronto, 1980). For a discussion of medieval ideas about sexuality and the '(un)natural', see J. Boswell, Christianity, Social Tolerance, and Homosexuality: Gay People in Western Europe from the Beginning of the Christian Era to the Fourteenth Century (Chicago, 1980), ch. 11.

ing for the absent beloved, and bereaved spouse in need of philosophical or theological consolation. And in the Ovidian story, both love and bereavement are specified as heterosexual. In so far as we identify the narrator with Alcyone—and the poem gives us strong reasons to do so—we may retrospectively recast the narrator's distress as itself heterosexual.

The dream frame thus begins a process of sculpting the narrator's initially amorphous illness into a recognizable and conventional form—the form of heterosexual desire and loss—and it is this very movement, the narrator's identification with Alcyone leading to his (playful) reiteration of her falling asleep, that initiates the larger curative or therapeutic movement of the poem. Correction of the narrator's illness begins with a displaced, heterosexualizing specification of it. But just as the Alcyone episode leaves much unresolved regarding the possibility of a cure for the narrator's own melancholy—Alcyone after all dies in response to the dream sent to assist her—it also fails fully to resolve the problems of gender and sexuality raised by the narrator's illness. The heterosexualizing of the narrator through a certain identification with Alcyone only serves to intensify the problem of gender identification.[5] Specifying the narrator's melancholy illness as romantic and heterosexual involves the cross-identification of narrator with ancient 'quene' (65). If the Alcyone episode serves to allay anxieties raised by Chaucer's refusal clearly to attach his narrator to a particular sexualized position, it only serves to reinforce questions we might have about the narrator's 'masculinity'. (Gender-crossing also occurs in the Ovidian story in Chaucer's replacement of Juno's traditional female messenger, Iris, with an unnamed male messenger, whom some critics have identified as Mercury, 'the deity known for his ability to change gender when he pleased'.[6])

The Alcyone episode thus begins, but fails fully to carry through, a corrective specification of the narrator's position in relation to gender and sexuality. The work of the dream—as it moves the narrator out of stasis and passivity, into contact with a natural world, and finally into confrontation with the knight who externalizes his illness—is more rigorously to secure the narrator's heterosexual and 'masculine' identity. Indeed, the very same movement that works towards a correction of somatic disturbance operates to gender and sexualize the narrator. The movement out of the obsessive stasis of melancholy illness is a movement of masculinization, replacing traditionally feminine passivity with masculine activity. The entry into the conventional landscape of spring, where the 'sorwes' of 'wynter' (411–12) have been forgotten through the procreative force of Nature—'al the woode was waxen grene / Swetnesse of dew had mad hyt waxe' (414–15)—is both a movement out of the cold and dry of melancholy, away from the 'agaynes kynde' of illness, and a movement out of the non-heterosexualized, non-procreative position of the poem's opening, away from the 'agaynes kynde' of sexuality.

The bedchamber in which the dream begins is decorated with fictions that gesture both towards the masculine pursuit of war and towards the heterosexual and romantic:

> For hooly al the story of Troye
> Was in the glasynge ywroght thus,
> Of Ector and of kyng Priamus,
> Of Achilles and of Kyng Lamedon,
> And eke of Medea and of Jason,
> Of Paris, Eleyne, and of Lavyne.
> And alle the walles with colours fyne
> Were peynted, bothe text and glose,
> Of al the Romaunce of the Rose.
>   (326–34)

The action that ensues in the dream serves to bring the narrator into both the realm of masculine pursuit and the courtly love landscape of 'the Rose'. As the dreamer moves from his bedchamber to the hunt forming outside, he enters a realm simultaneously masculine and heterosexualized. The hunt is of course a conventional figure of the pursuit of courtly love[7] and, as is emphasized strongly in Chaucer's poem, it is at the same time a realm of male homosociality.[8] Countering the narrator's strong identification with Alcyone is his eager entry here into a flurry of masculine movement: 'I herde goynge bothe up and doun / Men, hors, houndes, and other thyng, / And al men speken of huntyng' (348–50); 'Ther overtok y a gret route / Of huntes and eke of foresteres, / With many relayes and lymeres, / And hyed hem to the forest faste / And I with hem' (360–4); 'Every man dide ryght anoon / As to huntynge fil to doon' (374–5).

As with the Alcyone episode, the hunt is cut short. But from here the narrator is propelled (via the whelp) to the 'hert' of the poem, his encounter with the knight. In part this movement, in which the 'hert' the narrator himself hunts down is revealed to be not a beloved woman but the sick 'hert' of the knight, works against the heterosexualizing thrust of the dream. As Hansen points out, 'the mysterious, liminally male stranger encountered by the questing dreamer', the lovesick and hence feminized knight, 'may be said to occupy a position filled elsewhere in romance by fairy ladies'.[9] At the same time, however, the encounter with the knight certainly continues the movement into male homosociality that the hunt institutes. And after the initial shock of having the presumed object of the hunt, the (courtly, female) 'hert', turn out to be instead the (courtly, male) 'hert' of the bereaved lover, the process of heterosexualization pursued, if incompletely, in both the Alcyone episode and the hunt, continues—and this time in a much more elaborated and complete manner. The potential homoeroticism of the meeting between narrator and knight (and hunted 'hert') is deflected, as so often, into a male homosociality that operates to secure a bond between men through the (fantasmatic) heterosexual exchange of women.[1] Here, the body of the dead woman, White, fictively (re)created within the male–male dialogue, is evoked to serve as an object of transfer between the two men. Her evocation, on the one hand, explains the mourning knight's illness, and presumably moves towards its cure; at

---

7. See Thiébaux, *Stag of Love.*
8. See E. K. Sedgwick, *Between Men: English Literature and Male Homosocial Desire* (New York, 1985).
9. Hansen, *Chaucer and the Fictions of Gender,* 61.
1. Cf. M. Ellmann, 'Blanche', in J. Hawthorn (ed.), *Criticism and Critical Theory* (London, 1984), 99–110; Hansen, *Chaucer and the Fictions of Gender,* 59; Margherita, *Romance of Origins,* 86; J. Ferster, *Chaucer on Interpretation* (Cambridge, 1985), 69.

the same time, it fixes the sexually questionable narrator's interest on the matter of courtly heterosexuality. The conversation between knight and dreamer provides a guide to the world of courtly love—tracing the process by which the (male) lover falls in love with, suffers for, approaches, is rebuffed by, reapproaches, serves, and finally is bereft of, the beloved lady.

Like the story of Alcyone, the knight's story, as it unfolds, condenses the lovesickness of a pining lover with the grief of mourning, and it makes both of these heterosexual. Again, as in the Alcyone episode, in so far as we draw connections of identification between the knight and the narrator, we have here a specification and heterosexualization of the narrator's initially undefined, amorphous illness. Indeed, the narrator's concluding gesture in his dialogue with the knight is one of sympathetic identification: 'Is that youre los? Be God, hyt ys routhe!' (1310). And this seems to be precisely the required gesture to complete the movement of the dream. The frustrated and momentarily forgotten hunt with which the dream began is here reinvoked and judged conclusive: 'And with that word ryght anoon / They gan to strake forth; al was doon, / For that tyme, the hert-huntyng' (1311–13). And the forceful movement that the conclusion of the hunt then institutes—gesturing towards the public sphere of masculine action ('this kyng / Gan homwarde for to ryde', 1314–15) at the same time that it cryptically encodes, in its destination ('A long castel with walles white, / Be Seynt Johan, on a ryche hil', 1318–19), the heterosexual relation of John of Gaunt and Blanche of Lancaster that presumably motivates the whole poem²—reemphasizes the distance between the end-point of the dream and the poem's opening, with its hermetic bedchamber and its gender and sexual amorphousness.

The dream of the *Book of the Duchess* thus works to masculinize and heterosexualize the body of its ailing narrator. The correction of soma that the dream enacts—the tailoring of an at first amorphously defined body and its equally amorphous illness to certain naturalized designs of gender and sexuality—should not, however, be read as suggesting a full cure for the dreamer's illness nor even a neat solution to the poem's gender and sexual complications. After all, the movement I have just described, while it allows the hunt to be declared complete, and while it suggests that the dreamer no longer remains in his initial, paralysed, position, still leaves him in sympathetic identification with the ailing figure of the knight. This is a figure who, paradoxically, serves to bring the narrator closer to masculine and heterosexual positions at the same time that he enacts illness—and specifically the feminized illness—of the courtly lover who, perhaps improperly, over-values the beloved object of desire (as the dreamer suggests to the knight, 'I leve yow wel, that trewely / Yow thoghte that she was the beste / And to beholde the alderfayreste, / Whoso had loked hir with your eyen', 1048–51).

While the knight's self-revelation in the courtly narrative of 'White' may operate therapeutically, the full therapeutic demand—that he detach himself from the lost object of desire, that he recognize (in Ceyx's consolatory words) that 'in . . . sorwe there lyth no red' (203), that he pursue the Boethian movement towards consolation hinted at repeatedly in the dialogue between knight and narrator ('But ther is no man alyve her / Wolde for a

---

2. See F. Tupper, 'Chaucer and Richmond', *MLN* 31 (1916), 250–2; id., 'Chaucer and Lancaster', *MLN* 32 (1917), 54.

fers make this woo!', 740–1), that he transcend, leave behind, attachments to the body and the bodily—remains unmet. The complex medieval Christian ideology of body—one that embraces a 'proper' (masculine) gendering and heterosexual positioning of the male body—also recognizes that a truly masculine attitude towards body pushes beyond embodiment, towards spiritual transcendence. * * *Implicit in the path towards the masculinization and heterosexualization of the amorphous, ailing body of the poem's narrator is the understanding that the masculine, heterosexual body, while the body proper for a man, is itself a temporary position, and one that the truly masculine Christian will move beyond, striving for a 'virile', disinterested detachment from body. Alongside the strong thrust towards correcting the gender and sexual positioning of the dreamer operates the dreamer's own urging that the knight should recognize the deceptive and fleeting nature of bodily attachments. Chaucer thus represents the dream as not just bringing together medical and moral discourses to enforce a certain somatic correction that is at the same time a correction of gender and sexuality, but also adding to this already complex mixture the recognition of an imperative to transcend soma. At the same time that the dream maps out a therapeutic movement towards the correction of body, it suggests that the proper valuation of body and bodily desire might necessitate a rejection of body altogether. But the poem carries through this particular double movement only to a certain point; the hunt is complete only 'for that tyme'. At the conclusion of the *Book of the Duchess,* circularity reasserts itself. The narrator promises to write his dream down, and that promise reminds us that the moment of writing, the present tense of the poem's opening, while posterior to the dream, represents the dreamer as apparently unaffected by his successful falling asleep and the dream's corrective action.[3] Indeed, it is the morning after the dream that he 'fares the worse' (99) in sympathetic response to reading of Alcyone's distress and death.

The rejection of body is a position that no one in Chaucer's poem, with the exception of the dead Ceyx as he speaks the words of the gods—not Alcyone, not the knight, not the narrator or his dreaming self (despite that self's attempts to voice certain consolatory Boethian ideas)—is able fully to attain. At the core of the poem's final irresolution are certain unresolved, perhaps unresolvable, questions that, indeed, Chaucer would return to repeatedly in his poetic career, most notably in the poems of the Marriage Group: How to participate in love without falling into a feminized position? How to (hetero)sexualize the body without overvaluing it? How to mandate sexual desire and at the same time devalue that desire? While, as I have suggested, the dream, with its access to both spirit and soma, is an appropriate place to raise such questions, and while the dream of the *Book of the Duchess* does effectively work through certain complex issues about the body and its proper positioning, ending with a strong movement out of the landscape of melancholy and a certain 'straightening' of gender and sexual anomalies, it also reasserts, in its final circularity, the problems of body and melancholy illness, suggesting that the correction and (re)valuation of soma must, for embodied human beings who are also spiritual subjects, be worked through over and over again.

---

3. Cf. Bronson, '*Book of the Duchess* Re-opened', 868.

Geoffrey Chaucer: A Chronology†

The Historical Record	Literary Production
1327 Edward III becomes King of England.	Chaucer led an active public life, and thus there are far more records to document his life than to link his individual poems to specific dates or events. To be sure, we cannot always be certain of the significance of the life-records: Does "raptus" mean rape or abduction? Was the poet's financial situation secure or precarious? Did his royal affiliations put him in danger? At the same time, we have a surprisingly large amount of information about the fourteenth-century courtier's biography. In contrast, much of the evidence used to date his poems remains speculative and internal to the texts themselves. The dates below are reasonable guesses and often cover the span of many years, during which the poet may well have been working on more than one poem or translation. His habits of revision and his tendency to leave works unfinished also make a firm dating of the poems complicated. All of his major poems and translations are listed here, though not individual Canterbury tales that were begun before he had that major work underway. The only short lyric poems represented here are those that are included in this
1337 Beginning of Hundred Years War between England and France over the French Crown.	
1340–45 Birth of Geoffrey Chaucer.	
1347–51 First wave of plague ("Black Death") sweeps over Europe.	
1357 First life-record of Chaucer, serving in the household of Elizabeth, Countess of Ulster.	

† Based largely on Martin M. Crow and Clair C. Olson, eds., *Chaucer Life-Records* (Oxford: Clarendon P, 1966).

1359–60 Chaucer captured and ransomed in Hundred Years War; carries letters to the Earl of Ulster from Calais.

1360–66 Gap in the life-records: Chaucer perhaps serves at royal court, receives legal training, or attends university.

1366 Chaucer travels to Spain; by this date, Chaucer is married to Philippa Chaucer (née Pan).

1367 Chaucer in the pay of the royal household of Edward III.

1368 Death from plague of Blanche, Duchess of Lancaster, wife of the English prince John of Gaunt.

1370 Chaucer journeys overseas in the King's service.

1372–73 Chaucer travels on royal business to Genoa and Florence.

1374 Chaucer leases house above the Gate of Aldgate in London and becomes Controller of the Wool Custom; granted life annuity of 10 pounds by John of Gaunt and daily pitcher of wine by Edward III.

1377 Richard II becomes King of England at age of 10.

1377–81 Chaucer sent to France to help negotiate for peace and for a possible marriage between Richard II and the French princess Marie.

1378 Daily grant of wine (see 1374) commuted to annuity of 20 marks.

Norton Critical Edition and whose dates are the subject of reasonable conjecture. Further information on dating the lyrics can be found in the notes to the individual poems.

1368–72 The *Book of the Duchess*.

The *Romance of the Rose* translated before 1380, probably before 1372.

1378–80 probable date of the *House of Fame*.

1380   Chaucer released from the charge of rape ("raptus") of Cecily Champain.

1381   The Peasants' Revolt.

1382   Richard II and Anne of Bohemia married.

1380–82   probable date of the *Parliament of Fowls*.

1382–86   probable date of *Troilus and Criseyde*, translation of Boethius's *Consolation of Philosophy*.

1385–89   Chaucer serves as a Justice of the Peace for the County of Kent.

1386   Chaucer elected Member of Parliament from Kent; gives up his house in London and retires as Controller of the Wool Custom.

1385–88   possible date of "Anelida and Arcite," "Chaucer's Words to Adam."

1387   Death of Chaucer's wife Philippa.

1388   "Merciless Parliament" and triumph of Lords Appellant mark crisis of power for Richard II; Chaucer surrenders his annuities to one John Scalby.

1389   Chaucer appointed Clerk of the King's Works, putting him in charge of numerous repair and construction projects.

1391   Chaucer resigns as Clerk of the King's Works.

1391   Begins writing the *Treatise on the Astrolabe*

1394   Death of Queen Anne; Richard II grants Chaucer a life annuity of 20 pounds.

1386–96   The *Legend of Good Women* (two versions of the Prologue, nine tales, in progress).

1396   Richard II marries the seven-year-old French princess Isabelle.

1387–1400   *The Canterbury Tales* in progress.

1397   Richard II grants Chaucer a "tun" of wine per year (amounts to a reasonable daily allotment).

1398   Richard II banishes Henry Bolingbroke (one of the Lords Appellant, John of Gaunt's son, and the future Henry IV).

1399   Richard II deposed. New king, Henry IV, confirms Chaucer's grants with an additional 40 marks per year; Chaucer leases a house in the garden of Westminster Abbey.

1400   Date on tomb in Westminster Abbey records October 25 of this year as the date of Chaucer's death.

1399–1400   "The Complaint of Chaucer to His Purse."

Selected Bibliography

•indicates works included or excerpted in this Norton Critical Edition.

Any such bibliography is bound to be incomplete, due to the abundance of good work that has been done on Chaucer's early and minor poetry and on the dream vision over the past several decades, not all of which can be included here. The studies listed below offer a beginning list of readings, chiefly based on work done over the past fifty years. For additional current sources, see the excellent annotated bibliography published with each annual volume of *Studies in the Age of Chaucer* and available online in an electronic database managed through the University of Texas (http://uchaucer.utsa.edu).

MODERN EDITIONS, TRANSLATIONS, AND FACSIMILES

Chaucer, Geoffrey. *The Book of the Duchess*. Ed. Helen Phillips. Durham, Eng.: Durham and St. Andrews Medieval Texts, 1982.
———. *The Canterbury Tales: Fifteen Tales and the General Prologue*. Ed. V. A. Kolve and Glending Olson. 2nd ed. New York: W. W. Norton and Company, 2005.
———. *Chaucer's Dream Poetry*. Ed. Helen Phillips and Nick Havely. London: Longman, 1997.
———. *Chaucer's Poetry: An Anthology for the Modern Reader*. Ed. E. T. Donaldson. 2nd ed. New York: John Wiley & Sons, 1975.
———. *The Complete Poetry and Prose of Geoffrey Chaucer*. Ed. John H. Fisher. 2nd ed. New York: Holt, Rinehart and Winston, 1989.
———. *The Complete Works of Geoffrey Chaucer*. Ed. Walter W. Skeat. 6 vols. Oxford: Clarendon P, 1894.
———. *The House of Fame*. Ed. Nicholas R. Havely. Durham, Eng.: Durham Medieval Texts, 1994.
———. *The Legend of Good Women*. Ed. Janet Cowen and George Kane. East Lansing: Colleagues P, 1995.
———. *Love Visions*. Trans. Brian Stone. Harmondsworth: Penguin, 1983.
———. *The Minor Poems: A Variorum Edition of the Works of Geoffrey Chaucer*. Ed. George B. Pace and Alfred David. Vol. 5, Part 1. Norman: U of Oklahoma P, 1982.
———. *The Parliament of Birds*. ed. Steve Ellis, trans. E. B. Richmond. London: Hesperus, 2004.
———. *The Parlement of Foulys*. Ed. D. S. Brewer. 1960. Manchester: Manchester UP, 1972.
———. *The Riverside Chaucer*. Ed. Larry D. Benson. 3rd ed. Boston: Houghton Mifflin, 1987.
———. *Troilus and Criseyde*. Ed. Stephen A. Barney. New York: W. W. Norton and Company, 2006.
McGillivray, Murray, ed. *Geoffrey Chaucer's Book of the Duchess: A Hypertext Edition*. CD-ROM. 2nd ed. Calgary, Alberta: U of Calgary P, 1999.
Norton-Smith, John, ed. *Bodleian Library Manuscript Fairfax 16* [Facsimile]. London: Scolar P, 1979.
Parkes, M. B., and Richard Beadle, eds. *Poetical Works, Geoffrey Chaucer: A Facsimile of Cambridge University Library MS Gg.4.27*. 3 vols. Norman: Pilgrim Books, 1980.
Skeat, Walter W., ed. *The Works of Geoffrey Chaucer and Others* [Facsimile of the 1532 edition of William Thynne]. London: Alexander Moring, 1905.

LANGUAGE, RECORDINGS, AND EDITING

Baugh, Albert C., and Thomas Cable. *The History of the English Language*. 5th ed. New York: Routledge, 2002.
Benson, Larry D. *A Glossarial Concordance to the Riverside Chaucer*. New York: Garland, 1993.
Blake, Norman F. *The Cambridge History of the English Language: Vol. 2, 1066–1476*. Cambridge, Eng.: Cambridge UP, 1992.
Bowden, Betsy. *Chaucer Aloud: The Varieties of Textual Interpretation*. Philadelphia: U of Pennsylvania P, 1987. [Includes audiotape.]
Burnley, David. *A Guide to Chaucer's Language*. London: Macmillan, 1983.
Cannon, Christopher. *The Making of Chaucer's English: A Study of Words*. Cambridge: Cambridge UP, 1998.
The Chaucer Studio Recordings. <http://english.byu.edu/chaucer>. Includes audiocassettes of the *Book of the Duchess* (1988), the *Parlement of Foules* (1986), and selections from *The Legend of Good Women* (1997). Available at a reasonable price by writing to Paul R. Thomas, Dept. of English, Brigham Young University, Provo, Utah 84602-6218. <PaulThomas@byu.edu>.

Davis, Norman, and Douglas Gray et al. *A Chaucer Glossary*. Oxford: Clarendon P, 1979.
Fisher, John H. *The Emergence of Standard English*. UP of Kentucky, 1996.
Gaylord, Alan. "Imagining Voices: Chaucer on Cassette." *Studies in the Age of Chaucer* 12 (1990): 215–38.
Horobin, Simon. *The Language of the Chaucer Tradition*. Cambridge, Eng.: D. S. Brewer, 2003.
———. "A New Approach to Chaucer's Spelling." *English Studies* 79 (1998): 415–24.
Horobin, Simon, and Jeremy Smith. *An Introduction to Middle English*. Oxford: Oxford UP, 2003.
Kökeritz, Helge. *A Guide to Chaucer's Pronunciation*. 1961. Toronto: U of Toronto P, 1978.
Mooney, Linne. "Chaucer's Scribe." *Speculum* 81 (2006): 97–138.
Oizumi, Akio, ed. Programmed by Kunihiro Miki. *A Complete Concordance to the Works of Geoffrey Chaucer*. Vols. 5, 7, 10–12. New York: Olms-Weidmann, 1991.
Ruggiers, Paul G. *Editing Chaucer: The Great Tradition*. Norman, OK: Pilgrim Books, 1984.
Smith, J. J., ed. *The English of Chaucer and His Contemporaries: Essays by M. L. Samuels and J. J. Smith*. Aberdeen: Aberdeen UP, 1988.
Tatlock, J. S. P., and Arthur G. Kennedy. *A Concordance to the Complete Works of Geoffrey Chaucer and to the Romaunt of the Rose*. 1927. Gloucester: Peter Smith, 1963.

BIOGRAPHIES AND GENERAL REFERENCE

Akbari, Suzanne Conklin. *Seeing through the Veil: Optical Theory and Medieval Allegory*. Toronto: U of Toronto P, 2004.
Armitage-Smith, Sydney. *John of Gaunt*. New York: Barnes and Noble, 1964.
Bennett, J. A. W. *Chaucer at Oxford and at Cambridge*. Oxford: Clarendon P, 1957.
Brewer, Derek. *A New Introduction to Chaucer*. London: Longman, 1998.
———. *The World of Chaucer*. Cambridge: D. S. Brewer, 2000.
Calin, William. *The French Tradition and the Literature of Medieval England*. Toronto: U of Toronto P, 1994.
Collette, Carolyn P., and Vincent J. DiMarco. "The Matter of Armenia in the Age of Chaucer." *Studies in the Age of Chaucer* 23 (2001): 317–58.
Copeland, Rita. *Rhetoric, Hermeneutics, and Translation in the Middle Ages: Academic Traditions and Vernacular Texts*. Cambridge UP, 1991.
Courtenay, William J. *Schools and Scholars in Fourteenth-Century England*. Princeton: Princeton UP, 1987.
Crow, Martin M., and Clair C. Olson, eds. *Chaucer Life-Records*. Oxford: Clarendon P, 1966.
De Weever, Jacqueline. *Chaucer Name Dictionary: A Guide to Astrological, Biblical, Historical, Literary, and Mythological Names in the Works of Geoffrey Chaucer*. New York: Garland, 1988.
Doob, Penelope Reed. *The Idea of the Labyrinth from Classical Antiquity through the Middle Ages*. Ithaca: Cornell UP, 1990.
Economou, George. *The Goddess Natura in Medieval Literature*. Cambridge, MA: Harvard UP, 1972.
Gardner, John. *The Life and Times of Chaucer*. New York: Random House, 1978.
Gray, Douglas, ed. *The Oxford Companion to Chaucer*. Oxford: Oxford, UP, 2003.
Green, Richard Firth. *Poets and Princepleasers: Literature and the English Court in the Late Middle Ages*. Toronto: U of Toronto P, 1980.
Howard, Donald R. *Chaucer: His Life, His Works, His World*. New York: E. P. Dutton, 1987.
Jones, Terry, with Robert Yeager, Terry Dolan, Alan Fletcher, and Juliette Dor. *Who Murdered Chaucer? A Medieval Mystery*. New York: St. Martins P, 2003.
Kelly, Henry Ansgar. *Chaucer and the Cult of Saint Valentine*. Leiden: E. J. Brill, 1986.
———. *Love and Marriage in the Age of Chaucer*. Ithaca: Cornell UP, 1975.
Lewis, C. S. *The Allegory of Love: A Study in Medieval Tradition*. London: Oxford UP, 1936.
Magoun, Francis P., Jr. *A Chaucer Gazetteer*. Chicago: U of Chicago P, 1961.
Minnis, Alastair J., with V. J. Scattergood and J. J. Smith. *The Shorter Poems: Oxford Guides to Chaucer*. Oxford: Oxford UP, 1995.
North, J. D. *Chaucer's Universe*. Oxford: Clarendon P, 1988.
Olson, Glending. *Literature as Recreation in the Later Middle Ages*. Ithaca: Cornell UP, 1982.
Pearsall, Derek. *The Life of Geoffrey Chaucer: A Critical Biography*. Oxford: Blackwell, 1992.
Spearing, A. C. *The Medieval Poet as Voyeur: Looking and Listening in Medieval Love-Narratives*. Cambridge, Eng.: Cambridge UP, 1993.
Wack, Mary Frances. *Lovesickness in the Middle Ages : The Viaticum and Its Commentaries*. Philadelphia: U of Pennsylvania P, 1990.
Wallace, David. *Chaucer and the Early Writings of Boccaccio*. Woodbridge, Suffolk: D. S. Brewer, 1985.
Wallace, David, ed. *The Cambridge History of Medieval English Literature*. Cambridge, Eng.: Cambridge UP.
White, Hugh. *Nature, Sex, and Goodness in a Medieval Literary Tradition*. Oxford: Oxford UP, 2000.

BIBLIOGRAPHIES AND ESSAY COLLECTIONS

Boitani, Piero, and Jill Mann. *The Cambridge Companion to Chaucer*. 2nd ed. Cambridge, Eng.: Cambridge UP, 2003.
Brewer, Derek, ed. *Geoffrey Chaucer*. Athens, OH: Ohio UP, 1975.
Ellis, Steve, ed. *Chaucer: An Oxford Guide*. Oxford: Oxford UP, 2005.

Gaylord, Alan. *Essays on the Art of Chaucer's Verse*. New York: Routledge, 2001.
Hammond, Eleanor Prescott. *Chaucer: A Bibliographical Manual*. New York: Macmillan, 1908.
Peck, Russell A., ed. *Chaucer's Lyrics and "Anelida and Arcite": An Annotated Bibliography, 1900–1980*. Toronto: U of Toronto P, 1983.
———. *Chaucer's Romaunt of the Rose and Boece, Treatise on the Astrolabe, Equatorie of the Planetis, Lost Works, and Chaucerian Apocrypha: An Annotated Bibliography, 1900–1985*. Toronto: U of Toronto P, 1988.
Pugh, Tison, and Angela Jane Weisl. *Approaches to Teaching Chaucer's Troilus and Criseyde and the Shorter Poems*. New York: MLA, 2006.
Quinn, William A., ed. *Chaucer's Dream Visions and Shorter Poems*. New York: Garland, 1999.
Rose, Donald M. *New Perspectives in Chaucer Criticism*. Norman: Pilgrim Books, 1981.
Rowland, Beryl, ed. *Companion to Chaucer Studies*. Rev. ed. Oxford: Oxford UP, 1979.
Schoeck, Richard J., and Jerome Taylor. *Troilus and Criseyde and the Minor Poems*. Vol. 2 of *Chaucer Criticism*. Notre Dame: U of Notre Dame P, 1961.
Utz, Richard J. *Literary Nominalism and the Theory of Rereading Late Medieval Texts: A New Research Paradigm*. Lewiston: Edwin Mellen, 1995.
Wasserman, Julian N., and Robert J. Blanch. *Chaucer in the Eighties*. Syracuse: Syracuse UP, 1986.
Watts, William H., and Richard J. Utz. "Nominalist Perspectives on Chaucer's Poetry: A Bibliographical Essay." *Medievalia et Humanistica* n.s. 20 (1993): 147–73.

DREAM POEMS AND THE VISIONARY IMAGINATION:

Barney, Stephen A. "Allegorical Visions." *A Companion to "Piers Plowman*. Ed. John Alford. Berkeley: U of California P, 1988. 117–33.
Brown, Peter, ed. *Reading Dreams: The Interpretation of Dreams from Chaucer to Shakespeare*. Oxford: Oxford UP, 1999.
Cherniss, Michael D. *Boethian Apocalypse: Studies in Middle English Vision Poetry*. Norman: Pilgrim Books, 1987.
Davidoff, Judith. *Beginning Well: Framing Fictions in Late Middle English Poetry*. London: Associated U Presses, 1988.
Dinzelbacher, Peter. "Vision Literature." *Medieval Latin: An Introduction and Bibliographical Guide*. Ed. Frank Anthony Carl Mantello and A. G. Rigg. Washington, D.C.: Catholic UP, 1996. 688–93.
Richard K. Emmerson and Bernard McGinn, eds. *The Apocalypse in the Middle Ages*. Ithaca: Cornell UP, 1992.
Erickson, Carolly. *The Medieval Vision: Essays in History and Perception*. New York: Oxford UP, 1976.
Hieatt, Constance B. *The Realism of Dream Visions: The Poetic Exploitation of the Dream-Experience in Chaucer and His Contemporaries*. The Hague: Mouton, 1967.
Kruger, Steven F. *Dreaming in the Middle Ages*. Cambridge, Eng.: Cambridge UP, 1992.
Lynch, Kathryn L. *The High Medieval Dream Vision: Poetry, Philosophy, and Literary Form*. Stanford: Stanford UP, 1988.
———. *Chaucer's Philosophical Visions*. Cambridge: D.S. Brewer, 2000.
Nolan, Barbara. *The Gothic Visionary Perspective*. Princeton: Princeton UP, 1977.
Piehler, Paul. *The Visionary Landscape: A Study in Medieval Allegory*. London: Edward Arnold, 1971.
Reed, Thomas L., Jr. *Middle English Debate Poetry: The Aesthetics of Irresolution*. Columbia: U of Missouri P, 1990.
Russell, J. Stephen. *The English Dream Vision: Anatomy of a Form*. Columbus: Ohio State UP, 1988.
•Spearing, A. C. *Medieval Dream-Poetry*. Cambridge, Eng.: Cambridge UP, 1976.
St John, Michael. *Chaucer's Dream Visions: Courtliness and Individual Identity*. Aldershot: Ashgate, 2000.

SOURCES AND ANALOGUES

•Alain de Lille. *The Complaint of Nature*. Trans. Douglas M. Moffat. New York: Henry Holt, 1908.
———. *The Plaint of Nature*. Trans. James J. Sheridan. Toronto: Pontifical Institute of Mediaeval Studies, 1980.
Altmann, Barbara K., and R. Barton Palmer, eds. *An Anthology of Medieval Love Debate Poetry*. Gainesville: UP of Florida, 2006.
Andreas Capellanus. *De amore et amoris remedio* [includes English translation of the *Art of Courtly Love*]. Trans. P. G. Walsh. London: Duckworth, 1982.
•Boccaccio, Giovanni. *The Book of Theseus*. Trans. Bernadette Marie McCoy. New York: Medieval Text Association, 1974.
———. *Theseid of the Nuptials of Emilia*. Trans. Vincenzo Traversa. New York: Peter Lang, 2002.
•Boethius. *The Consolation of Philosophy*. Trans. Richard Green. New York: Macmillan, 1962.
•Boffey, Julia, ed. *Fifteenth-Century English Dream Visions: An Anthology*. Oxford: Oxford UP, 2003.
•Cicero and Macrobius. *Commentary on the Dream of Scipio*. Trans. William Harris Stahl. New York: Columbia UP, 1952.
•Dante Alighieri. *The Divine Comedy*. Trans. Allen Mandelbaum. New York: Alfred A. Knopf, 1995.
Froissart, Jean. *An Anthology of Narrative and Lyric Poetry*. Ed. and trans. Kristen M. Figg and R. Barton Palmer. New York: Routledge, 2001.

Gower, John. *Confessio Amantis*. Ed. Russell A. Peck. New York: Holt, Rinehart and Winston, 1968.
———. *The Major Latin Works of John Gower*. Trans. Eric W. Stockton. Seattle: U of Washington P, 1962.
Guido delle Colonne. *Historia destructionis Troiae*. Trans. Mary Elizabeth Meek. Bloomington: U of Indiana P, 1974.
Guillaume de Machaut. *The Fountain of Love and Two Other Love Vision Poems*. Ed. R. Barton Palmer. New York: Garland, 1993.
———. *Jugement dou roy de Behaingne and Remede de Fortune*. Ed. James I. Wimsatt and William W. Kibler. Athens, GA: U of Georgia P, 1988.
———. *Jugement de roy de Navarre*. Ed. and trans. R. Barton Palmer. New York: Garland, 1988.
•Jean de Meun and Guillaume de Lorris. *The Romance of the Rose*. Trans. Charles Dahlberg. Princeton: Princeton UP, 1971.
Langland, William. *The Vision of Piers Plowman: A Complete Edition of the B-Text*. Ed. A. V. C. Schmidt. London: J. M. Dent & Sons, 1978.
———. *Piers Plowman: A New Translation of the B-Text*. Trans. A. V. C. Schmidt. Oxford: Oxford UP, 2005.
Lydgate, John. *Fall of Princes*. Ed. Henry Bergen. EETS OS 121–24. London: Oxford UP, 1924–27.
•Ovid. *Heroides*. Trans. Harold Isbell. London: Penguin, 1990.
•———. *Metamorphoses*. Trans. Charles Martin. New York: W. W. Norton and Company, 2004.
Skeat, Walter W., ed. *Chaucerian and Other Pieces*. Supplement to *The Complete Works of Geoffrey Chaucer*. Oxford: Clarendon, 1897.
Symons, Dana M. *Chaucerian Dream Visions and Complaints*. Kalamazoo Medieval Institute, 2004.
•Virgil. *The Aeneid*. Trans. David West. London: Penguin, 1990.
•Windeatt, B. A. , ed. and trans. *Chaucer's Dream Poetry: Sources and Analogues*. Woodbridge, Suffolk: D. S. Brewer, 1982.

LITERARY CRITICAL AND SOURCE STUDIES

Astell, Ann W. *Chaucer and the Universe of Learning*. Ithaca: Cornell UP, 1996.
Barney, Stephen A. "Suddenness and Process in Chaucer." *The Chaucer Review* 16 (1981): 18–37.
Bethurum, Dorothy. "Chaucer's Point of View as Narrator to the Love Poems." *PMLA* 74 (1959): 511–20.
Boardman, Philip. "Humanism and Language in Chaucer's Dream Visions." *History and Humanities: Essays in Honor of Wilbur S. Shepperson*. Ed. Francis X. Hartigan. Reno: U of Nevada P, 1989. 239–51.
Brewer, Derek. "The Structure of Chaucer's Imagination in His Earlier Poems." *L'imagination médiévale: Chaucer et ses contemporains*. Paris: Publications de l'Association des Médiévistes Anglicistes de l'Enseignement Supérieur, 1991. 19–31.
Burlin, Robert B. *Chaucerian Fiction*. Princeton: Princeton UP, 1977.
Chance, Jane. *The Mythographic Chaucer: The Fabulation of Sexual Politics*. Minneapolis: U of Minnesota P, 1995.
Clemen, Wolfgang. *Chaucer's Early Poetry*. Trans. C. A. M. Sym. London: Methuen, 1963.
Davenport, W. A. *Chaucer: Complaint and Narrative*. Cambridge: D. S. Brewer, 1988.
David, Alfred. *The Strumpet Muse: Art and Morals in Chaucer's Poetry*. Bloomington: Indiana UP, 1976.
Dean, Nancy. "Chaucer's Complaint, A Genre Descended from the *Heroides*." *Comparative Literature* 1 (1967): 1–27.
Desmond, Marilynn. *Reading Dido: Gender, Textuality, and the Medieval Aeneid*. Minneapolis: U of Minnesota P, 1994.
Dinshaw, Carolyn. *Chaucer's Sexual Poetics*. Madison: U of Wisconsin P, 1989.
Edwards, Robert R. *The Dream of Chaucer: Representation and Reflection in the Early Narratives*. Durham: Duke UP, 1989.
Ferster, Judith. *Chaucer on Interpretation*. Cambridge, Eng.: Cambridge UP, 1985.
Fradenburg, Louise O. " 'Voice Memorial': Loss and Reparation in Chaucer's Poetry." *Exemplaria* 2 (1990): 169–202.
Fyler, John. *Chaucer and Ovid*. New Haven: Yale UP, 1979.
•Green, Richard Firth. "Chaucer's Victimized Women." *Studies in the Age of Chaucer* 10 (1988): 3–21.
Hansen, Elaine Tuttle. *Chaucer and the Fictions of Gender*. Berkeley: U of California P, 1992.
Huppé, Bernard F., and D. W. Robertson, Jr. *Fruyt and Chaf: Studies in Chaucer's Allegories*. Princeton: Princeton UP, 1963.
Kean, P. M. *Chaucer and the Making of English Poetry*. Vol 1. London: Routledge, 1972.
Kiser, Lisa J. *Truth and Textuality in Chaucer's Poetry*. Hanover: UP of New England, 1991.
Knight, Stephen. *Rymyng Craftily: Meaning in Chaucer's Poetry*. Sydney: Angus and Robertson, 1973.
Lawton, David. *Chaucer's Narrators*. Cambridge: D. S. Brewer, 1985.
Mann, Jill. *Feminizing Chaucer*. 1991. Expanded ed. Cambridge: D. S. Brewer, 2002.
Martin, Priscilla. *Chaucer's Women: Nuns, Wives, and Amazons*. Iowa City: U of Iowa P, 1990.
McGerr, Rosemarie. *Chaucer's Open Books: Resistance to Closure in Medieval Discourse*. Gainesville: U of Florida P, 1998.
•Muscatine, Charles. *Chaucer and the French Tradition: A Study in Style and Meaning*. Berkeley: U of California P, 1957.
———. *Poetry and Crisis in the Age of Chaucer*. Notre Dame: Notre Dame UP, 1972.

Patterson, Lee. *Chaucer and the Subject of History*. Madison: U of Wisconsin P, 1991.
Payne, Robert O. *The Key of Remembrance: A Study of Chaucer's Poetics*. New Haven: Yale UP, 1963.
Peck, Russell A. "Chaucer and the Nominalist Questions." *Speculum* 53 (1978): 745–60.
Pratt, Robert A. "Chaucer's Use of the *Teseida*." *PMLA* 62 (1947): 598–621.
Schless, Howard H. *Chaucer and Dante: A Revaluation*. Norman, Pilgrim Books, 1984.
Sklute, Larry. *Virtue of Necessity: Inconclusiveness and Narrative Form in Chaucer's Poetry*. Columbus: Ohio State UP, 1984.
Strohm, Paul. *Hochon's Arrow: The Social Imagination of Fourteenth-Century Texts*. Princeton: Princeton UP, 1992.
Taylor, Karla. *Chaucer Reads the Divine Comedy*. Stanford: Stanford UP, 1989.
Wimsatt, James I. *Chaucer and the French Love Poets*. Chapel Hill: U of North Carolina P, 1968.
———. *Chaucer and the Poems of 'Ch'*. Cambridge: D. S. Brewer, 1982.
———. *Chaucer and his French Contemporaries: Natural Music in the Fourteenth Century*. Toronto: U of Toronto P, 1991.
———. "Guillaume de Machaut and Chaucer's Love Lyrics." *Medium Aevum* 47 (1978): 66–87.
Winny, James. *Chaucer's Dream-Poems*. New York: Harper & Row, 1973.

RECEPTION STUDIES

Bennett, H. S. *Chaucer and the Fifteenth Century*. Oxford: Clarendon P, 1947.
Boffey, Julia, and Janet Cowen, eds. *Chaucer and Fifteenth-Century English Poetry*. London: King's College Centre for Late Antique and Medieval Studies, 1991.
Boswell, Jackson Campbell, and Sylvia Wallace Holton. *Chaucer's Fame in England: STC Chauceriana, 1475–1640*. New York: MLA, 2005.
Brewer, Derek, ed. *Chaucer: The Critical Heritage*. 2 vols. London: Routledge and Kegan Paul, 1978.
Ellis, Steve. *Chaucer at Large: The Poet in the Modern Imagination*. Minneapolis: U of Minnesota P, 2000.
Green, Richard Firth. "Women in Chaucer's Audience." *The Chaucer Review* 18 (1983): 146–54.
Krier, Theresa, ed. *Refiguring Chaucer in the Renaissance*. Gainesville: UP of Florida, 1998.
Lerer, Seth. *Chaucer and His Readers: Imagining the Author in Late Medieval England*. Princeton: Princeton UP, 1993.
Pinti, Daniel, ed. *Writing After Chaucer: Essential Reading in Chaucer and the Fifteenth Century*. New York: Garland, 1998.
Spearing, A. C. *Medieval to Renaissance in English Poetry*. Cambridge: Cambridge UP, 1985.
Spurgeon, Caroline F. E., ed. *Five Hundred Years of Chaucer Criticism and Allusion 357–1900*. 3 vols. 1925. New York: Russell & Russell, 1960.
Strohm, Paul. "Chaucer's Audience." *Literature and History* 5 (1977): 26–41.
———. "Chaucer's Audience(s): Fictional, Implied, Intended, Actual." *The Chaucer Review* 18 (1983): 137–45.
———. "Fourteenth- and Fifteenth-Century Writers as Readers of Chaucer." *Genres, Themes, and Images in English Literature from the Fourteenth to the Fifteenth Century*. Ed. Piero Boitani and Anna Torti. Tubingen: Gunter Narr Verlag, 1988. 90–104.

ANELIDA AND ARCITE AND THE SHORTER POEMS

Boffey, Julia. "The Lyrics in Chaucer's Longer Poems." *Poetica* 37 (1993): 15–37.
Chance, Jane. "Anti-Courtly Love in Chaucer's Complaints." *Mediaevalia* 10 (1988 for 1984): 181–97.
———. "Chaucerian Irony in the Boethian Shorter Poems: The Dramatic Tension between Classical and Christian." *The Chaucer Review* 20 (1986): 235–45.
———. "Chaucerian Irony in the Verse Epistles 'Wordes Unto Adam,' 'Lenvoy a Scogan,' and 'Lenvoy a Bukton.' " *Papers on Language and Literature* 21 (1985): 115–28.
Cherniss, Michael D. "Chaucer's *Anelida and Arcite*: Some Conjectures." *The Chaucer Review* 5 (1970): 9–21.
David, Alfred. "Recycling *Anelida and Arcite*: Chaucer as a Source for Chaucer." *Studies in the Age of Chaucer, Proceedings 1, 1984*. Ed. Paul Strohm and Thomas J. Heffernan. Knoxville: New Chaucer Society, 1985. 105–15.
Edwards, A. S. G. "The Unity and Authenticity of *Anelida and Arcite*: The Evidence of the Manuscripts." *Studies in Bibliography* 41 (1988): 178–88.
Fichte, Joerg O. "*Womanly Noblesse* and *To Rosemounde*: Point and Counterpoint of Chaucerian Love Lyrics." *Studies in the Age of Chaucer, Proceedings 1, 1984*. Ed. Paul Strohm and Thomas J. Heffernan. Knoxville: New Chaucer Society, 1985. 181–94.
Horvath, Richard P. "Chaucer's Epistolary Poetic: The Envoys to Bukton and Scogan." *The Chaucer Review* 37 (2002): 173–189.
•Lenaghan, R. T. "Chaucer's Circle of Gentlemen and Clerks." *The Chaucer Review* 18 (1983): 155–60.
Moore, Arthur K. "Chaucer's Lost Songs." *Journal of English and Germanic Philology* 48 (1949): 196–208.
———. "Chaucer's Use of Lyric as an Ornament of Style." *Comparative Literature* 3 (1951): 32–46.

Norton-Smith, John. "Chaucer's *Anelida and Arcite.*" *Medieval Studies for J.A.W. Bennett* Ed. P. L. Heyworth. Oxford: Clarendon P, 1981. 81–99.

Reiss, Edmund. "Dusting off the Cobwebs: A Look at Chaucer's Lyrics." *The Chaucer Review* 1 (1966): 55–65.

Robbins, Rossell Hope. "Chaucer's 'To Rosemounde.' " *Studies in the Literary Imagination* 4 (1971): 73–81.

Ruud, Jay. *"Many a Song and Many a Lecherous Lay"*: *Tradition and Individuality in Chaucer's Lyric Poetry.* New York: Garland, 1992.

Scattergood, John. "Social and Political Issues in Chaucer: An Approach to 'Lak of Stedfastnesse.' " *The Chaucer Review* 21 (1987): 469–75.

Stallcup, Stephen. "With the 'Poynte of Remembraunce': Re-Viewing the Complaint in *Anelia and Arcite.*" *Feminea Medievalia I: Representations of the Feminine in the Middle Ages.* Ed. Bonnie Wheeler. Cambridge: Academia Press, 1993. 43–68.

Wimsatt, James I. *"Anelida and Arcite*: A Narrative of Complaint and Comfort." *The Chaucer Review* 5 (1970): 1–8.

THE BOOK OF THE DUCHESS

Anderson, J. J. "The Man in Black, Machaut's Knight, and their Ladies." *English Studies* 73 (1992): 417–30.

Blake, Norman F. "The Textual Tradition of *The Book of the Duchess.*" *English Studies* 62 (1981): 237–48.

Bronson, Bertrand H. *"The Book of the Duchess Re-opened."* PMLA 67 (1952): 863–81.

Butterfield, Ardis. "Lyric and Elegy in *The Book of the Duchess,*" *Medium Aevum* 60 (1991): 33–60.

Davis, Steven. "Guillaume de Machaut, Chaucer's *Book of the Duchess,* and the Chaucer Tradition." *The Chaucer Review* 36 (2002): 391–405.

Diekstra, F. N. M. "Chaucer's Way with His Sources: Accident into Substance and Substance into Accident." *English Studies* 62 (1981): 215–36.

Donnelly, Colleen. "Challenging the Conventions of Dream Vision in *The Book of the Duchess.*" *Philological Quarterly* 66 (1987): 421–35.

Ellman, Maude. "Blanche." *Criticism and Critical Theory.* Ed. Jeremy Hawthorn. London: Edward Arnold, 1984. 99–112.

Friedman, John Block. "The Dreamer, the Whelp, and Consolation in the *Book of the Duchess.*" *The Chaucer Review* 3 (1969): 145–62.

Hewitt, Kathleen. "Loss and Restitution in the *Book of the Duchess.*" *Papers on Language and Literature* 25 (1989): 19–35.

• Kruger, Steven. "Medical and Moral Authority in the Late Medieval Dream." *Reading Dreams: The Interpretation of Dreams from Chaucer to Shakespeare.* Ed. Peter Brown. Oxford: Oxford UP. 51–83.

Morse, Ruth. "Understanding the Man in Black." *The Chaucer Review* 15 (1981): 204–08.

Palmer, J. J. N. "The Historical Context of the *Book of the Duchess.*" *The Chaucer Review* 8 (1974): 253–61.

Peck, Russell A. "Theme and Number in Chaucer's *Book of the Duchess.*" *Silent Poetry: Essays in Numerological Analysis.* Ed. Alastair Fowler. London: Routledge, 1970. 73–115.

Phillips, Helen. "Structure and Consolation in the *Book of the Duchess.*" *The Chaucer Review* 16 (1981): 107–18.

Robertson, D. W., Jr. "The Historical Setting of Chaucer's *Book of the Duchess.*" *Mediaeval Studies in Honor of Urban Tigner Holmes, Jr.* Ed. John Mahoney and John Esten Keller. Chapel Hill: U of North Carolina P, 1965. 169–96.

Shoaf, R. A. " 'Mutatio Amoris': 'Penitentia' and the Form of *The Book of the Duchess.*" *Genre* 14 (1981): 163–89.

Spearing, A. C. "Literal and Figurative in *The Book of the Duchess.*" *Studies in the Age of Chaucer, Proceedings 1, 1984.* Ed. Paul Strohm and Thomas J. Heffernan. Knoxville: New Chaucer Society, 1985. 165–71.

Taylor, Mark N. "Chaucer's Knowledge of Chess." *The Chaucer Review* 38 (2004): 299–313.

Travis, Peter W. "White." *Studies in the Age of Chaucer* 22 (2000): 1–66.

Wimsatt, James I. *"The Book of the Duchess*: Secular Elegy or Religious Vision?" *Signs and Symbols in Chaucer's Poetry.* Ed. John P. Hermann and John J. Burke. University, AL: U of Alabama P, 1981. 113–29.

———. *Chaucer and the French Love Poets: The Literary Background of the Book of the Duchess.* New York: Johnson Reprint Corp., 1972.

THE HOUSE OF FAME

Benson, Larry D. "The 'Love Tydynges' in Chaucer's *House of Fame.*" In *Chaucer in the Eighties.* Ed. Julian N. Wasserman and Robert J. Blanch. Syracuse: Syracuse UP, 1986. 3–22.

Bevington, David. "The Obtuse Narrator in Chaucer's *House of Fame.*" *Speculum* 36 (1961): 288–98.

Boitani, Piero. *Chaucer and the Imaginary World of Fame.* Cambridge, Eng.: D. S. Brewer, 1984.

Cawsey, Kathy. " 'Alum de glas' or 'Alymed glass'? Manuscript Reading in Book III of *The House of Fame.*" *University of Toronto Quarterly* 73 (2004): 972–79.

Cooper, Helen. "The Four Last Things in Dante and Chaucer: Ugolino in the House of Rumour." *New Medieval Literatures* 3 (1999): 39–66.

David, Alfred. "Literary Satire in the *House of Fame*." *PMLA* 75 (1960): 153–59.

Delany, Sheila. *Chaucer's House of Fame: The Poetics of Skeptical Fideism*. 1972. Rpt. with a foreword by Michael Near, Gainesville: UP of Florida, 1994.

Edwards, A. S. G. "Chaucer's *House of Fame*, Lines 1709, 1907." *English Language Notes* 26 (1988): 1–3.

Eldredge, Laurence. "Chaucer's *Hous of Fame* and the *Via Moderna*." *Neuphilologische Mitteilungen* 71 (1970): 105–19.

•Evans, Ruth. "Chaucer in Cyberspace: Medieval Technologies of Memory and the *House of Fame*." *Studies in the Age of Chaucer* 23 (2001): 43–69.

Goffin, R. C. "Quiting by Tidings in the *House of Fame*." *Medium Aevum* 12 (1943): 40–44.

Hagiioannu, Michael. "Giotto's Bardi Chapel Frescoes and Chaucer's *House of Fame*." *The Chaucer Review* 36 (2001): 28–47.

Irvine, Martin. "Medieval Grammatical Theory and Chaucer's *House of Fame*." *Speculum* 60 (1985): 850–76.

Koonce, B. G. *Chaucer and the Tradition of Fame: Symbolism in the House of Fame*. Princeton: Princeton UP, 1966.

Kordecki, Lesley. "Subversive Voices in Chaucer's *House of Fame*." *Exemplaria* 11 (1999): 53–77.

Leyerle, John. "Chaucer's Windy Eagle." *U of Toronto Quarterly* 40 (1971): 247–65.

Overbeck, Pat Trefzger. "The 'Man of Gret Auctorite' in Chaucer's *House of Fame*," *Modern Philology* 73 (1975): 157–61.

Ruggiers, Paul G. "The Unity of Chaucer's *House of Fame*." *Studies in Philology* 50 (1953): 16–29.

Shoeck, R. J. "A Legal Reading of Chaucer's *House of Fame*." *University of Toronto Quarterly* 23 (1954): 185–92.

Steadman, John M. "*The House of Fame*: Tripartite Structure and Occasion." *Connotations* 3 (1993): 1–12.

Steinberg, Glenn A. "Chaucer in the Field of Cultural Production: Humanism, Dante, and the *House of Fame*." *The Chaucer Review* 35 (2000): 182–203.

Vance, Eugene. "Chaucer's *House of Fame* and the Poetics of Inflation." *Boundary* 27 (1979): 17–37.

THE LEGEND OF GOOD WOMEN

Aloni, Gila. "A Curious Error? Geoffrey Chaucer's *Legend of Hypermnestra*." *The Chaucer Review* 36 (2001): 73–86.

Cowen, Janet. "Chaucer's *Legend of Good Women*: Structure and Tone." *Studies in Philology* 82 (1985): 416–36.

Delany, Sheila. *The Naked Text: Chaucer's Legend of Good Women*. Berkeley: U of California P, 1994.

Eadie, John. "The Author at Work: The Two Versions of the Prologue to the *Legend of Good Women*." *Neuphilologische Mitteilungen* 93 (1992): 135–44.

Fisher, John H. "The Revision of the Prologue to the *Legend of Good Women*: An Occasional Explanation." *South Atlantic Bulletin* 43 (1978): 75–84.

Frank, Robert Worth, Jr. *Chaucer and the Legend of Good Women*. Cambridge, MA: Harvard UP, 1972.

Gaylord, Alan. "Dido at Hunt, Chaucer at Work." *The Chaucer Review* 17 (1983): 300–15.

•Hansen, Elaine Tuttle. "The Feminization of Men in Chaucer's *Legend of Good Women*." *Seeking the Woman in Late Medieval and Renaissance Writings*. Ed. Sheila Fisher and Janet E. Halley. Knoxville: U of Tennessee P, 1989. 51–70.

Kiser, Lisa J. *Telling Classical Tales: Chaucer and the Legend of Good Women*. Ithaca: Cornell UP, 1983.

Kolve, V. A. "From Cleopatra to Alceste: An Iconographic Study of *The Legend of Good Women*." *Signs and Symbols in Chaucer's Poetry*. Ed. John P. Hermann and John J. Burke. University: U of Alabama P, 1981. 130–78.

Kruger, Steven F. "Passion and Order in Chaucer's *Legend of Good Women*." *The Chaucer Review* 23 (1989): 219–35.

McDonald, Nicola F. "Chaucer's *Legend of Good Women*, Ladies at Court and the Female Reader." *The Chaucer Review* 35 (2000): 22–42.

Percival, Florence. *Chaucer's Legendary Good Women*. Cambridge: Cambridge UP, 1998.

Phillips, Helen. "Register, Politics, and the *Legend of Good Women*." *The Chaucer Review* 37 (2002): 101–28.

Rowe, Donald, W. *Through Nature to Eternity: Chaucer's Legend of Good Women*. Lincoln: U of Nebraska P, 1988.

Sanok, Catherine. "Reading Hagiographically: The *Legend of Good Women* and Its Feminine Audience." *Exemplaria* 13 (2001): 323–54.

Simpson, James. "Ethics and Interpretation: Reading Wills in Chaucer's *Legend of Good Women*." *Studies in the Age of Chaucer* 20 (1998): 73–100.

Taylor, Beverly. "The Medieval Cleopatra: The Medieval Tradition of Chaucer's 'Legend of Cleopatra.'" *Journal of Medieval and Renaissance Studies* 7 (1977): 249–69.

Travis, Peter W. "Chaucer's Heliotropes and the Poetics of Metaphor." *Speculum* 72 (1997): 399–427.

THE PARLIAMENT OF FOWLS

Aers, David. "The *Parliament of Fowls*: Authority, the Knower and the Known." *The Chaucer Review* 16 (1981): 1–17.

Bennett, J.A.W. *The Parlement of Foules: An Interpretation.* Oxford: Clarendon P, 1957.

———. "Some Second Thoughts on the *Parlement of Fowls.*" *Chaucerian Problems and Perspectives: Essays Presented to Paul E. Beichner C.S.C.* Ed. Edward Vasta and Zacharias P. Thundy. Notre Dame: U of Notre Dame P, 1979). 32–46.

Benson, Larry D. "The Occasion of *The Parliament of Fowls.*" *The Wisdom of Poetry: Essays in Early English Literature in Honor of Morton W. Bloomfield.* Ed. Larry D. Benson and Siegfried Wenzel. Kalamazoo: Medieval Institute, 1982. 123–44.

Bethurum, Dorothy. "The Center of the *Parlement of Foules.*" *Essays in Honor of Walter Clyde Curry.* Nashville: Vanderbilt UP, 1954. 39–50.

Boyd, David Lorenzo. "Compilation as Commentary: Controlling Chaucer's *Parliament of Fowls.*" *South Atlantic Quarterly* 91 (1992): 945–64.

Frank, Robert Worth, Jr. "Structure and Meaning in the *Parlement of Foules.*" *PMLA* 71 (1956): 530–39.

Gilbert, A. J. "The Influence of Boethius on the *Parlement of Foulys.*" *Medium Aevum* 47 (1978): 292–303.

Harwood, Britton J. "Same-Sex Desire in the Unconscious of Chaucer's *Parliament of Fowls.*" *Exemplaria* 13 (2001): 99–135.

Hill, Ordelle G., and Gardiner Stillwell. "A Conduct Book for Richard II." *Philological Quarterly* 73 (1994): 317–28.

Jordan, Robert M. "The Question of Unity and the *Parlement of Foules.*" *English Studies in Canada* 3 (1977): 373–85.

Kelley, Michael R. "Antithesis as the Principle of Design in the *Parlement of Foules.*" *The Chaucer Review* 14 (1979): 61–73.

Kiser, Lisa J. "Chaucer and the Politics of Nature." *Beyond Nature: Expanding the Boundaries of Ecocriticism.* Ed. Karla Armbruster and Kathleen R. Wallace. Charlottesville: U of VA P, 2001. 41–56.

Leicester, H. M., Jr. "The Harmony of Chaucer's *Parliament*: A Dissonant Voice." *The Chaucer Review* 9 (1974): 15–34.

Lynch, Kathryn L. "Diana's 'Bowe Ybroke': Impotence, Desire, and Virginity in Chaucer's *Parliament of Fowls.*" *Menacing Virgins: Representing Virginity in the Middle Ages and Renaissance.* Ed. Kathleen Coyne Kelly and Marina Leslie. Newark: U of Delaware P, 1999. 83–96.

McCall, John P. "The Harmony of Chaucer's *Parliament.*" *The Chaucer Review* 5 (1970): 22–31.

McDonald, Charles O. "An Interpretation of Chaucer's *Parlement of Foules.*" *Speculum* 30 (1955): 444–57.

Olson, Paul A. "*The Parlement of Foules*: Aristotle's *Politics* and the Foundations of the Good Society." *Studies in the Age of Chaucer* 2 (1980): 53–69.

Oruch, Jack B. "Nature's Limitations and the '*Demande d'Amour* of Chaucer's *Parlement.*' " *The Chaucer Review* 18 (1983): 23–37.

Peck, Russell A. "Love, Politics, and Plot in the *Parlement of Foules.*" *The Chaucer Review* 24 (1990): 290–305.

Piehler, Paul. "Myth, Allegory, and Vision in the *Parlement of Foules*: A Study in Chaucerian Problem Solving." *Allegoresis: The Craft of Allegory in Medieval Literature.* Ed. J. Stephen Russell. New York: Garland, 1988.

Quilligan, Maureen. "Allegory, Allegoresis, and the Deallegorization of Language: The *Roman de la rose*, the *De planctu naturae*, and the *Parlement of Foules.*" *Allegory, Myth, and Symbol.* Ed. Morton W. Bloomfield. Cambridge, MA: Harvard UP, 1981. 163–86.

Scattergood, John. "Making Arrows: *The Parliament of Fowls*, 211–17." *Notes and Queries* 49 (2002): 444–47.